Orphana

Level 2 Becoming Unaware

Table of Contents

Chapter 1 | The Prophet's Game 1
Chapter 2 | The Dimensions of a Human Experience 26
Chapter 3 | Sound is the Primary Basis for Creation 54
Chapter 4 | The Symbol of the Game 77
Chapter 5 | The Planet's Third Eye 103
Chapter 6 | Perceptions Around the Polarities 127
Chapter 7 | The Illusions of Time 154
Chapter 8 | The Game of the 3rd Dimension 182
Chapter 9 | The Role of the World Ego 207
Chapter 10 | The Game of Ecstasy 229
Chapter 11 | The Divine Union of Spirit 264
Chapter 12 | The Voice from Nowhere 298
Chapter 13 | Your 'I Am Guardian Angel' 312
Chapter 14 | When Egos Play the Human Game 358
Chapter 15 | Group Souls are Gathering 380
Chapter 16 | Manifestations Created by Thoughts 405
Chapter 17 | The Initiations through Conscious Awareness 437
Chapter 18 | When the Distortions Become a Battle 462
Chapter 19 | The Effects Fragmentations Create 500
Chapter 20 | The Elemental Rules of Matter 527
Chapter 21 | The Law of Karma & Love 556
Chapter 22 | The Prophet's Orphanage of Souls 583
The Jaarsma Tree 620
The Jaarsma Tree 621
About the Author | The Ascension Journals 622

Books by Nadine May

Awakening to the Ascension Series
Novel 1. The Reality Shifters – 2018 (Ingrids Journal – Romance)
Novel 2. Orphanage of Souls – 2019 (Richard's Journal – Romance)
Novel 3. Vanishing Worlds – 2020.(Annelies' Journal – Psychic awareness)
Novel 4. Parallel Realities – 2024 (Tulanda's walk-in Journal)
Novel 5. Riddles of the Prophet's Game – 2025 (POWAH – the Guide)
The Language of Light – workbook in Full colour 2021
The Language of Light – workbook in Grayscale 2021
Meditation on the Language of Light 2021 (Full colour)
Seven. Doodle Symbology journals on the 7 Chakra channels in full colour or greyscale
The Body Codes of Light – workbook—(forthcoming)
The Self Employed Housewife book 1 – 2018 (novel)
The Self Employed Housewife book 2 – 2022 (novel)

The story of the Jaarsma Clan and their awakening was downloaded over a period of twenty years. Orphanage of Soulmates was published in 2003 and republished in 2019 this award-winning novel was twice updated.

Published by: The Power of Words SA
Contact Details:
Website Author https://nadinemay.company.site/
Author's blog : the End of Time: https://nadinemay.com/
Novel Blog : https://allrealityshifters.wordpress.com/
The Language of Light workbooks and journals: https://lightworkerjournals.wordpress.com/
ISBN – SKU 978-1-0672285-2-1
EBOOK ISBN 978-1-0672285-3-8
Previously published by Kima Global Publishers.
© Copyright Nadine May 2019
Cover Art by Author Nadine May
World rights by Author's. Except for small passages quoted for review purposes, no portion of this work may be reproduced, translated, adapted, stored in a retrieval system, or transmitted in any form or through any means, including electronic, mechanical, photocopying or otherwise, without the Author's permission

Acknowledgements / Dedication

This second stage of the Jaarsma family's awakening journey has become more accurate for Robin and me. Although this is a visionary fiction novel, I could not have written it without the documented material available to us all, be it through books, articles or videos on the internet. Many authors of articles have enriched my life with their personal or professional outlooks on the subjects I've included throughout this novel.

Often, books come into my life that I intuitively know I need to read while writing Richard's journal. My own experiences during Dreamtime made up for the rest.

Without Robin, this work of fiction would not have been possible. There are some details that I have chosen to use, particularly concerning the Ascension computer game that brings Annelies' decoding workshops to life. An inspired mind must still develop this software. As a novelist, I have creatively formulated visions that felt appropriate to me. I awaken at the same rate as the characters envision. Once my thoughts are printed and published, there is no guarantee that I will still perceive the truth the way I wrote it. The Science of Consciousness is a movement of intelligence and is always subjective. This second awakening novel serves as a mirror through which the reader can participate in the awakening process.

My years of research took me on several roller coasters with many different beliefs surrounding the questions: where we came from, who we are and why we choose to incarnate.

In 2001, I served as the book stylist and cover designer of Kima Global Publishers and travelled with Robin to many book fairs. During those years, we kept up our Spiritual science studies. Our motto was to make a difference in people's lives.

After my dear soul mate of 22 years, Robin Beck, my publisher and the love of my life, passed from this physical reality, I asked for guidance, especially to finish my soul purpose project, writing about our awakening to our ascension through the genre of visionary fiction.

Robin was the kindest man alive. He died in January 2023, and it broke my heart. I thought the best was behind me, but during the staggering weight of despair and unforeseen circumstances, I needed to regain control of my Soul purpose by finishing writing the visionary five-stage novels about the Jaarsma Clan. That meant to republish all my books.

The duality of our lives and the power of perception gave me a chance to look back in wonderment and gratitude. It is that awareness that I try to bring with this novel, and at the same time, my grieving lifted.

Dedication

I dedicate all my visionary fiction writings by acknowledging Robin Beck, who, during the month before his passing, started writing the first pages of the fifth novel in the Awakening to our Ascension series: The Prophet's Game.

Nadine
November 2023

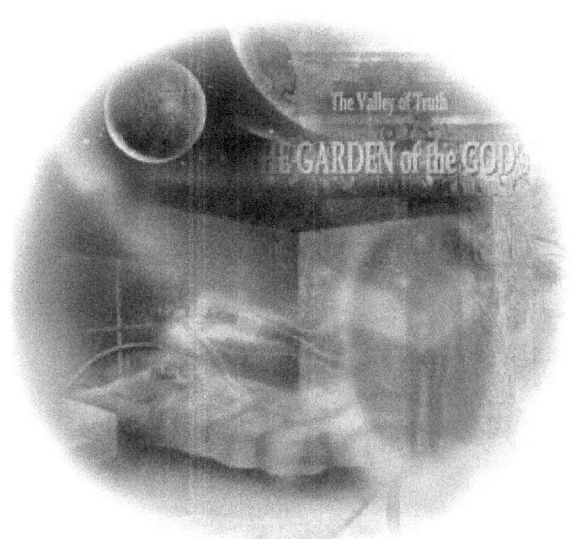

Preface by Tulanda

The Editor
I Will once again present Richard's awakening journal, like Ingrid's, to the elders on my parallel home planet during our Earth time as a novel by telling a story that can transport the reader towards a 'higher evolved reality'. My sole purpose has been to re-create their journals into works of fiction that are not realism or fantasy or a novel of ideas, but more a projection of a reality that calibrates on a level my elders like to perceive our 'manifestations 'on Earth can ascend towards.

Many collective souls will awaken as the Earth awakens and set on a journey to return home. The Language of Light symbols left behind by our ancestors will assist them in this endeavour. Our solar system originates from these ancestors, who were perceived as gods but were angelic beings from the Elohim.

Hans and I have overseen the editing of the twenty-two divine songs (the Tablets) to synchronize the latest interpretations with the ancient Sumerian texts in Mesopotamia.

These tablets are published on the same blog and website as the excepts in Ingrid's journal. https://allrealityshifters.wordpress.com/richard-de-jong/

Namasté

Tulanda / Liesbeth

Prologue

To you, the reader, I Am that part of you who IS and KNOWS. With deep respect, I salute all your spirit sparks for the courage to have incarnated during the closing of this coming cosmic cycle. The plant, animal, bacterial and mineral life forms who have all chosen to explore a physical reality with the help of the four great elemental beings within your universe have all requested to ascend.

<For many on the awakening journey, these times are not accessible. For humanity to leap into higher consciousness, I was allowed to participate in the transfiguration of your solar system. Although Spirit has continuously resided throughout every creation, it has now chosen to lift the veils that have kept its presence in this realm from being fully known. Out of love of Spirit, the forces of light are now infiltrating this Earthly system. Because each human being contains the whole story of our universe within their soul library, reflecting all that ever was or has been. Every human being will face the challenge of their spiritual awakening through their physical existence.

<When your planet started integrating her first 144 Language of Light tonal frequency qualities, these ideographic symbols showed us two pathways. One direction was regressive, and the other was a forward-evolving pathway. The planetary soul had started her resurrection process before the ascension began. Likewise, the reader will also stand on the brink of significant changes. Like humans, the Earth's planetary soul reflects all that was or has been through its five-sensory form. It knows that every action is a cause that simultaneously creates an effect.

The Matrix - *(not the movie)*

<The matrix is an intercellular substance created by the Power of One. This life force is named Ether on Earth. (This

is also the ether double light body of every human being.) This creative energy force links all conscious live streams or spirit sparks as one - constantly evolving. Thoughtforms on all frequencies use this life force to evolve or regress through the seven rays that oversee your physical galaxy.

<Many planetary bodies in your universe had to realign themselves to emanate a particular frequency towards your planet to stimulate specific characteristic signatures. These 12 signatures became known as the 12 archetypes. That was how your science of astrology was born.

<The birth of the planetary ego influenced all living expressions as they entered her auric field. Divinely inspired souls that experienced the same fragmentations then chose to incarnate between 25%-75% of soul energy into a physical human form and through many other parallel lifetimes. Due to the time zone band around the planet, humans translated the word parallel as their past or future lifetimes.

<Like the human left and right brain, the Earth has a northern and southern hemisphere. The human population is affected by nine planetary soul aspects associated with the 12 archetypes. One's ego drives these characteristics and can significantly impact one's mental and emotional state.

<As the planetary soul evolves to a higher keynote, all live streams residing on and within her body must develop during the resurrection process.

<We of the Angelic Spiritual Council observed your planet's preparation for the ascension, knowing that incompatible energy pockets —manifested as undercurrent frictions now being released would cause significant distress. Various fallen angels and group souls had devolved into a lower frequency, leaving behind distorted life forms called humanoids. They produced conflicts within the immortal etheric chromosomes of the genetic blueprint of the human race when they embody them.

Instead, distortions on a cellular level took control over our human creation.

<I was one of these 'ascended masters' that could not evolve further unless the souls (our brothers and sisters) that have embodied our human creations woke up!

<We had reached the point where we thought we had achieved everything; instead, we overlooked the pollution within the human energy field that corrupted cellular memories. When we found out, it was too late. We had not progressed together as a divine group soul. In our unawareness, we had exploited the splendour of our group soul's knowledge by sharing it with other creations already infected with a virus. Many humans have become technological animals. Our karma was great.

<When the Collective Angelic Spiritual Council granted your planetary soul the opportunity to ascend towards a faster vibrational universe, we saw that most souls that embodied a human form, 'our pride and joy,' were heading for self-destruction, just like the primordial race of many ages ago. The Jaarsma Group Soul was permitted to inhabit 144 human forms to fulfil the Divine Plan for humanity, both within and outside of embodiment, and ultimately return to the Primary Source.>

Love POWAH

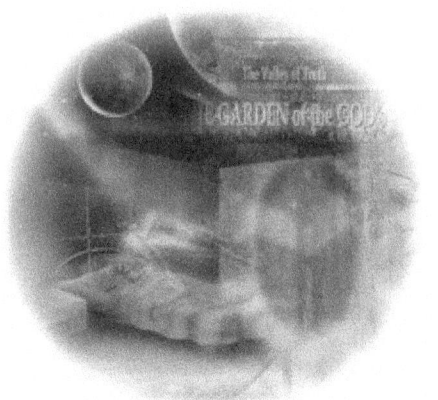

Cast of Characters.

The Jaarsma Clan represents a Soul group. The people of the Jaarsma Clan learn about the various density vibrational frequencies through the 22 Tablets about "Program Earth"(published on the internet) to prepare themselves for a new 5th-density level Earth reality realm.

Richard de Jong' – Orphanage of Souls journal
Theo de Jong:-Late Brother
POWAH:-Spiritual Guide
Sascia Barendse:-Richard's girlfriend
Sammy de Jong:-Richard'sDaughter
Ellie de Boer:-Richard's ex-wife
Ben & Leo Jaarsma:-Uncles
Mien du Toit:-Aunt
Sonja du Toit:-Niece
At & Jock du Toit:-Cousins
Debbie Barendse:-friend/ sister of Sascia
Vinny Jaarsma:-University friend
Trevor Zwiegelaar:-Colleague

The Pannekoek-Coffee bar
Connie de Wit:-Coffee bar assistant
Jeroen Barendse:-Twin brother of Sascia
Nel Hartman:-Kitchen staff

The Power of Words Bookshop
Yolanda de Wit:-Manager/Connie's mother/Participant
Fred Jaarsma:-owner/Connie's uncle
Quincy Hartman:-Fred's partner
André Jaarsma:-The detective

Ascension Workshop
Annelies Zwiegelaar:-Facilitator - Vanishing worlds journal
Liesbeth Jaarsma:-also known as Tulanda/Participant- Parallel Realities journal
Ingrid Barendse:-mother of Sascia/Participant Reality Shifters journal
Hans Jaarsma:-Annelies' adopted son /Participant
Gerrit Jaarsma:-Participant
Niels Jaarsma:-Participant
Zola de Boer:-Participant
Ed Barendse:-Ingrid's brother-in-law/Participant
Toon Haardens:-Ingrid's husband/Participant

Half-way House

Peter Spark:-Manager
Helen van Houten:-Peter's wife
Harry Brinks:-Owner of Pleasure Park
Tieneke de Beer:-Art therapy teacher/ daughter of
Harry Brinks:-Wealthy friend of Annelies
Dirk:-Pilot
Otto Jaarsa/Jill Spark:-(Buttercup Valley)

Chapter 1
The Prophet's Game

Holland (Utrecht)
Richard de Jong leaned forward so as not to miss a thing the lecturer said. His casual, longish, wavy dark brown hair held back by a rubber band gave him a cool look for a man in his late thirties. He hid the fact that he was a lecturer in ancient languages by his dress code. His notebook resembled a child's scrapbook. Scribbles of symbols that made sense only to him became alive in his mind.

"Ladies and gentlemen," the lecturer concluded. An electrifying wave transfixed the audience as he continued. "We are collectively embarking on a great voyage in our time where we make decisions that can reshape life as we know it completely." Mr Trevor Zwiegelaar, an archaeologist in his late sixties and a well-known charismatic speaker on alternative subjects, held his audience in a mental grip with his eyes, paused, and continued.

"Through deciphering the many ancient tablets that have come to light, we know that 'the wars of the Gods' reveal paradoxes which forced researchers to acknowledge that reason alone cannot give all the answers. As students, teachers, archaeologists, and scientists, you must reconsider all previous discoveries, including beliefs and dogmas, to regain true freedom."

Richard's heart pulsated from awe. The radical lecture confirmed his speculations. The speaker responded with compassion and dignity to some rather blunt questions throughout his presentation. Many referred to the strife, war and violence that had become a global issue, especially the fake virus the whole world was treated by and bullied with. After all the disclosures on evils and the withholding of technologies that followed, he expressed absolute disbelief in the behaviour of the human population worldwide.

"How fortunate we are to experience these times," the speaker concluded. He made a perfectly timed dramatic pause by lowering his head as if deep in thought. The audience, made up of various age groups, waited in suspense. At last, he gazed straight into the spellbound assembly hall, he said.

"Let me disclose a simple riddle that humbled me."

He turned and drew a giant oval sphere on the whiteboard, and inside the centre, he drew a circle. A buzz of bewilderment filled the auditorium. Trevor Zwiegelaar waited for people to quieten down, drew breath, and his powerful voice expressed his devotion to the subject matter when he said:

"Ladies and gentlemen, I urge you to engrave this symbol on the template of your memories because science alone does not possess all the answers." Everyone waited in suspense. Richard was amazed at how Trevor made his outrageous theories so plausible.

"There will be a tremendous acceleration in our awareness due to merging the physical and the spiritual sciences. This union will collectively transform our world for the human race's advancement."

Mr Zwiegelaar returned to the whiteboard and filled in the smaller solid circle. A symbol appeared that began to look like an eye.

"The greatest secret about our human species lies in a symbol that we must study on our papers. We must understand that only through the Power of One can we as humans overcome the distortion within our genetic blueprint. Each cell within us contains the intelligence of the whole and only one presence from the invisible realms in our DNA's intelligence. The 'I AM' divinity always manifests itself impartially towards the light. From the ONE and to the ONE, we shall return. The rest is pure contemplation." The speaker strode purposefully off the podium and out of the room while the crowd sat in stunned silence.

Meeting a friend from University days

Vinny Jaarsma, a close friend from university, peered silently at Richard over his wire-frame spectacles.

"Well, Richard, what he said must have been right up your alley?" Richard smiled when they shuffled out of the lecture hall. He was known to his friend as the linguist who had a mission to experience first-hand what had transpired in ancient Egypt. Still, deep in thought, his tall, lean, strong body moved in the queue as if time stood still; Vinny's remark confirmed that his friend was still sceptical, although Vinny had made bewildering comments during the lecture. His psychology background and following Freud's ideas were still obstacles.

"I hope Mr Zwiegelaar will have the time to look at my interpretations." The public that left the auditorium were all still in a mental daze. Vinny was a psychologist with a flair for extracting information from the unconscious of his clients with a cunning charm, especially with women. They had known each other since high school and stayed in contact.

"Vinny, why did you react when Trevor said, "Our 'perceived' realities are transitory dream pictures that we project in time and space?" It surprised him because Vinny had always been more interested in what he called straight psychology.

"My father believes that we all live in a hologram of our creation. His hypothesis captivated me and made me rethink some misleading philosophies I had allowed myself to believe. My dad is a forward thinker and has developed some interesting theories lately." The buzz of voices almost drowned their conversation."

"I must admit, I've never taken seriously the idea that we humans were originally visitors from another solar system, but now, after hearing Mr Zwiegelaar's astounding evidence, I'm not so sure where I stand anymore."

Richard waved at some people outside the hall when he thought he spotted Wim, Zola's partner from a decoding workshop he attended. The weird guy, somehow Wim, gave him the shivers, but he had no idea why.

"Where are you off to now?" Vinny asked

"Back in Apeldoorn, the coffee shop is bustling. Thankfully, my capable assistant is now running it part-time so I can prepare my four-part lecture on the mystery of the Sphinx, starting on Wednesday. And you?"

"You're kidding. Did the faculty rent a lecture hall to you? Gee, I'm impressed." Vinny looked at his watch. "I'm meeting Sascia in Amsterdam in two hours; I must hurry. She'd attended a talk on the photon belt timelines and the solar flares that had everyone speculating. She's good company. This time, I sure hope I make out with her tonight!" Vinny grinned, slapping him on the back. His friend's typically jovial casualness didn't fool him. When they arrived at the car park of Utrecht's Parapsychological Institute of the State University in Utrecht, Vinny's cell phone rang.

"Dr Jaarsma speaking", as Vinny opened his vintage sports car door; he was glowing when he responded, "Hi gorgeous, how was the talk?" Vinny's new girlfriend must be unique. Their conversations with women had guided him through his divorce. Marriage? Never again. To commit to one woman had only given him grief. Vinny smiled when he passed his cell phone to Richard.

"Tell Sascia what Trevor Zwiegelaar was like, will you?" It was a pity that Vinny's cell phone was an old model. It showed no visual portrait of the caller.

"Vinny... what are you up to? Did you go to Trevor's lecture?" He waited for more juicy questions, but none were forthcoming.

"Hi, Sascia, Vinny has been bragging about you. What do you want to know about Trevor's lecture?" Her voice triggered him into action, and to prolong the conversation, he sprinted to his yellow Honda.

"Was the lecture really about time travel?" Her voice carried a charming but somewhat intellectual tone. He threw his notepad on the back seat of his untidy car and closed the car door just before his friend could return his cell phone. He grinned at his slick move.

"Is that what he told you? Well, that is not far off the mark; call it inner space travel. Vinny told me you attended a talk on the photon belt and timelines. He said that's your interest. I've not met any other women that are." He ignored his friend knocking on the car window as he settled in comfort.

"Goodness, many friends are interested in learning about alternative topics. Where is Vinny?" He laughed at his friend's frantic behaviour outside. Slowly, he opened the window. "He's trying to get his cell phone back but must beg first."

"You are Richard the Egyptologist, aren't you?"

"That's me. What was the latest outcome of the Solar flares?" He was genuinely interested.

"I've read that it is likely to result in a possible breakdown in our telecommunications and that more earthquakes, floods and fires could erupt around the world, not to mention the fake pandemic rumours!" Sascia replied. Then Vinny got hold of his cell phone.

She sounded like an interesting girl that could probably hold stimulating conversations. Good luck to his friend.

"Sascia, I promise I'll see you in two hours." Vinny's eyebrows rose at her response. Richard would love to know what she had replied. Telepathy would have come in handy. He asked Vinny where he had met a girl interested in solar cycles. They were the last left in the car park. Dark clouds drifted across, darkening the pavement.

"I met Sascia at the opening of Carla's first sculpture exhibition. Gorgeous girl, tall, slender with just the right proportions. Yep, she's the one." Vinny glowed with anticipation of the coming evening. He was lucky, especially when he thought of Carla Visser, Vinny's first wife, whom he had divorced by mutual agreement. Richard's four-year marriage ended in arguments and strife. After their divorce, his only regret was that he hardly saw his little girl, Sammy.

"What about the nurse you told me about?" Vinny reminded him. Richard's eyes were roving over the parking lot, searching for Wim, whom he had spotted in the lecture hall.

"Debbie, lovely girl, but not for me. She is too serious for my liking."

"Are you waiting like I have been for the lightning to strike? I tell you, that's a myth." Vinny's tone made him recall his friend's wedding story. Two years previously, Vinny had been caught by surprise when he spotted a stunning blonde while he was dancing with Carla, his new bride! When their eyes met, he experienced a depth of emotion he'd never known existed – as if lightning had struck, were his own words. Vinny had claimed that it had not been a superficial infatuation. He couldn't make it to Vinny's wedding because his brother had been diagnosed with terminal cancer.

That had plunged him into a deep depression. After Vinny's divorce, his friend admitted for the first time that the dance floor incident at his wedding had occupied his mind far more than he thought...saying that that was why his marriage to Carla had disintegrated within six months. After his disastrous marriage, he had no illusions about love at first glance.

"What makes you think Sascia is the one?" Since Vinny had blamed his divorce on the fact that he had constantly been thinking about the mystery girl at his wedding party, he confided that after his mysterious encounter, something had happened that had created a sense of loss.

"I know, don't remind me. I've never found out who the girl was on the dance floor at my wedding. She was gone before I could probe."

Over Vinny's shoulder, he spotted Wim climbing into a green Opel. He would love to chat with him, although he was mysterious. Something about him triggered his energy levels. Very quiet, as if there was something else listening at the same time. Not like Wim's girlfriend, Zola de Boer, a flirty, light-hearted female who could dress to kill.

"Now that the practice is successful, I want to settle and start a family. Strangely enough, Sascia reminds me of her, not in looks, but in character." his friend was half muttering to himself as he climbed into his vintage sports car and waved goodbye.

Sudden hunger pangs reminded Richard that he had skipped breakfast and now lunch. Before driving home, he must get something from Utrecht's Station Mall.

Driving Home to Apeldoorn

After he collected his lecture schedule at the faculty office, his mind drifted back to the talk. Gosh, if what Trevor Zwiegelaar had explained held truth, he'd better look at his research material.

Richard took the A1 to Apeldoorn while the thought-provoking topic of 'Chambers and Passageways into the Future' lingered. The same Trevor had spoken over the radio a few weeks previously. Occasionally, Theo, his brother, mentioned the name Trevor Zwiegelaar when they used to have beer on the balcony of his flat in Apeldoorn. The memory of Theo's passing made him turn on the radio to distract his mood.

Heavy raindrops started to hit the car roof when the radio announcer interrupted the popular hit tunes from the nineties with a special bulletin...

"**Building developments at the Pleasure Parks construction site in France have stopped due to the kidnapping**"...

He almost didn't see the car in front making a last-minute decision to slow down to make a left-hand turn. He pushed his brake pedal flat on the floor to avoid a collision. The word 'kidnapping' still lingered when his adrenalin rush settled down. The windscreen wipers worked ferociously through the downpour when radio Utrecht filled his car interior again.

"**This violent incident has been the result of trouble that has been brewing for a while. These new events will probably expose many disturbing facts about the whole area of the estate, which is now under investigation by Interpol and the Green Peace movement. The rumours of high deposits of gold that had shown up in the readings of two geologists recently could have triggered the latest development.**"

Gosh! Ingrid Barendse worked for Pleasure Parks. He met her at the genetic decoding workshops he joined in April. He recalled the aerial photo on the CD she had given him to look at a few weeks back.

An announcement about Trevor Zwiegelaar arriving at the studio...but a call on his cell phone muted the radio, so he missed the introduction of Trevor Zwiegelaar. Damn!

"Richard speaking."

He now needed all his wits about him driving through a torrential downpour. He got distracted by the electronic billboard, which kept flashing the revolving words.

Philanthropist shot; fighting for his life! -

Then Connie's voice came over the car speakers. "Richard, do not forget to pick up the shopping from Nel."

Connie de Wit, a vibrant nineteen-year-old, was his assistant in the coffee bar The Pannekoek, which he managed for his aunt Mien Jaarsma, who was on holiday in South Africa.

"Thanks; I'll try to collect Nel, our cook's request, on the way home; see you tomorrow." When he ended the call, the radio rang alive again...

"Currently, a full-scale search is underway for the kidnappers, causing the postponement of construction of a sizable dodecahedron-shaped dome..."

Trevor's masterful voice was under distress.

"Mr Zwiegelaar, have the kidnappers made any demands yet that will explain why" ...

He lost the rest of the conversation when a truck hooted a loud warning to a cyclist about to cross the intersection in the pouring rain.

"We wish to make our listeners aware of the impending changes in Earth's electromagnetic energy flow. Much more is at stake at this particular site in France, and what has happened now with the...

" His radio again disconnected, regardless of an incoming call he had blocked...It was Connie again; he could see it by the number. Oh well, he'd phone her from the flat.

" Our goal is to uncover various conspiracies cleverly concealed from the masses. These revelations will ultimately impact all of humanity. We aim to inform the conscious and aware public and question the strange practices people have been engaging in for centuries."

Richard knew what the man was referring to, but what did the Pleasure Parks complex have to do with the whole affair? He had spoken to Ingrid over the phone about this new building site. His radio was affected by the thunderstorm because it started to crackle.

"So, a holographic island will be installed at the resort, generating quantum energy waves to promote a deeper sense of self-awareness for visitors. This hologram island aims to awaken visitors to new levels of awareness?"

Oh no! His radio crackled again, now that the interviewer had asked something interesting...

"To explain the origin of your current source of chi, which is electromagnetic energy in nature, we must delve a little into Earth's history. Millions of years ago, earth's energy supply was only magnetic" ...

Frustrated, he turned his unstable car radio off as he knew it was affecting his driving. Ingrid Barendse had shown an image from her laptop at the coffee bar. It was a photo taken from a great height. It showed a crop-circle pattern on the ground that resembled the Eye of Horus, a well-known Egyptian symbol. It covered the whole estate where 'The Pleasure-Parks holiday resort consortium was building the new leisure complex. The photo had aroused his curiosity.

The enormous geodesic dome, as they had in Cornwall, would cover the whole eye image. Ingrid spoke to him last week, and she mentioned that there were problems with the dome and that her boss's house, Mr. Brinks, had been robbed. He was curious about the connection between the kidnapping and the person they took.

He switched the radio back on when he arrived in the street where he lived to hear the radio announcer thanking Mr Trevor Zwiegelaar for his willingness to talk at such short notice.

Richard's flat in Apeldoorn

At his late brother Theo's flat, he stumbled over a pile of clothes for the laundrette; all he could think of was the aerial photo with that symbol. Clothes, books and more paperwork muffled a penetrating ringing sound. Gosh, he did need to clean up! Which reminded him of Nel's juice extractor and her shopping, which he'd forgotten to collect.

"Richard speaking," he gasped after locating the portable phone under the pile of papers. All he heard was heavy breathing. Sensing someone swearing momentarily, but then he was cut off. That was all he needed: a wrong number!

His whole body was stiff from sitting at the computer for four hours. He almost knocked his coffee mug over his keyboard. He decided to check his e-mail and go to bed. An email had just come in, and he was startled to see the name T. Zwiegelaar.

——- Original Message ——-
From: "T Zwiegelaar"
To: <R de Jong:;>
Subject: Thank you
Dear Mr de Jong

Thank you for the invitation to your lecture on the seventh of this month. I'm sorry that I cannot attend as I will be in Zurich that day. First, I would like to express my sadness about the departure of your brother, Theo de Jong, whom I greatly admired. He was a diligent researcher and an expert in his field. A relative told me that you are following in his footsteps. I was disappointed to have missed your trip to Egypt in October last year. I heard it was well organized. I met your father long ago in Egypt and would like to get acquainted with you soon. I will contact you shortly to discuss your fascinating interpretations. Thank you for sharing your unusual insights.

Regards.
Trevor.Zwiegelaar

Talk about coincidence; the man knew both Theo and his dad! He suddenly remembered that Annelies' maiden name from his decoding workshop was also Zwiegelaar. It was a very uncommon name. They must be related.

After making himself a late snack, he returned to his brother's PC to look up some files to support his coming lecture. The rain had stopped, and the sounds of frogs applauding Mother Nature triggered his spirit of adventure. He would have loved to reply to Trevor, but his intuition told him to go to bed, so he disconnected his phone.

Whenever the anticipation of a dream journey overcame him, he knew he would meet Theo during his astral travels. This year, he conducted most of his historical research in the early morning hours after jotting down his dreams upon waking up. These days, he moved out of his body quite naturally compared to the first time.

He vividly recalled the first time he had experienced consciously leaving his body. Just before he drifted off...the dot within the circle came into his mental view...Theo and his memory took over...

• • • •

Something unusual was going on inside his body. It seemed as if he were loose. He felt almost as if he were getting smaller, and yet another part of him was getting larger. His body became a tingling sensation. The vibrational feelings that penetrated right through everything startled him at first...but... when he found himself suspended in space and saw his body still on the bed...feelings of sheer terror gripped him. As he suspected what happened, he felt his heart palpitate. He had read about astral travelling, but he was nevertheless stunned...

The room appeared very bright, as if the evening sun shone! This weird awareness grappled him as he grasped that he saw everything simultaneously! Then, a robust and merry laugh from somewhere told him he was not alone. A grey substance that took on a human shape became increasingly accurate. For a second, he wondered if he was dreaming because Theo looked the same as when they had last been camping together. He somehow sensed that Theo was enjoying his surprise.

"What happened to me? I surely did not die?" His thoughts shouted in silence. The figure of a man who looked like his brother came closer and placed his hands on his forehead. Theo's hands...felt very real...and firm! His emotions somersaulted, questioning if this was for real!

"Theo, is that you?" Feelings of great joy overwhelmed him. He was shaking his brother's shoulders to satisfy himself. Theo was alive!

"How are you? What are you doing? Why am I here? Did you help me get out of my body?" His mind raced, not comprehending what he was seeing.

"Hi buddy, I had to give you plenty of shuffles! Don't worry, I'm fine and having a great time, as you will see for yourself."

Had he honestly heard those words? He again looked back down at his own physical body lying on the bed. There he was, apparently asleep and seemingly unaware of what had happened! Then something changed in his eyes! His body on the bed looked darker and felt queer and faint, as if nothing was solid anymore. Was he moving into his own body? His mind had to get used to new surroundings, adjusting to the unfamiliar scenery. A faint luminous glow came from his physique, which spread through all the flesh and even the sheets and became transparent. It was a weird sensation. He was staring right through his body!

"Yep, this is how you would look if you already had X-ray eyes. Clairvoyants have these perceptions developed, and there are many degrees and stages. Our fleshly form is condensed energy that moves in a grid of vertical and horizontal flowing pulsations." When Theo placed his hands over his forehead again, Richard saw that his body was getting fainter and more ethereal looking, and it extended further outside his skin, which he found rather beautiful. Something was in constant movement while he heard a penetrating beat of what, his heart?

"Well, yes and no. You observe your life force as a moving, pulsating current. This essence of life flows through the living ether like your blood that runs through your veins!" He bent closer. His body on the bed started to look ghostlike. The shimmering light-blue/green colour that was once his flesh became tiny interlaced threads that, like a spider's web, took on the shape of a human form. Peering even nearer, he saw millions of conductor tubes through which a pale blue/green light raced backwards and forward. Was that him?

"You bet everything that uses chi: humans, animals and plants all have these life force currents that activate matter. Everything is energy! it's your double or... let's call it the etheric double, which acts as a conductor." With astonishment, he observed the incredible beauty of his body but from a very different viewpoint. He was pretty satisfied with his six-foot medium-frame physical form. He had an almost constant-suntanned look, and women loved his thick, wavy, dark-brown shoulder-length hair, but this!

"Theo, is my mind seeing this? Where is my mind, in the past or...?" Oh, all his book reading had not prepared him for this phenomenon. "Richie, learn first to see your etheric form as an elemental being."

He was so confused; how real was all this? "Richie, before I left, I was given a glimpse of how I would assist you from behind the veil."

Did he hear Theo speak? Amazingly, he saw clouds of grey mist shapes passing by in his bedroom!

"Come, I will show you. Let's take your new experience slowly." Theo took his hand and almost pushed him inside one of these formless shapes that seemed to move past them. He was startled at what he saw. A misty human shape was appearing inside these ghostly shapes. Like his own! What he saw must be the essence of a being!

"You've got it. The etheric body contains the sensory or physical body, like a core. This essence is the densest in vibration." When he looked back at his body, suddenly, everything looked smoky. What was happening?

"Hey, now we are looking like ghosts!" Gosh, how weird!

"Richie, I will try to answer all your questions and introduce you to POWAH, but you must first get familiar with your inner space travel arrangements. I'll help you stimulate your holographic sight, an extension of your physical sight. Once your mind has adjusted, it will start interrelating what you experience from now on." He kept thinking about how he got to do it...having an out-of-body experience. Was he inside his dream?

"Richie, you can come directly to this plane of consciousness where I will be waiting. Now, you must look back into the etheric plane, directly below it, for a better term. Watch!" Wow, everything seemed to light up, like rays of coloured lights, interlacing, mixing, separating, and blending. It reminded him of kaleidoscope patterns. Even the grey, smoky substance when he peered at Theo's astral body was complete in every detail. Even what looked like clothes were glowing like a light bulb.

"Are you going on a hike somewhere? I see you are wearing your hiking clothes?" Was Theo for real?

"Oh, am I? Gosh, I've given no thought to what I was wearing," Richard marvelled at how they conversed. It was as if he was talking to himself, but mentally.

"Theo, did I unknowingly make that up?" The way they communicated astonished him.

"Yep, your mental body immediately manifests your thoughts on this plane. In your physical reality, it's called telepathy. On the fourth dimension, the mental field translates thoughts into *colourful, moving symbols. So be aware!* Any thought projection materialises in the astral matter, but it's nothing like physical matter; it is much finer and much higher vibration. Here, every thought creates astral matter, whereas on the physical plane, what one sees with one inner sight – if empowered by strong emotion, turns into physical matter. "Were those his brother's thoughts he heard? He could feel that his life force was pulsating from pure awesomeness.

"You are still 'the doubting Thomas', aren't you? Where do you want to go?"

"Go where?

"I don't know. I'll leave it to you," Theo formulated words silently. Seeing him alive and standing in his bedroom filled him with a sense of certainty that anything was possible. However, he hesitated to move, unsure if it was real. When he saw Theo leaving through the window, he hoped his brother did not expect him to travel along!

"Buddy, get used to the idea that the force of gravity is gone on this astral plane!" He saw Theo's swirling energy form, shooting out colours as he moved. Theo laughed. Richard got used to the idea that his brother could read his thoughts. He observed that some colours moved with him as well.

"You are confused between our auras, but I am impressed with yours. I sense that you haven't found the right partner yet." Theo's proper girlfriend remark made him mentally squint intently into the atmosphere.

"Tell me, what do you see?" while trying to distinguish between the eddying colours of his light bubble and the brilliance of his brother.

"Richie, on the higher astral planes, your soul blends with the mental and emotional planes. Those colours you see mingling are your emotions. You will learn about that in the decoding workshop *you will soon join. Come along, let's go."* He felt Theo's hand in his. Suddenly, the sensation of travelling at high speed followed. As they moved away, many formless shapes passed by.

"We call them earth souls; leave them for now. There is much to explore already." Then, a void of nothingness engulfed him; he clutched onto Theo for dear life.

"Theo, I would like to get back again!" Hoping his brother would understand.

"You are attached to your physical, bud, aren't you? Stop worrying, look!" a thin glowing coil danced behind him like a kite tail in the wind. So, it was true! It was the silver cord he had read about! The sense of incredible speed, for there was no headwind or any resistance at all, abruptly stopped! He sensed a seriousness coming from Theo.

"Before we go any further, I want you to think and observe, then ask yourself, 'Who are you?'" For a second, he felt numb, and then he knew.

"I'm all of this simultaneously!" Theo's eyes filled with love. He intuitively knew he'd passed a test.

"Yes, you have; it's of the utmost importance that you are awake to this state of being. If you were not, your Soul would not have been strong enough to travel in these inner spiritual realms while having a physical body." As he heard those thoughts, he felt himself glowing, as if he had become light.

"Buddy, you have just created a light body to travel in, congratulations. "Really? How did he formulate a light body?

"It's through a love force. You must first strengthen this experience to recall the adventures of your spiritual journeys. Let's go!" Again, a sensation of speed overtook him.

"Astral matter must give your mental body the impression of terrific speed. Here, it makes no difference because we travel by thought!"

"*Whose thoughts?*" he pondered when suddenly he observed tall houses over. Rotterdam! He recognised the harbour! But the period was wrong. The streets reminded him of old photos. And should it not be dark? After all, it was evening.

"*Now, now come, there is no night or day here. What you see is heavenly light. Those in physical embodiments, their astral part is asleep when they are awake in the sensory world. Soon, you will join Annelies's body codes of light workshop and learn more. For now, let's go and do some inner space exploring,*"

This woman, Annelies, must have been an exceptional friend. He wondered if Theo could see into the future because, looking around him, it looked like a scene from the past.

"*Gosh, Richie, there is no concept of time; Time is an adaptation to speed! Past and future aren't separate locations. Our Over-Soul stores our genetic records of a physical incarnation with the Akashic record keeper, which is your Higher Self.*" As those thoughts penetrated his mind, he wondered if his Soul was as aware of this realm as he was mindful of the physical. Theo mentally replied.

"*Annelies' decoding workshop will help you observe your akashic libraries to reconnect with your genetic lineages consciously. Her workshop is all about a card game with a difference; it's to awaken star seeds, light workers and walk-ins. I will gradually explain the difference between the three conscious embodiments and the many other dimensions. Don't ask any questions just yet. Let's first see how well you can move your butt in the astral.*"

Wow, he marvelled at how real it all appeared. The harbour city's pavements were busy, but this did not make any difference to Theo as they joined other pedestrians. Whenever he wanted to jump out of the way, he kept losing his sense of balance. Theo just walked through people! He had to try it, but the idea was strange! Richard saw a woman walking towards him hurriedly;

whoosh! he did it! ... It felt like he was passing through a small, formless cloud of mist. One minute, he was in it, then through it! He was slowly getting the hang of it!

When Richard peeked at Theo, he observed a different set of clothes! His brother grinned.

"So, you noticed? I was wondering how long it would take. I changed because the moment one thinks of an outfit, it immediately manifests." Richard thought of his ex-wife, Ellie, who was obsessed with clothes. Gosh, she would have had fun here!

"That is where she remembers it from,"

"What do you mean?" Did others do this but never tell him?

"Everyone visits different levels of the astral planes during sleep depending on the awareness level of the dreamer, but most don't remember any of it because the Soul is confused by the first lower levels with distorted thoughts. That's why nightmares or confusing dreams discourage the Soul from investigating." Richard knew that it could mean many things when he recalled dreams or just the symbols, but to experience it like this made it so much more real!

"Richie, I'm preparing you for our coming assignment. Don't ask too many questions; experience what you perceive for now. Later, it will make more sense. Remember, time is not an issue as everything happens now." Theo had placed his hands over his eyes again for him to focus on his mental eye, as he called it. Suddenly, he was drawn inside a tubular vortex, again moving at a terrific speed.

"What I'm showing you is from the Akashic records of an individual Soul within our ancestral lineage. We are observing the records of one embodiment upon the Earth plane. Just observe." He saw a stocky man in old-fashioned mining gear bending over what looked like mummies.

"That's right! During World War II, thieves stole mummies from royal cemeteries on the west bank of the Nile across from

Luxor." Where was this old, dark, and dusty workplace? It was not in the Valley of the Kings. He wondered what was so special about these rows of mummies. It was fantastic to be an observer. The older man was carefully removing the bandages!

"Watch for the gold foil sheets that are underneath. This English archaeologist knew that the symbols on these ancient, fragile sheets, dated before the original Sumerian pictographs, contained important information about our genetic lineages." Very carefully, the man removed the foil. It was so brittle; He was puzzled about deciphering the embossed writing on the brittle surface. The man didn't have the equipment they had today. Did Theo mean that these mummies dated back to before the Archaic period?

"Yes! Remember that I always searched for recorded scripts on what happened during the last cosmic closure."

"No, not really. Richard remembered an old historical record inscribed on palm leaves inherited from their dad. What he saw now was completely different.

"All these embossed sheets have the Language of Light symbols engraved, which we now know are dated from an earlier Atlantean age. Did you know that the Old Babylonian dialect remained undocumented until much later?" Theo's excitement was contagious. With fascination, he studied the walls of the cave. Where were they? It felt as if he was somewhere where centuries of experimentation on human and animal bodies on the wall of the cave. Gold-painted glyphs that portrayed part human and animal figures were everywhere.

Looking back at the older man, the dust and grime of centuries were gently removed from a broken sheet under the bright floodlight of the miner's lamp onto the man's forehead.

"Every Soul passionate to awaken through the physical form will have to activate their immortal, etheric double, the original

blueprint." That sounded like a mammoth task. He wondered if the archaeologist knew they were watching him.

"*No, but nothing is a secret. Look closely.*" His mental eye could see the bending man had a yellowish moving mass that merged with other darker colours mixed with flecks of grey and black.

"*As you can see, his auric field corresponds to every thought and feeling as it gathers information. Richie, please remember what you saw when you wake up. Practice remembering! That's the most difficult challenge to master. Only then will you strengthen your etheric body*" How would he know if it was not just a silly dream?

"You will intuitively know. Learn to recall where you have been during dream time. When you travel back through the denser distorted maze of thought projections from other dreamers, the nearer you get back into your fleshy butt, the thicker the distortion." Theo's explanation encouraged him to touch the fragile-looking gold foil sheets. A Deja-vu reflection flooded his mind for a split second when he saw one of the symbols.

"*You will find that the symbols were of a primal seed language. We never considered that they were songs.*" Had he seen those gold-embossed sheets before?

"*Yes, you have.*"

At once, Theo made him recall the photos! They had suddenly appeared, so Theo had said. How could he have forgotten how laboriously they swatted over them together? His emotions accelerated.

"*Richie, we were recalling our experiences from a long-gone world. It withstood the test of time.*" What stood the test of time? Had Theo found out what was on the gold sheets? It felt like he was being drawn back to his body when he recalled his childhood. From the day his father took him into the Great

Pyramid at Giza and other temples when Richard was only four and Theo sixteen, Richard had been fascinated by ancient pictographic languages. Still, it felt like he knew the message! He heard Theo's mental chuckle.

"At some point, you will obtain the knowledge you are searching for, and I assure you that it will be at the appropriate time. Someone stored ancient knowledge, made of gold, in pure crystal skulls...." Now it was getting more fantastic. Crystal Skulls! If Theo knew the message, why didn't he?

"These crystal skulls carry the codes of this creation. Their information will awaken you to realise who you are and who you are not. Richie, this assignment for both of us will start soon."

He was still mulling over Theo's mental voice when he was back inside a spinning tube again, travelling at a terrific speed.

As he moved to a near-awakening awareness, he recalled that Ingrid had spoken about a guide named 'POWAH' who had contacted her through the computer, of all things! But she had been timid about revealing her experiences. After one of Annelies ' ascension workshop classes, they had all been having coffee at the Pannekoek.

He realised he was floating above his body and slipped back with a terrific jolt.

• • • •

As he stretched while looking at the clock... 7:30 a.m., he was stunned about his dream! It all came back! The old-fashioned clothes of the man, the mummies! Had he experienced an almost identical dream but had not remembered it before? Gosh, a lot had happened since that first astral travel experience, especially when his brother introduced him to POWAH, an Alpha and Omega council spokesperson for the Ninth astral sector. That's what Theo had said.

He remembered seeing and hearing Theo, but the rest was vague. He recalled Theo telling him his assignment on the second level of the body code of light's workshop had begun.

Traffic noises from early risers penetrated his mind while lying between his rumpled sheets. He still pondered in absolute disbelief. He did it! He knew that the vibrations that felt like gooseflesh worked! It had truly separated him from his body! He wondered how many other people used a similar technique.

He took a deep breath and tried the remote viewing skill. Theo taught him to remember what he would call a lucid dream.

The clear image of hieroglyphic symbols embossed on the golden sheets stirred his brain into action.

Three years ago, Theo told him that he had received six photos through the post. There was no sender address, but he recalled that they both had swatted for hours over each image of an enlarged palm leaf with symbols they thought were ancient Egyptian. Was the text unfamiliar because it was a seed language?

That thought got him. Theo had assigned a unique number to every photo he had stored. This detail was something that he remembered clearly. He got up, stumbled to the kitchen, switched on his juice maker and peeked through the vertical blinds. It was sunny.

Theo had assigned a unique number to every photo he had stored. This detail was something that he remembered clearly. A piece of paper with Theo's handwriting was attached, along with a title linked to a website with his name.

Tablet One

He recalled the symbols on the header to read: - The Prophet Game [1]

---

1. https://allrealityshifters.wordpress.com/richard-de-jong/tablet-one/

Each paragraph starts with a symbol, translated by Theo de Jong—to be a letter of the English alphabet, especially the third paragraph. It almost reads like poetry. He wondered who created the link to an online page.

< This symbol C I give my memoirs freely within these 22 tablets for the perfection of the whole so that the etheric blueprint will soon sing like an illuminating carol. >

Wow! He was flabbergasted. It had taken them ages to translate each symbol into the text that followed, but they could never understand it. As he read it repeatedly, he was amazed by the genetic map referral he thought to be the palm prints in everyone's hands! The symbols looked familiar.

They reminded him of last year when he had participated in a mind-drawing doodling course with Tieneke de Beer. She had often mentioned the Language of Light.

His analogue drawings started to look like the pictorial symbols from the Egyptian temples, but he could still not link this message.

Because they had fascinated him for as long as he could remember, he disregarded his mind-drawings. Theo must have got it, but he never shared it with him. He knew that Theo had explained it.

In his dream, was Theo implying that 'they' wrote the ancient symbolic text? He must have meant their swatting two years ago! No wonder Theo always appeared happy and content and readily accepted his diagnosis. He must have had a terrific revelation. When he intuitively heard,

"Everything that has manifested has a purpose." Trevor Zwiegelaar's lecture kept reminding him that they were all participating in the prophet's game of creation itself.

In his mind, he saw the magnificent and colourful Hieroglyphic drawings on the temple walls of Nubia when he heard the words, *"Undisputed evidence from a wealth of meticulously recorded sources verifies that together, the human race originates on planet Earth during her five previous evolution stages, arriving at the fifth post-Atlantean age.*

Chapter 2
The Dimensions of a Human Experience

Apeldoorn

The sun had disappeared, and threatening clouds guaranteed more rain as Richard drove to the Pannekoek coffee bar. The electronic billboard above Yolanda de Wit's bookshop with the heading: **'Pleasure-Parks new site in France has been sabotaged.'** got his attention.

The radio announcer who had interviewed Trevor the day before and the newsflash above **the 'Power of Words'** bookshop sign made him think of Ingrid again! He parked his Honda and sprinted past 'Pleasure-Parks complex. The coffee bar's phone shrilled for his attention as he disengaged the alarm censors. It was the wholesaler. He confirmed a large grocery order to be delivered the next day. The Pannekoek was getting busier towards the weekend due to many visitors to the palace Het Loo. It is one of the many popular tourist attractions near Apeldoorn. Connie had left everything from the day before in perfect order.

"Richard, please open, I'm getting wet!" Nel Hartman, his kitchen manager, called through the glass front door. She had joined his staff after his aunt had phoned from South Africa, asking if he could use her. His aunt still lived in South Africa while the farm murders were going on. He often wondered why she had not returned earlier to Holland during the bad times; He kept updated about what was happening there.

Nell was a close friend of his aunt, who had lost her job and was made redundant. Nell was in her early sixties, short and dumpy with a sense of humour, an absolute gift. She introduced many interesting new dishes. Because of her enthusiasm, employing her started to pay off. Aunty Mien would be pleased when she returned from South Africa in September. Now that the business was picking up, he needed to look for more help. Nell was commenting about the weather and asking about the juice extractor he was supposed to bring when she stacked her umbrella away. He made a weak excuse for his slip-up. Nell disappeared into the kitchen, shaking her head.

Connie was a bubbly, pretty girl but far too young for him. He would turn thirty-seven in August, which made him question his feelings towards Debbie Barendse, a stunning blonde with the most bottomless blue eyes he'd ever seen. He wasn't madly in love with her, which, for a change, had prevented him from sleeping with her.

He later wondered if he knew what being in love was like. It had been a short, passionate affair with Ellie that ended in her getting pregnant. When he took Zola to the movies, she reminded him of Ellie, coquettish and needy, even if she was interested in the same immortality philosophies. With her, the topic of immortality was probably just a buzzword she hooked onto for kicks. Not him. Although believable enough, he had always suspected that ageing and dying somehow smacked of a lie. What was the point of creating a species meant to evolve but within a ridiculously short lifespan? Even the scriptures mention that the human race lived for hundreds of years at one time.

The women who were all participating in the same ascension workshops, as Annelies called it sometimes, were, like him, genuinely inspired by her theories. He had joined Annelies' genetic decoding classes three months ago, and he especially enjoyed the women's company just as much as the few men, except for Wim and Zola. Those two were somehow out of place.

Vinny's new girlfriend's voice had triggered his curiosity, but she was taboo, being his friend's girlfriend. So...was he turning into a firm bachelor?

While he took the chairs from the tables, Nell asked, "Richard, when is your friend Liesbeth going to update the menu?"

"Oh, I forgot. Are there any more dishes you want to add?" Nell passed her the list they had discussed.

During the tour last October, he'd met Liesbeth Jaarsma, a very handsome, tall, dark-haired woman, in Egypt. She also lived in Apeldoorn. She was a freelance editor for a few magazines and had introduced Ingrid to him. Liesbeth, apart from Theo, made him curious about Annelies' unusual ascension workshops. Theo had always talked about Annelies, which reminded him that he would soon take over from Ingrid, writing a journal on the second level of Annelies Zwiegelaars' workshops. Gosh! Hadn't Theo said that his assignment on the second level had begun?

A brassy-looking female with a young boy and an older woman entered the coffee bar. The young woman reminded him of Zola. At first, he had been flattered by Zola's flirty behaviour, but her daring outfits and her neediness got to him. She was not his type. He turned on the music to liven up the place and went to the pantry while they decided what to order.

Nell poked her head around the kitchen door, reminding him to order olive oil because they were getting low.

When he returned from the pantry, he saw the flashy woman snooping behind the counter while the youngster kicked against the steel safe on the floor.

He was furious. The brassy girl looked familiar, but the heavy layers of face paint distracted his memory. He got rid of them quickly, catching the two in their snooping act. The older woman threw the menu at him and followed out the door.

He calmed down as he mulled over his dream. Last week, he confided to Liesbeth about his remote viewing abilities during Dreamtime. Many people would have been sceptical, but she accepted it as usual. He did not need to prove anything to others, only to himself, but she was the first woman friend he could be himself with.

As he switched on his aunt's old Pentium, the USB stick beside the monitor reminded him that Ingrid had never returned to fetch it last week.

He'd better take it home. Something about the images made him uneasy, but the phone stopped his brooding.

"The Pannekoek"

"Oh...Richard, have you heard?" Debbie's agitated voice cried out.

"Heard what?"

"Mom was kidnapped yesterday!"

Ingrid... kidnapped?

"What do you mean?" It was not like Debbie, her daughter, to be melodramatic, almost bordering on hysterical. Abductions belonged to the movies, after all!

"It all happened yesterday afternoon an hour away from Paris." sobs punctuated her words, and she gasped when Debbie related her mother's ordeal. The word 'kidnapping' and shooting on the radio and the bulletin newsflash jolted him back to Debbie's story. The philanthropist! Could it have been Toon Haardens, Ingrid's boyfriend, who got shot?

"Debbie, where are you phoning from?" The nerves in his gut tightened.

"I'm at the hospital. I'm on duty in the children's ward. I'm getting off at five, and then I'll revisit Toon. He's still in intensive care. Oh, Richard, I never knew about Mom and Toon. Toon is still very weak, and they all worry he might not make it. My sister dropped all her work and has gone up in a plane this morning with mom's boss, Mr Brinks, to take aerial photos of the area where she got abducted." Debbie's despair rubbed off. He liked Toon and Ingrid. He wondered what karma was playing out, thinking of Annelies' theories.

"Debbie, I'll contact Annelies. Can't I phone you back?"

"I don't know. We are not allowed cell phones in the wards. I will contact you after work. Annelies stayed with Toon all night while we stayed at Mr Brinks's home. I feel better for phoning you. Annelies, Toon's half-sister, told us not to say anything to anybody, but I needed to speak to someone, and I know you attend the same evening classes as my mom." Debbie's voice was quivering. Gosh, she must be near breaking point. Toon adored Ingrid. They seemed to have an attraction for each other that one could only dream about.

As he dialled Annelie's home line, he realised that all this had happened the previous day! Hans, her son, answered and called Liesbeth on the phone. Ingrid's lovely face flashed past his eyes. He could still not grasp that she was involved in any criminal plot.

"Hi Richard, can you come over?" Liesbeth's voice gave away her concern. He was so startled at her sudden request, and for a moment, he pondered what she was doing at Annelies' house.

"What, now? I've just spoken to Debbie, Ingrid's daughter. I've only just heard about the kidnapping. How is Annelies taking it?" Meaning that her half-brother, who seemed seriously wounded from a shooting that had landed him in intensive care, must have raised some questions for her.

The people in their Friday evening group had all become very close, almost like the family he had never really had. Apart from the decoding activities, which were fun, their discussions on immortality topics made him feel closer to Theo, whom he still missed big time.

This Friday's reading with Annelies will likely be postponed due to sudden disruption. He was still immensely curious how Annelies, with the help of POWAH, had written a genetic decoding method that could awaken them to full consciousness. At first, he had difficulty with POWAH, the higher guide entity. Still, gradually, he opened to the idea that there could be various levels of awareness within Annelie's unconscious mind that occasionally spoke through her as if it were a separate entity from her.

Her workshop had sounded wacky at first. Without Theo's involvement, he would never have gone for Tieneke's mind-drawing course and never heard about Annelies.

"Richard, I cannot talk over the phone. Can you come now? We need your help." Hans asked this time. Gosh, what did they need him for?

"Annelies stayed at the hospital late last night. She has just phoned to say that she will be home soon." Richard suspected Hans, Annelie's adopted son, was going out with Liesbeth. It seems that the speculations about his relationship with her were unfounded. How could he possibly be of any help? His thoughts turned to his lectures because his intuition said he would be unavailable. Where that strong idea came from was a mystery, but the hunch was very real. Cancelling this late was not appreciated. He knew Annelies would question him later but decided to take the risk anyway.

No wonder why Connie had not arrived for work! He knew she would be at her mother's bookshop around the corner.

After serving a customer coffee and cake, he dialled 'The Power of Words' bookshop. Yolanda, Connie's Mom, answered, and he asked after them both.

"Oh, Richard, sorry for not letting you know that Connie has been with me, but the phone has been going crazy since the police informed us about Toon and Ingrid. Annelies just phoned and asked if Connie could attend the coffee bar because she needs you. I have no idea what, but here is Connie." He could hear the tears in her throat.

"Richard, isn't it awful! Uncle Toon is terrible! Annelies asked me to help you out! She wants your assistance on something. Shall I come now and work the whole day?"

Connie's otherwise bubbly personality sounded gloomy. She showed up twenty minutes later.

Liesbeth asked him how much he already knew when he arrived at Annelie's house. He told her what he had heard from Debbie and the newsflashes. Both Hans and Liesbeth shared what they learned from Annelies. Richard was stunned at the details of Ingrid's abduction and ruthless treatment, which smacked of an American movie!

"What can I do?"

"Richard, you told me you can regularly project your consciousness out of your body?" Richard looked intently at her serious face as he sat across from her on the leather settee. He was unsure what she hinted at or how well he could direct his mental travelling. It did not always happen when he wanted it to, either.

"You want me to look for her? I have to know where to look. I'm never sure how accurate my memories are, but I'll give it a try."

"Thanks. We overreact somewhat to the horrible events but are all at wit's end. Any suggestions on how we could find Ingrid?"

"No, not really. I can project my mind out of my body and deposit my consciousness into my etheric double, as some would call it, but how would I look for Ingrid?" Hans consoled her, noting that those two seemed to be hitting it off well. Liesbeth was a beautiful and intelligent woman, but somehow, she was unapproachable. Hans didn't seem to have any problem on that score. Although older, he appeared to have uncanny pearls of wisdom and poise he knew he lacked.

"Richard, Hans and I can help you, but I'm unsure how to explain."

"Try me! I mean, clarify!" He'd wondered if it was possible to ask for Theo's help. Could one do anything from the other dimensions? But then why not try it? Until now, he had never succeeded in remembering anything valuable without Theo's help.

"Richard, both Liesbeth and I have discovered a frequency band where there is a peak of uncontrolled thoughts that emanate from all living forms on Earth. We can move to that point of those frequency zones with our minds and bypass them." He tried to grasp what Hans meant.

"We found out where we can pass through all the human mind activity zones to enable us to reach the light pulsations Ingrid is naturally projecting."

Hans's face suddenly reminded him of the heretic pharaoh Akhenaten except for the thick mop of white hair, which created an odd feel to the already bizarre conversation. All he could do was frown in puzzlement.

"Richard, Ingrid and Toon are in constant telepathic communication. We can connect directly to their Earth-related human mind projections. Ingrid is projecting powerful pulsations because she is pregnant! We can create a thought-form doorway, but please don't ask how! We'll tell you one day, but not now." Liesbeth's air of sophistication that Nefertiti, Akhenaten's wife, carried appeared odd next to Hans' wild look.

"Ingrid is pregnant!"

"Please don't even mention it to anybody. Annelies only told us because of the urgency of the situation. Toon promised Ingrid to keep it a secret until she had medical confirmation. He proposed to Ingrid umpteen times."

"Do her children know?"

"No, and don't you tell them."

"What do you both mean by a doorway?"

"Mmm, are you willing to try? We're unsure if our effort will do any good, Richard, because nobody has ever tried what we have in mind. Would you be willing to let us use you? "Hans was also having doubts while Liesbeth's eyes looked pleadingly. Richard observed how unusual these two were. Hans was what one would call a genius. His looks also reminded him of Trevor Zwiegelaar. There was a similar bone structure with a long nose.

They heard the front door, and Annelies and a man walked in. Annelies' otherwise charismatic posture seems worn out, but there was a glow on her face when she introduced Ben Jaarsma, her husband. Hans greeted them both with affection.

"I'm glad to meet you, Richard. I hope you can be of some help." Ben's penetrating stare made him doubt even more if he could.

"Liesbeth, I have heard about you driving home in the car. We are all very proud to have you in our family." Ben's remark was loaded with a sound of surprise while holding her hands. He was the same height as Annelies, with cropped grey hair and eyes that confirmed an active mind. Richard wondered where he had been all those weeks. Annelies wanted to know if Liesbeth and Hans had already spoken to him.

While they all helped themselves to coffee and bread rolls that Annelies had prepared in the kitchen, she brought them up to date. Joris, Toon's young Labrador, showed his pleasure as he patted him. Liesbeth said that Joris knew something had happened to Toon.

"Early this morning, Toon seemed stable, but his doctor was not pleased. He's out of intensive care and in a room on his own but still attached to the latest life-support unit. Toon was alert enough to send Sascia, Ingrid's daughter, the photographer, and Harry Brinks, Ingrid's boss, up in his aeroplane this morning to fly over the site where he lost the van with Ingrid. It was to take aerial photos. We just came home to pack some fresh clothes and drive back to stay at Harry's place again tonight." Ben and Hans were comparing notes while Annelies withdrew into herself at the breakfast counter.

"Harry and I.... let's say we are very old friends. When Harry received a call from one of the kidnappers in the middle of the night, he heard Ingrid screaming. According to him, the creeps were physically abusing her! I don't want to even think about it. He had to get two missing flash drives from Ingrid's office. Ingrid and Toon's lives are in danger if he does not immediately respond." Annelies' tears said the rest. Liesbeth held onto Annelie's clenched fists. Harry Brinks owned the Pleasure-Parks holiday consortiums that much he knew from Ingrid.

Ben returned from outside and asked if Hans could give her an energy boost. Richard wondered what sort of treatment that was. The name Sascia made him recall the sophisticated voice of Vinny's girlfriend.

"Annelies, did Harry...Mr. Brinks get the flash drives?"

"Yes, he did. Ben went with Harry to copy sets and add a message with an infrared tracking device on them. Harry deposited them at the appointed meeting place. He was lucky they did nothing to him. I haven't told Toon any of this as he would only get more determined to walk out of that hospital to fly his plane. "They were all silent for a moment, digesting the latest developments.

"Annelies, have you also been telepathically in contact with Ingrid?"

"Yes, Toon and I can intercept her thought projections with the help of Liesbeth." Annelies glanced affectionately up at her. He was fascinated with their mental communications.

"Ingrid is over her fear, so her barrier is gone, but she is in pain. We have to find her soon. I hate to think what those creeps are doing to her. By the way, the police have no idea that we are in communication, and nobody must ever find out, as that could be dangerous for Ingrid." Annelies' despairing voice while resting her elbows on the kitchen bench overwhelmed everyone. It was so unlike her.

"Annelies, may I use one of your bedrooms? I have never done remote viewing during the daytime, but that shouldn't make any difference. I only hope I'm as focused as I can be. I'll see if I can reach my brother."

Annelies took him to a spare bedroom. The first item that greeted him was the large Star-map painting above the double bed. It reminded him of the ceiling paintings on the roof of the tombs in the Valley of the Kings in Luxor.

"Take as long as you need, and if you fall asleep, that's okay too. Richard, have no expectations, focus. Theo and I had long discussions about many things. Did you know his interest in the castle's history that became the Prinsengracht Hotel?" Annelies' was staring out the window, but her voice revealed a closeness she must have had with Theo. The rain had cleared, and the sunny view streaming into the bedroom calmed his nerves.

"Theo often talked about you. I became interested in your ascension workshops, but he never spoke about the hotel's history. I didn't know until recently that Connie, your niece, is connected to the hotel., but Theo told me about your card game.

"Really?" Annelies stared into space as if she was far away while he took off his shoes and sat on the bed. She asked how Theo had been before he left. She and Ben had gone over to Australia during that time. He told her how Theo prepared him to accept his choice to leave when he still appeared healthy. That was the hardest, not being there for him at the end. It was still difficult to reconcile himself with Theo's decision to book himself into a clinic. In a way, he had felt left behind, deserted.

"After Theo had gone, I went into a depression. He contacted me months later while I was trying to fall asleep. I've never been out of my body before, and as my mother had died of Leukemia, I felt rather left behind, I suppose." Gosh, what made him so sentimental?

"How old were you when your mom died?" Annelies sat next to him on the bed.

"I was twelve. Theo lived in India then but came home and cared for my father and me. My father joined my mother six months later. Without her, he lost the will to live. I moved in with my aunty Mien, who owns the Pannekoek coffee bar." Annelies's eyebrows shot up.

"You are related to Mien du Toit?" Richard observed how her dark-brown eyes were expressing some revelation.

"Mien du Toit is my mother's sister. I never knew any other family members because my parents lived mostly overseas. My dad was a historian stationed in Africa and later Egypt for many years. We all came back to Holland when my mother became ill. I was about ten, and Theo was then already twenty-two." Annelies listened attentively.

"The first time I met Aunty Mien was when she visited my mother in Holland. She had emigrated to South Africa with her children after her divorce. Later, she came back to live in Holland with her daughter Sonja. That's how I came to live with her."

"Richard, did your mother or aunt ever talk about her other two brothers?"

"Not really; I knew I had another family because Aunty Mien mentioned her twin brothers, who she visited due to a fake pandemic scare that was threatening to control the human population on a massive scale mentally." He shrugged his shoulders. His resistance to digging into old family memories still prevailed. After he moved in with Theo before he left, they sometimes discussed why their parents cut ties with their family.

"Richard, Ben, my husband, is one of the twins! He's your uncle!" Annelies' distraction by that revelation became serious again as she returned to the matter of Ingrid's plight.

"Richard, I'd better leave you now, but one day, I will show you the names I have discovered on the chart of a family tree I showed you all in class." As she said that, Annelies stared up at the star painting.

"Now, more puzzle pieces are slotting into position," she murmured.

When Annelies left, he was too stunned to think straight. Was Annelies referring to the star-map painting? Ben was his uncle? He had a family he never knew about right on his doorstep.

As he lay in his underpants on top of the duvet, arms under his head stretched out, his thoughts reeled. How could he establish what was valid that he recalled from his dreams? Theo used to warn people not to enter into the super sensory realms boldly without proper training. He was very adamant that if someone was weak in his willpower to control addictive behaviour in the physical realms, lack of talent to make a valid assessment in the etheric realms could be unsafe. He warned about entities that would infuse the unaware soul with fantasy images useless to that person's awakening. He was so aware of his doubts he wondered if that was an obstacle. Having never attempted to travel astrally at someone's house and during daylight, he wondered if it would work, so he focused on his breathing.

• • • •

He knew he had fallen asleep because it was getting dark, and someone had pulled a blanket over him. He focused again on his breathing until he felt familiar pins and needles going over into the vibration that gave him a feeling of spinning, and then he rolled and whirled out.

He knew that he was more than a physical body, more than physical matter, and deeply desired a complete understanding of the energy systems in which he felt so consciously immersed.

"I'm asking the supreme Source of All for protection and guidance at all times from any source that might provide me with less than I desire," he prayed, still somewhat apprehensive at the same time, marvelling at his ability to transform his consciousness into his etheric copy body, as he called it. It still amazed him that he could be free from his physical tomb.

The room had an airy feeling, very different from his flat. The smell of the woods nearby was far more potent, and he heard more natural sounds than traffic. Theo said there appears to be more distortion between one's dream-time experience and the memory of it as recorded just before waking up when living in built-up areas. He stared at the ceiling as he recalled Theo's explanations. The distortions or veils by thought forms activate the illusion of the third dimension. The denser the population, the more unintelligible dream recollections were. As a result, little has value unless the higher self is awake enough to bring it clearly into the conscious mind. He read that dreams are sent through the silver cord from the light body via the etheric body back to the physical form for interpretation. Theo called the subconscious mind a storage space that edits and distorts the experiences. It still baffled him to think that what he called reality was an illusion.

• • • •

"*Hey buddy, will you stay in your mind or focus on your etheric manifestations?*"

Theo's familiar vibrational signature startled his contemplations. His shimmering light bubble overpowered the room. As always, his mind soared at the freedom. The memory of mummies flashed past him for a split second, but then Ingrid's plight took priority.

"*Theo! Can you help me find Ingrid?*" His anxiety for Ingrid's predicament flared up.

"*Richie, there are many forms of unconscious acts which damage one's multidimensional body.*" Theo plunged into a sombre mood. What was he implying? "*Richie, there are things you need to know before we look for Ingrid. I'll take you to POWAH's classrooms first.*" Theo was wearing a white robe.

"*Are we going to a Greek seminar?*" he joked as he followed him out of the room.

"*Very good! Take my hand; we will be joining many others. Some are like you, astral travelling, and some come from…oh, never mind, come.*" They left Annelie's home like two birds. The sensation of speed and a subtle breeze as if he were travelling through air enveloped him. He decided to try imagining himself wearing the same robe. The sensation of blending himself with Earth's elemental realm was extraordinary. Merging with the plant kingdom had an almost drowning effect. Trees and shrubs became a sea of moving entities. What a strange awareness to feel his energy field blending with forms he knew as plants.

A vague humming sound alerted him into a state of attentiveness. Suddenly, they were other light beings. Theo's nearness gave him tremendous comfort; he felt like an angel.

"I like your tunic; it's very sexy, I must say," Theo's chuckle made him look down. His robe only came to his knees, which wouldn't do so, so he visualised it longer. Suddenly, the centre podium lit up. The humming sound receded until it was dead quiet. He could hear his own... what, pulse? An astonishing light being appeared. The energy that POWAH emanated was phenomenal, not to mention the sound.

"Those are soundwaves from the Language of Light. They will telepathically formulate into symbols or words. Richie, listen to the tones without expectations. Just be aware of their feelings. "He followed Theo's advice. The melodies became images at first, then a voice.

—*Beloved ones, greetings from the God/ Goddess of light. Together, let us hold our focus on Gaia -Earth. My temple has many dimensions, but regarding the present transformation on Earth, let us focus on the physical, etheric and astral levels, which will soon unite, creating a new consensus reality.* —

POWAH's glance triggered a sensation. He received an instant download of information flooding his mind.

"Richie, spiritual science is only given in a language of symbolic signs. Those who wish to learn to communicate with their soul energy must first learn to understand this symbolic language."

Was that the idea? The shapes he visualised through hearing their sounds became a thousand words. He now started to understand how a mind drawing could do the same. Were the shapes and movements filtered into his mind through sound?

"*POWAH speaks from the realm where ideas originate from.*" Theo's explanation stunned him.

"*You say the Language of Light reflects our feelings stored in pictorial images?*" Was he translating the sounds the same way as he would when looking at art or listening to music?

"*Yes, I like your interpretation. In your journal, on the second level of the awakening journey, you must write about how a new set of rules awakened you to play the game of life.*" Theo's mental beam, or so he thought, catapulted him back above his body. What rules was Theo referring to? Again, he heard the musical soundwave that his mind translated into a sentence...

< *Human beings can tap into their power by remembering their divinity. Your soul will slowly awaken into the many different dimensions and reconnect with the fragmented parts of all that makeup YOU. Through the Language of Light, you will become aware of the genuine oneness with all that is. By knowing you can have it all, you activate your supra-sensory soul vortices and your chakras, so they once again will rotate and resonate with the universal pulse that manifests this holographic illusion you all call reality.* >

He could take it all in on a certain level, but how does one activate chakras? He didn't even know or feel them...or did he?

<*When you dream, your consciousness taps into the universal mind. With practice and diligence, your higher mind can translate this information. Your sacred service is needed to work with the many power points activated on the planet. The mighty vortex in both hemispheres must be re-opened so that many initiates can ascend through this porthole, which bridges many dimensions.* >

Was he hearing all this? Was this for real? Was POWAH speaking about the eye symbol? Theo nodded. He saw so many different light bodies around. Some were more transparent, others...more...solid. Were they like him, out of their physical body?

< There is much before you, and with visionary eyes, I see that many of you will have to release attachment cords with your intellectual or religious beliefs that have taken control over your beings. Many are searching for truth but miss it. I also see great joy and salute and bless you for what you have all dedicated yourselves to. In physical embodiments, you will soon see that everything in the third dimension still reflects the complete manifestation of the god/goddess of all that is. >

Richard truly felt an immense unconditional love coming from POWAH. The unity with everyone as if they belonged together made his spirit force accelerate in bliss.

< Through your efforts to map the ascension journey, the planet will ascend towards a faster speed, and nobody will be left behind. You will soon know how to reactivate a magnetic link with other star systems. One can no longer fantasize about something without manifesting it in this lifetime. Violent beliefs or fantasies will materialise almost instantly in the physical, as you have all experienced recently. There is no longer a delay between cause and effect due to the corrections in the speed of time. >

Gee, there was still a lot of violence on the planet! So, a faster speed created the illusion of experiencing a shorter time? *"Yes, you could say that. We are now going back into the future."* Theo's choice of words made the following message more apparent.

< Ascending beings must utilise their thoughts to clear their internal belief systems. Establish an inner landscape rather than indulging in external physical fantasies. Ascending beings must release any identification with their false self. Through clearing away belief systems, one will manifest one's ascension. >

POWAH's light evaporated in mist spray, and the humming sound quietened.

"Theo, the porthole POWAH is referring to, is there a connection with Ingrid's abduction and Pleasure Parks?" he beamed at Theo. The CERN Organization for Nuclear Research Large Hadron Collider sits near and beneath at a depth of around 328ft (100m) and runs around a 17-mile (27km) tunnel. The aerial photo on her laptop reminded him of this place. Then again, he wondered, where was he? He felt so formless, mingling with forces he had never been aware of.

"Come, our work has started. I know you have trillions of questions, but observe for now." After a while, he heard noises in the distance and simultaneously perceived a pinpoint of light from which irregular energy waves came at him. For a moment, his mind got confused. This pulsing energy was almost too much to take in a while, intermittently broken by occasional quick flares like disorganized patterns of magnetically drawn colour waves. A strange mixture of emotions surged through him into the commotion. Lots of people in hospital gear were all rushing in the same direction. Nobody noticed him, but he felt Theo's hand pulling and then recognised him. He saw Toon leaving his body while life-support systems and people surrounded him. The colours around Toon were very bright.

"Toon, leave it to them; you wanted to be with Ingrid. Now come." He could feel that Theo emanated deep compassion, which helped Toon over his fear because he thought he was dead. A similar sensation of moving at an incredible speed followed.

"Toon, you are not dying, but your consciousness is, for the moment, detached from physical reality. Your physical body is having a mild heart attack, so it is operating on an automatic basis. Your alarm and alert system will call you back when needed. Come!" He was aware that Toon was mentally squinting at him.

For a moment, Richard thought that he saw a glimmer of recognition.

"*Richard, is that you?*" Theo alerted him not to respond. A patchy grassland with a small winding stream that twisted like a snake and sparkled in the late reflection of a light source similar to the sun appeared. Where was he?

Then Theo proceeded towards a building that had seen better days. The mildew on the walls and a metal staircase in the basement appeared dirty and run down. Toon looked distressed. He wanted to say something, but then they both saw her. Ingrid was shivering despite a ragged blanket draped around her. She worked at a keyboard. As he noticed a bra lying on the dirty floor, Toon must have seen the same because he was telepathically projecting.

"*Oh, no, Kitty, love.... what have they done to you? I'm with you. I can see you. Oh, love, what are they wanting from you?*" He felt Toon's overwhelming anxiety as he tried to touch her but went right through. That shocked Toon to the core of his being while Theo stood aside, watching.

"*Snooks, are you all right? Why do I feel as if you are near me? Oh, Toon, please don't let me think you are...dead. Toon, I love you! Please come back!*" How did she know that he was near? Ingrid dropped her head on the keyboard. Her blanket slid off as her agonizing sobs shook her body. He saw that her torn shirt hung open. For one horrific moment, he thought of rape. Feelings of helplessness when he saw that Toon was trying to comfort her overwhelmed him with misery. Why would Ingrid think that Toon was dead? Theo then beamed.

"*Toon, you have had a mild heart attack. Now you know that you have to take care of yourself. Look after your physical body. Don't take it for granted.*"

Richard felt that Toon needed to return; he didn't want to be dead, and before he knew it, Toon was gone. He wished he could somehow reach Ingrid because she looked so lonely in that hovel. Had she been sexually assaulted? Theo took what felt like his hand, and they floated up through the roof of the broken-down building.

"*Theo, what is going on? Why has this happened? What sinister plot is this? Does it relate to the images I saw on Ingrid's laptop? What do they expect of her? Theo, I have to know!*" What could he do? He didn't want to leave her there!

"*Calm down, believe me, everything is a manifestation of divine will in action!*" The feeling of deserting her created such enormous, gripping guilt. Was that all in his mind?

"*Theo, I can come to terms with being unable to bring clarity through thinking about Ingrid's situation, but could thinking about it never bring any satisfaction?*" The further they were away, the more he felt hopelessly sad for not doing anything.

"*Richie, your soul trusts natural thinking; don't ever doubt your thinking.*" Thank goodness. The idea of not thinking was unbearable.

"*Buddy, people rarely truly think. It's their created false self that does. Their personas most often just run the same thought forms past their minds. You must develop originality in your thinking. Go beyond the thoughts that jump into your mind; it will strengthen the awareness of your human soul, and it will ignite the real you, a cosmic being, your Spirit I AM.*" He knew that Theo was far more aware and prepared him with patience for something. A feeling of peace drew him back to the sensory world, but again, the mummies hiding the golden foil sheets took him mentally back to the other dream.

"*I'll take you on an akashic record trip another time, but for now, I think your body is calling you, and hey, try to remember,*"

Those were the words ringing in his ears when he felt a strong magnetic pull. As he approached his body, no sooner was he near to it than he was back in again with the unnerving feeling of having dropped from a great height with a full bladder!

Annelies' house

He woke up to an unusual silence, totally devoid of traffic noises. How long had he been asleep? Had he consciously been away from his body? The early sunlight was streaming into the bedroom when he saw a towel, a toothbrush, toothpaste, a pen, and some paper, probably supplied by Annelies. He recalled the vision of Ingrid's torn shirt and her bra. They had brutally ripped it off. Feelings of anger erupted while jotting down more images. While frantically writing so as not to forget anything, he heard sounds coming from the hallway and a knock on his door.

"Richard, are you awake?"

"Yes, I'm coming." First, he made for the bathroom. When he returned, Liesbeth and Hans held hands in the guest bedroom doorway.

"Richard, my mother was called in during the night; Toon had taken a turn for the worse." Hans's voice was still husky and had a charged emotion.

"Yes! I remember that part! Toon had a heart attack." Both their eyes widened from surprise. Hans' hand went through his thick ash-blonde hair from anguish.

"Gosh, my Mom was shocked and could not accept Toon dying. I'm glad my dad came out of his undercover assignment to be with her." Hans's father was undercover! Was Ben with the police? He noticed that both Liesbeth and Hans were...listening. ... Then they looked at each other, smiling. Richard intuitively knew it was good news.

"Is Toon out of danger now?"

"Annelies just told them that Toon had woken up and has already been dishing out instructions," Liesbeth breathed in a relieved tone.

"Gosh! Just like that! Gee, I have to learn to become telepathic. It certainly beats cell phones any day. He followed them both to the kitchen; it was still early. Hans let Joris the Labrador outside so he could chase after something.

"Hans, what did you mean that your Dad was undercover?"

"He's connected with Interpol on a freelance basis, investigating what might be underneath the Pleasure Parks estate drama. We were only told about this when you had already slept."

"Richard, where can we contact you during the day? We have to find her soon." Liesbeth was, like him, anguished about Ingrid. He somehow had to be able to connect the basement of an old warehouse to the area where she was being kept hostage. He told them what he could remember, including the scene with Ingrid. *I'm hoping he was not just making it all up.*

Joris' wet nose nudged him when he was allowed back into the kitchen. He relayed some of his dream time memories with POWAH. Both showed great interest.

They were fascinated with his explanation when he told them about the musical tones POWAH projected, translated into words. He settled onto a high chair while Hans tackled the coffee machine.

"Please, Richard, tell us more."

"POWAH spoke about the many dimensions. During our awakening, we will reconnect with our fragmented soul parts. Like Annelies told us in her ascension classes!"

"Yes, our souls are only partly projecting into this living hologram we call our physical body. It mainly gathers fragmented experiences that it already knows. As you know, we have many pockets of blocked spaces in our grid formations."

"Liesbeth, you mean our soul is not projecting all of itself into our physical body?"

"Oh no! That is not possible. We...our soul...that is...is from a timeless realm...It experiences many parallel lives, and our soul is simultaneously projecting in all of them." Hans joined the conversation as he poured the coffee. His mind was staggered.

"Richard, the human physical form, which reflects our genetic ancestral heritage as well as our soul's choice of what to experience within this creation, dropped so enormously in vibration, especially in this galaxy, that the distortion that set in is phenomenal." He noticed that Hans and Liesbeth had very similar ways. Their bodies appeared very different, but...what did those two have in common?

"We share many parallel lives and one Over-Soul." Gosh, did he think this just now, or what was that? Did Hans mean past lives? Did he suddenly give himself answers?

"Richard, a soul connects with its multidimensional self on different planes for many reasons. One is for...mmm, let's say revising." Hans smiled as he said this, knowing he needed to stack this information in some order. What did he mean, revising of what?

"What are you two talking about, and how do you know all this?"

In the distance, a rooster announced a new day. He hoped Connie and Nell had a quiet day at the Pannekoek and had closed early yesterday.

"Souls that have been incarnating upon the Earth for the past 100,000 years fragmented into many planes of reality," Liesbeth added.

"Really? You mean we live many other lives at the same time?"

"Mmm, each plane has been compartmentalised and cut off, allowing each human experience to have little memory of anything other than one current physical world. This fragmentation resulted from many "declines in consciousness," Liesbeth did not drink coffee but sipped warm water instead.

"Richard, revising is a clearing process on a higher level of consciousness. Like our personalities that have to release negative thought forms, our soul or auric field also collects many distorted thought forms. "He still had great difficulty absorbing it all. Liesbeth smiled as if she could read his thoughts.

"Through re-casting, our soul field unites with lost soul particles and releases foreign energy frequencies. The result is that we start to remember parallel lives, which some call past lives. We call this the beginning of ascension." She explained while Hans gave Joris his breakfast.

"You mean that recasting is a correction in the distortion of a soul?"

"Yes, you got it. Also, such a connection allows for a purification of all experiences that the human soul has had within the lower dimensions." Hans noticed that Joris was getting agitated about something.

"Richard, you can experience conscious dream time. Remember in one of our first classes with Annelies when she talked about people who naturally had out-of-body experiences?"

"Yes, I recall that Annelies said I was the dreamer."

"Mmm, so you heard that. Ask Annelies why when our classes start again. Was there anything else you remembered that POWAH said?"

"Yes, I recall something about a mighty vortex in our hemispheres that must open for initiates to ascend through and that this stargate will somehow create a bridge into the other dimensions!" Hans' eyes turned up, creasing his high forehead into a frown.

"Lizzy, it's the hologram island under the large dome within the new Pleasure Park complex. I now see what my dad is involved in. Of course, he is investigating the Astral star-ship near the building site!" The ringing doorbell startled him.

"What do you mean by the starship? Who's creating or rather designing this hologram island? Do we have such technology?" As he spouted those questions, Joris jumped up against Hans to remind him that someone was at their front door.

"Richard, your questions would take rather a long explanation. All I know is that my Dad's twin brothers Leo and Trevor are investigating a rather secret spacecraft, as you can imagine." Hans took Liesbeth's hands in his.

"Lizzy, let's tell Annelies what Richard told us."

"Richard, when this rather distressing time has passed, we will answer your questions about us," Liesbeth promised as they both glanced at each other. Joris's excited bark disrupted their conversation, and Richard felt that the three became a crowd, so he said goodbye, leaving through the kitchen door that led to where his Honda was parked.

When Richard drove back to his flat in the early morning, he realised that this was the most bizarre family, including Trevor! Were they all off-beat? He never heard of an Astral star-ship. He was surprised that that kind of news had not leaked to the media. He was somewhat envious of Liesbeth and Hans' closeness to each other, like Ingrid and Toon. He knew that one either attracted a soul-agreement relationship or a karmic one. He was starting to see the difference.

The usual traffic outside calmed his otherwise fairly balanced nature, which was still in an uproar of the kidnapping affair. That had indeed thrown him into a state of chaos. Assimilating everything was tough for him, especially his family connections. As he entered his street, he visualised POWAH and mentally saw this figure of light again. Such rapture came over him that he almost drove right past his flat.

As he opened his front door, one of the six photos that revealed the gold embossed sheets was lying on the floor. Startled, he wondered, had he dropped it? Surely, he would have seen it when leaving his flat? Had someone been in his flat? It was one of the six photos Theo interpreted two years ago.

At the back, the words in Theo's handwriting made him shake again in awe. He looked at the symbols Theo wrote on the top to use as a guide for his translation from the photos. He remembered that each symbol stood for a letter...but it looked like the symbols on Annelie's wall! How did Annelies know these symbols? The title of the second tablet translated into The Many Dimensions of the Human Game[1]. The link is on the page of this tablet.

Tablet Two -

< *Ye who read my message, watch thy thoughts when spoken out loud.* —*Thy vibrations through the breath will manifest many worlds throughout.* >

Theo must have translated the six photos repeatedly because they read very differently. They never knew where the images came from. He never looked at them again after Theo left.

Theo had refused any treatment, and now he could understand why. Not that he had started to look ill. On the

---

1. https://allrealityshifters.wordpress.com/richard-de-jong/tablet-two/

contrary, Theo must have had a clear head to translate the unfamiliar symbolic text all over again. He looked in the file for their previous translations, where they used the symbolic conversions that appear on the Rosetta stone.

He got it! In Theo's handwriting, the words were like a string of beads.

When our elders acknowledged that divine creator beings within the core of the matrix were trapped, Humanity's creation held the key. We observed how the devastating battle between the celestial fallen beings that fought for control of the ninth sector, known as the Pesh Meten, destroyed our star. The war in the heavens fragmented the nine passageways that linked humanity into the intercellular substance of the matrix. When this crucial Star-Lane shattered, including our magnificent celestial ship Grenova-, our group soul that would embody the human creation she was carrying, splintered into lower frequencies.

He was stunned at his dream's synchronicity and what Hans had said about the Astral star-ship. Reading both interpretations brought up quite some memories. At the time, they were both very mystified. This time, Theo must have used a different method. He'd always wondered who the Group Souls were that came from a different universe and who had left this text behind.

His emotional attachment cords with Theo were still firm. Would he ever be free of that heart-rendering feeling of loss? He, of all people, shouldn't feel so separated.

His moment of daydreaming was interrupted by an early morning phone call. He wondered who it could be!

Chapter 3
Sound is the Primary Basis for Creation

Richard's flat

As Richard picked up the phone, there was silence...but intuitively hearing..."Go to your PC" he suddenly wanted to switch on Theo's old computer to check if he had an e-mail. He was startled when Theo's WhatsApp icon flickered to announce a text. He never or rarely used that app. Theo had because he had found it suitable if one wanted to chat. A short message appeared on his screen.

Dear Richard,

Anneies suggested that I communicate with you in this manner. I hope I can give you some guidelines for your journal that will assist with your transformation.

We all know that in ancient times, the king was also the high priest, and the temples were the seat of scientific knowledge. The rulers, pharaohs or kings were often worshipped and seen as gods. Our readings from the ancient tablets clearly explain why the battle between the Creationists and Evolutionists makes such a separation between people.

With the "Fall of Man" expression, due to genetic experiments, the consciousness of humanity became distorted and infected with belief programs. Before a significant geological cataclysm during the Atlantean epoch, the human creation could access the cosmic memories within its DNA. Your interpretations surrounding the Sphinx coincide with ours.

Trevor.

Why would Annelies suggest Mr Zwiegelaar contact him through WhatsApp? The acknowledgement of his research into the mysteries surrounding the Sphinx, which he'd prepared for next week, uplifted his spirits after all that had happened. The kidnapping affair had absorbed his mind entirely. The informality, calling him by his first name, established a friendship he had missed ever since Theo left. Richard knew nothing about genetic science except that humans, according to scientists, have two strands of DNA. He decided to respond.

Good morning! It was a surprise to find your message on my brother's PC. I was drawn to it amazingly. Congratulations on your excellent lecture about "The Past Is the Future" and your input on the wars of the Gods. You certainly stirred your audience. There are many different explanations about the "fall" of man. I'm interested in knowing your interpretation. He typed it with two fingers.

History seems to have repeated itself with fear-mongering, so-called fake pandemic predictions, and fraudulent indoctrination.

Trevor immediately responded because the Whatsapp box flashed again in the corner of his screen, and the following text appeared.

Good, you got my thought beam! Richard, it appears that a nuclear bomb or a colossal satellite plunged into our planet, which shifted its frequency to an even lower vibration approximately 9,500 years ago. This explosion was 100 times more potent than the one dropped on Hiroshima in 1945. Recent discoveries suggest that the human lifespan has significantly decreased from 500 years to less than a century, the current average lifespan. This information is crucial because it sheds light on the genetic and cellular changes we are experiencing due to the photon belt and the shifting of timelines expected to occur in the next decade.

He gasped, resting back on his office chair, thinking. Theo, an evolutionist and a mystic, had gathered vast amounts of theoretical data about the same topic for years. He combined Rudolf Steiner's writings for humanity and planet Earth with his theories on Babylon. He always said that the name Babylon was more a "code word for Rome"! Theo's end-of-day prophecies were becoming more and more intriguing and relevant.

Did the gold foil sheets reveal this catastrophic event Trevor just mentioned? But then, where did this nuclear device come from? Violent space wars have been a common theme in science fiction movies. Were they nearer to the truth than all the religious dogmas?

He asked a minister the same question once when Aunty Mien insisted that he should go to Bible classes when he was about twelve. They were discussing Lot's wife, who had turned into a pillar of salt because she had looked back over her shoulder. With today's space programs, he wondered if the world's future was approaching the same destruction. Or was the solar system, including planet Earth, ascending towards a higher dimension? There has been a lot of speculation on this 'belt' of light particles. He wondered how Trevor connected a nuclear explosion that had happened 9,500 years ago with the photon belt theory and shifting timelines.

He knew and read in articles that Earth is becoming a 5th-dimensional planet due to an exchange or neutralization of polar forces. Something to do with the Photon Belt? He recalled POWAH talking about both hemispheres.

"How do we know within ourselves physically that this photon belt theory is real? What genetic changes are you talking about?"

He clicked on the 'send' button next to Theo's name. Should he edit it or not? He pondered what Trevor's views on the genetic engineering experiments that Theo believed in might be. They often discussed topics like the cloning of animals that happened today and compared it with the creation of a slave race in ancient times. When an article about how researchers at the Oregon Regional Primate Centre modified a baby rhesus monkey's genetic makeup, Theo suspected that today's scientists were repeating the same genetic experiments that the 'high priests' in Atlantis had done.

Richard, in our current human form, the cells are continuously replaced, as you know. But evolution seemed to fall well short of perfection. For example, human lungs are pretty impressive organs but pale compared to how bird lungs work. When a vulture sucked into the engine of a plane years ago, it was flying at 11264 meters! Because our air passages end in two-way lung air sacs, not as much fresh air reaches the deepest parts of our lungs – unlike the tubes of bird lungs – where air flows in one direction. When we go through the resurrection process by expanding our conscious awareness of who we are, the new cellular changes triggered by the photon belt phenomenon will activate the memory of our original cellular frequency. This cellular memory no longer deteriorates or dies but rejuvenates itself.

He saw that Trevor was typing again.

Have you ever wondered why we feel so disconnected from our true selves? It turns out that our original frequencies have intentionally been tampered with through an artificially created virus.

Flash flashes of his dream suddenly jumped into his mind—the scene on the dirty-looking walls. While pondering, he recalled that Annelies had mentioned a cellular conversion process during her decoding classes.

Can we prevent significant errors in evolution? Some scientists think so. By understanding the causes, we can take proactive measures. What do you think?

Annelies had asked him what subject he'd studied besides Egyptology. His direction was more in cultural anthropology, which concerned the study of languages or rituals.

Children's running feet outside his flat complex reminded him of Sammy. His eight-year-old was in bed with the measles so he couldn't speak to her last weekend. He typed a reply.

Trevor, do you know if we are, through these cellular changes, even more affected by bacteria and artificial viruses? How are they getting them to spread? Or has our DNA design already gone wild?

He'd thought again about Theo's discussions on gene-mixing. He often mentioned that childhood diseases, like measles, were examples of how the human DNA design had degenerated.

Thinking of children, he'd received Sammy's first e-mail during her computer class at school. He was so chuffed at his little girl's achievement that he'd replied at once, but he had heard nothing back. With fascination, he watched how Trevor's words appeared back on his screen.

The gradual deterioration of our organs and bodily functions, caused by cellular mutations, is the primary reason for ageing. While I think every virus will eventually reappear in a different form, I am not knowledgeable enough in the medical field to expand on this idea. Annelies will provide more information on this topic in her third-level journal. We will also share more details about the awakening process on our website soon. Annelies uses a different name to refer to these celestial lower beings as fallen angels.

He stared in stunned silence. Good grief, was Trevor also referring to the Pleasure Parks project? He seemed to know all about Annelies' decoding workshops! His mind cartwheeled back to his interpretations of the crop-circle image Ingrid showed him a few weeks ago. From a great height, he saw the Egyptian symbol of an eye and wondered about its significance. With two fingers, he typed...

"Trevor, I have the aerial photo of the new Pleasure Park site in France, where they are building another holiday resort. An image resembling the Eye of Horus symbol appears below the surface. It can only seen from a great height. When you write about a hologram deck, are you referring to that site?"

Ingrid hadn't collected the CD last week, and her abduction ordeal had begun to stir a wave of inner anger he didn't know he had.

Richard, what is happening at the site in France could be seen as a mirror reflecting the dark energies in action within us all. I'm convinced that an attempt to stop the activation of this ancient wormhole is the cause of what has happened. We suspect that the rotation of this wormhole will again establish a connection with the world of antimatter. Because most of us have been under the influence of the global centralization of power known as the new world order, the plot of the Illuminati for decades, we've lost this knowledge. Ask Theo to take you through the Akashic records, especially during Ra 10,000 years ago, just before the atomic destruction.

Trevor's reply gripped him. Was Trevor implying that the kidnapping affair was a decoy? He felt pretty exposed when Trevor referred to his remote viewing abilities. He was not ready to let his bizarre skills out to the world. His wormhole and anti-matter theory baffled him, but Richard would look that up before admitting it. He admired Trevor's nerve in coming forward with the most outlandish theories, but was he prepared to do the same? Annelies must have contacted him while he was sleeping at her house.

The morning noises below his flat told him it was time to open the coffee shop. He was still stunned that Trevor knew about his contact with Theo! He recalled Theo mentioning to a colleague that Trevor Zwiegelaar was heavily into conspiracy theories.

"How did you know about Theo and my out-of-body experiences? I'm very uncomfortable broadcasting my dream world for fear of being seen as a freak."

He already felt that his way-out interest affected his social interactions with others.

"Do you genuinely suspect that we are under some form of mind control? All of us? I mean, are we all under this influence now?" He added before he clicked on the send button.

The words "an ancient wormhole" reminded him about a vortex-porthole POWAH had talked about in the transmission Ingrid had shown him. It was getting late, and the traffic noises got heavier.

Last night, Annelies told me about your lucid dreams. I recall that Theo had some interesting theories about parallel universe awareness. Richard, we are all vibrational patterns of interacting frequencies that our mind converts into a holographic form. However, yes, I respect your need to stay incognito. Various inter-dimensional beings who can appear in any form can still control us. They dwell in our energy field and drain our Chi through our personas, ego or, as Annelies calls it, our false self. Ask Theo on your next astral journey. I must go, but let's keep communicating through WhatsApp for now. But soon, we need to move to other channels, knowing who owns and controls WhatsApp.

Regards Trevor.

He was glad for Trevor's last note. More and more, the imageries of past lives flashed into life. The feelings associated with them were true of being controlled. His life had become more tangible in his mind as if he had an inner world that was just as accurate as the outer world! He could also relate to Trevor's perceptions, no matter how bizarre when his mobile phone rang. It was already after eight. Connie's face flashed before his eyes.

"Richard, I cannot open the coffee shop this morning because my mom is too upset. Do you mind?" He told Connie that Toon was out of danger.

"Richard, they think it's my dad...He could be involved...I can't believe it, but Annelies told my mom they suspect my dad has been the middleman from the start." He could almost feel her tears gushing through the handset.

"My Mom is so ashamed that she doesn't want to speak to Ed Barendse, Ingrid's brother-in-law. They have only just met, and she likes him, but...Oh, Richard, what if it's true? My father used to work for Pleasure Parks; My dad left Pleasure Parks without my mother's knowledge. What if my dad was the one that shot Toon?" Her distress matched his inner uproar. Good grief, did Yolanda feel...guilty?

"Love, that is not any reflection on either of you; crimes are often family-related. There must be far more behind all this than we know." Connie had always sounded plagued when she mentioned her father on two occasions. He wondered what made Annelies suspect her father's involvement. He tried recalling what he'd seen beside Ingrid in that dreadful place, but his memory was foggy. Connie replied that she would call him back at the coffee shop after speaking to her mom...

Back at Work

The Pannekoek shop had no appeal for him this morning. The abduction affair had taken on a new dimension when he returned his juice to his PC in his flat. What did all the side effects mirror for all of them? Ever since he started to focus on the possibility of awakening to full consciousness, his life had taken a different turn. Previously, on his free days, he would ensure that he had dates lined up to enjoy female company and what could follow.

Ever since he joined Annelies' group, he has felt fulfilled. After Trevor and Connie's call, his concern for Ingrid and why her Dad kidnapped her occupied his mind. He searched for any possible reason that could be more sinister than just pure human greed.

Ever since the warning of a fake pandemic and the US election fraud, I had been avoiding watching the local news, never knowing what was true and what was manipulation propaganda. He could not believe that Dutch people, known to be more outspoken and upfront, would fall for the manipulation by scaring people of what was to come since it was so depressing. He was frequently astonished that many people could not see that the banking systems still had complete control over the monetary energy force that humanity had created as a tool for exchange, even after the talk about a financial reset. He had hoped things would change, but apparently, that takes time. No one was excluded from its powerful grip unless you lived a monastic lifestyle. The news on TV showed how the people on the African continent instigated massive killings for food and water. Even they have been sucked into the greed virus, as Theo used to call it.

He sincerely hoped Connie's father had nothing to do with the sexual abuse.

He ignored the traffic outside as he gazed at the flame on his PC screen saver. His mind hypnotically drifted off. He felt weird, as if he were suddenly getting smaller. An energy ripple, like gooseflesh, travelled slowly up from his feet into his right leg up on one side, past his ears and down on the other side, making him feel as if he were leaving his body, but this time he was more conscious of what was happening!

Somebody grabbed him by his shoulders. The jolt resulted in an adrenaline rush...then feelings of being free,...suddenly... whoosh!... He felt himself separating! That had never happened while he was wide awake!

• • • •

"Are you in fear of leaving your butt while it's not lying down?" He saw his body slumped over his keyboard, worried about his body's comfort and stifling the stack of questions while worried that his physical body would get uncomfortable. The objects in his flat became transparent, as if everything had a rhythm of different vibrations. Theo was near because he sensed rather than saw him.

"Theo, why did the kidnapping happen? How can any negative and almost violent behaviour be of any good?" Ingrid's plight absorbed his mind, but they had disappeared into a mist before he knew it.

"Richie, only on one's Over-Soul level is one's greatest potential known. Our journey of awakening is very often affected by facing our dark side. Sometimes, we need to experience certain situations outside of ourselves so that we can acknowledge them within us and release them through forgiveness. Many can do this through their dream world." He didn't like the dark side...

"Which dream world? This one, or when I'm awake? How do I know the difference?" This time, he followed Theo away from his flat without hesitation while the morning traffic was in full swing. For the moment, he felt a strong pull back to his body slumped over his keyboard because he needed to get to the coffee bar... but then...

"Come, don't be worried about time; let's first deal with what is most in your mind." They were now floating over very familiar scenery. *"Prepare for an event I have called to assist with, but remember well that time is irrelevant.*" He recognized the buildings, and the dreadful oil smell almost suffocated him ...without any warning...he heard loud noises of hooting and...the screeching of brakes of an old-fashioned car, which gave him a rude jolt! A big solid thump followed! It was amazing to watch how two cars from the nineteen forties crumpled in the collision right before his eyes in slow motion!

He looked aghast at the wreckage whilst a crowd of people gathered around. The ambulance and fire engine noises in the distance affected the pulsations of the maze of colours whizzing at great speed around everything. He was observing an accident that must have happened during the forties, but the coloured sparks puzzled him...

"Those are the many emotions revealed by the auras of everybody around the accident. People are unconsciously attracted to a scene where death could appear as if they want to connect subconsciously to the world beyond. Now, look!" What he saw next was so unexpected that he had difficulty taking it all in—a cloak of dense matter from the two bodies inside the car aimed to wind itself around them. Then, two people climbed out of the wreckage. Was that their astral form? A thick, foggy substance completely enveloped their bodies in a funnel of moving matter that appeared from nowhere. They must have thought they were all right as they looked around them in a daze. The couple stared at each other with an intensely miserable look. By their expressions, he could see they saw themselves simultaneously inside the now crumpled-up cars while they were out of their bodies!

"Sisca, are you all right?" the man tried to call out, taking her hand as he moved to her side."

"Steven, why are we still in the car?" pointing to the couple inside.

Theo approached them, and Richard knew his brother gently coaxing them to follow. A glimmer of understanding came over Steven when the clinging grey matter, which had partly enveloped them before, suddenly started to disconnect and fall to the ground, evaporating into smoke and dust.

Then Sisca sobbed hysterically as the same thing happened to her. Steven looked very troubled. Theo took them both by the elbow, away from the fear and horror of the accident, and told Richard to come out from the scene to the countryside near the woods. Like a snake, Richard saw a little stream winding down to a bridge in the distance. The couple was very upset about leaving their baby son of only seven months, whom Steven's parents were looking after…He felt himself move away from them…he experienced absolute blackness as if he was in a void…Feelings of timelessness overcame him when a glowing point of light came nearer. His mind searched for an image to feel tangible when he saw two brilliant figures. Gradually, he felt the full effects of their radiation…The young woman from the car crash was talking to the two light figures…Was it the same Sisca?… Her lovely face and hair gave off a golden copper glow against the simple garment of white silk. The radiation she emanated awed him. She was standing in bright sunlight. Her eyes were bottomless; her lips did not move, but a cheery chuckle startled him.

"You don't remember me, do you?"

"I thought for a moment you were the woman called Sisca who died in a car crash, but you can't be" he projected as he came closer.

"And why not?"

"You look…different … I mean. …are you reading my mind?"

"I thought you were going to help?"

"Help?" With what?

His thoughts reeled as he recollected that his physical body slumped in front of his computer in his flat; how long had he been away? Where was his brother?

"Right behind you, buddy, I've told you! Everything happens simultaneously!" It took a while before he could see Theo, wearing a beautiful robe of many shimmering colours that made him feel quite drab in their presence.

"Now, where did that feeling of unworthiness come from suddenly? You look wonderful to us, and we have some work to do, remember?" What did his brother mean by 'us'? Were more people going to help him find…Ingrid?

"Both Liesbeth and Hans have contacted me. They are hovering behind you." Was Sisca implying that the two light bodies hovering above Sisca were?...

"Those are two compelling mind projections. Both Liesbeth and Hans are what is called walk-ins. But even for them, playing the awakening card game will help to clear the side effects of the dense electrical magnetism of this third dimension. They are now observing the halls where many souls summoned for incarnation go. The selective karmic board granted Sisca, as you know her, permission for an embodiment through the parents of our genetic lineage. Toon and Ingrid," he saw that Sisca was communicating, but with what? … Was that what some mind projections looked like?

"But then they must know where Ingrid is. "Then Sisca turned to address him.

"Richard, I have been partly responsible for the attraction and the bonding of both Toon and Ingrid. In my last incarnation, I was the mother of Toon. Ingrid belongs to the same genetic tapestry and is a twin soul, meaning they share the same Over-Soul. Their *souls agreed to bond their physical forms in communion once they both were aware of the divine union within themselves...In this incarnation, Toon and Ingrid's souls must serve to benefit humanity. It was an opportunity not to be missed,"* Sisca telepathically conveyed.

"But... how is this all going to help Ingrid?"

"*Look around you! What do you see?*" After some concentration, he saw a landscape surrounded by woods, a small curving river and an old and run-down building in the distance. Sisca pressed how important it was for him to remember this scene when the noise of a plane engine circling over the area disrupted his attention. The two light figures had disappeared.

"*Richard, both Toon and Ingrid had to experience their conscious transformation sooner because my physical body, which is growing inside Ingrid, is just at its beginning stage. It has not yet entered her womb.*" On hearing this, he almost reeled back to his body. Was the lovely woman that was speaking saying all this?

"*Yes, Richard. My future body still travels in her fallopian tube while my biological cells multiply. There has never been a more significant time to be born into the physical world so close to its major transformation into a 5th-dimensional reality.*" "Wow! Were more people so eager to get trapped in a physical tomb? Would he remember all this, he wondered? The smile told him that she had read his mind.

"*Before my soul's blueprint codes arrive in her uterine lining for shelter and nourishment— you call it the implantation—the alteration in my cellular metabolism will impact all facets of Ingrid and Toon's lives. Her dietary preferences and attunement to my vibrational patterns will significantly alter their emotional and mental capacities.*" Richard was still astonished. Was this woman implying that she would be the baby Ingrid was expecting?

" *Richie, remember this moment and look up the third tablet translation under the S of sound.* Theo beamed just before the scene became foggy...

Suddenly, he felt the pull of his body calling him to his still-slumped form in his chair...when...whoosh! he was back...

• • • •

As he stretched himself, he noticed the time on his screen. Had he fallen asleep for twenty minutes? It was only half past eight, but he suspected he had had an out-of-body trip. Images that were so bizarre tumbled in his mind. He remembered his parents were killed in a car crash and then with Theo, Sisca, Toon's mother! Gosh, it came back to him. He must ask Toon about the car crash. That would confirm that his out-of-body trips were for real.

Sisca had talked to him about her next incarnation, which would occur through Ingrid!... Oh, how was he going to assimilate all these garbled recollections? It was all overwhelming, especially about Liesbeth and Hans' light bodies! He felt stiff all over, but more flashes of his short dream came to mind. He flimsily typed whatever he could remember. Did he remember the part about the baby? It sounded beyond comprehension. Had he just made it all up? Suddenly, in the back of his mind, the letter S jumped up....

He rushed to look under the S in Theo's files, hoping to find the translation of the third tablet. With trembling fingers, he found the envelope. Theo had already written the title at the back of the print: **Sound is the Primary Basis for Creation**[1].

Tablet 3

---

1. https://allrealityshifters.wordpress.com/tablet-3/

Inside his laptop, he clicked on the link. It took him to a page, and he saw all of Theo's older third translations. He remembered some of the...yes, this was it!

<As each sound wave vibrates, a tonal expression of the source of all—Will manifest greatness into the world of the exceptional. >

He now remembered that they could not establish a complete sentence. Each tablet on a photo had taken Theo weeks to translate. He started feeling somewhat better emotionally because Theo must have known all along, even before his parting, that he would find his translations one day. In the last five years, they have had many discussions about the origin of the human species. Theo even linked the ancient monument, the Sphinx, with his theories. Theo suspected that the lion/human monument, the Sphinx, was built as a reminder of visitors who were fully conscious beings that belonged to a different epoch.

Theo's inserts were beneficial, especially the harmful thought part. Gee. Would he ever be free of attachments or negative thoughts? He had to focus on today's responsibilities and prepare to open the coffee shop as it was already late. Reluctantly, he slipped the photo and envelope back into the file.

The memory of the sounds from his dream from POWAH rang in his mind under the shower. As the water cascaded over him, he recalled that Tieneke explained that gold and silver emanated a single, dual, tri, and quad tones of the Language of Light. When she said it, he recalled that Theo once speculated that the elements of silver and gold resonated with the tones of photon energy particles. As he soaped himself, he recalled Theo explaining that the photon belt is Earth's mirror. It will reject any energy particle that does not resonate with the thought form of her Great Central Sun. At the time, Theo's philosophies often eluded him.

He now grasped why humans experience that any destructive thought comes back to them. Seeing planet Earth as a being, planet Earth must match her gold and silver tones to pass through this photon belt energy. So, if one perceived the central sun as planet Earth's higher self, which Theo thought was Venus, then maybe other planets and stars must have combusted in attempting to enter this photon belt without adequate preparation. What a wacky thought. Hearing that the sound was the primary basis for the creation game, he speculated that whoever left the golden foil sheets behind saw life as a creation game. He was still standing under the shower when his landline rang. While dripping water everywhere, he grabbed the portable phone.

All he heard was a hazy, rasping sound of someone breathing down the line.

"We are on to you", a squeaky male voice threatened. The forbidding tone brought on visions of Ingrid's predicament. The hateful energy that gushed through the phone took away the amazement he felt before. The dialling tone announced that the owner of the voice had hung up.

The Pannekoek

When Richard opened the coffee shop, the phone's alarm and insistent ringing inflamed his anger. If that threatening individual had followed his movements, he would have given him something to brood over.

"What did you remember?" Hearing Liesbeth's voice softened his heart.

"I hear your chuckle; tell me how you know I had another out-of-body experience at my flat this morning?" The crockery trembled when the thunder erupted after a flash of lightning. Crumbs, was this rain ever going to stop?

"You remembered! Good! We were successful in locating you. "Gosh, Liesbeth confirmed his dream vision. His vivid reflections tumbled verbally out his mouth like a waterfall that rushes over rocks. Richard was glad nobody in the coffee shop overheard him detailing his bizarre lucid dream. Liesbeth said she would hand the phone to Hans.

"Richard, you were a great help, and we both thank you."

"Have you found where she is?" Hans responded by asking him if he had anything on for today. Nothing would stop him from participating in the search for Ingrid. He was too bewildered about the bizarre circumstances to be just a bystander. Their telepathic communications still astounded him, and their confirmations of his unusual talent increased his intent to fully awaken to a higher awareness level, whatever that took.

"Hans, are you both going to visit Toon?" Ingrid's predicament and Toon's gunshot pulled him back to the reality of the kidnapping.

"Yes, could you join us? Sascia will have her aerial photos in print by this afternoon, and she'll take them to Harry Brinks' estate in Utrecht." Vinny's girlfriend, Sascia, the intellectual one, again jumped into his mind. It made him curious about Ingrid's other daughter, who had the same name. When Hans described the estate, Mr Brinks, Ingrid's boss, must be wealthy. They both said their goodbyes as he got his directions until the afternoon.

When he joined Annelies' classes, he was more at home with them than he had ever felt with other people. The Friday evenings, once filled with dating, were now filled with exciting activities he would have avoided years ago... The awakening bug had caught him.

Nell Hartman had not yet arrived, but the aroma of her freshly baked 'stroopwafels' from yesterday still hung around as he took the chairs from the eight tables and filled the coffee machine. He spotted three telephone messages in Connie's handwriting on the counter. The faculty, the wholesalers and Aunt Mien all phoned. He wondered what his aunt called for. Yolanda, Connie's mother, answered when he dialled Connie's number first. He asked her about the card game she had played the previous Friday with Niels Jaarsma and Zola from their Friday workshops. He knew her mind would be more occupied with the deplorable kidnapping affair, but a change of topic might be just what she needed.

"Richard, it was very thought-provoking. It also makes me realise how cunningly the illusion of our creations deceives us. I now realise I never really let go of my emotional attachments. If we are moving into a new paradigm, gosh, the things I still mirror in my life!" The silence that followed revealed Yolanda's distress.

"The card game also has a light side, and I could laugh at myself so I could learn not to feel guilty, but this sinister criminal affair is quite a test for me. I've tried to shield Connie from her father's activities as much as possible, but it's pretty hard on her. I'll call her for you. See you soon." Richard could sense that Yolanda's anguish went a lot deeper.

He overheard Yolanda telling Connie that Uncle Fred, the bookshop owner, would come past soon after he had seen Toon at the hospital. Fred Zwiegelaar was Annelies' brother. Annelies' parents fostered Toon, so they grew up together. It must be even more horrible for Connie and her mother to have their father and ex-husband involved in such a negative way.

Nel was late, so he started to go over his shopping list while cradling the phone in the crook of his neck.

"Richard, I'll be there after lunch. Did you find my note?" Connie's bubbly nature had gone. He reassured her he had while wondering if he could again ask her to take over for the day.

As he changed the grocery order and looked up Aunt Mien's phone number in South Africa, Nel arrived, drenched from the heavy rain still pelted down.

"Jock du Toit, can I help you," a voice with an Afrikaans accent answered. He chatted to Jock, asking after the family. He'd heard a wind-chime in the background when Jock was calling his mom. He'd never been back to South Africa, but Theo had told him something about the garden route in the Western Cape with its prehistoric forest.

"Hello, my boy; I'm glad you phoned back quickly. You have a very nice and helpful girl called Connie. Is she special?" Richard had to smile at her rapid questioning; his Aunt was forever matchmaking.

"Business is picking up, and I need to look for more help, especially during the holidays. Aunty, no such luck about the girlfriend part, but I promise I'll let you know if I have found the right woman. What can I do for you?" Nell fluttered her eyelashes at him as she stacked more packets of stroopwafels on the counter.

"Richard, you'd better!" his Aunt chided. "Listen, we heard about the kidnapping and shooting saga that involved Pleasure Parks in France. I know Harry Brinks, the owner. He is a close friend. We heard through the grapevine that Nick du Toit, my ex, could be involved, but I don't want to contact him, in case I'm mistaken. Do you have any idea? I thought maybe you might have heard more about it?" Richard was speechless; she'd never talked about her ex-husband.

"Aunty, what do you mean by 'involved'? I know both Toon and Ingrid very well. I've never met Harry Brinks, but I'm meeting him this afternoon."

"Well, well, have you ever! I had this strong intuitive feeling about contacting you, and now I know why. Richard, please use discernment over this whole affair. We are related to the Jaarsma family. I will do some snooping and contact you again through e-mail. Give my love to Harry and Nell, will you?" She said goodbye without any more explanation of her ex's involvement.

He had not used the opportunity to tell her about her brother, Ben Jaarsma, because Connie had walked in behind three customers who all wanted to buy stroopwafels. He could see that she'd been crying. He hoped the heavy rain would soon clear up. Sunny weather made the world a lot brighter. There were no customers at any tables, for which he was glad.

"How is your mother taking it?" They hugged. He felt clumsy, but what else could he say? Connie's wet, long blonde hair looked charming as always, even when she wore it in a ponytail.

"She was fine until the police arrived. How much do you know?" Connie's expression of helplessness screamed for a friend. He told her he had been with Annelies and had met her husband, Ben. He didn't tell her about his unusual involvement. He also needed to pay attention to the work from the faculty and prepare his four lectures, not to mention his aunt's coffee shop. He knew too well how easily he could get involved and forget his other priorities.

"What did the police want?" The squealing threat over the phone this morning was hopefully not her dad. The meaning behind the threat, "we are on to you," still made no sense.

"Oh, they asked questions we could not answer. My parents got separated for the last two years before their divorce settlement, but I can relate to the way my mom must feel. You know, partly responsible. I overheard her talking to Aunt Tieneke, saying things like, 'If only she'd paid more attention to him!' Grrr, my dad is a gambler, and he drinks! I've lost count of what else." Richard froze when she mentioned the 'what else' part. He knew from Ingrid that Tieneke de Beer was the daughter of Harry Brinks. Most of the people in the Friday group had attended her mind-drawing classes. He suspected they were all handpicked from Tieneke's list to join Annelies' ascension group. The image of the Jaarsma ancestral tree chart from the orphanage Annelies had spoken about in one of her classes came to mind.

"You have no brothers and sisters, have you?"

"No, thank goodness. It's only my mom and me. My dad had been married before but never told us anything about them or his three sisters. I'm not surprised that he fell out with his family. My grandmother from my Dad's side came from the Jaarsma orphanage. My father never talked about his family, but my Mom always inquired about my grandmother, which often ended in a fight. I could never understand why she wanted to know anything about this orphanage in the first place." Connie sighed.

They were interrupted by a whole bunch of young kids. The two adults in charge ordered pancakes with cherries and cream for them all. Nel was quick, and Connie served them. He shared his family connections with her when she returned behind the counter.

"Connie, a lot seems to surround this orphanage. Even my family could be associated."

"Really? My mom has always been fascinated by family stories. When Aunt Annelies and Uncle Fred bought the castle, which used to be the orphanage, they renovated it to become the Prinsengracht Hotel. We came to live at the back. I must show the garden to you someday."

Connie told him about her plans and the hotel college she would enrol in in August. His mind hovered over how attractive she was, and he could see her managing that stately place one day.

"So, I must find other help before you leave to return to college?"

"Mmm, if you want to find someone to take over from me, yes; it will also get busier now, during school holidays.

"How are you for this afternoon? I must go to Utrecht to re-schedule my lectures and visit Toon in the Hospital. Could you stay here and close early, say around six? I'll ask Nell to open up in the morning."

"That's okay with me. Why don't you go now? Uncle Fred wants to see what I'm doing. You don't mind if I show him around, do you?"

"Mind! You're kidding! I'm lucky to have you helping me out! Thanks, and I will look out for some help for you." Connie seemed to have forgotten about her father for a while, and he would not bring it up again.

The Pannekoek was buzzing with customers when he left.

Why was his life suddenly so...what was the word...timeless? Should he take the weird, unpleasant phone calls seriously? How could Connie's dad be involved?

He started to understand, or rather suspect, that the Jaarsma name stood for something. What, he could not yet come to terms with. The group soul theory was still too vague, too unscientific. He was still greatly influenced by the idea that concepts that are not scientifically proven could be primarily false! But then he also knew most schools fail to teach a wide range of subjects, including ancient history and other more spiritual sciences.

He was struggling with his thoughts while driving on the freeway, making him ponder about being multidimensional. He could almost be at two different locations mentally. He must accept that honest criticism often directs his mind. Knowing at the same time that his inner knowledge, from his memory, must hold a more complete picture of the history and science of humankind as it evolved on the face of this Earth. He could accept that the pyramids could be an interplanetary communication system, especially in Egypt. But why the Jaarsma name seems to pop up everywhere remains a mystery. Questions...Questions...

Chapter 4
The Symbol of the Game

Utrecht
As an afterthought, Richard decided to go via his flat to pack an overnight bag. He contacted the faculty by phone at his flat and had a hunch to check his e-mail before going to Utrecht. There was one message with an attachment from a Ljgroup in France. He has never heard of them! It could be spam, but it was intriguing, so he opened it.

——- Original Message ——-
From: "ljgroup" Ljgroup@gold.fr
To: <J de Jong:;>
Subject: you need this map
Dear Richard,
One day we will meet. Take this map, which will be a guide with the interpretations Theo left behind under the word consciousness. Very unpleasant developments have come to light, which tends to happen when you deal with human behaviour that gives way to abuse. And no, we are not spamming!..
Regards from Leo Jaarsma

Gosh, unpleasant developments; that was an understatement, considering what had happened to Toon and Ingrid. He remembered that Leo Jaarsma was Ben's twin brother, the brainy one. His sudden family connections made him feel more involved.

He clicked on the attachment icon, and a roadmap appeared. After encircling two places on the map, he decided to print out both messages plus the map and take it to Harry Brinks' house.

This Leo must have known Theo about the photos of the gold foil sheets! He seemed to get the interpretations of each tablet in sequence.

He searched through several of Theo's files under the word consciousness. There were several files until he found one with the photo he now recognised. The eye symbol he knew as the Eye of Horus was still faintly showing. Once again, a piece of paper is attached to the back of the photograph. The handwriting was Theo's but had no title this time. Instead, the same envelope had a chart of the Language of Light alphabet with a note!

Last year, around October, when the weather was miserable, Theo persuaded him to join Teineke's mind-drawing group for a long weekend. She had sent him a personal invitation by email. Because Theo mentioned her, he decided he had nothing to lose. Mind-drawing for two days had unlocked so much that he was never the same again after that creative weekend.

There, stacked under a pile of papers, he immediately recognised Theo's handwriting! He had used Tieneke's chart to translate the title of the fourth tablet! He saw it was pretty simple once the symbols changed into letters.

The result was that the Eye is the Symbol of the Evolution Game.

<Richie, I was given a universe history map before I left. During the reign of Ra, The Eye of Creation was a symbol of worship before the most recent cosmic shift before the last cosmic shift. Our ancestors might have been infected on a cellular level by humanoid creators from the outer world, personified as a deity called Horus. When I translated this musical tablet, I realized how destructive all fantasies or desires can be.

As you know, I had to experience this physical world, and I'm somewhat dismayed by my experiences in the flesh. When Annelies shared her visions about her card game, I realized that she held the knowledge of genetic science within her cellular memory. I chose to help her. We were the last initiates transported back to the previous epoch of Atlantis..

Love Theo

Theo's admission of fantasies or desires astonished him, especially the part about the previous epoch of Atlantis. Hadn't Hans mentioned an Astral ship? He recalled a discussion that the human creation had been sabotaged by what Theo called the mind of the matrix, starting with Mars many thousands of years ago. At the time, he had found Theo's explanations challenging to grasp. Theo had mentioned dates around 35,000 years ago when, again, an intervention changed the projections or the script for this creation.

It was once again something to do with their DNA. He also mentioned that he had read of an international team of astronomers a few years previously who had reported that an unidentified planet was lurking in the outermost reaches of our solar system. Was that an Astral ship, but spotted physically?

His theory that each creation had a script, like a movie script, was thought-provoking. In Annelies' decoding classes, he became aware of the actual sciences of Alchemy, but Theo's explanation brought to light what he had overlooked before. To recall prehistoric history, one had to roll up the film or script of this creation before one came to the beginning. Theo had always lived in an alchemical world or was thinking of some aspect of alchemy. Alchemical symbolism circled his life; he had much in common with Annelies.

Richard recalled that Theo had always expressed an unbroken strength and self-confidence in his contemplations, which he still lacked.

Theo's note at the end revealed an inner struggle that his condition must have brought on. He was equally disturbed about the fantasy part of the human mind. His soul must have chosen to pass from this dimension, but why could he not be healed? And where did he go to spend his last days?

With a heavy heart, he was surprised that the title The Eye is the Symbol of the Evolution Game[1] was a computer hyperlink in Theo's new translation of the symbols.

---

1. https://allrealityshifters.wordpress.com/tablet-4/

Tablet 4

< *Thy world is a mirror of heaven above—The divine patterns within thy eye reflect the world of Love..* >

He found their first translation when he opened Theo's interpretations on his laptop under a folder titled consciousness. "Click on the link Annelies created to read it online." He heard internally. He was tempted to go online but looked at the time.

< *If pockets of density or attachments are not released during transformation—humanity's physical body will reflect like a mirror and feel diseased.* >

He put Theo's file away for later studies and left for the Freeway toward Utrecht.

Utrecht

It took some effort to find Harry's estate without a satellite navigator. He had to ask around until he found the driveway leading to a stately home.

When he arrived, Debbie appeared from the side of the property. She must have seen him coming. He was glad she was there because he'd never phoned her back. After a hug, they walked hand in hand through an impressive hall leading into a large lounge. The room was elegant, with large windows from floor to ceiling.

A distinguished-looking man in his mid-sixties approached them and introduced himself as Harry Brinks.

"I'm delighted to meet you, Richard. Annelies told me something about your talents, but I do not understand it. If Annelies and Toon find it important, I have no problem with it. But please come through. We are studying the aerial photos Sascia took."

When he entered the large room, Richard spotted a young woman on the floor surrounded by many photos. Annelies and Hans were poring over the prints. As she turned and looked up, he was struck like a thunderbolt in his solar plexus when he observed how gracefully she disentangled her long legs from under her while getting up like a dancer.

The incredible image of Ingrid, but a younger version, greeted him. He was spellbound; what a dish! He was magnetised when their eyes met.

"So, I finally meet Debbie's Richard!" Sascia commented while she looked him over, showing approval. He sensed that she felt the same attraction when they shook hands. Her eyes were like Ingrid's, a luminous green with a speck of light brown, but she was a lot taller than Ingrid or Debbie. He thought he recognised the tone in her voice but rejected the idea. He didn't want to let go of her hand. It felt as if he'd known her from far back. He knew that he flirted, happy for being still taller.

The front doorbell announced Sascia's twin brother. He was taller than his sister and had the same features that resembled Ingrid. Jeroen Barendse's sleek hair covered half the front of his face, but his easy manner settled his emotions. He tried to calculate their ages, knowing Debbie to be Ingrid's youngest, and he was twelve years older than her.

"Richard, will you look at these photos?" Annelies brought him back to reality, and he joined them on the floor. The photos were good; Sascia knew her work, but how would he ever recognise anything? He remembered the map from the e-mail and excused himself.

As he sprinted to his car, the sun was peeping through patches of blue. The fragrance of drenched foliage, plus his encounter with Ingrid's other daughter, invigorated his spirit as he walked back with the map and note from Leo. Richard felt a strong sense of purpose rekindled after Theo's departure. Sascia took the map while he handed the typed letter to Annelies. Both Ben and Harry peered over her shoulders at the email.

"Where did the e-mail come from?" Harry Brinks' alarmed tone reminded everyone of Ingrid's plight.

"Richard, what did the interpretations say?" He stayed quiet, seeing Annelies staring at Ben. In his mind, he scanned Theo's explanations on the symbol of consciousness while they all waited for his reply. Theo had also revealed an intimacy between them, so what should he say?

"I'm guessing that the position of the large dome in Pleasure Parks resort in France has a connection with the interpretations. It said an inter-dimensional passage must be activated, meaning it's like a wormhole that runs between this and another universe." The blank stares from Ingrid's children and Harry made him feel ridiculous. How was he to explain that you must bypass the intellect and listen to the heart's intelligence to grasp that the pictorial eye symbol was a cosmic device? Annelies winked and mentally responded.

"Thank you for reminding me that words convey information, but symbols evoke understanding." He thought Annelies projected these words momentarily, but he shrugged it off.

Ben left them to make a call on his cell phone while Richard's eyes were scanning Sascia's aerial photos.

"Yes, I recognise something!" He almost fell on top of Sascia as he tripped over her legs. He grabbed the map to take it into the full daylight. Sascia followed and stood very close. Her body perfume stroked his senses. What was wrong with him? He had never reacted like this with any other woman!

"Yes, it appears the same", he murmured, recognising the small stream near the woods with the bridge and the building that appeared in the distance. Could it be?

"Annelies, I think this is where Ingrid is! Why was the circle drawn with a number next to it?" Upon seeing the marking close to the building, he was surprised.

"Sascia, can you remember where you were when you took that photo?" Annelies asked.

"Yes, I made marks on the map similar to the one Richard received over the e-mail. I followed our route as we flew over some scenery and marked the map to connect them with the photos. I'm pretty sure I can find it again. What are we to do now?" Sascia's penetrating stare revealed a fighting spirit.

"Mr Jaarsma, can't we involve Interpol by giving them this information on the building?" Jeroen appealed to Ben, who came back into the lounge.

"Interpol knew about us taking photos, so let's get on with it ourselves. Harry, what's the detective's name again?" Ben asked. The atmosphere in the large lounge reminded him of a suspense thriller. A housekeeper brought in some refreshments. This household was very wealthy, as having servants was rare.

"André Jaarsma will be here in ten minutes; I hope they are taking this seriously," Harry remarked as he helped himself to the sandwiches.

"Toon would have already gone to that spot to investigate; what are we waiting for?" Sascia called out, which forced everyone into a corner.

"How far is it by car?" Both Jeroen and he responded at the same time while he carefully examined the map again.

"It is near the Belgian border, approximately one hour from Maastricht," he muttered. It would still take quite a few hours, so they had better get a move on, hoping her children didn't suspect how serious their mother's situation could be.

"Okay, we'll make copies of the photos so Uncle Harry can keep the originals for the detective. Who is going with us?" Hans asked as he got up from the large leather sofa.

"I have to start my shift this evening, so I'll be with Toon," Debbie said reluctantly. Then, everyone was motivated to act.

"We'll go with you, the three of us, I mean, Jeroen and Sascia?" Richard eyed the twins, and both nodded. Harry took Jeroen to his study to make photocopies of the map while Annelies spoke to Toon on her cell phone.

"Toon feels it will take too long, so he'll contact his pilot because the plane is still at Soesterberg. He knows a landing strip near the area; a car will await you. He wants to speak to all of you," Annelies handed her mobile to Sascia. The mood was gloomy.

"Toon, have you heard from mom?" The tremor in Sascia's voice made his heart melt.

"Moved? Toon, did she know where to, and why?" Sascia listened while the rest waited in suspense, passing the cell phone to him as a tear travelled down her nose. Toon's voice was weak, but his willpower made up for it. Toon thanked him for his help and shared that he felt sad because of his medical contraptions. He urged him to hurry and not to wait for the police but to take a satellite phone with him to keep him informed. Then he asked for Jeroen.

Toon's energy was nothing like that charismatic power he displayed on one Friday evening at the coffee bar. He gave the phone to Jeroen, who had just come back. Annelies looked worried.

"Did Toon say anything more about Ingrid to you?" Annelies whispered while Jeroen was listening. Ben was still talking on his mobile.

"No, but" ...Sascia was on the couch with her head in her hands. He kneeled in front and took her hands while gazing into her beautiful eyes. All he wanted to do was to cuddle and hold her close. Debbie had not once stimulated the need to comfort her like that; why? Did that mean he was not capable of sincere compassion?

"Sascia, what did Toon tell you?" Debbie joined them.

"Toon said that mom 'telepathically' told him that they were preparing to leave the place and that she had no idea where they were going." Sascia wiped away her tears as his hand stroked her cheek slightly. She held onto his hand, which made him glow.

"Are they communicating telepathically?" Debbie exclaimed in awe. Richard was thinking about the second circle on the map that appeared at least a few miles apart, wondering what the circles stood for.

He called Connie on his cell, explaining that he would not be back and that she must close up early. Connie was very understanding, and Uncle Fred was with her.

"Annelies, do you want to speak to your brother?" Annelies was visibly surprised as Sascia took her photos and stuffed them into a large bag.

"Who is Fred?" Jeroen whispered as they walked out. He promised to tell the twins about Annelie's family in the car. He glanced at Sascia, whose worried expression made him want to squeeze her.

Debbie left simultaneously and hugged him outside next to the car, thanking him for his support. He felt very guilty. He was kissing Debbie, but he was attracted to her sister.

Hans drove Harry's Mercedes towards Soesterberg while the rest waited for André, the detective, to arrive. Liesbeth, who had just turned into the driveway, waved at them with her thumb.

"She must know where we are going, but how?" Sascia called out. Richard glanced sideways at Hans, who must have known what he was thinking because he suddenly heard *"I told her"* clearly! Was it his inner dialogue again, or could he return a thought? When he was in his remote viewing mode during dream time, he had no problem as long as he focussed his thoughts. *"Yes, you can, try it,"* Richard's amazement at hearing this telepathic made his heart leap.

"Richard, who's Fred?" Jeroen asked again from the back. He told the twins about Fred being Annelie's brother and the uncle of Connie, the girl who ran the Pannekoek coffee shop when he gave his lectures." Ingrid's children didn't know Annelies or any of the Jaarsma family. Hans never participated in their conversation, so he told them what he knew.

Hans was a good driver; they had a good time on the freeway. It was just before peak hour, so they would probably make it to Soesterberg before four o'clock.

"Richard, tell me about your lectures. Debbie told us you've studied ancient languages." Jeroen asked from the backseat. He turned around to respond.

"My lectures are on a freelance basis, meaning I structure a set of lectures on a specific ancient temple slate, tablet or scroll, like the one I cancelled yesterday, which was the first of four lecturers on the mysteries of the Sphinx." As he explained, he observed how Sascia curled up, resting against her brother. Richard wished he would be the one she was resting against. Could Vinny be her boyfriend? He hoped she wasn't.

"Really?" Sascia suddenly sat up straight.

"When is your first lecture, and what is it called?" she asked. Their eyes held briefly, and a seductive uproar spread like fire.

"Egyptian Mysticism and how the Rosetta Stone broke the code of hieroglyphics."

"You mean everyone can listen to these lectures of yours?" Sascia asked.

"Yes, the university promotes the events, welcoming university students and outsiders. All you have to do is register at the faculty." Their unspoken chemistry was incredibly stimulating.

"So, you're saying that you are not like a teacher that students must attend. You don't give tests, and nobody gets a diploma after attending your course of four lectures." Jeroen concluded.

"That is correct. However, suppose someone is interested in studying archaeology or ancient languages, as I did. In that case, they can write a research paper based on my lecture and conduct further research. This way, they will receive academic credit for their work. But, unless they write a best-selling book, they won't make a significant amount of money from it.." Jeroen asked how he interpreted the hieroglyphs because they were so symbolic.

"Yes and no. The hieroglyphs encapsulate an intuitive knowledge through an image in the fullest sense."

"You mean a symbol represents an idea?'

"Yes, like the icons in your PC, they convey and represent many words."

"Richard, Liesbeth told me that you met her in Egypt on an excavation above the temple of Hatshepsut." He turned to Hans, who was driving.

"Yes, I replaced my brother who...left this world a year ago. The sponsors asked me to take over from him so the tour could proceed." He still had difficulty accepting Theo's death.

"That must have been hard! Sascia remarked her eyes softened when he turned around.

"Gosh, you resemble your mother a lot. I'm sure you've heard that many times."

"Toon did. It was the first thing he said when he saw Sissy at the hospital...I wonder how Mom is?" Jeroen hugged her, and Richard could see that these two were very close. He wondered what unique bond twins have. Sascia must have related to him when she said it was hard for him to take his brother's place. Richard looked sideways at Hans, wondering if he was in contact with Liesbeth... "*Telepathy has no barriers or distance but requires a strong mental connection on a magnetic wavelength.*"

Richard again wondered if he had mentally picked up something – like at Annelie's house.

"*Hans, Ingrid is under some emotional strain at this moment. Toon can't reach her, which makes him less receptive. It must have something to do with the move.*"...He heard that thought beam very clearly, but was it directed at him or Hans? Or was he speculating these words in his mind while they were driving? At last, the sun had broken through and baked the shining bonnet of the highly polished Mercedes as Hans moved with haste on the freeway just on the speed limit, passing other traffic.

"*Richie, it's me; Hans can also hear me. Psychic hearing mixes the reception of extrasensory signals expressed as a word, a sound, or some form of language, like what you hear when you talk to yourself. Because psychic hearing manifests itself as inner mental dialogue, most people are unsatisfied until they completely understand how it manifests. They're being analytical.*" The late sunshine and the engine purring created a timeless moment. Everyone was with their thoughts. Did he hear Theo, or was his mind making all this up?

"*I heard Theo as well, Richard!*" He still was not convinced that he was not playing tricks on himself. He mentally beamed

"*Hans, can you start drumming on the steering wheel if you hear me?*" He wondered if it would work. Hans was steering the car around a big truck, and after he overtook it, he glanced at his watch. Suddenly, his fingers started to tap on the steering wheel!... Richard felt all glowing inside; he wanted to believe it was real, not just coincidence.

"*Now, are you satisfied?* "Wow! ... that was very clear, like a voice! Was he satisfied?

"*Richie, you have heard others think for a long time but have interpreted their pondering as your thoughts. You have been interpreting that psychic echo for so long that it is in your thinking as coming from YOU. Most of it came from others! When you were a child, do you remember that we used to talk like this, without speaking?*" Richard's mind reeled, thinking back to when they used to know that some of Dad's friends in the army base were lying because they could sense their thoughts, which contradicted what they had said aloud! He had...

"*Richard, direct your listening attention inside your head above your ears rather than towards specific outside sources! This will heighten your sensitivity*". Did he hear that coming from Hans? He tried to follow Hans' advice, but how did he know where or from whom the voices came?

"*When you call me, shift your attention inward and focus on your temporal lobe area. Send your love to me on a beam of light, and I will be listening and...buddy, if I am busy with something, I will let you know. Practise it on Sascia!*"...

Did he imagine a chuckle coming from Theo? He would try it out, ask himself, or instead, his higher self some questions first. Sascia was in his vision when he glanced at the rearview mirror. Gee, he was attracted to her.

"*It's mutual, that's why.*" Okay, he wanted to hear that, so surely it must be his wishful thinking,

"I did not ever feel about Debbie that way. Why? he projected to himself. *"What feeling?"* Richard wondered if he would get honest answers.

"When I look into her eyes, I get drawn right into them. I want to know more about her. I want to be with her. I want to touch her, and I want to...Gee, I'd better stop." He felt pretty silly having this conversation with himself. He hoped Hans was not listening in!

"*What if Sascia was?*" That thought spurred him to peer sideways; the grin on Hans's face made him suspicious. They were silent in the back. Indeed, he did not formulate that answer. He almost knew he did not.

"*How do I best get along with her? How do I get her to like me or even to want me?*" he beamed, holding his breath while observing her in the rear-view mirror....

"*Gosh, could Richard be direct and truthful to me? Laugh, make jokes with me, and work things through with me. Would he be gentle with me when I have to do something new? Could I trust him?*" Richard was stunned. Was he hearing this? Were they Sascia's thoughts? Hearing this gave him a different perspective on what she would be like. His focus was again within his head, just above his ears, while sending a message back to her.

"*Sascia, please ask me something.*" He waited in suspense fully and saw Hans peering in the rear-view mirror at Sascia. Had she heard his question?

"*Richard, how do I make you. Oh, this is silly, I'm kidding myself. I wish I could do with Richard what mom can do with Toon. How would I?*"...Richard was astonished. Was this how he had been speaking and replying to what he heard mentally, to himself? Her eyes were closed as she leaned against Jeroen.

"*Sascia, wait until I finish speaking, even if I'm still thinking. I find it helpful when people ask me questions that help clarify my thoughts. I love a good discussion, but I hate confrontations; laugh with me and share.*" he could think of millions of intimate things he would love to tell or share with her. He had to resist turning his head to see if she responded.

"Richard, what drew you to study ancient languages?" He gasped. Sascia's question surprised him so much that he had to turn around first. Did she have him on? When her green eyes laughed, his heart jumped. Both of them in the back were waiting for his reply.

"I always wondered if our Egyptian ancestors had not already discovered the secrets of life, and if they had, would they not want the future generations to know about that? So, what if they left that information behind in a symbolic language for generations? Then, it would be important to be able to translate them. I have always enjoyed unravelling mysteries. I lived in Egypt as a child, and my father and brother Theo studied ancient scripts. They interpreted many hieroglyphics on the temple and tomb walls. I followed in their footsteps."

Nobody had interrupted his rather lengthy explanation. He suddenly realised why he was always so drawn to the hieroglyphics on the walls of the temples. He was most drawn to the study of Hatshepsut in 1478 BC but couldn't understand why. Somehow, he wondered if there was a connection between him and the 13th Illuminati family. The first twelve heads of the world order are known, but who was the 13th?

"Richard, are Egyptologists scientists?" Sascia questioned. He turned to have straight eye contact with her when he replied.

"It's rather a sacred science because Geometry is sacred. Art is sacred. Your photography is a sacred science, not so?" Their eye contact became sacred momentarily, and her smile dimpled her cheek.

"I recall Debbie telling me you worked as a photographer for a newspaper. Did you take off from work to be with us now?" His question hit the mark because her eyes expressed a flutter of doubt about whether she had broken some rules.

"I never liked working for the newspaper, and I would like to be freelance like you, so I resigned from my job," she said as if she had just decided.

"Well, you are a good photographer, so I'm sure you will get work, or at least you'll have fun. Are you going to stay living in Amsterdam while you are freelance?" He knew he was flirting as he was talking to her while Jeroen watched the traffic.

"Gosh! he's flirting!" Gosh, what a thrill if he could read her mind. He'd better go slow with her.

"Well, my boyfriend would not be happy if I left Amsterdam. He tried to stop me from resigning, but I have decided. Maybe I won't go broke in the first two months, and if I do, Jeroen has to put up with me at home for a while." Sascia teased her brother with a twinkle in her eye while pushing him with her back.

He got a jolt in his solar plexus when he heard about the boyfriend. Had she said that on purpose? What made him think she was available? She could be Vinny's girlfriend, after all.

Before he realised it, they had arrived at the small airport. Sascia directed them to the hangar where the plane was waiting. A short, stocky man in his forties walked towards their car.

"That's Toon's friend and pilot, Dirk, who looks after his plane," Sascia whispered. Richard had never been on a private plane, so he would enjoy the experience, to say nothing about the seating arrangements! Hans sat beside Dirk in the front while Jeroen sat in two seats alone, and Sascia sat in the window seat beside him.

The intimacy he felt with her he had never experienced with Debbie or even his first wife, Ellie. When he saw Debbie for the first time, he took to her; it was mutual, but nothing like what he felt now. He recalled Vinny's story of meeting the girl of his dreams at his wedding, but...what if Sascia was Vinny's girlfriend? Richard could never grasp how, at your wedding, you could meet someone else, but now he could relate to that story. He now knew that Debbie would never be his future partner.

What if this attraction happened again, or if it was not mutual and Sascia was in love with her boyfriend?

As he peered over Sascia's head to look outside, he realised she had fallen asleep on his shoulder. He moved his position so she would be comfortable and studied her face from above. She had long, curly eyelashes, and her hair had an apple fragrance. She was wearing jeans with a T-shirt that stretched over the rounded outline of her breasts. He had already observed that she was well endowed. He hoped she would not wake up if he moved his arm so she would lean against his chest more. He lifted her gently by her shoulders and got an arm free to embrace her when she moved! ... He thought she would wake up, but she settled more snugly into the crook of his arm. Hans turned and grinned.

"How did you manifest that so quickly?"

"How long is the flight?" he beamed back. Hans was wearing one of those headphones, and he talked with the pilot, then glanced back at him over his seat.

"You're in luck, mate; you can have her on your lap for at least thirty minutes, then we must be on the lookout!" Richard felt ecstatic at being awakened to this new way of communicating. He was not complaining and grinned back.

Sascia's arm and hand were gradually resting on his leg, and as her soft rhythm moved her chest, feelings of an erotic nature started to challenge him. Her quiet, steady breathing accentuated her full lips; gosh! ... if only he could kiss her softly first, he would open her lips...

"Richard, you'd better stop this." ...he heard Hans' warning. He was annoyed with his imagination. Jeroen was leaning against the window on the other side, dozing. Both of them must have been lacking sleep and being emotionally frazzled.

• • • •

After a while, he also felt sleepy, but the flight itself was quite a novelty. He leaned in, gently stroking her hair. He breathed in the scent of apple blossoms as he applied more pressure, resting his weight on her head and settling into a familiar rhythm. As the gooseflesh travelled through his whole body, he knew what was happening. Could he stay in this position?

Then... he saw.

Theo...nodding. Looking at his familiar face, a deep affection for his brother awakened his need to please.

"Buddy, thank you again for your devotion, but I hope you are here because it pleases you?" What pleased him the most was the feeling of being connected this way. He would not miss their journeys for anything, hoping he would always be back...in time...

"Theo, in our etheric bodies, we aren't limited by time, space or size, are we?" They went straight through the walls of the small aeroplane, which gave him a flutter where his solar plexus should be. He could sense Theo's secret chuckles but didn't respond because he already knew that the part that travelled away was an extension of himself.

"That's right; we are travelling through morpho-genetic fields where all essential ideas first concentrate into an etheric mass." Did Theo mean that he never went anywhere? He was everywhere all at the same time? After swift movements, they viewed the continent from afar; Richard could see the whole province just over the Belgian border. Then he saw it! The symbol! The eye of the creation symbol was evident from a far distance, but the closer they came, the more confusing its outlines became.

"Theo, we have arrived at the location of the new park's large dome. Shall we go inside? Then, in a flash, mentally, he saw the photo from which Theo had translated the fourth tablet. The same eye symbol had been visible!

"Richie, since the end of the Lemurian times, many colonies of people occupied huge underground cities. This civilization was fortunate enough to avoid the kind of catastrophic events that could damage people's souls." Theo pointed to the centre of the eye, and a funnel appeared that drew them in. A spinning sensation of timelessness followed. In the end, he saw what looked like an opening of a lens, and the next scene reminded him of the Colosseum in Rome!

"Richie, other civilizations co-exist within our 3D electromagnetic energy grid program. We move our conscious awareness in and out of those parallel realities so they appear to be physical."

What did Theo mean by saying there is such a thing as civilisation within the earth?

"Richie, the inner sun concept is a metaphor for our inner light—connection to source—our soul." Was Theo implying that there was an inner world but not in a physical sense? Other people must have visited this place, calling it Shambala and getting their ideas from there. He could live with the idea of ancient tunnel systems but buried cities beneath the surface, which was a bit much.

"You are right. The architect of the Colosseum remembered this amphitheatre from his dreams, but this is not Rome; we are in the inner world. But for now, we will call what you see the planetary Over-Soul's mental classroom projection. We have received an invitation to take part in an intervention. Look!" The sensation of standing in an arena, looking down over rows of seats, gripped his attention. What intervention would POWAH reveal?

"Pay attention to the topic so you can write about it accurately." Many light-beings were all gazing at a brilliant laser ray in the centre. The imposing entity, POWAH, was again quite spectacular. The mere vibration of himself animated his tunic of an intense electric blue. POWAH's eyes scanned the gathering, and Richard imagined that his gaze reached into the depths of each inner being. Sounds of clear voices in perfect unison charged the area. POWAH's glance rested on him for one moment, and the familiar tones formed the words in his mind.

<*Dearly beloved, when you all embrace and work in unity, silently and freely, each one in their particular way will experience liberation within. You are all here to prepare yourselves and your fellow beings for the space-time overlap intervention soon upon you. You are preparing a pathway so others can follow.*>

The most awe-inspiring spectacle of blinking stars reaching out into the silken darkness of fathomless space surrounded them all. The Milky Way appeared in all its glory. In the prime of her life-span that had become a home to various kingdoms, Planet Earth spiralled nearer into his mental vision.

<*The resurrection for a new earth is already in process. Those souls who have come into this incarnation to gather lost knowledge missing from their Akashic records choose to do just that. Those who seek light through colour and the fundamental basis of all matter are rooted in sound.*>

Streams of soft rose-red flares burst into a fireworks display, forming brilliant layers of colours around the lonely planet, like an onion. Layer upon layer of shades of intense beauty settled around the floating sphere.

When the sound of harmonic vibrations penetrated his light body, Richard began to grasp how one could attract each tonal frequency into one's auric field.

"That is how matter and anti-matter created a passage through time and space, through sound and colour!" Theo beamed.

< *The Language of Light has always been your original communication medium. "Tiamat" used symbols, tones, and vibrations but was destroyed. Please keep this information in mind.,. The crystal skulls on your planet are the storage conductors of these pure sounds. They hold the memory of the Language of Light within their crystal consciousness. It is necessary to place these crystal skulls on the inter-dimensional passage to reopen the sound wave realms. These crystal skulls will re-activate the magnetic force field around the planet. From the planet's inner sun, portholes will re-open. Each of you here who has been guided by loved ones who have passed over into other dimensional realms during these transformation times will again remember who they are.* >

POWAH's message brought his consciousness back to his task. He could still not quite grasp how it was all accomplished, but one day, he would. Of that, he was sure.

"Music is a universal language. Try to hold the sound of the Language of Light in your upper memory levels so you can describe them to others." Theo beamed.

< *The honour granted to me to be with you during these momentous times has inspired many souls in the upper dimensions to join you all in the oneness and wait for you all to wake up from your illusionary dream. The increased photons in the planetary atmosphere will activate dormant, subtle glands in your biological form, such as your adrenal glands, hypothalamus, pineal, and thymus glands.* >

Richard hoped with all his heart that he would take the memory of this experience with him as he slipped back into his body, wondering what the veil consisted of that blocked it off.

"Destructive fear-based thought forms. Richie, every human being unknowingly adds to this energy veil on a moment-to-moment basis. That is the simplest way to explain this

veil. Each realm is divided by energy veils." Gosh, but how come he seemed to bypass this veil when out of the body? A grey fog clouded his vision, but the pure sounds that seemed far away strengthened when he saw their colours through his inner eye.

"Richie, remember that dimensions are realms of consciousness that define a vibrational frequency range through which you can project mentally. Creating your light body on this level of your resurrection and playing the awakening card game will synchronise your brain modes. I will be with you through this balancing process, helping you obtain the highest vibration possible within your body."

When Theo mentioned the brain hemispheres, he knew the second level of Annelie's awakening card game dealt with two cards. A left and right-hand card revealed encoded information derived from the lines in the palms of their hands. He hoped he was up to this task. Writing about the left and right hemispheres and the different functions they perform still haunted him.

<*Mastering inner harmony allows for greater group harmony, which is essential in this period—man's natural being lies not in his outer but inner world. When the Language of Light's 144 symbols are consciously integrated, over 50% of harmful thought patterns are transcended at all levels of reality. During this second stage in your awakening process, you must embody the first ten tonal harmonic Language of Light tones in your auric field.* >

Did the others in his Friday evening class still remember all this information Annelies spoke about because he didn't? He recalled the mind-drawing workshop Tieneke gave, but he was never aware of the depth and importance of their mind-drawing symbols then. Liesbeth and Hans seemed to know, but what about the people he encountered daily?

"Richie, many people are aware, but on an unconscious level." Theo beamed with the sweep of his arm. Was he suggesting that some of the light beings were unconscious?

< *Throughout many falls in consciousness, the human creation slowed down in speed. A "whole" soul was too high in pulsations or speed to embody a slower, denser form. Only fragments could represent a lower subtle form. These fragments formed Group-Souls, who in turn divided into fewer Over-Souls. This further division brought the pulsation down to the 6th and 5th realms* >

Richard was curious about the origin of POWAH as he received information through reflective images. He could sense the streams of energy around him without seeing them. As he focused on each colourful energy field, they transformed into human-like forms.

"You can guess, can't you? We are all part of this soul." Was Theo implying that they were POWAH's creation? They lived, or had they been in POWAH's mind field? But…how real was that?

< *Over-souls are often divided into individual souls incarnate into the physical plane. However, due to the limitations of the human form, the individual soul becomes further fragmented and separated. Some parts of the individual soul incarnate into the subtle bodies of a human form, while other fragments become personality aspects. The non-individualized element of the soul becomes the energy link between the human spirit and the higher self. It is with this higher self that I am currently communicating.* >

POWAH's brilliant light seemed to merge with them all as he addressed the gathering of light beings.

"Richie, when an evolved species from an outer universe started to seed their implantations into the human species, unexpected genetic distortions occurred. On a soul level, complete forgetfulness *trapped us into a cycle of reincarnation."* Theo's mental projection about reincarnation triggered many inner visions until POWAH's voice brought his focus back.

<*Dearly beloved, many souls were lost between incarnations when their soul particles became personality aspects in repeating incarnations. When personality aspects are in complete control of the human form, they are inclined to merge with other personalities in small and medium-sized groups while having a human experience. These groups, in turn, are more easily controlled by a group soul from an outer universe. The attempted solution did not improve the loss of consciousness.* >

For an instant, the visions POWAH showed them looked familiar. Did he remember flashes from his past?

"Richie, some evolved souls, who were then seen as 'Gods' by our ancestors, were shattered group souls who tried to return home through the force field of others. It is even happening now. That is where the vampire stories come from."

He now started to understand how difficult it is to translate energy images into words. Words make forms out of what is formless.

"You may need to make multiple trips to gather your records. However, it's important to remember that all creations come from the source of everything. Richie, remember that the fourth-dimensional records of planet Earth are in etheric computers. These records must be re-embodied to balance both hemispheres within the human form." Theo directed his attention back to when they decoded the Sumerian texts. Then, they speculated that Ra was a force or Group soul. Was Theo also not all that aware of the truth? Again, the sound waves took hold of him when his brain translated them into words.

<Learn from your dream time and stay sovereign in assessing life around you. Feel our unconditional love for all that is in all. Live like a God/ Goddess in the physical form. >

In a flash, it was over; POWAH had gone. These sessions never seemed very long, but he always felt fully charged afterwards. How would one go about finding this lost knowledge just through dreams?

"Richie, we'd learned that the Lyran culture came from a parallel universe. They created this inter-dimensional portal for us to become galactic space travellers. Aeons ago, vast amounts of radiation slipped through this portal, bypassing Earthman. POWAH mentioned beings from an outer universe. Their involvement gradually shortened the human life span. Our human form shrunk from a normal height of 8 to 10 feet to barely 5 to 6 feet." The stadium opened its concealed doors, and all etheric bodies dressed in colourful tunics left. Theo beckoned him, and he felt a sensation of speed again when the thought of time gripped his mind!

"Buddy, we are moving in consciousness. There is no past or future, only now. Time is a fabrication of man." Could that be true?

"You mean that nothing I see is there? Is everything just a mental projection? Are we not real...individuals?" What he had seen and felt was very real to him!

"Richie, practice remembering what you heard and saw." He then experienced an urgent warning... it felt like a tremendous jolt, followed by a shock...

••••

"Richard, Sascia, wake up; we are near the area! Sis, get your photos." The urgency in Jeroen's voice rang in his ears while the sensation as if he was falling, startled him. His jolt made her eyes shoot open. Suddenly, he was wide awake! ...

Chapter 5
The Planet's Third Eye

France

Sascia stared in bewilderment, blushing, while still in Richard's arms. He couldn't resist flirting, but the magic moment disappeared when she got her photos out of her bag...

The scenery below clearly showed a freeway. The sun was still up. Thank goodness for the extended daylight in the summer; it was around eight in the evening. Dirk, the pilot, was talking to the air control over the mike. It was impossible to have a conversation with him due to the noise. Hans pointed at their headphones above so they could hear Dirk explaining where they were. Sascia showed him one of the air photos. He recognised Pleasure Park's site by the three big lorries, but they were not flying high enough to see the eye symbol. The photo on Ingrid's disc appears from a much greater height.

"Now watch that road; it follows in a winding turn; you see that dip there? That is where Toon would have almost gone over if Peter had not stopped him...Now, follow the road and keep on it. They lost the Volkswagen with Ingrid at this location."

The small plane was tilting sideways. Dirk pointed out landmarks as everyone strained to see. Richard tried to remember the scenery from his dream state.

Dirk circled a few times over a large area and pointed at the fuel gauge to Hans. Then he saw it, and it felt like he had deja vu! He peered closely over Sascia's shoulders through the window, pointing at two buildings hidden in the woods. You could see part of it; even the stream was there. There was a back road leading into a densely wooded area.

Richard looked at the map he printed out from the e-mail this morning. All three were straining their eyes when Jeroen spotted a small dirt track, and then nothing...until they flew over an open area where the road continued into a long winding lane with an occasional fork in the country road that led towards the main service road...As they flew further, all they saw was greenery, and suddenly, they all spotted a large country estate. It looked like a large house with smaller buildings in a horseshoe shape.

It had a swimming pool with deckchairs and a tennis court. He was looking for a run-down building, which they must have already passed.

Hans asked Dirk to turn and fly over what looked like a health resort.

"That is where Ingrid is, I know it," Hans exclaimed

"What is that place?" Sascia called out. They circled twice over the estate when Dirk pointed again at the fuel gauge, and they flew away from the large property. Richard felt confused and worried that his dream vision did not match this reality. Sascia was crying in silence. There was no sound; just a tear came down her creamy cheek. The headphones made her whole being small and vulnerable. He took her hands in his. Jeroen also looked strained from anxiety for their mother.

Dirk was talking to the ground flight control staff. As they landed on a small airstrip, Dirk sighed with relief because his fuel had been low. The little plane came to a complete stop, and the backdoor swung open.

"Come people, the car is waiting," a tall man in his late thirties with a short-cropped hairstyle and olive complexion called out from the back of the plane. Jeroen was the first to move. He took Sascia's big bag with her equipment and followed her to the aircraft's rear. There was a cool breeze, and the late evening sun was creeping behind the mountains in the distance, still showing a spectacular light beam in the sky; it was a beautiful evening. Hans introduced them to Peter Spark, a relative who seemed to live in the neighbourhood.

"Did you people see anything, something that could give a clue where she could be? I heard that Ingrid has moved to a different location.." Peter's French look matched his emotions because he was agitated when Sascia showed him the map Richard retrieved from the e-mail.

"Peter, do you know of any large estate like a retreat, a health farm, or something else?" Dirk's chubby but solid appearance represented stability when he joined them after seeing the plane. He pointed at the map, more or less where Hans seemed to feel that Ingrid had moved intuitively. That must have been why the run-down building from his dream had not come true.

"It looked like a large building with a swimming pool and tennis courts from the sky." Sascia's voice sounded tense, causing both Peter and Dirk to react.

"Gosh, nobody ever hears anything about that retreat, but we all know it's there. You do not see many people visiting that place. We think it is a hideout. I'm surprised that it never has been investigated; I've heard... Sorry, I'm rambling on... Dirk, I'll keep you informed by phone. Let's drive down there; it will take about twenty minutes."

Richard knew that Peter was holding back information. After they dumped their bags in the boot of the BMW, he joined the twins in the back. Hans seemed sure that Ingrid was there, and they all trusted his hunch. While driving toward the estate, Peter told them what he knew about the place.

"There are lots of hypotheses about who seems to stay there. The local community speculates that it is a hospital where experiments occur."

"What do you mean?" By Jeroen's tone, Richard knew that Peter's insinuations made them both jump to conclusions. Jeroen started to pull his finger joints when Sascia grabbed his hands. Peter drove the BMW down the winding secondary road devoid of traffic.

"I never had any reason to investigate the retreat, and I'm sure Ben would know if something sinister was going on. Hans, what do you know?" Peter glanced sideways at Hans, who never replied because they were suddenly at a T-junction behind a delivery truck. Hans directed Peter to follow closely behind the car into the private driveway of the estate. Hans had been silent during the whole drive, concentrating. There was an electric tension in the air. They all knew they were driving on property that didn't welcome them. Richard felt Sascia's hand slide into his for comfort.

Large electric gates opened, and Hans calmly ordered Peter to stay behind the delivery truck. A man came out of the small gatehouse and was about to stop them when he suddenly looked dazed. He shrugged his shoulder and closed the gate behind them.

"Didn't he see us?"

"He thought he did, but I projected an empty lane behind the truck, so the man thought he was seeing something that was not there."

"Hans, that is a neat trick! You hypnotised the man!" Peter acclaimed in awe while following the truck, which took a side turn into a narrow lane. They all spotted what looked like the main building appearing on their right. The gardens were well-kept, and the place looked affluent but uninviting. There was not a soul to be seen... how extraordinary.

Peter drove up in front of the main entrance and stopped. A wide forecourt with concrete steps spiralled up to large closed double doors. Substantial potted plants decorated the imposing entrance.

"Peter, you stay in the car; I need the rest. Now, remember! Remember that the people inside will not understand what we are doing here, so let's play it by ear. I will soon know from reading their minds if Ingrid is there." Jeroen took his sister's hand, and they joined Hans in walking up the concrete stairs. They stepped inside the foyer because the doors were left unlocked. Everything looked very impressive. Soft music was playing in the background. They all approached the front desk occupied by a stern-looking woman who immediately started to shout at them in French.

Hans spoke calmly in her dialect, which he couldn't understand.

"Richard, check the register while I'm probing her thoughts. I've just asked if a lady of Ingrid's description has arrived here in the past twenty-four hours to see if she is denying anything."

The woman waved her hands at the doors, gesturing for them to leave, when he spotted a register book. He swiped it from the counter and turned a page back while Jeroen peered over his shoulders. The woman started to shout!

The last entry was not legible, but the number 22 was marked. Jeroen reacted as if he knew instinctively that his mother was held captive in that room. Sascia pointed with great agitation at a glass door that revealed what looked like a long passage. The twins pushed it open and called out for their mother.

The agitated woman spoke on the phone while Hans tried to calm her. Both Jeroen and Sascia were banging on doors by now. He followed them but realised they needed keys. He ran back just in time to be held by a man in a white coat who had suddenly appeared from nowhere.

"Hans, we need keys; the doors are all locked!" Jeroen called out.

A man was holding on to him with a firm grip when his anger exploded, recalling the scenery of Ingrid inside that basement. He knew that there must be something sinister going on with Ingrid's abduction, the whole Pleasure Park affair, and now this place. As they wrestled, his head was sideways when he spotted the star painting on the wall. For a split second, he was so stunned that he didn't realise the man had slackened his grip. Then he let go of him and sat in a chair, looking somewhat exhausted.

He saw Hans staring at the man while passing him three card keys. The woman behind the counter looked equally dopey. Hans must have used a hypnotic spell on them. He sprinted back to where Jeroen and Sascia were talking through the door.

Jeroen snatched the cards and slotted them in. The last one clicked ...When the door swung open, they all saw Ingrid fall, but Jeroen caught her just in time.

"Mom! Are you okay? Are you hurt? Oh, your face!" Both Jeroen and Sascia were clinging to her. The heart-rending relief and the emotional stress of the last few days poured from Ingrid's cry of surprise while she squeezed them both. He detected a blue and purple bruise on her cheek. Ingrid looked strained and worn out. All had tears running from relief that the ordeal was over.

"I see that I have a whole party rescuing me."

Her choking voice broke when she recognised who had joined them to look at the commotion.

Jeroen carried his mom through the passage while Sascia retrieved her bag. Ingrid said she could walk, but no one wanted to hear. He took Ingrid, who was surprisingly light, from Jeroen when they descended the steps. The two people in the foyer did not attempt to stop them. Peter jumped out of the car and hugged Ingrid. He settled her in the back seat while handing her his mobile.

"Hello...Toon...are you there?" she whispered. Richard observed Ingrid's face, which expressed pure anguish about Toon.

"Toon, thank you." She started to cry... again for my children. It was such a surprise. Was Debbie there?" Ingrid was listening while her tears were streaming down.

"I'm fine, love, really, but how is Toon? Please, Debbie, is it bad? He sounds so weak?" They all held their breath. Did Ingrid know that he almost died?

Peter was driving away from the resort while Hans hypnotized the person at the gate again. It opened when they came near, and they went away fast, following the winding lane again.

"Peter, is it too late for Dirk to fly us back tonight?" Ingrid pleaded. Peter looked at her in his rearview mirror.

"We will arrive at midnight, Ingrid; you cannot visit him then anyway; they won't let you near him."

"Toon, have a good night's sleep; I'll be there as soon as possible," she spoke softly. A weak smile appeared on her face... Suddenly, Ingrid let go when Sascia hugged her mother.

"Oh, Mom, what have they done to you?" Sascia softly stroked Ingrid's face. Sascia's leg was against his. Being so closely squashed between the twins in the back seat felt good.

The image of the star painting still haunted him. Something Theo had said in his dream tried to come to the surface. What would Annelies know about it?

"So, you spotted the painting; I will get to the bottom of this, don't you worry", Hans beamed. No sound had come from his lips, but Peter seemed aware of their mental communication.

"Toon is a wonderful guy, Mom; where did you find him?" Sascia asked. Jeroen grinned.

"What makes you think Mom found him? I think he found her!" That cleared the whole atmosphere, and for the first time, Richard noticed they drove past beautiful scenery.

Peter mentally asked Hans what went on inside. Hearing that activated him to beam, *"Yes Hans, tell me, what did you do to them inside?"* When he saw Peter glancing at him in his rear-view mirror in surprise, he felt light-hearted. He could do it! Just like Liesbeth and Hans. All his reading and searching for some form of truth of why human life was how it was all started to fit in.

Their communication was just like he communicated with Theo, but how could he not hear Sascia's or Jeroen's thoughts or Ingrid's?

"Hey! Have some patience; you're not that good yet! They are not projecting their thoughts in the first place. The twins' minds are closed until you have more practice. Ingrid is mentally too frazzled." Richard sensed Hans very clearly as if they were talking aloud. He knew there had been no sound or words. Was Hans implying that Ingrid was telepathic, but due to stress, her mind was not functioning to participate in their mental interaction?

Ingrid seemed to know where they were going. She explained that she had visited Peter, his wife Helen, and their children last weekend with Toon when they had flown in from Buttercup Valley. Sascia asked about the place when they drove into a private country lane towards a beautiful large chateau with a thatched roof and many outbuildings. A sign that was hanging from a tree caught his attention.

"Half-way House" ... B&B.

By your choice, dwell you now in the world you have created. What you hold in your heart shall be true, and what you admire most, you shall become...

A blonde woman who looked like Yolanda appeared when Peter pressed the horn. Peter introduced his wife, Helen van Houten, who openly cried from relief as she hugged Ingrid.

"We have had three, no four of the worst days ever. Even the children picked up that something terrible had happened. They are impossible." Helen's shaky voice uttered while wiping her tears away.

"Are they already asleep?"

"Not Timmy; you know he is very telepathic; we had great difficulty keeping stuff from him. He is troubled about Toon. He can't come to terms with it."

Richard was amazed at Annelie's family. These people were equally unusual. He encircled Sascia's shoulders slightly, realising that it almost became natural to him. Ingrid introduced her twins and him.

A cocker spaniel greeted them with a wagging tail, especially Ingrid. Hans, speaking to Dirk on his cell, arranged a time early the following day to fly back to Holland.

He liked the place; it felt very inviting. He saw what looked like hothouses at the side of the main building. He would walk around before they left, wondering if any guests existed.

"The people who stay here all work in the vineyard; it is a rather special B&B. It all belongs to Toon, who wants to use it as a halfway house for people attracted to community living," Peter projected, replying to his thought.

"You need some practice, so I peeped into your mind. Did I have your permission?" Peter beamed again when they went inside the main house. He overheard Helen asking Ingrid who he was. While Peter waited for his mental response, he peeked to see if Sascia heard her mother explaining his and Debbie's relationship.

"Yes, please let me practice. You are running a B&B as well, aren't you?" He pictured the words visually to give them a mental focus.

"Yes, we do, and we grow tropical plants in hothouses. I'll show you around after dinner." Just like that. No sounds or words.

Helen asked them if they were hungry, and Jeroen suddenly remembered that none had had any supper. Helen grinned, pushing her bottom lip out as if to say,

"Mmm...Richard, you are far more interested in the other daughter." Had she projected that?

Gosh, he needed to be aware of his thoughts! He could almost sense what Helen was thinking, but she was not projecting to others. They had all been silent while Ingrid and Helen talked.

After supper, Hans returned with a young boy of about six or seven who ran to Ingrid in the tastefully decorated lounge and climbed on her lap. When they left the table, he joined Sascia on the large sofa.

He saw that Ingrid had a way with children but wondered when she would tell the others. Then, he suddenly knew he needed to focus on something else mentally. Ingrid was very telepathic and would know he knew about her pregnancy!

Peter asked him about his studies after Hans had told him about his lectures. Peter was an entertaining host who seemed to know a fair bit about the history of Europe, especially Italy, from around the Middle Ages. Peter asked if he knew that the Duke of Florence ruled Florence until 1537 and was keenly interested in ancient manuscripts.

"Yes, it was well known that Cosimo de Medici was safeguarding the books on Thoth-Hermes. He believed that they held the secret of immortality. My brother researched the entity called Poim Andrés, who claimed to be an Egyptian with the knowledge of Ra." The cave where he'd seen the mummies flashed past for a split second. Peter was fascinated by historical artefacts; you could see that by the decor. When Hans recited hieroglyphic symbol quotations that sounded vaguely familiar, it had never occurred to him that Hans might know about Theo's translations!

Ingrid explained to Helen about Debbie, who was with Toon, and how Richard met her at the coffee bar when Debbie was home for the weekend. He looked up to see if Helen's response to her gave away his attraction for Sascia, but Ingrid didn't react.

Peter carried Timmy to his bedroom after falling asleep on Ingrid's lap. He heard people talking outside toward the outbuildings, wondering how many were working at the Cup of Gold Half-way House.

After coffee, Hans told them to break up their evening party. He would have loved to stroll in the garden with Sascia, but she followed her mother upstairs. Ingrid insisted she could climb the stairs herself, but everyone could see her ankle hurt.

Peter took him on a tour of the hothouse and showed him to his room inside an extension of the main building. An envelope had arrived for him from a courier. Helen thought it was for B&B guests, but she had to cancel because of the shootout and kidnapping.

The envelope with his name on it was lying on the bed. Inside was a photo. He gasped in surprise, for it reminded him of his dream! How did...Again, the eye symbol came up. Peter had said that a courier had delivered it... but from whom? Theo must have given his interpretations to someone who knows far more about what is happening. On the back of the photo was a sheet of paper titled "The Planet's Third Eye Game"[1] written in Theo's handwriting, but it again had a computer hyperlink.

Tablet 5

< *The mind field of men modulates mental energy into physical energy fields— for deep in the essence of matter are many mysteries concealed* >

He typed the Tablet title into his cell phone to read Theo's message and the rest of POWAH's fifth Tablet.

"Richie, after experiencing an out-of-body incident, I spent much of my time remote viewing and eventually comprehended the oneness within everything. I knew that the rhythm of the verses was tonal projections from POWAH's group soul. I saw that each vibrational sentence carried the identity of pure potential. I observed that many more universes are within the one source of 'All That Is.' Through the verbal movement, they are projected and hidden in the verse. During a cosmic out-breath, explosions rocked the nothingness of primordial essence, pushing it outward. Creation evolved into a movement as more galaxies were born within the two parallel universes."

Love Theo

He realized that Theo, besides the text, wanted to share his visions, but there was too much to take in. It wasn't easy to follow Theo's reasoning. He knew Theo had many out-of-body experiences during his last weeks in the flat. He always thought that one had to be ill or very spiritual to slip out of one's body. He knew he was neither, so what enabled him to do it so quickly?

He never remembered if he had questioned Theo about these photos when he travelled in his light body during Dreamtime. Was the message on these golden sheets left by people from the past or the future? Or...had Theo's brilliant mind unravelled the magical religion of the earlier Egyptians?

After taking a refreshing shower and climbing into bed, he realized how exhausted he was from all the emotional events. He knew that the moment his head hit the pillow, he would finally be able to relax and be free from his worries.

---

1. https://allrealityshifters.wordpress.com/richard-de-jong/tablet-5/

• • • •

Familiar vibrations took hold of his body within two minutes of lying down. He lifted or levitated by thinking about a thick rope he was pulling himself up with. Where that idea of the rope suddenly came from, he had no idea, but he was suddenly overwhelmed with a sexual urge. He tried shutting it off, feeling embarrassed.

"*Well, hello again! I see that you found the right girlfriend! You activated your primal higher frequency!*" Theo's mental comment was embarrassing. He beamed, asking what he saw, as they left the Halfway house guest room.

"*Want to know what that energy does and how powerful it is?*" He was not sure if he had heard correctly.

"*Oh, come on. Let me show you what a higher frequency charge looks like. If you deny yourself something on the physical plane, it will hound you in the astral; haven't you learned that?*" He detected Theo's humour, and he didn't think of it as funny; it was very humiliating, more likely.

"*What do you mean?*"

"*Buddy, Sascia sexually stimulates you, are you not?*" Richard felt emotionally naked. Were there no secrets anymore? He did wonder what sex would be like in the astral, in his light body.

"*Do you want to find out?*" That shocked him no end, especially coming from Theo. What was he suggesting?

"*I'm being practical; we have a lot of work to do, so you'd better release some unbalanced charges you have accumulated. Come.*" Good grief, was Theo taking him to a heavenly brothel? The relatively heavy, cloudy substance that had surrounded him cleared away. A group of people stood in a circle on top of a shimmering spinning disk. Streams of orange and violet were occasionally flaring up like flames. They were both invited to join in. They seemed a friendly bunch, and a female offered her hand.

He took it, but when she moved closer, the mere nearness of the woman reminded him of Sascia and in a momentary flash, a sex charge followed. At least, that was what it felt like. The woman stepped away from the disk, and another equally attractive female shape, and the same thing happened! He experienced a giddy electrical-type shock followed by a shooting flame. The person even thanked him, and his urge was gone! That was it! He wasn't even that aware of who they were. He wondered if this was where sex dreams came from.

"You need to learn the rules of the fourth dimension, Richie. What happened is more like eliminating a waste product you have accumulated while physically conscious. Soul energy does not resonate to these lower astral planes." Theo's explanation brought on embarrassing visions. He linked food waste products with lavatories. Indeed, sexual energy must have more functions than that.

"Oh, yes, sexual, erotic energy is fundamental in the development of group consciousness. Many people greatly misunderstand and abuse it, especially during the Atlantean civilisation. Because consciousness is multidimensional, any sensual energies form a connection link to all of who you are." Richard had to ponder this, but he would still love to know how Sascia felt towards him. As he looked around him, he saw many spinning disks. Like a dancing flame, the energy that covered the spinning surface crackled. What was that?

"Richie, as the kundalini energy rises in the nervous system along the spinal column, your greatness of self-expression and physical joy seeks to create more and more energy." He saw that the spinning disks slowed when the orange-violet flame dropped to nothing. There were no people about it. It was calm and peaceful.

"Now, watch what you see." Weird, he suddenly saw people having a trance party in the same spot! The rhythm of the beat flared the colourful force up into a charge again. The disks were spinning. He could see that this created feelings of a union in the dancing crowd. Wow!

"Now, watch what you see next. When it is an overspill of energy, and this biological urge charge is not released, manipulative and abusive sexual practices on the physical plane are the result, and it creates an inflexibility that can turn into addictive patterns." In absolute amazement, he saw how the beat started to influence the people's dancing. The disks began to wobble. What he saw next was people who were having sexual orgies. Electrical charges of a different nature entered the scene.

"This vibration of what we call lust underlies all addictions and does not serve." As he heard Theo mentally lecturing, they moved away from the valley where the spinning disks were. His thoughts went back to the times when he had sex. Had he been abusing this need to have sex?

"Yes, I'm afraid so; the opportunity now exists to move beyond just genital sex because human bodies evolve due to the increased electromagnetic field potential in the physical form." He heard Theo's remark, but when he saw another landscape with revolving disks, he noticed that what he saw as disks were more like vortices. He was enchanted by Theo's face when they moved closer, and he watched for confirmation.

"Isn't it beautiful? They are the elemental spirit sparks. They are the essence of life." All he saw were fairies and more fairies. He now understood where artists got their creative imagery from. It felt like paradise. He suddenly found himself surrounded by flickering, luminous beings that showered him with rose petals. Deep within a burst of laughter, he could not stop shaking his

whole being when he saw that Theo, his serious brother, was given wings.

"*One learns to honour all life forms, including oneself. In honouring oneself, you allow your inner light and love to shine.*" Theo stepped inside one of the vortices, and the fairies were gone. The wings disappeared, and instead, the music of the beat he had heard before clothed him with love. That's the only feeling word he could find to describe his feelings. He was curious about what Theo experienced, so he stepped into another spinning vortex and for a moment, he felt a sexual charge. Instantly, great feelings of peace, like after making love, came over him. Richard still felt that religion was mainly responsible for condemning sexual practices by proclaiming them to be sinful. How could this feeling be wicked? Did Theo imply that he should not want to have sex anymore?

"*Richie, the irony is that when someone focuses his life on spiritual things, then the kundalini energy is even more activated to rise past the sacral chakra, thereby stimulating the sexual energy.*" Theo stepped away from his spinning funnel as if he had just had a shower. His brother looked radiant. Like him, he now knew that the feelings from the heart had embraced him.

"*Richie, before the sexual energy can go into the heart chakra where love, compassion and dedication are activated, you must become aware of its power and direct it appropriately.*" Theo made gestures to follow him on a narrow path into the woods. Tremendous guilt gripped him. He knew that he had been guilty of acting out purely from a sexual urge in the past. He was not looking for any spiritual meanings then.

"*Theo, is it the same for women?*" He knew that the women he had had sex with had all been very accommodating. As he mentally asked Theo about women, they were suddenly surrounded by lovely young women running side by side, leaving very little room for them to walk.

"It's interesting that you ask because I also wanted to know that. What I've learned so far is that women generally confuse the sexual urge as being love because their primary instinct is to nurture." He wondered where the passing women were going. They seemed to be in a hurry. Theo sat on the fallen tree trunk surrounded by tree ferns and other foliage. It felt like they were in a semi-tropical forest.

"Where men are actively following the sexual urge to impregnate externally to take possession, women passively give of themselves internally and more emotionally to nourish." While Theo mentally beamed this, further away from the path, he became aware of a large circle of kneeling monks meditating. Richard wondered, does giving up physical temptations lead to sexual abuse? Were they not blocking a natural process?

"Yes, they are. Men are generally more blocked in the heart chakra because women are allowed to exhibit their feelings more. I know you will learn more of this misunderstood energy on the other levels of Annelies' decoding card game, but we are joining the others for a special gathering." As he pondered whether to choose an intimate relationship or to pursue higher knowledge, the images of Sascia replaced the praying monks.

"Richard, when you have successfully passed this sacral energy vortex and turned this urge to the awakening of yourself by activating the heart chakra, then you are evolved enough to experience a truly loving relationship with an opposite polarity and your sexual interaction with someone equally as evolved becomes a cosmic experience, providing both parties are motivated by the same course." Theo must have picked up on his thoughts in that last mental beam. Had Sascia the same urge to awaken fully? Most people didn't believe it to be possible.

"Let's join POWAH's classroom. I'm sure you don't want to miss that!" They got up and followed the same path others had passed before. Theo stopped after they had walked for a while, pointing at an opening through some thick foliage. Many people were resting or lying in a large gathering area. He would describe it as a large crater in the ground.

"What does this classroom remind you of?" He truly pondered. All he could come up with were the spinning disks. A lush green carpet of various mosses, grasses and wildflowers overgrew this one. In the centre was what he would call a...sun disk. Theo nodded while making gestures that they should sit down. He felt as if he had been here before.

"You have many times. Remember the temple we think was built by Amenophis I and Thutmosis III?" His mind reeled. What came to mind was Horus, as a solar warrior god. He noticed that there were lots of birds around. As he looked at the people, the faces around him had one thing in common. All beings come in many sizes, shapes, densities and vibrations, but all have a shared feeling of devotion, which seems to grow into a build-up of expectancy. Many more people sat down on one of the many levels of natural steps. They were all waiting for POWAH's arrival. Somehow, he knew he never answered Theo, but like the others, he felt at peace just by being there.

There he was, like a light flash! POWAH was gazing about at all the faces that turned toward him. You could feel his tremendous outpouring of love energy.

< *Greetings in the oneness of our source. I stand amongst you with great honour. Whatever transpires upon your planet has an impact throughout the Cosmos. We are grateful to each of you who contributed by breaking your mind free from worldly bondage and limitation in your created world of the senses. Your planet is preparing for her ascension during your*

next hundred years and beyond. Earth will re-locate into what we call the Cosmic consciousness realm of spirit that is everywhere at once, beyond time and space. Some of you have already experienced what that is like! >

Richard knew that was for him; at least, that's what it felt like. *"Richie, there are Group Souls who are more interested in retaining the world of illusion."* What came to mind was written on the last tablet. 'Masters were they of great secret wisdom.'

"Their control over many civilisations, regardless of the imminent warning of change, kept human consciousness ignorant. Even the predictions of such change, throughout the planet to many individuals and now through cyberspace, still do not stir the human population." Gosh, that was true! He received plenty of emails that all said the same thing.

< *You, who incarnated on Earth, must recognise that you represent the most significant challenge because of the intensity of duality in your thoughts. You all have chosen, on a soul level, to experience the process of choice. As you become aware of who you are, your focus is challenging for many. To be confronted with ancestral karma is not easy, but if you all persevere, you will see a greater perspective of this duality, and you will be less governed, less caught within its pull* >

POWAH was looking straight into his eyes. He was very aware of POWAH's love that abundantly showered over them all when he spoke.

< *You of the earth are in the battle of light and darkness. In your ancient days, the colony on Earth was awake to the divine essence of truth. The struggle for control came about because of the energy of those who were good and those who had forgotten. The battle of what you call Armageddon has happened a long time ago. The result was a drop in vibrations*

throughout the physical world of matter and in the celestial spheres surrounding your beloved planet. >

As he took it all in, POWAH's words triggered memories so vividly that, for a moment, he wondered where coincidences came from. The real truth behind everything he saw and heard still eluded him completely, but POWAH's pictorial explanation brought his mind back to what was said.

< When you descended, the hanging garden cities descended into the lower spheres and created a black hole for different civilisations from other universes to come through. This black hole was surrounded, protected, and glorified because it brought power to those who controlled it. It created a passageway, an opening between cosmic dimensions. That brought on the law that every effect has a cause. Many co-creators used this cosmic law to their advantage, as seen in your society today. >

Richard suspected that POWAH was talking about the eye symbol. He found the black hole phrase fascinating, recalling what Theo had written at the back of the photo: that beings from other universes had created a false intervention that still eluded him. Utilising radioactive and electrical currents to override the planetary Over-Soul's thought form was equally wacky.

"Richie, the experience of decay or even death was never a part of the human blueprint. It was to be an ageless existence that ended with a conscious choice to end the physical incarnation." Theo beamed. Looking around, he thought he recognised some faces listening to POWAH with riveted attention.

< As your galaxy is rapidly approaching the permanent closure of this cycle and you all enter the age where cosmic rules apply, you need to be prepared for a whole new set of rules. The holographic mind of the human species has to adapt. In the

history of this planet, there have been several significant cycles that were close to evolving into a higher vibratory octave. Still, we only saw it fail globally because of the interference of the dark thought forms that fully control the human ego. >

"Within the coming years, it is anticipated that a small number of earth's populations will move into the next dimension during the resurrection of the planet." Theo beamed. Richard pondered if he would be among that small number of people when he suddenly made eye contact with POWAH.

< *By the earth-year 2025, your beloved planet Earth will move fully into the Photon Belt, and most of humanity will have complete liberation. The significant lessons are the detachments from time and space. The highest purpose of service will be to awaken human consciousness to the oneness of cosmic reality. I hold each of you in the light of that perfection.* >

POWAH's energy slowly evaporated as if he had dreamt it all. Richard was overwhelmed. He wished he could write it all down while in his light body. The journey back into his physical body could still wipe out the information.

"Richie, the entry into the photon belt will help you all connect to parallel worlds simultaneously. Because your mind is still so used to evaluating things that the five physical senses have detected, This awareness will be considered fanciful and ignored." Richard contemplated Theo's message. His five senses must play a significant part in the awakening process. How was he otherwise going to know the real from the fantasy? The stillness that settled in after POWAH's message, which sounded like the music of the spheres, stilled his mind after everyone had gone.

"Are you blaming our five senses?"

"Richie, your biological body is aware in motion and is always a part of the eternal field of awareness at the source of creation." Theo guided him out of the rows of seating. The large circle slowly changed its form. He was getting used to becoming part of the surroundings. Why did he feel more limited when in his physical body? Observing the world through the five senses must surely be the obstacle.

"Buddy, it is difficult to express the ONE from the perspective of the current state of distortion. Your limitation is the exact opposite of being inside of ONE. Inside ONE, you know and can access all records of all experiences of all aspects of the ONE; therefore, knowing is unlimited, and creative potential is unlimited. That is as close as we can express such a state of being. Individuality leads to limitation; therefore, there is no Individuality per se as you know it, as it is a part of your distortion." Gee, he thought, if we have this need to be individual, will we never experience this oneness? He liked seeing himself as an individual.

"But you are multidimensional. Your DNA's intelligence operates simultaneously in the past, present and future and on many parallel levels. The many planes surrounding Earth split into many vibrations. Our soul lives through many different parallel lives simultaneously." Liesbeth mentioned parallel bodies, but he still had difficulty embracing that idea. Why could he not access the other so-called lives? Or did he? They seemed to be in a tropical valley; simultaneously, he was sleeping. At least his body was.

"At this moment, you are in two places at once, not so! One is the visible, sensual world, where your body is subject to all the forces 'out there, but if you are standing under the shower, your consciousness doesn't get wet! When we were bracing the heat in Egypt, it did not melt our memories!" That is all very well, but why are we unaware of them if we live simultaneously in many parallel universes? His mental perceptions seemed unequipped to deal with opposite dimensions of space. He speculated if it

had to do with speed. Theo's mental signature permeated his mind again when he heard his response.

"Richie, the word 'coincidence' means being drawn together at the same point. Events are never a pure chance, as some would have us believe". The soul's energy force interacts with many other individuals multi-dimensionally." Richard pondered what dimensions meant. Might it have to do with speed?

"During the fourth level of Annelies' card game, you will have learned much more about the planetary inner eye when you play with your three highest body cards. Soon, many more will awaken their holographic brain codes, restoring all memories from when they were asleep. Because you live out your stored images from your distorted genetic grid patterns, they are responsible for manufacturing your version of time."

One evening, Richard's friend Niels, from Annelies' workshop, shared his belief that his memories are in his body fat. Niels realized that no matter how much he dieted, he wouldn't be able to lose weight unless he let go of the past.

"Yes, that's right. Toxic memories can accumulate inside the human form. How often do we try to run away from something that is part of ourselves?' 'It is incredible how Theo always replied to his thoughts. He could feel Theo's emotions, and for the first time, he realised that even his brother was recalling what it was like to have a physical body now that he had none. Would one regret it? That brought on a whole lot of other questions. Would Theo incarnate again? But then he would not be there for him...

"Richie, the human species has to overcome this time-bound illusion. Try to remember the eye symbol and what it stands for." Both were walking in a familiar garden, and he recognised the hothouse Peter had shown him. Gosh, that was sudden. They were back! As he looked at Theo, a blinding light that came from Theo's forehead reminded him ...of what? ...

"Richie, remember, the I AM of you and me are not a body!" was Theo lecturing him again? He knew his ego was hooked on being an individual. Was it just his ego that wanted Theo all to himself, even at the end? Would he ever have had this astral travelling experience if it hadn't been for his help? A hot feeling between his eyebrows made everything vague. *"Don't you get too attached even in the astral light body? Let's get you back to yours again. Don't you feel the pull? I can see it"* ...All he felt was as if he fell again from an incredible height. He broke out in a sweat and... suddenly, he heard noises ... children's laughter woke him up...

Chapter 6
Perceptions Around the Polarities

Half-way House

The sun was streaming into his room when Richard heard Timmy calling his younger sister Karin in the hallway, telling her they were allowed to wake up Ingrid. Helen warned them to be discreet and well-mannered.

In the shower, he recalled his sexual encounter during his out-of-body trip! It returned to him in broken bits; not all the images made sense. Recognising his indiscretions in the past, he was happy he'd never slept with Debbie. Now he knew he'd like to share his thoughts and feelings as he did with his brother and with a partner! He wanted a loving relationship where he could be flirty and have fun at the same time.

Sascia was still on his mind, but he would approach her differently, more like a friend. If he could release his sexual urges during his sleep, well, so be it.

It was after seven when he left his room. Outside, the sun was already peeping through the enormous old trees planted after the chateau construction. Last night, Peter showed him the dining room the guests used for breakfast.

He passed some people on the way to the main house who asked after Ingrid and Toon. He wondered what kind of jobs they were doing. He felt an immediate affinity with them. It was a community where you know that the people all have a similar interest and are doing something about it. He now grasped enough about community living to realise that Toon and Ingrid were forerunners in building an infrastructure where people of all backgrounds could sustain themselves in a very empowered and utopian society. He wouldn't mind being part of that in some ways.

As he entered the large dining room with a panoramic view over what looked like a vineyard, he saw that Sascia, Ingrid, Hans and Helen were already having breakfast in the far corner. Sascia's hair was still damp. She looked fresh and crisp as the morning dew. He couldn't resist flirting. She blushed, which made him lightheaded so much for his intent.

He helped himself to breakfast from the sideboard and joined them. Ingrid was telling Helen about Sascia's photography. He winked at her, knowing how mothers can brag about their children. Helen asked if Sascia could shoot photos for a pamphlet advertising the halfway house and their visions.

"I would love to. I'll contact you after I have resigned from my job with the newspaper." Helen told them they had a small publishing business on the premises that could help her with printing the brochure. He wondered what else they were doing at Halfway House. Last night, Peter had given him so much to think about concerning community living. He only showed the hothouses, which was his passion, but they met quite a few others who all seemed to have jobs to do, although it was already late.

The more he looked around, the more he was astounded at the setup. They called the cup of Gold Half-way House, but it was more like a small village on a large property. Very well organised. Toon was the principal benefactor, but Peter told him the halfway house had started making a profit. Peter had begun to explain their currency idea, which reminded him of his student days when worldwide economic and social changes were high on the agenda. He remembered that about seven years ago in Rotterdam, only 'Let's Credits' were acceptable when one shop started offering goods and services to the general public. You had to become a member to make a purchase.

Jeroen joined them for breakfast while Timmy and Karin bounced around him for his attention. Both Sascia and Ingrid were their favourites until they spotted him. Karin reminded him of Sammy. He asked Timmy if he played games on a computer.

"You're kidding! Please don't encourage him to show you any games. Timmy has also discovered how to send emails." Peter remarked as he joined them. Ingrid told a story about her receiving flowers from every florist in Apeldoorn and its surroundings.

"Gee, that must have cost Toon a small fortune!" Hans remarked as he patted her on her shoulder. He saw that Ingrid was suddenly anxious to get going.

They said their goodbyes, and Peter drove them all to the small airbase where Toon's plane stood waiting to take them back to Holland...

At 11 am, Ingrid arrived at the hospital. They left after receiving love and concern from Annelies and others in the corridor. They all wanted to be a fly on the wall when Toon had Ingrid back, but Hans dropped Jeroen, Sascia and himself off at Mr Brinks' house, where their cars were. The three had lunch at Harry Brinks.

When they parted, Jeroen drove to his grandfather's steel firm in Mijnsherenland to tell him that Ingrid was all right. Sascia was parked next to his, so he asked her where she was going.

"Back to Amsterdam, I suppose. I would love to visit Toon, but for now, my mom will want him for herself." He could feel her reluctance to drive to Amsterdam. He needed to reschedule his lectures at the faculty and see how Connie was doing in the Pannekoek.

"I'm planning to visit Toon this evening. He asked me to come before we left yesterday to search for your mom. Why don't you come with me? We will visit them both together. I'm sure that your mom will be staying with him at the hospital. She will probably have to have some medical attention herself." He hoped she would feel the same as he did, not wanting to part company. They were outside waving at Jeroen, who had driven away.

"Richard....have you contacted Debbie yet?"

"Tell you what, I'll phone her now, and we'll have dinner at the hospital before we visit Toon and your Mom tonight." He wanted to take her with him and drive off anywhere, but he had lots to do himself, like confronting the faculty.

"All right, I'll see you at the hospital around six tonight?" Her cheer and smile made him melt on the spot. Sascia climbed in her car and waved at him, saying she decided to go home to her mom's place to get some fresh clothing and confront her boss by phone!

"Why don't you come past the Pannekoek, and we'll drive back to Utrecht together."

"Maybe I'll do that, see you!"

After he explained to Wil, the secretary at the university, that Trevor Zwiegelaar had asked for his assistance with the latest developments on the Pleasure Park abduction of Mrs Barendse, she didn't ask him any questions. She was even keen to reschedule his lecture. He was amazed. His connection with Trevor Zwiegelaar seemed convincing enough to overlook his late cancellation. The freeway was clear of traffic, and he returned to Apeldoorn.

When he arrived at the Pannekoek late afternoon, Connie wanted to know everything. Nel also appeared from the kitchen with questions. Both were relieved that Ingrid was fine and Toon was improving, according to Connie, who had just spoken to Hans.

"Hans asked me if you could phone Harry Brinks when you arrived; it was urgent." He was about to dial Harry's cell number when Sascia entered, and his heart leapt.

"So, this is the place where Debbie met you! What a cosy coffee shop! I've never been here!"

"Gosh! You're just like Ingrid, but taller," Connie introduced herself.

He felt rather sheepish for being so captivated with her. Nel looked spellbound at Sascia when she came back from the pantry.

"I've never met your mother, but you remind me of my previous daughter-in-law's sister. It's incredible."

"Who's she?" Sascia asked when Nel went back to the kitchen. When Sascia climbed on a barstool in front of the counter, he could only stare at her shapely body. The dolphins jumping around a yin-yang sign on her t-shirt tucked into her jeans accentuated her curves. Connie bragged that Nel was an absolute gem in the kitchen, and only yesterday, Nel had told her that she had worked for Toon's firm! They both kept looking piercingly at him, waiting for an explanation.

"I didn't know." He felt reprimanded for not knowing Nel's previous employer!

"My aunt appealed to me to employ her. She phoned me from South Africa one day and asked if I could do with some more help in the kitchen. They are good friends." Nel came through with more newly made stroopwafels that were in great demand. The aroma penetrated the whole coffee bar, but none of them asked who her previous daughter-in-law's sister was.

"Sascia, does your mom have a sister?" He asked when Nel had gone. Sascia frowned and mentioned her aunt Quincy, who was going through a divorce.

While he was serving a few customers, Connie and Sascia were chattering as only women can do, and when the phone rang, they both ignored him completely.

"The Pannekoek", he answered while observing Sascia artfully. The person at the other end startled him. It was Toon! His voice was much stronger, and he remarked how relieved he was to have Ingrid safe with him again. Toon asked if he could fetch some papers from Annelies since he had heard from Sascia that they would visit them together.

Sascia was peering at him as he rang off. He wondered what papers were so important that he had to bring them. Connie was busy explaining the directions to the palace 'Het Loo' to English tourists. He excused himself to get something from his flat before leaving for Utrecht. He'd explain Toon's request later. Connie would close up early; she needed to be with her mother, who was still getting over her ex's possible involvement in the kidnapping.

Her husband must have seen him coming when he arrived at Annelies', Ben. It was strange thinking of him as an uncle.

"Trust Toon to start scheming when he has his strength back!" Ben remarked when he followed him through to the kitchen.

"What's Toon up to? He asked me to get some papers?" Annelies looked up over her glasses, grinning at Ben.

"Love, tell him, but Richard, you keep it to yourself, you hear!"

"Toon will ask Ingrid to marry him at the hospital chapel. He has asked me if I could contact your uncle Leo, who has a marriage licence to do the traditional ceremony." Ben handed him an envelope.

"He's a minister?" He felt pretty good hearing the uncle part.

"No, not really in a traditional sense.... Ooh, I almost forgot; Leo gave this envelope to me for your journal. I believe you are having supper at Harry's before you and Sascia visit them, not so?" Gosh, he never phoned Mr Brinks back. He was about to ask Ben what role Leo played when Annelies told him to hurry; she was eager to know Ingrid's reply because of the organising involved.

Annelies walked with him to his car. She was glowing as if a massive load had left her. Joris the Labrador playfully raced towards a bird. He was growing; only a few weeks ago, he saw him on the first level during the last decoding workshop.

He felt excited as he had Sascia all to himself during their drive to Utrecht and back to Apeldoorn! Before he collected Sascia from the coffee shop, he quickly tidied up his front seat, throwing all the papers in his boot. He was eager to see what was inside his envelope but was already late. He placed it behind his visor for later. Leo must be some interesting man. Theo had often mentioned him, but only now, when snippets of his dream came back, did he wish he had been more attentive. He hadn't written his dreams down since the search for Ingrid began.

They had a good time on the freeway back to Utrecht. Sascia's perfume penetrated his nostrils, filling him with a delight he'd never experienced. He knew this was not an unknown pattern but stronger than ever. This girl was so charming that he had to restrain himself from being coy. She asked a lot about his interests but cunningly became very evasive when he wanted to know about hers.

"Does your boyfriend know that you are going to resign?" She was staring ahead; her thoughts were miles away, and he could feel it.

"Richard, the decoding workshops Annelies gives, do you...I mean, can people? Do you believe we may be physically immortal?" He could so relate to her feelings of doubt. He knew it in his heart to be the truth, but even after all his out-of-body experiences, his logical mind challenged him constantly.

"The rituals practised before c.12,000 BC were eventually transformed into funeral ceremonies. At some point, these rituals may have been misunderstood by later generations and interpreted as funeral ceremonies. In my preparation for the talk on the Sphinx, I gathered ample evidence to support this possibility of transfiguration." Sascia was nodding. He wondered how much she... *he'd love to...I knew it, and I felt it to be true. Oh, I feel so lucky to...* He was somewhat startled at his gradual sensitivity to hear her think, but it stopped as they drove up to Harry Brinks' estate. Had he just now experienced telepathy? He still had no straight answer about a possible boyfriend that she had fleetingly mentioned in the plane. Sascia jumped out before he could probe again.

Both Hans and Liesbeth came strolling hand in hand towards them, making him wish he could take hold of Sascia's hand.

"Why don't you? I'm sure she doesn't mind."

"Hey! What about some privacy? What makes you say she wouldn't mind? Are her feelings for me like mine for her? Tell me, please," he beamed back as they gathered in the dining room. He watched both their facial expressions for any signs of rapport.

"You'll have to do your courting. We promise to keep any information confidential." Liesbeth projected as Hans pinched her in her waist. His joy knew no bounds. Sascia knew

something was happening between them, but she quickly looked away when he winked. He saw her reaction when he flirted. To know that she was not entirely impartial for him gave him hope.

Richard apologised to Mr Brinks, explaining that he had got an urgent message from Hans asking him to phone him and that he had tried. Harry never disclosed what the urgency was all about.

Tieneke, Harry's only daughter, who facilitated the Language of Light mind drawing workshops, was helping the housekeeper lay out a buffet of seafood, meat, salads and various delicious dessert goodies. He was once more amazed at the timing of meeting up with her again.

At the table, Tieneke asked if he still wrote down his amazing dreams. He explained to Sascia that he had attended her long weekend workshop last year and that Tieneke got him to write down his first thoughts when he woke up. He had never known that Mr. Brinks was her father until now. He recalled that Tieneke had a daughter in the twenties who had sometimes interrupted her mother during her mind-drawing class.

His plate was loaded with snacks when Debbie arrived. She kissed him while welcoming the rest. Debbie entertained them all with stories of Toon and Ingrid. While he was listening, he noticed that Sascia was very quiet. In between organising the catering staff, Tieneke asked about his studies. She also had a keen interest in archaeology.

"Richard, the Egyptian hieroglyphs on the temple walls are full of references to the sacred eye and the sun disk, not so?" Tieneke's question on the eye symbol jogged his memory. He never considered it like that, but Horus's eye often appeared throughout ancient Egyptian texts.

"The vivid ritual scenes could all be related to the resurrection or reawakening of Osiris, the god within."

"Who is Osiris, a king or pharaoh?" Debbie asked.

"Osiris is the father of Horus. In a duel with his evil uncle Seth, Horus lost his eye. After being crowned as the divine king of the Osirian Kingdom, Horus embarked on a journey to the underworld or astral realms to find the soul and body of his father, Osiris. Horus delivered his father's lost eye to him, which revived Osiris from his lifeless state.." He loved telling metaphysical tales that, in reality, disguised a different story.

"This is all a myth, not so?" Sascia's eyes were glinting as if she heard an inner joke. He was relishing a piece of chicken when he winked at her. He knew that they were all waiting for his reply.

"Yes and no. The Eye of Horus became an important Egyptian symbol of power and even to this day is represented on the U.S. one-dollar bill." Harry opened a drawer from a wall unit and produced a dollar bill!

"Is the New World Order not an expression used by the Illuminati, signifying the coming world government to establish a universal regime over the world?" Harry responded.

"Yes, remember that Roosevelt was a member of a secret society called the Ancient Arabic Order of Nobles of the Mystic Shrine (Shriners). He attained the grade of a Knight of Pythias. The Order of Nobles and Mystics claimed to be an offshoot of the Illuminati." Hans replied.

"The eye symbology is a reminder – announcing this "New Age of Horus," Liesbeth added.

"That is our time, not so. The time of the great awakening?" Sascia asked in general.

"According to my brother Theo, the afterlife is populated by numerous angelic spiritual beings who aid the deceased on their journey towards resurrection. Many like me are on a quest to uncover the transmission of ancient Egyptian texts and later Hermetic teachings to Gnostic sects. I suspect that the writers of the hieroglyphs presumed that we, the interpreters, would know that they told, through a pictorial text, the tale of the fall of consciousness in man."

"Mmm, that's a way to look at it." Sascia nodded.

"In the past, archaeologists have tried to interpret the symbols in a linear mode of thinking. In the Egyptian text, I suspect that, like the eye shape, the owl and the symbol of a shaft, those symbols refer to our written word ascend, or the place of ascension." Sascia was genuinely taking it all in.

"I speculate that the golden capstone that is missing from the tip of the pyramid has a connection with this whole passage in the text," he added, feeling stimulated to speculate. Hans mentioned that the star Sirius represents the goddess Isis, the mother of Horus. The five-pointed star symbol denoting the hieroglyphic name Sept suggests that the start of humanity, the birthing phase, happened within the womb of Sirius. Both must meet through the missing capstone to open the secret chamber. He looked at Hans in amazement. Was that the connection of the star Sirius with the disappeared capstone? He wondered if Hans had ever read Theo's interpretations.

"*Oh yes, many scientists have speculated that the Great Pyramid represented a star in Orion's belt, Zeta Orionis. The eye of Horus represents the original seeding of the human race.*" Was Hans projecting all this? Did Hans know of many more secret chambers that exist below the Sphinx? What would their purpose be?

"*You will find out; be patient*", Liesbeth beamed smiling. The more he observed Hans and Liesbeth, the more he got the feeling that they were not from Earth. It was a weird idea, and he rejected it when it entered his mind. Harry excused himself from the table while the housekeeper cleared it. Coffee was served in the living room while he tried to recall Theo's translations. He wished he could chat with Hans, but time seemed to be against him as always.

Debbie had to take a phone call just before leaving for the hospital. She explained that her friend's brother had been in an accident and she had to meet her friend. When Sascia asked where the accident had taken place, Debbie explained that the motorbike accident had happened a few months ago, but her friend's brother had died last week of his injuries. He felt sad for Debbie, who always seemed involved with people's misery. Sascia walked with her sister to the parking bay at the side of the house. Hans and Liesbeth were driving home, so only they would visit Toon and Ingrid. It was already after seven.

"Richard...what is your relationship with Debbie?" Sascia asked after they both had been silent during the drive to the hospital. Before answering that one, he wanted to think. He tried to sound genuine. Somehow, blurting out his infatuation was not appropriate... He drove in silence, and when he pulled into the hospital grounds and found parking, he turned to her in earnest—the cooler evening made her shiver because her nipples started to show.

"Debbie and I have a special friendship. I admire her dedication to her work and humour at things in general. But...I'm not in love with her. *I've fallen in love with you, girl.*" he beamed, dazzling her. She blushed. Usually, he would have acted on his urges and attempted to hold her or at least touch her. Thank goodness she jumped out of the car before he could act impulsively. As he took Toon's envelope from behind his visor and locked the car, he heard, "*You gorgeous hunk, I'm not falling for your flirting so easily.*" his sensitivity startled him. Was he hearing her think? When Sascia turned her head while running to the lift, he saw that she was laughing!

He was waiting to jump into the lift before the door closed. They had the lift to themselves up to the fifth floor, and he lost his cool, pressing Sascia into the corner of the lift to kiss her soft lips. He could feel her breast pressing against him. For one second, she responded as she slid her arms around his neck. The saliva on her tongue triggered his brain into such arousal he knew he had to cool it.

When the lift stopped, they parted just in time as the door opened, and people came milling in. Crumbs, he hadn't planned to do that! He had promised himself to go slow.

Sascia ran down the hall and knocked before opening the hospital door of Toon's room. As he walked in, Toon settled beside Ingrid in the same bed! Although the room had a second bed, they preferred to snuggle up together.

"Hi, mom! Gee, you look a lot better, and Toon? Has he slept? I brought you some clothes. I hope I chose the right ones," Sascia rattled off. He saw Ingrid raising her eyebrow at her daughter.

"Are you coming down with something?'

"No, Mom, stop fussing. I feel great." By her shaky voice, he knew Sascia was only recovering from their intimate embrace. He handed Toon's letter to him. He was still on a drip. He gazed sideways at Sascia, but she ignored him. As Toon read the letter, he saw a big smile when he looked at Ingrid, who was suspiciously eyeing him. Those two were very much in love. Ingrid asked what Toon was hiding from her. He captured Sascia's attention through eye contact, just in time to observe that she was still trembling!

"Will you marry me?" Toon firmly asked Ingrid, passing the letter. Ingrid's eyes turned a brilliant green as she opened the paper to read what it said...her expression said it all.

"What, here? In the hospital? .... Oh, Snooks, yes I will." As Ingrid gently hugged Toon, he grabbed and squeezed Sascia's hand, who was taken entirely by surprise.

"Mom, Toon, I'm so...I don't know...happy for both of you, I guess. What a surprise! Toon, how did you arrange that from your hospital bed?" She let go of his hand to hug them both.

"Did you know about this, Richard? Toon, what have you got to say for yourself? I can see on your gloating face that you know more about this scheme." Ingrid's accusation made Sascia equally curious about her mother when she gazed at him.

"I'm only the messenger boy. Toon, I did as you told me to do, and Ben printed this letter out on instructions from Leo. You also need this paper to get co-operation from the legal people." He handed over more papers that Ben had given him.

Both women were whispering to each other, and before he knew it, he was dragged out of the room by Sascia, who, while walking to the lift, demanded to know how he knew that Toon was going to propose to her mother while she hadn't! He had to grin at her sudden bossiness. The sensors opened the lift door for them. When he stepped in, for one second, Sascia hesitated, looking to see if anybody was following them, but he was not having any of this. He activated the sensor and, taking her by the arm, pulled her inside. When the door closed on them, he took her in his arms. She was about to talk, but she almost lost her balance as he kissed her. The way she kissed back revealed plenty. If it was not for the very short time in the lift, he knew they would both easily get close to the point of no return.

"Rich, I can't, I mustn't, I'm in a relationship...and you and Debbie." All he could do was hold her close. The lift opened, so they were not alone anymore. They ran to his car, her hand still shaken from pure jubilation.

"Moppie, I've...fallen in love with you," was all he could stammer when they were inside.

"But Debbie, she loves you, I know... and...I have a boyfriend...oh, I don't know...Please, Rich, give me some time to think this over; I'm so confused; I need time to sort my life out."

He didn't know what to reply; all he could think of was Sascia mentioning a boyfriend. He knew this was the right girl for him, but he didn't want to push her into anything. They had only met three days ago, but it felt like he had known her much longer.

After their silent drive to Apeldoorn, each with their thoughts, she told him that she had officially resigned from her job at the paper. She had talked it over with her mother. She would come home to stay for a while and see if she could make a start at photography freelance. Suddenly, his idea of writing a symbolic dictionary that would translate ancient texts from an ascension theory point of view became more real. To have photos of old artefacts that would bring his lectures to life bubbled up into his conscious mind. Ideas were flooding into his brain. Somehow, he knew that she would be in his life. He would have to be patient. He needed to prepare for his first lecture on the Sphinx, scheduled for the next day.

He dropped her off at Ingrid's house and walked her to the door. He was about to remind her how she responded to him, but the front door opened, and a chic lady greeted them.

"Richard, this is Quincy, my mom's sister." He shook hands with an exquisite woman who reminded him of Debbie in a way. He wondered if she was Nel's daughter-in-law.

"Quincy, mom said yes. They are getting married at the hospital!" Sascia's excitement covered up her feelings towards his romantic intentions.

Her aunt was immediately on the phone to Annelies. Both women were focused entirely on the wedding planning. In the meantime, he requested an excuse, and Sascia walked him to his car. She inquired about his talk the following day and addressed him as Rich. He pulled her into the bushes beside his car, asking her if she would attend his lecture. He was shaking all over.

"I will try, I'll"... and a kiss smothered the rest. Richard couldn't resist feeling her body quivering against his once more. Boyfriend or not, this girl had to become his, and he was sure of that! Before she could object, he let her go and drove off, knowing he had unsettled her far more than she wanted to admit.

When he arrived at his flat, all his senses were sharper than ever. His joy that Sascia had shown her feelings for him gladdened his heart. He emptied his car, retrieving the letter Ben had given him from Leo.

As he opened his front door, the silence was more noticeable than ever. He wanted a companion again. His short, disastrous marriage to Ellie did not overshadow his thoughts this time. He now knew what he wanted in a partner. He would like to share his connection with Theo with a woman. Would Sascia be the one? He had never before been so serious about another relationship. He hoped there was more than just the sexual attraction between them. Could he have it all?

After putting on some music, he settled himself in Theo's favourite chair and peeped inside the envelope. The photo revealed a thin gold sheet wrapped around the mummy's leg. How did he? Did he make that up? He remembered from a dream how the older man had pulled the gold foil sheet, wrapping it away! He wished he could remember where the cave with the mummies was.

It would take him hours to translate the symbolic text, but on the sheet of paper stuck at the back of the photo, he recognised Theo's small but neat handwriting.

As you can see from the photo, this sheet was more damaged. However, the Akashic records showed me how initiations were practised well before the 1st dynasty. ...

He wondered how, through remote viewing on the astral plane?

The Lion (Sphinx) temple was a tribute to a highly evolved species in another time zone. They visited our universe through a magnetic tunnel that later separated them from their universe. They had the knowledge to control the life span of the human species. Their message projected that the human species' spiritual intelligence became out of balance...but the priests misinterpreted it from the 1st dynasty.

Was Theo serious? The magnetic tunnel eluded him. It sounded like a science-fiction script.

Every human being is a co-creator in the most total sense. Every person is a co-creator. We learned to awaken and heal seven passageways linking us to the matrix. Annelies and I learned to activate and heal the seven pathways connecting humanity to the matrix. When the giant geodesic dome is positioned directly over the eye symbol, it will act like a hemispheric synchronization temple. The patterns of light and sound played out within the dome will become a tuning fork to balance the male-female, electromagnetic aspects within the planetary body.

He had no idea what Theo was implying, but Annelies must know. He must soon show her all of Theo's letters as he gathered them for his journal. From the link, he was eager to read online about **Perceptions around the Polarity Game**[1] on Theo's laptop.

Tablet 6

< In a time long forgotten, we opened the energy vortex of the planetary third eye—It revealed nine other space zones within the essence of matter that had passed us by. >

---

1. https://allrealityshifters.wordpress.com/tablet-6/

His mind could hardly grasp what Theo had uncovered. Whatever happened that resulted in the kidnapping and shooting must have somehow made a connection with what Theo translated in tablet six. How and why eluded him, but he would do almost anything to find out.

He was so awake that he cleared some of his brother's drawers. He had been meaning to do that for so long.

An old photo drew his attention. There was a photograph of a woman sitting upright in a three-cornered chair. She had a middle parting in her hair and a crown of plaits around her head. Her high-necked satin dress was embroidered with beads but looked quite uncomfortable. The person looking at the picture wondered why Theo kept the photo of their grandmother. He had never shown much interest in family history before but became curious ever since Annelies had referred to Aunt Mien as family. Surely Aunt Mien knows that Ben was Annelie's husband? How come his aunt never talked about family when they lived with her? He should give Aunt Mien a call, especially to ask about her first husband, who might be involved in the whole kidnapping affair. He had not told Annelies since a vague insinuation would not be a good enough reason.

He felt a strong need to start throwing some old stuff out. Too many memories needed to be released. A new life had begun, and he knew his habit of holding on to things would clutter his manifestations.

He spotted another old photo of his parents with the Giza pyramid in the background. They looked like a happy couple. His mom was heavily pregnant with him; Theo stood beside them, holding his father's hand. He remembered so little about them. He had asked Theo about another family once when they were on a camping trip five years ago. All he knew was that the family disapproved of their parent's union. Theo remembered his father once saying that he had an older brother who also had married a Jaarsma girl, and their parents felt one Jaarsma in the family was enough. He was wondering why they had never explored their family connections.

Gosh, his lecture on the Sphinx! He should have worked on it tonight, but he was frazzled and couldn't be bothered now. He dropped like a sack of potatoes onto his bed whilst drifting off to sleep, visualising a long mirror floating above him. Maybe he should have mirrors on his ceiling...

• • • •

He saw himself in this mirror, lying in bed...He was amazed at the ease with which he lately seemed to float out as if he only then came to life. Theo was already waiting for him and took hold of his hand to stabilise himself because of the incredible experience of being free!

"I know, just before I left for good, I had many out-of-body experiences. That created such peace, knowing I could release my attachment to my physical form." Richard was glad for his brother's sake but realised how selfish of him to be so depressed not having him around physically. But why did he leave him to stay with strangers? That still left feelings of hurt. His intent to fully awaken became more vital each day because of that.

"Theo, if we don't have to physically perish to be able to 'travel' out of the body, why can't I remember more clearly what I've experienced so I can write about it?" Somehow, there was still that blank space of forgetfulness when he returned. He had to admit that the sexual experience during his dream helped, but...

"Buddy, stop fretting. Let go of past feelings. They served a purpose; it got you motivated, not so?" Was that why he left before he died? As they travelled away from Apeldoorn, streams of colours that moved while making patterns ignited his curiosity.

"Richie, I'll take you on a journey that will startle you even more. I've only recently been there myself, so don't ask any questions yet; trust me." It was hard not to ask about the light waves.

"Richie, science has already discovered that everything is of light waves and that different devices send out waves that become physical matter." He wondered if dreaming was made up of these light waves. All this was indeed still a dream, but he was beginning to wonder if living and experiencing life through the five sensual organs was not a form of dream state!

"Yes, the world of matter is also a reality-dream in the picture-making energy world. As long as the person allows the will of the lower ego to overshadow his higher self, the material world or plane becomes a tricky playground. When you learn to create a reality you consciously want, you become in control of your destiny."

While his mind was mulling over which questions he would ask, Theo placed his hand over his eyes.

"No questions yet; I want you to carry on observing!" Slowly, the colour waves and patterns gave way to a person who was gardening; it could almost be…Annelies?

"Yes, she is well-balanced and makes a good subject for our next adventure." He was curious what his brother was on about; it was a good subject for what? Was this Annelies? Not that she looked the same, it was more her energy, it had the same…charisma? He would refrain from asking, and as he watched, he waited. He became aware of a much greater form than completely encompassed Annelies. It vibrated as if this was more the energy that made her the woman she was! She was a mighty female, but not physically so much; it was in her energy. Annelies reminded him of POWAH energy-wise. Was it the depth of her knowledge that she expressed through her feelings?

Theo took his hand when they drifted inside her pulsating etheric form. The colours were streaming around him...how...could he be..." *Yes, I know it isn't obvious to you because even astral matter seems solid. You are practically clutching yourself to me for dear life,"* Theo's humourous beam made him relax.

"Are you ready?"

"Ready for what?" he projected in alarm when he felt like they were shrinking!... The gigantic energy field of Annelies gradually changed into a beautiful and mysterious pulsating sea of colour waves surrounding her forever fainter physical form!

"You are still regarding her as a human body! Leave that behind. We are all just energy." This time, his vision slowly grew more apparent, and the subtler substance of the life force within her etheric form became more visible vapour. Many colours gradually intermingled and waved in a rotary movement.

"What you are seeing now is what a very well-trained clairvoyant can see; focus your eyesight from the physical to the etheric and then from the etheric to the astral," When he heard an incredible sound like a powerful organ, he grabbed Theo.

"Please remember we are in an astral form as we are passing through her heart," This mental statement shocked him to the core. He jumped out of his light body from the noise when her beautiful etheric heart came into view. The thumping sound came from her life force! The pulsations looked like neon wires on fire.

"It looks a bit like Las Vegas, don't you think!" Theo chuckled. Her heart began to fade when he became aware of the golden light.

"That is the doorway to the goddess within, but we are here to go into the brain's convolutions. I just wanted you to feel her like this, to prepare you for what is to come!" As he quieted his growing excitement, the scenes on the temple walls started to have a different meaning for him.

"*Richie, observe because you need to know this for your journal.*" He saw what he would call a sun, a beautiful glowing fireball. Its many rays were flowing out, glowing. It created the effect of a great chrysanthemum made from living streams surrounded by many planets. Was he looking at a solar system?

"*How magnificent! Where are we?*" He was in rapture, seeing fireworks of such beauty. Nothing had ever impressed him more.

"*This is the centre of life. You see her pituitary gland, where her spiritual life force flows. That is why they call it the thousand-petalled lotus. Each petal connects her with an aspect of her cosmic multidimensional life. We are honoured to look into her akashic records because she is from our genetic soul lineage.*" He was astounded. Did they all have these fireworks? It felt like space. Was this what he imagined the cosmos looked like?

"*Theo, I'm so ...overwhelmed. Will I remember all this? I thought the pituitary is like a kind of telephone exchange where every experience and effort of thought is registered. "* He had read that somewhere.

"*Yes, it is, but we are privileged to see an important experience from her soul's library come.*" He felt a sensation of a breeze, and when he focussed again, Richard immediately remembered where he was, or so he thought. In its original state, this land of the 'gods' must have been paradise. He marvelled at the white marble pyramid high above the cove's water. Then, he saw crafts of different descriptions parked around the island. At least that is what it looked like."*They are waiting for the last initiation before the closing of the pyramid.*" He stood in the late sun watching. He was so enchanted by the splendour of it all that he almost missed the teak and ebony barque that sailed past them when he spotted her. A nearly golden girl stood at the rail with one hand shading her eyes from the sun while the other held onto the railing. Two strong guards were watching her.

"She has been chosen as the final initiate to be initiated with the high priest and priestesses before they seal the entrance.."

The girl wore a sea-green Egyptian sheath, revealing one shoulder.

"*Yes, this is the same soul you know as Ingrid.*" He was awestruck as he saw a very tall, magnificent-looking woman who suddenly appeared when what looked like a group of devotees had parted. He could sense that Theo wanted to reach and touch her, and for one moment, her eyes seemed to lock onto Theo's because her smile expressed warmth that made even his heart melt.

"*Theo, is she able to see us? Anneliese', is she special to you?*" He became very aware of the two of them looking at each other in genuine adoration.

"*I love her more than myself. She represents life to me. She is my twin half. Richie, I've taken a vow to aid all humankind if it lies within my power, especially if it is the will of the source of All That Is, to assist her in her soul purpose.*" He heard his brother's inner passion for this woman for the first time. Was that why he never married? Suddenly, calls to the rushed crew to perform precise manoeuvres for the landing created feelings of dread. The girl he now knew to be Ingrid moved off the barge and knelt gracefully in front of the tall, splendid figure he knew to be Annelies. Both climbed up the granite steps, which looked like thousands of feet had already polished them.

"*Where are they going?*" He could feel Theo's longing to be with her.

"*To the temple of Horus. They are both priestesses responsible for preparing the crystals within the temples. The ruling son of man in this period in Egypt detected a major universal problem they could not correct. They discovered an inter-dimensional "tear" between our third and neighbouring fifth-dimensional universe.*"

What did Theo mean by a tear? There was an atmosphere about the place as if everyone was ready to depart!

"Richie, the cause of the "tear" was created by one of the many nuclear wars that other civilisations within third- and fifth-dimensional realities had manifested over time and has caused the neighbouring fifth-dimensional beings to fall into our third-dimensional reality." He was still not getting that war as we know it, as what happened in Hiroshima had happened before. Everything looked very fresh and beautiful; the plants were of a beauty that he'd never seen. The temple of Horus was at least in its prime.

"Yes, man is repeating the same pattern, but this time, the human race will not be allowed to cause any more nuclear destruction. The spiritual leaders then decided to halt the initiations until they found a solution to the problem at hand."

Why? What does that have to do with the initiations? He then recalled the ten interpretations from the photo. The link to his physical body made him roar back in an instant until he felt a grip behind his neck.

"Please concentrate on the fact that human beings are multidimensional. The beings responsible for the nuclear destruction merged biologically with human bodies, leading to various problems. Some fallen beings came from other creations and wanted to inhabit human forms. That has caused a drop in the vibration of human creation. As a result, many female initiates preparing to become 'givers of life', like Annelies and Ingrid, failed. The result for them was that they physically died rather than transcending the shortened life span." He was more and more confused at what Theo was projecting.

"You mean they are going to die?" He beamed in anguish. He wanted to follow her through the long passageways where the walls were heavenly decorated with scenes of drones of people

who all seemed eager to walk the path Ingrid and Annelies were going to take. Could he warn them?

"*No, they will experience a failed ascension. These fallen angel beings, not aliens we now understand, became a serpent creation. They embedded themselves within the human genetic grid formations through their knowledge about advanced genetic engineering methods.*"

"You're kidding! I thought that was all a fabrication in the mind of men?" Again, he was observing the initiation ceremony. Was what he saw next a reconstruction, a simulation of his mind? A funnel opened above both Annelies' and Ingrid's heads, creating an opening into the sky. Gigantic objects were flying overhead, throwing massive boulders upon the Earth! The explosions were deafening. A thunderous roar wiped away the funnel over their heads as the boulders exploded.

"*Richie, the mind of man is like a sensitive reception panel. For the stronger energy impulses, because the five senses influence its translations, the mind translates these energies into images.*" Amazingly, he watched how the same funnel became the radiation of light. The priest raised an Egyptian cross and held it in the blazing funnel.

"What are they doing, exorcising?" He had heard Theo's theory but wanted to absorb what he saw."

"*Not totally. Watch.*" A lot of commotion around the altar where the priest stood became clear. The priest himself changed or shapeshifted into a …serpent? Was he seeing a movie in his dream? Both Ingrid and Annelies looked lifeless. People came forward and gently picked them up. A crowd in white linen robes wanted to touch the two dead bodies. Despite their attempts, they were unable to do so. Instead, an imposing figure came forward and stretched out his hands. Blue light streamed from his fingers into the two bodies. Both Annelies and Ingrid stood up and kneeled in front of the healer. His face was so familiar for a moment that he thought Hans had picked up the serpent and thrown it into a jar containing a red liquid.

"*They must return to lower dimensions before the inter-dimensional tear is closed.*"

"What do you mean, the serpent?"

"Now, look." Instead of a liquid, it solidified into a copper-coloured rod.!

"What is that?"

"That is a copper substance that can carry living brain cells." The copper rod was gone, and Annelies and Ingrid were honoured for their contributions.

"What is happening to that rod?" He could not forget that, at first, it was the priest, then the serpent was put into a jar with a red liquid and out came a rod.

"They knew the law of alchemy we have forgotten. We now live in the time age for that to occur."

Richard was utterly baffled; this was new to him. The many discoveries around genetic engineering that had taken place during previous civilisations had not prepared him for this. The serpent story completely confused him.

"Gee Theo, I don't understand. What do the serpents embedded in our holographic grid formation mean? What, all of us, too?" The serpent image in the Bible is a translated symbol from an earlier script. During Annelies' first 12 weeks of the decoding workshop, he had been sceptical.

"Buddy, you have seen more than enough for one journey. We will be back here and join her in their preparations. But now you must return. Write down what you remember, and don't worry if you don't all grasp it for now. It will come at the right time, believe me."

Again, he felt his brother guiding him away from the scene. Did he recall witnessing this all through Annelie's pituitary gland? They had never attended any of POWAH's gatherings this time.

Even if he remembered this journey, he would probably disregard it as complete nonsense. But it had been so real!

"It's the duality of human perception that causes distortion. You will understand it one day; I know you will." These were the last words he mentally recalled when he heard noises outside his flat.

Chapter 7
The Illusions of Time

Richard's first lecture on the Sphinx

The traffic on the freeway to Utrecht was heavy, and the rain made it even worse, going bumper to bumper. Richard took a bite of his breakfast apple while changing to a lower gear. He hated driving like this; his windshield wipers were doing overtime. Richard had to reschedule his appointment with the wholesaler on the way to Utrecht. He had run out of time.

This morning, a man called, claiming he had received some photos of his lecture on the Sphinx and had to collect them from the office. He was too surprised to respond as it was an unusual request. He tried to ask for more details about the photos and the person he was speaking to, but the caller hung up in an irritated tone.

He let Nel open the Pannekoek and leave earlier for Utrecht in case there was some truth in this special delivery. He should be prepared for his public lectures as they tend to have a life of their own. Connie will arrive later due to her involvement in the wedding preparations. He hoped everything at the Pannekoek would go without a hiccup. It was getting hectic, so he needed more help than Connie.

He felt stressed after an unusual phone call. While driving to the faculty, the car radio's music was interrupted by a news bulletin. "Good morning listeners, I've just heard from our correspondent, who is following up on the abduction and release of Mrs Ingrid Barendse, that the philanthropist Toon Haardens, who during the kidnapping affair got shot, has asked Ingrid hand in marriage. The wedding will take place on Sunday the 9th, at a special request, at the hospital where the couple is recuperating from their ordeal.

The following tune, 'Are you awake', is played for Ingrid and Toon at the request of a family member, the Egyptologist Trevor Zwiegelaar! " The announcer added.

Trevor must still be in Holland. Upon entering the lecture building, Wil de Wit from the front office informed him that a package had arrived for him. After fetching his parcel, he went to the cafeteria for breakfast and studied these photos. Students from all walks of life mingled. It was a hectic, frenzied atmosphere, even during the holiday season. Some students were having a debate while others were poring over notes.

Two clear close-up colour prints showed the same embossed symbol markings as Theo had translated. He was genuinely annoyed that whoever had them delivered hadn't bothered to turn up. For the first time, he saw that the Hieroglyphic text was hiding other embossed symbols. He had not seen that before. The buzz around him faded in the background when he attempted to interpret what he thought to be the Sumerian text. Since this was such a strange coincidence, considering the other photos, he approached with caution. But...the buzzing cafeteria noises ruined his concentration.

"Hi, Richard!"

"Vinny!.Gee, hi." He was glad to see him but suspected that the same Sascia could be his girlfriend. He should find out.

"What are you doing here?" he asked instead. Vinny joined him with a steaming mug of coffee.

"I'm meeting Sascia. She will be attending your lecture on the Sphinx. I was in Utrecht, so I thought, why not? It sounded interesting enough." Vinny's eyes peered over at the photos.

"Mmm, where is she?"

"She'll be hereafter one-thirty; we'll have some lunch first. I was hoping you could wait until you meet her; she reminds me so much of the girl from my wedding. Sascia is going to a banquet this evening, but I'm sure we'll have time to chat after your talk."

He was invited to Toon and Ingrid's wedding reception, confirming they were interested in the same girl. He suspected Sascia had contacted Vinny after leaving Ingrid's house but knew she hadn't mentioned him since Vinny was unaware of his involvement.

"What meanings do these symbols have? Are you translating them for your lecture?" Vinny held one photo up high.

"Someone had them delivered for my attention. It's very irregular. I've made some notes, but whoever left them should not be impatient. I'm not about to rattle interpretations off from just a glance." After his lecture, he planned to meet Vinny, who spoke on his cell.

Upon arriving at the auditorium, Richard noticed the place gradually filling up. This lecture hall is primarily reserved for guest speakers, often called lecturers. He couldn't fathom why he was selected to speak here. He proceeded to check his laptop, the microphone, and the overhead screen to ensure that everything was working correctly. He was getting used to lecturing in the public eye, but the butterflies would never completely disappear from his stomach. Could he again captivate an audience sufficiently to make his talk come alive? What he was about to disclose was controversial, which often triggered confrontations.

The chatting voices died down when the overhead lights went out due to the programmed timer set at two o'clock. The doors would lock automatically from inside so no one could interrupt the lecturer. It was a great improvement. He used to be so sidetracked by late arrivals.

"ARE THERE SECRETS HIDDEN UNDERNEATH THE SPHINX?"

He opened his talk with the same question seen on the screen and got their immediate attention while the Sphinx's 3D image projected on the wall made the audience gasp. The rows of seats up front were full. He could make out the first three rows going up; the rest disappeared into the darkness.

He moved next to the Sphinx, which towered above him for the audience to focus on. He found that explaining his last trip to Egypt as a travel adventure was easier to follow than when he merely lectured about the mythical stories far removed from his audience's daily lives. His explanations came alive with the backup of some tremendous 3D images from his recently updated laptop. Before he knew it, he had delivered the bulk of the information. He gathered his notes, tidied up and sighed that he was ready to receive questions.

He fully understood most people's fascination with a highly skilled civilisation that suddenly appeared in the region around the middle of the fourth millennium BC.

"Sir", someone stood up in the middle of the row on the left and asked a question. He peered to see who was talking to him.

"Please, call me Richard. Can you repeat your question?"

"Richard, could you tell me if the archaeologists have established who first built the Sphinx?" Tricky question. Speculations were always dicey if people took them for facts. He repeated the question in case others missed it.

"Please remember that interpreting symbolic text, particularly those predating the Babylonian civilization, requires research, knowledge, and intuitive perception skills influenced by various factors." He showed an artist's impression of the Giza pyramid. Next, on the screen, he placed the pyramid of today.

He reminded them that the artwork was an impression only, not fact.

"Like many others, I also concluded that the Sphinx might be older than the Giza pyramid." He showed some great pictures from his last expedition in October last year. It had been a successful trip. The sweltering heat at the Valley of the Kings had not dampened anybody on his team.

"My studies of the hieroglyphs, including the 'ceiling of stars' section, confirm the same idea." He knew that was not a direct answer to the question, but how far should he speculate?

"So what are you saying?" the man questioned. He felt inspired to delve into somewhat uncharted territory.

"I understood it to be a civilisation called Myrex that constructed the pyramid of Giza approximately 15,000 years ago. But then some calculated it even to be 18,000 years ago. The Sphinx is again a lot older. It seems likely that a very advanced civilisation that seemed human and or non-human must have lived on or visited our planet, however bizarre that might sound." "Richard, you mean aliens?" A burst of laughter rippled through the audience. He had expected that.

"I prefer to call them our Human ancestors but not from another universe." Now he got them. Other people interrupted the giggles of some, who were eager to hear more.

"Richard, who are the Myrex, and are they human?" There was still some laughter, but most people were seriously interested. He waited before answering.

"When we use the term human, we mean our species. Many researchers now accept that other co-creators must have visited planet Earth. But I'm not so sure about that." Theo called them fallen angels that had shapeshifted into reptilians, but that was still too controversial.

" There seemed to be five previous epochs, as I call them, each representing a human civilisation but not how we understand that to be. Throughout the following three lectures, I will explore my thesis." He hoped that would keep them satisfied for now.

"Richard, scientists say that the erosion pattern on the Sphinx indicates that it was carved at the end of the last Ice Age when heavy rains fell on the eastern Sahara. They speculate that it was perhaps 12,000 years ago. Are you saying they are out?" A man in the back asked.

"No, I didn't say that. It depends on the calculations and interpretation or the illusion of Time." A girl in the front jumped up.

"Richard, you mean that we were first both animal and human?" He came on tricky ground here. How was he to explain that there could be a possibility that the human soul could have shapeshifted into any form? It was too far-fetched to include in this hypothesis, but so what? It would spice up his lecture.

"Yes, who knows? This ancient monument, he pointed at the Sphinx on the screen, was probably built just before an ancient Sumerian civilisation prospered way back around 12,000 years after the great destruction that shifted earth's polar caps. That catastrophic event probably only left a memory of their shining legacy. The monument has scars with water running past its body so that it could have disappeared during the great flood. But that is still open to discussion." He heard a murmur coming from the audience. Many raised their hands. He nodded to a woman in the middle.

"Was that during the flood of Noah?" Someone else added the last civilisation of Atlantis theory.

"Probably."

"Richard, could you tell us what you think was the purpose of building the Pyramid and the Sphinx?" A man in the front asked.

"Ever since the days of the ancient Egyptians, who constructed their sturdy pyramids to last for eternity, human beings have been preoccupied with the means for assuring everlasting life. I strongly feel that that was the original purpose." Suddenly, an inner vision flashed before his eyes. In between the paws of the statue, an underground entrance appeared...Its great bronze doors at the end of the well-worn steps opened wide... Was he daring enough to speculate on a dream vision he had months ago? Everyone was waiting for his response...

"It is speculated that the great Sphinx is above a laboratory with its main entrance hall facing the river Nile."

"Still the doubting Thomas, are you?" For a split second, he froze and stuttered.

"Under the monument between the Sphinx's paws, many suspect a steep chiselled-out staircase leads into a large chamber. This chamber holds an inner temple where rods of living fire, like laser beams, were used for initiations and experiments." He showed pictures taken from science fiction magazines, which he modified as he perceived it.

"There seem to be two underground tunnels leading from this temple towards the Great Pyramid. One pathway leads to an evolutionary process of the initiate, which has evolved and has a magnetic nature. The other pathway leads to de-volution when the initiate is out of harmony with its original blueprint due to a radio-active distortion in their energy field." His explanation triggered a buzzing response; he was stunned at himself. He'd never done this, but hearing Theo's remark created bold courage.

"I believe that many of the magnificent monuments all over our planet, including those in Egypt, were built to commemorate the time when our ancestors, considered to be "human gods," walked the Earth. They possessed great secret knowledge about the mystery and meaning of life, which they took with them when they departed, either through natural causes or a physical ascension process." The slides he showed were of the many initiation practices. The images on the walls of the Temple of Hatshepsut. "

"Richard, you mean they travelled away in a spacecraft?" He expected that. Lots of hands were in the air. A vision he saw in his mind influenced his reply.

"The hieroglyphics deal with Celestial battles between fallen angelic 'gods' fighting among themselves, is another interpretation."

"Richard, go back to the chambers or laboratory below the Sphinx. Could these 'initiations or experiments,' as you call them, be imprinted or recorded into our DNA?" This question came from a familiar voice high up in the dark.

"Yes, why not. I perceive that to be the case. The question is, how do we decode that information? Or, which path did our ancestors take?"

His PowerPoint presentation on the screen produced a slide that showed the human form with its subtle bodies at various stages.

"Probably both pathways are embodied within our cellular memories. Some of the hieroglyph symbols seemed to tell stories of a process used for funeral rituals. Still, a new thought has taken hold of many researchers that the vivid drawings could also tell of the process involved in regenerating the physical body cells." He showed an artist's impression of a rejuvenation chamber.

"That would interest a lot of ladies, I'm sure." He had all their attention.

"Richard, could these experimentations have been of a genetic engineering nature?" A man on the right asked. He put a new image on the screen showing a suggested map below the Sphinx, indicating that the chambers or laboratories could be hidden deep under the Sphinx. He used images from science fiction movies to make it more realistic.

"You mean they were medical labs where genetic engineering experiments took place like we have today?" The sound of everyone whispering almost overpowered his voice over the microphone.

"It is possible that the underground chambers beneath the Sphinx were for rejuvenation and cloning. The assumption that it was for burial is likely incorrect, as the wall drawings depicting such rituals come from a much later period," he added, knowing Ben had asked the question.

"Richard, did the early Egyptians recall any knowledge of the Atlantis period?"

"Yes, especially the knowledge of medicine."

"Richard, the Greeks retained the Atlantian legends more than other cultures. Is that correct?" Richard could have sworn that sounded like Sascia. He tried to see, but it was too dark. There was something wrong with the lights. It never used to be this dark.

"Yes, that is true because of the memories Plato seemed to have. That propelled his mind to keep it alive."

"Richard, was it Socrates who was the channel and was Plato the one who recorded it? That was Vinny. He recognised his voice.

"Yes, that is correct, but the interpretation of Plato is important to us today."

"Richard, the man-animal figure, were they more advanced than us?"

A young girl in the front row had been waving her arms frantically. He thought of the different fallen angelic beings with their shapeshifting abilities. They could have interfered with human genetics. Theo's interpretations from the foil sheets crossed his mind, but that would be too difficult to explain in one lecture.

"Probably through the science of alchemy." He showed a Star Trek movie image showing how different beings worked together on the Enterprise.

"Where did all that fantasy come from if not from our genetic memory?" Annelies commented from the upper row.

"Yes, I suspect the fallen angelic 'gods' could have been exploring and applying genetic experiments with animals and even people as we do now. We need to ask why?" That triggered another reaction. An electric tension filled the auditorium.

The Sphinx's origin and purpose remain a mystery. Some speculate that the original head or mask was of a feline cat. He concluded. There were so many stories around the Sphinx; he'd better cool it.

"Richard, could you attempt to translate the two photos left for your attention?" A high-pitched male voice from the back row asked. He could not identify identifiable features; the man appeared even more shrouded in darkness.

He placed one of the photos on his overhead scanner, showing the slates in full view on the screen. He looked over his notes and responded.

It is an unusual request, but I'll try it. I would typically give it more attention, but I'll take the photos home since someone left them for me to study."As he pointed at each symbolic image, words came into his mind.

"The pyramid's...inner chambers...hold and protect the Earth records...Something about a device," he stopped and referred to his notes. There was complete silence.

He followed the row of symbols on the screen with his marker.

"I'm speculating now, but there's something about the... use of the H...crystal...codes of the human...THALAMUS. It is situated... under the...Sphinx, ...the great Pyramid...formless." He pointed at the different symbolic drawings...

"Something about...magnetic tunnels...It is the symbol of the capstone with the eye of Horus...At least, I think it is." Richard was stunned, thinking of the other translations of the eye symbol. While peering at the one photo, he remembered seeing this gold foil sheet before! It came back very clearly! The vision from his astral travel journey with Theo, as did the mummies, came to mind!

"To the gentleman in the back! Do you happen to know the interpretation before you asked me?"

A shuffling noise came from the back, and there was no response to his question. Someone was leaving through the back door, which was unusual.

"Richard, if the Sphinx symbolically represents the face of divine intelligence, please read the second photo for us. It might want to tell us something?" *"These two photos have disappeared from Leo's laboratory; please be discreet and always keep them on you."*

The silence in the lecture hall revealed that he had everyone's riveted attention, but Ben's telepathic warning unnerved him. He replaced the first photo on the scanner.

"When...porthole...opened...alternating...gravitational fields... released? Humanity can consciously...connect...twelve energy...vortexes...world...connected...Pyramid

Sphinx....Man...will...have...reached...threshold...where...ene-rgy...vehicles next...evolutionary...station."

Richard was mentally tired. There was far more, but he had had enough. He needed to be careful. Many could take his words very seriously. Interpreting any symbols was tricky. He felt very responsible for the attention his audience gave him. He needed to investigate these photos in more detail to respect that trust. He kept seeing a vortex or spinning disks as he interpreted the symbols, but it gave him no clue why. Many tried to get his attention, but he felt physically drained.

"My time is over, but I will continue with the translation at home." The crowd applauded, but he was still glad it was over. He promised to have more information on the two photos and would share it in his following lecture. He had a good audience, with no heated debates, thank goodness.

During the last question, an older man sidetracked Richard, causing tension to arise from the back instead of meeting Ben.

"Richard, thank you for that fascinating interpretation you gave just now; I'm impressed. I know that Tibet-India and Israel-Sinai areas correspond to the two hemispheres of the human brain. I liked what you translated about the THALAMUS. I know the mystery of our human species lies in our holographic mind!" He peered with interest at the man. Not many people saw the mind as a hologram.

The crowd that gathered around started to suffocate him. Richard was mulling over what the man had said about the mind as he walked out of the lecture hall with him. Was that why he had to write about the brain's two hemispheres? He shook the man's hand and hoped to be at his second lecture.

Many people asked individual questions, and when the last person left outside the hall, he wondered if Vinny and Sascia were still waiting for him. His spirits lifted as he saw Sascia outside, leaning against a gigantic tree.

"Hi, I knew it was you asking about Plato." He looked into her brilliant eyes when Vinny appeared behind the large tree.

"I see the two of you know each other already?" He detected an undercurrent vibe.

"I've waited for Sascia to tell you."

"Rich, I loved your lecture," Sascia said, interrupting what Vinny was about to say. "I'm very impressed. Debbie never told me that they were so interesting." She connected her arm with his, letting Vinny know that they were very familiar with each other. All he felt was confusion. Why had Sascia not told Vinny everything?

"Since when do the two of you know each other?" Vinny pressed. He sadly sensed Vinny's sudden coolness.

"Richard is a family friend and my sister's boyfriend." So she hadn't told him about the chemistry between them. What game was she playing?

"Well, I must say, you are better acquainted with Sascia's family than me! Where are we going? The relief when Sascia mentioned her sister was so obvious it made him feel more guilty than ever.

As he left the venue, people lingered outside and asked about the date of his following lecture.

"There you are, that was quite a performance," Annelies said *"Keep those two photos safe, will you!"* Ben beamed.

"Trevor will be impressed," Annelies added. Their sudden appearance created a diversion, especially as Sascia was between them, hooked onto their arms. Annelies observed Sascia and Vinny with great interest. Sascia introduced Vinny and asked Annelies when they would have to arrive for the dinner Annelies and her aunt Quincy organised in honour of Sascia's mother's wedding that evening.

"We will expect you both at seven or just before. Vinny, you are welcome to come along. I'm sure Ingrid would love to meet you." Vinny had made other plans and expressed disappointment, but his father had asked him to watch over his sick cocker spaniel while attending a wedding function himself. He waited for Sascia to say something. Annelies reminded Ben that Quincy was alone, and they said their goodbyes. He patted his briefcase as an acknowledgement of Ben's mental plea.

As they walked towards the parking bay, Richard remembered that he knew of a coffee bar around the corner, so he suggested leaving their cars behind. It started to drizzle. He kept his briefcase with him when they ordered.

Vinny asked him all about his trip to Egypt in October last year. His sudden interest was most peculiar as if he was avoiding the fact that he knew Sascia.

Vinny, of all people. Why could he not have been someone else? Why did he not go and look for that girl at his wedding he described so longingly? What was he going to tell him? That he was attracted to his girlfriend? He caught Sascia's eye, but she looked away. Gosh, what was he going to do? After they had an apfelstrüdel at the coffee bar, Sascia followed him in her car to the hospital grounds' reserved dining room on the outskirts of Utrecht while Vinny drove off to Barneveld, where his father lived.

Later in the evening, he felt miserable and disappointed as he drove through the rain past Zeist on the freeway back to Apeldoorn. The whole banquet had been a strain. He had very little chance to talk to her during dinner. He had a suspicion that Sascia had been avoiding him the whole evening.

After hearing from Annelies that they had all been at his lecture, Debbie wanted to know why she had not brought Vinny to the dinner. Sascia didn't comment but said that she hadn't known that Richard had known Vinny from her college days. When Debbie asked about Vinny, he told her about their friendship and Clara Visser, Vinny's first wife. Sascia knew that Vinny had been married before, but not to Clara, whom Debbie seemed to know! When Jeroen overheard part of their conversation, he said Vinny could not have been sincere in withholding such information. He hated Jeroen's insinuation that Vinny was not honourable. Debbie needed to defend his friend, which somehow changed the atmosphere. He felt it appropriate to tell them about his divorce. Debbie knew about Ellie, but he was not sure if Sascia did.

Sascia had chosen to travel back to Apeldoorn with Annelies and Ben, leaving her car with Debbie. Quincy, Ingrid's sister, seemed to have partnered up with Uncle Fred and Yolanda. Connie's mother was captivated by the brother-in-law of Ingrid, Ed Barendse, a friend of Toon living in Australia. Jeroen told him that their grandfather called his uncle home to do with the steel construction business. He was left to drive back on his own.

When he arrived at his flat, he was down and tired. A part of him wanted to travel away from his physical body to escape the loneliness. Sascia's sudden coolness had affected him more than he wanted to admit to himself. He was angry at himself for falling again for the same pattern. He remembered how depressed he was when Ellie left him.

Since his mind was too troubled to go to bed, he checked his e-mail. There was a letter from Trevor.

——- Original Message ——-
From: "T Zwiegelaar"
To: <R de Jong:;>
Subject: Thank you

Dear Richard.

I know your lecture will be successful, and Ben and Annelies will be present. Leo handed me Theo's interpretations after the photos went missing from his lab. He wants you to study the images first. The thieves must have missed Theo's interpretation of the photos. When you connect with Theo during your dream time, we would love to know what he is doing. Please keep the photos secure.

Trevor

He clicked on the attachment, and Theo's familiar handwriting appeared on Wordpad. He must soon ask Leo, Ben's twin brother, how he possessed the two photos and Theo's writings and where Trevor fitted in. The title '**The Illusions of Time during the Game**'[1] was intriguing.

Tablet 7

< Fourth, I came out of my body by moving in the illusion through time—Strange were the sights I saw on my journeys, but I learned that all is divine. >

After reading Theo's translation online numerous times, he was rather chuffed at his attempt to decipher this rhythmic message derived from one of the photos. But if it was published online, was it Trevor who posted them online?

He needs to let go of the negative emotions that might hinder his ability to dream consciously. He was angry at himself for being so affected by Sascia. Vinny was a good friend. If something was outstanding between him and Sascia, he had to trust that it would all work out.

He placed the two photos in Theo's file in his briefcase. Tomorrow, he would gather all Theo's work and keep it safe under the counter at the Pannekoek. Recalling Ben's warning didn't help his mood. He made himself a hot chocolate drink to feel better as he crashed into his unmade bed. He had adopted that habit from Ellie and wondered how she was doing.

---

1. https://allrealityshifters.wordpress.com/tablet-seven/

• • • •

After a while, when the vibrations didn't happen, he kept visualising himself sitting up with his feet resting, touching the carpet floor.

Out loud, he told himself..that he would wake up from his dream...while in the dream...Then he started to visualise lying down, while he was also at the same time sitting up!... Then, he heard very clearly. *"Are you finally ready?"* Every time he saw Theo, it was a joyful experience.

"I did it!" He mentally shouted!

"It was about time. Come, we have a lot to cover." Why the hurry, he thought as he looked back at his sleeping body. Suddenly he remembered his last dream trip!

"Theo.....about Annelies and Ingrid, what happened to them?" He became aware of a strange sensation that made him tremble. Feelings of dread came over him. Had the stolen photos and Sascia's aloofness affected him so much that emotionally, he was what, unstable?

"My brother, your moods affect the separation of your light body from your physical body. Your uncertainty and lack of self-worth affect your ability to free yourself. You have hindered your exploration of the higher etheric levels because of emotional pollution." Theo was straightforward but saw that the energy cord keeping him connected with his physical body was shaking. He felt infiltrated...as if some polluted thought form had infected his field. What a thought!

"Theo, can we visit someone in their bedroom when they are asleep?" A plan was forming in his mind. He could do nothing about the intrigues around the photos, but his emotions needed healing.

"Richard, your thoughts control your experiences. Are you prepared for that?" What was Theo implying?

"Richard, remember your emotions will be evident! By the way, what are you going to wear?" Theo's humorous *"Wear?"* made him suddenly aware of being naked! At least the amusement Theo emanated made him feel better. He remembered that he could wear anything, so he dressed in his black polo neck jumper and jeans."
"Yes, she will like that." How did Theo...
" Oh, Buddy, come on! Your thoughts are all over you! Yep, just thinking about her. You should do it, but you don't visit someone in their bedrooms; that's private!" How?.... Where else would he see her?... They left the flat. Theo always seems to have a plan for where to go.
"Richie, your subconscious is revealed through the colours swirling around you. You are giving yourself away with your thoughts and feelings. It will reflect on all your multidimensional levels. Remember, your feelings will be visible, and so are the feelings of others!" He never thought...but then he would know her feelings too? Well, why not? He could not be that wrong, surely. He felt rejected when he saw her driving away with Annelies and Ben to Apeldoorn after dinner, cool and distracted. It still hurt. He'd never been like that. Was he more sensitive than ever? Looking around, he wondered if he was part of a game. Where was he, anyway, in a park? Everything looked neat and organised. The flower beds and shrubs that encircled the sloping lawns reminded him of a gardening magazine.
"Richard, remember that life is like a game; the holographic reality you have chosen to take part in through a specific soul character, but you have to take responsibility for any thought forms that are not yours." Theo was lecturing him again. He only wanted to know why Sascia had been so aloof to him.
"Richie, you are getting more sensitive. Your true self, your Higher integrated self, observes life outside your energy field,

watching it all happen. It means that when your real self is in total control of what happens, you are in charge. You can prefer to stay within the game or leave the game just as you wish. Learn to use your free will."He remembered Annelies once explaining how the card game would make them realise they could observe themselves outside the game. She explained that only part of your consciousness is experiencing the game.

She suggested they take out an old movie called The Matrix if they had not seen it.

"You've got it; which script will you play?" He knew he wanted Sascia's affection, her love, her...but was that the right desire to have? Suddenly, he felt the familiar whoosh... and...when the misty substance cleared, there she was!... At least the young woman surrounded by flowers and shrubs looked like Sascia as she walked towards him on a green grass carpet! She was beautiful!...she was wearing something, gosh...it was almost transparent. He looked around for his brother. Were they alone? Did she see him as well?

He got closer, and she moved towards him! Wow! She was almost more beautiful in her astral body! He could see everything! Her surrounding colours were vibrant, and her breasts were perfect as she moved. His arousal was very real, especially when he gazed into her eyes.

"Rich, is this a dream?" They were standing very close. Her eyes had a dreamy look. He never realised one could feel erotic passion while in the etheric or astral plane! Sascia was probably having a dream, but would she remember it? Would he remember? Was this all his imagination? Was this just a sexual fantasy?

"Rich, hold me." Good grief, what was stopping him? His sexual passion while caressing her body flared. It felt so real! He knew it was just a dream. ...Her breasts were so...soft round, and

even her nipples were...as his solar plexus. Hers were touching; he experienced a feeling of fulfilment so wonderful, so exquisite, no normal orgasm could have compared with this ecstasy. He felt completely at one with her! It also almost pulled him back into his physical body.

It took a moment before he realised he was on his own! Where was she?

"*Happy now?*" Theo stood next to him in a shimmering multicoloured robe.

"Theo, did you see her? Was she not gorgeous? Or did I imagine it all? Was it a dream? Would she remember?" The many questions piled up while he was recuperating from his astral lovemaking cleared all his previous depressing cobwebs.

"*I know you will remember.*" Theo beamed humorously.

"*We empathised, realising it was necessary so you would remember your dream when you wake up. You have been too intellectual.*"

Was he too mental? Was that why he kept having to question everything?

"*You've been infected by thoughtforms from negative inorganic entities that trigger feelings of doubt. So much so that for you to be able to remember the inner planes during your out-of-body dream state, you need to experience real feelings. Your objective left-hemispheric thinking mode otherwise keeps discarding your dream journeys.*"

He tried to understand what Theo meant by thought forms from inorganic entities. Indeed, his intellectual side kept questioning everything he experienced, but what was wrong with that? What did Theo mean by infested?

"*Richie, many people will challenge you on all levels. It is good that you have become aware of the invasion in your energy field. It's good that you question everything you do and always are discerning at all times."* He knew he didn't take all his dreams seriously.

"Practise meditation before you go to rest. People who are very subjective in their spatial right hemispheric thinking are far too easily influenced by what they see and feel. They end up where they don't want to be. Come, I'll show you where that can be." He saw groups of people effortlessly moving away from the flowering green grass scene. Some were in pairs, and some formed larger groups that were having...crumbs...orgies? Did all these people have sexual dreams?

"Yes, It can be addictive; remember that!" Richard never even thought you could have an addiction in the astral plane! He became aware of a strange smell of overheated bodies. It became repugnant when he saw men and women lounging like animals during the mating season. It's not what he wanted; this was not what he experienced with Sascia! These people had no regard or feelings for each other.

"Theo, why did you say I needed to have this experience with Sascia?" It left an almost distasteful sensation behind when they left the scene."

"Why, do you think I remember the dream better? Because of the feelings? I would remember feeling better. So I might remember the rest as well?" Now he got it. His feelings would back up his intellect!

"Yes, that's it. You will realise how important it is to trigger your brain cells into remembering your wanderings. It will enable you to recall invaded thoughtforms and release distorted energy pockets that are not yours. It is essential in the resurrection process. Come, you are ready for your next lesson; follow me." The scene around them started to go foggy at once, gradually giving way to a new one. Again, it was first misty, and then the surroundings became very different.

"Richard, the soul planes are divided into many spheres, levels, or sub-planes. Remember when, on one of our previous astral travel journeys, you saw the buildings from above with the stream and the bridge and knew that you were looking for Ingrid?" He remembered it when they were flying over it with the plane.

"That was the first astral level close to the physical plane. It is not where the soul dwells. Your subtle bodies, extensions of your multidimensional soul consciousness, have access to these realms. Some people can see mentally at this level while in their physical bodies during their awake states. More will soon. That's why it is so important to play the first level of the card game with the Language of Light cards together with your first five awakening cards."

He had been reading many esoteric books that recorded seven spheres of consciousness in the astral world, each less material than the next layer. Did that mean that he was only aware of one dream reality? Metaphysical science has always fascinated him. He was keen to see a relatively close reflection between the Sumerian information left behind by an ancient civilisation and the spiritual sciences that he could not ignore.

"There are many more spheres or realms, but for now, this will do. Richie, just now, we were passing from one sphere, where Sascia was experiencing her dream with you, which is closer to the physical plane, into the next, the second sphere following into the third, where we are now".

The next scene was familiar, but for the first time, he saw what appeared to be a gathering place in the shape of an open auditorium. It was filling up with lots of people of all races and colours. Men and women were all wearing different swirling garments that didn't look solid, like on the physical plane. The colours changed as they moved. Some men wore loose, multi-coloured fitting clothes or silk shirts and wide trousers while others wore tight-fitting, very stately uniform-type outfits.

Many wore impressive buckles, clasps and other jewellery ornaments. All the magnificent creations revealed the thoughts and feelings of each individual. What was he wearing, jeans and a T-shirt, how plain and boring was that? Were all these people astral travelling like him?

"Richard, many places in the dream planes are for people who come to learn and listen. Some are in the physical like you." He pondered that POWAH must be several dimensions beyond the third dimension.

"That is an understatement. There are many levels, even on this third solar sphere. This beautiful entity must lower its vibrations to bring its message well-loved by all. POWAH can materialise in a physical or, in this case, a light body. He always astounds us by the beauty he surrounds himself with, purely for our benefit. In your and my thought process, Richie may appear as human, or as you saw him as an energy ball, but he has evolved beyond needing any form."

A melody beyond description filled the whole scene. He felt a common spiritual devotion emanating from everyone as if he was a part of one combined life stream that was now entering their present.

A very tall, towering person appeared in the centre, first as a transparent image that became more solid, looking ageless. POWAH's wavy golden hair hung on his straight, broad shoulders, shining like burnished gold. He was wearing a simple white robe. He wore a crystal-studded waistband that highlighted his slender waist. His vibrant aura swirled around him in a multitude of colours and shapes.

"Who does he remind you of?" Was Theo implying...Was this not POWAH? As he watched in awe, the face suddenly reminded him of Akhenaton, the Pharaoh who had impressed him the most. He felt an exquisite emotion going through him, like a warm feeling of bliss, nameless but still indescribably meaningful, as if he were part of the forever-changing living colour symphony. It must be home, he thought. The harmonious vibrations of music spun around him like a dynamic, harmonious passage in consciousness that gave him a deep, incoherent emotion. The choirs formed by human voices echo in a song of celebration.

< Beloved Children of the One Universe. I welcome each of you in Love; my temple exists on many dimensions, but regarding the present transformation on Earth, let us focus principally on the physical and etheric levels. Soon, these two shall unite, whereby all its etheric (heavenly) perfection will be tangibly manifest in form. My heart swells with joy that the power of love is reaching out to your planet, Earth, in the momentum of the Divine plan. >

The chorus burst into a song of praise. Where did the music come from, he wondered. Who was singing?

< In terms of the coming transformations, the force field of your aura bodies will expand due to our intervention plans starting to take effect. Everything you think, feel, say, or do will be recorded. You are the future of Earth, bringing her past into a glorious eternal moment where the one source of love, wisdom and power dwells. >

He could feel that message's vibration engulfing him like a lover's embrace. He could see that everyone was affected in the same way. Was this an illusion, too?

< You have all chosen to take command of your five subtle bodies and taken full responsibility for keeping these bodies in a feeling of tolerance, harmony, purity, love, happiness, joy, and understanding. All these qualities already emit a great light needed to prepare the shift into the second vibration level of the awakening process. It is to your greatest advantage to secure the

conscious cooperation of your physical, mental, emotional and intuitive creative bodies >

POWAH's powerful voice was not heard but felt like a mental message that captivated every fibre of his being. Theo smiled. He became aware of a fragrance, a perfume as if...the words! Did he hear them or... Did his mind translate the sounds, colours, shapes and movements into words?

< The fall of man resulted in a separation between his two modes of thinking. This polarity created the illusions of the world of cause and effect. Your right and left hemispheres spun out of balance. Only shattered, fragmented soul energy particles could incarnate a biological form. The birth of your personality came about to form a bridge. It was to prevent the human race from completely disappearing as a species. >

Did he translate this correctly? Was it his ego that saved the human species from extinction? What a thought!

< Gradually, over aeons of time, the powerful projections from the personalities were responsible for the limitations that you experienced. These thought forms created a foetal membrane, which resulted in forgetfulness. On many past or parallel worlds, this caused great suffering, resulting in an even slower vibration for every life form that evolves on Earth. >

The workshop of Annelies flashed past his mental vision. They would soon make three more cards on this second level. He looked forward to their creative experience. Making something like their own cards had a similar effect as hearing POWAH speak.

< Due to the coming of the electromagnetic null zone, your new genetic structure will gradually change. Great transformations will awaken your soul's memories. Recent global events can and will also trigger memories that create chaos and despair. These painful thought forms are unlocking

and will manifest in your physical world for you to release them. You all are here because you have chosen to be on the planet at its last stages before her cosmic shift >

Richard still could not imagine how it would happen. Most people were not even remotely aware of any changes of this nature. Or were they, but would memories or visions from other lives make them dysfunctional in this society if they believed them? Theo nodded.

< You who gathered here are to act as transmitters of this higher frequency as the global awakening process is quickening. Glands and hormones that allow one to experience unity between the intellect and intuitive sides of oneself will be re-cast. These broken connections between your hemispheric lobes will once again come into balance. These changes will vary from person to person depending on the level of evolution within that embodied soul >

Richard was so aware of the powerful love when he felt POWAH's glance in his direction. The eye contact felt like an embrace. He has started to understand why churches where people sang and danced attracted crowds. It uplifted them the same way, but did it last?

< My dear, it all comes down to your level of awareness. So, please stop thinking that you are separate from me. Soon, we will be together in the impersonal realm where the threefold nature of our creator, expressing all power, wisdom, and love, dwells. This realm stores all activities as successive images in a multiple-image hologram. You can access past, present, and future records from any point in the Thalamus chamber, the hall of records present within each individual. >

One last vivid, violet-coloured flash, and it was all over. The final word, Thalamus chamber, lingered on. He would have to ask Theo...

"Buddy, POWAH meant that each image is like a frame in a movie. A hologram is nonlocal, like our astral and soul planes. This awareness will only occur when your higher mind has polarised within the soul's consciousness. Richie, you are very privileged; no physical eye could have looked at his form through physical eyes even for a second, for such was the dazzling intensity of the brilliance. It would have blinded you instantly." He then heard a ringing, piercing sound that brought on a burning heat, stinging his eyes. Suddenly...he was falling...When he hit his pillow, the fall made him gasp for air...

• • • •

His eyes shot open, and the sun was warm on his face. He remembered something about eyes not being able to see! His body was aching as if he had been on a hike. It felt stiff, cold and limited, like a tomb. He tried to remember! He knew it was necessary.

Did he recall Theo saying something about a game? And the feeling! He experienced a feeling of making love. Suddenly, he remembered Sascia! He recalled...seeing Sascia wearing a transparent robe of some sort. He probed further into his dream, trying to remember! Did he make love to her?

Had that been for real? Through sheer concentration, he remembered more..., a powerful voice... and seeing many people that were all listening to that voice. The music! He remembered some of the things he heard...The words..."*You are to act as transmitters of this higher frequency as the whole process of your awakening on a global scale is quickening. New glands and hormones awaken to unite intellect and intuition, repairing and linking brain hemispheres*".

He knew he could not make that all up; new glands? He felt happy that he could bring back visions from his dream. But why the stiffness? It felt like he had been busy during his sleep, but time was an illusion. His phone rang as his alarm went off...

It was Sunday, this afternoon. Toon and Ingrid would get married... When he got to the phone, a high-pitched male voice attacked like a sound blaster.

"This is a warning! We are on to you! The next time we come into contact, it won't be pleasant."......a dialling tone announced a disconnection...

Chapter 8
The Game of the 3rd Dimension

The Wedding

Richard's only suit made him feel like a clown all dressed up. For Vinny, this was everyday attire; for him, it was like a straight-jacket. The last time he wore it was to his wedding, which did nothing for his mood.

Nel had offered to look after the Pannekoek as her morning shift. She would close the coffee shop after lunch so he could attend the wedding party.

He got their answering machine from the coffee bar when he phoned Ingrid's house. Sascia must have already left for Utrecht. The snarling remarks through the phone this morning didn't help his feelings of disappointment. He had no idea what they were implying, wondering if someone had their numbers mixed up. When the phone rang again, he let Nel answer it. He went to the pantry to write a grocery shopping list for the following week.

At least it promised to be a sunny day. Nel called him from the pantry to say that Connie was on the line.

Nel served coffee to two English customers. Connie asked if he wanted a lift to Utrecht. Her mother was at the hotel with Ed. He was so down that he made a pathetic excuse. He tried to drive up silently, hoping to recall anything from his out-of-body experience that would lift his spirits. That blasted phone call had stripped his dream memories. All he remembered were spinning eyes.

"Go on, you'd better leave; you'll be late", Nel warned as she took the keys from him so she could lock up after two. It was quiet on the freeway, and he had a good time.

As he arrived at the hospital's side entrance in Utrecht, he noticed a group gathered outside a small chapel. Upon looking inside, he saw abundant flowers.

Annelies, Ben, Sascia and Debbie were standing in a group talking with Quincy, Ingrid's sister, and he joined them. He tried to ignore Sascia, but he failed when he felt how she casually took hold of his arm while greeting the others as if nothing had happened. Sascia introduced him to Ed Barendse, Ingrid's brother-in-law, while bragging about his talk on the Sphinx. Ed's Australian accent soaked his Dutch words, giving them an unusual sensation of power and directness. It reminded him of Toon. The same joyful approach to life he so admired as if they had shed any fear of failure.

Far in the distance, he heard an ambulance approaching the casualty section. A soft breeze cooled the warm summer day. It was a joyful occasion, and he felt his spirits rising.

He took hold of Sascia's hand, and while they were strolling between the many arriving guests, he asked how her boss had reacted to her quitting her job. She pulled away and rested on a low wall while stretching her long legs. She wore very smart slacks with a matching jacket. She looked stunning!

"Oh, he shouted at me for not doing my job by disclosing the photos I took during the flight over the estate of Pleasure Park; he reminded me that I was still in his employment while I took my days off. Now he wants to have my last report with photos on his desk by tomorrow," she sighed. He was about to put his arm around her when Debbie joined them on the low wall. Debbie was dressed in sky blue, complementing her slightly rounder and shorter figure. She looked very elegant and elegant, like Quincy, Ingrid's sister.

Richard pondered what solution he could devise to help Sascia, feeling she didn't want to write that report. Annelies had told him about the detective handling the abduction case and the blackmailing Mr Brinks had to endure. Maybe she should involve the detective with the report and do some investigation on her own. She could be the one talking to her mother instead of strangers. He suggested that idea to her. People were slowly streaming towards the entrance of the chapel. He followed both sisters into the chapel.

"That's a clever idea, thanks," Sascia whispered. A powerful fragrance from the massive arrangements penetrated his nostrils the moment they walked in.

"Gosh, who did the decorating, and what flowers are they? Do you girls know?"

"I've seen them in Peter's hothouse in France," Sascia replied in awe. Of course, Peter had told him that Toon imported the giant cup of gold creepers from South Africa.

"Mom told me that she got to know Toon through a story about flowers. Remember that Toon owns a landscaping firm."Debbie said as the chapel was filling up. They had to squeeze closer on the bench to let more people sit down. He sat between the sisters, and Jeroen joined them with the twins' grandfather. Both Sascia and Debbie greeted him with affection. On the opposite side, Annelies, Ben, Fred and Quincy took their seats. Ed, Yolanda, Connie, Peter, and Helen followed behind when the music announced the couple.

He spotted Niels with a woman he'd seen with Ingrid in the Pannekoek. She reminded him of Vinny's first wife!...then he saw Gerrit, Zola and Wim arriving. They were all from Annelies' ascension class. He was surprised to see Wim. They must have got back together again. Zola gave Sascia a hostile look when they got near. Sascia frowned back at her. Gosh, Zola stood out with her bright, flashy clothes. All the men stared at her as she sat; she loved it. He smiled, knowing that she was harmless, just arm candy.

Many people were still arriving when a bald man in a long white tunic appeared upfront, displaying two large candles. Hans and Liesbeth sat on the right in the first row. They were directly behind them in the second row.

Ingrid and Toon came in hand in hand, both looking radiant, smiling at everyone. Ingrid was wearing an elegant blue outfit. Behind them, Timmy and Karin bounced like rabbits, already throwing rose petals from their baskets as they climbed onto the bench next to their parents. He could sense that Ingrid's daughters were very tense. Sascia was tearfully staring into space, holding her own, while Debbie's tears ran down her cheeks. He took both sisters' hands and squeezed Sascia's slightly. She responded, which made him glow all over. He wondered about their father. He knew Ingrid was a widow.

The ceremony was very moving. What a difference compared to other weddings. Richard liked the way his uncle Leo conducted the whole service. He peered sideways at Sascia, who was now smiling.

When Toon, being Toon, responded to Leo's final closing by smothering Ingrid with his devotion, the whole congregation laughed. It was the most impressive wedding ceremony he'd ever witnessed and would stay with him for a long time.

After the ceremony, Hans took Toon away while people surrounded Ingrid. Ingrid glanced, worrying at Toon because he looked very pale.

"Is Toon all right, do you think?" Sascia asked her sister. But then both Toon and Hans appeared again, and he looked fine, taking Ingrid's hand while he walked her outside.

The music 'Are You Awake' played loudly over the loudspeakers. Toon whispered something to Ingrid just before they climbed into the white Mercedes waiting for them and drove off...

"Richard, do you know where they are going for their honeymoon?" Sascia asked when they all left the hospital chapel. The twins and Debbie waited for his reply.

"What makes you girls think I should know?" Sascia ignored his reply. She told Debbie he had delivered the papers to Toon at the hospital about the wedding.

It was the first time he saw Jeroen wearing a suit. He grinned when Jeroen kept shrugging his shoulders inside his jacket.

Connie asked if they would join them for an intimate gathering at Uncle Harry's residence. Both Ingrid's daughters stayed with him when Niels approached them with Carla; she had changed. She was fat! Years ago, they had socialised when he was married to Ellie. They used to hang out together.

Carla was equally surprised that he was there. She explained to them that she and Ingrid worked for the same firm. He thought that Debbie and Carla knew each other because of how they greeted Sascia, but Carla never spoke to each other. Everybody from Annelies' class was standing outside the chapel, and he suggested that whoever wanted to follow him to Mr Brinks's estate. They all took him up on his offer.

"I think Jeroen has taken a fancy to Connie if you ask me." Sascia chuckled when they drove off. Both girls sat in the back since his briefcase and laptop took up the front seat.

"Richard, were you at Carla's wedding, Vinny's first wife?" Debbie asked. He peered in his rearview mirror at Sascia, who gaped at her sister. He told them about Theo and why he never married. Debbie asked after Carla, and he told them he knew Carla as a sculptress years ago. He mentioned that more for Sascia's sake when he recalled Vinny telling him he'd met Sascia through one of Carla's exhibitions. Sascia shrugged her shoulders and admitted that she had never made a connection between them at the time and that she now realised how little she knew about Vinny. Sascia's eyes locked for one moment in his rearview mirror.

"*I still think you are the most gorgeous woman I've ever met,*" he beamed, wishing she could communicate with him that way. He noticed a dimple on her cheek; did that mean she heard?

"*Gosh, I have fallen for him. I must talk to Vinny; he will be so hurt!*" While he was still savouring Sascia's thoughts, Debbie told them she had been at Vinny's wedding. Debbie's involvement with Vinny's first wedding surprised him. He never knew she knew Vinny!

"You were? But, I never heard you mention Carla, Vinny's first wife." Sascia replied, confused. Debbie told them that she had known Carla years back but had lost contact. She never knew that she was divorced and that Sascia's boyfriend Vinny was Carla's ex.

Debbie's story hit like a bombshell. When he turned into the imposing driveway of Harry Brinks, he asked her how well she knew Vinny. Many cars had already arrived. When they arrived at the west side of the property, Debbie's reply went unheard by him. Ben approached him with Trevor Zwiegelaar in tow. He was about to introduce Sascia, but she disappeared.

"Well, I'm glad to meet you in person on this happy occasion finally. Ben told me your lecture went very well, but the man connected with the two photos disappeared. I'm glad you had a good response." Trevor was Ben's age, about mid-fifties, with features similar to Hans's. Trevor appeared to be an outdoor man who would spend most of his time digging around ancient excavations around the world. He looked very fit and ageless.

"Ben, where did the happy couple go, not back to the hospital?" Trevor asked.

"Oh no! Harry hired a barge, and the wedding couple are sailing on the Rhine for four days before returning home. Toon still needs medical aftercare, and Ingrid has offered to finish her work for the Pleasure Park complex. I admire Ingrid; she hasn't avoided helping Harry despite her difficulties and is still working with him until the project is completed."

Ben and Trevor were discussing police business while gorging themselves. The tables were laden with lots of goodies. The catering staff were walking around offering drinks. He wondered where Tieneke, Harry Brinks' daughter, was because he recognised her daughter. He was rather shocked at Henny's appearance. She was dressed very tarty, with lots of makeup and bright dangling jewellery. She acknowledged him with a faint smile when he asked after her mother. She shrugged her shoulders. She seemed angry. Her eyes looked sulky when she looked over his shoulder at someone. Had he seen her recently? The episode at the Pannekoek where he chased the young boy with a very informal-dressed woman...gosh, it couldn't be, surely?

He felt a slight pressure on his back when Tieneke greeted him while changing a plate with cheese for a new one on the table. Henny ignored her mother when asked to help the catering staff. Tieneke looked stressed. When both Ben and Trevor complimented her on the food, it brought on a smile, but her eyes stayed troubled. Their brilliant blue colour matched her blouse. He introduced her to Trevor. Tieneke excused herself when a catering staff member asked if she could come to the kitchen.

Ben was called away, so he chatted with Trevor, who asked about Tieneke's work, which he'd heard about from Annelies. He seemed quite charmed by her. Richard scanned the crowd for Henny, but she had gone. He let the incident slide.

"Richard, I need to talk to you about the Pleasure Park's hologram deck soon; the smouldering unrest is not resolved as you can imagine. The police and Interpol are still searching for Ingrid's kidnappers, but I'm leaving for the United States tomorrow evening." Trevor replied to his questions.

An excellent dance tune started the party, and he wondered where Sascia was. Trevor was a fascinating person with strong convictions but was quite challenging to contradict.

"Richard, I'll contact you in two weeks," Trevor said goodbye to a few people when Hans bumped into them. The buffet was crowded with people.

"Uncle Trevor, give Richard some chance to dance with the girls, *I'm sure that's all you want to do,*" Hans beamed. Trevor eyed Hans with fondness. He spotted Connie and Jeroen dancing, but both sisters were nowhere to be seen. Annelies joined him while eating a snack from the smorgasbord spread, asking when it would be convenient to reschedule his reading. She explained that before they could play the first level of the awakening card game, she would go over their 22 spacings with each of them. Toon and Ingrid would be back next week, so she wanted to organise their game evening before they started on the second level. He made a time for next Friday. Harry called her away, and he was on his own.

Suddenly, Zola was hanging on his arm. She asked when he would drive to Apeldoorn because she wanted a lift. He made an excuse, telling her she had better go home with Wim and walked away. He was rather proud of himself. In the past, he would have fallen for her plea. He felt almost sorry for Wim.

Sascia was talking to a familiar man on the other side of the room, and he overheard the man telling her to leave the editorial up to him and he would speak to her boss. It must be the detective, and Sascia introduced him. Ben broke into their trio when he asked André to come with him, so they were alone. She looked exquisite, she must have changed because it was the first time he'd seen her in a dress. It reminded him of his dream. He asked her to dance and they joined Yolanda and Quincy with their partners on the dance floor that had been erected especially for the wedding party. Sascia felt so precious while moving with the music, wondering if she remembered her dream. He could feel she was slowly joining in the rhythm of the music as he held her close. Again, the oneness from his dream was profound ... very...

"Rich" she looked up at him. "Do you...remember your dreams?" she whispered close to his ear so only he would hear. Gosh, if only she knew. Or...did she remember? He whispered back what he recalled, and he could feel her quivering. He pulled her closer, knowing that now everyone could see they were dancing far too intimately for a casual couple.

"Rich...what about...Debbie...let's stop...I"...and all he could do was ever so slightly nibble on her ear. The dance floor became heaven just for them. Her body moved at one with his. It took a while before he became aware of the pressure on his shoulder. Debbie observed them with a confronting look.

"Sis, I have to talk to him, so get a drink; you'll have him back just now," Debbie said firmly. She was not on a warpath because she pulled a clowning face at her sister when she steered them away from the dance floor. He felt very overpowered by the female species. Debbie looked up, observing him; her clear blue eyes were open.

"Richard, I know you are in love with my sister, so you two don't have to be so elusive; it's written all over, but I need to know something. This Vinny, is he in love with her too?" he was, for a moment, lost for words.

"I think he thinks he is…but, no, he's not," he answered slowly. He knew that that was probably the most clumsy excuse for his wishful reasoning.

"What makes you say that? Do you think he still loves his first wife, Carla?" The dance floor was getting crowded.

"Oh no, he never really was; he already knew that on his wedding…say, why all these questions?" It was challenging to have a conversation as the music was getting louder. Before Debbie could reply, a great commotion from the house disrupted the party. Nobody knew what was going on except that something was brewing. André, the detective, approached him while speaking on his cell phone. He looked serious. Connie, Yolanda, and Fred were explaining something to Annelies that shocked them. Connie suddenly stood next to him, grabbing his hand.

There has been a break-in at Pannekoek. Nel is attacked, and our bookstore is ransacked. The thieves were likely searching for something. André just received a phone call from the police in Apeldoorn." Connie's expression said enough. He felt sick to his stomach. All he could think of was Nel. Connie was seething with anger. The music had stopped, and Harry made an announcement. André asked him and Yolanda if they could return to Apeldoorn to identify if anything was missing. He offered to drive them back to Apeldoorn if needed. Sascia walked towards him. She overheard Andre's offer and grabbed his hand. The atmosphere changed from a happy light activity buzz to a heavy, overloaded electric energy, making everybody in the room feel rattled and attacked.

Sascia, Jeroen, and Connie would drive back in his car with him, and Fred, Quincy, Ed, and Yolanda followed them in Fred's Mercedes. Debbie stayed in Utrecht because she would be on duty the following day. Carla and Niels stayed with Debbie, which made him feel good. He knew she wanted to be with them, but she had commitments she took very seriously.

When they drove away, he suddenly recalled the aggressive phone call that morning! It must have been meant for him after all! He should have mentioned the incident to André. He was relieved to be behind the wheel. The stillness of the car gave him a chance to think, and he raced through his mind, searching for any clue as to why or who had broken into the coffee bar. He couldn't bear the thought of Nel harmed in any way.

"Rich, what could they have been looking for?" Sascia interrupted his thoughts while sliding her hand onto his knee. Connie and Jeroen were talking in the back.

"I wish I knew," he covered her hand and drove to Apeldoorn in silence...

He dropped Connie and Jeroen off at the bookshop and drove to the coffee bar.

The glass door of Pannekoek's coffee bar close to the handle looked shattered. The till bolted onto the wall, was empty and torn off the wall. The computer was still on, but they couldn't get past the password. They would have been out of luck if they were after money, only getting away with a hundred Euros. Nel was taken to the emergency room due to shock. The police were looking for fingerprints and preventing people from looting or wiping off the evidence. He heard from the police that the bookshop was even more messy. Whatever they were after, they pulled every bookshelf down. The police took statements from all of them.

Connie and Jeroen came back from the bookshop, shocked. He wanted to see for himself. Sascia walked with him to the Power of Words shop around the corner to see how things were. Fred and Yolanda were in shock from the vandalism. The feeling that overwhelmed him the most was the violence, especially towards the books.

It was already after six when he drove with Sascia to Apeldoorn's clinic to see Nel while Jeroen and Connie offered to stay behind in the Pannekoek to clean up.

Thank goodness Nel was fine. Her anger saved her. A couple started to disrupt everything behind the counter when Nel was still in the kitchen after she locked up. Hearing a lot of noise, she courageously yelled at them as she ran out of the kitchen, holding a knife tucked into her apron. The man had dropped his mask as he grabbed her around the throat, taking the knife away. Nel started to scream, which alerted a passer-by. The woman yelled at the man to leave her alone and ran for it. He followed her after he tried to kick the steel safe door open under the counter but instead hurt his toe. The couple must have been at the bookshop first. Whatever they were looking for did not satisfy them, so they came to the coffee shop. The police had taken Nel's statement, and she would visit the police station for a photo identification session the next day. Nel told them that the detective André inquired whether the woman's name was Iris, but she was unsure and didn't know. Sascia was tremendous and very affectionate towards Nel, hugging her to calm her, which he would never have been able to do the same way.

Nel had no intention of staying at the hospital. After being discharged, they drove her back home to Hoenderloo. Her late husband, who had been a caretaker at the national park de Hoge Veluwe, had passed away four years ago.

Nel lived on her own with a tomcat in a charming free-standing bungalow. She was still shaky, vividly repeating her ordeal, describing how the couple had tried to get into the computer. The woman wore a veil, but she saw a glimpse of the man when she started screaming, and he dropped his mask.

She gave a rather alarming description of the man. He suspected that they were connected to Ingrid's kidnappers. What could they have been after?

It was Nel who alerted the police after the intruders left. They were there within three minutes. Someone else had reported that the bookshop's open door was damaged and the big glass doors of the Pleasure Park offices had also been tampered with.

After Nel settled in and they checked around her house, she insisted they had coffee with her. It was already after seven o'clock, so he felt restless, wondering about his flat, so they both excused themselves. He suggested Nel stay home the next day since the coffee shop could not open early.

Sascia insisted on joining him in going to his flat first before he dropped her off at Ingrid's home. They talked during the drive about the flash drive with the crop circle. Sascia was very intrigued by the whole story.

"Do you think they were looking for Mom's flash drive?"

"I have no idea. I know that the architectural drawings on the dome were also on that stick. I think I took it home, but I'm unsure what I did with it. It was in the coffee bar behind the counter..." He told her about the phone call that morning. Sascia was shocked.

As they walked in, he saw that his flat was in chaos, not his making. It astounded him that people could have so little regard for other people's property. His outrage slowly settled as Sascia phoned the police on her cell. He moved in a daze towards his PC. All the disks, old tapes and papers were scattered everywhere.

"Rich, what else could they have been looking for?"

"I have no idea. I'm looking for the flash drive, but it's not here." He knew that the intruders were after something, but what? Sascia kneeled next to the upturned box with the scattered old photos he had been clearing out the other day. The mere fact that they ruffled through his stuff outraged him. He felt like he had lost everything important to him. Thank goodness that his laptop with the...envelope with the photos! That must have been it! The two photos!

Ben had warned him to keep them in a safe place. The flash drive was nowhere, and when the police arrived, he couldn't tell them what was missing apart from his speculation. He now hoped that the flash drive was in the safe at the coffee bar. Sascia reported his nasty phone call.

After the police had taken fingerprints of everything that seemed out of place, Sascia prepared a light snack in his kitchen—having her around made such a difference. Only this morning, he felt miserable and wished she would stay. He was observing her as she moved to make tea. When their eyes locked, he saw that she swooned for a second as he came closer.

"I...do you...want tea or something stronger?" They were standing very close, just gazing at each other. His arms slipped about her waist, and he drew her to him, kissing her eyes, cheeks, and lips. He slid his hands under the strap of her dress, sliding it off her shoulder. He could feel her firm breasts against him, the wondrous curve of her body. He wanted her desperately...Her trembling, as he was stroking the side of her breast, then suddenly stopped.

"Oh Rich, not yet, I'm...it's too soon," she was shaking when she stepped away, rearranging her dress. He managed to stabilise his urges, but when Sascia looked at him with such love, he almost lost it again.

"I'd better take you home. It's already after ten, but oh, Moppie, I never felt that way about Debbie; please believe me." They stood close.

"I know, me too, about Vinny, I mean," she whispered. This time, the heat of the moment blossomed into a warm and intimate togetherness. Now was not the right time, but soon it would be. He drove her home, and before she left the car, she showed him with her soft, sensual kiss how much she wanted him.

It was getting dark as he drove back to his flat. His depressed mood of this morning had vanished. The vandalism in his flat and the coffee shop did not dampen his spirit. He was in love! His joy knew no bounds.

He parked his car behind his neighbour's green Opel. They had also just arrived. He wondered if they had been home at the time of the break-in. Bernie and Jane, a middle-aged couple, had been living next door for as long as he could remember. They were naturally shocked to hear what had happened. They had been away visiting their daughter for the whole day, so there was no point asking them if they had heard anything.

Gosh, was he tired! As he opened his flat front door, things looked much better than they had two hours ago. Sascia had helped him with most of the mess.

He picked up the shoebox from under the coffee table and gathered the scattered family photos. He was about to throw them back into the box when he saw a fancy airmail letter with a watermark of a picture of a luxury cruise liner addressed to Theo. It was open, and his curiosity got the better of him.

Dear Theo —The Fairstar

I've gone with Ben to Sydney without saying goodbye when you get this letter. When you told me that you were going through with your disappearing act, I couldn't accept that you would leave us. I know you are at peace parting from this world, but as you know, I'm not. The sorrow rises within me, imagining what you must go through, saying goodbye to your brother. I keep asking why we could not write this decoding workshop until the end. POWAH explained your decision, but I'm still wondering why.

Ben knows about us and what we share. I love him with all my heart, and he is a great partner, but his job gets to me. I've repeatedly warned him that his attachment to Interpol will affect our marriage, but he needs to dig deeper into the intrigues Trevor and Leo have dragged up on that old historical site in France. The fact that Leo is involved makes me hold back from reacting, but if only they could see the energies they mess with.

My half-brother Toon invited us to visit him in Brisbane. At least Ben is getting away from his desk job, which he hates. Toon paid for this world cruise; what a treat. The food was outstanding, the entertainment in the evening was excellent, and the weather was good. Well, I had a tan, and Ben turned a darker pink. The next port we are berthing is at Perth. I will post this letter to your old address. I hope your brother gets it to you if you have already gone. I know we will always be together, but I want it all.

My dear twin soul, I need to share my outline of the first level of the card game. How am I ever going to attract people to be the guinea pigs? I will have to leave it up to you know who.

Remember the aspects of the 22 spacings we have worked on together? I've projected the spacings over a watermark of Toon's auric field that shows the triple chakra vortices. You know the one I mean. It's incredible how the Language of Light symbols and their interpretations are already in place, based on what I've seen in Toon's aura.

As you know, Toon allowed me to use his astrology and numerology information to practice. I'll share it with him when we arrive in Brisbane. Amazingly, your paradigm-shifting theories intertwine with the cutting edge of physics, evolution biology, information theory, and the Vedic teachings; it all comes together.

My love, I'm rambling on. I received the new proposed plan for Pleasure Parks from Harry through the mail, and there it was, just as I had seen it in my visions! The spread of the cards. After I scanned the image and took out all the detailed info that was not applicable, I left with just the suitable layout to help each player interpret.

Oh, I miss our discussions on how our two ideas dream of our existence and that we are collectively God's but unaware of it. Those two understandings come alive through playing our cards.

The whole layout uncannily resembles a drawing of an Egyptian eye symbol. You would have loved it. The 22 pyramids that will each hold the Language of Light cards reflect our two ideas. Tieneke's plan to let people first create their private dream home with their Language of Light cards was brilliant. I still have to work out the five levels of understanding, but Tieneke will help me. I hope it is going to work. Trevor has offered to help out on the website. Like the well-known tarot deck, using your cards to awaken the dreamer's creative field is a suitable medium.

The first level of the card game is still relatively easy to play and mainly deals with our present life issues. I'm already looking forward to the next level, and POWAH regularly speaks through me.

How I interpret the next stage of all the ancestral lineages is still a mystery, but as you know, it is revealed to me at the right time.

My dear, dear soulmate, I'm missing our talks. With you, I have a rapport that is so special; I hope that we can keep communicating even when you have gone from our realm. Ben is calling me to get ready for our evening dinner.

I'm looking forward to seeing Toon. My love, my thoughts are with you.

Always yours A

He was speechless. Had Theo read the letter just before he left? He never suspected that Annelies and Theo had such closeness, but he vividly remembered Annelies from a dream. He was suddenly inspired to start writing it all down. He would start on his journal this minute, describing what he recalled from his first dream journey.

It was past eleven when it became dark outside. Richard loved the long summer days. He filed Annelie's letter away with the photo he found under the letter G, which stood for the game in Theo's files. Suddenly, he turned to stone. The two photos! They were still in the Honda with his briefcase and his laptop. The intruders had looked into the files but had been distracted by something. He sprinted to his car to retrieve his laptop and briefcase from his boot.

When he returned, he pulled out the file with the first photo. He read Theo's first interpretation of the tablets about the prophet's game at the back. An old used CD he'd never seen before fell out. The disk was marked; 'Orphanage of Souls.' in Theo's handwriting.

He took it to his PC, which still had a CD drive. He was so eager to start his assignment that he slotted it in at force, hoping the disk would still work, but Theo's old PC didn't come on! The power was there; he checked the main electricity board, and everything was on. Flipping hell, the prowlers! They must have done something. Thank goodness for his laptop, but it had no CD drive. His was the latest model. He knew that the PC in the coffee bar had one. It was late, but he was wide awake!

The streets in Apeldoorn were quiet. The soft, drizzly rain promised good weather for the next day. He parked near the back entrance. There was nobody around. Sunday evenings were always special to him. When he came to stay with Theo after his divorce, on Sunday evenings, they would have a beer on Theo's balcony, weather permitting.

The computer still worked through Windows Explorer, but he needed an access code. He wondered what Theo would have called it. He typed in Richie, and it worked! It showed two files, named Tablet 8 and the other file called; 'Becoming Aware of Being Unaware.' As he clicked the yellow folder, the 8th tablet opened in Wordpad. Thank goodness because the shop's PC had only two programs. One is for the bookkeeping, and one is from the VVV with info on all the tourist activities in the Netherlands. It had no word processor.

As he opened the document, he was amazed at how he managed to get the tablets in the correct order. That was indeed a mystery to him. He stared at the 8th tablet without a photo titled The Eye of the Observer Game.[1]

Tablet 8

< I knew that far in the past, before Atlantis became my home—some priests used dark magic, calling up beings from an unknown realm >. ... The rest was gone, but Theo had left a message for him.

Dear Richie, Leo, Trevor, and I believe energy vehicles hold the original human genetic code frequencies beneath the Sphinx. They think activating

---

1. https://allrealityshifters.wordpress.com/richard-de-jong/tablet-eight/

these codes through the crystal's eye will trigger readings on the Astral portal on the celestial belt behind Mars during the next cosmic shift. Despite this, I was concerned about the warning of the realm of darkness behind Mars.

So many things suddenly started to fall into place. Why the world was in its state, and why each person needed to experience a wake-up call, no matter how painful or traumatic. Why does the word fantasy not mean natural, but how accurate was the physical world?

He made himself a cappuccino and clicked on the other file. Suddenly, the PC cut itself off! It had fallen over again. He checked the plug, but everything was working. It was already well after twelve. He would look at it tomorrow. The rain had stopped, but a breeze blew from the east, promising more rain!

At his flat, he dropped everything and went straight to bed. He was in the right mood again. He knew that made all the difference with his out-of-body trips. As he was relaxing, he imagined his light body stretched above him as if he saw himself in a mirror...

• • • •

When the early sensation came over him, he knew he would soon be free! ...When Theo took him by the hand, he felt again this unmistakable sensation of speed...

"Richie, I'm taking you on a different journey this time since your vibration is speedier and happier. Don't be alarmed." The unmistakable feeling of being drawn into a funnel still had not prepared him for what he saw next! How awesome. It was both beautiful and weird. All around him were eyes spinning in all directions to a point of light!

"Richie, when I decoded the fifth tablet and saw a visual projection, I felt overjoyed." He could imagine. Where was he? He had a sensation of being pulled back toward his physical body for a moment.

"We are now taking the mystical travelling route the shamans use. Describing this journey in words is complicated, so hold onto the visuals instead." The point of light became almost too bright for him when they got nearer.

"Remember that the eye symbolises consciousness you could only see from a great distance. Look!" He saw nothing at first, and then a thrill of surprise at the change of scene made him call out! *"Are we going to visit a star?"* They were heading towards a bright light.

"Richie, this burning ball of fire is our Sun; look away from it." For a moment, he only saw a significant cluster of other planets, like they were swinging freely around the burning ball. He recognised what he thought was planet Earth because he could still decipher its outline of land and sea, even at this great distance. The scene below him gradually took on a strange and beautiful significance. Like a cobweb, he perceived it as a ball caught in a pulsating web of colourful living electrical fibres. *"Theo, how fast are we moving? I can never feel that there is any effort in our movements."*

His mind could still not grasp that he is only a conscious particle of energy.

"Yep, we are just that. That's why we can move faster than electricity; you only have to think, and you will be there." He gazed at the miniature country scene below when his mind and eyes adjusted to the new focus. The only way to describe how the next panorama came into play was as if he were observing everything through a giant telescope that could zoom in on whatever was happening on Earth or the universe.

"I saw the birth of two universes that could not exist in the same environment. New galaxies were born within those two universes. These ejaculations became a new beginning of each solar system within a galaxy that embodied the same matter or anti-matter particle." Theo's revelation eluded him, but…as he watched,

meadows became mountains. Buildings that were on flat land ended up on mountaintops or plains. Deserts became water areas. Mountains again sank into the water or became valleys. Land masses moved apart or moved together. Some just broke off and plunged into the oceans. Was the planet moving?

"Now you see how I started to grasp the oneness within everything. I saw that each vibrational part carries the identity of pure potential through oneness." He still did not grasp...then...when they moved closer...he saw long lines of people going into caves and holes in the Earth while other groups stepped into an unusual-looking craft and flew away. The various crafts took three distinct forms. The largest one was cigar-shaped. Another was saucer-shaped. The third one looked like an upside-down oval dish.

"Are these the flying saucers people have seen? What are these people doing, and where are they going?" He was mesmerised by the scenery. Was he part of it? Was this all for real?

"They are mining! Again, we are looking at the holographic akashic records of our ancestors from the last period, which we call the Lemurian age. Everything belonging to the external world of the senses is subject to time, and time destroys again what has originated in time." Theo pointed at a large group of people that moved into what appeared to be. Their forms. Had they evaporated? Or, had they become part of the Earth? They changed shape while doing it! Some forms changed into water or air, while others merged with the landmasses if you could call it that—feelings of. Loneliness and separation suddenly overwhelmed him. How strange...why?

"I know; I reacted as if I was left behind." The entire vision entranced him with the action as if he were there! But where was he? *"This vision is from POWAH's akashic record of when the Eye of the Observer was a living revolution organ within the planetary*

chakra." His thoughts somersaulted as if all his emotions were spinning. Were they observing the soul library of POWAH?

"*Yes, I've been told that the higher angelic beings who walked on the planet have hidden their experiences and wisdom in many human forms through the qualities of the Language of Light.*"

"*What do you mean?*" He wished he understood it

"*Their qualities have become part of our soul's experience. Their vibrations connect the physical form to the spiritual realms. It is that aspect of our soul that creates our spiritual connection.*" He couldn't fathom what Theo was implying; all he saw were ring-like vortices, one opening up after the other while he was speeding inward. Toward what? Was he in a hologram deep inside Earth? As he was grabbing for Theo, he knew that...he was formless.

"*Richie, this dimensional porthole was left behind around the planet in many places. Throughout ancient mythology, they influenced many civilisations who all told the story of the creation of our species according to their perceptions.*" He wished he could write it all down now. How was he ever going to describe this accurately?

"*Oh, Theo, look! They look like the clay figurines found at ancient excavation sites. But... they look like the people we saw! Had they been wearing goggles on, like our astronauts? Where are they going?*" Then, next, he saw what appeared to be palaces and temples. They were surrounded by hanging gardens with gates that displayed drawings of winged bulls and chariots. He knew they were tables of astrological forecasts. "*Remember when we studied these treasures and their written records? You will soon have to lecture on these artefacts, so be observant.*" When Theo reminded him of his rescheduled lectures, he almost leapt back. He knew his body was calling him.

"*Theo, what would happen if man reached cultural levels that included airborne craft technology like these?*" Gee, could man shape-shift in the past?

"*Yes, some could, but still, what took place is the same as today; they fought among themselves. Ancient tales tell many stories of the yearning to pursue the divine connection followed by the idea of an afterlife.*" They left the scene at a speed that made everything smaller. When Richard looked back again at the awe-inspiring garden city surrounded by a beautiful setting of an undulating valley with grounds that were gradually sloping upwards until it reached a row of hills in the distance, he realized that this community was constructed in circular patterns, with an inner circle that served as the location for ceremonies. As he observed the community from a broader perspective, he noticed that it resembled the shape of an eye. It was clear to him that this garden village was intentionally designed in the shape of an eye. "*Now, what do you see?*" He heard Theo ask while he was scrutinizing the scenery in its changing movements as if he saw time go by...Then...as if he was soaring up fast away from the garden below...velvet darkness with blinking lights settled his vision. He was back outside!"*Theo, are we inside the Earth?*" There was no mental speech responding to him. His inner eye focused into dark space towards the planet when he recognised the aerial photo of Ingrid; it was the same, without the roads, freeways and buildings. This scenery was bare of any signs of civilisation.

"*The planet's third Eye rotates its inner configuration to draw in light energy for a higher purpose. It's the jewel, very like our own third eye. The five levels or spheres represent our five subtle bodies.*" Richard was still baffled.

"*Theo, if they had such knowledge, I still cannot understand why they experienced a fall in consciousness?*"He always thought that if you knew and understood something, you would act in a way that would not go against what you knew to be the truth.

"Richard, in those times, people who knew that the sacred tonal sound language became distorted due to genetic and cellular cloning mixing. They knew that they had created cosmic karma." He tried to recall Theo's first interpretations. They were very different to the rhythmic sentences. Why?

"Richie, remember to look at the back of my drawer in my study. I left most of my work from the last two weeks there." The mentioning of the flat again almost pulled him back to his body. He still had millions of questions. He beamed them all. About Annelies, Ben and Trevor, the lot.

"So Trevor remembered, good!" Theo's thoughts, like replies to his, helped him formulate some structure within his mind while he took in the visions around him.

"Richie, the veils of illusion will soon be lifted through activating the 'Filters' between the subtle bodies of planet Earth and the filters between the inter-dimensional portals." Theo seemed to think he would remember this dream and even see some logic. He already knew he would be unable to reason what he had seen.

"The fact that we are holographic projections will trigger our holographic mind into full awareness. It is necessary to detoxify or release the dark forces within the human physical form to awaken the original blueprint fully.." Annelies' first 12 weeks of workshops came to mind. Had she been aware of all this already? "Buddy, we've seen enough for the moment. I took you on this shaman's journey to stimulate your right-side consciousness."

"Did it? get stimulated, I mean." They were approaching the building where his flat was. He knew that he would be back in his body at any moment and remember very little. "Richie, practice your remote viewing when you wake up. Remember that you are still a player in the material game." He knew that his dream journey stretched his imagination to the limit. He constantly had to battle to stay grounded. *"Richie, for humanity to contact the subtle or inner worlds, you must expose your reader to their intra-terrestrial centre where true alchemical science is known. Your reader has all the knowledge already."* All he could think about were eyes, lots of them...

Chapter 9
The Role of the World Ego

The Power of Words Bookshop

Richard woke up with a headache, which left him feeling dreadful as if the person or persons who had violated his private space were crawling in his head. He wondered if that could be true. He reckoned that his headache stopped him from remembering any dream travel. All he recalled was the movie The Matrix but with eyes. Maybe he needed glasses? He fancied phoning Sascia. Hearing her voice might get him out of his foggy state.

Jeroen's sleepy voice tripped feelings of embarrassment for behaving like a lovesick schoolboy. Sascia had informed him about the break-in that occurred in his apartment. He was glad that his mother and Toon were cruising down the Rhine on a boat. Later that morning, Connie, Jeroen and Fred would help at the bookshop, clearing up the mess.

He could hear a commotion, and Sascia's voice made his heart leap. She asked if he had any interesting dreams, and he chuckled, wishing he did.

"Did you?" Her giggling stirred his fantasy. He tried remote viewing to see what she was wearing.

"What are you up to today?"

"I need to drive to Amsterdam to clear out my desk at the newspaper and see to my cat Ginger." He wished he could come along but needed to write a report if anything was missing and prepare for his following lecture. He tried picking up her thoughts, but all he imagined he heard was: "I don't think Jeroen's old t-shirt will charm him." He knew anything would please him so long as he could explore the contents.

"When will you be back this evening?" She was vague about that and left her landline number in Amsterdam. They chatted some more until Jeroen called her away. It was something about Quincy, who was staying with them.

He phoned Nel, who insisted she came in this morning when he told her about his flat. She wanted to work instead of being alone at home. He rang Fred's bookshop because they opened before nine and made arrangements with Connie that he would join them and bring Nel's famous sandwiches around half past ten.

He jumped into the shower and ran the cold water tap until his skin lit. He rubbed himself dry vigorously and shaved, feeling better already. Theo had been shorter because he had to bend while looking into the mirror. His wavy hair was getting long. He tied it at the back and slipped into a pair of jeans, noticing his muscles still rippled beneath his T-shirt. His spirits were up, the sadness cloud gone. He hoped that Nel was there before he prepared breakfast; his stomach was growling.

The mess behind the counter was a reminder that the computer had crashed. All the accounts and Aunt Mien's files were in there. The backup hard drive did not save anything. The place was quiet, apart from one person in the corner who was sipping his Cappuccino. The burglary attracted some curious people, and a passer-by asked what had happened to the door when the man from the glass company was busy repairing it.

He tried the computer again to see if it would start. It did! He re-entered the old CD, typed in the code Richie, and clicked on Theo's file titled Becoming Aware of Being Unaware.

Richie, I will have already gone when you find this old CD. I don't know when you will read this message, but let me explain this decoding card game I have worked on for a few years with a dear, close female friend, Annelies. I have always been very discreet about my relationship with her. We were friends in South Africa, but she is married now.

We met again years ago at a dinner at the Prinsegracht held in honour of Trevor Zwiegelaar's successful excavation in Egypt. We once again clicked immediately.

Annelies was entirely in tune with my theories about the possibility of physical immortality. When you read this, you might have already met. The decoding classes were written by hand when she asked me for help with the card game. We spent many evenings together when Ben, her detective husband, was on a case. He knew of our mutual interest and would sometimes join in. His contribution to the deviousness and manipulations people get sucked into was of great help to our project. I was told that you would become one of Annelie's guinea pigs and take on the second assignment.

The PC fell over again. Gosh, how annoying now that things are falling into place. He never knew that Theo had been so involved with Annelie's project.

Nel told him that the sandwiches were ready to take to the bookshop. She loved telling people of her ordeal, and she didn't mind being on her own. He took the CD from the PC and put it near his keys. He would read the rest later after someone looked at the computer. Nel would phone him when the coffee shop became too busy for her to handle.

Yolanda and Fred's bookshop was still in a mess. Connie was sorting out the magazines that were all in one heap. All the shelves were back up, and the police had left. Their PC had also been tampered with. Jeroen was trying his computer skills out to see if he could get it running again since both Fred and Yolanda were lost so far as that was concerned. All their older music CDs were scattered, but so far, not a thing was missing. Whatever they were looking for, they gave up searching and moved to his place.

"Gee, something is trying to steal all my genetic records. Isn't that weird?" Yolanda commented. She was on the floor picking up books. That's a feeling he could relate to! He had felt equally violated when he was in his flat, especially when they went through his family photos.

"That's what happened on an etheric level", Fred replied as he reviewed the inventory. Annelie's younger brother's whole persona commanded respect. He carried dignity as a second skin. He was no military man but a modern philosopher with a distinguished manner and witty humour. He had the same dark, cunning, penetrating eyes as Annelies.

"Really, by whom?" Yolanda asked as she leaned against the counter, twisting her long blonde hair in twirls. She was in her early forties with a voluptuous look that could fool many men looking for a shallow affair. He knew better. She was earnest and easily hurt.

"What do you think?" Fred challenged while devouring Nel's chicken sandwich with relish.

"Piet? But I've released him! He's not any more in my..."Yolanda peered around, looking for Connie, but Jeroen and Connie were far too engrossed in each other to hear their conversation. Piet, her ex, was one of Ingrid's abductors. The police have been unsuccessful in making any arrests so far.

"Why are you saying that? You mean he is still connected in my... auric field?" She looked at Fred with dismay.

"What did the game tell you last week?" The backup hard drive did not save anything. The backup hard drive did not save anything. The backup hard drive did not save anything.

"Gosh, you're right; I kept getting the brokering card! Annelies said it was a warning. I even thought that...well, right after the game, I met Ed, Ingrid's brother-in-law and...I thought"...

"That he was the one you must be aware of! You'd better, but not for that reason." Yolanda was blushing as she gave Fred a playful shove.

"Fred, what about you? It's your bookshop?"

Fred shrugged his shoulders. He agreed that, on an energy level, he could follow Annelies' dark forces theory.

"Richard, how do you feel? About your flat, I mean?" Fred asked while reorganising the front desk.

"The same as you both." Annelies once explained how she could see, on an etheric level, how people's emotional attachment cords with others or goods, no matter from which realm, were often torn or shredded. It was especially so with people who had experienced a shock. Can you see that, too?" Fred calmly observed him while he emotionally recalled his inner rage that someone had the nerve to go through his goods.

"Richard, what do you think has created an attachment or etheric cord in your field? "Yolanda asked before Fred could reply. He told them about the phone threat and his suspicion about the two photos. He explained the lecture incident and what Ben had told him. That didn't tell him anything as explicit as Yolanda's possible hook into a distorted reality, but it reminded him of his feelings this morning.

"Did you tell the police about the phone threat?"

"No... I didn't take it seriously enough, I guess."

They were all lounging around when the alarm suddenly went off. Everybody jumped.

"What the"...

"Well, I must have scared something away, or are you expecting the intruders back?" Ed's booming Australian accent greeted them in a buoyant style. Yolanda blushed when Ed openly showed his affection by sweeping her up around her waist while telepathically beaming, *"I missed you."* Richard was stunned that he had intuitively overheard him. He presumed they were unaware of his newly acquired sensitivity, so he kept it to himself. Fred was on the phone with the security firm, reporting that the alarm was faulty. Ed asked if anything was missing since he felt not at all responsible for any brokering. Yolanda's eyes shot up.

"*How did you know we were?*".....Yolanda beamed at Ed

"Discussing information brokering? I didn't. I had a long discussion with Annelies and Ben last night. Toon used the same theories but could never make himself as clear as Annelies. I've learned more last night than I have in years. What a woman." Richard was fascinated to see Yolanda and Ed in love. They must have done something right.

"*Thank you for reminding us, Richard.*" As he looked up, Ed raised his eyebrows and winked.

"I believe you also have been paid a visit by the scoundrels. Do you know what they were after?" Yolanda filled him in about his phone threat. He added that Ingrid's flash drive was missing and that he was glad to have left his laptop and briefcase in the boot of his car. Richard liked Ed. He was cheerful and caring but still unsure if he had heard the telepathy.

When Ed talked with Connie and Jeroen, he could see that Connie liked him too. He was glad for Yolanda. A new relationship would do her good. He knew in his heart that he wanted a relationship that would include a telepathic connection.

"Listen, people, have we not been too calm about what is happening? First, there were problems with Mr Brinks' firm. My father updated me on how seriously Pleasure Parks had been jeopardized in its development when they started on the project in France. It comes very close to home when one's employees and business associates are brutally wounded. Now, this vandalism. The repeated violence seems to have a ripple effect because it is spreading to all our family members. What are we not seeing?" Ed had them all thinking.

They were all gathered in a circle among the books piled high on a low coffee table, waiting to be sorted. Yes, it started to feel that they had been like sitting ducks. Fred tore a sheet from a roll of brown wrapping paper and spread it out on the counter. He drew a circle in the centre, representing the troubled building site, with lines like a spider connected outward. Above the lines, Fred wrote the names of each possible association with the Jaarsma clan. Each one of them could come up with a brainstorm idea. He added his speculation and Ingrid's speculation about the symbol. He included the telephone threats, which were still a riddle, but no doubt it would all become clear one day.

Yolanda mentioned Annelie's board game graphic, which coincidentally reflected the eye symbol. Ed knew a lot about the drafting background and the reports his geologist had supplied them with concerning the blasting. He remembered that there was talk of gold and iron readings at the building site, which Ed confirmed. Fred mentioned Nick du Toit and Roelof de Beer's involvement. He added his Aunt Mien's first marriage with Nick du Toit, including her suspicions. Fred asked when she would be back. He had not seen her since his university days. Connie added her dad, and Jeroen reminded them of the resort where Ingrid was held. The atmosphere had changed into a unified effort to recognise what was happening.

"For our next move, I suggest a family meeting. We should also invite the detective. What's his name?"

"André Jaarsma, and what about Hans, Liesbeth, Peter and Helen." He added them to the list. Jeroen mentioned Sascia and the pilot, Dirk. He could be of help. Connie suggested Nel since she had seen one of the intruders. The list was getting long, but everyone realized how vital each role could be in the affair. Fred included Leo, Ben, Trevor, and Quincy without question. Ed asked him what he could add to the mystery surrounding the layout of Pleasure Park and the Egyptian symbol.

"You mean the Eye of Horus?"

"Yes, what do Egyptologists say about that symbol?"

"There are many different viewpoints. At Giza, the golden capstone with the eye symbol had a special reference to the star Sirius in the constellation of Canis-Major." he shrugged his shoulders, adding, There was a rumour that the capstone would return to the pyramid at the turn of the millennium, but it never happened. He still couldn't see what connection there was with the France project...He knew that the dreams he recalled were very descriptive, but he was not ready to appear like a freak. It was still all too bizarre. Fred started to draw the eye symbol while Yolanda found a book on the same subject.

"How do we connect this eye symbol and what has happened in France and here? My mother informed me about the various changes to the dome's drawings to achieve optimal acoustics. Could that mean anything?" Jeroen asked. Gosh, he remembered something. The laser beams! It had to do with sound. He had dreamed about a vortex...inside the centre pupil of the eye. He mentioned his sudden hunch, but nothing made any sense. Ed and Yolanda started to collect every book they could find on the eye of Horus symbol. Even a children's book on hieroglyphics was practical.

"Let's ask everyone on our list to write down their impression of what is happening in their own words. It will be amazing to see what comes out. Then we'll organise a meeting place to apply more brainstorming. It is a somewhat unorthodox way of solving a mystery, but the whole affair is bizarre." Ed suggested.

The phone rang, and Annelies reminded them that Trevor was about to be interviewed on the radio for a particular alternative program in Hilversum. They were all eager to hear that, so everyone dropped their work. The bookshop was closed for business. He hoped Nel would cope on her own. This morning, the Pannekoek was also quiet.

They must have missed the introduction and the first question because Trevor's voice answered the interviewer.

"Yes, during the millennium celebration, it's been speculated that a golden capstone with the symbol of Horus would return to the pyramid at Giza. We know it never happened; our time has not yet arrived for that to happen."

Startled, they all looked at him, thinking the same thing: synchronicity?

"Gee, I wonder what the question was. Why the sudden interest in the capstone?" Jeroen whispered. They all waited for the interviewer's next question.

"Trevor, we have heard some rumours lately. We learned that gold and iron were found at the Pleasure Park's building site. Secondly, someone has anonymously sent us suggestive information that there could be a connection between the area and the Great Pyramid of Giza. Could you please provide us with more information on this matter?"

Nobody spoke. They all looked at each other in amazement. Fred made a shh sound past his index finger for silence to hear Trevor's reply. He wondered who fed the radio station information.

"The only connection I can think of at this moment is that there is a vortex or tunnel or crater beneath the site that acts like the Bermuda triangle....but to connect that with the symbol of Horus, well... I'm just contemplating, so don't quote everything I say as gospel, but here we go. The capstone symbolised the transformation or the departure of the ruling Pharaoh. Suppose that the sun-god Ra-Atum underwent initiation in the ascension chambers. It is a translation from the Benben stone, by the way."

Fred looked up the Benben stone in the index from the book Secret Chamber by Robert Bouval. He tried to recall what the tablets were saying.

"This sun god, Ra, climbed the ladder to ascend to heaven, but instead, the departed king's soul, identified with Orion's constellation, was sent back to its creation. We doubt if the pharaoh ever physically ascended, but who knows? He could have shape-shifted into a mythical bird, the Phoenix, associated with Orion. To our ancestors, this planet always seemed to have appeared at dawn. You must remember that perceptions differ greatly depending on which epoch you think you translate any text."

They were all looking puzzled. Where was Trevor leading them to? Fred and Ed both made notes. He was stunned by how Trevor's reply reminded him of Theo's translation.

"You've lost me. What connection is there with the French site where so much has happened during the last weeks?"

He wondered how Trevor was going to respond. The interviewer's directness must have been a surprise because Trevor took some time to reply.

"We have to accept that the ancient builders of the temples in Egypt had been keepers of a powerful wealth of science. We suspect that the science of physical immortality was one of them. Some monuments on our planet are unique not only in their architectural grandeur and precision, but they also have a powerful spiritual and unconscious effect on people from all walks of life."

Trevor was probably stalling or getting his thoughts into order because he still didn't know where he was leading. Again, the translations from the eighth tablet flashed before him.

"Like the Vatican, which holds the main repository of ancient books associated with Christ and the Bible, the Pyramids are often mentioned in the Sumerian tablets and the book of Thoth. All the writings maintain that the architects were divinely inspired messengers, and I say, all were, and still are, diversions of the truth, but at the same time, truth is often hidden among controversial contemplations."

Fred got up to look for a book. When he returned, he saw it was on Thoth's story. The last sandwiches were gone, and Yolanda made coffee for everyone. He sensed that Trevor was avoiding any speculations surrounding the French project.

"Trevor, the media has always been interested in the spectacular phenomenon around the explorations and research at the Giza necropolis. Is that not because most of these people seek enlightenment and peace?"

The interviewer allowed Trevor time to think. Was it to formulate what he wanted to hear? The interviewer had done his homework.

"It has always saddened me that some well-known Egyptologists underestimate others who are scientific researchers and mystics all rolled into one. We speculate that the man-gods that visited our Earth belonged to a higher evolution. Some might have come to Earth to accelerate the evolution of humanity."

Richard wondered what Trevor was leading up to. He thought of POWAH, a member of the Alpha and Omega council and the spokesperson of the Ninth sector. That's what Theo had told him at the beginning of his out-of-body adventures.

"You have often mentioned the word ascension in your articles. One of the rumours is that the resort in France will hold the first holographic platform, whatever that is, for that same purpose: to ascend from this 3rd dimension. I can't take this too seriously, but I have researched; there is speculation that intra-terrestrial centres have been active since the primordial times. These points on the planet are powerful in the redemption of matter. What are your thoughts on that?"

Richard was impressed with the interviewer. He knew of active nucleus points, which are the Bermuda Triangle but under the Pleasure Park complex. That's a thought.

"Yes, these centres are the connecting links to supra physical planes. They can have extensions on the surface of the planet. We know that true alchemical science is there to fulfil the Earth's evolutionary aims."

They were all frowning at him. Ed shrugged his shoulders when Yolanda whispered something. Connie shook her head at Jeroen.

"Thank you for that explanation. Our researchers have speculated that these intra-terrestrial centres were beneath the paws of the giant Sphinx monument in Egypt in primordial times. That's why large halls or initiation chambers are leading toward the Pyramid. Might those have been more like laboratories? Are they excavating the area? Trevor, could you elaborate on that"

The interviewer was well-read on the subject. Richard was now waiting in anticipation of what Trevor would say next. They were going back to Egypt now. So, what was the connection with the French area?

"To my knowledge, no secret excavation has occurred inside or outside the plateau at Giza. Let's go back to the golden capstone with the eye symbol. It has a special reference to the star Sirius in the constellation of Canis Major. Suppose most of the human race's original seeding happened on the star Sirius. In that case, Sirius, the fifth nearest star to our solar system, and Horus, who, as a symbol, represents the divine star of origin within us all, indicate a beginning to me. Sirius is often associated with the magical birth of humanity. The phoenix is the celestial sign that marked the vehicle for the renewal of life and order."

Richard suspected that Trevor was trying to take the interviewer away from France permanently.

"Richard, are they exploring additional chambers or tunnels in Egypt?" Ed beamed. He shook his shoulder. Excavations were always going on, especially in the Valley of the Kings.

"Have the tunnels under the French site been exposed to the public?" he beamed back, wondering if Ed would respond.

Ed shook his head. Fred pointed at the magazine rack, passing a magazine from the stand with an article on the Giza Pyramid by Trevor Zwiegelaar. Is the Pyramid of Giza a galactic remote control device? The interviewer pressed Trevor for more information about Pleasure Park's involvement.

"Are the rumours correct? Have heavy deposits of gold been found?" the interviewer pressed on.

"Good grief. Who in the hell is spreading those rumours around?" Ed beamed.

"I would like to inform you that there is currently a full investigation taking place in France regarding a recent kidnapping incident. Additionally, I would like to share that three more lectures are scheduled on the mysteries of the Sphinx in Utrecht next week. The lecturer, Richard de Jong, is an associate of mine, and I had the pleasure of knowing his brother and father, highly regarded Anthropologists. I am thrilled to hear that Richard has translated some newly discovered tablets dating back to an earlier Sumerian civilization, and it is his responsibility to bring public awareness to the fact that we live in extraordinary times. I have elaborated on this topic in my latest article in the 'Archeological' magazine."

"Ed was reading the article while Jeroen peered over his shoulder. Hearing his name mentioned was daunting. He never saw it as his job to awaken public awareness. They all looked at him. The interviewer asked Trevor to provide his thoughts on the document given to him.

"Trevor, the text says, "O RA, make the womb of the nut pregnant with the seed of the Spirit. The text below had the word "Benben" scribbled underneath. The person who sent us information mentioned that it refers to genetic engineering experiments?"

Trevor cleared his throat before replying. The image of the resort where Ingrid had been held hostage flashed before his eyes. "

"I know someone is trying to divert people's attention towards many controversial rumours. I am partial to that, but I would like to know who this person is that you refer to all the time."

They were all waiting to hear who it was that would speak next.

"It's important to keep having a deep admiration for the human body the way it is. We are in for the time of our lives and individually and collectively responsible for what happens to our species. Much of what we spoke about, especially the energy vortex centres, is not to be found on any physical level, but through them, humanity receives its evolutionary impulses."

Someone was trying to get into the bookstore. Fred managed to persuade them to come back the next day.

"I will address your initial question. The term 'Benben' has a sexual connotation in the texts, a mythological depiction of how our ancestors seeded our race. At present, many individuals carry the same genetic lineage as star seeds, and they will reveal to us how the human genetic code hides alchemical science. We are in a phase where evolutionary impulses are triggered, and the ancient text seems to narrate stories about the end of times. It is unclear whether it refers to theirs or ours. I recommend attending Richard de Jong's public lectures to know more."

They were all looking at him. Fred held up his thumb. After hearing Trevor advertising his lectures, he was pretty shaken. Trevor was quite courageous in exposing his ideas in this manner.

"Where can a person look upon all this information if you can't make the lectures?"

Trevor told them about their website. Jeroen wrote it down so he could look it up later.

"With the help of our five senses, the human mind configures atomic and cellular activity. This pervasive wave-motion in our hearts will again commune with the cosmos. Our DNA stores sufficient data about our multidimensional lives. Ancient scientific knowledge about the Soul, the Self and the body (including DNA) is all encoded in myth and legends. Our collective transformation is imminent, but for many, this awakening will mean the end of our Earth's history."

Trevor's closing comment reminded him of Annelie's class. She often mentioned how each tissue in the body has individualized frequencies. Trevor informed the listeners that Mr Zwiegelaar was requested to avoid making further speculative comments about the French site due to recent unsettling incidents. Fred switched off the radio.

"Well, that was quite a tug and pull between them. Has anyone any idea who's feeding these rumours about these mysterious centres to the radio station?" Ed asked. None of them had. They all asked him if he knew what Trevor was talking about. He had to get his mind right on that one. He said that he was just as puzzled. Gosh, it was all happening! He was keen to work on his lectures instead of returning to the Pannekoek. Before he shared the interpretations with the others, he would use them in his journal! He told them about the first eight tablets and that Annelies would explain the content of the tablets after her journal was finished on her website, ' ascension-workshop'.

He asked if Jeroen could look at his PC since he seemed to know his stuff and said cheerio. They all needed to get on with daily chores, and he wanted to go back to the PC to see if it would open again to read what more was on the old CD from Theo about the card game.

Ed reminded them that they planned to meet again to follow up on his idea about gathering information surrounding the criminal elements.

Nel managed well on her own. The computer was on, and he inserted the CD with his password. He wanted to know what Theo had seen during his last dizzy spells.

I knew I would always be a part of the group creating this map but from a different realm when the workshop participants were to write about their journey of awakening to map out this relatively challenging path. When you read this, you may be surprised, or maybe we have already connected through your out-of-body experiences. I hope it's the latter, as it will make it easier to explain what follows...

The screen suddenly went black... That was it. Richard would wait for Jeroen to take a look at it. He took the CD out and put it in the safe. Then he saw the flash drive that belonged to Ingrid. The intruders must have been after it... He regretted not having taken a closer look at it, but he had left his laptop and briefcase concealed under the seat of his Honda. Maybe not the best place, but nobody would think he would keep valuables in his old car. For now, he has returned CDs and sticks to the safe.

While serving two customers, Richard wondered what he would discover about himself through this card game. Everyone had a dark side he knew all along, but to be confronted with the aspect of oneself you might not like must be challenging. Would these centres Trevor mentioned purify physical matter?

Connie and Jeroen arrived after lunch. Connie showed Jeroen around and introduced him to Nel. He was amused at how she took over. While Connie helped new customers, Jeroen looked at the Pannekoek's PC.

"Connie told me you are looking for part-time help during the holidays. Is that true?" What was he implying? Jeroen was punching the keyboard, and it looked like he knew what he was doing.

"Are you offering your help?" Connie joined them, and her blue eyes were like Yolanda's, large and enchanting. When he asked Jeroen about his family obligations, Jeroen replied that it would be part-time and he would regulate it with Connie if that was alright with him. Jeroen was still studying in Eindhoven. As far as he knew, Jeroen had also worked for his grandfather's steel firm. Jeroen said he could do with the extra cash. More likely, he wanted to be with Connie, but it was true that he wanted more time for himself. He wanted to work on his journal, so they agreed on pay and hours. Jeroen got the PC working but warned him to back it up. He speculated that the CD hardware could be faulty. When he slotted Theo's disk in, a small screen reported an error. What now?

"Those CD's are no good." Jeroen sniggered. "They don't last. Was it important?" He was disappointed, wishing he had saved it on the hard drive. Jeroen tried several times but had no luck.

He asked after his sister. Jeroen didn't know when Sascia would be back. He said she didn't want to give up her flat since it was impossible to get such a good position overlooking the many canals in Amsterdam. When Jeroen left, he phoned Sascia at her flat, but he had gotten her answering machine.

It was busy today. By now, more people had heard Trevor on the radio. When customers discovered who he was, some people were amazed. Some people had followed the kidnapping saga. Connie froze every time someone asked her what she knew. He told her to go back to her mother's shop. He and Nel would manage. Connie was still very concerned about her dad's involvement.

The Star-map

The rest of the week dragged on. He hadn't seen Sascia but had spoken to her over the phone. She had resigned, but her ex-boss had made it difficult for her. He had been in contact with André Jaarsma and wanted an exclusive on the whole Pleasure Park affair. Sascia got him to agree that she would do it on an utterly freelance basis for a month if he decided to include extra money so she could pay someone who would collaborate on the write-up of the Pleasure Park developments. Her boss knew that Sascia would have the exclusive rights to the story with her connections. He was rather impressed with her business sense.

He needed to prepare for his second lecture scheduled for next week. Since Trevor's radio interview, his Sphinx topic has become popular.

On her way to the Prinsegracht hotel that morning, Annelies dropped off an envelope with a flash drive for his journal. Next week, he would see her for his reading. He had to stay focused on his coming lecture, but he was nevertheless looking forward to the reading with Annelies. He wanted to discover what she knew about Theo's work and the Tablets and who was sending them. The card game was postponed for a week after his reading.

He had missed his dream journeys. Since he started writing in the journal, his dreams have stopped. At least there was no memory of any. He had gathered all the information from Theo's translations with the photos for his journal and what he could remember from his previous dreams. He started meditating again, but keeping a coffee shop running started to unbalance him. He wanted to do his best but felt torn between obligations.

Back at his flat after a busy day at the Pannekoek, he went back to his laptop. The C drive in Theo's PC was beyond repair. The prowlers had tried to open it by force. He rearranged his desk while reviewing his translations from the two photos. Ever since the break-in, he has carefully kept them inside his briefcase. It was apparent that Leo, Trevor, and probably Ben knew much more about what was happening, but they were not forthcoming. He needed to spend much more time deciphering the symbols for his understanding.

His home office was full of drawings and diagrams arranged on the floor, so he knew what was what. He opened Annelie's envelope with the stick inside. He tiptoed between the papers to his laptop and opened the flash drive.

Two files appeared. One was a TIF file titled Star-map—the soul lineage of POWAH. It intrigued him. His Photoshop program opened the same image he had seen in Annelie's house and at the entrance of the place where they found Ingrid. Again, the star painting reminded him of the ceiling of stars in the tomb chamber of Unas, except for the image of the goddess Nephthys. He must ask Annelies if she knew who painted the original. The other file must have the translations from the ninth tablet. Now more than ever, he wanted to know if Trevor had been with Theo before he passed on. Theo had again translated this slate with the title, The Game of the World Ego[1].

Tablet 9

<When the Gods and Goddesses returned to the planet after the flood—a new reality was created by merging their blood.>

To read the rest, he now needed to visit the blog page, but He was always keen to read the letters Theo left behind for him.

Richie, Annelies and I have concluded that this tablet provides insights into how our personalities differ from our higher selves. We have started better understanding how our soul experiences life through these nine aspects. Annelies will share these aspects with you so you can note them in your journal. As you read them, you will soon realize the crucial role of personalities in the grand scheme. It's incredible to see how these nine

---

1. https://allrealityshifters.wordpress.com/richard-de-jong/tablet-nine/

types are reflected throughout the continents on our planet. We all now agree that historically, the pyramids on our planet were used by spiritual initiates to enhance the speed of human cells to transcend the experience of death. This process converts a physical embodiment into an etheric light body code. Unfortunately, this process failed before the closure of the last cosmic cycle. Each continent has its distinct signature that is now prepared for its reawakening. This is the resurrection our planet is currently involved in. This significant shift will impact any life form that merges in speed with Earth's energy changes.

Love Theo

He pondered how the continents and their civilizations on Earth reflect nine personality types. What was Theo telling him? Nothing made absolute sense. It seems that many beings walked the Earth; that was clear, but what did they know that humanity had forgotten? Was he ever going to find out?

The decoding classes of Annelies had prepared him somewhat on how to intuitively map the universe with himself, thereby reflecting his level of awareness or state of consciousness, but seeing himself as a more extraordinary being from his Earth-based perspective was challenging.

It was already after ten; he wondered if Sascia was home at her flat. When he redialed her number, all he got was her answering machine.

He was restless. He wanted to go to sleep so he could leave his body. He knew he wanted to escape, but from what he had no idea. He had no inspiration to work on his journal, and nothing on the TV interested him. As he stretched out on his bed, he tried to do some remote viewing.

Before he even tried to visualise her, he found himself staring at the ceiling, and the goosebumps ran through his body. He kept imagining that Sascia was like him, lying in bed. In his mind, he saw a smile appearing on her sleeping face. Did he wonder why? He kept practising remote viewing. Before he knew it he was gone.

• • • •

Would it be possible to see her in a dream again? Theo's breeze of joyful vigour made an impression on him.

"Theo, do you know where she is?" he beamed.

"I'll show you where. Come." He heard and sensed Theo's energy, which seemed to merge with him as he followed him. In a flash, he became aware of scenery so different; it amazed him how real it all looked. He heard children's laughter coming from behind thick bushes. The air was crisp and clear, like he was high in the mountains. He could even see patches of snow on the sloping hills all around. Was Theo again showing him glimpses of a parallel world?

They approached a group of children of all ages. They were unaware of their presence, and he had been one of them before he knew it! He knew that he was experiencing a parallel physical life. Was his soul showing him another physical experience?

In this life, he knew he was a teacher of sorts! He felt older than the other children, around sixteen. Their clothes looked weird. They reminded him of the winter gear tribes who lived in the Himalayan mountains.

"Very good, see, you do remember. Now, for the moment, merge with the boy you are in this life. I'll be waiting."

As he did so, he felt an acute weariness, as if he was grieving! A young girl hung on his sleeve. She begged him not to go while the other children yelled at him. He wanted to brush his little sister away. How could she understand? He had nothing to live for. He might as well go to the city. Teaching them lost all joy now that Savina was gone. His sweetheart of fifteen was promised to a wealthy merchant who had arrived to claim her. Savina had run to him in tears three mornings ago. Her sparkling green eyes were full of horror. Life was cruel; why could his family not have the money her father needed to keep his land? He wanted to take Savina and make a run for it, but where to? The monastery was the only place they could go to, but then they would be separated. Girls were not allowed.

Yesterday, he had wanted to follow the caravan this merchant had travelled with to fetch his bride. He had been up since dawn, waiting for them to pass their village. When the sun had appeared from beyond the mountains, he knew they must have taken a different route. He was too late to catch up with them without being prepared. He would die of cold, and Cathy had made great demands on him that morning. She had been the last child his mother gave birth to. He had lost two little brothers and one sister who had all been younger than him. His dad was the village teacher who knew all about the mountains, their secrets and death traps. All children between the ages of five and fifteen were required to participate in outings, some after school and others after completing their chores.

He had taken the educational activities over from his dad, but his mind was not on it today. He wanted to die. The numbness from losing Savina had created a void he didn't know how to fill. The emotional pain he felt so shook him; life without her was unbearable.

His outing trip class was finished, but Cathy, his sister, never stopped crying because he had told his parents that morning that he would enter the monastery to become a priest. At least he would learn something. His mother had only nodded, and his father never took much notice of what happened around him these days. He had lost his sight due to a fire accident. The spark had gone out of him. Nobody cared for his dad except for Cathy.

His sorrow gripped him like a vice. He knew he was disappointed at his dad's lack of control over his life. His dad had become grumpy, unreasonable and even mean.

When he became aware of Theo, who guided him away from himself, he wondered if this had all been for real.

"Richie, a soul has to go down to the very roots of its being to uncover the Love that is never lost." Shucks, does it have to be so painful?

"Yep, I know. There can be much suffering in love." Theo's mental empathy brought him back to the present.

"Richie, the beautiful thing about consciousness growth is that when you give it up, you get it all back." Had he given it all up? Was that me? Why did it always appear in his past if he was someone else while dreaming? On these inner planes, he felt detached from the lives he must simultaneously be having. In the

physical, everything was solid, and he felt very attached to his surroundings...Theo was watching him, and he knew that he had read his thoughts. They were resting on a grass lawn in what he would call a park. By now, he knew it was often just like a stage or setting for his mind to comprehend.

"During my out-of-body experiences, before I left my human consciousness known to my ego for good, my inner being had gone ahead." Theo beamed.

"What do you mean gone ahead? You mean my journeys on different realms while I still live in a physical body?" Conversing with Theo in this way created far deeper feelings of receptiveness. Was it because they were without weight or gravity?

"No, not quite. You still have many attachment cords, grounding you into the physical experience. It would help if you kept grounded to explore the awakening process. Our inner travel journeys are to create an effective link between physical and astral-emotional consciousness." When Theo beamed that for the first time, he could justify his eagerness to experience his dream travels.

"Richie, your inner being shifted for you to see more broadly. Do you feel any discomfort?" Theo's question rang in his ears as he stretched his body. Something in his neck was throbbing, but then it went away. He was trying to hold on to his dream's last flashes of conscious awareness.

"Richie, universal life is a mathematical game. Each civilization reaches a maximum development point, then it will vanish." As he stared at the ceiling with those thoughts, he woke up.

Chapter 10
The Game of Ecstasy

The second lecture on the Sphinx
Just as Richard closed his front door on the way out, he heard his phone. He was hurrying to the Pannekoek before driving to Utrecht for his second lecture, but his curiosity was too intense; he was hoping it was Sascia, but it was Aunt Mien.

He told her about the burglary and updated her on all the developments, assuring her that Nel was alright after her ordeal. He asked about her family since he was born in Bulawayo in Rhodesia, now called Zimbabwe. His parents had moved six months later to live in Durban, South Africa, for two years before his dad was back excavating Cairo. He would one day love to visit South Africa and Zimbabwe to pick up his energy roots. His flashback stopped when he heard his aunt telling him that her ex was involved with a real estate dispute related to Pleasure Park's upheavals. His aunt asked if the name Roelof de Beer had come up at all. She had been sniffing, as she called it. Theo had spent a lot of time with her in South Africa while he was at university. He described her as a people person who is compassionate, witty, and adventurous.

"I don't think so, why?"

"You are in contact with Annelies Zwiegelaar, are you not?"

"Yes."

"I know she is a close friend of Tieneke de Beer, Harry Brinks' daughter, the owner of Pleasure Parks. Tieneke and Roelof de Beer have one daughter called Hennie." In a flash, the tarty young woman at Ingrid's wedding came to mind.

"My source told me that Hennie is having an affair with a Jason van Hattum. Boy! Is he an undesirable character!" He wrote the name down.

"Richard, this Jason, he's a gambler and takes on unlawful jobs to pay for his gambling debts. He is at least thirty years older than Hennie. He has a wife somewhere with two grownup kids called Paul and Iris." The name Iris prodded his mind. He asked who his aunt's source was, but she avoided a direct reply.

"Roelof de Beer is also a gambler. I suspect he is blackmailed. He was surprised by how much she knew, as she had always been a very sociable person interested in people, but now she had become a detective. That Tieneke's family could be involved was a shock. Nothing about Tieneke convinced him that she knew more than she let everyone believe.

She was a vibrant, loving person and a close friend of Annelies, he now learned, but her daughter did fit the bill.

"Aunty, this Iris. I remember that Nel told the detective handling the case that the man called the woman Iris; what do you know about her?"

"Well, the rumour is that she is involved with Piet de Wit. I hate telling you all this, but Richard, don't get involved with that bunch. I always hoped Yolanda would leave her husband. She could do much better, and I am sure Annelies always felt the same, although we rarely spoke to each other." His aunt astounded him. The way she mentioned Annelies made him wonder. Who told him that Theo and Annelies only met during the renovations of the Prinsengracht? Had Theo and Annelies been lovers when they were much younger? Something must have happened that caused a rift between Mien and her.

"Aunty, about your ex, are you still in contact with him?"

"Well, my boys are. I hate to say this, but my ex-boyfriend Nick has always tried to outwit Harry Brinks. When Annelies wanted to purchase the Prinsengracht, the orphanage where my parents and grandparents grew up, Nick did everything he could to outbid them, but he lost! Annelies' family had been in the hotel business for a long time, and she and her brother Fred wanted to turn it into a hotel." He never even suspected that his Aunt knew that much about Annelies. The fact that Ben, her husband, was related to him and that his aunt seemed to know things about his own family he never knew put things into a different perspective. He wanted to ask her more but couldn't get a word sideways.

"Harry, who had a crush on Annelies, managed to outbid Nick and sold it to her for a lower price. I remember it well because Patricia, Harry's wife, was involved with Nick then. She was furious with Harry. I overheard their conversation when we were divorcing in the seventies." Peak-hour traffic sounds alerted him that his aunt could go on forever.

"Richard, Annelies, Fred and Harry are good people, but watch the others, they are dangerous. I thought you should know. I feel responsible. I owe your mother that much, at least." What she meant by that last remark might mean nothing, but it got him thinking. André, the detective, believed every life event was personal. The groundwork had been laid for a long time, but André could not understand it.

He told his aunt that he had met her twin brothers and hinted about his lecture in Utrecht while she rattled on, unaware that he needed to hang up.

"Richard, my mother had a twin sister called Kitty. There is a fascinating story going around that surrounds the girls who grew up in this orphanage. They all took on the name Jaarsma. It would appeal to you, I think. Theo and Annelies were always digging into the background of the Jaarsma sisters, as they called them.

Bingo. They knew each other from way back. He managed to find parking behind the coffee bar. He was lucky no cop spotted him talking in his cell while driving with one hand on the wheel.

"I will tell you all about Nick and the intrigues that I wanted nothing to do with in the past when I am home in September. I know from At and Jock that Toon Haardens, who helped them to start their community in the Western Cape near George, got shot. How is he? Do you know?" Richard never thought his cousins were into community living and that they knew Toon.

"He married Ingrid at the hospital chapel last week, remember? I was at their wedding together with Ingrid's three children." His aunt rattled on while he was listening in his parked car. Her phone call must have cost her a small fortune, but she seemed to need to tell him all about a family he never really knew much about. She was glad he'd reconnected with them after Theo's departure.

"Oh yes, both At and Jock would like to know that you were at Toon's wedding. Richard, this Ingrid; what is her surname?"

"Barendse" He remembered her maiden name from their last workshop as it appeared on her decoding chart.

"Richard, when you see her, ask her if her father's name was Eddie van der Linden. I know something about him, but you must go to Utrecht, good luck with your lecture. Richard, Jock asked if you have a recording of your lecture?" He told her that it was all taped. She told him the date of her return in September and that Sonya, his cousin, would come along.

After she hung up, he pondered the name Jason van Hattum. He had plenty to think about and tell Annelies about his connections with the Jaarsma family, which she probably already knew.

He sneaked inside the back entrance of the Pannekoek. Connie was on the phone with her mother as she waved at him.

Jeroen took an order from a customer, and later, Connie showed him how to make cappuccinos. It was a sunny morning. The coffee shop was busy; many people visited the' Het Loo palace.' Apeldoorn was very popular with tourists in the summer months.

He overheard Jeroen telling Connie his mom and Toon had returned last night. Graphically, he explained their telepathy. They would gaze at each other in silence. It was very embarrassing because their expressions made him and Sascia want to eavesdrop without luck. Jeroen thought his sister had picked up something, but he didn't. Connie glanced flirtatiously at Jeroen.

"My mom is very telepathic; I don't think I am. Aunt Annelies tried to teach me, but I think I'm mentally lazy" Hearing that Sascia was back in Apeldoorn made him delay leaving for Utrecht, so instead, he phoned Ingrid's number.

By a stroke of luck, Sascia picked up the phone. They chatted, and he asked about her plans. When she told him she was about to drive to Utrecht for his lecture and to her flat in Amsterdam, a brilliant idea jumped into his mind.

"Sascia, have you ever thought of having a photo exhibition?"

"Oh...Yes, I had one in Amsterdam and four other photographers; why?"

"Well, an idea came to me last night: the walls of the Pannekoek are bare! What about hanging some of your work here? If you want to sell, put a price on it! What do you think?"

The silence gripped him with suspense.

"I could? Do you think that people will look at them? I could try it, but most of my work is in Amsterdam...but...I like the idea."

He suggested that he fetch her on the way to Utrecht, and after the lecture, they would drive to her flat to get her portfolio. They should be back later in the evening.

"*Gosh, he is moving fast. I only need my portfolio, but can I take him into my flat? In my heart, I want to, but...!*" He jumped with glee as he picked up her thoughts.

"*Moppie, I promise I will do nothing you don't want me to do.*" He beamed, knowing instantly how challenging that would be. Sascia consented to his plan. He left the Pannekoek to pick her up, feeling invigorated at the prospect of her company.

The traffic on the freeway to Utrecht was heavy again. He felt Sascia observing him, so he grabbed her hand. He knew that he should think about his lecture, but instead, she intoxicated him.

"Rich, I....spoke to Debbie just before you fetched me. I told her why I was joining you."

"What was her reply?"

"She wanted to know if Vinny knew."

"Sascia, I've taken Debbie out quite a few times, but I never felt the same way I feel about you...so...I never slept with her." He peeked sideways. He knew he scored a mark.

They drove in silence. Richard remembered reading somewhere that women usually chose partners and that men were made to believe it was all they were doing! He wondered if she had.

"Did you know that Vinny had been married before?"

"Oh, yes, I met Vinny at an art function when I wrote an article with photos of a sculpture exhibition. I just never knew that the sculptress was his ex-wife."

"Mmm, I feel that Debbie knows Vinny."

"What makes you say that?"

He had to concentrate on the road as they came to the off-ramp to Utrecht. It was jam-packed, being a student town. Not all universities have started yet, but many lectures are open to the public during the holidays.

"We had a drink at a bar after he was newly married. I think Vinny did have a few too many, and he was depressed, but…I still remember exactly word for word what he said, "Richard, you know what depresses me the most? I met the girl I should have married on my wedding day."

"Really! What makes you think it could be Debbie?"

"Well, he described her as a gorgeous blond with sky-blue eyes. He was earnest. I asked him if he knew her, and he said he never found out. He was referring to The Cinderella story with the glass slipper! You know why and when I remembered this incident again?" Sascia stayed silent.

"When I walked into Harry's lounge in Utrecht and saw you sitting on the floor surrounded by all your photos, I knew we connected." He waited for her response. When he saw her, he knew he wanted her as a partner. How uncanny was that?

"Gosh, if he only knew that the moment I saw him walking in with Debbie, I wished I was her." As he drove into the university parking lot, he heard her thoughts! He parked, switched off the engine and smiled, then kissed her.

"We'll have to continue this conversation after my lecture." He meant her thoughts. Sascia had no idea how serious he was about her.

The lecture hall was packed. He hoped Sascia got a seat up front because he didn't see her. Some people already wanted to ask him questions before he had even started! Wil, the faculty secretary, suddenly appeared as he was about to begin. The lights had not yet dimmed because he could still see back—the noise of many whispering voices filled him with anticipation.

"Ladies and gentlemen, we've been overwhelmed with phone calls since the radio interview with Trevor Zwiegelaar. I speak for our faculty when I say we are very pleased that Richard will again entertain us with two hours of gripping and thought-provoking tales of antiquity. We know you are all somewhat squashed; our apologies. Please only ask questions when Richard has finished his talk." She introduced him by rattling off some of his personal information he never knew was on their file. Both Theo and his dad were mentioned. The doors closed after she walked out.

ARE THE PYRAMIDS ON THE PLANET USED AS ENERGY "CONVERTERS"?

As he projected the title of his talk on the screen, he scanned the audience for Sascia. He had worked through many late nights to prepare for his talk, but if he'd known she would be listening, he'd...He better get on with it.

"Is there a universal supercomputer system that stores all of the information on every deed, word, feeling, thought, and intent that has occurred at any time on our planet; where would those records be found? Many scientists, Egyptologists, and Archeologists are all wondering about that. That is also why you all are here, no doubt."

After a broad sweep of his arms during that long introduction, he switched the laptop projector on, knowing that the kaleidoscope graphic of the Mitchell-Hedges Crystal Skull would grab everyone's attention as it did his when he found it on the Internet. By enlarging it, he knew it would be an ideal background as he shared his contemplations for this lecture.

After everyone quietened down, he carefully managed to ease a few Egyptian symbols into each facet of the Crystal Skull. It again created a reaction he expected.

"This is what I imagine a holographic mind looks like. All the necessary information is left within each facet. Now, let's create a movement." The audience's soft whispering stopped when a spectacular new spectrum of colours and patterns appeared.

"A complete change occurs, but still the symbols are there; it's just a different viewpoint of the same information." He explained his thoughts on being a holographic being. Together with images from trees and animals, he shared his thoughts about how each mind resides within the auric field that surrounds an organic life, be it human or otherwise. He spoke about various writers who all took great courage and time to decipher the many pictorial records our ancestors left behind. He loved mentioning that each writer and reader, including him, had a unique way of perceiving the world of reality. Each contemplation created a visual shift, which he demonstrated graphically on the screen. That got everyone's attention.

"Let's remember that every living organism has the same holographic, kaleidoscopic-auric field and that each facet holds a major experience engraved as a code called DNA." He showed them slides of printed images taken from Aker's book. The pictorial symbols projected a descriptive resurrection scene. He knew that many in the audience were eager to ask questions, but he managed to stall them long enough for him to finish his talk. People who demanded to be heard always created a dilemma. Who would he respond to first? He started in the front row, nodding to a heavyset man with long hair.

"Richard, much stress is laid upon studying the hieroglyphic language. Is that not so?"

"There is no such thing as a hieroglyphic language, but you are right about the symbols. It prepares the translator uncannily to grasp inner recollections about the symbols from their memory. I call it intuitive reading. There are two complementary methods of thinking: our analytical and analogical modes.

Depending on which thinking mode is applied, many difficulties can arise in the reading." Gee, he should base his following lecture on the different meanings; it could make for an exciting talk.

"Richard, are the Egyptian officials not upset that there is so much speculation on the fact that people of a much higher culture and education came to Egypt and used the underdeveloped locals as slave labour after the destruction of Atlantis?" A gentleman from the middle row asked as he stood up. Suddenly, he spotted Sascia in the row before him. He winked, but she had just turned her head to the man. Richard was glad he was in Holland and not back in Cairo while he replied to that question.

He admitted that some officials were having problems acknowledging this. He reminded everyone that religious rituals very often became dogmatic and destructive. He remembered how Theo had been dismayed at the backstabbing and blackmailing that seemed to be the order of the day. How difficult was getting an exploration permit after Theo left this world? The SCA had withdrawn the permit, but at the last minute, they changed their mind. Typical of the Egyptians. He loved their don't worry, be happy attitude, but they were the most devious when negotiating and bargaining.

"Richard, there seems to be a dispute about the original builders of the Sphinx. Can you elaborate on that, please?" A woman asked at the back.

"Something did happen around 10,500 BC, but I suspect somebody had already built the pyramid at Giza." He remembered from his dream that the pyramid had been sealed after the initiations. Could that have been at that time, just before the great flood? A man and woman in the last row were both asking for his attention, and he asked the crowd for some silence to hear their question.

"Can you repeat that, please?" He recognised Annelies, who stood up and took a sheet of paper from Ben, who waved at him.

"Richard, we both know of your late brother Theo's work. He speculated that the temple of Deir el-Medina near Luxor contained an almost complete scene that forms a ritual that describes the survival of the physical form through frequency conversion. Do you know his thoughts on the hall of record theory?" Good grief, so far as he knew, Theo wasn't sure about finding a physical Hall of Records legend.

"Theo studied the books of Thoth, the god of wisdom. Thoth later became known as Hermes, the keeper of knowledge. Theo thought that only observational knowledge could open the door to immortality. He believed that the truth of the four three-dimensional models could direct the human mind towards its inner world. My brother's interpretations from the Hermetic texts clearly say that man must reflect on earthly matters and raise consciousness to travel in the company of the spirits. Does that answer your question?" Annelies nodded, and two more questions aired before he could take a break.

"Please, one at the time. I'll try to answer each of your questions, but I'm afraid these must be the last." It brought on a heavy protest, but he concentrated on the last two people in the middle of Sascia.

Their eyes met for a moment, and he felt a direct link.

"Richard, many ancient texts contain evidence from a much earlier source; what are your thoughts on that?" He and his brother believed in several periods throughout the ancient texts.

"Yes, you are correct. We talk about at least thirty dynasties, from the first in upper Egypt during the development of Jericho. This first time might be the golden age. The second age seems to be during and after the great flood. The thirtieth dynasty is around the time of Alexander the Great, around 330 years before Christ. He nodded at the last person, hoping the question would tie in with his closure.

"Richard, when I look at your kaleidoscope image, I think of the mandalas the Buddhists draw in coloured sand. Is there a connection?" He was so surprised he could not have asked for a better question to finish his lecture.

"Those mandalas symbolize the universal mind and the state of realisation or awakening. There is a link between Giza and the temples of Angkor. Excavations have proved that all the ancient temples act as active instruments where initiations into immortality through the science of sound and colour was practised" He switched off his laptop, and the lights came on. Before his mike was disconnected, he decided to remind his audience about his next talk.

"Next week, in the third lecture, we will discuss the newly discovered tomb of Nefertiti, wife of Akhenaten." He closed his laptop, collected his notes, and put them back in his briefcase.

Sascia, Annelies and Ben joined him below on the podium when the crowds left the hall.

"Richard, congratulations, I would not have missed it for the world. Leo, Toon and Trevor asked me to get a copy of the recording, and Leo asked me to give you this." Ben stood between both women with arms draped around their shoulders as Annelies handed him a blue envelope. She eyed Sascia, asking if they had any plans after his talk. He loved listening to her explanation about her portfolio.

"Fast work, I'm impressed", Ben projected. Annelies' dark eyes beamed a grin.

"You see your mirror, don't you?" With Annelie's mental reply, Ben laughed and took her by the hand. They said their goodbyes.

"What was that all about?' Sascia queried as she took some of his equipment off him so he would not have to take two trips to the car. He responded with a smile, rejoicing at the prospect of going to her flat.

On the way to Amsterdam, they listened silently to his music collection.

"I'm looking forward to seeing how and where you live in Amsterdam." He beamed.

"I bet he is keen to see where I live. I hope I can keep a cool head." He picked up on her thoughts. They were almost off the freeway, near Amsterdam's city centre.

"What are you stopping? We are not there yet?" He parked off the road and leaned towards her.

"You know why! You can read my thoughts, can't you? I just heard yours!" Her expression gave her away.

"My mind tells me to stop; otherwise, my heart will take over later, and I don't know if I will then keep my promise!" He beamed while keeping her in his gaze. Their eyes conveyed their thoughts.

"You mean when we are in my flat?" She remarked slowly.

"Yes...You know that is what I mean." Their eyes merged as he pulled her towards him, kissing her half-parted lips. Her body was quivering. She responded passionately, and it triggered his arousal.

"Oh, Moppie, you have affected my whole world, but I want more than this; I want to know the real you!" His hands travelled under her top, her skin so smooth... but she pulled back.

"Oh no. I am not that easy." Her thoughts shrieked at him while she giggled.

"Richard, what did you mean by 'your mind" He glowed, seeing her take a deep breath as she tried to hide her feelings.

"Moppie, you want me as much as I want you!" For a moment, her eyes became soft and alluring. The passing traffic outside created a perfect privacy screen.

"What did your mom tell you about Annelie's card game?"

"Gosh, how am I keeping my voice...he makes me all shaky..." He stroked her lips with his finger, and she reacted by nibbling them.

"That you are writing the journal on the second awakening level, about the Left and Right hemispheres and the personality cards," she answered, trembling, as his fingers continued tracing her ear lobe, following her neckline lower down, clearing her top away from her shoulder.

"What more did she tell you?"

"I love looking at your lips moving, Moppie; keep talking to me." Sascia blushed, and he knew she was becoming receptive to his thoughts.

"Mom told me that the Right Hemisphere was the nurturing garden of the mind, where all heart-based emotions like compassion, kindness, love and true inner joy are experienced and expressed."

"Oh, Rich, please, don't." Seeing her arching her back, he couldn't stop himself when he moved his arm behind her.

"Very good; what more did she tell you?" She dazzled a smile while trying to keep her calm.

"The Left hemisphere is where the intellect is developing 'the seeds of our reasoning."

"Oh, those eyes," he heard when he nibbled her earlobe. Again, her scent aroused him big time.

"Annelies explained that thoughts like seeds grow there to maturity and store new information..."Oh, Rich, I...not here." He was slowly stroking her breasts...

."Go on, what did Annelies tell you?"

"Rich, please, I can't think"...she was trying to squirm away as he explored.

"In the left hemisphere, we logically observe this physical world." She giggled, trying to take his hands away.

"That's right, where our senses are...translated ready for planting into the Right Hemisphere".He finished her sentence with a groan. Her eyes had become all soft while his hands were exploring. The stretchy fabric moulded around her raised nipples when she inhaled. "I am practising using my whole brain here", he whispered. "My intellect, my logical mind, told me to stop the car."

"Sure, so you could be all over me." He heard her thought! His joy in their mental connection knew no bounds.

"Oh gosh, I'm falling for this guy." Her eyes laughed, challenging him.

"Moppie, my thinking mind wants to experience kissing you first.....before my Right Hemispheric mode will join in by adding my emotions of arousal, knowing I would lose control because it is very ready to participate!"

Sascia was quivering.

"Rich, please"...she wriggled, pushing him away. She adjusted her clothes while peering outside. The car had all steamed up inside.

"How can I hide my feelings for him now?". He heard.

"You are saying that if you let your Right hemisphere mode think, your emotional feelings will take control, and you would lose control?'

"Absolutely!" he laughed, pulling her against him just one more time, feeling her upper body as she arched back.

"Richard, this mental discussion we are having is partly telepathic, not so?" As she stroked his hair, he could already feel himself coming as he pressed his forehead between her breasts.

"Moppie, my eyes only have to travel over your body, and different feelings enter it. I want to love you as well as make love to you. Do I make any sense?" Her face turned serious.

"I...think so...Oh, you make it very hard for me to...let's get to my flat and get my portfolio."

"Is that a proposition?" He laughed, knowing he had cornered her.

"Oh! No...I think...you promised, remember?" Sascia wiped the steam away from the window as he started the car, and she gave him directions to her little apartment. He'd better keep his cool. He got dizzy thinking of his opportunity.

Integrating the Left and Right hemispheres simultaneously would be the one thing I'd love to do with you sexually." He beamed while manoeuvring his Honda through the sea of bicycles. When he parked his car where Sascia told him to, he took his laptop, briefcase and the blue envelope from Annelies and followed her up the steps. What would that do to combine physical, logical, spatial, emotional and mental? Richard wondered if Sascia had been reading his mind all the time. She opened a front door from the street.

"Did you say anything?" Sascia turned before stepping inside up more stairs.

"You heard me!" The noises coming from the other doors in the passage made her run up the stairs, and he followed her, admiring her bottom.

"I'm just contemplating, nothing more." He said, laughing. Was he not just like any other male who entered the apartment of a female to whom he was enormously attracted, anticipating the possibilities?

Sascia greeted a couple as they passed their open door. Many families lived in similar narrow but high typical Amsterdam houses. Sascia's apartment was an attic. She entered her key in a bright, dark-blue door with gold trimmings. The door handle and letterbox were brass with her name above the letterbox.

Richard was amazed at the cleverly decorated little apartment. Everything was visible, but you could still recognise the kitchen corner, her dining room corner, and her tiny living room, which ran into her bedroom. She had a double bed covered with pillows and teddy bears! Richard saw a door leading to a bathroom and a balcony overlooking Amsterdam.

"Sascia, you must keep this place, it's wonderful!"

"Yes, I know, I love it, but I'd better make some money to pay the rent, and I must spend some time here as well; otherwise, I could lose it."

"Really, who would know that you…?"

"News travels fast, and if you don't work in Amsterdam? I don't know; I was on a waiting list for two years before this became available. Would you like some coffee?"

Her apartment had a happy feeling. It was small but very intimate. Noticing Sascia was nervous as he stood behind her, placing his hands on her hips and kissing her neck.

"Richard, you promised!" He sighed. His mind said to stop it, but his feelings told him something else!

"All right, you win; where is your portfolio?"

"Behind the bed, you can see it sticking out, see the black handle, just pull it out." Mmm, was she stalking him? The bed was pushed against the wall, so he had to lean over to get to her portfolio; he pulled it onto the bed and started to unzip the sizeable black cover. The black and white photos, of which some were mounted, astonished him. He recognised one. It must have been taken out of the plane when she flew over the area where her mom had been kept hostage.

"Sascia, don't ever sell this one." He held up the photo.

"It has no good memories for me."

"But that photo made me remember where they had taken your mother."

"Yes, I realised that; how was that possible? How did you know?"

"Moppie, what did Annelies tell you about my involvement in the search for your mother?" His eyes were drawn to her naked belly as she reached up for some mugs.

"I asked Annelies if I could do my 22 spacings with Mom's help. I'm interested. She told me that you can transport your consciousness away from your body. I read about astral travelling, at least its theory, but I have never experienced it. At least, I think not consciously." She ground the coffee beans as he made himself comfortable on her bed. He saw that her clock radio said 17.30. and he wondered if he should order pizzas to be delivered.

"Would you like to learn to astral travel?"

"Oh yes, I realise there is so much to learn and do when your body is asleep at night. I realise that if you can do that!...

"There is no ending?" She beamed.

"No ending to what Moppie?" Richard looked at her. He froze.....suddenly he knew that he had lived with her before! The girl standing in her tiny kitchen corner was once a woman he had loved deeply.

"Dying does not separate us from the ones we love." He remembered hearing in his dream.

"What's wrong, Rich? You look like you have seen a ghost?" She asked as she walked towards him with two steaming mugs.

"I just remembered something. Trust me, it was no ghost!" He gave her a piercing look that made her blush.

"Do you want to learn it? I mean out-of-the-body travelling?"

"You mean it can be taught?" She handed him his coffee.

"I think so. I had some help, but yes, the problem is that you have to fall asleep without going to sleep."

He patted the bed for her to join him. "Not to mention sharing your bed; that would be an option."

"Did you have help?"

"Yes, Theo, my brother who passed on last year. He was permitted to help me." He gazed at her.

"I would love to astral travel with you, merge with you in a union that is so wonderful that even having sex in the physical, however pleasant, is nothing compared to that experience." Sascia's whole body language revealed that she picked up his thoughts. Her eyes were wide open, startled. She placed her coffee next to him on a low side table and sat on the other side of her bed, deliberately changing the subject by talking out loud about what photo to take and whatnot. She asked him for advice. Then she stopped...

"Rich, we... I think"...The amazement on Sascia's face gladdened his heart.

"Are we having a telepathic conversation?"

"I know we have. I'm so pleased. The more reason I have to make love to you."...lying half on her bed wishing she would join him instead of sitting on the edge.

"Moppie, why don't we order some pizzas and have them delivered as it is already late? After dinner, we'll take all the photos and sort them in my flat." He had no intention of wasting any more time sorting photos. Before getting the phonebook, she asked if he didn't need to be back to close up the coffee shop. He phoned Connie on his mobile to see if she could manage herself since Jeroen was with her. The thought of staying over and driving back with her tomorrow was even more tempting. Would she? Sascia got up to play some music after they ordered pizzas. The atmosphere in her small hideaway den became quite romantic.

"How long have you been taking photos like this?" He liked her sensitivity to the children's black and white prints; they were very striking. The more he saw of her work, the more he felt a love for her welling up inside. This girl was so suitable for him. He wanted to share his life with her. She was already an independent woman with no illusions of fantasy dream weddings or external means to make her feel good about herself, unlike Ellie, who always needed his assurance about her appearance.

"Richard, how will we find out if Debbie is the girl Vinny was talking about?"

"It's important to you, isn't it?" Sascia frowned as she drank her coffee. He picked up a photo of Sascia sunbathing on a sailing yacht.

"Who took it?" She looked stunning, topless! He sensed that she was embarrassed as he was admiring her nakedness in the photo.

"Ronald. Took it three years ago." They both heard the knock on the door. It was the pizza man, and both tucked into them as she prepared her small table and opened a bottle of Rosé from South Africa. He asked about Ronald, trying not to pry. He loved her music and realized that he saw no computer.

"We had been going out for five years. Last year, we both broke it off. Ronald wanted to sail the world, and I chose to stay. I had to choose between taking this flat or going with him. At the time, I felt miserable that he didn't want to stay on for one more year, but now I realise I was not really in love with him." As she stared into the distance, he knew more to come.

"He drowned six months after he left." He didn't know what to say. Thank goodness she hadn't been in love with him, but it still must have been hard.

"Sascia, has Vinny been here?"

"Yes, twice, to pick me up when we went out." I know what you want to know!"

"Did you?" He projected. Her glint made him go warm all over.

"I never made love to anyone in my flat ever. Happy?" She beamed as she got up to clear the table. He returned to the photos on the bed. When she joined him lying down, she rolled sideways to look at him, resting her head in the cup of her hand. He smiled, intuitively knowing they had arrived at their moment of no return.

"Now I know why I was never ready to have a sexual relationship with Vinny. I was not connecting with my right hemisphere!" She giggled. Not that he would have held it against her, but did she know how special she was to him?

"Moppie, I want you. I was hoping you could share your life and my flat with me. My flat needs you in it to make it a home." As he beamed his proposal, he gazed into her sparkling green eyes.

"I would love to share your life with you, help you with your research for your lectures, or whatever you do. Make milkshakes with you!" She seemed to project back while holding her own. He was sure he heard her thinking.

"Would you make love to me here? In your flat." Their eyes were making foreplay so erotic he almost lost it.

"You want to practice using both hemispheres?"

"Absolutely" He moved the photos away to be closer.

"Is the right hemisphere not the feminine side of the brain?" Her voice quivered. She was lying on her back, looking at her ceiling.

"Yes, it is called 'the garden of Eden" He whispered. "*Are you ready for some seeds to be planted?*" Knowing she knew what he was implying.

"*Mmm. Are the seeds ready for planting? Don't you need the right conditions? Like the right season and the right temperature.*"She chuckled at her mental imagery, challenging him big time. He slowly moved his hand under her top, which had parted from her jeans. He was holding her with his eyes while pulling her top off. The sight of her nakedness as he caressed her breasts brought on her moaning. He was getting close.

"Do you want to? Are you ready? Or must I stop?"

"I have already made love to you before you know?" he whispered as he unzipped his jeans with her help.

"Oh Rich, I... I want you ...He knew he could go further, but she would never admit that. She was stunning, slim, but voluptuous at the same time. He felt her hands on his back, pulling him closer.

"Oh, Rich, I have been dreaming of making love to you." She murmured, quivering.

"Moppie, that was for real, believe me." He had great difficulty holding back just a while longer. Sascia's movements became a physical symphony, and he admired her body when she thrust her hips up. She was as eager for him as he was for her. She gave herself, so ultimately, they both moaned from ecstasy at their union.

A warm, glowing feeling of utter relaxation settled in, happy that he made her part of him. He didn't want to move off her. Her eyes sparkled as she was smiling up at him.

"Rich... that was the best sex I ever had."

"*Believe me, you were...incredible*" he beamed.

"Moppie, what I feel is more than just lust. You are so gorgeous, beautiful and sexy, but I want to love all of you."

"*Our lovemaking was like a piano concerto.*" He mentally added. She giggled, giving away that she heard his admission. Observing her nakedness and playing with her nipples made him feel very fortunate.

"Please, would you move in with me in Apeldoorn? You can get started on your own and keep this little apartment on. I'll help you with the rent. If your freelance work takes off after my lectures in Utrecht, we'll stay in Amsterdam. We'll live here." He waited in suspense. Then they heard a woman's voice. Her neighbour handed Sascia a ginger cat, who started purring when Sascia took him in her arms.

"Thanks, I came home to fetch something. I wasn't aware that my kitty was with you."

She closed the door and stood with the cat, holding it away, saying, "What will I do with you? You are going to fight with Mom's Fluffball, I know!" Miiiaaaauuu is all she got as a reply.

"Do you have a basket or box for him?"

"What have you got in mind?"

"Well, since you are going to live with me, he'd better come along as well; what is his name?"

"Really! You don't mind?"

"Not if you come with the package!" Sascia paused. He could see she was thinking about what he'd said.

"*I'd love nothing better, sharing in his research, sleeping together, making love, and doing my own thing but.... am I ready?*" He was ecstatic; her thoughts were so clear to him.

"You are sure about this?" she asked.

"What about the cat or you?" he replied, tugging her by her waist as her cat jumped.

"What am I going to tell my mom?"

"Don't worry, they will get used to it; what's his name?"

"Ginger. Rich, I love you, you know" Her lips met his softly, eagerly. He never realised that being in love with someone could be like this.

"Why do you think I want to take care of you?"

"I don't need taking care of....but.... I'd love to share your life...oh, keep doing what you do"...Sascia then made him stop.

"I never will have enough of you!" He beamed longingly.

"I know," she giggled, "but we have the whole night. What's in the blue envelope Annelies gave you...or is it personal?"

"Good grief, I forgot all about that!" She prepared Ginger's dinner while he looked inside.

A stick fell out as he pulled out a large print. It showed an image of Earth taken from a great distance. The satellite photo triggered the memory of a dream. Whoever created this very high-tech computer image vividly displayed the combustion of energy around the planet. He knew the shattered, colourful facets surrounding the Earth were to reflect a message. On the sticker on the flash drive was written 'The Shattering World Ego'. Sascia joined him on the floor on her rug, leaning against her double bed as Ginger curled up on her lap.

"Who took this?" He told her about the first photos Theo received three years ago, the letters from Theo after he was gone and how the interpretations had left him without any doubt. Like his brother, he also concluded that their ancestors had left behind a legacy. Their information was very applicable to these times. He turned his laptop on and showed her some of the previous interpretations he had received.

"This envelope with the print came from Leo. I now realise that Leo and Ben knew where Theo must have been until his death. My brother had left his later work with them, knowing I would get it when writing the second journal."

"Gosh, how uncanny. Mom showed us the excerpts from POWAH she received through her e-mail and the post box. Jeroen had asked Toon lots of questions. Toon told us that the twin brothers Leo and Ben had been researching this information for the last ten years and that Trevor had only recently joined them. He seems to be the I.T. specialist. It's all to do with the holiday park, not so?" He shared his experiences, and the time flew by. Sascia picked a typed letter up from the floor. It must have fallen out of the envelope when he removed the print.

"May I?" He cuddled her, enjoying their intimacy while reading the letter over her shoulder as she nestled against him.

Dear Richard

When the time came, I promised Theo I would send you the interpretations he decoded from the following fragile golden foil sheets.

The ninth and tenth tablets were quite a revelation to us. Because logic is absent in these symbolic metaphysical mysteries posed by ancient cosmogony, the texts of the initiations can be read and studied in two ways, as you know. The esoteric teaching of ancient Egypt was what present-day science offers us today. We are standing before a riddle that could be of the most incredible wealth in the history of humanity if we use the right key to open it. So far, we have learned to read symbolic writing, but have we grasped which of the twelve constellations? We are beginning to believe that the mystical writer of the texts was describing all the nine perceptions simultaneously. Now, we are questioning which of the seven planes or spheres he was coming from. When Leo channelled the piece on the shattering world ego, many questions arose from this information. Theo must have figured it out before he left us. He had given us strict instructions to feed you the tablets individually. We know you connect with him, so we leave it up to you to decide what your reflections are when combined with your dream travel experience. I will contact you soon.

RegardsTrevor.

"Oh Rich, how I dreamed of living with you, sharing as mom has with Toon..." In his joy hearing her mentally say it, he wanted to make love again.

"*You like it don't you?*" Her blushing face gave her away. She giggled as she rolled away. She ran into her small bathroom, and he heard she had turned on the shower. It was already after eight, but it was still light.

When he joined her, she was already standing under the water. When he held her slippery, wet body pressed to his, he came on again. She draped her arms around him as he grasped her buttocks. She was again ready for him. Waves of excitement washed over them, and before he knew it, he penetrated her, bursting through with a sweet release while they both had a climax.

Richard was happily cleaning the bathroom while Sascia lit candles. It was getting darker. She burned some incense while moving around stark naked. The thought of spending the whole night with her dazzled him.

"Richard, you know what the time is?" In all the frantic shuffling, he must have dropped his watch somewhere. When he saw it lying next to the bed, next to a photo of a small child, it suddenly made him think!

"Moppie! I never thought!..I never used anything".

"Sascia laughed. You mean your intellectual, logical mind deserted you?" She pulled his towel away and used it as a rope around his neck as she kissed him.

"Completely".

"I am on the pill, but I must admit, I now realize how easy it is to be careless!" He stroked her hair, which was still wet from the shower.

"Whatever happens, you will tell me, won't you?" Sascia raised her eyebrows in surprise as she leaned against her kitchen counter. He pulled her up on the counter, and she draped her legs around him.

"What made you ask me that? Why would I not tell you?"

"Oh, someone I know mentioned that he had no idea who his father was." As he was still dreamily looking at her nakedness, familiarizing himself with every square inch of her body, she stretched out, arching her back.

"Don't you worry, you will know. Tell me about Sammy; how old is she?" He told her about his marriage to Ellie, why they broke up, and that he regretted having so little contact with Sammy. He passed her the long, colourful caftan she pointed at hanging on a hook. He admired the result as she draped it around herself, knowing she wore nothing underneath. It reminded him of the Egyptian paintings.

"Imagine falling pregnant at my mother's age?"

"Mmm, she knew it the moment it happened, the conception, I mean."

"How!"...Sascia stared at him in amazement.

"How did you know that?"

"Oh...I have so much to tell you. Did you ever wonder why I was involved in finding your mother?" He picked up the blue envelope that was lying on his laptop.

"You were helping Annelies. I never quite knew how, but it was almost like you had been near her in your sleep?" Sascia put on another music CD when there was a knock on the door. Both looked at each other, thinking the same thing, Vinny? Sascia looked around the flat, tying her caftan. He hastily pulled his jeans on before she opened the door.

A stranger handed her a note and then left, and she read out loud:

PS: Leo asked me if you would acknowledge his channelled message from POWAH in your journal. I thought I sent it to you by email. Let me know if you received it and what your intuition tells you.

Trevor

"Did you get such an email?"

"Not yet. Can I connect my laptop to your phone?" Sascia showed him where the phone jack was, and they both stared at the screen when his mail came into his inbox. Leo wanted him to cut and paste this message titled 'The Matrix', in the prologue of his journal. As he read it a few times, he noticed that the style differed from Theo's letters. This was not Theo's style. Sascia asked if he had read any of her mother's excerpts. She felt that there was a similarity.

"Gosh, I have to read that a few times." she pondered over Leo's channelled excerpt from POWAH titled The Matrix. He would love to meet his uncle, who performed in Ingrid's wedding ceremony in person.

"Have you written your journal yet?"

"Gosh, no. I've just started. I'm so busy with the coffee bar and lecture preparations. I must also decide what to do for money when Aunt Mien returns."

"Rich, what did you do before? I mean, what job did you have?"

"I taught history at a primary school in Delft. After my divorce, I quit teaching to help Theo with his research and became a guide on the tourist trips he organised to ancient temples worldwide. That became so lucrative that he employed me full-time. He sold the Sacred Site touring business to devote all his time to his research. I became his assistant."

"You must have had a great time with your brother."

"Believe me, I did, especially the research. We both had had enough of the tourist business. Some people you meet on those trips are complicated to stay civil with." Especially one particular woman who had her eye on him. She had even sneaked into his hotel room while her husband was asleep! That was their last trip together. Theo was often so bored and spaced out, although he never complained.

Sascia opened a jar of fruit for dessert, and he indulged in her homey atmosphere.

"Rich, what's on the disk? Could it have a connection with your personality card? Mom showed me her cards from Annelie's workshop."

"Probably. I'm not all clued up about psychology; you might come in handy."

"Let's look at what's on the flash drive, then we'll call it a night."

Her proposition of how they would spend the night made him want to leave the laptop and get to bed, but she had already slotted the stick in. He nibbled her earlobe as she sat on his lap. There were two files on the stick. When he clicked on the file that read the tenth tablet, a note from Trevor preceded the now familiar rhythmic translations.

Ginger was purring and complaining as he disturbed him when his arm encircled Sascia's waist. They both giggled at the title. He had not seen the photo of this tablet, so he could not practice and compare his interpretations.

Richard, we didn't change anything in the paragraphs Theo left for you. In ancient Egypt, we know that the symbol of an animal often reflected vital characteristic habits in its mating customs. That is why he must have chosen the title of The Game of Ecstasy[1].

Tablet 10

< *Because of the waveform properties of pure white light, the mind field of man can expand its light body during the night.* > They had to read the rest of the channel's message by clicking on the link.

Underneath was Theo's letter.

When you receive this, you will have played the first level of the card game or will soon. Later, you will start to decode your second level. Remember that the concept of "light" is the most misunderstood term. Light is the force

---

1. https://allrealityshifters.wordpress.com/richard-de-jong/tablet-ten/

of reclamation, stewarded by the power of creation. Light is nothing less than life itself. It is LOVE. The symbols within our hands explain that the right hand modifies destiny and that the lefthand bears the inscription of predestination.

Love Theo

"Gosh, Rich, do you think Theo knows I will move in with you?" He laughed at how her mind worked.

"Man will encounter more sexual energy force" She squirmed from his lap as he became familiar. Richard sensed that Sascia was bursting with questions. He looked at her studious expression, which he had started to love so dearly, and waited. She scrolled online back to all the Tablets under the symbol images.

"Rich, what does POWAH mean when he says that ideographic Language of Light symbols shows two pathways?" He could not stop squeezing her first, recalling their lovemaking.

"When I first learned to grasp why our forefathers used only symbols, I wondered if the writer was a scientist who used a more logical approach or if they were true mystics. There is a great difference."

"You mean because of their thinking, purely in pictures or visions? But...don't we all think in pictures?"

"Yes, originally we did, but the birth of mythology happened when we translated the images into fantasies. The result was that we programmed the information away in words." He was unsure if that was right but intuitively knew he was close.

"Mmm, your bother, was he a mystic?"

"Oh, yes, no doubt. Theo could crack a joke with anyone; believe me, he could fit in anywhere, but he could also trot out theories from his soul awareness."

"You must miss him?" She pressed her lips under his jaw and he could feel her naked body through the thin wrapping that had become rather loose. He told her how Theo left and how depressed he was when he heard that he had gone. As she cuddled him from pure compassion for his pain, she again stirred a great longing. The fact that they would spend the night together made it easier to keep talking. It had started to get dark outside, and the candles and the soft music made their togetherness even more sensual.

"Rich, what does that mean? Embrace all 12 archetypes. Or is that too complicated to explain?"

He was surprised that she thought it would be too difficult.

"You know of the twelve zodiac signs?"

"You mean, in astrology?"

"Yes, but not the characteristics, more the spiritual sciences." Sascia's frown made him think.

"Our brain produces human thought, but cosmic thoughts reflect our whole being. Some say that the 12 cosmic spiritual hierarchies influence them." Sascia's frown told him that she was trying to assimilate it all.

"Vinny once explained his counselling techniques, using nine personality type outlooks that we each have plus their associated characteristics, making it a threesome unity called the ego."

"Mmm, the nine becomes twelve, but..". *"Where are my thoughts coming from? How can we read each other?"* Sascia gazed, beaming. He took a while formulating an answer; all he saw in his mind's eye was how their holographic mental bodies mingled, vibrating on identical waveforms.

"Our thoughts enter into the brain to be translated." He had difficulty getting across what he meant.

"You mean our brain does not think; it is just a reflector...like a mirror is if we see our face as a reflection?" He kissed the tip of her nose while being very proud of her.

"We are also a reflection of the cosmic thinkers. On this ascension path, as Annelies calls it, we learn to bring all the twelve outlooks together and learn the task of spiritual science related to ourselves. Will you be joining us?" Sascia encircled him.

"Try to stop me."

"I'd love to join this path with you, even if it means releasing addictions...so long as...we can"....He glinted, knowing what she was implying.

"Making love means you don't want to give that up?" Her expression became so severe he had to laugh.

"We can make love on many levels, you know." Her eyes ...like deep pools... the depth... made him swoon.

"You mean during...when we dream?" He heard her think when he remembered how they made love on the astral plane.

"You were so lovely, so" ....He closed the laptop; he had had enough. The other file on the shattering world ego would have to wait because the scent from her closeness had entirely distracted him.

"Rich, all this..." She picked up the print from Earth above.

"It's so fascinating! I also want to wake up in my dreams, I want to...please teach me." He slowly disrobed her as she blew out the candles. He carried her to the bed. The night sounds from outside merged with the energy of their highly charged fields, celebrating their union.

• • • •

As Richard gazed into space, Sascia's hideaway became transparent. She lay in the crook of his arm while his conscious awareness was suspended away from his physical form. Their naked bodies were still intertwined from their lovemaking. As he hovered above, he wondered how he could help Sascia move out of her body. He saw how millions of energy strands were floating away from them into swirls of smoky moving waveforms.

"Richie, she's already out, look!" As he focussed on her sleeping posture, he became aware of the glittering spider-web thread that disappeared in the distance.

"Where is she?' He could feel Theo's energy signature before his brilliant light body appeared.

"Theo, why can't most people remember their dreams?" He thought back to the time he never recalled any, and then suddenly, he started to have his out-of-body experiences.

"Richie, your soul needs to enter more energy into the physical realm instead of hanging around in the ethers." Good grief, how would he stop hankering after his dream time? He knew that the few days he remembered nothing of his dreams had troubled him. The freedom to travel wherever his mind took him was genuinely exhilarating. Was he becoming addicted? He pondered over Theo's remark about his soul hanging around in the ethers when Theo's energy field took on a form he recognised. He followed Theo away from Sascia's den, passing the canals of sleeping Amsterdam. There was movement from the street people who hovered near Amsterdam's shopping district.

"Richie, there is no need for this style of living, but the drug intake is still addicting many users." Young people were huddled in alleys. They were all plastered with intoxicated poisons of some kind. There was hardly any soul energy there.

"The home of the mind of all things implies a domain that, in its holographic form, manifests many parallel life visions like a string of beads. In one life, one could be an alcoholic or a beggar, and in another, a king or tycoon both simultaneously." Theo's explanation created visions of many soap bubbles that swirled around. Had he become the bubble blower? With every move, a transparent sphere unfolded...

As he peered closer, he merged inside one bubble and saw her before he knew it. She was dressed in a white, transparent, flowing dress, and her long, dark, braided hair was tied together with a large, golden, fan-shaped tiara. She looked the same, but he could see by her makeup that she was Egyptian.

"Richie, your etheric body is a holographic template transmitting between your thoughts and energy fields. The collective consciousness of your Higher self and Soul forms a dynamic relationship between all your subtler bodies. It is in a timeless realm" As he heard the words, he became part of the vision and drowned within her gaze. When she offered her hand, as they touched, an electric shock ran through his arm as if he was connecting to a part of himself that had separated.

• • • •

He knew that he was the artist her father had commissioned to create a sculpture of her. Her enchanting beauty was so captivating he was tongue-tied. He guided her into the sunlight to capture her outlines as she leaned against the fountain. He drew a breath when he walked back to the marble rock and gazed back. She scooped water with her hands and let it run down her bare arm. During that act, every detail of her body was as precise as if she was standing naked! Her faint smile gave away that she knew the effect she had on him. For one moment, their eyes locked. He kept admiring her openly to see if she was that unaffected by his observation of her nakedness. When she looked away, he knew she was not wholly immune to his stare.

He slowly started chiselling away as he followed the contours of her proud, uplifted chin into her neckline, observing her raised arm as she studied the water drops that ran down past her elbow into the valley under her arm, wetting her gown that stuck to her shapely breast. He worked fast before the sun would slide behind the temple. He knew with regret that his sculpture was a gift for her future husband, the pharaoh's son, but in that timeless moment, their mutual attraction was forever registered in his soul memory as if...The image faded.

• • • •

"Theo, was that Sascia? Did I lose her again?" He swallowed to gain control of himself. He remembered that in a different dream, the girl called Savina had created a void he didn't know how to fill. What had happened then? Theo was nowhere because he had not replied.... He was getting near the point of waking up. He recognised Sascia's building, where her hideaway den appeared as a haven of cosiness and love.

He wondered if she was still fast asleep. He hoped he would be as clear about his out-of-body travels as he was now...There was so much to learn. He knew they would penetrate the veil that separated them all from the world of spirit. With that focused thought, he would try to wake up next to her.

As he revelled at the prospect of her naked closeness, feeling her curves next to him, she turned. Theo's last words still lingered in his mind while his hands explored her soft roundness. *"Our ancestors have passed on their beliefs and concepts of truths through the thought forms that created our physical bodies; remember that."*

Chapter 11
The Divine Union of Spirit

Amsterdam
As he peered at her lovely face, he realised she had been awake for a while. Looking around Sascia's flat helped him to orientate where he was.

"Am I still dreaming, or is it all for real?"

"I know, I feel the same. Gosh, Rich, I think I remember my dream!"

"Really? Tell me."

"It's all bizarre. You know the story of Lot's wife in the Bible when she turned into a pillar of something when she looked back?"

"You mean when she turned into a pillar of salt when she fled from the destruction of Sodom and Gomorrah?"

"That's right. What do you think the story meant?" He had to think long on that one.

"What has this got to do with your dream?"

"I'm somehow trapped into this pillar or block."

"Mmm, could it have been a marble block a sculptor is about to carve?" He wondered if their consciousness had tried to bring back a similar memory. As she entered back into her body, her memory seemed vaguer, and so her rational mind added whatever information there was in her unconscious to reason it out. Sascia's deep pause kept him in suspense.

"Gee...you know, I get the feeling that someone was trying to trap me into a piece of stone...but, how did you know?... I remember feeling so hurt..." Sascia sounded as if she had experienced the same emotional pain he had. He could hardly contain himself but knew he could not share his memory yet. He didn't want to put ideas into her mind that might not be there.

"Can you get into the feeling?"

"I don't want to create something that is not there." They were both distracted when his cell phone rang. He saw by the number that the call was from South Africa.

Aunt Mien asked how things were. He had plenty to tell, including everything about his new flatmate. He winked at Sascia while answering all his aunt's questions. Hearing himself speak about Sascia made him feel shy. She showed a gleam of satisfaction. When he hung up, his suggestive glance to make love was greeted with an equally inviting expression. Suddenly, she rolled on top, and he allowed himself to be seduced.

He phoned Connie before she left home to ask her to open the Pannekoek. Over the weekend, they opened earlier. He'd arranged for Connie and Jeroen to work his shift. It would cost him double, but it was worth it.

They stayed at her attic apartment for most of the day. He marvelled at her view. Amsterdam had such a different vibe compared to Apeldoorn. Nearing the evening, they went out for a stroll up and down the many canals and for the first time in months, he felt as if a new world had opened up for him.

It was already nearly midday when they left Amsterdam. It had taken a few hours for Sascia to pack as many belongings as possible. She had to phone a few people, see her mail from his laptop and cancel a few appointments.

They drove in heavy traffic towards Apeldoorn. As his fingers tapped to the beat of the music 'Timeless' on the steering wheel, the whole interior of his Honda was engulfed with joyful energy. Sascia very intimately rested her hand on his leg. Ginger was in his cage in the back seat, peering at him disgustingly. Sascia's portfolio and a suitcase were piled next to him. It gladdened his whole being, knowing she was moving in with him. He looked forward to sharing his life with someone he could relate his experiences to. He realised he wanted to be in a committed relationship with her, for she was beautiful, creative and intelligent.

"Richard, I have to talk to Vinny soon. He thinks I am in France, I feel sad for him. I know we did not ever have...what we have...but I wish he would find that girl he was so captivated with. It would make everything so much easier."

"Moppie, I have a strong feeling that things will work out the way they should. If Debbie happens to be that girl, let's be innovative; how could we bring them together without them knowing?"

"Well... Vinny is often in Utrecht. Could they not run into each other with our help?" He pondered her idea.

"Rich, are we not interfering? Do we have the right to meddle in others' lives?"

"Yes and no. If life is like a game, then we make the moves. Gee, I would love to be around when they meet. We know that Debbie is the girl if we see and feel a spark between them. If not, then nothing is lost."

He turned past Amersfoort toward Apeldoorn and grabbed her hand, which rested on his leg. Sascia turned the radio on when suddenly a news bulletin intercepted their space:

This is radio Hilversum, Roger speaking with the latest update on the Jaarsma mystery. In the early hours of the morning, police made a breakthrough as a result of a shooting incident that took place near the railway line outside Genk in Belgium. Police reports revealed that there could be a connection to the kidnapping of Mrs Barendse that took place".

While driving on the freeway, there was sudden static on the radio due to a passing lorry. The radio seemed too temperamental; however, once Richard turned off the highway, the radio station came back.

Our local police have been working with Interpol to uncover some unsavoury real estate deals involving a large Chateau used as an orphanage in France during the Second World War. There is some speculation that, at the same time, it was used as a secret hiding place for artefacts and other valuable pieces of artwork. We will keep you updated on the mysterious events surrounding the now-famous cult called The Jaarsma Clan.

Both were stunned into silence. He could feel her panicky thoughts when Sascia took a deep breath.

"Oh, Rich, what is going on? Why are they calling the Jaarsma Clan a cult?" her voice quivered; that last comment also took him aback. He switched the radio off. Whatever happened, he would not allow any vibes playing on the frequencies of fear to enter their private space.

"Moppie, any group which deviates from Biblical, orthodox, historical Christianity teachings are often branded with the name Cult. Annelies created the Jaarsma Clan name as a genetically linked family clan, not a cult." He squeezed her hand while steering. They were in a traffic jam and moving very slowly. It would take them much longer to reach the turnoff for Apeldoorn.

"I know, that's what mom said. I always thought that a cult is more like a group of people who claim to know the only way to God, or enlightenment, or whatever."

"You can call all the major world religions a cult," he replied with a tone of distaste. Thinking about some people he met over the years who make you feel that everything outside their religious group is 'of the devil' or 'unenlightened.'

"Moppie, let's not react to what the man said on the radio. We know that there are many ways to reach happiness, etc.. Still, many people will use thought reform or mind control techniques to gain control and keep their members, especially when a group of people have a pyramidal authoritarian leadership structure with all teaching and guidance coming from the person/persons at the top." As he replied, a big lorry suddenly swerved in front of them.

"So...you don't think POWAH could be such a person?"

"Good grief, no, I don't ...think so. He was about to hoot at the intruding driver in disgust while Sascia's question lingered.

"It never crossed my mind, and...there is absolute evidence that none of the people who ...let's say, belong to the Jaarsma Clan have behaviour patterns that are abusive or controlling. As I perceive it, a cult is when a group of people adopt a group mentality."

"But Richie, don't you feel that there is a sort of bonding among the people who join Annelies' workshops?"

"Mmm, yes... but in a cult group, people are not permitted to think for themselves apart from the group and only accept what they are told. Annelies hates it when someone agrees without individual input to the contrary." He needed to focus on driving because another car was trying to pull in front of him.

"Have you been present when people in her class didn't agree with her?" He recalled that Wim often tried to challenge her, but Annelies had always respectfully responded to his usually rude remarks.

"I wondered what they said about Mom." Sascia was trying to find the same station back on the radio while he shook his head, wondering what secret hiding places they referred to.

"Moppie, have you ever heard of an orphanage in France? Do you think they mean the halfway house? I know that the Prinsengracht Hotel in Apeldoorn used to be an orphanage. That's where the Jaarsma name came from." He told her how he discovered that his family was related to Ben and Leo. When she heard her mother was kidnapped, Sascia shared her first dealings with Harry Brinks. When she spoke to Annelies, she quit her job and offered her skills by taking photos from the small plane.

"You know Rich, even Mr Brinks seemed absolutely in the dark, but I wondered lately about Annelies' husband Ben...It must be severe when they talk about Interpol's involvement. Rich, is it all connected, your burglary and the bookshop?" Richard recalled what Aunt Mien had told him: that her ex-husband was dealing in real estate! Could that be the connection? He told her about his aunt and her family in South Africa.

As he finally turned off into Apeldoorn, he parked in an alley behind the coffee shop to give her a big cuddle. He had forgotten what it was like to be in love. He knew their relationship would mature into a more relaxed pattern, but he enjoyed every moment of their romantic attraction for now.

"Oh, would this feeling of...total infatuation last? I know I love this man with all my heart." He knew that she felt as he did, completely besotted. Suddenly, a vision of a statue crossed his mind. With it came the pain of losing her.

"Oh love, share my life, my love and everything that lies ahead of us we share." As he beamed, he knew she had heard his plea. Her pupils widened, and a smile broke through as she kissed the tip of his nose.

"I will" She whispered. They just sat momentarily intertwined in each other's space while the traffic zoomed by.

Walking hand in hand into the Pannekoek pantry from the back entrance raised Connie's eyebrows. It was buzzing with customers. Jeroen was behind the counter, making milkshakes for a family with four children who occupied a table in the corner. It was getting busy during the school holidays.

"I appreciate that you could both work my shift. We have been delayed." He felt rather silly looking at the time. It was already getting to four o'clock!

"I bet." Jeroen grinned. Richard wondered if they had heard the radio news and if he should tell them. He looked at Sascia, who shook her head.

Connie would be distraught; her father is still missing, remember. Gosh! Was she projecting? No customers needed them when Jeroen returned, so Sascia explained their photo gallery idea. Nel greeted them and disappeared back into the kitchen.

"Connie, can I ask you another favour?" He followed her into the pantry. He was starting to feel bad asking her to stay on.

"Have you brought your photos?" he heard Jeroen ask.

"They're in the car. We will review them tonight and start hanging them up in the morning."

"Aren't you coming home?" Richard overheard Jeroen asking as he helped Connie carry fresh containers of ice cream to fill the fridge.

"I am moving in with Richard."

"Mmm... I see. Richard, you made a big score. I consider my sister a good catch." Jeroen thumped him on his shoulder while Connie beamed a smile.

"Jeroen, what would Mom say do you think?" Richard was amused that Sascia was still apprehensive about how her mother would react.

Jeroen laughed and simultaneously said goodbye to a customer he seemed to know. He looked back at his sister with a gleam.

"After you left, when we had breakfast outside on the veranda, Toon said, "Kitty, I can see you in Sascia more every day. I bet you she won't be coming home tonight." Jeroen mimicked Toon very well. Connie laughed. Sascia stared at Jeroen, blushing. He tried not to laugh, thinking back at how much she had tried at first not to give in to him.

"What was the favour you were going to ask?" It was almost five o'clock. They would close at seven.

"Would you mind if we drop Ginger the cat at my flat? He is still in the car with Sascia's bags. I'm not particularly eager to keep him in the car too long. And if the two of you could lock up? I know it is a bit of a cheek; you two spend more time there than I do."

"You're in luck; we are going to the movies after eight." Jeroen said, "We will close up. Sissy, I'll look forward to seeing your photo gallery tomorrow."

When they arrived at his block of flats, he tried to remember in what state he'd left it. He was not the tidiest, so he hoped he'd made up his bed and cleared the dishes. As he turned the key, he grabbed hold of Sascia as she was about to walk in.

"I know this is ridiculously old-fashioned, but if it's all the same, I like its meaning." He picked her up and stepped through the door.

Richard's Flat

He woke early, with Sascia snuggled up close. He didn't remember any dreams, but as he observed her, fast asleep, he marvelled at her body, which was made for love. Yesterday evening had been total bliss. He marvelled at her soft skin, her rounded hips and slim waist, and her breasts… Sascia stretched, which made Ginger complain; he was curled up in the hollow of her back. When the phone rang, it was just after seven! He picked up before Sascia was completely awake.

The line was silent…but he sensed someone at the other end…When he repeated his name, the phone switched to an engaged signal. He tried to feel the energy that had connected with him for a moment, thinking of his other phone calls lately, but he didn't want to become paranoid.

He tiptoed to the kitchen to make tea and got online on his laptop. Something told him that there would be an email for him. He sensed that something was brewing, but he couldn't pinpoint what.

———-Original Message ———-
From: "T Zwiegelaar"
To: <R de Jong:;>
Subject: eleventh tablet
Dear Richard,
The ancient Egyptian symbols reveal their concern about their world during their last age, just as we are today. The serpent symbolizes our dark side, and the Eye of Horus symbol, encircled by the serpent, is intriguing. Our ancestors used the snake symbol to represent the dark force that has trapped man's unconsciousness in forgetfulness. Add this information to your journal.
Regards Trevor.

The traffic outside was in full swing when Sascia brought two steaming mugs of tea to his study. She read Trevor's email as she sat on his lap. When he scrolled back to Trevor's letter, he hadn't seen any more photos of the fragile gold foil wrappings. Why was it that when Theo was still around, he had been scrutinising the symbolic text on what appeared to be an old palm-leaf manuscript? These photos appeared much later. Where was it now? Theo had it. He's seen it. That had been before he moved into Theo's flat. At that time, he was still depressed by his marriage breakup, so Theo's fascination with symbolic scripts had not grappled him as it had now.

It must have been Theo who left the explanations with them on Word Perfect. He was almost sure that Theo had spent his last weeks with them. He thought the title, The Divine Union of the Spirit, was appropriate. Sharing these interpretations with someone as interested as him about the tablets made all the difference.

"Have you started on your journal?"

"Yes...sort of, but it's hard. It has an effect on my preparations for my lectures."

"How come"

"I'm not sure, but it's almost as if a part of me is holding back acknowledging the information I recall from my dreams."

"Ha, I know what you mean. Almost daily, when I do my daily chores, a part of me moves in an observing mode. I'm dying to read this eleventh tablet. Let's click on the link. How many do you think are there?" Sascia's natural perfume so close to him almost clouded his thinking.

Tablet 11

The Divine Union of the Spirit[1]

< *When the sky swallows the sun each evening and appears again at dawn—the north and south emerge as one body to reform.* >

Translated by Theo de Jong

"Rich, how thought-provoking! It is indeed like a riddle. Who originally wrote it, do you think?"

"That's still a mystery to me. Theo also doesn't seem to know. Let's see what is in the attachment."

It was a personal note from Theo. How he could've known that he would write a journal was still a mystery.

"Rich, didn't you tell me your brother left before he got ill?"

"Yes, Theo never told me where he was to spend his last days ...I now suspect it must have been with Leo and Trevor."

Dear Richie, As I was interpreting the symbols from our ancestors so you can add them to your journal, it reminded me of the fire initiations we both attended on the astral plane.

"Do you know what he means?" Sascia asked in awe. His mind was racing through his mental filing system to recall his dreams. Suddenly, an event flashed before him, but it was too vague to elaborate; he would instead just read on...

---

1. https://allrealityshifters.wordpress.com/tablet-eleven/

I know it must still be a mystery why I choose to leave my work behind this way. It was the only way I could assist you without interfering with your truth like our ancestors did by forcing us to decipher the rich language of images for our awakening. The external world cannot show the truth; it can only mirror what is already within us. The nine aspects will affect each embodied soul that resides within an energy field of a human form. Contemplate this riddle before we meet again.

Love Theo.

"Gosh, it feels as if he is speaking to you now, doesn't it!" Sascia's awe at the content was a relief. He would have hated it if she lacked enthusiasm.

"Gosh, Rich, I want to do the decoding workshop you and my mom have done to play the awakening card game on the first level with you. Do you think Annelies will let me?"

"So you no longer think Annelies is the head of a cult, do you?" he grinned as he said it.

"No, I realised Mom and Toon never lost their ability to socialize outside the Jaarsma Clan. Toon has many friends who would never understand what we are into. Mom too. They are both very grounded, I'd say.

"You can only ask. Phone Tieneke first. We were all recruited from Tieneke's mind-drawing classes."

"Really? I must tell Mom. She is still puzzled how she was contacted."

"You mean POWAH's excerpts?"

"Yes. Twenty-two."

"Oh, I thought Toon knew. Surely Annelies knows? Or at least Leo, who happens to be my uncle." After that remark, Sascia wanted to know all the details about his family.

The Pannekoek

It had been a busy day. The coffee shop was getting more traffic since people had heard about his lectures. The change in the type of customers amazed him. More and more people who came into the Pannekoek for refreshments or a light meal seemed to use the venue as a meeting point. Often, he joined in discussions about metaphysical subjects. He learned a great deal from his new friends. Sometimes, Sascia or Connie would join in.

"Rich, when is your Aunt coming back?" Sascia asked when they drove home after they closed the Pannekoek. She would leave early in the morning to join her mother, Ed, and Yolanda, who were all flying on Toon's plane to France.

"In September. I think the twentieth, why?"

"I just wondered. How would your aunt be with the new crowd coming to her coffee shop now?"

"She'd love it."

Sascia's luggage was ready in the hallway. Toon would pick her up around seven.

"I will miss you", he whispered while snuggled up in bed.

"Oh, I do wish you could've come with us. I'm also very sorry that I will miss your third lecture."

• • • •

It took far more effort to leave his body consciously. Was that because Sascia shared his bed? He observed her breathing softly. Watching her sleep brought on feelings of gratitude. Pure joy flooded his whole being, recalling their lovemaking. It almost felt like his life had just started when he shared it with her. Could that make him co-dependent on her? He hoped not. There was so much to learn together. So much to share. He wished he could share his dream time as well.

"What, still stuck on limitations?"

Theo's breeze of joyful vigour exalted his own. Looking back at the sleeping couple, he saw a smile on Sascia's sleeping face. Did he wonder why?

"*I'll show you why. Come.*" He heard and sensed Theo's energy, which seemed to merge with his as he followed him. When they were leaving the bedroom, the setting he saw next looked like nothing he'd seen before. When Theo guided him into what looked like a courtyard, he wondered, as always, if this was all real. He asked about his other lives with Sascia. The first one he recalled was when he seemed to live near the Himalayas.

"*Richie, a soul has to go down to the very roots of its being to uncover the Love that was never lost.*" Blimey, does it have to be so painful?

"*Yep, I know. There can be much suffering in love.* " Theo's mental empathy brought him back to the memory of the boy he once was.

"*Richie, the beautiful thing about consciousness growth is that when you give it up, you get it all back.*" He thought he had given it all up.

Then...instantly... he was back into the boy who felt he had nothing to live for. By the scenery, he knew that they had entered the monastery. It was as if everything his mind projected belonged to the same self. The long studies, his fellow companions, and his daily chores created many experiences of being in the eternal now moments. He knew at that moment that real love blossoms and remains.

"*Now you know that the optimal future is always generated from the free-flowing, non-expectant present moment.*" Was he hearing Theo speak because the monk who worked in the field next to him appeared to have telepathically communicated to him...

"*Every thought, feeling, and communication can add to the world's loving energy field. Being aware of this can shape your life with love and service.*" More and more, the fact that he was only pure consciousness became real. His unconscious mind held many lifetimes of experiences. Was his soul tapping into them? He experienced being an observer as well as the by-now older boy.

"*Richie, the law of karma makes it possible to restore equilibrium to the imbalances that have collected.*" He still didn't like the word karma. Since he started writing in his journal, this karma issue has been playing in his mind. Did he want to know if one ever reached beyond the law of karma?

"*Richie, when humans still create material values that generate either abundance or scarcity, depending on the quality of their needs, their DNA codes are governed by karma.*" As he heard Theo, or the other monk, mentally replying to him, it helped him to assimilate it all. He suddenly knew that Theo had been his teacher in that life. He had asked the same question before! He had devoted that life to spiritual studies. While he was partly aware of being a monk, he realised that through being an observer now, he was mindful of Theo, who was simultaneously his teacher.

As he thought of Annelies' explanations, he knew he was dreaming. She kept repeating that they were awakening their original immortal body's genetic code program through the decoding workshop.

"*Theo, how can we upgrade or awaken our original DNA codes?*" He tried to remember what he had learned as a monk. He wanted to know if dreaming is a way to access learned lessons.

"*I asked myself the same questions. I learned that as we grow and expand in consciousness, our understanding of the law of karma changes.*" Theo took his hand, and he felt himself again moving at speed.

"*Richie, remember how we speculated that to create life, the universe had to develop a new technology to store the data for physical forms of this universe. This technology is what we call the genetic DNA code.*" As he heard Theo's telepathy, he remembered their debate. They were drinking a yoghurt shake, especially created by Waleed, Theo's Egyptian friend, who consistently joined them on their tours. He became aware of a soft breeze that seemed to wrap around them like a funnel as they looked upon a crop glyph's sheer beauty and precision.

"*Theo, remember that you were speculating that our genetic DNA codes are patterns of matter itself that are chemically repeated over and over again on a tiny scale?*" Theo nodded as they observed the symbol of Horus's eye emerging in a field without any signs of buildings or roads.

"*What has that got to do with how our law of karma changes?*" Theo pointed at cornfields in front of his eyes like a movie screen. Multitudes of patterns of crop circles appeared one after the other.

"*Richie, the study of sacred geometry is the study of the genetics of the universe. These seemingly simple patterns of triangles, squares, pentagons and all the rest are the building blocks of all other patterns in the universe. These are the universe's genetic codes for the setup that has created our solar system.*" He always wondered how physical creation had come about.

"*The energy used to form crop circles is translated through an electromagnetic 'musical scale'. All forms of energy are just different wavelengths and frequencies played out in different geometries. I showed you this so you can remember how we like to play with colours and patterns.*" In an instant, he was back at the monastery. He saw how they chanted while creating beautiful patterns with coloured sand.

"*The genetic DNA code of this evolutionary cycle will soon be replaced by a new one that will go beyond the level of matter. That is what the crop glyphs are telling humanity: that great changes are happening soon.*" He couldn't comprehend what Theo meant by the new genetic code, but he knew he had learned much during that lifetime. If it was true, then his life as a monk was the most awakening. He had devoted his life to studying an inner world where Spirit and Soul dwell.

"Now you know that all the soul's experiences are never lost." Did Theo mean that that was why he now consciously awakened to his multidimensional existence? Did everyone on Annelie's ascension path awaken as he did? It must be, thinking of Debbie's sudden skill in Psychometry and Sascia's telepathy.

"Yes, you are all learning to quieten the chatter of inner voices stored in the EGO file. By bypassing the human rational subconscious mind, a new world will materialise." I am wondering how many people remembered their dreams. And what happened to the love of his life? Was he both the monk and simultaneously the Egyptian artist or Richard?

"My brother, your mental storage field still has lots of programmed distortions stacked up for you to deal with and release. I know you don't like karma, but then you must question what the word ignorance stands for darkness?... Because you are on this transcending journey, you are now learning how to play the human game". Well, he could go along with that. While he was interacting with Theo, the thought of Savina lingered...Could it have been Sascia?

Third lecture on the Sphinx

Connie and Jeroen would run the coffee shop in the afternoon when he left for Utrecht to give his third lecture on the Sphinx. Sascia had left early the previous morning with her mom and others for the halfway house in France. Tieneke, who gave the Language of Light workshop, was already there with Annelies. They had set up a joint workshop. He would have gone too if it had not been for his lecture, but people had found his email address on Annelies' website. Richard advertised his talks with specific dates and times.

Soon, they would play Annelie's awakening card game. They were all keen to experience it after doing her first twelve-week workshop.

Sascia's freelance work started to take off. She would do much work for the Cup of Gold Halfway House in France. She was also, with Quincy and Ed, participating in Annelies' second evening group on a Wednesday evening.

He was looking forward to tomorrow afternoon when Annelies would do a reading for him. Sascia, Ed, and Quincy see Annelies straight after they come back.

In her absence, he had worked on the layout for his journal. He would approach it the same way as if he was writing a thesis. He hoped to read Ingrid's journal soon after Liesbeth had edited it into a novel manuscript.

The auditorium was packed full. The doors closed before more people tried to get a seat in the already overcrowded lecture room.

Is the Pyramid of Giza an Interactive Dimensional Transporter Machine?

Behind the question, on the screen, he showed and narrated many images, especially pictures of the antechamber that takes one into the King's chamber, which looks like a massive machine to anyone with some visionary insight. He shared how the King's chamber radiates an atmosphere of exceptional energy and power. He impressed his audience by saying that the Sphinx is still the world's most significant single piece of sculpture. He linked his talk to the speculation that the Sphinx reflected a race that lived on this planet in pre-dynastic times. Then he showed the unusual oblong heads of Akhenaten and his family. He shared his speculation that there could be a link between this royal family and the mysteries about their knowledge that have puzzled all the scientists, historians and philosophers alike.

"Last year, deep in a dark tomb in the Valley of the Kings, my brother's hunch was right. We discovered what we believe to be the remains of the Egyptian Queen Nefertiti, the wife of Akhenaten, the Queen of the Nile." The large image of this gorgeous woman dominated the podium. When the giant screen projected a domestic scene with Akhenaten, Nefertiti and four of his six daughters, he added that today, in some esoteric circles, it was speculated that Akhenaten could be the same soul that incarnated as Moses, Hermes, Thoth, and Oedipus. This idea stirred some people in the auditorium.

"Nefertiti is a real enigma. We speculate that she was part of a royal harem or a Mesopotamian princess before she married Pharaoh Akhenaten and became co-regent of Egypt." Then he did something he knew would bring another reaction. He took Nefertiti's face and moved it over the face of the Sphinx. A remarkable thing happened. Both faces merged as one. He left it at that.

When question time arrived, most people were fascinated with the mysterious figure of Nefertiti.

"Richard, how old ...no... when did Nefertiti live...how long ago?" A young boy in the front asked. He could not have been more than thirteen or fourteen years. He asked for his name.

"Ronny, this very controversial figure, was born around 3,200 years ago. Very little, if anything, is known about her early years. Only when she became Queen around 1352 BC did her fame travel far and wide."

"What was so special about her?" The older girl next to the boy asked.

"Well, apart from her beauty, it was because of the revolutionary religious practices that she became infamous. The royal couple turned their backs on the centuries of tradition by shutting down the famed temple at Karnak." he showed a slide of himself standing under the famous archway.

"Richard, what does her name mean?"

"The beautiful one has come." He recalled how angry the Council of Antiquities became when Theo broadcasted the images before they were released through the official channels. Theo had always been fascinated to find proof of the couple that had made countless enemies among priests and nobles.

"Richard, they say that she could have been the most ruthless woman of the ancient world; what are your thoughts on that?" A man in the front asked. He had heard it all, but his intuition told him a different story.

"People who are cultural creatives are often labelled as either saints or villains. Many believe that Akhenaten and his family fell victim to plotting and foul play. Remember that even in those days, like today, criticism in any form against the ruling power, the priests in those days, is seen as rebellion. Whatever the case, she had a powerful influence over her people which must have pissed off the ruling priests."

Many questions were about Trevor's radio talk. He was glad he had prepared some answers to questions he would have asked.

He was surprised to see Wim in the audience when he packed up. He was about to call him when he disappeared into the crowd. He would never have guessed that Wim, of all people, would show an interest in his subject. He had been very sceptical when he had joined Annelies' first ascension workshop. He always wondered how he got to be part of the group. It must have been Zola who talked him into it.

He missed Sascia. They phoned regularly, and he heard much from her about what went on in France with Toon's community projects. He wondered if they ever discovered what happened in that resort where her mother had been held. Life had a fast pace. She would return on the 27th after going to the Buttercup Valley with Toon and Ingrid. Aside from his research, the coffee shop took up most of his time. Lately, he was increasingly drawn to get back into teaching, but when they phoned him to cancel his following lecture without any valid reason, his hopes for a more permanent teaching post in Utrecht were squashed.

Annelies' reading

Sascia returned from her trip to France and would help Nel in the coffee shop while he went for his reading. The weather was sunny and warm as he drove into Annelie's driveway. There was a quietness about it, as if no one was home. He saw no cars parked outside. The fragrance of recently cut grass had activated millions of insects to have a feast. The grating sounds he made on the gravel broke the stillness when Joris, the young Labrador, started to bark inside the house.

Annelies organized private sessions for each of them before they met the others to play the awakening card game, as she called it. He was curious about what that entailed. After an abundant greeting from Joris, he followed him to her conservatory, where large tropical plants with a waterfall feature set the mood for an enjoyable late afternoon. He wondered where Ben was as she poured him a tall ginger beer.

"*Ben is driving Ingrid and Toon to Schiphol, but they will join us next week.*" Annelies mentally replied, at least he thought so. There was still a lot of doubt in him surrounding his telepathic abilities.

"Where have they been?"

"*You are getting better, aren't you?*" she beamed. He grinned. He was becoming accustomed to the idea that his own impressions were thought waves transmitted telepathically by aware individuals.

"*Toon has to attend a business conference in London with Hans; Ingrid is with him for the ride, I guess.*" he heard clearly.

"*Annelies, I get a strong hunch about what you, Hans, Liesbeth, Ingrid, Toon, and lately even Sascia project mentally, but there are no other people yet. Why is that?*" Annelies' dining room table was covered with the Language of Light cards he remembered from Tieneke's workshop.

"You are mentally not yet that focused. It takes time for your brain to pick up thought waves that your rational mind can form back into words. I imagine your neuron pathways must re-program a connection link with each magnetic thought wave it perceives. You must ask Theo." Annelies was dressed in different shades of blue. Her flowing robes created a majestic impression.

"You knew Theo very well, didn't you?"

"As well as you can ever know someone. We used to talk about ascension subjects. He wanted to develop a study course on the artwork of intuitive symbolism our etheric realms could translate. After he left me with all his notes, I was so overwhelmed. It required so many days in the library to complete Theo's task that I approached Tieneke instead.

"Did Theo ever meet Tieneke?"

He only did it once, but he loved her approach. Richard said that his work was almost done."

"That must have been just before he left?" Annelies nodded.

"Tieneke and I embarked on a study course on alchemical symbolism; that's how the decoding classes came into being. He was very special to me, but you must know that." Annelies' voice went soft as she poured more ginger beer. Should he share his dream, especially the part of her and Theo? Annelies raised her eyebrows but stayed silent.

"Please show me your 22 spacing and your five awakening cards on your vibration sheet, then we can proceed," Annelies asked if he perhaps had any of the Language of Light drawings with him. He had looked for them everywhere.

Last night, Sascia helped look for them while she was tidying up what was now their office. He wasn't sure if he kept them. At the time, his symbols had not triggered any particular message. He realised he was not as aware then as he was now. Sascia had joined Tieneke's evening classes to be trained as a facilitator. She told him how much fun they had when she, Ed and Quincy joined Tieneke's long weekend workshop at Half-way House. He would love to have been there with them. The coffee shop was quite a bind. Annelies read his sheet while he tried to pick up on her thoughts.

"Theo, what do you think? Has he found his direction yet?"

"Theo? Is he?"...he almost dropped his glass. Annelies looked at him with a glint.

"I was just checking. Have you brought your first Symbol cards?" Blimey, for a moment, had him fooled. He handed in his work from the first decoding class and waited in anticipation as to what would come next.

"Richard, your unconscious has an attachment cord with the numeral 22 energy within the matrix. No wonder you were the one chosen to write on the second level. You hold a tremendous volume of information that your soul needs to share." She paused for a while and looked into Tieneke's Language of Light book.

"Your soul qualities of prosperity and unconditional love will back up your instinctive quality with an inner strength." Annelies looked up.

"I can see great changes like a relocation before his real work has started." He was sure he sensed her thinking about him relocating.

"What do you mean by the energy within the matrix?"

"All in good time. You will know it," she beamed. Joris' nose was nudging him for attention. His big brown eyes indeed expressed the quality of unconditional love. He was growing by the day.

"Richard, you must fully embody these two Language of Light frequencies to activate your immortal light body and your Soul Purpose in this life."

"Which ones?"

"The Language of Light tones that emanate the power of your intuitive nature and inner strength. Let me see your spacings again." Annelies studied his grid-sheet. The stillness in the house captured his attention, still thinking of what she could have meant by the energy within the matrix. So, was his soul purpose not activated because he lacked inner strength?

"You have already awakened them, but you would have strengthened those two soul qualities if you had known what you were doing during her mind drawing workshop." He topped his glass with Annelie's favourite ginger beer when she looked up to see if she had his attention.

"Your soul purpose vibrates on the tonal frequency of unity consciousness, and the motivational strength of perseverance with a quality of unconditional love backs it up." What did those three aspects do for him in his daily life?

"We will soon go into your Akashic records, but I first want to see your chosen path."

Annelies' reading was fascinating. He started to see what Tieneke was trying to do in her workshop. While they were doodling and mind-drawing, the realms where thought dwells became physical. Last night, Sascia had shown him her symbols. When he studied her drawings, he realised how resistant he had been in the previous year. Women seemed to go for that sort of thing much more quickly. Only now did he see the wisdom behind it. What a pity that he had been so ignorant.

"Richard, your soul seems to enter through the seventh pathway, which means you must overcome the fear of knowledge. The gift of this path is to embrace unlimited cognition, so you see, don't look for answers outside of yourself; you have it all stored within your genetics." He wondered how this information was written inside his palms as he looked at his hands. He hoped to learn more in their second decoding workshop.

He was a seeker of knowledge; that was true. Thinking of his lectures and the fear that was always there just before he started his talk must be what Annelies was referring to. It was more like the fear of misinterpreting the ancient text or not knowing enough. Her often staring into space reminded him of her mind-reading ability. He asked her if it was wrong to have so many questions.

"Richard, when a person stops asking questions, they are either so wise, they need no longer to play our material game, or...they have forgotten why they were born." Annelies had some thought-provoking things to say about his five awakening cards. She asked if he was having a birthday party on the 24th of August. He had never given it a thought.

Annelies handed him a booklet as she got up to answer the phone. The cover showed the Language of Light symbols that flew through waves of colour around a human skull. It was an awakening manual titled The Eye of the Observer Simulator awakening manual, level 1. He was supposed to paste his five awakening cards inside the booklet, including his Language of

Light cards from Tieneke's class. He'd decided to do them all over again when Sascia gave her first mind-drawing classes with the help of Tieneke's Language of Light book.

Upon returning from her phone call, Annelies inquired about his internet access. The number 300 was his access code so he could download the PDF file explaining the card game's rules on the first level. Annelies shared that she had worked them out with Theo's help. Now he understood the link. It was a pity that the old disk with Theo's explanation was damaged.

As she let him out, Joris escaped, chasing anything of interest he could spot in the driveway. She gave him a large blue envelope from Leo and Trevor. It was to be included in his second journal. He placed it under the seat and waved at Ben, who turned into the driveway as he drove back to the coffee shop. He hoped that Connie had been coping on her own in the Pannekoek...serving customers with Nel in the kitchen.

The Card Game

Finally, they had a quiet moment in the coffee bar. Despite the cancellation of his lecture, the coffee shop was busy with people of all backgrounds over the weekend. Sascia returned and reminded him to look inside the envelope Annelies had given him for his journal. He found a flash drive that could only come from Theo. When he opened it, he was so glad to see that it was the same file he'd found in Theo's folder, the faulty one!

He had already read the first half, but Sascia read Theo's letter Becoming Aware of Being Unaware over his shoulder after she sold a print.

"Gosh, you know. Your brother left you more in this way than if he had given you all this information before!"

"I suppose so. I just wished I had been as aware as I feel now, but I suppose I was still far too caught up in the illusion of everyday events to have been receptive to all this."

"I know. If I had read this a year ago, I would probably not have been as riveted as I am now."

Dear Richard, It was necessary to have her workshop participants write about their awakening experiences to map this relatively tricky path. I was told I would always play a part in the mapmaking group but from a different realm. When you read this, you will either be astonished, or we will be in contact through your out-of-body adventures. I hope the latter will make the following explanation easier for you."

Two customers interrupted their readings. Sascia was getting very good at making coffee. Connie had the day off. Nel had stayed on when he went to Annelie's reading so Sascia would not be alone. When Sascia came back from serving a customer, they carried on reading.

Richie, each player must create their Language of Light deck on the first level of the card game. It is essential for the shift in thinking. Each Language of Light symbol with its qualities is there to help the players re-observe themselves, knowing they are playing the game of life. They must know this perceptional observation to become an ascension initiate in the etheric realm. We had been working on the card game rules for some time and concluded that the players must make the end rules. This freedom releases one's intuitive nature.

"Gee Rich, how uncanny. Do you get the feeling that Theo is standing watching us?"

"That's quite possible. If we feel that he must be." They both looked up when a group of tourists arrived. They were Germans. The leader of the group asked him for directions to the Prinsegracht Hotel. After his explanation, he sold all of Nel's remaining stroopwafels to them, and they left. They were both keen to read on. Sascia was eager to learn as much as she could now that she had joined Annelies' workshops.

All the instructions on the Language of Light symbols have one thing in common. Any individual who is either a record-breaker mentally, emotionally or intuitively or a physical grid-breaker would be exposed. We concluded that all of us are destructive in one form or another. It is primarily unconscious, but the game triggers these damaging patterns, and the player has to be diligent enough to recognise their dark side.

"Wow! What is a grid or record breaker?" Sascia asked him. He had no idea, but there was no doubt they would learn that during the game.

"Rich, I can hardly wait for Wednesday. He scrolled down to the next page.

The ancestral texts we have uncovered reveal some astonishing information we have incorporated. The awakening card game is both a space travel guide, an awakening tool and a tuning fork to prepare the initiate for the ascension journey from the physical into the etheric Lightbody. Both Annelies and I knew that we, with the help of POWAH, had created a card game shaped by and informed with alchemical and emblematic symbolism that could take our conscious awareness into the next evolutionary cycle.

"Gosh, you know, now I understand why my mother was so engrossed in her workshop with Annelies when she met Toon." Sascia and Ed were decoding with Annelies to join the game on the first level.

We are both very humbled by this cosmic code device. The story about our creation, the birth of our planet with the Garden of Eden, and the great flood, those stories were all left behind by our ancestors so we would remember why we embodied a human form during these times. The first level will activate the light body of the player so that the initiate can consciously navigate the non-physical realms to prepare themselves for the second level.

Nel interrupted them, asking where all the stroopwafels had disappeared to. She was rather chuffed when she heard that a group of tourists bought them all. She wrote an extra shopping list for the wholesaler that came around once a week. He immediately phoned them so it would still be delivered today.

A customer summoned Sascia regarding one of her photos taken in France. The woman recognised the Chateau from her childhood. They both listened with amazement when she told them that it used to be an orphanage. *"We were right! I must ask Helen about it."* she beamed. Sascia told her about the B&B, and the woman was keen to see what her previous home looked like today.

• • • •

After they closed the Pannekoek and returned to the flat, They were both keen to read the last section of Theo's letter.

Each player will also activate their five psychic sensors by bringing into consciousness the talents and skills the initiate's soul has accumulated over aeons.

When you read this, I hope you will soon play the card game for a trial run. It will guide you in your map-making, and I hope to read about your journey on the second level of the etheric realm. The star map plays a significant role in this evolution card game; more will be revealed at the right time. Please go through the old photos I left for you in my box. You will find some clues you need to know to find your place on this star map created in 1888.

Good luck on the game's first level, "Getting Motivated to Become Aware."

Love Theo.

"You know Mom and Toon have been studying this Star map. She seems to have an uncanny explanation of how she suddenly knows who is who. Toon sometimes makes jokes saying that she probably painted it."

"Really? But I thought Toon knew much more about who was behind all the mysterious appearances of unusual documentation because of Annelies."

"No, apparently not. Toon told us over dinner one night that Annelies knows even less than Hans and Liesbeth. They are truly a lot more aware than we are. I almost think they are ...from another world."

"Wow, that is an exciting statement; I know what you mean. What did Toon tell you about his adopted family? I got the feeling that he was away a lot."

"Yes, but Toon is Annelie's half-brother. Did they not grow up together?"

"Yes, they did, but Annelies is ten years older and led quite a turbulent life." He was suddenly mentally far away. Incredible, he had an aha moment.

"Moppie, now I am beginning to grasp what Trevor meant when he said: Let me disclose a riddle so simple that it humbled me." He opened his laptop and searched through his notes.

"What are you talking about? Who is Trevor?" she had followed him into what he called Theo's room, which was almost like a sanctuary to him.

"Remember when I spoke to you over the phone for the first time?"

"Oh, you and Vinnie attended a lecture on time travel?"

"No, not really." He tore a page from his notepad and drew a big oval; inside the centre, he drew a circle.

"Apart from looking like an eye, what is so earth-shattering about this eye symbol?" Sascia asked.

"Eye symbols have a foundation of understanding in the ancient and indigenous traditions of the Earth. Remember that our knowledge comes to us through memory. Theo's work was to decode ancient texts to understand why our forefathers had very advanced technology withheld from later civilizations."

"Was it? I mean, are we today not far more advanced in science and technology than, I don't know, say 2000 years ago?"

"I'm talking about at least 12000 years ago. Some glyphs show a sacred symbol called the "God's Eye" through the Native American ways of thought. The knowledge that comes from our memory is a far more complete picture of the history and science of humankind because we are the observers; after all, we are now at a period that we can awaken from our creations."

"You've lost me."

"Many people will say that our concept is not scientific and, therefore, mostly false, but now I have to accept that the pyramids make up an interplanetary inter-dimensional communication system.

"Rich, what triggered your mind suddenly? You are very distant, almost as if you are somewhere else. Oh...gosh... were we supposed to be at Mom for dinner?"

"Yes Yes,... I suddenly recall the pupil of our eyes and the symbol Trevor drew on the board at one of his lectures. He explained that the black hole was revered and protected because it conferred power to those who controlled it. It created a gateway, a portal between cosmic dimensions, and was responsible for the law that every effect has a cause."

"Are you talking about the crop circle eye symbol, the image you see when you fly over the Pleasure Park resort?"

"Yes, the same. I now see how Theo and Annelies came up with the idea for a card game. Sorry, Moppie, I get this way when I suddenly get inspiration. It's like being on a mental roller coaster. Let's go."

They were about to leave for Ingrid's house when the phone rang. Wil, the faculty secretary, told him that his last lecture had been moved again up to next month. No explanation was given, but he didn't want to ask her. He was somewhat relieved. He had been so occupied with his journal, especially when Liesbeth asked if she could have his first draft. He promised to give her his unfinished journal soon. He had ample time to work on his last lecture about the Sphinx. When they closed the back door, the phone went again. As he picked up, there was just silence again. He could feel that someone was listening. After repeating his name, he hung up.

"What was that all about?" she asked

"No idea?"

"Do you think you should report it?" Sascia asked in an uneasy tone. He thought of the other phone incidents but didn't want to fall into a mental trap that would spoil his evening.

"I'm not to be bullied into feelings of fear; let's just ignore it."

They were invited for dinner at Ingrid's house. Toon and Ingrid would be leaving for New York the following morning.

"Gosh, Moppie, you never mentioned that your mom was having a party? He had to find a parking space further down the street.

Half-way House

Last evening, they celebrated Ingrid's upcoming birthday. Connie, Jeroen, and Debbie were there. So were Liesbeth and Hans. Annelies and Ben were away, so Joris was staying with friends.

Ingrid had expressed joy seeing Sascia as happy as she was with Toon. It reminded him about their plan to get Vinny to meet Debbie. Matchmaking had never been his thing, but Sascia insisted they were meant for each other. Ingrid's sister Quincy and Fred came around for drinks after dinner. There had been some trouble down the street where they lived. That was why there were so many cars parked. Toon had gone snooping to find out what the commotion was all about, but even Ingrid's neighbour, who owned an old ugly duckling car, was also in the dark. Why there were surveillance cars with people in them who were seemingly bored, according to Toon, remained a mystery. Toon tried reading their minds, but nothing was there, he whispered after Ingrid pleaded with him to get back into the house. She was still not her old self. Her kidnapping ordeal had left some scars after all.

Last night after dinner, when Toon showed their latest office equipment, he drooled at the speed of their computer, not to mention the large screen. Ingrid still worked for Pleasure Park, but when they were in Apeldoorn, she did her job mostly from her home office.

Last night had been a natural family gathering. He had never known what a family was like. He remembered lots of travelling and illness when it came to grownups. Theo was his only family. Lately, he wondered how it would have been if Theo had been still with them. Apart from the impression that he had been a monk in a past life, he had not recalled any more dreams as vividly as he would like.

Theo's flat.

Sascia stirred next to him, turned over and went back to sleep. Last evening, he was sure that he wanted his own family. Monastic life was not for him. He hoped that Sascia would take to Sammy. It was his turn to have her with him next week. This time, there would be the three of them.

He marvelled at how he had attracted her in his life, especially having her moving in, which was a miracle. Ginger, Sascia's cat, was purring as he moved his leg away from under the blankets.

"Pssst, don't wake her up." He whispered. Ginger stretched himself with a look as if to say, you do your thing, and I do mine. He needed to work on his upcoming lecture before the rest of the day was occupied with mundane activities that paid the bills. Evidence of their last night's lovemaking, after they had come home from Sascia's mother's birthday party, made him look back at the gorgeous female that shared his bed."Lucky dude" he sighed and tiptoed out of the bedroom. It was going to be a sunny day. Noises from the outside stairway into the street told him that research time was short.

Sascia's untidy desk under the window reminded him of Ingrid and Toon's expression when she presented her handiwork.

Sascia had framed one of her favourite pictures from Buttercup Valley taken on her last trip to France. She gave it to Ingrid at midnight on her mother's birthday. Toon and Ingrid seemed to hold special memories about the spot Sascia immortalised. Sascia could not stop talking about Toon's community project over dinner, telling them she had flown to the Buttercup Valley in the Rhaetian Alps straight after Tieneke's weekend workshop. Sascia showed him on the map that it was near Lichtenstein.

Sascia told Debbie about the Talent Exchange currency they used at Half-way House, and they all gathered in Toon and Ingrid's study so that Toon could show them the offering list on the internet. Then, while Toon was encouraging them all to sign up online, he suddenly remembered a dream. They were all in the office when he had urgently asked for a paper and pen.

In a flash, he again recalled a death-like stillness about him while he read what he wrote last evening. He again heard subdued sobs as if some people were weeping, but the mourners were invisible. Where were all the people who were grieving as if their hearts would break?

Why would he dream of stationed soldiers acting as guards, and why was he now thinking that a crowd of people had surrounded him? Last night, he asked Hans if nightmares were ever flashes of things to come. Hans had reminded him of something that Theo had mentioned.

"Everyone visits different levels of the astral planes during sleep depending on the awareness level of the dreamer, but most don't remember any of it because the soul is muddled by the first nine levels that are rather compressed with distorted thoughts. That's why nightmares or confusing dreams discourage the soul from investigating." It all came back to him.

He had no idea why he now suddenly experienced how the brightness of the snow in the Alps had blinded him, or so it seemed...and he could not remember Theo in this dream either.

Chapter 12
The Voice from Nowhere

Theo's investigations
He had to squeeze past the furniture clutter to get to his desk. Last night, while everyone was outside on the veranda, Toon gave him the flash drive telling him that the message was uplifting and mind-blowing, so he wanted to see it there and then, but the commotion outside took Toon away to investigate.

Interacting with financially wealthy people often made him feel a lack of abundance, and he still had not gotten used to the idea that he was included in a family circle due to his relationship with Sascia.

Ginger appeared and jumped on his desk. That was new, too, having a cat around. He slotted the stick into his laptop. He heard that Sascia was up and about. With great anticipation, he sat on the edge of the settee.

"Hi Brother, when you listen to this recording, I'll be long gone, but I know that you will soon receive the twelfth interpretation. Where I'm heading for, time is of no concern, but in your world, the constriction that time has will have more and more of an impact on your lives if you don't overcome it."

"Rich, who is speaking, I was wondering"...she mumbled while putting a breakfast tray on the coffee table. He had clicked on the pause button.

It was her turn this morning to prepare breakfast while he was supposed to work on his journal.

"Who is it?"

"Toon gave this flash drive to me last night," Toon asked if he was in direct contact with Trevor Zwiegelaar, a colleague, and he replied that they had emailed each other.

"Who is the voice? I thought for a moment it was you speaking to yourself."

"He settled back on the couch, tapping her to join him, enjoying Sascia's coffee while admiring her long legs. He was hungry. Smelling toast reminded him to look at the time. They had to open his aunt's coffee shop at ten o'clock because Connie would be late.

"It's Theo" he replied with some emotion in his voice. Sascia's stare of surprise reminded him of her mother, Ingrid. Gosh, she so looked like her mom. Ingrid still worked for Pleasure Parks, but ever since her abduction and Toon's recovery from a bullet wound, she did her job mostly from her home office.

"Did Theo make this recording before he left?"

"Probably."

"I just heard the beginning." When Theo had decided to leave, moving away from everyone who knew him, to pass away somewhere on his own, he had been devastated."

"You mean he knows how far you are with your journal and about your translations on the ancient text?"

"It seems that he is aware of my involvement with Annelies' awakening classes, yes."

"You mean her ascension workshops."

"Well, yes, whatever. Let's listen."

"While it would take too long to explain why I left you and for what reason I moved in with Leo and Trevor in France, I always knew that you will be in contact with them through Annelies. I asked Trevor to pass my recording to you in any way he deemed fit, time-wise. As you hear me now, I know that we have already connected long before on the Astral plane."

There were static noises in the background as if Theo was having difficulties with something.

"Rich so much has already changed in your life. When you hear my voice, I often wished I could have been part of your life in the physical, but being with those two extraordinary people during my last months on the planet has been such a gift. I've grown so speedily in my awareness that it has become a lot easier to let go of my Earthly connection cords. The simplicity of Trevor's ten-dimensional holographic model of the world, although striking, strengthened my observation mode ever faster. I took it in as if I'd known all along that your Earth life would end up being a very good one. I was privileged to have observed two geniuses at their best. Everybody's favourite parallel universe, the internet, comes into the picture. You will soon have interaction with his invention, but know that his multiple dimensions are purely at a speculative stage as of yet. Despite that, Trevor's 'simple' viewpoint has many fascinating connections, not just to leading-edge string theory and physics, but also to the average person's common sense knowledge of how the world works."

"What is he talking about?"

"Don't know, maybe a new way of thinking about time and space." He paused so Sascia could feed Ginger since he had been nudging for attention.

"You mean what Trevor talked about a month ago?" she questioned when she returned from the kitchen.

"I didn't connect it, but who knows it could be." He clicked to carry on with the recording.

"The paradoxes of time travel, music, and memory are all multidimensional and programmed into the planetary matrix, but the implications of Trevor and Leo's discoveries on time have barely begun to be explored. Besides hosting an animated tour through the ten dimensions, at the Valley of the Gods resort, which Toon will soon be involved in, Trevor's 10-D idea is very imaginable in any direction."

"Where is the Valley of the Gods?" her question stayed unanswered. He had no idea and looking at the clock there was no time to even discuss it. If they want to be in time to open the Pannekoek, they had better hurry...

"You said it, a new way of thinking about time and space. How fascinating"

"Trevor and Leo have created a mirror that allows many people to see elements of their belief systems embedded into their energy fields. Their computer game program reaction has completely exceeded our expectations."

Theo's timing in mentioning the paradox concept was exceptional, considering his interpretations of the symbols they had pored over years ago. Still, looking at the clock, he needed to make a move. Sascia made signs suggesting they listened to the recording at home in the evening. She took their dishes to the kitchen, but he couldn't resist hearing more:

"Rich, I have to go back to a time, while you were away when I was visiting Annelies at home. While we discussed reincarnation, fate and free will, including the existence of God, during that discussion a black rock spontaneously appeared in Ben's living room from out of the blue. We were all blown out of our minds, seeing a phenomenon we then could not fathom. I kept this from you for very good reasons. We were told to do so. The possibility that consciousness spans multiple dimensions was proven to us most unusually. The compelling idea that UFOs, ghosts, and other apparently "paranormal" phenomena may be the best evidence in proving that the nature of dark matter and dark energy is for real will be useful. I then had no problem anymore showing them evidence of the unseen influence of a higher dimension."

"Rich, are you coming?"

"Yes, yes." Reluctantly he switched Theo's recording off and followed her out of the front door.

What Theo had said about the nature of dark matter and that dark energy is for real, had kept him unfocused on his daily routine in the coffee bar. Most of the people who came into the Pannekoek were still totally ignorant of the warnings that were all around.

He began to suspect that TV presenters had been scripted about climate change, energy consumption, and rising sea levels that could significantly affect human mortality, not to mention financially. The diversity in people's attention about their reality was in itself proof that nothing was real.

Theo's recording

They sat cosily on the settee and waited for Theo's voice to fill the living room.

"We both know that higher dimensions exist while in a dream state, but I was present during their discussion, and you will soon find out why I left this recording. For you to hear it when the time was right."

There was a long pause, and he was about to check when Theo spoke again.

"While Ben suggested that the mysterious appearance of the rock reminded him of a novel, Annelies' brother Fred suggested that the ten sefirot of Kabbalah also represents the hierarchical gradations of divine creation. We then contemplated that a two-dimensional being, or a square, that has an encounter with a three-dimensional being, or sphere, could be a shaking experience. So, the concept of an alternate dimension, like a 4th or far higher dimensional perception, to an audience that might never pick up a book on cosmology, string theory, or quantum geometry, those discoveries will truly blow minds. Richie, soon the world as you know it will change drastically, provoking plenty of philosophical and spiritual inquiries."

There was again a pause, but he waited.

"I leave you to it and hope that what you have heard might one day sprout into an idea that you already know all there is to know. We will meet again soon."

"What was all that about? Why, what is the message? Let's look."

He knew that they had the same idea: emails. He lately always checked his e-mail the moment they arrived at his flat in the evening. While Sascia prepared Ginger's food, he downloaded two emails, both from Trevor.

——- Original Message ——-
From: "T Zwiegelaar"
To: <R de Jong.> Sent:
Subject: tablet 12

Dear Richard, This twelfth interpretation made us all aware of a mirror, reflecting what is in our mind. Theo's translations are almost poetic. The Language of Light symbols describe the five Initiations with such vigilance any other translator would have completely missed the essence of their meanings. It reveals the spiritual depth that the artists held about the soul. From an external perspective, love and passion have consumed these concepts. Our entertainment activities have distorted them by projecting the barrenness of what love is. Most humans find themselves in a state of darkness and experience loneliness before they leave this world. Ancient Egyptians knew opportunities were lost due to a lack of zest for life at the soul's departure just before physical death. Leo and I will soon show you where Theo redid the last of the 22 translations. In the meantime, listen to the tape Toon gave you. It will make no sense to you immediately, but I'm sure Theo had reasons for you to listen to what he had to say. Don't worry about the prints that were stolen from us. Each one has a different role to play at these end times.

Regards Trevor.

They were both surprised when Trevor mentioned the photos and the symbolic text he was supposed to translate. They had been stolen from his flat last month. Ben must be in daily contact with Trevor. So there were 22 Tablets.

"What do you think he means about the roles we each play at the end of time?" Sascia had read his mind.

He opened the following email. It was another translation from the fragile golden sheets still visible in the photos. He still had no clue where they had been discovered. Sascia urged him to read on while she snuggled up on his lap. The link retook them to the Tablet 12 webpage. Together, they peered at Theo's translation titled The Initiation Game[1].

Tablet 12

Translated by Theo de Jong

Richie, karmic intelligence arranges things for us the same way that the brain coordinates and organises the functions of our organs. A directing mind will reflect us, many times multiplied. The effects of your soul's good deeds while shaping every painful experience toward growth will increase happiness. Remember that.

Love Theo

Sascia asked him questions he had often pondered over as they re-read the eleven interpretations from Theo repeatedly.

"This spiritual Christ force will activate every biologically created life—In man... That is the first time I read Christ," Sacia commented,

---

1. https://allrealityshifters.wordpress.com/tablet-twelve/

"When I translate the pictorial texts, I usually get visions. I don't know if that is anything to go by. Still, when I read that Annelies' ascension or transcending path catalyses our physical manifestations, I began to learn how much our daily thoughts manifest in the physical. The word Christ must mean a higher spiritual consciousness."

"You mean the thoughts one has about an 'intent' is what makes it so?"

"Yes, I imagine that our bio-gravitational fields are changing. I think that our thoughts have such an effect on the cellular level. When we awaken more and more about who we are, we penetrate that idea into the nuclei by pure thought." The visions of shapeshifting came to mind as he spoke. Sascia pondered. "Gee...you mean like they do on Star Trek when they are beamed up?"

"Who knows? Sometimes, movies are ahead of us, like any science fiction story. Our mind-fields must tap into these possibilities; Annelies calls them causal planes. Awesome, hey?"

"It's amazing, but what are these causal planes?" she asked

"It's a realm created by our daily thoughts about the future realm."

"You mean it is a fantasy realm?"

"In a way, yes, a high spiritual plane of existence. However, as Theo says in his recording, The Paradoxes of time travel, music, and memory, all multi-dimensionally programmed into the matrix, can be misinterpreted. The implications of Trevor and Leo's discoveries have barely begun to be explored." Sascia pondered on this as she rested her head on his shoulder.

"Rich, our lovemaking. It feels like...a sensation of golden sunlight spreading through all my body's fibres!" Her voice trembled as she spoke. He gently stroked the hairline on her neck.

"*My entire body trembles in waves of rapture during our physical union.*" He could see when she smiled that she had read his mind. When their eyes melted, he could read hers. "Rich, will it stay? I mean, will it always be like this for us? Do you think so?" The joy of their telepathic experience filled his entire being. "I now know that I always yearned for this complete union. I feel that our relationship goes beyond the joining of the flesh. Like Toon and your mom have."

"In the stillness when they both mentally communicated, timelessness set in....

• • • •

When Sascia was fast asleep, he settled himself in, to slip out. The thrilling pulsations that rippled through his body told him that he would soon be free. At first, the mental sensation that he was out of his body settled his sense of equilibrium. Then, images that first seemed to appear as streams of colours started to form into shapes. Where was Theo? Had he suddenly arrived at what looked like ancient Egypt by himself? When he observed the scenery closer, he got a feeling that he was not in Egypt at all. He saw what looked like a tropical island.

"*This is what Annelies calls the causal plane.*" Theo's mental beam settled his uncertainty. He marvelled at the aesthetically laid-out gardens. He saw massive Egyptian sculptures among glass-shaped pyramids that created an all-over fairyland effect. Somehow, this felt like it was in the future. He knew Annelies had once explained that the causal plane was a 'test run' reality that projected 5 to 6 years ahead. Then he remembered why the place looked so familiar! Annelies gave him a preview of the image of the card game layout during his reading. This place had the same feel as if she had photographed a miniature copy of this scenery. This was far more real because he was part of it. Like a hologram. Had the card game become a hologram in his mind?

"Not so fast, but yes, in several years, people will visit these healing temples, depending on the maturity of their etheric visions. You have just been granted a preview." He recognised others! Ingrid and Toon strolled with a jumping toddler whose long, thick, light blonde curly hair sparkled like golden reflector beams. Her bright little face spoke with delighted rapture. Her big blue eyes flashed cries of wonder as she telepathically addressed her parents. Then he spotted Sascia, and his mouth flew open. *"There you are, Rich. Come, I can't wait to hear what POWAH is going to share with us."* she beamed at him. His emotions spun. Sascia was massive! Her slim waistline had gone! Instead, it appeared that at any moment she might go into labour, delivering at least twins! *"How wise, Annie. Now he has something to write about."* he heard Theo mentally project to Annelies. He looked at Theo's loving expression when Annelies joined them. Where had she suddenly come from? Sascia dragged him over a wooden bridge that spanned a turbulent waterfall. On the far side of the lake, small boats were heading for the same island they had arrived on. It was almost like a reunion. People came by air in a balloon, over water in a dinghy and overland. There were many different ways to reach the centre portion of the area.

Why did he have a feeling that... *"Theo, it reminds me of the Pleasure Parks project in France."* The island was above the centre of the eye symbol that could only be seen from a great height. A massive tropical island covered the centre where the pupil would be. Colourful birds flew in abundance among the giant cycads and tree ferns. The fragrance was influential, as if every flower bloomed, spewing pure perfume at each other. It was indeed a tropical paradise. The magnificent promenade, which reminded him of the temples of Karnak, blended in with the fountains decorated with rows of Sphinxes.

He knew now that the enormous project of Pleasure Park would see its completion. He wished he had had a hand with the architecture, even if the monuments and pillars were probably all imitations of the Egyptian monuments, but they looked great. Many people like them entered a sizeable open-air auditorium. He could still see the tops of glass pyramids between the natural wall that lush tropical plants formed. Gemstone-quality seating arrangements decorated the magnificent open-air gathering place. Laser beams of colourful lights were directed towards the centre, dominated by a massive fountain feature. He tenderly helped Sascia to sit down. Her protruding top-heavy belly dominated her otherwise lean neckline. Her glowing face made him melt like butter. Her slim hand slid into his as the place was filling up. He thought he had spotted Debbie with a group of children momentarily. Then, the water from the fountain transformed into a being of light resembling a genie from a bottle, drawing everyone's attention to POWAH's presence.

<*I'm very privileged to be amongst you all. I have already met some of you, and I will say greetings to those who are here for the first time. First, I must congratulate the animal and plant kingdoms for this beautiful display resembling the Garden of Eden.*

Due to your awakening period, many similar light centres are now appearing all over your planet. Your mental projections are slowly shaping your environment back to what it used to be.>

They did it! All that has been written about has come true! The unrest and wars that seemed to have overtaken the planet in the first years of the twenty-first century had taken their toll, but many people had broken away from that lifestyle. They had had enough.

< We are aware that many cannot yet access this sanctuary. You know that it is only reachable in the new consensus reality. Due to the entrapments of forgetfulness, some couldn't make it. Because of this sad state of affairs, we will first beam thought forms of unconditional love to the beings still bound in the illusion of 3rd-dimensional consciousness. >

"Theo, how far is this in the future?" If he could recall this dream, he wanted to know its year.

"Richie, wherever you have created this reality, it's all in the mind. At all times, the total truth lies within the ethers."

Why could he create anything with his unconscious mind while others, who seemed fully conscious, did not need to make this paradisical sanctuary?

"Richie, when you look at something, you're in a dualistic relationship to it. You become the observer when you look upon the world from a space of no judgment." He could still not grasp that this projection was purely in his mind.

< Loved ones, you have all been incompletely forgetful, and there is still much inner work to establish this sanctuary permanently. If many souls of like mind exclusively project peace and harmony, your planet will speedily Transcend into a higher 5th-dimensional reality. If there are still pockets of energy fusions that cloud your brain cells in all your mind fields during your dreams >

He wondered what happened to those pockets, as POWAH called them.

<Many guides have offered their assistance during your soul's recasting moments. You have all worked hard during your dream state; now is the time to bring your awareness into the conscious, awake state, as humans would call it. The small

children that are already born, or soon to be born, will have memories of many divine realms, and they will share them with you.>

At that last statement, Sandra, Ingrid and Toon's little girl clapped her hands joyfully. It was self-evident that she was very aware already. Sascia reacted with laughter as she allowed Sandra to rest her ear on her tummy to listen. It seemed ticklish.

< If couples who have reached an awareness of inter-dependence have, before this incarnation, requested to be united with their twin for service, they will be the forerunners of the valid marriage. It is a union between the male and female, each of whom has matured within themselves. Those souls who have brought their inner polarities into balance first are ready for their twin union. That had never happened during the last days before a previous cosmic shift. Some isolated cases have been noticed over the centuries, but this is becoming more of a possibility in your age. >

Sascia squeezed his hand. If this was all in the future, would she remember this when they woke up? He peered sideways at Theo and Annelies, who looked ageless. Her glance at Theo at that moment revealed their affection for each other. What happened to Ben? What happened to all the people who were not here? *"Richie, it will be stored in their subconscious. Some of it will filter through like a dream. You have been especially privileged. Like you, annelies will also recall this consciously, but she has learned not to disclose too much. This is to protect the visions. Dark forces are still roaming through all your auric fields to stop this causal plane event from happening. They are slowly losing control. That is certain death for them, so they will do anything to stay alive."* Theo's warning made sense, but he never liked the idea of the dark forces. What was a dark force anyway? Something that brought on pain and suffering? Or was it something completely different? In his mind, he could hear POWAH speak of twin souls. The people around him were strolling as if they were all on a Sunday picnic. Where did the voice come from, from the fountain? POWAH's image seemed to be formed by the water spray.

<*It has been brought to my attention that some of you will soon take on an embodiment to join your parents on their physical ascension. It is both a joyful and, for some, a temporary separation. Remember that all is one. There is no separation in the truest sense. Only when one takes on a physical form does the soul feel separated when not fully awakened. If the awareness of these souls is full-blown, there will be a dimensional bridge that others can cross at all times on the ascension path>*

The energy of POWAH withdrew.

Sascia was pulling at him when POWAH's last words were still lingering.

"Rich, gosh, I think I've started! I felt it, a contraction!" His concern for Sascia became so great it tore him away from the feelings both Theo and Annelies suddenly projected. Their sudden anguish at their separation startled him, but the prospect of becoming a father made him jump back.....

. . . .

He woke up with a massive jolt. Sascia was already awake. The sensation of falling from a great height next to Sascia was such a shock he nearly forgot that he... " Hey, what's with you? You look like you have never seen me....are you okay?" He was confident that he had again seen a possible future. The words still rang in his mind... *"Rich, gosh, I think I've started! I felt it, a contraction!"*...It took a while to orientate himself to which reality he had woken up in. He placed his lips on her tummy to make sure. "How do you feel? Are you ready for a new day?" It was still early, just after seven. Sascia's soft curves were a stimulating sight.

"You are flirting; I know that look. Was it a great dream?"

"Absolutely, and you were in it." Her nakedness became irresistible. Her lush lips tantalizingly parted. He accepted the warm invitation while his dream lingered in the background...

Chapter 13
Your 'I Am Guardian Angel'

Annelies' Awakening Card Game
"Rich, have you seen my file where I kept our genograms?"

"Moppie, we worked on them after we closed the Pannekoek. Remember?" Did you take your work home with you?"

"I'm sure I did." She looked everywhere. Tonight, they would play the first level of the awakening card game. It seemed like months ago that others played it. During April, his awakening had truly set in when he joined Annelies' ascension workshops, as Sascia insisted on calling them. The concepts, the approach to life in general, and his new communication skills have changed his perceptions of life. He met new people, and some were even family! And... he met his partner for life, at least in this lifetime.

Annelies asked them to see if they could bring their genogram or what they knew about their family tree. She wanted to see if they were on the star map painting. Sascia had done hers from her Father's side since her mother would bring her side of the family to the class. Richard knew that his father was a lot older than his mother. He was born when she was already in her late thirties.

"The file might still be in the car." Her flirty look told him plenty. *"Thanks"* she responded. It was unusual for her to forget where she had left her things. Sascia fed Ginger while he had another look around. He hoped they did not have to go back to the Pannekoek. Outside in the street, as they got inside his Honda, he spotted her yellow file that had slid under her seat. For some weird reason, he felt like he was being stared at. Lately,

he often thought that somebody was watching them. He kept it from Sascia. Lately, he was unsure if he imagined it or had become more sensitive, but he had no skill to interpret his hunches.

On the way to Annelies, he felt like a child going on a school outing. He had been wondering for ages how the card game would be played. Throughout the week, Sascia repeatedly guided him in drawing the Language of Light cards. She had purchased another one of Tieneke's journal manuals, and they had spent great evenings together listening to good music and insights.

Sascia's uncle Ed's car pulled into the driveway behind them. He was surprised to see Yolanda, another family member, knowing she had already played the card game with the others from Annelies' decoding classes.

"Mom's back!" Toon's BMW was parked in the driveway. He must ask how New York had been. America was still sliding deeper into an economic depression. Europe, too, was feeling the financial pinch. Most people had to budget for things they could easily afford previously. He certainly had to.

Fred, Annelie's brother, opened the door. He was surprised to see the bookshop owner since he had not taken part in her workshops.

Yolanda and Sascia chatted as only women can. Ed greeted him in his flamboyant Australian manner. Together, they saw the sign on Annelie's workroom door when they greeted the others.

The Initiation Game on the First Level

DESIRING TO BECOME AWARE was written in bold letters underneath. Richard felt so glad to be back again. Lots of drawings from herAnnelies previous class were still displayed on the walls. More people had recently joined Annelies' decoding classes. Sascia told them Tieneke planned to exhibit her work with hers at the Prinsegracht Hotel. He was proud of her.

Annelies' illustrations on the wall spoke many words. A drawing of colourful funnels that streamed away from the chakras of a couple blended into the forest background. Finally, his curiosity about the card game was to be satisfied.

The large oval dining room table was covered with a transparent vinyl sheet, indicating where they all had to be seated.

Most of them were there. Liesbeth, Hans, Ed and Yolanda, Toon and Ingrid. Her pregnancy must have benefits because she looked radiant, even at her age. Three couples, four if he included, had found a spiritual mate to journey together in each other. Niels and Gerrit just arrived. There was no sign of Zola and Wim.

"*Rich, it's true what the tablets are predicting.*" Sascia beamed. All the telepathists in the room heard her because they wanted to know which tablets she was referring to. He explained Theo's interpretations. Ingrid was amazed at the content, telling them all how, in a way, it related to the excerpt she received from POWAH. She asked Annelies if he could share them with the group before he handed his second file to Liesbeth, who replied mentally.

"*Ingrid POWAH's excerpt from Jour journal is published online*". Ed asked some interesting questions while Annelies was gathering up their genograms.

"When will you tell us where each of us might be placed on the star map?" Yolanda asked. Annelies said "soon" and asked him if he could bring Theo's interpretations of the first eleven tablets and if Ingrid would get the first eleven excerpts before they started on the second level of her workshop. She wanted to read them before she shared what she knew about the Star-map. For now, they would have to be patient.

Sascia asked her mom how her sister Debbie was. There still was no opportunity to figure out how to get Vinny and Debbie together.

"She's gone to Greece for ten days to chill out," Toon replied. He felt terrible about not contacting her. The few times he had tried, but she had been on duty at the hospital. Not that they were ever an item like he was with Sascia, but they had gone out many times.

Ben must have gone back to France to be with Leo and Trevor. Due to Theo's video, he knew they were busy with a project, so Annelies seemed to be on her own as usual. What was so special about France was still a mystery to him unless it had something to do with CERN. Ingrid told them that Pleasure Parks had started preparing to construct the dome again. He suspected Pleasure Park's new holiday complex was connected with Trevor and Leo's project, but that was just a hunch. Instead, he asked Toon about New York.

"Sascia, Helen asked when you are coming to the estate to take photos of the children?" He telepathically overheard mother and daughter conversing while Toon told him about New York.

Ingrid helped herself to Annelie's ginger ale while waiting for Sascia's reply. The idea of Sascia going away again gave him a jolt. He was annoyed that he was reacting so pathetically. He chatted with Niels and Gerrit, whom he had not seen since Toon and Ingrid's wedding, to stop him from eavesdropping mentally.

"I know you have all been looking forward to playing the card game, but before we carry on, I want to remind you of two breathing points during this first initiation level."

Annelies demonstrated that by inhaling, they can take in and exhale to release all that is past and ready for release. He sensed that she was stalling for time. She sorted the facilitator's backup and instruction cards while watching her watch. She asked if they all printed their ascension manual from the internet. Trevor had created a blog for Ingrid's first journal.

"I know we have been through quite a disturbing time with Ingrid's abduction and what followed, but this is probably a good opening to the card game. I have learned a lot about my habitual patterns that came rushing to the surface in recent weeks." Annelies was again wearing one of her colourful caftans. Richard noticed that women her age could still emanate a sensual charisma that younger women lacked. What was that experience?

"You know it is only a month ago that all our good intentions collapsed around us!" Yolanda sighed. They all agreed.

"Okay, let's start with the introduction. We'll go over the rules again of this first level." Each person was seated and instructed where to place their cards.

"As you all know, the ascension game is just a tool to awaken us from our consciousness slumber. Each of the five stages is so designed that each player's unconscious mind will learn how to communicate with your sub-tangible physical world — the quantum world of all possibilities."

"Can you prove mind over matter with the card game?" Ed asked.

"Ed, yes, the marriage of our unformed mind and matter can assemble itself into something tangible, as your mind drawings show. The game or your interaction with it is just a tool to let you all know how your progress is shaping up."

"Annelies, can we see each level as an awakening stage?"

"Yes, Niels, through our card vibes and their Language of Light qualities, we will discover what addictive thought patterns we might still hang on to." They were all listening to Annelies while she moved around.

"The five levels of the game are meant to activate our sensitivity thresholds subconsciously and consciously," Liesbeth added. By now, most of them knew or presumed like him that Hans, Annelies' stepson and Liesbeth were far more awake.

Annelies returned each form they had filled in at the beginning of their decoding classes. She also passed on their twenty-two spacings chart, except that only the three lower chakra funnels of red, orange and yellow were in colour, being the first level of the game.

They were all studying the five sense organs with their colour vibrations when Annelies asked if each would place their five present awakening cards with numeral vibes into a round dish in the centre of the large table.

"Those five vibe cards are linked to your five senses. You will understand what I mean later." Annelies kept looking out the window as if she was waiting for someone, but then she took the centre dish away, and the eye symbol appeared. Only now did he recognise the park-like landscape printed on a thin, flat vinyl sheet. There were five ways to cross the water to reach the island in the centre. Then, Annelies replaced the bowl containing their five awakening cards with a large perspex pyramid that now covered the black pupil of the eye. He wondered if the card game was more of a board game.

At that moment, someone had arrived; Joris the Labrador made that very clear. Annelies seemed relieved as she left the room.

"What is ...Ben doing here?" Toon mentally remarked.

Ben walked in with lots of equipment. Between each couple, he placed a flat computer screen. Niels got up to help Annelies with a huge flat screen that fitted on a shelf against the wall. They were all surprised.

"Are we going to pay for a computer game?" Sascia asked

"Sort of, but with a difference. Bear with me; you are all guinea. Pigs," Annelies replied as she looked up at Ben and explained further.

"Two visionaries, Trevor and Leo, have developed a groundbreaking tool that engages with our mind, body and spirit. Your game is an "Inner-active" computer journey that integrates with state-of-the-art 3D graphics, video and music. With this big screen, which is linked to Annelies' computer in her office, and the smaller screens, Trevor and Leo, with help from other developers, have created software that interacts with Annelies' card game."

He was impressed by what an expense must have gone into this setup. *"Well worth the investment, I'm sure."* Sascia's telepathic reply to his thoughts earned her a wink from Liesbeth. Both she and Hans seemed the least surprised.

"Until now, biofeedback technology that interacted with each player had not been invented yet, or not that we know of, but both Trevor and Leo hope that their technology will not only interpret the interaction each player has unconsciously with the sub-tangible dimensions but that the responses will interpret your results."

Suddenly, when the giant screen lit up the room, the landscape scene vividly reminded him of the aerial drawing of a resort Ingrid had shown him long ago. That was it! Even the eye drawing was perceivable.

He noticed Ingrid and Toon glancing at each other.

"Now you know where I got my inspiration from at that meeting, Annie's platform! Look at the island, right in the centre where the pupil is." Toon beamed. Ingrid nodded her head in amusement.

All the screens in front of them came up with the same image. Wow, very impressive. Especially when he saw Sascia pointing at the winding road, and to the amazement of all, the image came alive!

When Annelies started to wave her hand near their screen, seven cottages appeared on the outskirts of the landscape. When he pointed to his small screen, the same landscape appeared, with many coloured footsteps heading past different signposts, such as plants, flowers, shrubs, or even trees. They all came into view as he touched the screen.

"Tell me, Snooks, what did you see first, this image or the designs to build a holiday resort which has given us so many hassles?" Richard couldn't wait to learn the meanings behind these footsteps while picking up on Ingrid's mental dialogue.

"Kitty, I seem to remember a setting that enchanted my mind, I just..." Annelies peered at Toon, waiting for more. They were all silent. Toon's frown revealed that he was somewhere else. Both Hans and Liesbeth nodded at each other.

"Toon, let the flashes come back. What you remember is no fantasy. We have them all the time." Hans beamed.

"Really? You mean, what I keep seeing as a mental vision is not just imagery?" Toon's disbelief reminded him of the flashes he had woken up with this morning.

"When do you know what is of value?" Toon asked out loud

"Toon, phantom visions have plagued many in our history. The philosopher Democritus purposely blinded himself to hold on to his visions. He studied under the Babylonian priests and even the Hindu Brahmans." Fred, Annelie's brother, replied when he came in with refreshments. He remembered that Fred was an expert on ancient lore and had a fascination for old books and scripts. He should tap into the man's mind for inspiration for his following lecture.

"By now, we all know that we create our reality when we wish for or intend something. On your small screen, the couple's auric field and the colours that stream from each chakra, those vibrations will reveal this incredible phenomenon to you all."

"You mean our mind over matter?"

"Yes, Gerrit, the game will prove it to you. Your decoding card numbers interact with the big screen. From those results, you will learn how numeral vibes regulate or influence your thoughts, emotional states, etc."

"But...we are born with most of those numeral vibrations. Do you mean they are a program in itself?" Sascia asked.

"You mean that the card game lets you know how you're doing on our smaller screen?" In response, Annelies changed the scenery on their smaller screen, showing them how to interact with each chakra on the big screen. Soon, everyone was deeply engaged in how their screen interacted.

The images and some of the buildings reminded him of a virtual reality computer game where players also encounter breathtaking scenery. It also incorporated mythology symbols and elements of the classic hero and heroine's journey.

"Gosh, Annelies, I'm so impressed." Ingrid, like the others, was mesmerized by the unusual layout of the park-like setting, which invited each player to find a pathway towards the centre island of the Landscape. When they were told how to fill in a form adding the individual numbers that they would see on their first-level grid sheets, he peered at Sascia's. She and Ed had been decoding their 22 spacings with Annelies during the two previous weeks.

"Now, as you can see on your screens, seven funnels are linked to our chakra points. On this first level, we are dealing with the three lower consciousness awareness centres." On the big screen, Annelies moved seven different geometric forms under each of the seven medium-sized pyramidal shapes among the creative scenery. This again triggered his uncanny visions from his last dream.

"Richard, did you perhaps link with Trevor's virtual reality game? In man, hyper-communication will mean that one suddenly gains access to information outside one's knowledge base. He is at this moment writing the software for it. We hope that soon people will be able to play the game in Cyberspace."Annelies mentally asked. He sensed the other's attention, waiting for his telepathic reply.

"I had a dream that felt like a glimpse into the future. In the dream, I was addicted to a virtual reality game that allowed me to receive knowledge from various fields. The information was verifiable, and I could recall it from the morning. It was like receiving a whole encyclopedia during the night.." His thoughts projected the imagery.

There was a moment of silence before Annelies carried on. She explained what Richard telepathically shared and added that being addicted was a warning.

"What I arranged on the screen are the seven major ascension temples. Each pyramid temple must be seen as a doorway, and each chakra holds the key to each temple. Each temple links you on all the multidimensional levels."

"Richard, Trevor is working on an idea that in cyberspace, we can create a new form of group consciousness, namely one in which we attain access to all information via our DNA without being forced or remotely controlled about what to do with that information. I saw some of his simulations that are very creatively displayed." Annelies telepathically replied. Whoever the artist was who created the digital imageries, this interactive card game was a work of art. Ed also asked in admiration who the artist was.

"Ed, it's a combined effort with Theo, Richard's brother, Leo, Trevor and me. The rest was done at Harry's design centre. I was somewhat alarmed at the A. I technology that might be able to interfere, but they were sure that was not possible. We are working on the etheric levels through this game. Tieneke has been a great help in creating the illustrations that Trevor scanned back into his computer."

"I never knew they could do this in their art department," Ingrid commented.

Annelies moved fifteen smaller pyramidal shapes around the big park with the help of a mouse. They then appeared on the various bridges, picnic spots or other reflected recreation places. Everyone was excited and fascinated at what they would learn about themselves. Was this game telling them that everything around them was just an image their minds had created, showing that even this digital simulation was part of an illusion?

"Richard, visionaries often catch a glimpse of a greater life. It's their mission to share with others what the future holds in preparation for the next evolutionary step. If humans regained a link to a loving group consciousness field again, they would have far more control over their god-like power to create, alter, and shape things on Earth! Many people are collectively moving toward such a group consciousness." Hans beamed

"There are now twenty-two ascension temples on the layout on the big screen. The fifteen smaller temples represent our rational mind-sets which connect with our brain's limbic lobes." Annelies explained further.

Gee, hearing Hans' revelation on group consciousness but having no clue about what lobes Annelies was talking about, how awake was he?

"Don't worry, Richard, you will know about it when we play on the second level." Annelies' telepathic reply settled his nerves. If she had such trust in him, why should he worry? Liesbeth winked. Her expression glowed with understanding.

"If this is only the first level, I wonder what the other levels have in store for us," Toon remarked.

"All the temples hold a question, quotation or message that is retrieved through the five geometric-shaped objects on the right of your small screen."

"Look. they represent our five senses."

"Toon, Trevor and Leo are still working on the second level of the game." he heard while each couple typed in their own five awakening card vibe numbers. Sascia showed him what to do when the decoding form appeared. She seemed to grasp the idea of interaction faster than he did.

"In one of the five senses at the bottom of your form, type in your other card number vibes and sit back, relax or stretch. During this virtual reality game, we can all walk around if needed, providing all attention is given to the person who's playing at that moment."

Annelies walked around while they were all filling in forms.

"We can all learn from each other. There are no win-or-lose situations. The game is not about competing. It's so created that players can become aware of their mental and emotional blockages within their energy field." Annelies checked if they were all ready to start.

"There is a pathway each must follow and complete before each player is ready for the next level." Annelies looked at Yolanda, who looked flushed.

"You tell them, love, you wanted to play it again." They were all waiting for Yolanda's reply. Ed playfully embraced her, which seemed to give her an opening to share why she wanted to play the first level again with the group.

"I did not finish the last game, and I was asked not to tell you all that these computer screens were part of the game either, but it seems that I have far more understanding of the dynamics behind it all this time. Expressing a good intention for others is as healing as doing it yourself. So, Annelies suggested that I do the game again. I now know very clearly why. My feelings of rejection and judgment I had against myself and my ex kept coming up. I never realised that I had been so hard on myself, either. That evening, just before Toon took Ingrid to France, I almost didn't turn up for the dinner Liesbeth and Hans had organised for Ingrid." Yolanda's brilliant blue eyes were flirting with Ed, who turned and glanced at Ingrid.

"*I always knew that dinner was a setup. Were you responsible for the family gathering or Toon?*"Ed beamed to Toon. Ingrid laughed in response to her brother-in-law.

When he heard the sound of a key in the front door, and Joris reacted like a bullet from a Winchester, he was glad of the break. After abundant greetings in the hallway, Ingrid's sister Quincy joined them. Quincy was dazzled by the spectacular scenery on the wall. Fred introduced her to Niels and Gerrit, who had been very quiet during the evening. Both Fred and Quincy had been invited to watch the game as observers. He'd heard from Sascia how they'd met each other just before her mother's wedding.

"I need to review the game rules with you all again, so I'll use my first level sheet as an example." Annelies arranged her setup while talking.

"The recycling bins on the bottom left of your screen are there to release or remove programmed addictive ego-files that are of no use. The footsteps on the big screen represent our thoughts that lead to our manifestations. You are all familiar with the Universal Language of Light symbols, reinstating your connection to the God/Goddess within. As I said, the small temples hold our 'software programming,' as Trevor calls it."

"Our computer language does reflect how our brain works. Very creative of him." Hans added.

"Yes, I can see that his influence is greatly felt throughout the game," Toon remarked with glee. Liesbeth got up to change the music, which was playing softly in the background.

"As you can see, on each form on your screen, there is a button next to the five senses illustrations. That's where you click on, and the same Language of Light symbol will appear, showing you which soul quality you have already earned during this lifetime."

He started to get the hang of the rules of the game.

"But this button will also flicker to tell you where we can lose or give them away." Richard knew there had to be a win, some, and some loss of interaction. He noticed that only the first ten Language of Light symbols were used. Annelies must have read his mind.

"The first ten Language of Light qualities are the most powerful tonal vibes, especially on this first level. Each player must earn at least three different symbols. Those symbols are the most helpful in your awakening. You all keep those vibes throughout the game. You probably already know your soul's purpose if they have the same numeral vibe as any of your first three soul numeral vibrations on your decoding sheet. I mean, through what medium you can best serve."

Annelies was reading her ascension manual when Quincy got up and whispered something in her ear. Annelies nodded and glanced at everyone while Quincy disappeared from the room.

"Each player will take a turn. Annelies selected a cottage with a red roof. She then clicked on her Tetrahedron-shaped red symbol from the left of her screen, which showed the number four. She then moved it with the help of her mouse on a pathway towards a bridge on the big screen. They all followed what she did on the screen on the wall.

"Is there a reason you have chosen both the red symbol and a red-roofed cottage?" Ingrid asked.

"Oh, yes, each geometric shape belongs to one of the seven cottages, remember? The colour Red links to our Base chakra on your screens. Now study your Language of Light cards; see they all have an extra symbol in the corner." Annelies held up the second Language of Light quality card with a star in the corner.

"I wondered why these symbols appeared on our Language of Light cards," Sascia commented.

"The orange geometric shape represents our kundalini life force or sexual energy."

"The yellow geometric shape reflects our creative inner willpower internally and externally." She showed a Language of Light card with a question mark in the corner.

"Gosh, you all must have had fun creating this computer game!" Ed remarked as he took a spare ascension manual from the side table.

"Yes, it has been most rewarding for us all, and it still is. When you are inspired by some extraordinary project, dormant forces, faculties, and talents come alive. We are still working on it. Remember, you are all guinea pigs, including me."

"What do you mean? Have you not played all the levels?"

"Sascia, no one has as of yet. Because each move shows a mirror reflection of the state of our mind at this moment, we all learned how we often create our distortions. I have played two levels, and we will start on the third level soon. But...we have all been dragged back due to the recent dramas. All of us, excluding Theo, fell back in vibration." Everyone was silent for a moment. It was so easy to get trapped in illusionary dramas that seemed so real. He was somewhat surprised to hear her mentioning Theo.

"Richard, Theo had to keep realising that this game was also part of his illusion. This simulator platform on your screen is just a tool to break free from the thought-created realm in which we are all trapped. Whenever many people focus their attention or consciousness on something similar, like having the intent to ascend, Theo believed that an ordered group consciousness can affect others outside the group consciousness!" Annelies beamed.

Annelies had chosen red, the first addiction level that he knew dealt with fear, issues of survival or security, as well as being the foundation level of their emotional and mental health. He had done his homework using Tieneke's Base Chakra journal in between his chores, or it was more the discussions he had with Sascia till late. Women seem to know these things by instinct.

"I use any opportunity to be shown an addictive thought pattern I might still hold on to. It will be embedded in my auric field. So I chose to work with my base chakra vibe." Annelies landed in front of a flower bed. Yolanda got up, took the flower card dish from the side table, and passed it on to her. Annelies took one card.

"The elemental kingdom reflects the base chakra in the flower's stem. Like them, be grounded at all times. Be in your body." She read out loud. To him, she was the most grounded person around.

"That was quite a good example. I have been very...up in the clouds lately." Annelies grinned.

"Oh, tell us, why?" Fred asked as he got up to massage her shoulders.

"Oh, when Ben phoned last night, firstly to let me know that he would deliver your screens in time, but he also shared that he's been researching on a personal matter." Fred lifted his eyebrow as he glanced at Toon, who reacted similarly.

"Annie, what are you two up to?" Toon beamed. Annelies took a deep breath as she moved her mouse, ignoring Toon's query.

This time she arrived at a small temple near a recycling bin with a question mark. A dragon symbol appeared when she moved her mouse over it. Very neat.

Fred passed her the dish from the side table with dragons on them. Annelies took one card and turned it to read the wording. She was silent for a moment while they all waited.

"**Universal Law is what it is; it does not always align with man's desires.**" Annelies heaved a sigh as she placed the card back in the dish. He wondered what she was hiding. He picked up feelings of sadness, but there seemed to be a mental screen. Fred gave her a hug and winked at Toon.

"Annie, give it up. Remember, when you let it go, your reward will be well worth it." Annelies moved her mouse again, ignoring Toon's advice. He wondered what she had to give up.

"Now I have landed on a spot without information, so the next player joins the game. We will always go clockwise." Annelies explained.

Quincy came in with a tray of goodies. Drinks and snacks were always in abundance at Annelie's house. He sensed that she was upset about something. Liesbeth sat next to her, and she took her blue geometric symbol with the number sixteen. Richard knew the others had avoided Toon and Annelies' mental interaction.

Liesbeth started from a blue-roofed shack near the water. Richard looked it up in his ascension manual, and it was called the Icosahedron shape, which was associated with taste. Liesbeth moved her mouse past a rowing boat that held a recycling bin, but her sixteen steps moved her towards the bridge. She landed right inside a small pyramid on the opposite embankment.

"Now, as you all see, when I move my mouse over the pyramid, a green flowerpot with roses appears."

Yolanda handed the bowl with green cards with roses on them from the side table. Liesbeth took a green sense card." Liesbeth's eyes shot up. Everyone was in suspense.

"**Take a deep breath; your heart chakra will trigger any addictive fear-based thought forms within your lower base chakra. Take a red addiction token for processing later.**"

Yolanda passed the bowl that said; red addiction tokens. Her card read, "**Don't deny others their hurt feelings.**"Richard spotted the identical icons on his screen. There were seven icons on both sides. When he highlighted them, names like security, sensation, power, love, oneness, awareness and cosmic bliss files popped up. On both bottom corners of the small screen, the two recycling bin icons must be there to eliminate any programming if you got the opportunity, he suspected. How neat.

"*Practice that you are pure consciousness, Richard. Opportunities are there all the time.*" Hans beamed from across the table. That might be easy for him to say, but he felt sluggish. Also, he doesn't want to lose his identity.

"Annelies, surely don't we all want to take painful feelings away from a loved one?" Ingrid questioned Liesbeth's addiction token.

"Mmm, Liesbeth, what do you feel? Can you relate what it reflects to you?"

"Well, I have to think of a situation where I have this urge to save someone from emotional pain...I can think of many." Liesbeth looked at Hans, who nodded.

"We knew that Ingrid was physically safe when kidnapped, but her soul's need urged her to experience the energy from a higher level. I had great difficulty keeping this knowledge from Toon because of his fear for Ingrid." Liesbeth turned to Toon beaming:

"*Toon, my fear came up when reminded that if a dark force were to use its mental power over a unified civilization, it would have control of the energies of its home planet as a natural consequence. And that includes all-natural catastrophes!*"

"Thinking back, I did not trust everything happening for the good of all. Meaning I still have a control issue." While everybody was waiting for Ingrid to say something, he was sure he heard Liesbeth's mental confession.

"You mean when you told me that you felt Ingrid would be alright, you used your power to control me?" Toon asked.

"Well, I did, didn't I?"

"You took away some of the fear, that's true. I trusted you to know, so... instead, I started to order everybody around me. You gave me enough energy to retake charge; what's wrong with that?"

"So what or how did I help you?" Toon was frowning.

"I'm very good at escaping pain; I just take control. I need to be in control to feel I'm in control, something like that?" Richard could relate to both of them. What's so bad about making someone feel they are in control?

"*No, it is not, so long as you don't take away someone's inner ability to deal with the fear themselves.*" Annelies projected. Richard started to recognise that their telepathic undercurrent dialogue, which happened on a subconscious level, reflected a mental mirror. Inner thoughts seem to run sideways with the spoken word.

"I know what you are all thinking, but remember, during our awakening, it is of paramount importance that we are at all times aware of our programming and addictions, even as understandable as this one. Remember, Liesbeth's rational mind created the illusion that Toon's fears were real!"Annelies reminded them. Ingrid listened attentively, Ed frowning, and Toon munched away at a snack while nodding.

"Where does compassion fall under? Did Liesbeth not show compassion?" Ingrid asked.

"Oh yes, she did. I have and still am very guilty of the same projection. Because we are more aware and sensitive than most, we must control others with kindness. It's unconscious, I'm sure." Richard was still confused, but he let it go. He hoped he would grasp the more profound meaning later.

Annelies took over the role of facilitator and told Yolanda to sit down. She would supervise the game. Hans joined them on the big screen, and Ed, Ingrid, and Toon followed. When Sascia chose the orange star symbol, Annelies held out the bowl. They all laughed at her cottage. It was a double-story Wild West bar. Sascia moved her mouse in six places and landed her in front of a bush with bees. She dipped into the bee bowl and read out loud: **My assignment is to be industrious while helping nature cross-pollinate. What is yours?** Annelies looked at Sascia, who shook her shoulders. They were all waiting to see what would come up. Nobody spoke. The scene on the big screen created an illusion that they were the actors on a stage. At the same time, the human form encapsulated in layers of colours on each small screen showed how, through vibrational colourings, they interacted with the big screen.

"Care to share what thoughts or feelings this message triggered?" Annelies asked. Sascia sat staring, and a grin appeared.

"Pregnancy! Wow, that makes me feel insecure...my freedom is gone, how do I earn enough money when...gee, where did that all come from?" Her hands covered her mouth. Richard was so startled at her reaction. He still knew nothing about what went on in her mind.

"Is that a block in her security centre's base chakra?" Ingrid asked. Annelies looked at both their smaller screens. Nobody said a word, and we all waited for Sascia to reply. Sascia was pondering. The two male and female images on their screen showed how a wave of brilliant shooting colours interacted between them. He peered at her small screen in anticipation.

"Why would I feel that way, and how do I get rid of that feeling?" Sascia's apprehensive response triggered similar feelings in him, but why? And how clever that the screen seems to interact with feelings! Annelies pointed out that the orange footprints on the large screen connected to the two life cards. It could reveal a program that says pregnancy means poverty.

"You mean a memory from a past or parallel life has surfaced?" Richard asked because he could not get the dream out of his head where Sascia, his beloved, had died in childbirth. Only now had the dream popped up! He remembered dreaming it long ago before he even knew Sascia! In that life, her pregnancy only brought sorrow.

"Yes, most probably both your feelings stem from another incarnation. That is why bringing back soul intuitively memories is so important."

"Richard, please share your dream with her" Annelies had read his mind!

"In one of my dreams I...Sascia died giving birth."

"Really? You never told me." Sascia joined in.

"Well, I only now remembered the dream. I was despondent and...I remember that I ended up as a beggar." He wondered if some of the others mentally heard them because he only heard his inner voice.

"Feelings of emotions often create mental veils to stop other thoughts from entering." Liesbeth beamed.

"Can anxieties be programmed in our DNA, from our parents, going back to our forefathers?" Ingrid asked while she quoted; 'The sins of our father'...They all knew the scripture passage. It suddenly dawned on him how mentally polluted they all were on the subtle levels.

"Ingrid, all superconductors can store light and thus information; that is how the membrane of each biological cell that makes up the human body stores information," Hans mentally replied.

"Sascia, just let the feeling be there for a while. By the end of the game, you could well have an answer and be able to release this thought form for good." Annelies winked, nodding for him to take his turn. He was glad the music in the background kept him focused on the big screen. He decided to choose the same orange symbol to start with. As he dipped into the orange bowl, the card with the number 8 showed him how many footstep moves he could take with the mouse that placed him near the same Wild West saloon. No message! Toon made an ambiguous comment, and Ingrid gave him a poke. He ended two footsteps from a small temple with a spewing dragon inside. Toon said in a loud voice that it triggered many visions in him. He asked if that counted.

"We will all see when it is your turn." Ed chuckled as he urged Yolanda to take the mouse. He would have to wait for his next turn to find out what the dragon had in store for him. By this time, they all were present at various places on the big screen, either on the outskirts, on the water, on one of the bridges, or on the middle island. No one had yet landed in one of the prominent ascension temples. It became pretty interesting when the interaction between them started.

When his turn came again, he moved past the small dragon temple and towards a yellow recycling bin with an ear symbol.

The game told him to stop. Annelies held out the yellow bowl with the ear symbol cards. Toon sighed in disappointment. He selected a yellow release card that said; **Any feelings that stem from co-dependant or sensation addictions must be released.** When the card directed him to change to the yellow pathway while keeping his release card in front of him, Richard already knew why it was that message. He moved and crossed Sascia's orange path. Annelies explained that they must now all observe and learn. Both he and Sascia peered at their screen, and their sacral chakras were spinning like mad. They giggled, thinking the same thing.

"If players land on a crossing of footprints, that means that both players have come together to work out karma, or they have a soul agreement, or the synchronicity is a sign of being aware. Richard, you are both in a transition spot, meaning you must wait for your next turn."

Richard was mulling over his release token. It said he had to let go of feelings kept alive by control issues. His feelings when Ingrid asked Sascia when she would be going to France again made him realise his addiction! In his dreams, she was taken from him twice. Was his addiction the need to hold her with him? Sascia winked.

"Mine are the same; that must be our karma we have to work on; what do you think?" He was astonished. That was it! They needed to grow interdependent. Only then could they indeed be soul partners?

"You are so right, love, but there is so much I want to share with you." They were distracted by Yolanda's call of triumph. Yolanda earned herself a Language of Light card when she was the first to land in one of the prominent temples. The yin and yang symbol on the card dealt with relationship issues. Annelies asked how many footsteps she had to move because the card

said relationships. On the side table, she grabbed her ascension manual. From the section with the same symbol under the number 8, she read out loud;

"**Everything you have ever experienced has led to your being who you are now. You have earned a Language of Light vibration of Divine Union by releasing your search for happiness through relationships. You may eject any release card if you have any in your sensation temp file. If you don't have any, another player is holding on to your karma.**"

"*Take it back, dear.*" Annelies beamed. Yolanda looked puzzled.

Annelies peered at Yolanda and walked behind everyone to look at their screens. He then saw that Ed had two release tokens. Yolanda's expression changed to amusement as her lips parted. She looked into Ed's eyes. Then he clicked.

"*I knew it; I never needed to do anything creative to escape boredom; it's your karma!*" Ed beamed his revelation at Yolanda. Both Quincy and Fred, as clairvoyant observers, must have picked up something in their energy field because of their laughter. Yolanda was as pleased as punch.

"*My love, with pleasure. With you, I will never be bored; I will release that addiction token in the next round, you'll see.*" she mentally replied when Ed gave her the tokens that belonged to her.

Toon poured everyone a drink after Ingrid scored a Language of Light card. She shared her experience with everyone when, in her deepest despair, cold, kidnapped and lonely in that basement, POWAH's text brought her back to her senses. She experienced what being in the moment was all about. What was so amazing was that the feelings that went along in that moment were of monumental peace. Liesbeth and Hans both agreed.

"At that moment, you operated from your fifth chakra level of consciousness. You realised that you had nothing to be afraid of." Annelies reminded her. Ingrid gaped in surprise and pointed at their small screen.

"It was a miracle, but the feeling didn't last long. Soon afterwards, I fell back into my security illusion level again. I can see that now." All could see that Ingrid was re-experiencing her ordeal again. Toon was about to smother her with his love, but he held back.

"Annie, I can so relate to her; I feel what she feels. I see what her mental eye sees, I hear her thoughts, can't I share?" His expression said plenty. "You know, I wish it were as easy to release hating as when it started," he added with sadness.

" Snooks, the fact that you care is enough."

"She's right; your loving energy pulls her out of her three lower consciousness levels. You don't have to do anything." Annelies said, smiling.

"Men, in general, have great difficulty withholding from fixing things, don't they?' Ingrid remarked with humour.

Liesbeth gaily pushed Hans, and he agreed; rescuing a damsel in distress was a typical trademark of the male human species. When Toon gained a release token that said that abundance is a natural state, they all laughed, agreeing that must surely be someone else's karma. When it was his turn, the yellow footsteps on the big screen stopped him.

A yellow Octahedron shape associated with air directed him to his first large ascension temple after Sascia. Again, they shared. Hers had been all about the art of listening. She had earned a Language of Light card because she had learned to let go of her idea of how to make money. Annelies was reading his explanation from her ascension booklet. **"You have learned to go beyond the limit of this dimension ordinarily imposed by form. It will change the way you relate to life."** Sascia was all ears.

"Annelies, is that a referral to his out-of-body-travel abilities?"

"Absolutely! Not so much travelling, we all do that. It's in the remembering of the visions where his skill lies." Annelies looked around and them all. "We all must aim to remember any dreams when we wake up. Write them down so we can read over them later".Richard knew Annelies had always given him full credit for what he had told her; why could he not give that to himself? There was still always a doubt as to the reality of his memories.

They played the computer game with their cards for nearly three hours. It was the most awakening game Richard had ever participated in. He learned a lot from the others, and in Sascia, he found a soulmate, playmate, teammate, and now an ascension travelling partner. He fully expected that they would have their moments, but at least they were both willing to observe their addictive programmed patterns.

Next week, they will start on the second level workshops, making the two hemisphere and personality cards. Annelies reminded them all to come early to scan their palm prints. She explained that their palm print could be used as a DNA map, like the human aura image on this game level. She would explain what that meant.

Ed, Ingrid's brother-in-law, had decided to stay in Holland until the end of the year. His father needed him in the steel business. He would move in with Yolanda, and she planned to join him when he went on business trips. Sascia arranged to join Toon on the fourteenth when he planned to fly to see Peter and Helen. Both Ingrid and Toon wanted to look at the progress of Buttercup Valley while she shot photos at Halfway House and helped Tieneke facilitate a Language of Light workshop. He could not join them again because of his preparation for his coming lecture and the Pannekoek.

Annelies' ascension - workshop classes

Pulling up to Annelie's driveway, they noticed Toon's BMW parked at an odd angle, making the driveway packed.

"Look at that, what a way to park!" He could squeeze his Honda next to the BMW halfway into the hedge. He'd have to get out from Sascia's side.

"I guess Jeroen has parked it." Sascia tickled his ribs.

"Moppie, watch out."

"Are you threatening me?"

"Big time," he whispered as he slid his hand inside her thigh.

"That's very... intimate!" A loud hoot broke the spell. Connie's yellow beetle parked them all in as they exited the car.

"Can I park here?"

"Hi, sure, why not? We will all leave at the same time, I'm sure."

"Is Jeroen here?" Connie's eyes lit up when she recognised Toon's car.

"You see, Jeroen drove the BMW."... Sascia was about to defend her brother's parking skills when the front door opened. Joris' usual welcome suddenly changed into a loud bark. It was so unexpected; they all looked around to see what Joris saw, but they didn't. Toon followed Joris as they stepped into the hallway.

"Who are you barking at, boy?" Toon kneeled to peer under the Jeep to see what seemed to grip Joris' attention. The deep, low growl alarmed them all. Joris was about to take a sprint at a figure that suddenly ran from behind the Jeep and jumped over the hedge when Toon grabbed his collar.

"Ts...okay boy...good boy..." Joris' whole body was trembling from the adrenaline rush that had taken control of him.

"What ...did you see who that was?" He asked. It happened so fast that the figure was nowhere to be seen.

"Do we inform the police?" Connie shivered.

"Go inside, all of you. I will get someone to inspect the neighbourhood. Let's not alarm the others." Toon's frown told him that he had taken the incident seriously. Ever since the tablets started to arrive, he has become increasingly aware of the separation between different worlds.

"I know just what you mean." Toon beamed.

Class 1

On the door, in big letters, was written;
THE TWO MAPS REVEAL OUR SOUL CONTRACT.

As they entered Annelies' workroom, Toon closed the door. He understood why Sascia was so impressed with a man with a vision. Toon's dedication to his community projects was remarkable. How fortunate that a man like him existed to invest in people who weren't scared to follow his soul's passion no matter how controversial. Toon never showed off how wealthy he was. The plane gave it away, and he seemed to own a lot of real estate, but otherwise, he lived with Ingrid in a very modest house.

He felt different this time when he arrived to participate in Annelies' workshop. He remembered how sceptical he had been on the first introduction evening.

"You were, weren't you!" Annelies beamed with glee.

"You knew?"

"Sure, most people would be too, if they weren't exposed to inexplicable phenomena. So wipe that look off your face." Annelies trip to France must have done her good. She had a nice golden tan.

"Come, let's join the others. We were waiting for the two of you to arrive".

Everyone was there: Ed and Yolanda, Ingrid and Toon, Niels, Zola, Gerrit, Liesbeth and Hans. He wanted to ask where Wim was, but he held back. They all sat around the large oval conferencence table. Two places were kept open for them. Jeroen and Connie said their goodbyes. Jeroen had waited for Connie. They were going to see a late movie after helping Fred and Quincy with a function at the hotel. The small screens were gone, and so was the big screen.

"Jeroen, please stay alert..."

"Mom, we are fine. Relax. Stop worrying. Have fun with the others. We are joining Annelies' first decoding group next week." Toon whispered something to Jeroen when he walked them back to Connie's old Beetle.

"What was all that about outside, Richard?" Ingrid beamed. They all waited for him to speak up. At least whoever heard Ingrid's mental question.

"Joris must have seen a cat. He went quite berserk as we arrived." Sascia mentally replied, shrugging her shoulders.

"Well, Richard, congratulations, Sascia has awakened her telepathic skills," Ed grinned like a Cheshire cat.

Sascia had met Niels, Gerrit and Zola at her mother's wedding. Zola ignored him. He was not sure how to handle Zola. Sure, he took her out a few times in April when she was fighting with Wim, but that was all. She was not his type.

"Richard, what happened between you and Zola? Has she come on to you?"

With relief, he saw that Sascia was too involved in talking to Yolanda to pick up Annelie's telepathic question.

"I'll tell you later". Niels was taking all their palm prints with a scanner he had brought with him from his computer shop. Toon said that Niels had upgraded most of Annelies' electronic hardware through their alternative monetary system they named the Talent Exchange Program.

Annelies asked them to bring their five awakening cards from the previous workshop, including the Language of Light cards they had made with Tieneke. The mood relaxed after everyone had their left and right palm print in front of them. The Language of Light symbols on the walls strongly reminded Tieneke. On the table, large cards showed all different types of shaped hands. He could already see which shape hand he didn't have.

"As you all know, the two cards with your palm prints are used in the second level of the ascension game, along with your personality card. When I was sort of instructed to study palmistry, I never thought that so much could be revealed in the palms of our hands." Annelies showed them some cards that had already been reduced to the size used in the game. A few Language of Light symbols appeared within the hand palm. He wondered who they belonged to.

"*Theo's. We've worked it out together remember?*"

"*Really!*" He took a closer look at the sample card.

"Annelies are we doing the left-hand tonight?" Zola asked. Annelies replied that they would first establish what type of hand and fingers they had. She showed them how to measure their palms and fingers. Very soon everyone was busy. They all laughed at how Toon decided if he had an earth or fire hand.

"Remember that the four classes do not make you a palm reader."

"*Oh, what a shame. I was already contemplating learning an extra skill I could add to my offering list.*" They laughed at Toon's mental suggestion. He must investigate Toon's currency idea more. Sascia had mentioned it to him several times.

"All of you will learn enough about palm reading to recognise how your habitual patterns have become part of your outlook on life. Especially if they are held over a long period."

By now, they all had grasped how to establish what type of hand they had. He had a water hand. Sascia had an Air hand.

Both Toon and Ingrid had fire hands. Annelies found that very amusing. He hoped he would learn why.

"Our hands, like our feet, are the endpoints of our physical body that receive the impulses from our brain. They are translated and registered as lines and markings in our hands, like the star, a cross, squares and triangles or a grid" They were all peering at their palm prints.

"Annelies, the markings, do they connect with the symbols we have used in our mind-drawings?"

"Sascia that's quick of you to make that connection. We will get to that later. After we have linked the five elemental cards with the shape of our hands and further divided the type of hand with the seven chakras, things will start to fall into place. I'm getting ahead of myself. Let's first establish whether we have a square or a rectangular hand. The way I told you to measure will tell you which."

Annelies showed them how to determine if their hands were small or large in proportion to their body. Gerrit told them that handwriting analysts often found that small-handed people had large handwriting.

Toon's prominent name on his sheet made them look at his hands. They all noticed that his hands were bigger than theirs, but then his body was large. Niels had big hands too. Gosh, and his name was written in a small, neat corner of his page.

"I'm left-handed. Is there a difference when we read palms?" Ed asked.

"All of you follow me, interweave your fingers and thumbs. Ed, which thumb is on top?"

"My right thumb."

"That means that your right hand is your ruling hand when we analyse your way of thinking." Annelies walked behind them when she talked.

"In most people, the left hemisphere is the more personality-based centre. That is the most dominant when perceptions are formed." He peered at Sascia's hand compared to Ingrid's to see if he could see by the lines what Annelies explained.

"In all of us who are right-handed, if the left thumb is on top, the left palm print reflects what we have chosen to be to express ourselves. Ed's thinking modes are reversed. His left thumb is also on top, so he reads his left palm the same." It was fun to be relaxed and play, while learning something he would never have given any attention to. Zola kept asking lots of questions while the rest of them just followed Annelie's self-explanatory charts.

"Zola, by dominant, we mean the hand you write with. The word ruling means which thinking mode is the strongest when we make our choices in life."

"Gosh don't we make things complicated. Why not call it our writing hand instead of our dominant hand," irritably remarked.

"I'll suggest it to Tieneke to explain the difference in the ruling thinking mode, which in most of us is accessed through the hand we don't use for drawing, our non-dominant hand," Annelies replied.

"Am I the only one that is different?" Zola asked again. Her voice and body language told him that she seemed to think it was less worthy.

"*Very observant Richard, take that into consideration, will you*," Annelies responded to his thoughts.

"No, Zola, my left objective hemisphere also rules my thinking. Let's not let our beliefs get in the way. It has much more to it than just those two categories."

"Hans is right. Throughout this workshop, we aim to understand how the genetic map on our grid is encoded.

Whatever we have accomplished or desired to do can be found in our writing hand, which seems to deal more with our conscious mind.

"I see, and this hand is the most influenced by our personality type, right?" Yolanda asked.

"Yes, the readings from our other, more passive hand can tell us more about our genetic inherited traits. I've been to several palm readers, and each has a unique approach to describing my character from an angle I had never seen before. " They were all studying the charts that helped them get to grips with what Annelies tried to teach them.

"Annelies, do the lines in your hands change at all?"

"Yes, Ingrid, they do. Lines and markings change over time. They can reflect a new attitude in life. Or our health can influence palm patterns or... Our heart line, representing our emotional attitudes, can change over the years." Toon found this very intriguing and was sorry that he didn't have their palm print from ten years ago.

"That's ticklish!" Ingrid cried when Toon traced her lines.

"Shock can reflect in the hand... or lots of grief," Annelies added.

"Is everything written already in our palms?" Zola asked. They were all somewhat surprised. Hadn't Annelies already explained that lines change?

"She needs to talk for the sake of being heard. It will show in the reading. Observe the length of her fingers.." He peeped at Sascia to see if she had heard Annelies.

"Annelies why... is Zola jealous?"... It was the first time that Sascia used her telepathic skills on someone else. He could feel the difference! It was so very...mental.

"Ask Richard." Sascia glanced at him.

"Let's go back to our decoding after our coffee break" Annelies suggested. Sascia grabbed her papers together and completely ignored him during the coffee break. Her body language was all cool and hurt. He tried to stay away from Zola – who seemed to have skin like an elephant. She kept hanging around him. He was as cool as he could be without being rude.

Gerrit asked about his lectures, for which he was grateful because Zola finally drifted away. From the corner of his eye, he saw Annelies talking to Sascia. He tried to pick up what they were discussing, but Gerrit was talking and couldn't hold two conversations simultaneously. Women!

When they were all returning to their seats, Sascia asked him to swap places. Before he knew it, she sat in between them, which was fine with him.

"I heard your boyfriend Wim is interested in Richard's lectures!" Sascia asked Zola, who didn't respond. He was surprised that Sascia asked. He'd told her that Wim was in the audience at his last talk but that he was gone before he could say anything to him.

"Theo, Richard's brother and a dear friend of mine, discovered that palmistry originated in India, not Egypt, and corresponded to the seven different planetary hands and planets that rule the zodiac. We have translated the seven planets into the seven chakras. After establishing which elemental energy your hand reflects, look at the seven-shaped hands on the table."

"What happens if you swing from one shape to the other." Liesbeth could not decide if she had a fire or a water hand. Hans had an air hand. Annelies had a look and said that Liesbeth should take the ether element. It reflected balance. Annelies showed them how to choose the three different finger settings. He was amused that there was so much in the structure alone.

He never gave much credit to the palmistry, but he became increasingly fascinated.

Sascia seemed to have overcome her sudden coolness towards him. He'd better tell her that he had taken Zola to the movies a few times.

"You'd better!" She shot back at him

"Richard, watch out for these firewomen." Sascia tried to give Toon a fierce look. She had overheard his mental contribution.

Annelies took them through the mounts within their hands, and he was astounded by how much more information came up.

"Let's do the four major hereditary lines before we finish for the evening. They are formed in the first sixteen weeks after conception. They reflect the genetics that our soul has chosen to incarnate in. They are the life, head, heart and fate line."

They were asked to colour them with four different colours on their two palm print copies so that they would stand out.

"Is a long lifeline an indicator of longevity?" Zola asked.

"No. However, it can reveal the quality of your life but not the length of it."

"Mine is broken." Yolanda cried out.

"So what. Remember the life line is not a dead line" He realised that although he was never involved in palmistry, some beliefs had also crept into his subconscious.

"Annelies, can I share my idea about who and what we are regarding a program with you and the group? I'll keep it short." Gerrit asked. They wondered how to keep that topic short, but Gerrit was well-liked.

"I'm all ears."

"Okay, here goes. When we go on the internet, we look at cyberspace. From our screens, we can travel to any place in cyberspace. The quality of our equipment and online connection determines our lifeline into cyberspace." Gerrit let that sink in. They were all attentively listening.

"Let's say that Cyberspace is the universe of all that is. Or like an energy field with full creative potential to create anything. There is nothing outside of cyberspace. We search throughout cyberspace, and when we come to a site that interests us, we move into someone else's website." Annelies was busy scribbling what Gerrit was expressing."What would you compare someone's website with? A solar system? We know that in that website we will find, or hope to find, information we might want to download into our computer." he carried on.

Toon joined Annelies in the drawing. Gerrit watched to see if he still had their attention. Hans and Liesbeth were smiling, and Ed looked thoughtful. Zola held an expression of indifference, whereas Ingrid and Toon were all ears.

"What does our computer stand for?" Sascia asked.

"Our auric field, the body of our soul," Gerrit replied.

"What, that sounds too...sacrilegious!" Yolanda commented. He tried to grasp what Gerrit was leading up to.

"Try not to translate my contemplations; it's just a way of observing our reality from a different angle."

"Okay, I'm sorry, go on"...Yolanda apologized.

"Our auric field carries all the information from our solar system and more, but it is restricted by the channel it uses to download information."

"Why?" Niels asked.

"It's fragmented. Our soul's energy field only uses a section of its magnificent power and can only enter our reality through our etheric body."

"You've lost me. Can you please return to...our computer". Ingrid asked. Annelies patiently waited for Gerrit to carry on while observing everyone. He wondered what she was seeing.

"Aha..... it depends on the quality of the life force that establishes a link into cyberspace," Niels confirmed.

"Yes. This life force is the spirit. There is nothing wrong with the essence of the spirit, there can't be, it's part of all that is. Part of the field that holds our full potential, but let's say that"....

"Don't lose yourself, go back to your original thought. You were on the right track." Hans suggested. Gerrit closed his eyes for a moment, gathering his thoughts.

"We download the information we want from cyberspace, and it is now on our PC's hard drive because we have stored it in a folder. Our hard drive is our unconscious mind." Gerrit paused..."If we have the right program, we can open the information we have just downloaded and see it now on our screen." Annelies carried on doodling, and so did Toon. Both drawings were completely different, but he could read them both.

"Say we decided to print out the information, it becomes a hard copy."

"The information becomes physical!" Sascia replied.

"Yes, or, say we change the information and then print it out, we have a different version in hard copy."

"Aha, but...we can't ever change the hard copy... it will get used...become old and get thrown away!" Zola added. He was surprised. She mentally stayed with them. Gerrit smiled.

"You are right, but remember that we can repeat many prints so long as the spirit is active." Gerrit waited for anyone to respond.

"Gerrit is right. We can change anything by our thoughts and actions. Then, our cellular molecular DNA can be re-programmed with different information. Our physical bodies are always changing on a cellular level." Annelies looked in awe.

There were so many elements that came to his mind, he tried to stay with the surface idea.

"Gerrit, where do you put the operator of the computer in your theory?" He asked. Gerrit had taken his glasses off and stretched. He smiled.

"Thank you. I see the operator as the creator god in the making."

"So the creator god, meaning us, who is now looking for a way to go back to the source, must first awaken and reprogram all our energy bodies with the body codes with flawless information so that it can change into a hard copy... so it can evaporate itself?" They all laughed at his analysis.

"I can see it already. I've just added the information from cyberspace to my database. After restoring the last missing link, our project has all the necessary information. It's so marvellous...instead of printing it out...me the operator...is staring into the screen...the feelings, when you have this 'aha' moment, is spreading into and through my genetic database"....Niels' eyes went all glassy. They were all silently watching someone having an inspiration.

"*Mom, can you see how his auric field is shimmering from ecstasy!*" Hans beamed. Gosh, he now wished he could see. They were all watching Niels. Suddenly, the first sentence from the 12th tablet started to get more precise. *Behind every physical form is an elemental spirit in action—they project a form into being to express the divine as a fraction.* Annelies' facial expression told him that she had picked up his thoughts.

"I'm still not getting it." Zola broke the spell.

"Gerrit thanks for your wonderful insight." I'm sure many of us are enriched by it, if not somewhat confused. But that is also good. Now and again we have to step out of ourselves to look back at our own illusion. Next week we will look at our main hand-lines and markings in order to make our two-hemisphere cards. During the week please download the information from our website that goes into your booklet."

They all responded in hysterics at the synchronicity when she mentioned the word downloading. Nobody had responded to Zola.

Annelies asked if everyone would bring their geniogram information on their family tree again the following week. She added that in connection with the Star-map, she would share that with the class in the sixth session. For the next hour, they all looked at and learned about the map of lines in their hands. What a revelation....

On the way home, they were both savouring the evening. It was already past eleven. There was a slight breeze coming in through the open windows. There was hardly any traffic on the road.

"Rich, I'm sorry for reacting to Zola's behaviour."

"What made you change"

"Annelies."

"Oh... are you going to tell me why?"

"No, it's women's stuff, except that she made me look at myself."

"Okay, I'm sorry too for not telling you I'd taken her out a few times."

The fact that they went home together still thrilled him to bits. It didn't matter to him that Sascia might have to deal with the feelings of jealousy Zola had triggered in her.

He saw that her eyes lit up when he was about to plant a kiss on her nose.

"You read my mind. That is what Annelies pointed out, my jealousy! How did you?"....

"I didn't, but I heard your telepathic question loud and clear when you asked Annelies why Zola made you jealous."

"You did? You mean I did...I asked myself where these feelings came from as I looked at Annelies. You mean I used telepathy, too?"

"You didn't know? It was all over the room. Your mom, Toon, Hans, Liesbeth, Ed, Yolanda, Annelies, and I all heard you." Sascia blushed.

"Really?"

"Yep, now you know that your thoughts are no secret anymore. At least some of them are not. I'm still learning to tell the difference."

"Rich, I'm sad you will not join us tomorrow."

"I know, so am I. If it were not for my lecture, I'd make a plan, but I know I will join you one day. Especially when Aunty Mien is back."

"But that is only next month!"

"I know, but my lectures are important. I hope to get a permanent post to get an income when the Pannekoek falls away." Ginger greeted them with a long miaow when they opened his front door. Sascia had fed him just before they left. She picked him up and walked through to their office.

"Pssss, did you feel lonely? Oh...I know...we have no time for you." Ginger was purring against her shoulder. He could feel that she was somehow not all that keen on his idea of a teaching post; why, he couldn't tell.

"Rich, what is involved when you get a teaching post? Is it time?"

"It all depends. I hope to get a full-time post so we can keep your flat and have enough money to get you the dark room we discussed."

"But sweety, ...I might spend a lot more time in France...I wish you could see what they are doing there." He wished that too, but he could not see what there was to do for him in a Half-way House project. When Sascia reminded him that she was leaving for France early in the morning, he felt unfortunate. Again, she would miss his fourth lecture. He knew that she had listened to his tape more than once, but it was not the same and she knew it.

"Rich I am sorry you know...I get paid...and love what I can do there." He was not sure what getting paid in Talents did for paying the rent on her flat, but he was not in the mood for an argument. Suddenly Sascia was crying.

He knew that she had read his mind. He took her in his arms. Ginger jumped off her shoulder.

"Moppie, I'm worried that you will lose your flat. You can't pay the rent with Talents." He felt terrible for making her sad but didn't know what else to suggest. He knew if he stayed in his chosen subject, he could teach. He certainly didn't want to ever go into the tourist business again.

"Rich, do you like teaching?" He shrugged his shoulder as she waited for an answer.

"Gosh, if I had the money to pay the bills, I would love to do what I do now. Prepare a set of lectures and get paid for them. But it's far too irregular to live on."

"How does Trevor do it?" She seemed to feel better because she hugged him. He often wondered about that. Trevor had many lectures and radio interviews lined up. Public speakers can get good money. He said as much which seemed to satisfy her.

"Let's see if there is any email. I'll make us a coffee shake while you have a look. I'm sure tablet thirteen must be waiting for you."

"Now you're talking! He kissed her and started his laptop. As they expected, there was an email from Trevor. Sascia came back with two coffee shakes and a stroopwafel each. They shared his office chair as they stared at the subject title: Your I Am Guardian Angel. As he opened Trevor's email, he looked forward to the translations of the 13th tablet. He hoped that the information he had gathered would be useful for his upcoming lecture

—- Original Message ——-
From: "T Zwiegelaar"
To: <R de Jong:;>
Subject: Your I Am Guardian Angel.
Dear Richard and Sascia,

I know you want to see the photos from which Theo translated what he calls the 13th tablet. Toon phoned me an hour ago, and I will give them to Sascia when she is here with Peter and Helen at the Halfway house. I heard from Ben that there is some progress on the whereabouts of Piet, Yolanda's ex. Everyone is beginning to accept my theories about the Jaarsma Clan. Good luck with your coming lecture. It's incredible how this 13th tablet coincides with what we speculated surrounding the crop circles.

Regards Trevor.

"Rich, I still wish you could join us. Didn't Trevor meet Tieneke at Toon and Ingrid's wedding?"

"Yes. He liked her."

He had heard from Yolanda that Tieneke's husband had had a heart attack and was ill. Her husband used to be a subcontractor for the Pleasure Parks project. He tried to remember his first name. When Sascia said de Beer, he remembered! Of course, Roelof.

Sascia opened the attachment with the title, which was a link: Your I Am Guardian Angel Player- Created the Game.[1]

Tablet 13

---

1. https://allrealityshifters.wordpress.com/tablet-thirteen/

When the translator of my coded text activates the symbols of Sirius— our patterns will re-appear on planet Earth through thy cornfields to stimulate the mind of the genius.

Translated by Theo de Jong

Richie, these four wave-form frequencies are known as BETA, ALPHA, THETA, and DELTA waves. The two Hemisphere cards we introduced play a significant part in your awakening. When I translated this message, I knew by then who had written the text because the I am within me recognised the signature. Remember the power of RA?

Love Theo.

"Rich, what is the power of RA?" He knew it had to do with the power behind sacred geometry and the flower of life.

"Moppie, Theo is referring to a prime language of reality. I think Annelies uses the same, or a similar, system when she talks about a grid system."

"What are you talking about?" Vaguely, he recalled something about a dimensional tear that resulted in a loss of consciousness. He shrugged his shoulders. He was supposed to remember something, but what?

"Moppie, I'm not sure. I suppose I don't remember all my dreams." He was fascinated to read about the pandora's box, which was full of surprises.

"Is the text referring to the Sphinx?" He was impressed that she got the same idea he had.

"I would say so. But what is hidden under the paws is still pure speculation." Sascia yawned as she asked, "It has to do with human virtue. What could that mean?" He had no idea. It could refer to work of great merit or a woman's virtue. With that thought, he gave her a big hug.

"Moppie, I'm bushed. Let's go to bed. You have to get up early. Have you packed yet?" Sascia shook her head.

"I think I'm not going."

"Moppie, please don't cancel going because of me or what I've said or thought. Let's go to bed and set the alarm; we will talk about it tomorrow."

• • • •

When Sascia was fast asleep, he got up to quench his thirst. It was already well past midnight, and the traffic outside had gone quiet. When he got back to bed, he marvelled at the sleeping girl. He wondered if she was dreaming. Very carefully so as not to wake her, he lay beside her. Her rhythmic breathing made him sleepy.

He wanted to find out what had happened after he had made a sculpture of her. He tried to think back to the last moments he could still remember. He knew with regret that his sculpture was a gift for her future husband, the pharaoh's son.... Suddenly he was out...

"*Hi there, I heard you call.*" Theo beamed.

"*What call?*" He could not remember calling him.... Only vaguely was he aware that he was...dreaming...for he belonged to forty household servants chosen to escort the soon-to-be-queen on her long journey to her new home. He was selected to accompany her on her journey as her private tutor in the arts. As he rode his camel close to the princess' camel, on which she was perched high and hidden by an enclosed throne, the desert wonderland that was dotted with huge, pure white rocks blinded his eyes. Vegetation was extremely scarce; just here and there a dry shrivelled-up shrub. The caravan of sixty camels came to a halt. She whispered something to him, but her private physician then summoned him. He rode to the front following the physician's slave, who ran barefoot beside his camel.

When he entered the physician's tent, he found that he had made a potion for the princess. He was to pass it on to her when he finished her statue. It was to help the princess with her nausea.

He waited until after her tent was up for the night before going to her. Their secret love affair went unnoticed, so they thought— until later in the journey when her private physician again summoned him, but this time to her tent. The princess appeared to be pregnant! This compromising situation brought a gripping fear to the whole household. He knew it to be his child.

Feelings of both joy and fear for her well-being gripped him when he was ordered to travel ahead with the gift. Her marble statue would hopefully distract the new pharaoh so he would not become too impatient by the long delay. The high priest decided to postpone their journey until the baby was born. No one ever questioned who the father was.

He knew that it was the last time he would ever see her. His grief during the rest of that life from losing her, because he had heard that she died in childbirth, had broken his spirit.

What they did to him a year after her death didn't make a lot of difference to him. When, on the instructions of her physician, they burned his eyes out, his skills as an artist became obsolete, so he ended up begging to stay alive. His shimmering light body was shaking. The feelings he had just encountered affected him, so he wondered where this emotional pain was stored.

"Richie, you have just observed the extensions of your soul's records. It proves the immortality of true love. Simultaneously, we can also feel the heart-rending pain that is stored away. It is within us all." He slowly settled back into his Lightbody, realising that becoming an explorer of the many planes of consciousness required courage.

Theo, in his typical way, requested him to follow. He knew now that his mind could create many experiences, but he was still having difficulty grasping this nonlocal world of pure consciousness.

His Lightbody shattered due to a shrilling noise...He gasped from shock when he felt himself falling into a bottomless pit. The noise penetrated his whole being, which took his breath away as his head hit the pillow with a thump.

It was the phone...He grabbed the receiver to stop the noise. There was no one at the other end...Gosh, what a dream. He knew he had dreamed before that Sascia was pregnant and that there was a loss involved that resulted in great sadness. He should've tried to change the dream while he was dreaming, make her have the baby, and live happily ever after.

It was very early in the morning, but there was enough light to see that Sascia was still fast asleep.

Chapter 14
When Egos Play the Human Game

The Pannekoek
Sascia's picture gallery was a great success. He was proud and happy for her. Their life routine worked well between them.

"Richard, it's your Aunt on the line," Connie called out over the noise of the milkshake machine. It was hectic. Visitors had hit the town. From the pantry, he saw Sascia discussing photographic work with an older woman in the corner.

"Hi, Aunty. When are you due to arrive in Holland?"

"I will arrive with Sonja on the 23rd of next month. Will you be fetching us at Schiphol?" He assured her that he'd make a plan.

"Richard, I'm looking forward to coming back. Crumbs, I need to get busy again, especially now that Nel's bragging about your changes." He was glad that he had Nel's approval.

Mien told him that her ex had pitched up on their doorstep a week ago. He was inquiring about her nephew, the Egyptologist. She was very suspicious since Nick had never shown any interest in her family.

"Since when has Nick been interested in ancient history?"

"He's not. He's after something. I know I was right about his involvement that led to the burglaries. He also seems to think you know what is happening with the Jaarsma brothers in France. Look, he was very cagey. Mostly, I read between the lines so to speak." He heard his aunt speaking to someone in the background.

"Richard, Jock just told me that Toon must be careful. He seems to think that someone is paying Nick to investigate Toon's business."

"Really? What makes Jock think that?" Mien replied by passing the phone to her oldest son Jock.

"Hi mate, I heard from Toon that you're involved with Ingrid's daughter." Sascia joined him behind the counter after she had said goodbye to her business client.

"Are you still talking to your Aunt from South Africa?" He winked, grabbing her around her waist, while Jock was telling him that his dad didn't seem to be even slightly interested in his communal project, saying that the powers that be would not support community schemes. Not even in South Africa. When Sascia wormed away from his embrace, be beamed;

"Tell you later."

"Richard, my dad turned sour when my mom and I mentioned Toon's name," Jock admitted. There was a silence as if Jock was hesitant to say more.

"He warned us that we would get into trouble. I had a big argument with him so I didn't see him leave. He was driving a fancy car and was bragging about buying property. Where he gets his money from is a mystery to us. My dad is a resourceful man, but the cash he was throwing around was obscene. Someone is paying him to get at something, we would love to know what." He also questioned what Nick du Toit was after.

"When my dad was here, he got a call from someone in Holland. It was to do with property papers in connection with Harry Brinks, mom's friend." Jock was called away so his aunt came back online.

"Richard and Nick poked around while he was in the Eastern Cape, especially about the talent exchange system, which also triggered snarly remarks. Jock was trying to explain to his dad how it helped lots of people who were crippled by the interest rates at the banks, but that only brought on more derogatory comments. We think he's up to something." Both Connie and Sascia were making signs, wanting to know what his aunt said. When Mien asked after Jill, Peter's stepmother, who was Nick's first wife she astonished him.

"You mean the same Peter who runs the Half-way House project?"

"Yes, that one. When Jill married Otto, Peter came to live with them. I learned from Harry that Otto and Jill live in Buttercup Valley. You must have met them?" He tried to remember. He had heard of Otto because he had been a speaker at a Zürich conference, but the name Jill drew a blank.

"Richard, what worries me is that Nick knew a lot about your comings and goings. Someone must be in contact with him, either directly or indirectly."

"Really, why...what is so special about me? I've got nothing to hide. I can't think of anything that interests someone like Nick." Both Connie and Sascia were listening in.

"My boy it has to do with your research work and maybe even Theo's. I know you were very depressed when Theo left. He did come into the coffee shop just before he died and gave me what looked like a small key. I'd forgotten all about it. I put it in the safe." He immediately wanted to look, but his aunt kept talking.

"Sascia, please open the safe for me."

"I'm in contact with Harry through email. Harry is very down. He is looking for a buyer. He wants to offload Pleasure Parks altogether. We speculate that Toon will take it over if only to secure the Pleasure Park's resort in France." She chatted some more about her family while he peered into the safe. At first, he saw nothing apart from his aunt's papers and a CD...right at the back there was a very small cross with something that looked like a screw shaft on a metal ring.

"Aunty I found it, the key. Did he tell you?"

"No. As I remember correctly, Theo said he would write to you. I was very busy then, so it might have slipped my mind." His aunt carried on about Sonja who wanted to know if he could find out if she could do nursing in Holland. She was fully qualified. He promised to email Debbie's contact details.

When he hung up, it suddenly dawned on him. Next month! What was he going to do for money? Sascia's freelance work only started to happen but would not help them with any bills. They both wanted to keep the flat in Amsterdam but the rent was high. They could purchase it if they had the capital, but they couldn't. Thank goodness Theo's flat was paid off.

"Well, well, what was that all about? You have been on the phone for at least an hour!" Sascia's laughing eyes wiped his worry away.

He strung the little key on a chain around his neck. He asked if Connie knew Otto and Jill after he told them what his aunt and his nephew Jock talked about.

"Peter's mom and dad, of course, I do; they are part of the family from Mom's side. Helen is my mom's sister."

"Gosh, I can't wait to see everyone's family tree." Sascia's enthusiasm for Annelies' workshops was catchy. He wondered where Jeroen was as it was nearly six. Jeroen would come to help Connie out until closing time. He had been at his grandfather's steel business with Uncle Ed to do with the project in France. Jeroen knew the ins and outs behind the new holiday park, so he could probably confirm his aunt's suspicions.

"What do you think, is Nick is after Toon's money?" Connie asked. Sascia joined them after she finished with four customers.

"I'm sure it must have something to do with the takeover," Sascia replied when she returned some change. Nel came out of the kitchen with new stroopwafels. He passed on his aunt's greetings and told her she would return on the 23rd of next month.

"What take over?" Connie was all ears and so was he.

"Yesterday, Jeroen told me that Hans, Ed, Harry Brinks and Toon had a meeting at home," Sascia replied. "Harry wants to sell Pleasure Parks to Toon. Toon is not interested in the holiday resorts consortium, but he wants to make sure that the project in France is going well. He might be interested in taking over the whole land deal in France. Jeroen said that Toon has a different idea what the park should be used for." He was so surprised that she never told him anything, it almost hurt.

"Rich it slipped my mind to tell you, sorry," she whispered. "Remember during the game, and what your brother said in the video, he already knew about Toon being part of it."

"You mean they are changing the whole idea of the dome? Gosh, so my aunt is right. Toon is getting under some people's skins with his purchasing of land for his communities. I must say he is dedicated to his visions!" he said out loud, but he was far more impressed by Theo's predictiveness.

"Uncle Fred says that's why Hans is always travelling with him; he holds the purse strings,"

"Gosh, the man must be loaded; how did he make his money?"

"I'm not sure, I never asked. I still can't get over the fact that my mom married such an incredibly wealthy guy." Sascia asked Connie what Toon was like as an uncle since the man had such an inner joy for life. He was indeed a very optimistic, fun-loving person to have around.

"Uncle Toon never showed or acted any different than any other person in our family, apart from his humour about life. He has always been my favourite uncle. My dad couldn't stand him, but my mom always put it down to pure jealousy. My dad asked Toon for a loan once, but nothing came of it so I always thought he held a grudge."

"How did he get that rich?" he dared to ask. Over the noise of the milkshake mixer, Connie told them about her childhood experiences.

"He inherited most of it. Uncle Fred told me how rebellious Toon was in his early twenties. He had to be prepared to take over the massive fortune with all its assets, but all he was interested in was joining Uncle Leo on a pilgrimage. Uncle Otto and Trevor were his buddies. He wanted to live in a monastery like Leo."

"This Uncle Otto, he's the one who lives in Buttercup Valley, so they are all involved with Toon's communities? I mean is the whole Jaarsma....never mind I will ask Annelies."

When he arrived, Jeroen asked how much he knew about Egyptian architecture, but Sascia was eager to get to the supermarket on the way home, so they did not stay to talk. Jeroen couldn't have meant today's architecture. His vision of the city of Cairo only brought on images of unfinished buildings that were unpainted, unimaginative and scruffy! He must have meant the ancient monuments and temples.

"Rich, you've got an email from Trevor, can I open it?" Sascia's enthusiasm always charmed him. She had been helping him with his research for his lectures, so the tablets had become just as important to her as they were to him. Theo would have loved her for that alone. He joined her in the lounge carrying two iced coffees. It was his turn to make them.

"Where does Trevor work from, do you know?'

"I've no idea. Annelies once said that he was with Leo, who seems to live near Helen and Peter in France."

"Really? I must ask when Toon will be flying to Half-way House again. This time you must come along." Sascia was now regularly involved with the publishing business on the premises. Liesbeth had also started to give her photo artwork to do on her mother's PC at their office at the flat.

"Let's open the attachment and read the 14th tablet." The title, When Egos Play the Human Game[1], was intriguing. They clicked on the link and settled on the sofa with the laptop in front of the coffee table.

Tablet 14

Translation by Theo de Jong

"Gosh, Rich, there is so much to take in. I wish I had known your brother. I would have asked him what his feelings were about all this. I sometimes wonder who left these ideas to put into our written word. How accurate was Theo?"

"I often questioned it, but then I remembered Theo and his multi-tasking skills. He could hold an analytical debate with scientists on subjects so remote from his way of thinking, and he always made people think. Likewise, if you read Einstein's philosophy, you will know how deep his perceptions were. From both, I learned to keep my mind alert and allow my heart to evaluate." He scrolled down the link to read Theo's attached letter underneath.

Richie, this information that surfaced from my unconscious was such a revelation. I chose to seclude myself and take advantage of the quiet, recluse existence Leo offered me. I was determined to spend as much time alone as possible to study the ancient crystal skull we found.

When I studied the skull, after about an hour, meaningful visions would appear; while this happened, the skull seemed to disappear as the images became clearer. What I saw was how civilisations come and go. I saw a large landmass sinking into the water. The land did not sink all at once but in

1. https://allrealityshifters.wordpress.com/tablet-fourteen/

sections. I could see people moving in three different directions. These called hallucinations, helped me to translate the heavenly-coded scripts. The symbols were in clusters seemingly into ten quoting style sentences that had to carry a tonal frequency that flowed harmoniously. I now realise how the creator of these scripts, in some way, could be what we know as the Jaarsma clan. I suspect that POWAH is, or speaks on behalf of, one of the four great group souls who partook in the game of dreaming on a multi-dimensional scale called Alpha and Omega. The thought or idea is my creation, but...what if it is the truth?

Love Theo

The idea about the group soul was not so difficult for him to grasp, but POWAH being one? He stroked Ginger, who was purring on his lap.

"Rich, there was never any mention of a key in his letters, was there? I think you could be right. All the hassle might lead us to study the Star map. Look, I'll show you." Sascia had drawn up a family tree. He was pretty impressed. She would take it to their second workshop next week. He now saw a pattern he'd never seen before. Everyone gave Annelies their genogram sheet for the next class concerning their palm-print decoding.

He got up to show Sascia a picture of a crystal skull next to a woman named Anna Mitchell-Hedges.

"Gee Rich, they're for real! So there must be more?" Her comment made him smile. They were both very challenged by the far-reaching meanings of the tablets. Sascia told him she had a wedding to shoot after returning from France. It was not what she liked to do, but it would cover her month's rent in Amsterdam. Later in the evening, he worked on his journal while she read Tieneke's workbook.

When they were both snuggled up in bed after their lovemaking, Sascia wanted to try to stay awake while visualising herself out of her body. He had no idea why some people, like himself, had no problem and others did. As they lay in bed he was thinking of Trevor and what he knew about Theo.

"Trevor is the computer boffin isn't he?"

"Gee, you read my thoughts. Trevor's face flashed before my eyes. Yes, I think that he is mostly responsible for the e-mails we're getting." He marvelled at how his life had changed. Since his out-of-body travels and Sascia moved in with him, time had sped up....

• • • •

When he heard Sascia's rhythmic breathing...he knew that she was asleep. As soon as the goose-bump feelings travelled all over him he knew what followed would be the exhilarating feeling of leaving his body...He wondered why Theo had left him the little key...

"Richie, energy has many specific points of appearance. Every form of energy you become aware of is a channel through which the One Source flows." He gazed at what at first looked like a glowing spinning ball. The moment he thought that he heard Theo's mental dialogue, the image he remembered as being Theo appeared. Did Theo imply that...did he appear because he was in his thoughts?

"Richie it's the love you have for me that will create an opening through which the One Source Energy will flow." He stared at Theo's appearance, eyes, whole physical build, and again the camping gear clothing he seemed to favour. But then Theo always wore those clothes on their digs. Was Theo implying that as he thought of him, he became natural?

"Come, I'll retake you to a meeting on an even higher plane. Now that you are awakening more and more, meaning that more of your soul energy is participating in the human experience, you are ready to join us on this level." Was Theo taking him into a higher sphere?

"*Richie, you have been allowed to glimpse beyond the mental screen, which keeps most people from seeing beyond the veil of matter. This was to show you that everything is comprised of different intensities of vibrations in the luminous kingdoms of the spirit.*" He knew that he was in his mind, travelling in consciousness, but where was Sascia? Was she out of her body somewhere else?

The next scene was as breathtaking as some Theo had shown before. His mind translated it as if he was in some enormous cave made purely from the frozen, luminous white snow. POWAH's lecture had already started.

< *Your world is like a river where multidimensional cosmic beings can evolve. In surrounding oneself to the life of thought, the soul of man can genuinely inhabit a place in the universe of Spirit* >

Richard never saw himself as a soul. He realised that he only saw himself as human, trapped in a world of physical matter where the law of gravity permeated all things.

"*Richie, I've learned that for a soul to find the doorway into the physical world, a good preparation for understanding spiritual insights is the key for some to awaken.*" Theo's projection of the word key created an image in his mind of a smoky glass door that was suddenly crystal clear for him to slide open.

"*Yes, hold on to that image; it is in the repeated mental expressions of intent that the I Am can read the moods and attitudes of one's soul.*" That was new. Did his soul have attitudes and moods?

"*Oh yes, that is the adhesive that blends itself into the stream of cosmic existence.*" POWAH's message was beginning to trigger an understanding of what it meant to truly meditate. Focussed thoughts! "*You've got it; it is through occupying the soul with peaceful thoughts while excluding all other external thoughts that your rational mind has stored away. Feelings or memories of distorted programming often corrupt your powers of perception."* Theo's reply was helpful, but he needed to stop being sidetracked when he thought he recognised Sascia on the other side of the circular assembly hall. Theo often used the expression 'rational mind'. When he did, images of robotic science fiction beings often jumped into his vision. Did he wonder why? When POWAH'S glance beamed at him again, he heard the following words;

< *The spiritual world first appears in the soul through images. That is why it is so difficult to differentiate between illusions and reality in your realm. To experience the spiritual world, a person must learn about the many possible sources of illusions.* >

Gosh, how was he ever to do that? Images of humanoid-looking intelligence overwhelmed him.

"*Richie, patience; otherwise, you will be tempted to imagine the spiritual world as being like the physical, sensible world.*"

Theo's warning stung because he interpreted his dreams as experiences related to everything solid and physical. How could he ever step away from that? Were even the images of Sascia as an Egyptian princess an illusion?

"*Patience, buddy, value how your memories present themselves, but do not take them all literally.*"

< *My beloveds, prepare your souls for the pictures in your spiritual vision field. In your daily waking state, carefully develop the attitude that prevents you from getting trapped within your images. Rather, develop a supersensory awareness that is completely outside normal consciousness. The clearer you become about the flux of soul life through the physical, the better you shall understand clairvoyant consciousness.* >

POWAH's imposing light body evaporated as if he had never been there. The sounds that were by now familiar created a euphoric feeling he wished he could somehow record.

"Richie, some will. In these gatherings, some musicians have chosen the soul purpose to create the same sounds in the 3rd-dimensional world to trigger an awakening for many souls that cannot yet recall their dreams." Gradually the familiar scenery of Apeldoorn came back into focus. It was still early. Some early risers cycled to their destinations. What was their purpose in the bigger scheme of things?

"Richie, many awakening souls have been given different skills and talents to express our spirit world. Yours is to write and lecture on our ancestral information that is embodied into our cellular memories in the form of symbols." The traffic noises that announced a new day in this small city spurred him to write his journal. He was still in awe that he could clearly experience his dream state. Would others have the same experiences?

"Each person has a different outlook of what a spiritual world is to them. It is not anything remotely related to some religious concepts as you know. The evolution of our species is greatly hampered through any kind of belief system. To overcome beliefs of any kind will be the most challenging hurdle to master on this journey."

He observed two men pushing a broken-down car. Why did they wear a mask? Was the air polluted?

Market salespeople, who were all wearing masks, were setting up their goods, and a solitary dog was barking, to which other dogs replied. He wondered if he had also dreamed up these images of reality.

Theo said his goodbyes. He knew he would soon enter his body, but as he lingered, he knew with joy that Sascia would take part in their ascension path.

"Richie, learn to give each other the space to develop individually." Those were the last thoughts he woke up with...

Annelies' ascension workshop

They left the coffee bar at seven just in time to arrive at Annelies fifteen minutes later. They were running late because Aunt Mien had phoned again. She had wanted to speak to Nel, but she kept him on the line with more stories, this time all related to his dad. His mind was so occupied with all the questions he had no answers for. When they finally left, he truly hoped Annelies' workshop would relieve him of a nagging feeling he could not shrug off. Sascia squeezed his knee as he drove into Annelies' driveway. She must know that he was worried; first his aunt's speculations a few days ago and now some family history he had been oblivious about, then about Toon and his massive fortune, which made him increasingly aware of his nil bank account.

"I love you without a dime to your name." she beamed. He gave her a big hug. He had never thought he could feel this unsure and insecure. Where it all suddenly came from was a mystery but Sascia seemed to understand.

"Rich, I know you are worried. I know you have been wondering what you will do when your aunt is back." That was it. As usual, his child support to Elsie had been deducted from his account yesterday, and now that Mien had also given him a return date, something had snapped up.

"Moppie, it's not only the money. I can still carry on for a few months. But what am I going to do to earn an income after that is what I don't know."

"Mmm, I was worried that you think I will leave you because of your financial situation." He knew it had never entered his mind until she made that comment.

"I can always go back to teaching I'm sure. It's just that I wish I knew what I'm supposed to do...I feel so...I don't have a goal like Toon and Ingrid have, or Liesbeth, Annelies and the others. They all seem so... stable."

He snuggled up close, and Sascia held him tight.

"Oh... I do know what you mean. That's why you should look at the Half-way House. I got so inspired when I was there. When I listened to Peter and Helen and others moving to the Buttercup Valley, I knew I wanted to become part of that community. I'm unsure what I can contribute, but it will get clearer...but...I don't want to go without you."

"Is that what has been on your mind this last week?" He kissed her on the tip of her nose.

"Lots of things have been playing on my mind. We don't want to give up my flat in Amsterdam, but how will I pay the rent? Sure, the photoshoot has helped for now, but what about next month? Where are we going to live? How will I help out if we are more often at the Halfway House and you give your lectures in Holland?" She sighed...They both saw Ed when he came towards them from inside the house.

"Are you two to going to join us?" Ed asked as he opened his car door.

"We'd better go in but we will work something out." He kissed her and they grabbed all their worksheets.

"Is everybody already there?" Sascia asked Ed as they walked in. They were the last to arrive. Joris came rushing out when Ben greeted them. Richard was glad to see him. He was always away, which must be lonely for Annelies.

"We wondered what happened to the two of you?" Ben commented while whistling to Joris.

"After the workshop, we need to talk about the project in France." Ben beamed. Sascia wasn't listening telepathically.

Class 2

Big letters on the door stated;
THE MANIFESTATIONS OF MY CONTRACT.

"Hello, you two," Ingrid called out. Ed passed Yolanda her bag that she had left in the car.

"I'm sorry we are late. I got a phone call from Mien. She had so much to say, including when she would be coming back, it left us both somewhat frazzled." He said it, especially to Annelies.

"What did she tell you that got you both so unstable?" she beamed. Sascia must have heard her as well. She looked sideways at him when they took their seats.

"Are you going to tell them what you told me?" He was not sure if he wanted to alarm them all more than necessary.

"Richard, please speak to Ben during the coffee break about whether it has anything to do with Nick du Toit." With surprise, he looked at Annelies. He knew that both Ed, Toon and Ingrid beamed at Annelies for an explanation about Nick du Toit, but Hans suggested they should start finishing their second palm print readings for their two hemisphere cards.

"Last class we dealt mostly with the seven planetary shapes and textures on our fingers and we touched upon the mounts and symbols seen within our hands." He looked over his notes from last week, still wondering how their palm print told them what life script they had agreed on playing.

"It takes a very experienced palmist to see that Richard. If they do, they are not supposed to reveal it all without knowing the bigger picture on a soul level." He nodded to Annelies, and she knew he had picked up her thoughts.

"Remember, this is not a palmistry course; my workshops are a preparation for you to play the second ascension board game. With the three cards on this second level, you can see and recognise the personality and the script you have chosen to play."

"When are we playing the second level after we have made the three cards?" Zola asked. He felt there should be a break. Only two weeks ago, they played the game for the first time. He could easily do it over again.

"*I feel the same*" Sascia beamed.

"Let's see how we are going. Most of you probably need to find out what you have specially chosen to be your soul's passion." They all agreed to that. He was more at ease knowing that others like himself hadn't yet a clue what ignited their passion. He knew that his love had to do with the ancient texts and monuments on the planet, but how he was going to apply that in a way that would support his living conditions was still vague.

"*Richard, don't have any worries about that. Your higher self is very aware of your needs. Have faith.*" Liesbeth's wink told him that the message came from her.

"I want you all to try to read your palm print intuitively by dividing your left and right palm print into three zones." They were all using rulers and pencils. It was fun to be in a group that was so keen to discover things about themselves that would unlock the mystery of human consciousness.

The rest of the evening went fast. They made their two palm print cards during the following two weeks.

Richard's birthday

A whole bunch of kids occupied the Pannekoek. His eight-year-old daughter Sammy had persuaded her mom to drop her off with some friends. Surely what Sascia had planned for his birthday had not included all Sammy's friends?

"Daddy, can we have stroopwafels with ice cream since it's your birthday?" Before he could speak, Nel came out of the kitchen with a tray full of stroopwafels and cherries on top. Nel behaved like a grandmother, the way she fussed over her. He knew she had a son, but he was not sure if he was married with a family. Sascia had some errands to do and left him alone at the Pannekoek.

She had been very secretive early this morning. After they made love, she handed him a fancy-wrapped box with a shiny ribbon and a card. Her gift from the heart touched him. She had reduced and laminated his Language of Light cards and finished his booklet. He had been far too busy preparing for his lectures. Sascia had contacted Ellie to ask if Sammy could spend the day with them.

It was a beautiful day and they had planned to take the day off and take Sammy to the Efteling, Holland's most famous theme park.

Sascia walked in the door with a large wrapped parcel under her arm. Jeroen and Connie followed. They all started to make it obvious that it was his birthday, which embarrassed him.

"Sweety, I hope you like it. Hot from the press so to speak." As he unwrapped the large colour-framed collage, he was stunned. He saw himself on what looked like a giant movie poster! There he was, talking to a large audience while behind him on a big screen, the Sphinx, which had other shots of the pyramid of Giza, enhanced the title: **'The Garden of the Gods — The Valley of Truth**. Around the outside were more photos and text that announced all his four lectures about the mystery of the Sphinx with the dates. Sascia had wanted to give him a memento of his four lectures. He was thrilled to bits. Jeroen took his poster and arranged it where you could see it as you walked into the coffee shop.

Sammy loved the poster, too and made sure that every customer who came in knew that the man standing in the archway was her dad. When he hugged Sascia, he knew his eyes were moist.

"That is the best present I have ever received. Thank you." He whispered caressingly in her ear.

Sammy's girlfriend's mother arrived and introduced herself, explaining that her daughter and her friends had stayed over with Sammy for the night. Ellie had phoned her to ask if she could fetch them all from the Pannekoek, leaving Sammy alone with her dad. Nel got them all together and accompanied them to the Voyager Van that was parked in the front.

When Ingrid and Toon walked in, Toon stepped up to the poster and stared at it for a while before he said anything. He could see that Sascia was waiting for his reaction. Instead, he looked at Ingrid.

"That's it."

"What is, Snooks?" Toon pointed at his poster.

"The name for the park. The Garden of the Gods. I told you last night what I visualised." Toon was so enthusiastic that he had to be reminded it was Richard's birthday. Only Ingrid seemed to know what he was talking about. Toon applauded Sascia for her work with the words;

"My girl, I've got a job for you." He congratulated him for his lectures, which were so well advertised this way.

"Happy birthday!" Yolanda laughed, and Ed shook his hand when they came in. It was getting crowded. Sammy returned from saying goodbye to her friend, telling him Nel had gone to get something from the supermarket. She chatted to everyone as eight-year-olds do. Sascia showed her how to make milkshakes. When Niels and Zola came in, he suspected Sascia invited the ascension class.

"How did you guess?"

"I thought we were going to the Efteling" As he got that out, Liesbeth, Annelies and Hans arrived. Sammy pretended to be a waitress, helping Connie serve more fresh stroopwafels with cherries Nel had left in the kitchen.

One of his presents was a new radio for his car, a mug with his star sign, and a sweater. He was chuffed. Ingrid was entertaining Sammy, who had drawn a pyramid with herself in the centre of the back of a menu.

He behaved like a proud father, pasting her drawing next to the till. When Annelies and Ben joined the party, he was touched by the fact that so many people cared...It was lunchtime when Nel returned with a present from her, a new juice maker; how thoughtful. She said it was from his aunt as well. Then, the three of them left for the Efteling.

Later that day, they dropped Sammy off at Toon's office on the outskirts of Apeldoorn. He never knew his ex-Ellie worked for the Butter Cup Gardening Centre! He had been to one of Toon's enterprises for the first time.

Sascia was so impressed by it all – when they were taken on a tour around the place. It was strange to see that Ellie and Sascia got on so well. Ellie had put on weight, which strangely suited her. She had always been very skinny, which looked fine when she was young, but now she was far sexier. He wondered if she had seen someone, but he would not ask.

Sammy seemed to spend a lot of time in the front office. She proudly showed her that she could work the computer and had her email address. She reminded him of Timmy, Peter's son, who was about her age. Sascia greeted a young woman in the nursery as Sammy chatted her head off to him. He overheard that Sascia was very surprised to see her niece there. Her father, Oliver, Quincy's ex-husband, was involved with Ellie! What a small world.

They finished his birthday by going to see a late movie. When they came back to the flat from a long day full of activities, they both crashed into bed....

He woke early with Sascia snuggled up close, fast asleep. He marvelled at her body, made for love; yesterday was blissful. For some reason, images of that scruffy basement where Ingrid was a hostage still lingered in his mind.

Sascia started to stretch, and Ginger complained. He was curled up in the hollow of her back. When the phone rang, it was the crack of dawn. Who would phone this early? He picked up before Sascia was completely awake.

"Richard, I'm sorry to wake you so early, but something happened to Connie last night. I dropped her off at her mom's place after we'd been to the movies. Yolanda phoned me at five this morning! She is beside herself. She never came home all night. We are all up and about it, and Toon has already phoned André." Jeroen rattled in absolute despair. He had to shake himself fully awake when Sascia asked what was wrong.

"What time did you drop her off at the Hotel? I know they live at the back cottage."

"Something happened to Connie," he said as an aside to Sacia.

"Around eleven. I drove right in. All she had to do was to walk around to the back entrance! I should have walked her right to her door!"

"What do you mean?" Sascia sat next to him, trying to listen in.

"When did Yolanda miss her?"

"She thought she heard something during the night – she looked into Connie's room early this morning. She noticed that she'd never been home! We knew something was very wrong when she phoned me just now!"

"Moppie, what time is it?"

"Jeroen, how long is the Hotel open? Do you know?"

"24 Hours."

Sascia showed him that it was half past six.

"When I dropped her off, the restaurant had plenty of parked cars, so it must have been before midnight. Richard, do you think there is any connection? I mean, with the burglary a few weeks ago?" Jeroen's anguish said the rest. Sascia was listening in as she curled up behind him.

"Jeroen I have no idea. When and where is André meeting you? Will that be at the Hotel?"

"Yes, we are all going. André said he will be there at seven."

"We will join you as soon as possible. Jeroen, you must not blame yourself; here is your sister." While she talked to her twin brother, he had a quick shower. Feelings of unease started to make a knot in his stomach, knowing he tried to reject the thoughts surrounding the creepy caller.

"Jeroen, I know we will find her. Keep your cool, love." He heard Sascia's optimism while he quickly got dressed. Something told him to look at his E-mail.

"Oh...Rich...what do you think? Has she just gone somewhere without telling anyone? Has she been kidnapped, do you think, like my mom?" Sascia's worried tone gripped his gut.

"Moppie, we will know more when we talk to the others. He logged on to his email while Sascia got dressed. One letter, with the heading VIRUS was downloaded. He was about to delete it, thinking it was one of these tedious spam emails, when he read the text.

Unsubscribed As: Virus alert

Removal instructions are below -

YOU DID NOT TAKE OUR WARNING SERIOUSLY. WE SAID WE WILL ELIMINATE ANY VIRUS! WE WILL GIVE YOU ONE MORE CHANCE, SHE IS THE ANTIDOTE. RETURN THE MAP

TO ITS PROPER PLACE, AND WE WILL KNOW ABOUT ANY COPIES MADE. OTHERWISE, A REAL VIRUS DISEASE WILL SPREAD FASTER THAN YOU HAVE BARGAINED FOR.

It made absolutely no sense. What map?

"Richard! That's horrible." Sascia was shaking when the printer started to spew out the virus threat.

"I have no idea, but I'll show it to André. Are you ready? ... You look stunning!" She was wearing a navy mini-skirt with a matching top.

Chapter 15
Group Souls are Gathering

The Prinsegracht Hotel
There was hardly any traffic on the road. It took seven minutes to the Prinsegracht Hotel. So often had he driven past that hotel, and never would he have thought he would know the owners, Annelies and her brother Fred, one day. Toon's BMW just turned in, so they followed him to the back of the hotel, where Annelies and Hans were getting out of their cars.

Jeroen appeared, followed by Yolanda, who said:

"I'm so glad you're all here."

"Has André arrived?" Toon asked as he put his arms around her, beaming: *"They are looking for her love. Let's put our heads together and figure out what is going on,"* Ingrid whispered something to Sascia when the police car turned into the side entrance.

"Will you all come into the small dining room? We will not be disturbed there. Help yourselves to tea and take a seat." Fred suggested. Annelies and Hans followed them while Liesbeth stayed outside. It was after seven when André joined them.

The atmosphere was sombre around the big banqueting table. Nobody could accept that Connie could be in danger, but then Ingrid had experienced real violence, not to mention Toon.

"Okay, now we have to do some serious talking. I asked Mr Zwiegelaar for a place to meet and share ideas about what was going on. I believe that some of you already have some theories. Ed Barense will join us at any minute. He's collecting papers from the geologist who did the blasting for the dome in France." André looked directly at Yolanda, reassuring her that everything in his power was done to find Connie. Yolanda nodded. André took complete control of the informal meeting. He dreaded sharing the e-mail message, knowing it would upset Yolanda. Jeroen had not slept. Sascia was comforting her twin brother.

"*He is taking it hard, Yolanda. Please reassure him that he is not to blame. It must come from you.*" Annelies projected. Both Toon and Ingrid glanced at Jeroen as Yolanda leaned across, taking his hand in hers.

"Jeroen, I can feel your guilt; please don't. Rather help us find her, they must have followed you." Jeroen's eyes were moist from anguish; he cared for Connie.

André read his printout and showed them similar threats sent to Trevor and Harry.

André looked at him and asked, "Which map are they talking about?" The only map he could think of was the Star Map. He said as much, but nobody responded. He glanced at Hans, who must have also seen the Star-map at the clinic but was in his own world. He just sat there with his eyes closed.

"*Richard, I'm concentrating on her energy signature, don't interrupt me yet.*" Everyone was silent. Yolanda cried against Toon's shoulder, relieved that Hans was using his psychic skills.

"*Where is Liesbeth?*" Ingrid beamed at Toon.

"*She's meditating outside where Connie disappeared; I trust those two more than the police corps.*"

He telepathically beamed to Annelies about the star painting in the clinic where Ingrid had been held. Both Jeroen and André had no idea about their telepathic conversations. His intuition said that the email could refer to the Star-map. Somehow, he felt that they wanted something from him, but what?

Toon frowned when Annelies looked up at Ben, who had just walked in with Ed, the Australian. Ed sat down next to Yolanda after being informed about the topic of discussion.

Ben told them all a bizarre story about underground tunnels that had kept him away for the ten weeks he had been undercover. He showed them an enlarged map of an area near the Belgian and Luxemburg border, spreading wide, almost reaching Paris. His idea that the Star-map was involved was misguided. Ben's map seems more like it. He was intrigued by the intricate details of the underground tunnel system, which reminded him of London's underground.

"Were those tunnels never discovered when they built the Paris underground?" He asked in amazement.

"Yes, they were, but we guess they disregarded them then. We think that they are after a technical drawing." They all asked Ben what he meant.

"Back in the seventies, an archaeologist had discovered what he thought was an ancient burial site." Everyone was listening. As Ben talked, he said he wished that Theo was here. His detailed, comprehensive knowledge of the medieval period from that region would have come in handy. His attention was alerted when Ben mentioned 'mummies.' His dream about mummies came to mind.

"We were just as surprised to find several mummies the way the Egyptians did their embalming," Ben concluded. Annelies told them they had only recently heard about this burial ground, although Hans suspected foul play long ago. Annelies looked at him when she mentally mentioned the eye symbol.

"Theo knew about it. He joined Leo in his research, but I didn't know all the details." André, Ed, and Jeroen wanted to know more about this eye symbol when Ingrid reminded Toon. Annelies explained the appearance of the eye symbol she had used in the ascension board game. Toon added that the intricate designs in crop circle formations appeared more often near ancient sites such as Stonehenge, Avebury and other ancient burial sites.

"Is the area on the map a sacred site?" Ed asked.

"It could have been in prehistoric times, not so?" Sascia asked Hans.

"I only know of Al-Fatima. It acted powerfully as a centre to transmute matter in ancient times, where the true science of alchemy was safeguarded." Hans' revelation kept everybody spellbound. André was shaking his head. He wanted to know where this energy point was and asked if Hans thought it was around the same area.

"France is among the places still magnetically influenced today by this energy field. As we all know, Lourdes is known for its magical healing powers." He felt that Hans was on the right track.

"What are crop circles?" André asked.

"Mostly they are circles of bent down plants that appear mysteriously in fields at night, mostly in England, but lately they seem to appear around the globe. They don't always take circular shapes but make conglomerations of circles, hemispheres, lines, and many other shapes. Many people differ in their origins; the explanations range from hoaxes to aliens to other supernatural forces such as radiation or ghosts." Toon was surprisingly knowledgeable about the subject. He remembered Theo's fascination with them.

"Theo always said that crop circles were often implicit messages left to the viewer to interpret." Annelies added to Toon's explanation. "They're also called pictograms or glyphs."

"What's all this got to do with Connie's disappearance?"

"Jeroen, we are looking at all angles. The parties responsible for all the criminal acts surrounding the building site of Pleasure Parks seem to have much more at stake. They also have means at their disposal that have prevented a large police force from finding them. That means bigger fish are involved. Connie is just one other lead." André said.

"But....we don't know for sure that she is missing, do we?" Ben said, implying that he knew a lot more. Richard wondered how much he shared with André. He noticed that André's stretched shirt revealed bunched muscles you only get from a good regular workout. Being in the police force must have its requirements.

"But she is.....Connie would never just not come home!" Yolanda remarked.

"Could the crop circles be a timing device, like a calendar?" He beamed at Annelies. It was as if something urged him to ask her that.

"That's an idea!" She got up and left the room.

Toon and Ingrid were comparing notes with Fred while Hans passed refreshments. He eagerly asked Hans what he had learned from his meditative insight, but he waited.

When Annelies returned with a Crop Circle calendar, they all looked at the fantastic patterns.

"Hans, have you picked her up yet?" Annelies beamed.

"Liesbeth thinks she is with her dad, who seems ill."

"Yolanda, you said yourself Connie would never just not come home without telling you, so someone must have seen her arriving and got her to come with them as she was about to go inside." André summed up.

"He's right, love. Remember, her dad is one of them. I'm sure he would not let any harm come to her." Ed beamed. Ben asked André if they knew Piet de Wit's whereabouts, revealing that André and Ben were not working together. Ed, Ben and Toon all picked up on his thoughts. He could tell. When André replied to Ben by

saying no, he aired his frustration with Interpol's secretiveness. André then asked Toon more about crop circles.

"Ben, is it true? Does Interpol hamper André?" Annelies beamed out loud for all telepathists to hear.

Toon told André that there was a proliferation of "insectograms" depicting scorpions, spiders, spider webs, and other insects in the crop circles.

"You mean the Nasca lines?" André interrupted Toon.

"Could be. Earlier, far back in 1993, there were more geometrical patterns. In the following years, the patterns suggested solar systems, asteroid belts, and other planetary connections.

"You mean there is a change in them?" Ed asked. He followed their conversation but waited for Ben to reply to Annelies telepathically.

"We don't know for sure, but we've decided that the primary formations are not of natural occurrence," Annelies said, shrugging her shoulders at Ben.

"What do you mean?" André, as a detective, seemed out of his depth. Richard was still trying to connect the medieval burial grounds with the Star map when his memory released a fragment of a dream about the English professor who had been studying the same gold foil sheets. Theo had mentioned that. He asked Ben more about the English archaeologist. Ben confirmed that this old Englishman had left many documents behind, of which some were from an auction of artefacts in London.

"Leo had found these papers of great importance. We know that Nick du Toit knew the professor because he grew up in an orphanage in France and had many meetings with him there. As we all know, Toon purchased land with the Chateau on it, and Harry won the bid for the rest of the estate, including the random buildings. Nick lost out like he did with the Prinsegracht hotel."

André asked Fred about that as Ben carried on.

"Toon turned the orphanage into a Half-way House community project, and we all know what Harry plans with his real estate. Leo and Trevor are still in the underground chamber, which has been transformed into a modern lab. Many fragile gold foil sheets were discovered there." That news blew him. That was it! When Theo left his flat in Apeldoorn to him, he must have joined Leo and Trevor to research the discoveries.

"He did, Richard. Theo asked us to wait for the right time to involve you. He had his reasons." Ben projected.

André reacted with contempt when he confirmed that they were referring to the same Nick du Toit who had a police record a mile long. The plot was thickening. His aunt's first husband was trying to sabotage the Pleasure Park project for sinister reasons. Richard was about to share his aunt's words when André aired his frustrations.

"This is getting out of hand. What's this Nick du Toit's involvement with your investigations?" André stretched his body and crossed his arms behind his head as he addressed Ben. André was getting frustrated, which was understandable since all their input made no sense. Thinking back to the Star map, Annelies thought it was a family tree that held the birthdays of the children born at the Jaarsma orphanages since there were now two.

"How can a map of an ancestral lineage be connected with all that is happening, Hans?" He waited in suspense to telepathically hear Hans' reply.

"Leo was right; the clue lies in our genetics," Ben responded while he peered over his reading glasses at Annelies.

"Mom, scientists are already using discoveries about our DNA to meddle with our genetics, thereby redesigning the human body." Hans had not said a word out loud, but he had heard his mental reply. Visions of the resort that could have been a private hospital where they had kept Ingrid sprang into his mind.

"Ben, Leo your twin brother is the genetic scientist who also performed the wedding for Toon and Ingrid not so?" Ed asked as he comforted Yolanda, whose whole body language affected them all. Ben told them that his twin brother studied alchemy in a monastery in Tibet after he qualified as a genetic scientist. Ben held his brother in high regard.

"What is Leo's connection in all this?" Fred asked.

"Like Richard, he is decoding these thin gold foil sheets that were like wrappings found near the mummies, at least that is what we speculate. We know that during the Egyptian civilization the priests who performed the embalming had scientific and genetic engineering skills that we have only just acquired ourselves." He still could not fathom that there could be any connection. If these mummies were found in Egypt, that would make sense, but in France?

"Leo told me that nearly 30 years ago, mysterious artefacts were found that led to one of the most intriguing scientific and anthropological discoveries ever made. A secret, unacknowledged department within Interpol responsible for lower friquensy technology assimilation took the discovery into their laboratory for their own agenda. How some of the papers ended up on an auction in the UK is still a mystery. This secret organization must know by now that we have found more artefacts and they are mad since they enjoyed complete anonymity until now."

Ben had mentioned an auction in the UK before, so more and more did it feel that his dream was becoming a reality, but he was not ready to share that as of yet.

"*Richard, will you share it with us during our second class?*" Annelies projected. Sascia squeezed his hand under the table. He would have to think about it.

"Ben, do you see any connection with this Star-map? Are we not talking about genetics here? This clinic where mom was held, what experiments are they doing there?" Sascia asked. Jeroen was clearly getting fidgety. He still blamed himself that they got to Connie. After all it was only a few weeks ago that they experienced a burglary and now this.

"Ben, when I was held captive, they....I mean the kidnappers were after something. I now try to bring back the moment when they were pressing me to change an architectural drawing. I thought it had to do with the structure of the dome, something to do with what I would call a soundcard. There is obviously far more going on, but why Connie? What does the threat mean and why send these threats to Richard?" Ingrid asked. Toon had his hand interlaced with hers on the table. Everyone was silent. Ben was about to speak when there was a knock at the door. Liesbeth walked in and handed Yolanda her own cell phone.

"Connie?" Yolanda was in an instant transformed as she was listening. Jeroen jumped up when she passed the phone to him over the table.

"You were right Ed, she's with Piet. Connie says she is fine but angry at her father for allowing them to threaten her. She's being used as a pawn." Yolanda sobbed as she spoke, turning to Liesbeth. He heard Jeroen asking Connie if she knew where she was.

"Do you know where she is?" Yolanda beamed at Liesbeth, who shook her head. André took the phone from Jeroen, but the connection had been broken.

"Did she phone you?" André asked Liesbeth.

"No. The call came through to Yolanda's cell phone, which I had on me."

"Richard, the words: YOU DID NOT TAKE OUR WARNING SERIOUSLY, do you know what they mean?" André asked while the others were talking, relieved that Connie was at least okay. Sascia grabbed his hand as if to say…*"He must not bully you"* He could only think it had something to do with the photos he received. He told André as such. The warning must relate to the burglary in his flat, but only his juicer was gone—not the two photos, which had been in his car at the time.

"Do you still have them?" André asked. He nodded.

"What would they have meant by the virus?" WE WILL ELIMINATE ANY VIRUS." Ed questioned.

"A virus could mean anything. It must have implied a computer virus. Their main function is to create havoc out of malice." Fred replied when he studied the printout. The atmosphere had changed but the word eliminate created a deathly silence.

"Why would Connie be considered an antidote for a virus?" Yolanda beamed in agony.

"Piet! He's the one that has created havoc, so they took her to blackmail him!" They all looked at Ben, who seemed to have some form of insight. Ingrid had started to shiver. They could all see that she was under stress. The memory of her abduction must have surfaced.

"André, we are going home. Annelies I'll speak with you later. Jeroen, you might want to stay and help André." Toon said.

He told Sascia that he had postponed the trip to France, which reminded him of his fourth lecture at two o'clock in Utrecht.

Ingrid was still shaking. Liesbeth and Annelies embraced her.

"*Love, release it all. You must let go of the thoughtforms. They are only harming the baby*" Annelies beamed. Sascia's eyes were moist....

"I could never understand how calm mom was after we rescued her. She must have bottled it all up." Sascia said when they left the diningroom and walked to the car.

"Do you want to go with her?"

"No, Toon will be the only one to get to her. My mom has always been a very private person. Toon is the only one who has broken through her barrier." He observed her serious face. Oh, he loved this girl. What is it that makes one person so unique? Was it just chemistry?

"*You both have soul agreements like Ingrid and Toon. Richard, many couples will transcend the old relationship paradigm, especially if they are both spiritually awake. You will still have to work through some personality issues, but as observers of your behaviour, you will help each other grow.*" Liesbeth responded telepathically.

André was called away and Fred needed to attend to matters at the hotel. It was decided that they would all meet at Annelies' home the next day. It was still a grave situation. Connie was still not free. Wherever she was, the police and Interpol were on the lookout for the abductors. They all believed them to be the same people that took Ingrid hostage. Jeroen stayed behind with Ben and André while Ed and Yolanda went to the back of the hotel with Liesbeth, Annelies and Hans.

It was after nine as they were driving back to the coffee bar that his cell phone rang. It was Will to tell him that his lecture was again postponed. He knew that a lot of disappointed people would visit the Pannekoek instead. Nel, sighed with relief when they walked in. She was already busy with breakfast customers. Before they knew it both he and Sascia were serving. Nel was stunned by the fact that Connie had been abducted by her dad's criminal buddies, but she also said that the father would not let any harm come to his daughter. He was grateful for her help in the kitchen.

The sunny weather attracted lots of people and the rest of the day passed quickly. When Nel let her two temporary staff leave, she wanted to know what the police were doing. Nel was angry. She liked Connie and asked after Yolanda.

The day had been so hectic, all he wanted to do was go home with Sascia and curl up. Sascia must have sensed his weariness.

"Can't we lock up early?" She suggested when Nel left. It was after five, the coffee shop was empty and there had been no word on Connie yet.

"Oh, let's go!" He had had enough. Business or no business, he was finished. He wrote an apology sign to hang outside and they were about to leave when the phone rang. It was Annelies arranging to meet the following morning early at eight, before he opened the coffee shop. That was great by them. Annelies asked if he could bring Theo's photos.

Ginger greeted them with disgust. They had locked him in the flat by mistake when they left so early. While Sascia prepared Ginger's dinner he checked his email from his laptop. He was hoping to hear something that could give a clue to Connie's whereabouts. Of the two e-mails he downloaded, one had no title and was addressed to himself.

Unsubscribe: R de Jong

Removal instructions are below -

RETURN THE TWO ORIGINAL PHOTOS AND THE INTERPRETATIONS IN A BROWN ENVELOPE TOMORROW AT

THE APELDOORN STATION AT 9 O'CLOCK ON THE SEAT NEXT TO THE CONDOM VENDOR, IF YOU WANT TO SEE CONNIE ALIVE! ANY POLICE ACTIVITY WILL BE NOTICED AND HER RETURN WILL NOT HAPPEN!
TAKE THIS VERY SERIOUSLY.

So they were after the photos after all, but why? He immediately dialled Annelies' cell while he opened the other e-mail from Trevor. He decided not to show this email to Sascia as of yet but print it out and show it to Ben first. Why burden her more? The threat would upset her now that her twin brother was involved. Annelies' voice-mail answered. She was not near her mobile. He phoned André and told him about the threat while Sascia was in the kitchen, then he started to read Trevor's email from his screen...

Dear Richard

As I'm sending you this fifteenth interpretation we were stunned at the timing of this information. We have been poring over Theo's translations and added some of our own suggestions. We have now realised with certainty that all the symbolic philosophic hieroglyphs from the ancient Egyptians on these slates are concerned with the external physical happenings during the last age. They reaffirm what they then knew and what we know of the photon belt. This, we feel is the age we live in. The serpent symbols represent our unconscious dark side because they talk about blind forces having to evoke conjunction, even the scriptures talk about the two paths. Those must also imply the two hemispheres of our brain.

Amazingly, the Eye of Horus symbol is encircled, like the symbol of the serpent who bites his tail. Leo is becoming convinced that our ancestors knew and used the snake symbol, or the beast, as a symbol to mean a dark force that has trapped man's unconsciousness field in forgetfulness. You can add this information to your journal. One day, I would love to read it.

Regards Trevor.

When Sascia prepared their coffees he tried Annelies' cell again.

"Let's open the attachment and read the 15th tablet." Sascia eagerly suggested. He had sent the threatening email to his printer and forwarded the email to André. When Richard scrolled to Trevor's attachment, he realised that he had not seen the photo of this slate, so he could not compare his impressions. It must have been Theo who left the tablet's information with them on Word Perfect. This time, Theo had to convert symbols and create a link to the title: Group Souls Gathering During the Game.[1]

Tablet 15
Translated by Theo de Jong

Dear Richie, as I was interpreting these rhythmic symbols from our ancestors so that you can add them to your journal, I was reminded of the initiations that we both attended on the astral plane. Do you remember? I know that it must still be a mystery why I chose to leave my work behind in this way. It was the only way I could be of any assistance to you without interfering with your truth; as our ancestors did by forcing us to decipher the rich language of images for our awakening. The external world cannot show the truth, it only can mirror what is already within you. The nine aspects within each auric field will affect each embodied soul that resides within an energy field of a human form. Contemplate this riddle before we meet again.

Love Theo.

"Gosh Rich, do you think it has something to do with the little key your Aunt put in her safe?" He was just as stunned by Trevor's email. He had kept it on a chain around his neck as a memento.

"So they, whoever they are, were looking for what Theo left for you?"

"It looks like that, yes." He wondered what could be such a secret that Theo went to the trouble to hide it until he was ready to find it?

When the phone rang he thought it might be Annelies but the call was from South Africa. Mien asked how things were. He had plenty to tell. As he winked at Sascia, answering all his aunt's questions and hearing himself speak about Sascia, it made him

---

1. https://allrealityshifters.wordpress.com/tablet-fifteen/

feel shy. The threatening email drifted into the background. His aunt had found out more about Henny, Tieneke's daughter.

After her call, André phoned his cell to let him know about tomorrow. He had to be at the Apeldoorn station as was instructed at 9, carrying a big envelope. He tried to speak softly so Sascia would not hear anything but she had read his mind when she beamed; *"Why did you not share that with me?"* He regretted keeping it from her.

When Sascia was reading the threatening email from the delete box, she was upset, cried and angry at him for not sharing. He received his first illogical female lecture. Not that he wished her away. On the contrary. He just realized how closed up he could be.

After a deep relationship discussion, they went to bed. They cuddled up close, but he sensed that she was not in the mood for sex. He knew enough about women to realise that their emotions when they were challenged, had to be nurtured back to equilibrium to react towards any amorous advances. Gosh, but making love with her would do wonders for his state of mind,...especially now that he was going to be used as bait tomorrow. Why could women not be the same...

"Rich, are you awake?'

"Mmmm what love" He was about to doze off...

"Please teach me to leave my body."

"But you already do. You just don't remember. Sleep overtook him as Sascia's voice vaguely lingered in his subconscious....

• • • •

He felt a hand pulling at him, directing him through a tunnel towards a light beam. As he entered what looked like green pastures, Sascia was at his side! He couldn't stop staring.

"*Rich, where are we?*" Good grief she was with him! Her auric field shimmered when her lightbody was formed. He was amazed at what he saw. Would she remember?... Where was Theo?

He saw what looked like a Swiss looking cottage in the distance. They were in a valley surrounded by snowy topped mountains. Large boulders that must have broken away in times past, created a rocky landscape higher up while wild flowers in clusters were growing on the steep slopes. The wintry crisp air released a dull sound that reminded him of snow-packed scenes.

"*Moppie, take my hand and we will investigate*" Together they were floating towards the cottage, which brought on great turmoil in Sascia's already exuberant state. "*Oh, It's Buttercup Valley!*" He hadn't been there yet so that was interesting.

"*Rich, are we real? Will I remember all this? Am I dreaming? Oh, look!*" He so remembered his amazement at his first time. Sascia pointed at a grazing deer that looked up, staring. Its brown eyes were filled in wonderment when suddenly its ears picked up. They heard it too as if the whole valley was communicating!

Children were running up the slopes laughing, so the deer leapt away. They had not moved, but it was as if the world around them had suddenly changed. The entire valley underwent an instant transformation and became a settlement...Buildings not there before appeared made from the same boulders half-buried in the land. The mountains were still there but without snow-capped tops. Sascia heaved as a child practically ran through her. A young woman waved, or so it seemed.

"*Does she see us, do you think?*" Sascia grasped his hand as if to reassure herself of his solidness. As they lay in bed, a sudden surge of energy overwhelmed them as if they were being drawn into a vortex. He could sense Sascia's confusion, so he held her tightly. He knew that their physical bodies were still in bed, but their consciousness had travelled elsewhere. However, without Theo, they both felt out of their depth. Eventually, the spinning sensation stopped, and hundreds of trees surrounded them in what looked like a tropical forest.

"*Rich are we still on the same spot? I mean did the world just change while we were in it?*" He was about to answer when a familiar sensation announced the presence of Theo.

"*Richie, the dependability of observation is much greater here than in your physical world of the senses. I see that you brought your soul partner along.*" Sascia stared as if she'd seen a ghost. Theo took her by the arm and guided her to an open space in the thick forest where a huge fallen tree with thick moss and toad-stools became a resting place.

"*I'm so glad that you have found each other. You can now both help each other recall the memories each of you will individually perceive.*" Richard could still not get over the awesomeness of their experiences, share his dream memories, which in itself would be of great benefit for his journal.

"*Theo, it feels all so real and normal to chat with you in this forest while we are asleep. Will it not seem like a nice dream when I wake up?*" Sascia's matter-of-fact approach brought on a smile. Theo tilted his head as if he was listening to the sound of a breeze playing music. More than ever did the wind feel alive as if it was communicating.

"*Theo how do we know we have observed and remembered clear perceptions?*" his thoughts asked. He knew that at first, he had denied his out-of-body experiences. He marvelled at the massive tree ferns and other plants unknown to him.

"*Richie, what you write in your journal is not infallible. Your perceptions can err. No man is free from error therefore one should never make judgments."* Sascia kneeled, touching the thick green moss carpet. It felt great seeing her in the astral. He hoped she would remember her dream.

"Come I will take you both through the akasha chronicles. It's time you learned about the first tribes or root races. Our ancestral records are stored in this prehistoric forest." He got hold of Sascia's hand and allowed the swirls of energy to take over. He sensed that Sascia was as troubled as he was at the beginning, but she never revealed a peep.

"She is not awake in this realm Richie. She probably will not remember anything, but hold on to her." Gradually Richard saw an unusual but spectacular landscape emerging. Green grassland was broken up by deep craters of barren rubble. In the distance, he saw what looked like a herd of...moving figures.

They came up out of the craters carrying boulders of enormous size. The weight must have been staggering. More and more people appeared. As they moved closer, he wondered if they were human because they looked rather black and very hairy.

"Richie, remember that your mind is translating this soul plane into an image unique to you. Just observe. I have to show you how some of our ancestors were de-fragmented to become a slave race".... As he looked closer he had difficulty relating to what he saw as being human.

"Some hybrid species called man were put upon Earth to start a new colony of stone cutters, miners and labourers. They were instead re-programmed to become servants or enslaved people for the lazy fallen angels who called themselves ' Gods.' This was no paradise by any means." Richard knew that some ancient text interpretations reveal all kinds of stories, more so than the hieroglyphs. Some speculated that life on earth germinated from the portion of the destroyed planet that had been blown apart. The wars in

the heavens were well documented but open to many different interpretations. Did a broken chunk of a dying planet really bounce into planet Earth, or was Earth the broken chunk?

"*Richie, so long as you remember that the original architect of our universe is a being that operated within the consciousness of pure light, all will be well. This inner journey will give you some clue that will help you understand what is happening today.*"What he saw next revolted him big time. He felt light-headed, almost giddy as he took in the details. People in groups acted like zombies. Even in mental homes, this scene would be disturbing for most of today's nursing staff. Some science fiction movie makers got quite close to projecting the horror they observed. So they must have been here in their sleep.

"*This is the result of genetic engineering. Grotesque aren't they?*"

Are they our ancestors? He saw some human figures with legs and horns of goats, some had scales and even wings or claws for feet. Some looked more human but most were very very weird. Gosh, that's where the scriptwriters of Star Trek must have got their ideas from.

"*That's it, in their memories they tapped unconsciously into their genetic lineages, but it is not for us to fear the truth.*"He could see what distortions did, but... why rake this all up? Was this a fantasy realm or what? He observed that the creatures were communicating but not through any verbal interaction. More like how animals related to each other. Unless they were telepathic but he picked up nothing.

"*What you see are indeed gross distortions. Richie, it's still necessary to retrieve these records of our ancestral lineages in a physical embodiment. These beings you see are still devolved co-creators like ourselves. Humanity must learn that there must never be interbreeding between different soulless creations.*" Did

Theo mean we created this? Were we the 'Gods' who experimented?

"*Yes in a way, we are their living ancestors. If you physically ascend, they ascend with you, and they retrieve all the lessons therein through your soul. For some on earth, the only means of burning off this karma is in dying.*" Gosh, if that's true, then there is even a service in physically dying.

"*That's right. Many people on a soul level know this, although not consciously. Many individuals sacrifice themselves for their future ascension, knowing that their lineage shall carry on and that all humans are ONE.*" As he observed the grotesque deformities, he felt great compassion, but he was still battling to accept that they were for real. Numerous TV programs expose people with handicaps that were just as bad, but...this was different.

A remarkable part human-part lion creature took a position high above on a plateau. As it gazed towards the horizon, his whole posture reminded him of the Sphinx. Was his mind busy translating or externalising what he perceived?

"*Richie this is what our world looked like about 200,000 years ago. Remember the stories of the Nefilim who came to mine gold.*" What he saw next reminded him of the X-file movies. Half-men half-fish beings seemed to live in and out of the oceans, but they nevertheless appeared to be consciously aware.

"*They are. They have found the passage that takes them to the halls of Amenti. You will soon remember how desperately the extraterrestrial king Akhenaton was looking for the same entrance.*" Vaguely he recalled a young man who became his confidant when he...

Suddenly Sascia commented that she saw the Lion King. The elegant massive creature emanated feelings of loneliness and despair, but at the same time, the beast emanated great love and wisdom. The 13th tablet flashed before his vision! Sascia thought she was looking at a Walt Disney movie, he thought of the Sphinx. His light-body was shaking from the idea that all this was an experiment gone wrong. Could it have been avoided? Why did he feel so sad?

"*Richie when this deformity is recalled from the akashic records, it's somewhat disturbing. It was due to the mixing of a humanoid creature. This resulted in the fall of consciousness.*" Sascia, who was suddenly wearing some kind of futuristic-looking uniform, moved among the creatures as if she expected them to greet her. Instead, they looked dumbstruck up at her, almost fearing her. Could they see her? It was weird observing how mixed genetic cloning turned out. Some beings were a part human part bird, or some appeared to have heads that looked like wolves heads.

"*Richie two separate races were involved in our creation, but then something went wrong. Remember that hybrids are incapable of reproduction. Aunt Mien will tell you African stories that originated from Gondwanaland.*" With riveted attention, he saw that some were aggressively communicating with Sascia. He wanted to join her but Theo stopped him.

"*This is how her soul can gather fragmented parts of itself. She will remember this event as a dream.*" One of the female creatures held on to a baby that seemed to look like a normal human baby. Sascia stroked its head and the child reacted like kids do when they are shy. She turned, looked at him and tears were running down her cheeks. He saw how her energy field was shaking.... Then she was gone....

"Theo, where is she?" It was like the whole scene went with her. Was it a vision from the future, or the past?

"*The soul will only retrieve akashic records it can handle. She will wake up with some memories of the dream, but only the feelings of the dream will have been downloaded.*" Theo's explanation did not tell him who or where Sascia was, instead he took him away to a quiet spot that was bare of any plant life. Was that also gone, destroyed? Had they ruined the planet with all their technology?

"Remember how upset some people were when we were having a campfire discussion? When I speculated that our common genetic inheritance came from a single ancestor between 150,000 and 300,000 years ago." How could he forget? Theo was answering questions from a chap who...

Suddenly a roaring spinning sensation took complete control of his mind...His light-body was intercepted by a physical body! The crackling fire woke him up. They were all sitting around the campfire. Theo was poking in the logs when he replied to a friend's question.

"These creator-gods could have been from a reptilian genetic stream called the serpent people who were already very gifted in the science of alchemy. They had created what we would call humanoids. I hope we, as humans, will never violate the cosmic codes of creation. And yes, the symbol of the serpent of the garden of Eden in the scriptures could refer to the same serpent." An aggressive muttering from an associate in their tourist business silenced the other six members of the hiking team. Russell, a very fit guy across from him who had joined the group at the last minute, blurted out:

"Hey, there is an area of the human brain known as the reptilian brain, how's that!" Everyone started talking at once. One of them stood up and walked away...Richard didn't know any of the people.

"I've read in Sitchin's work that the co-creator gods called Eridu or Anu seeded Homo-sapiens." a camper said. His mind stored so many questions. Like the others, he wanted to know now.

"Theo," he asked. "Why don't we remember any pre-historical fragments at all, or do we?" Everyone waited. Theo was silent. His eyes were closed, and his voice changed to a deeper tone when he answered.

"The geometric codes of the Tetragrammaton will soon trigger reactions within our DNA-RNA. The reprogramming of this world that has trapped us into our earthbound games of karma and cause and effect will soon be over." Nobody spoke a word. The fire had gone down to a smouldering glow...

In his voice, Theo added to it by saying that many historical truths have so long been obscured by dogmatic religious propaganda. In a flash, even while the dim light from the embers clothed them in a shadowy field full of unspoken thoughts... Theo continued, "When the shadows come out to play, absolute chaos will have its day."

"The many emotional mind games people have with their past renders them useless and depressed, or... holding onto an 'expectation of a future that is no more than a state of mind'. Those mind games, which are the shadows, make us incapable of moving on in life. A misunderstanding that"...as Richard stared into the fire, his eyes started to burn. The pain... Theo's words about shadows still lingered at the surface of his mind... But his eyes...were burning...it made him fall forward. Oh no!...not into the fire. With a jolt, he woke up. His heart was palpitating ...

. . . .

"Rich, are you awake?" Sascia's voice held such sadness, he wondered why. What had happened to him? He tried to gather all the images before they disappeared. His eyes felt scratchy.

"Richard are you alright? Gosh, I had such a horrid dream. I'm glad it was just a dream."

"Say that again, so did I." He could only remember that he fell into a campfire, the rest was clouded by the pain in his eyes. Gosh, the pain was so real.

"Tell me Moppie, what was yours. What do you remember?"

"I'm inside a movie house. I'm watching the Lion King, you know the Walt Disney animation. All around me some people are half human half animal. They are all yelling at each other. I tried to warn them. I don't know why, but suddenly Annelies appears and she takes one of the babies away who seems normal. I feel the pain of the mother. ...As if...It's my fault!"

"What is."

"I'm like a spy."

"Spying on what?" Sascia was quiet for a while. He was fascinated at her translation because it triggered visions from his dream which was different but similar, only Annelies never came up...

"That was it. I tried to stop the feelings of guilt."

"How. What were you feeling guilty about?"

"I don't know. Something to do with the child I took away."

"I thought you said Annelies did that."

"Yes, but I called her when I saw that there was a normal baby amongst the...herd...It was my job...Gosh Rich it was all so real! The roar of the Lion King scared me away." Gosh, he was stunned. Should he tell her that he thought it was the Sphinx? His dream was more than just a dream. He clearly remembered leaving his body. Intuitively he knew that he should wait until Sascia started to remember being out of her body.

"Was I in your dream?" he asked.

"Mmm...I think so, do you have a photo of your brother?" Wow! Did she remember Theo?

He got up and looked inside the box with photos of the one he took of Theo in his hiking clothes on their last camping trip.

Gosh, it was as if he was there when he woke up. He remembers staring into the campfire...

Chapter 16
Manifestations Created by Thoughts

Annelies' house

André phoned before eight to let him know he had already staked the railway station. Everyone was in place. André hoped that they would catch the person who was in contact with the abductors. He phoned Annelies to let her know. She was not pleased about him being used as bait but pressed him to call her when it was all over.

Apeldoorn station was bustling that morning. Trains to and from destinations slid along the platforms like bullets holding human cargo. Richard casually held on to a large brown envelope and sat down on the bench next to the condom machine. He knew and could feel that he was being watched. An older woman on the next bench was chatting with a youngster in tacky jeans and sneakers who had seen better days. The boy, around twelve, didn't want to sit down; that was obvious. The woman looked familiar, and so did the boy! He got up and left the envelope on the seat. He was about to go down the escalator when the same child came running after him, holding the envelope.

"Hey, mister! You left this; it's yours, isn't it?" Cocky brown eyes observed him like a hawk that was about to attack his prey. Gosh, he remembered. It was the same child that had snooped around behind the coffee bar counter. Reluctantly, he returned the envelope and decided to wait until it was nine, pretending not to recognise them. The woman got up, called the child, and stepped onto the train. When the train pulled away, he dropped the envelope again onto the seat, but this time, it slid between the seat and the wall. If someone had been still watching, they would have seen it. What now? The loudspeaker announced the next incoming train. He had one last glance through the railing toward the bench as he went down the escalator...

As he walked into the station mall and stepped outside onto the pavement, an adult male came running past, clutching his large envelope. Two men were on his tail. One shuddered to a standstill so as not to get run down by a delivery truck, while the other chased the motorbike that had pulled away like a bullet. The guy with his envelope had jumped on the back. Suddenly, a police car shot away from the taxi rank, and with screaming sirens, it followed the bike. Richard ran to the parking bay, jumped in his Honda and drove back to the Pannekoek.

Jeroen was displaying Sascia's photos on the wall according to her instructions. They both stopped when they saw him.

"How did it go? Did you see anything?" She showed relief that he was back. A few customers had already been served. He joined Sascia and Jeroen for breakfast and told them what had happened.

"I'm sure the old woman and the child were in on it," Jeroen remarked. They were interrupted by the phone as Sascia was about to question why.

"We got them, and the old woman too, including the envelope. The child was gone. We will let you know after they have been questioned. We want you and Nel, the woman who works in your coffee bar, to come to the station to look through some photos we have on file. In the meantime, stay alert because someone is bound to be mad."

Both Jeroen and Sascia grasped what André had implied. Jeroen switched the TV on to find out if anything was mentioned on the news. He phoned everyone and said he would not let Sascia out of sight. He knew that was what Annelies was concerned about. Any fear-based thoughts could be manipulated, so he concentrated on his last dream, which helped. It was obvious to him now. How easy it was to get trapped in a negative train of thought. What energy trail would that leave around them?

André had also asked if it was all right for the coffee shop to be closed between eleven and lunchtime. For some reason, he wanted Nel to join them and to tell her story of when she was apprehended at Annelie's house again. André would take her back to the police station so she could identify the older woman. He could come in later.

It was quarter to ten when he decided to go past his flat first, before joining the others. Nel reassured them that they would manage the coffee shop until Jeroen closed it at eleven to join them. He hung a notice on the door that the Pannekoek would be closed between eleven and one o'clock.

On the way to Annelie's house, he felt it would be a warm day. Last year's summer was so good that many people thought it was a fluke. This year, the summer had started late. Annelies' garden was tastefully landscaped by Toon's firm, The Buttercup. Being on the edge of the Value was a bonus. Annelies lived in a very affluent neighbourhood. He hoped to hear more news about Connie.

They were the last to arrive. Sascia was relieved to see Toon's BMW. She had been worried about her mom's sudden emotional collapse, feeling she should have been with her yesterday, but they both knew that Toon was the only one who had been through the same fear and pain as she. He would relate to her the best.

Joris greeted them with his usual abundance as he handed the abusive e-mail to Ben in the hallway.

They were all in the living room. Sascia hugged her mom, who looked happier when they joined Ingrid and Toon on the large leather sofa. Toon winked at both with his catchy charm.

"Sascia, I meant to tell you that you look radiant. Richard, you scored big; bless you both." Toon was mentally complimenting. Ingrid beamed him a big smile, making him glow into his toes.

Ed and Yolanda were talking to Liesbeth and Hans when Ben and André joined them. They all wanted to know how the station drama went. André had the two photos from the envelope with him, but he first wanted to hear his experience. André more or less told them the same story. The woman kept denying any connection to the boy or the envelope, but she had a record, so they planned to keep her at the Police station for as long as was legally allowed. There was no news yet about Connie.

After Nel and Jeroen joined them at eleven, André would take Nel to the Police station to see if she had ever seen the older woman. He was sure that it was the same older woman who visited the shop with the boy. The young woman had been heavily made up, but he was now equally sure it was Henny from the wedding party at Harry Brinks' house.

He told André what Mien disclosed about her ex and his connection with the granddaughter of Harry Brinks, Henny, who was wrapped up with unsavoury characters. This didn't surprise Annelies in the least but it nevertheless thickened the plot. Her mother Tieneke, was an attractive somewhat mystical independent type around her mid-forties, financially well off. Tieneke reminded him of Theo energy-wise. She expressed a lot of feelings in her artwork. He had been to an exhibition of hers called mind-scapes. They were mostly fantasy scenes. She illustrated children's educational books between her drawing classes. He couldn't imagine that she had anything to do with any of the intrigues.

André told them that the police from Holland, Belgium and France all worked together but there were no new developments. Ben added that both Leo and Trevor were close to a breakthrough but from a different perspective. André shared that he still had difficulty understanding Annelies' theories, but he shared that his half brother was into all of this. Whatever 'this' meant.

"André, your half-brother, what's his name?'

"Niels. We hardly ever see each other." They all were stunned, thinking of Niels from their evening group. André had the same Indonesian bloodline, so it must be true. He knew they all felt the same when Annelies probed André.

"My mom separated from my dad at the time when she was pregnant with Niels, who was not my father's child. We grew up together but when Niels went into computers and I joined the police we lost touch."

"André, didn't your fiancée Ula ever tell you that Carla, who also works for Pleasure Parks, that her boyfriend is called Niels? He owns a computer business and is in our ascension group." Ingrid revealed.

"Really? I have spoken to Carla, but Niels's name never came up. Ula did mention once that Carla's boyfriend knew Annelies. Mmm, when I was so involved with Mr Brinks' burglary, it slipped my mind."

"Niels told us that he never knew his father, did you?" Annelies asked.

"Oh no, my mom was always very cagey about her affair. We presumed that he must have been married. My dad divorced her before Niels was even born. I don't remember all this, but my mom told us that Niels' dad grew up in the same orphanage as her. I learned the other day that some of you grew up there, too." The star painting became more and more a focal point now that this orphanage had again come up. Annelies had said it was a family tree after all.

"My mom is working now in Spain, so I haven't yet asked her," André added.

"People, Hans, Liesbeth, Ben and I have been sharing our feelings about the whole affair since Ingrid was abducted, like Connie. I can no longer ignore the signs POWAH once warned me about. At the time, I could not fathom why I was discouraged by POWAH when I wanted to follow this path. He said that total dedication and pure intent are the requirements to follow this ascension journey, but... it could come at a price. He warned me that there will come a time when choices have to be made which are not easy." Annelies looked at Hans, who nodded for her to carry on. The silence in the room created a gloomy feeling. He always wondered if he was ready for Annelie's approach to life. Intuitively he knew that he had to face what she called the dark force within himself.

"Each one in this room who is participating in this ascension journey must embrace their unconscious addictions because dark forces have manipulated us."

"What does our unconscious have to do with it?" Yolanda looked grieved, so Ed cuddled her.

"Understanding the dark is a difficult thing. Most wish to deny the dark or believe that it is something outside of us, but in reality, there is a darkness of a destructive nature in all of us." Liesbeth's gentle voice softened the blow when she added: "I have, like many here in the room, learned that life is a mirror and what we all have attracted must be a reflection of ourselves".

"There is only one entity in this room," Hans added. For a second, Hans' subtle remark brought things into perspective when POWAH flashed before his eyes. He noticed that Toon wanted to say something but first looked at Ingrid for confirmation.

"Both Ingrid and I have come to a decision. For the sake of our child, the time has come for us to move out of this environment after the birth of our baby. We needed to look at what has happened to us. We have both done some soul-searching on those very thoughts. We need to do a lot of inner forgiving, and we both feel that living up in the mountains and helping Helen and Peter with the community will be good for us." Toon's statement stunned everyone. Were they leaving Apeldoorn?

"But Ingrid... what about Connie? How? ...Annelies, what does Connie's disappearance mirror to me?" Yolanda's sobbing choked them all. André was getting fidgety just as Joris started barking. They must all appear somewhat strange to him. He felt rather loony. He observed that a part of him always fought with his intuitive nature. Ben got up to answer the doorbell.

"I am well aware that we are all manipulated by people who have no interest in the well-being of others, but I can't see that leaving will resolve anything. I always deal with those people; does that mean I mirror that in my subconscious?"

They were all surprised at André's philosophical remark. Nobody had expected that. Richard heard Nel's chatty voice talking to Ben in the hallway.

"André, I know from your energy field that you are a soul with great integrity. You would not be here if you didn't. All in this room have the same...vibration signatures for the lack of a better word." André showed signs of embarrassment at Annelies' frank approach.

"That still means that we all have to take responsibility for what has reflected on us individually. You will most probably reach a time when you will leave your job. That doesn't mean you are running away. It means that your karma is finished with that kind of environment." Annelies held André in her laser-like stare.

Yolanda started to shake. She cried as she turned to Ingrid and Toon.

"I do understand. I can only speak for myself, but my attachment to Piet, who I thought I released in full, has been re-linked again through Connie. Ed and I have talked about the community in Australia, and nothing would stop me from following him and starting a group there, but how can I? I feel I'm not good enough." Yolanda turned to Annelies.

"Surely, after we all work through all five levels of the ascension journey, would we not have released most of our distortions?" Annelies shook her head. Yolanda looked dismayed up at Ed. He felt a long way off from the fifth level. Writing about the second stage made him aware of that.

"I'm so glad you observed that Richard, but remember that time is an illusion. We are already fully awake on a higher consciousness level," Annelies beamed. Yolanda must have heard her.

"I still have every intention of reaching the fifth level, but I know in my heart there is something, a belief issue I have about Piet, that I have not fully released." Everyone was silent when Annelies said that every person who has the motivation to follow this path has the full potential to do so no matter what.

"Sweety, are you saying you will not come with me because you have not finished with your ex?" He knew that many in the room had heard Ed's plea. Yolanda gazed at Ed as she squeezed his thigh.

"I will listen to my heart. If it's my soul's wish, I will know."

Ben introduced everyone to Nel while Jeroen returned Toon's car keys. Liesbeth approached Yolanda, clasping her hands, beaming, *"Good on you, truth resides within the heart; if you follow that, you will find your way home."* Ed was very proud; his eyes were glowing. He peered at Sascia, who winked at her mother. Women seemed to be far more aware of what went on with other women.

Nel uttered a strange remark when Toon got up to greet her. They knew each other. Ingrid's eyebrows frowned in surprise.

"Fancy meeting my former boss. Ingrid, I'm so glad you are fine after your horrible ordeal. I followed everything through the papers and from what Richard told us." Ingrid's utter amazement showed.

"Nel!... but...you were... fired!" she blurted as she looked up at Toon, whose face beamed astonishment. Nel was grinning.

"Well, I asked for it, I'm sure. What I do now is more my line; I'm grateful to have been given the boot. And very generously, I might add. Mr Haardens, take that surprised look off your face." Toon's grin cleared the air. Toon explained to the others that Nel was the receptionist when he took over the landscaping division. Nel told them with her usual chattiness that she got her future daughter-in-law to replace her. Sascia looked at him, beaming: *"Rich is she talking about Ellie?"*

Everyone relaxed when Annelies and Liesbeth brought in their favourite ginger beer. André used the opportunity to do his detective work, asking extensively about Nel's son and daughter-in-law, which surprised everyone. Nel was very talkative and proudly told them that her son Oliver was finally marrying his sweetheart of many years. They had a child together eight years ago when they were both married to different people. Jeroen interrupted her by confirming her surname, Hartman. He peered at his mother, whose mouth was gaping.

"Was your son married to Quincy, my sister?"

"Yes dear. We did meet once at a... funeral". Nel added that she regretted never having seen Kim, her older grandchild, grow up because she had lived in South Africa for many years before her husband joined the Parks Board in Leersum. Joris started barking again.

"Oh snooks, Quincy is going to be so hurt, she always wanted more children but Oliver point-blank refused. Now I understand why." Toon patted Ingrid on her knee. "Kitty, don't worry. Quincy will probably be happy for Oliver. Just imagine how it must have been for him all those years." Gosh another family connection! He couldn't take it all in but he saw that Sascia peered at Nel with an almost hostile look. When Fred came in they were all aware of his connection with Quincy.

Fred was introduced to Nel by Annelies, who beamed; *"Let's see if Fred is picking up something because Nel's energy field has suddenly changed. She knows him."*

"Well well we meet again. I recognised you from the Pannekoek when Connie showed you around." Fred's dignity seemed to always shroud around him like glue.

"Do I know you from somewhere else?" Nel asked. He could sense that Fred was suddenly more on his guard as he frowned at Annelies. Richard wondered what people who are clairvoyant can see. Annelies needed to explain because Fred's distinguished posture had become rigid.

"Fred, we only just discovered that Nel was Quincy's mother-in-law. Is Quincy joining us?" Fred shook his head. She had to see her health shop in Delft.

Nel chatted to Ingrid about her younger grandchild Sammy who had been practicing her email skills with the Buttercups orders while her mother was out of the office. He felt like he had been hit in the gut. Was Sammy Nel's grandchild? Annelies was observing him.

"Richard, what is wrong? Your field is shaking."

Nel's words: "They had a child together eight years ago when they were both married to different people," still rang in his ears. Did his marriage break up because Ellie was pregnant by someone else? He had been so happy when she told him she was pregnant, hoping it would bring back the attraction they had had for each other. Sammy was never his? Many in the room stared at him. Had they picked up on his thoughts? He saw suddenly in a flash what he had never seen before. Ellie's unhappiness. He could never understand the guilt complexes she displayed so frequently. Now suddenly it all made sense to him.

Sascia's hand slid into his, obviously aware that something was wrong.

"Rich I'm so sorry. Please let me inside. Don't close off." He was astonished at her sensitivity.

"Oh Richard, that must"...Ingrid leaned over past Toon and Sascia, touching him. Her eyes were so like Sascia's. Suddenly his joy for finding her released all the pain and hurt at that instant. He had never felt so free...

"Richard, go on releasing. That's one emotional attachment you will never have to carry with you anymore." Ingrid beamed.

"Rich, are you okay?" Sascia whispered. Her gorgeous eyes charmed all his senses.

"Moppie, for the first time I realise how lucky I have been, finding you!" Her confusion showed because she had picked up on his emotional shift.

Jeroen started to cough. He must have sensed a change in the atmosphere but he wanted to stay focused on finding Connie. He and Yolanda were both too absorbed in their distress to have been sensitive enough to feel other people's anguish.

André brought them all back to Connie's disappearance. Both Ben, Toon and Ed seemed to have a far deeper insight into the whole external affair than he and Fred had. He observed that most of them were also ignorant about the intrigues except for

Annelies, Hans and Liesbeth. They seemed to be aware of both the inner and the outer awareness levels.

André got up to take Nel to the station for an identification parade. He thanked Annelies for the intriguing way she showed him of looking at life and he thanked Ben for getting them all together. He talked to Jeroen as he guided Nel out of the room. Richard knew that André wanted to speak with Nel on his own. He didn't yet know that Ellie, her daughter-in-law had been his first wife but André was very observant, he probably understood more than he let on. André told them that he would keep the photos for a while. What for he didn't say, but he was reminded to come to the police station when he was free to do so. Back at the Pannekoek Richard planned to confront Nel about Ellie.

"Well, will someone fill me in on what I've missed? The energy is very electric after Toon's bombshell." Fred demanded. He told Fred and Jeroen what he had just discovered. Sascia's liquid eyes showed compassion but Jeroen stared in disbelief.

"Rich that must have been hard, hearing that..."

"That Sammy is not mine? Yes that was a shock. But I feel no different. She will always be mine. At least she was for the first eight years. I still feel that I'm part of her life. She will have a hard time herself. Knowing that...I wonder. Would they have told Sammy?" He looked around for an answer.

Nobody replied but when Sascia beamed *"I love you, I knew you would feel that way."* both Ingrid and Toon raised their eyebrows. Jeroen was the only one who was unaware of their telepathy.

Sascia's loving beam was like a regenerating tonic.

"My girl, your confession needs to be explored". Their inner connection became more established by the minute as he gazed at her.

"Do you all think that André wanted to interrogate Nel on his own?"...Jeroen asked Ben.

"You use a strong word young man, but yes you are right. André has some theories of his own. Detectives have a mind very much like psychics. They see further than most." Annelies looked at Ben when Ed asked what theories Ben was referring to.

"André thinks that someone has inside information on the Jaarsma clan, their whereabouts and who is vulnerable to whom."

"You mean someone knows why Connie has been taken...what do you mean? Yolanda is her mother!" Jeroen uttered in frustration as he pulled at his finger joints. Ingrid tried to stop him but he shoved her away.

"I think it is high time we looked at this whole mess in a different light. It is drawing us all away from our intent. Jeroen, this family (and you have become part of it), is being tested. Most of us have made an inner decision to explore waking up from the dream. Do you know what I mean?" Annelies asked in her kind but strongly directed tone.

"I think I do, from what mom told me. Connie and I have been talking about it a lot. It makes sense to me in some ways. I know Sascia has always talked till deep in the night with mom." Jeroen's whole posture changed when he admitted to psychic phenomena.

"Debbie is amazing; she has discovered that she can get images by only touching an object or someone. She has been inundated with people from the hospital. But she does not want to become a sideshow. So she clammed up."

"Really? Did she tell you all that?" Ingrid was taken by surprise, but it was Sascia's turn to gape at her brother.

"Why did no one ever tell me about Debbie? Did you know?" Sascia stared at him, but he only knew it from Debbie herself.

Toon told them what had happened at the hospital. All of them had forgotten that Jeroen didn't know about the baby. Jeroen expressed his disappointment at being left out as Yolanda threw her hands in the air.

"Gosh, I included, we seem to all live in our little world. Remember that Annelies shared with us what POWAH warned us about?" Yolanda seemed to get her perkiness back. Her whole energy felt stronger. More determined not to become a victim. That is how they behaved as if they had no say in what was going on. He saw that now. Was there a more extensive plan played out?

The doorbell rang, and Joris responded simultaneously. Ben got up while whispering into Annelie's ear. Liesbeth smiled and Hans winked back. Richard knew instinctively that Connie was somehow safe. He tried to listen to Ben in the hallway as Annelies addressed them.

"Alright, this is as good a time as any to share some of the information I was going to speak to everyone about before we played the game on the first level, but now that you are all here, I feel you all have to be reminded."

Yolanda told him that Wim had backed out at the last minute. Zola had been very upset so she declined to play the game on her own, but wanted to carry on with the decoding workshops.

"On our ascension path, while still living in this 3D reality, we have to recall all the physical memories our soul has accumulated. To achieve a higher level of consciousness, we need to integrate more soul energy into our etheric light body. By experiencing feelings, visions and intuitions, our soul can access the genetic records programmed over a long period. It is important to acknowledge that our DNA contains great distortions." Everyone was letting what Annelies had just said sink in.

"You mean we have to remember all our past lives?" Ingrid asked. Joris was now curled at her feet. When they all heard a familiar voice in the hallway Yolanda cried with joy. When Jeroen heard Connie, he ran from the room after Yolanda. He was so relieved to find out that she was never kidnapped.

"Sorry, Annelies, I didn't want to interrupt you, but..."

"Hold on to your question, Ingrid. Let's wait."

Annelies decided to call it quits. It was time to celebrate. The atmosphere had changed. Sascia squeezed his hand and all he wanted was to be alone with her. He had better not beam his thoughts; he had not managed to be that specific. He knew the others were, but he was sure they were both still open channels for everyone. Toon winked at Sascia, who gave him a push. Toon's throaty laugh, as he gobbled at pieces of cheese which Liesbeth had carried in, made him aware of Toon's acute mental alertness, which was quite remarkable. Yolanda was crying from utter relief. All of them became teary-eyed. Connie seemed fine but looked tired.

She told them all what had happened. Connie's story was gory, full of unpleasant remarks that were made to her when she was blindfolded. Her father had shouted at his buddies that if they dared touch her, he would expose a journal he had kept up to date. It first held all the names and dates of their business deals. They were at his lawyer if anything should happen to him. Piet was very ill, lying on a mattress in a shabby room. Connie was shocked when she realised how bad he was. Connie's vivid explanation had them all spellbound.

"Mom, I don't think he will live for long. Cancer has spread into his lymph glands. He is in great pain, and the woman who abducted me gave him morphine injections that made the pain go away." Ingrid asked if she could describe the woman. When Connie did so, she nodded at Toon. He suddenly thought if Iris could give morphine injections, she must have a nursing background.

"Can't he go to a hospital? Where is he?"

"No, he doesn't want to. Mom, he wants to die. I promised I'd come back if he wanted me to, but he said he had made up his mind. He told me all this in whispers when we were alone. He told me things about when the woman had left the room. He rattled off a date when this lawyer would open his instructions. He was rather dramatic but said he would ensure he was gone before that date." Connie sobbed as she relayed her experience.

"He said it would be at Christmas time," she added in a broken voice. Yolanda's tears were gushing as Ed held her. They were all rather shocked at Connie's sad story. No one deserved this ending, no matter what.

"Did he mention this lawyer's name?" Ben asked.

"Good grief, no. I was blindfolded and brought back to the hotel by the same woman who took me away to see him." Connie cried with her mother.

"She handed me her cell phone so I could tell Dad I was safely back."

"Was the drive long?" Ben asked.

"Oh, yes. It took hours. I think we were on a farm because of the smells. I never saw anything outside, and I was always with Dad. There were no windows." Jeroen said nothing, but he held Connie around her waist.

"Mom, when this woman jumped in front of me as I was about to enter the house, she showed me a photo of Dad, and then I knew it was real." Connie glanced up at Jeroen.

"Jeroen, you would not have been able to stop me from going with her if you had been there, so stop feeling guilty. I wouldn't have gone with her if she hadn't shown me the photo he always carries in his wallet."

Connie had aged from her ordeal; she was not the lively, bubbly young girl he employed. Instead, she was a young woman who had seen the world for what it was. Connie and Jeroen joined them on the sofa. Jeroen handed her something to drink.

"Humanity has reached a low level of consciousness. Connie has observed the physical manifestation of this low consciousness level. When abusive personality entities control the body, the soul tends to withdraw, and this can be reflected in the physical form." Annelies beamed. All he could think of was Theo. That could not have applied to him.

"Richard, don't analyse it. Theo withdrew for completely different reasons."

He looked at Hans, who was leaning against the wall.

"What reasons?" Hans asked if he would step outside for a moment. The sliding doors were open, and the sounds of buzzing insects, crickets, birds, and the aroma of heather and birch stroked his senses.

He felt good stretching his legs. The air outside smelled fresh and alive. Joris ran ahead, chasing butterflies. It was getting near to lunchtime.

"Theo had reached an awareness of full consciousness when he left. Do not ever think of him in any other way. His work only then started when he had reached a full awakening level of awareness." *"But why did he have to die?"* He screamed mentally. Hans looked with understanding but didn't reply. They were at the end of the garden. The Hoge Veluwemeadow stretched out into the distance.

"Richard, most of humanity thinks that ascension means disappearing into the next dimension. It is more transcending into higher consciousness, but humanity has fallen so low in

consciousness that they have to start in reverse. In the highest aspects of life, there is only unity consciousness without duality and illusions. Theo understood this, so he accelerated to a higher dimension through his etheric light body. He never physically died; Theo transformed."

He was aware of the depth of inner understanding Hans seemed to have, but it didn't comfort him. He was older than Hans, but he never felt that he was.

"You mean like the gears of a car. One being the slowest. Then, we reached a faster speed with the second and third gear, and the fourth gear was even faster. Is the fifth our top speed?" He was pleased with his interpretation. Hans laughed, his wild, streaky white hair giving him a mad professor appearance.

"Yes, that just about sums it up." Joris had joined them, sniffing each shrub to check where he should leave his scent behind.

"That's what tracing one's ancestry back is all about. Tracing one's ancestry involves releasing distortions in cellular-molecular memories to program a new genetic code." Hans grinned while inhaling the fragrance of the summer midday.

"Richard, on a cellular level, the motion particles have to spin much faster for more souls to embody our form. Both go hand in hand. More soul energy is needed to release the disunity manifestations. But the soul needs to experience them first through the etheric double. We live during a special time when that is possible for every human." Hans called Joris back. Richard mulled over his words. It was not a new theory, but how could one know how much of one's physical form reflected genetic distortion? Did the world they perceived be for real?

Sascia joined them, saying that the others were going home. He thanked Hans for informing him of the task and let the information slide into his subconscious for later contemplation.

Annelies reminded them about the third workshop planned for the following evening. He left for the police.

Sascia spent the afternoon with Liesbeth, preparing a presentation on sustainable living at the Halfway House. There was so much going on that he wanted to explore, but he seemed to be chronically short of time.

He did the whole evening shift on his own until nine after returning from peering through many photo records of female criminals. He did not recognise the older woman; the photos must have been old. It was quiet; every customer had gone, but he waited for Sascia before closing up. When Liesbeth dropped her off, they shared the events of the day.

It was after eleven when they arrived home. Ginger greeted them with a mmiiioooo. He'd found a playmate from two doors down. He would have liked to snuggle up and make love, but Sascia was keen for him to check his e-mail. ...

——- Original Message ——-
From: "T Zwiegelaar"
To: <R de Jong:;>
Subject: tablet 16
Dear Richard

This sixteenth interpretation made us all aware that it mirrors you. We heard that you have found your twin soul. Theo's translations are almost poetic. The hieroglyphs describe the fire Initiations with such vigilance. Any other translator would have completely missed the essence of their meanings. It reveals the spiritual depth that the artists held about the soul. From an external perspective, love and passion consume the original concepts. Our entertainment activities have confused them by projecting the barrenness of what love is. Most humans find themselves in darkness and experience loneliness before they leave this world. Ancient Egyptians knew about the trappings of our spark of light. Leo and I will soon invite you to show you where Theo found the 22 fragile foils. Don't worry about the original prints that were stolen from us.

As you know, we had Theo's interpretations. Take care and let the detective do his work. Each one has a different role to play during these times.

Regards, Trevor.

They both knew Trevor had received the same e-mail threats, so Ben had to contact Trevor daily. He opened the attachment, which was once more a translation. Sascia urged him to read it while she snuggled up on his lap. Together, they read the e-mail and clicked on the link with the title: The Fire Initiations during the Game.[1]

Tablet 16
Translated by Theo de Jong

Richie, this sheet section was easy to translate, but I wondered if it had a deeper meaning than just what one reads. When I asked for a revelation, I saw how people had to flee from the cities. I saw how the waters came out of the inner world and flowed back to it through only four openings. These centres are now power points that seem to have super-physical healing powers. This tablet was the last one I worked on before I left Apeldoorn. I shared my ideas with Annelies, who was told to reveal her genetic decoding knowledge to the initiates who have reached the third level of the ascension journey. I know the tablets are unclear, but I have discovered that whoever wrote them knew that. I will ask Trevor to show you where the crystal skull was found. Keep the key that you will have seen by now always on you. It will pick up your energy so that it can be energised.

Love Theo

As they both re-read the ten interpretations, Sascia was astonished about the key, and so was he. He was thrilled about how the fire element was translated. Sascia asked him how Theo knew what the symbols stood for.

"I imagine that our bio-gravitational fields are changing. On a cellular level, our thoughts have an effect. Theo must have had help to see further than most. When we awaken more and more about who we are, we build that idea into our nuclei by pure thought. Gee, why do I sometimes have a feeling that I said that before?"

"You mean you had a deja vu?" Sascia giggled. Her flirty glance stirred a fire in his belly.

---

1. https://allrealityshifters.wordpress.com/tablet-sixteen/

"Moppie, I had a deja vu when I first saw you. I knew you from many lives"...He was flirting back big time.

Their foreplay in the lounge ended up in passionate lovemaking until they had both fallen asleep in each other's arms on the sofa. Richard woke up from a stiff neck and carried her to the bedroom. Whatever life would bring, Sascia would always be the centre of his world. The gift of having her as a partner made it a joy to be alive. One day, they would probably make it legal for children to come into the picture. For now, he tried to live in the moment.

She murmured something in her sleep as he laid her down. He tried to listen, but her nakedness distracted him. He wondered if she was astral travelling. Would he be able to see it if he was out of his body?

· · · ·

He settled next to her, and when the vibrations ran through his body, he felt someone pulling at his toe! It almost made him jump back. Because he was getting so familiar with the procedure, he ignored it... When he felt the weightless sensation and mentally rolled over, he looked back at his physical body.

They were both naked. When he looked closer at their bodies, he again saw millions of tiny interlaced threads with a light blue/green colour. This pulsating pale blue/green light raced backwards and forward...Both bodies looked the same. Beautiful.

"Richie, many more people are becoming aware of a world beyond the veil of matter. Remember that everything is of different intensities of vibrations in the luminous kingdoms of the spirit." He knew he had heard that before, but then he was again travelling in his mind, travelling in consciousness, and he must have formulated those words back to him. But where was Sascia?

Theo, in his typical way, requested him to follow. He knew now that his mind could create many experiences, but he still had difficulty grasping a nonlocal world of pure consciousness...

"*Look around you.*" His mind must have formulated the aerial photo captured and stored on Ingrid's flash drive. But now it was different, more as if he was seeing the same scenery as it was...before... the age of this civilisation. He heard a sound so unusual it completely penetrated, as well as massaged him.

"*Experiencing hearing a formation put down in just the right place concerning its surroundings is stunning. It adds an extra dimension to a formation!*"

"Who's doing that, and why?" He was so enchanted, seeing a movement on the ground as if the soil with the trees and shrubs were all moving like it was driven by something. There was no wind, but it looked almost like an invisible storm was making everything shift. No wonder people thought there were other beings from other realities apart from our three-dimensional world.

"*Crop circles are like mouths that speak to us of the strangeness and depth of things. They speak to the heart more than the head and your soul more than the heart.*" he heard mentally.

"*Richie, don't believe that wind or plasma vortexes cause them. Rather, perceive it as a form of intelligence, a higher consciousness creating these patterns.*" He observed how carefully planned patterns suddenly appeared in the living fields underneath his feet!

"*It's a form of language, symbolism in its purest form. It's divine creation in full action! Previous creator gods have partially captured this divine power, but always remember that nothing exists outside God!*"

Theo took him within the eye pattern; it was so peaceful that he felt completely at one for a split second! This opportunity to contemplate with Theo while his body was sleeping was genuinely remarkable.

"*Theo, I've been thinking about symbolism and realise that lots of our perceptions are from our interpretations of the symbols we see, speak of, create in the form of words and even hear, feel and touch; not so?*" Looking around him, he now wondered who was, for obvious reasons, deliberately trying to get man's attention with this eye symbol. Was there an observer separate from themselves?

"*My brother, the human eye, like the symbol you see, is the symbol of consciousness. You know why!*" His brother gave an encouraging 'you're getting warm signal'. He was thinking of a circle that Trevor drew on the board of the lecture he had attended weeks ago...and they were inside!..

"*Yes, you are getting warm; all creatures, from the central suns down to mono-cellular beings, are built according to the symbol you see before you...the circle*"....Richard thought about the power of the one Trevor had drawn inside a circle on the blackboard. Then, his brother mentally projected.

"*God...manifests himself in the visible world as a dot within a circle; the pupil within the iris. It is at the point where the highest frequencies are. The energies radiating from that point form an idea, then separate. The 'between' towards movement creates the illusion of time. It is called divine creative power.*" Pondering over what he had just heard, he thought of God, constantly radiating. So what he saw around him, wherever he looked, even if his mind created it, was still all part of the one source, one energy force that permeates all. It suddenly took him back to a classroom where they were taught how to project in six directions.

"*Good, you're starting to remember. The scriptures have left out how, in Akhenaton's training, students were guided in their meditations to project out in six directions, then to connect the lines to form a square, then to form a pyramid and then to bring the lines down into a pyramid which we call an octahedron."* He was so thrilled that he remembered the rest. Even though it was just a mental image, the classes on sacred geometry returned to life.

"Theo, I get it! *What we call Ether is omnipresent and fills the entire universe! And we are all in it!*" So that meant that nothing could exist without being in this substance called Ether and without Ether penetrating it! That means all is Ether. Nothing can displace or dislodge the presence of Ether!

"Yes! *You see now that what we call Ether, the fifth element, stands above all manifestations of life. Why? because it rests in absolute equilibrium within itself.*" While Theo explained his theory, he could not take his eyes away from the planet's revolving, moving outer layer. He wondered how he would describe it from a physical angle. If it made no difference in what dimension or density of consciousness he perceived himself to be, some creative force manifested through different wavelengths, waveforms, and frequencies! But where does the human being fit into all this?

"*Some of the lower vibrations became what we are, co-creators.*"

Theo replied in thought. It was easy to forget all this when he was back in his physical body.

"Richie, *we are observing and experiencing what we would call a memory from our Lemurian past that has been brought back into your awareness.*" As he observed the landscape, nothing resembled any part of the world he knew. He was thinking of the area that held these underground tunnels; who built them? What it looks like today is in no way looking like this. This could very well be in the future or the past.

"*That's a good observation. Richie, there are places on the planet's surface that maintain a direct energy relationship with earthly waves. The pyramid was built on one of those waves, but it has been since the planet's 14th century. Solar shift, new planetary centres have been formed".* He stood up and walked over moss-covered ground that now and again released steam vapours. The sulphur smell in the air reminded him of naturally heated pools. Was this what the planet looked like thousands of years ago? Where are the people, the cities, if any? Suddenly, he stood on what looked like a disk spinning just above the surface. Then, at that point, his vision turned into a feeling because suddenly, he had an irresistible urge to move towards its centre. His mind created a vision as if he was inside a tunnel of sorts.

"Richie, I've discovered a network under the seas that was a passageway to the inter-terrestrial world." He thought of the underground tunnels, but this was more of a vortex. He recalled Theo's letter describing how he got visions by peering into a Crystal Skull. He knew that Theo read his mind, but he was alone when he stood peering into a bottomless pit where only pure vapour was seen curling up…He wondered what would happen if he stepped off the edge. It looked hot. The vapour could easily be a substance that could reach boiling temperature… He knew he was asleep in his bed, so the fear of being boiled alive should not grip him.

"Your mind has given it an appearance like a wormhole. You are looking at an electron." He still wondered if he should step in. Something drew him to do so, but why?

"What is an electron, some kind of particle?" he mentally asked.

"We know it as a primary carrier for electricity in solids, but the Crystal skull showed me that within this energy vortex, there are the elemental beings that create physical matter through the thought waves you are looking at." Was that what these were? Thought waves?

"You mean angelic beings?"

"Yes, that is how the human mind forms shapes that look like fairies or angels. So you see each lightwave that makes up a physical form allows our consciousness to become the architect of our inner world." He suddenly remembered the spinning disks. He had seen plenty of fairies in that dream journey. He wondered what this all had to do with his experience as a human being in a human body.

"Richie, I took you here for your soul to activate the memories of how we knew how to store divine power."

"What do you mean, store divine power. Like a battery? How?"Oh, he had so many more questions!

"Now now, all in good time, you will soon travel with me to the magnificent pyramid...the storehouse of that energy was utilised by spiritual initiates to gradually elevate the human form in vibration to transcend the experience of death. In the process, the embodiment was converted back to the original "crystalline." form This was accomplished over a twenty or more year time-frame." He had no idea what Theo meant by crystalline form.

"Richie your genetics hold this flame of remembrance. Once your ancestry was filled with magic, filled with the abilities of instant manifestation and teleportation and inter-dimensional travel. They left a legacy in the form of a crystal skull."

...in an instant, Theo brought him back to his physical body ... At first, all he saw was the pulsating fibre network of his etheric body that seemed to be in constant motion. He knew that Sascia was lying next to him but...she was not there...but...suddenly he observed how her light-body was hovering above her physical body, like his. Had she also just arrived back? She smiled at him. Before he could ask her anything she was gone. He noticed that her physical body started to move...

"Rich, try to merge consciously back in your physical body. I'm well aware of its limited perception ability according to the organs of sensibilities. I will keep reminding you of it, don't worry!" He hoped he would be as clear about his out of body travels as he was now. There was so much to learn.

He now knew that together they would penetrate the veil that separated them all from the world of spirit. With that focused thought he would try to wake up next to her; reveling already at the prospect of her naked closeness, feeling her curves next to him. When she turned, Theo's last words still lingered in his mind while his hands were exploring her soft roundness. Again he experienced a deja-vu.

"Because our biological ancestors have passed on their beliefs and concepts of truths through the thought forms that created their physical bodies, this time around your soul wants to explore being fully present in your physical body, remember that." He had such a pull, he tried to hold on to his awareness, but all he was aware of was his full bladder!

• • • •

When he came back from the bathroom, Sascia was watching him. He was about to explore her curves when the phone in the office rang so he gave her a morning kiss and got up to see who it was so early in the morning. Gosh, please no more drama!

He spoke to a woman who wanted to see him at the Pannekoek. Her voice was muffled as if she had her mouth covered up. When the woman carried on about working part-time in the coffee shop he was tempted to accommodate her. When he returned to the bedroom Sascia was already under the shower. He shared that a niece of Nel offered her help. Sascia gave him the thumb up while brushing her teeth. He felt sad. It was the first time they had no sharing of dreams, no snuggling or making love before the day started...

Annelies' ascension-workshop
Class 3

For a change, they were the first to arrive. On the door was written:

Our chromosomal blueprint

Annelies had decorated the walls with hands of all descriptions. From baby's hands to big man's hands to thin delicate hands. Each hand had a story to tell. Richard never realised the essence that was revealed by a palm-print alone.

Liesbeth and Hans came in after Toon and Ingrid. Joris made sure he was made a fuss off by everyone. Niels and Zola arrived with Ed and Yolanda in tow. Soon the large table was covered with sheets of paper with collected data from the two previous workshops.

"Annelies one's fate, is it engraved in your hands before you are born?"

"Niels, let me show you a PowerPoint presentation that so impressed me. Trevor is truly becoming a creative graphic computer boffin in his later years" When they all watched, suddenly his dream from a few weeks ago jumped into his mind. Why cropcircles had anything to do with the lines in their hands was a mystery, but looking at Trevor's creative video created a whole new perspective surrounding palmistry.

"Fate is always in your own hands Niels, but I know what you mean. No, the lines can change, sometimes rapidly, in response to a crisis."

They could see why—a human figure on the screen in the manner that clairvoyants might perceive them. The brain impulses were spread over the woman as she walked through a forest. You could see what she was thinking! Then, the camera zoomed in to take a closer look right near the surface of the palm of her hand. Trevor had tried to create a moving image similar to the one he remembered from his dream! He remembered the words, "Our biological ancestors have passed on their beliefs and concepts of truths through the thought forms that created their physical bodies," Annelies explained.

"So you are saying that the lines, patterns and fingerprints, are inherited?"

"Niels, our chromosomal blueprints are responsible for the shape of our hands, especially our fingerprint patterns. Remember that we are exploring our biological consciousness." Annelies wanted to see Ingrid and Sascia's hands. She explained how genetics do play a role. Her drawings and simulations to do with their grid structure that made up a human form, once again reminded him of his connection with the Christ-conscious being Akhenaton; who Theo said came from the star system Sirius.

"Look, many of the markings in Sascia's hand reveal a similarity to Ingrid's markings but you also see a great difference in the two palm prints."

They were all standing behind Sascia and Ingrid who were enchanted by the revelations they received. There were three magnifying glasses on the table. Toon grabbed one and started to inspect Ingrid's palm in great detail. He wanted to do the same but it brought on so many giggles from Ingrid and Sascia that Annelies broke up the party.

"Tonight we are preparing our two hand cards, while we are mapping our hands, meaning you are going to add all the markings on your two sheets." She pointed to the chart on the wall with all the markings that reminded him of their doodles. They were all working on an A4 sheet that would later be reduced to the size of a playing card.

"Gosh imagine that I would be the size of a flea. Then my biggest lines are the main freeways or highways and my secondary lines are minor roads." Sascia commented.

"Not to mention the mound, hills and valleys in your palm-print landscape," Liesbeth added. Hans seemed to enjoy himself. He knew that there was a lot of telepathy going on between them, but he also knew it was on a private wavelength. Hans looked up and winked, acknowledging his thoughts.

Annelies made them all work first on their lifeline. In no time he was involved with learning how to read the warning signs in his palm print.

Sascia was looking at his right hand when she took the magnifying glass and spotted a star symbol on his lifeline. She mentioned it to Annelies.

"Let me have a look. Mmm, Richard something major is in store for you at a certain time in your life. Something happens to you that directs a sudden rush of energy."

"Like what?

"That I can't tell you. Just keep it in mind." They all had to hold their hands up in the air and Annelies showed some interesting characteristics of each person in the room. Soon they were all looking at each other's hands. It was a playful relaxing time for all. Annelies had an interesting way of showing them what their fingers revealed.

Annelies went around looking at each palm print. She predicted that he would relocate. Somehow he had heard that before. Sascia wanted to know if she had the same signs.

"Gosh this would be handy for André to learn, I can just imagine how handy this could be for a detective," Yolanda remarked.

"Annelies, will you create a workbook like Tieneke's?" Ingrid asked. Annelies replied that she was planning to put their first and second workshop material into a book format when she was writing her journal on the third level.

"Could any one of us give workshops using yours and Tieneke's books?" Yolanda asked.

"I hope that one day there will be a program that would do your decoding for you, but now is not the time. For now, we make it a creative exercise we all love to experience."

During their break, Liesbeth and Sascia were discussing their plans to drive up to France together in Liesbeth's car the following day. He would be on his own again the coming weekend.

"Richard when will Mien be back in Holland?" Annelies asked. Niels asked what his plans were when he no longer had to run the coffee shop. He realised that he was not feeling good when he was asked that. He had no idea what answer to give. He responded by saying that he considered teaching full time. Annelies asked if he knew what he would like to do. He was honest in telling her that he would love to have a year off in which he could just write, research and read up on many things he had not had any time for.

"Just state that as your vision you want to manifest, and you will create it." she beamed. Richard understood it was probably just that, but he was not all that strong in visualising what he wanted.

Annelies was called to the phone...When they were packing up Hans suddenly got up and left the room. He sensed that something was wrong.

They all did because the atmosphere had changed. Liesbeth was sitting quietly staring ahead, listening.

"Lizzy, it's the hospital, Dad has been assaulted. I thought that Dad had taken every precaution to remain anonymous so he could not be traced. I'm now convinced that these artefacts in the tunnels

have been released against the wishes of a secret organization that probably has powers that even our government is unaware of. Will you let everyone know, Toon, mom..."

Toon got up and left the classroom. Ingrid and Liesbeth stayed behind to tidy up. He was stunned. Why had Ben been attacked?

"Gee Rich, how can anything happen to... Is Ben not a policeman himself? What do you think is going on?" She whispered. She must have also heard Hans' telepathic message.

"I'm sure we will find out. Will you still see Liesbeth tomorrow?" She never said or beamed she wouldn't, but then, Dirk is probably flying up and down. They all left after Ingrid promised to call them to let them know what happened to Ben.

"Oh Rich, will it always be like this...one drama after the other?" he heard her thinking when they walked to his Honda.

Chapter 17
The Initiations through Conscious Awareness

The Pannekoek
The coffee bar was buzzing with customers. The TV showed clips of earthquakes, tsunamis, and other natural disasters. Some were watching, but many people were coming in to discuss alternative topics. The Pannekoek had become a meeting place for the weird and controversial. He used to serve many people from Pleasure Parks, but only Carla and Ula, colleagues of Ingrid, stayed on as regular customers. Carla ordered a pancake with all the trimmings and sat at the counter to him. She was not worried about her weight and asked after Vinny, her ex. He explained that his friend had never returned his calls or emails since Sascia moved in with him. She shook her head, saying that he had it coming. He was unsure what that remark meant, so he let it pass.

Connie greeted her and told him she was visiting Ben this afternoon with Jeroen and Ed. He heard from Annelies that Ben had been released from the hospital the previous night after a thorough checkup. He was severely beaten up, but most of the injuries had been on the surface. A few cracked ribs would take some time to heal. The two days in the hospital with Debbie must have done the trick. Knowing Hans' healing skills and Debbie's abilities, anybody would recover fast.

André's fiancée, Ula a bright redhead, joined Carla at the front counter. It was their lunch break.

"How is Ben Jaarsma doing, Richard?" Ula asked.

"He's back home. I believe his injuries look worse than they are, thank goodness." He had heard from Toon, who phoned them after they'd got home from the workshop, that André had found him. Ben must have managed to infiltrate some stronghold near that clinic where Ingrid had been captured. He liked André. Richard felt that Ben should have taken him under his wing. He now understood that Ben was more a freelance operator and that André seemed to respect him greatly. Richard suspected that Ben had been holding back information. When he aired his views, Toon explained that Ben had experience in the black magic cult criminality levels that André didn't have. Toon added that Ben has great regard for André and has given him more leads than he ever would have shared with any other member of the police force.

"Niels told me that André, your fiancée is his half brother. I was so surprised. Did you know?" Carla asked Ula who shook her head while sipping a milkshake. Carla and Niels were an item, so he must have shared what had happened during their workshop at Annelies.

"Only last week André told me that Niels and he were close relatives. He was in such a state when he came home late around midnight. He had raced Mr Jaarsma to the hospital in his police van."

"Really! Do you know why he was so upset?" Carla asked. Both he and Connie were listening to the two women.

"Something to do with a syndicate that steals and sells artefacts. Interpol has only four people working in its stolen art and artefacts unit. Mr Jaarsma is one of them. André thought that Mr Jaarsma was beaten up because he discovered, or got near the stronghold of a western diplomat who has been smuggling objects for more than a decade. I don't think that was it though.

It was far more sinister, to do with a cult of some sort." Ula told Carla.

"You mean voodoo stuff, like black magic?" Carla winked, knowing his interests in esoteric subjects. Ula said that André never talked about his work, but this time he was out of his league... so to speak.

Their lunchbreak was over but he heard more news from their gossip than ever before. The story about the mummies became more and more plausible. What Toon had said about Ben now suddenly started to make sense. When the two women left, Connie shook her head in bewilderment and said goodbye as Sascia walked in.

"What, haven't you left yet?" He was pleased to see her but Liesbeth had already postponed her trip to France twice.

"Something is going on in France. The whole area is crawling with police and journalists. I came to tell you that Trevor will give a press release in one hour. Annelies has moved our workshop a day earlier so we can all leave for France on Friday. Rich, I so wish you could come too."

"You know that they have scheduled my fourth and last lecture for the next day; how can I?"

"I know, but they have cancelled often enough, can't you do the same?" It was tempting but it felt wrong to do that. The numerous people who had made plans to attend the last time but aired their disappointment of the cancellation through email, primarily an older man who asked such interesting questions. No, he couldn't. He also started to have a suspicion that someone higher up wanted to stop his lectures from happening. When the coffee shop was quiet again, he shared what he had overheard about the tomb raiders....

"Rich, Trevor's on, come, listen!"

Sascia turned the radio up. He'd just been to the kitchen where Nel was debating with a part-time helper, a young man with ambitious plans to start his own catering business. He could learn a great deal from Nel. He wondered if he was another one of her relatives.

"Good afternoon. This is Roger from radio Apeldoorn. I'm again honoured to have Trevor Zwiegelaar in our studio to tell us what is happening to do with the unrest around the Pleasure Parks building site."

The announcer explained the history of the unrest before asking Trevor to take over.

"Thank you, Roger. The reason why I'm glad to be on your program is that I need to alert our listeners about the looting that has been going on for years."

He wondered how they always got hold of Trevor to speak on the radio.

"You mean the hundreds of thousands of artefacts that have not even been documented by an overburdened cultural-relics department?" Roger responded. Richard was suddenly wondering if the rumours surrounding the underground gold deposit readings were on to something.

"That's right. A very good friend of mine has been working with Interpol for the last six years. He has been beaten up so we know that he must have got close to opening a hornet's nest, and we all know what that does."

"Has it got anything to do with the underground tunnels that were discovered during the blasting?"

"Yes, we have to go back for some years. We now suspect that during the first world war a very well known and very wealthy art dealer in London had managed to smuggle at least 22 mummies from the tombs in the Valley of the Workman. Probably in pure daylight. Remarkably, the Egyptian authorities at that time allowed such plundering to take place."

It was not that busy but he missed part of the interview by helping a customer. Sascia was glued to the speakers.

"How did it get to France?"

"It was purchased by an English professor who had a fascination for Egyptian artefacts. This professor lived in France during the second world war when the Chateau, which is now named Half-way House was an Orphanage."

"Is there a connection with the Prinsegracht Hotel here in Apeldoorn?"

Roger, from the radio, obviously knew that there was. It was getting busier, so when they both returned to the counter, Trevor thanked Roger for the opportunity to alert the listeners not to purchase antiquities without legal ownership certificates.

"Gosh Rich, what a story. What do you know about this English professor? Trevor said that his name was Karel de Jong, but that is a Dutch name, could he have been your grandfather?" The thought that a member of his family was responsible for getting stolen mummies into France was rather disturbing, but then nothing surprised him anymore.

Sascia was such a tremendous help; he would take her to an excellent movie to celebrate the fact that he would not have to spend the night alone.

Annelies' ascension workshop

"Rich, where are you?" Sascia was still waiting for him outside the flat when it had started to rain.

He heard her but the guy who was wearing a balaclava had him pinned against the wall with a knife to his throat. He could see that the man's eyes were bloodshot and angry. His breath reminded him of overboiled eggs.

"Call out and I'll slice your vocal cords." he hissed. They were outside his flat's door. He wondered if the neighbours Bernie and Jane were in. He couldn't remember if he parked his car behind their green Opel when they came home. They were on the way to Annelies when he realised that he had forgotten the printouts of the first sixteen tablets.

"Open the door and get the CD with the photos and all your brother's work, fast!" He knew that Sascia would come up any moment to investigate. He didn't want the creep to get her in his clutches. He knew that his briefcase was in the car. The CD was in the safe in the Pannekoek and André still had the photos. André was right, somebody got mad. What could he give the creep to stall him? With great effort to stay focussed he beamed; *"Hans, Toon, Annelies can you all hear me? I'm hijacked inside my block of flats."* He projected his thoughts so strongly, it brought on an instant headache.

The key opened his front door. He was dragged inside, while the knife started to cut into his skin. The guy banged the door shut with his foot. He was almost relieved. Sascia, who was bound to come back up, wouldn't know...

"We got your message. Keep him there," is all he heard.

"No games. Be quick, we've got your girlfriend just in case." That comment made him so mad, he kicked the creep in the groin while grabbing hold of the blade with his bare hand. When he heard the shots he was on the floor.

"Get away from the door," André yelled.

As the door burst open, three policemen came running in with drawn pistols, just like in the movies. He heard the sound of shattering glass coming from the kitchen. They were on the second floor, but the man must have gotten away.

"Rich! Oh, you're hurt!" Seeing Sascia unhurt was such a relief but when he saw that his hands were covered in blood, for a second he wondered if he had injured the guy.

"Rich, where is the blood coming from?" She knelt next to him on the floor. His whole flat was crowded with people. André helped him to get up.

"It's just a flesh wound in his neck," André remarked to Sascia who was crying. His one hand was bleeding the most. When he grabbed the knife away from his throat he had felt that he cut himself.

A paramedic inspected his neck, bandaged one hand and wanted to give him an injection in case of infection, but something told him to refuse the jab so they went away. By this time he was on the sofa.

The man, who was about to grab Sascia, was caught in the street trying to get away from the police.

"You were both very lucky. The neighbours saw what happened outside. They spotted a man coming from behind Sascia wearing a balaclava as she was calling out for you. Toon also phoned me on my cell when I was on the way home. How he knew about the abduction attempt is a mystery to me." André added. Sascia was shivering.

"Moppie, you're all wet, come close."

He grabbed a blanket off the sofa and draped it around her. André brought them both a cup of hot chocolate. The police left while André stayed with them.

"What were they after?" André asked.

"The same thing. The CD, the two photos that you still have...and oh yes...the creep said...all my brother's work." André paused. He recalled what Ula, his fiancée, had told Carla in the coffee shop. Did André think he has something to do with the stolen artefacts? When the phone rang Sascia jumped up to get it.

"Annelies we are fine." She told her what happened and that André was with them. Then she was listening.

"Rich, do you still want to go?"

"To Annelies' workshop, of course, and you?"

Sascia told her they would be there in twenty minutes and went to the bedroom to change. André asked him all the questions, including how Toon could have known. He reminded him of their telepathic skills. He didn't want to tell him what he heard from his fiancée, but he knew at least where André was coming from. André knew about his and Theo's past tourist business and realised he had been thoroughly investigated.

André said goodbye, saying that they must get together one evening. He was genuinely interested in their theories, and so was his fiancée.

Sascia was driving. She insisted. His hand was starting to throb, so was the cut in his neck.

"Oh Rich, how do we mirror all this violence?"

"Moppie, I don't think we must see it that way. We decided to map an ascension path, and like most journeys, there will be obstacles."

"What you mean is that the darkness is our obstacle?"

"I don't think so. The light could be an obstacle."

"How come?"

"I think that evolution means evolving through balance. Evolving or awakening our right side consciousness with our left side consciousness."

"You mean a united mind?"

"Yes. It's the united mind that can communicate with the universal mind. Or... our higher mind is starting to tap into an energy field that connects everything in the universe."

They arrived at Annelies' house. Joris must have heard them because something brought on his barking. Ingrid and Toon were the first ones to greet them. Mother and daughter did their thing while Toon greeted him with a heartwarming embrace. They were shocked to see the bandages on his hand and throat.

Everyone was glad the see them. Annelies told him that Ben would like to speak to him after the workshop.

"Where is he?"

"Still recuperating. Ben's in the bedroom. Come join us and let's start.

Class 4

THE JAARSMA MAP

When Richard read what was on the door, he knew he was in for a treat, but the first half-hour was taken up by all of them wanting to know what happened. He was grateful for their love and support.

"To my telepathic family, thanks for your listening skills, we would not be here if it was not for you all."

"Tonight we'll finish both cards with the help of the Star-map. I know you have all been wondering when our genograms were going to be used. But first, let me tell you a story."

After Annelies' extraordinary tale, she showed them her ancestral family tree with her grandmother, Katrina Jaarsma and her grandfather, Tim de Jong. She took another two sheets, showing only the outlines of her left and right hands. The night sky showed the shapes inside her hand on the new paper. Her significant life, heart, head and faith lines were still showing.

"Now I look at the symbol chart from Tieneke's Language of Light book. Look at the markings that I have in my palm prints."

They were all listening with rivetted attention because Annelies also showed them what she completed left and right hemisphere cards looked like.

"Now I have to intuitively think, what was my relationship with my mother." She drew the star inside her left palm print with the night sky as a background. Suddenly they all saw how she came to the constellations inside her palm prints. Inside her booklet, the palm print they worked on was reduced with written information next to it.

"Gosh Annelies, I must hand it to you. I can see how you linked each type of genetic relationship with your soul family." Gerrit was far ahead of him.

There were only three people he'd ever known in his physical life he'd call family.

"Richard, think back to when you were a child. *Stories that are told by family members are still all there in your organic filing system.*" Annelies beamed. He had vague memories about his grandfather who lived in France, but that might have come up only now, after the radio interview.

While they were all busy following Annelies' method, Niels told them that he and André, his brother, had spoken to their mother.

"Is she back from Spain?" Gerrit asked. They all looked surprised. Niels nodded, adding that both he and André wanted to know everything about their real father... They all waited...Niels was silent for a long time.

"Liesbeth, do you see what I see?"

"Yes, his field is stalling. Interesting when sudden revelations can release such emotional pain." The others who also heard their telepathic dialogue were all, like him, wondering who Annelies was referring to but nobody spoke. Gerrit asked Annelies if he could use the phone in Ben's study. Both Liesbeth and Annelies nodded to each other.

"Niels what did she tell you, we are all holding our breath here," Toon commented. Zola grinned. She had been very quiet the whole evening.

"My mom confessed that we are not half brothers. Her husband couldn't have children. They only found that out during her second pregnancy."

"Gosh Rich, just like Ellie and Oliver" Sascia blurted out. "Rich I'm sorry. That was out before I knew it."

Niels, Gerrit and Zola wanted to know what Sascia meant, especially Zola. During their coffee break, he told them.

Niels asked him how he felt, knowing his wife had cheated on him. He responded that if he had been more sensitive he would have known.

Gerrit came back looking like a different man. Niels confessed that he always felt guilty that André's dad left their mother because of him. Annelies warned that everyone in the room had to go through their resurrection process. The keys to their awakening were hidden in the energy that created feelings.

The rest of the evening they were all looking at each other's genogram sheets while working out the two different lineages. Richard was again stunned at their revelations. They were all unfolding into a plot so ingenious, how could they never have seen it? He had difficulty using his bandaged right hand, but the shock of his ordeal had practically gone. Sascia squeezed him under the table.

Gerrit asked them all to wait. He had something on his mind. That had been obvious the whole evening. Annelies nodded for him to speak up.

"Niels...I've just spoken to your mother..." Niels looked at him in total amazement.

"You know her?"

"Oh yes...very well indeed. Only tonight my suspicions were confirmed." Niels' whole posture shifted. All in the room felt a surge of emotion coming from him. Ingrid, Sascia and Yolanda reacted to his feelings with tears. Annelies and Liesbeth took deep breaths. Ed, Toon and he reacted sympathetically, while Zola started to giggle.

"Are you my dad?" Niels asked in a croaky voice. Gerrit could only nod in reply. They were all waiting for Niels' reaction. What Gerrit did next made them all teary-eyed. Niels was dumbstruck.

On the way home Sascia drove. His hand was sore, he suspected that he'd cut the muscles. They went past a chemist to get painkillers. The following day he would have to get it seen to.

"Rich, you should have asked for Hans to heal." He never even thought about it. He would give him a call since he wasn't going to France with Liesbeth and Sascia the following day.

When Sascia parked the Honda behind the green Opel they both recalled their ordeal. Sascia stroked his neck. The bandages were a strong reminder of how it could have ended.

"Let's drink some hot chocolate, and curl up in bed. Are you ready and packed for tomorrow?" he suggested before they got out of the car. She nodded.

When they walked inside, both of them looked around just in case. The window in the kitchen would have to be repaired. Sascia put her bags in the hallway while he made the hot chocolate. The plastic sheet in the window pane reminded him of their narrow escape that could have turned very nasty.

"Rich, before we go to bed, can we look at your mail?" he agreed and joined her on the sofa that now had a new cover. While his laptop went through its connection procedures they sipped their drink in silence.

"Rich, what do you think went wrong?"

He was trying to read her mind.

"You mean what got us trapped into the illusion of our realities?" She nodded.

When the title: When Myths Rule the Game appeared in the sub heading of an email, they were both became absorbed in the content.

——- Original Message ——-
From: "T Zwiegelaar"
To: <R de Jong:;>
Subject: tablet 17

Tablet 17

Translated by Theo de Jong

"Wow. Rich, how many people are aware of all this?"

"Probably not enough. On an unconscious level many, but consciously, I don't think so."

He was thinking of André and Ben, who were both involved in exposing the tomb raiders; the thieves and smugglers who were stripping away precious artefacts to sell them on the black market. He started to suspect that the author of the tablets knew that his message would be found, because of the illusion of time. The tablet stimulated his visionary faculties. For some reason he understood what the author was trying to do to the reader, but how he knew that was a mystery.

As he re-read the ten rhyming sentences, inexplicable images entered his head as if a new right-brain perception had been applied. He leaned back on the sofa while Sascia snuggled up. When the vibrations rippled through his whole body, he sensed that Sascia felt them too....

• • • •

Together, they drifted off...He knew...This time, they both would have an opportunity to become an observer of their soul's many incarnations...

They were levitating through thick, lush vegetation when a glimpse of the unmistakable shape of the great pyramid with an opaque brightness of a pearl, came into view. They both gaped with astonishment because today these ancient monuments looked so very different. Would he genuinely find out who had built them and why?

"Yep, you will. The pyramids were built by our ancestors from a parallel universe as you know already, but first, you must both observe how obstacles and diversities can hinder our evolution." His mind was mesmerised by what he saw next:...Sascia was enchanted. There was water all around...Everything looked neat and clean.

"Theo, is that what Egypt looked like, no deserts but green tropical growth around the whole plateau?" Sascia called out in surprise.

"I know we suspected a tropical climate, but the neatness is impressive" He responded in awe. Time was indeed not an issue here.

"Rich, are we going in?" Sascia's excitement was noted, for Theo's expression reflected amusement.

"Remember both of you, we are not part of their thought projections, only observers. We are observers of the mental hologram of our akashic records". Richard was flabbergasted. It was so like watching a movie and being part of it. Like being on a set, but he could still smell, hear, feel and see it all.

"Theo, what holds it together? If this is not 'real' who projects this for us to participate in?" Sascia asked. He wondered if it was some form of virtual reality game but that a bigger mind was controlling these thought projections. Theo looked at him but no mental dialogue had reached him. Richard sensed Theo's unease as if he recalled something alarming. He almost choked with fear when he remembered swimming underwater through a narrow tunnel... He knew that he had to go down further into an even narrower passage while his lungs were bursting...There was a gap above where the sunlight played a tricky illusion, but he knew it was more fearsome to reach for air. Then the crocodiles would get to him. This time he knew that he had to control his terror so he could join the others for his final initiation...

Then... it was over. He was free, walking in the open air...

"What? Did I, or we? Is this all coming from the one source? Was it all a game?" All around him, the scenery still looked like a tropical paradise. The air was even invigorating and pure! Theo sighed and shook his head. He sensed that he was supposed to remember something but what? They sat down between the flowering shrubs. Sascia was dancing between the flowers. He joined Theo and revelled at the peacefulness of it all.

"The more thought intensity that is expressed in a project, the more it expands. All illusions rely on emotional thought-beams of energy that is projected into an idea. This keeps it alive." Theo's metal beam sent him spinning back through time. Now he remembered. As he was lying in the sarcophagus inside the King's chamber during his last initiation, he had seen himself as Richard! At the time it had so confused him, he thought he had failed...

Sascia nodded to Theo, who explained how thought forms immediately manifest in the fourth dimension.

"Rich, that's what mom told me. She was always dreaming of community living and then Toon came into her life!" He heard her but he was still recovering from his awakened memories...

They were both distracted when they saw a very tall couple strolling past the magnificent garden. Sascia's comment escaped him when he heard that the colours of the flowers gave off a sound! They bloomed in such profusion as if he heard children's voices. As if the flowers were...but that was impossible, flowers don't talk or laugh...Sascia must have heard it too, she jumped up and bent closer.

"Rich come!" she waved at him as she laughed. He kneeled close to the flower. The fragrance and sound created a euphoric sensation. Wow, this was like a happy drug! As he looked around there seemed to be no form of transport whatsoever. Were they observing the past or the future?

"What do you think?" Theo's challenging beam, as he stroked a flower, interrupted his concentration. Sascia was running from one group of flowers to the next.

"I don't know... the past? Can they see us?" He meant the people who walked past. It felt like the flowers were responding to him! Theo's whole lightbody was shaking from mirth.

"Buddy, it is all a thought game! It's neither the past nor the future. It's just a projection that has been created by the thoughts and beliefs of our ancestors and plant-kingdom alike. Everything you see is all a figment of the imagination of the spiritual sparks that projected this as reality." Sascia heard Theo as well. Her light body shook from emotions of disappointment. He could see it!

"What do you mean? This isn't real?"

"As in our physical existence, some can see us, but most will not. It all depends from which hemisphere of the brain mode you are observing the world around you." He was confused. They were asleep, so what did Theo mean by ...Oh, there was such a great deal he didn't know or grasp. What he saw was so very real! Like Sascia, he wanted it to be real, but then, what did the word 'real' mean?

A group of very tall women were strolling towards the pyramid. They all balanced cut flowers in large baskets, either on their heads, like the African women do or on their hips.

"They are soon going to participate in an initiation celebration." Theo beamed to them both when he levitated away after them.

He took Sascia's hand and followed him. Theo directed their attention to a higher terrace where many people were standing in groups watching an artist that was painting the most intriguing symbols on great shining gold paper sheets. He gasped in astonishment. As he peered closer at the beautiful symbols, he saw that they resembled the ones on Annelies' walls in her classroom! Sascia was staring at the artist's face with an absorbed look. He was watching how the artist used a most unusual tool with his mind!

"Rich, is that you?" Sascia's voice held such a tremor. Nobody took any notice of him but goosebumps spread all over when he came close. He was drawn in by the artist, a man in his forties, although you could not pin any age on him. For a split second, he saw what the artist saw in his mind...Worlds flashed past him...Explosions, gunfire, a schoolbus that blew up, screaming children... Then the symbols that appeared three-dimensional came back into focus...How was that possible?... How did he do that?...

"Richie, evolution has had many side effects on our creative expressions. In our time-zone consciousness, this kind of art form, speaking in pictures has been lost. They became a symbolic language." Sascia grabbed him by the hand and pulled him away. Did Theo mean 'lost' like a memory?

"Yes, through your life as this artist you still held a full conscious memory of our original plan. You could merge your thought projections, and by painting these scenes as symbols, you tried to keep the memory alive. You hoped that your message would be found during the shift towards the null zone in the text cosmic age." Did Theo mean, that he wrote the tablets? He was the artist? Those foil looking sheets were just like...Gosh, the artist was painting the story of the tablets he'd just seen! The glorious colours and the in-between shades were quite breathtaking.

"Richie, listen!" He was alerted to a sound he had heard before! He looked around but nobody was playing any musical instruments nearby. Theo placed his hand over his and Sascia's eyes. Ever so gradually he became aware of a string of colours that moved around in patterns, like a dance...

"The colours are singing!" Sascia cried. The melody reminded him of sand on a metal plate. When sound was activated through the metal plate the sand on the plate would take on symbolic patterns. They reminded him of...Seeing the 'Mandelbrot'

pattern on a computer screen but these unusual melodies were like nothing he had ever heard before...

"What you are hearing is the Language of Light. Richie these sounds are the emotional thought projections from you as the artist." For a moment he felt dizzy from the feelings that came flooding into his Lightbody.

"They are portraying the forthcoming event."Richard heard Theo's words but he was seeing something else.

"Rich don't go, stay with me." He heard Sascia but Theo told her to let him go...

He went into an imagery spin. Lives flashed before him. He saw how magnificent the city of Akhenaten was. He was his friend, brother and teacher. He had helped to build Tell-el-Amarna. Richard gazed around at the indescribable beauty of the vegetation. Almost too perfect, especially the people...At first, they all looked ageless and healthy but something happened...The mushroom cloud they all observed in the sky said plenty. In horror, he saw how their etheric bodies incinerated just before their physical bodies took on a funny shape...He was pulled away by Theo...

"Richie, during the early Atlantian age our ancestors had many more active strands of DNA and could live a 500-year life span or even longer. Some carried this over into the next generation, but they experimented with the building blocks of creation."

He was back as an observer. The crowd watched him as the artist was striking in appearance very tall, and the women were beautiful, but some he noticed were identical! Were they triplets or?... Theo's explanation triggered many questions. Everyone looked so happy; what happened?

"Some are still clones, take a good look." Some women were...more docile than others.

"Rich, look at yourself. Your forehead is far more prominent than the others! His light body marvelled; he was impressed by the peacefulness. The Language of Light tunes was like a concert with everyone in rapture. The spectacle reminded him of an open-air pop concert, except this music was far more uplifting and harmonious. Birds of all colours and sizes fluttered around the upper levels of the terraces.

"Earth went through many cataclysmic changes and the few souls who tried to survive the cosmic shift were scattered over the planet. Many failed in their ascension during that time but they were still considered 'gods' We read about them in the Greek and Roman mythologies." Richard wondered in what period it was that this had all happened.

"Richie, you know that in the Old Testament, they were considered' gods' because of their different physical form and knowledge. They were the ruling hierarchy of the day. Remember what you asked me before?" Did he?...yes. The camping site. Something about geometric codes within our DNA, but...Theo guided them away from himself as the artist. He could have watched himself for ages. Something about the artist made him sad as if he knew his time was soon over. Why was that, he wondered, was this paradise or heaven?

"Paradise was a name the Greeks used to describe the upper regions of our soul planes. We will visit it another time. Like the genie in the story of Aladdin's Magic Lamp, in our innate faculties of perception, lies the ability to follow the thought processes that are inherent in all creation. Visions are only states of consciousness, which are often referred to as heaven."

He thought back to the beautiful scenery. How could all this knowledge have been lost, or had it? Were all these events stored in the hall of records, but due to a drop in conscious awareness, they were all lost for ages until now?

"Can you now see why; when the soul embodies various separate embodiments, the time lords decide the divisions through the manifestation of time" Was Theo implying that the choice was made all at the same time?

"Richie remember that 'time' is a conception. Time is created by the observer. The moment you observe anything in your physical reality, you create an image of it. " That idea instantly made him a question about blind people, unless...the other senses of hearing, taste, smell and touch also created an illusion of something solid.

"We suspect that the illusion of time helps us in a physical incarnation to maintain a sense of predictability to have a semblance of routine."...

• • • •

"Rich wake-up! We are late."
Late for what? What was her hurry? Where was Theo?...

"Sascia!"

"Yes, what?"...Gosh, his head hurt again! Then he heard the shower turning off.

"Sascia." He called again louder.

"Finally awake are you?" Sascia walked into the bedroom wrapped in a towel.

"You were in my dream, can't you remember anything?"

"No, but I woke up with the smell of jasmine. Boy that was real. What was so weird was that jasmine was talking to me. I must look up what flowers mean in a dream."

He was sorry that there was no time to discuss their dreams. He remembered the flowers that were singing. He knew it would come back to him when he worked on his journal. It often did.

The Pannekoek

That woman, where was she? For the first time, he couldn't wait for his aunt to come back from South Africa and take away the responsibility of running the coffee shop. To employ someone else at such short notice had not been on his mind, but when Sascia left yesterday morning he felt sad for not having spent some time with her over breakfast. Liesbeth had picked her up at seven. She had taken a lot more work on with Liesbeth, who ran a small publishing company from Half-way House. It was a long drive but she loved to explore the countryside on the way.

Jeroen and Connie were great when they worked together but they both had many other activities going on. He needed someone permanently to help his aunt when she was back at the end of the month.

"Nel, where is that niece of yours? It's already after ten, is she reliable?" Nel turned to him in surprise.

"Did Zola phone you?" He looked dumbstruck. Surely it couldn't be? Jeroen asked who Zola was. He was mounting Sascia's black and white prints from Buttercup Valley on the wall behind the till. Sascia's photo gallery was getting quite famous.

Connie greeted someone at the door, then Zola walked in. Jeroen's mouth gaped as he stared at the whirlwind of colours and glitter that had just arrived. She flirtily greeted everyone while Nel appeared around the kitchen door saying hello to her niece. Jeroen stepped away from his handiwork.

"Hi, haven't I met you...when was it...at my Mom's wedding!"

Connie's eyes were roving over Zola's outfit. He was speechless. Nel's niece! What next. Zola didn't at all look the type that would wait on tables. What was she up to now? He asked as much while he was working at the till. Jeroen balanced two trays full of dirty plates on his way back to the kitchen when Zola pleaded with him that she needed the money.

"What made you offer your help," Jeroen asked when he returned with an order. Zola simply confessed in a coquettish way that she had been fascinated with Nel's stories about all the intrigue, adding that she could do with a change of scenery. She was saving up for a trip overseas and since she knew Richard very well so why not. Somehow, Richard thought there was more to it. Her reminder that she knew him well had not gone unnoticed.

While they were chatting behind the counter, customers were coming and going. It was busy. The kitchen staff worked overtime on the weekend.

"Have you done any work like this before?" Zola was at least honest, saying that she had been a waitress on rare occasions to supplement her study loan. His intuition was screaming to say no, but what excuse could he come up with? He needed to leave for Utrecht. Reluctantly he asked if Connie could try her out for a few days. He told Nel in the kitchen that he would give Zola a chance since she needed the money, but if she had any other family connections that would suddenly appear on his doorstep, he would like to be informed beforehand!...

He was annoyed that Nel, who could be pretty chatty, didn't share anything. He had to drag Ellie's story from her. She admitted knowing that Sammy was not his, saying that Quincy had been far too airy-fairy for Oliver. They never had anything in common. She was sorry for Kim, her granddaughter, who had caused a lot of trouble to her parents, especially during their divorce.

Nel commented that it was the first time Zola would work for her money, but it might work out. Nel was a strange woman. When Aunt Mien came back, he would ask her how they had ever met. He couldn't understand why Zola never told them during Annelie's workshop that Nel was a relative, but maybe she didn't know that Nel worked for him.

On the way to Utrecht, his thoughts were crisscrossing from memories to the present. Music from Andréa Bocelli engulfed the interior of his Honda. Things had moved so fast since Sascia had moved in. So much had happened.

He had spent the whole of yesterday preparing for his fourth and final lecture on the Sphinx, which was still his favourite subject. It had been silent in the flat without Sascia, but he started to grasp why there was no evidence of a 500-million-year history of advanced life on Earth. The polar shifts must somehow have destroyed all synthetic objects. He wished he could've shared his ideas with her. How quickly can one get used to good company?

Last night, she had called from Half-way House. There were fifteen people in Tieneke's workshop. She and her mother helped Tieneke print out the manuals. She informed him that the entire day was occupied with the workshop. In the evening, she helped Peter and Helen plan activities for the Halfway House community. Her mom and Toon would fly to Buttercup Valley after the weekend. She would come home just before they did their first workshop with Annelies. He tried to hide his disappointment, which was ridiculous because he had been alone for almost two years. A few more days without her was not going to make a difference...

Although radio Hilversum played his favourite music, it still made him ponder. What was he going to do when his aunt was back? No sponsors were interested in funding another excursion to Egypt or Peru. He had applied to the faculty for a teaching post, but they had not responded to him. Everybody complained about money ever since Holland changed from the gulden to the

Euro years ago. Annelies had mentioned that, for the first time, the hotel was not fully booked this summer.

As he got nearer to Utrecht, the one o'clock news came on. The tomb raiders story was high on the news bulletin. The Middle East and Asia crisis and all the latest troubles reminded him of Babylonian times. It was clear that the world around him was in even greater chaos than ever before. Even then, materialism had disrupted living conditions. The more he thought about it, the more Toon's idea of community living seemed to be the answer. Or was that also an illusion?

What had Theo said about the illusion of Time? It reminded him that Annelies had asked him if he wouldn't mind writing an article for her website on the illusion of time.

When his cell rang, he pulled to the side of the road. He was not going to risk a fine. He switched off the radio. The last snippets of news about another ice chunk that had broken off again created a feeling of doom within himself. He hoped everything was alright at the coffee bar.

"Hi Richard, Sascia just phoned to ask if I would be at your talk this afternoon. It's my day off, so I'm just confirming when your lecture starts." Debbie told him.

"That's a surprise. How was Greece? I was surprised to hear you took a holiday." Debbie's usual chatter made him ask, "Are you interested in my subjects? I mean, you never attended my talks before."

"Well...not like Sascia, but I'm curious. Sascia phoned to ask what shift I was on. Ever since Mom's wedding, I have mostly been working night shifts."

He told her the date, and she chatted some more about Greece. She seemed happy and glad to be back at work.

"After your lecture, I will be visiting Tieneke's house. Her husband is very ill, and they asked for my help. What do you know about them?"

"Gosh, not much. I think he is a subcontractor of sorts. What do you have to do, do you know?"

He tried to remember if he ever met Tieneke's husband. He couldn't remember if he was at Ingrid and Toon's wedding. He asked her what she could do apart from her nursing skills.

"What everybody else wants, instant healing. I'm not sure I'm cut out for this work. Initially, I was excited about my ability to sense the body's needs, but lately, I'm unsure."

That was the first time he heard Debbie had psychic healing abilities. What psychic powers would she have that had been dormant before?

Debbie chatted more, and they arranged to have coffee after his talk. Gosh, he truly missed Sascia already. He promised to drive to Amsterdam after his lecture to check her post and see her plants. He would stay over and drive home early the following day.

It was about three months ago that he made love to her at her flat, but it seemed ages ago…

Chapter 18
When the Distortions Become a Battle

Utrecht
Richard drove into the parking bay near the lecture hall and recognised Vinny's sports car. He should talk to him, but Vinny had been so cool the last time they met on campus, just after Sascia had moved in with him.

People were already arriving, but he wanted a half-hour by himself, so he escaped to the cafeteria for the nurses, academics and staff. Vinny was speaking to a woman in the corner. Walking toward a table, he spotted Debbie, who had served herself lunch and was carrying her tray to an empty table.

"Hi, can you reserve a seat for me? I'm just going to say hello to a friend. As he approached Vinny's table, the woman got up and said goodbye. Vinny looked surprised to see him.

"I thought your lecture was cancelled?"

"Since when did you hear that?"

"On the radio! Haven't you been notified?" He shook his head. He had been at the coffee bar the whole morning. His cell had been charged, but nobody had left any messages.

"What reason was given this time, do you know?"

"You mean you don't know?"

"Know what?" Vinny's expression changed when he looked past him. He saw that Debbie looked equally glazed as she gaped back at Vinny.

"Well, well, if it isn't Cinderella!" Vinny remarked...

"It's you"... When they shook hands, he felt invisible.

That's why Sascia had asked Debbie to attend his lecture and meet Vinny. Gosh, trust women's instincts. It worked! For a moment, he forgot about his bizarre conversation with his friend.

"Richard, I've just heard from someone that there has been a bomb threat in your lecture hall," Debbie said with a flustered face.

"What?"

"That's right. The lecture by Richard de Jong has been postponed due to a bomb threat. I'm surprised they never contacted you. Please do sit down, both of you." Vinny eagerly cleared the chair next to him for Debbie. He was speechless. Had he prepared his talk again for nothing? The disappointment at not being in France with Sascia made it worse. He checked his cell phone for messages, but there were none.

"You're both sure?"

"Why don't you go to the office? Leave your stuff here. We will wait for you. I'll join Debbie for lunch." Vinny's eagerness to have Debbie for himself was evident; he would generally be annoyed, but how could he? He deserved it.

At the reception, Wil, the faculty secretary, immediately spoke into an intercom system, saying to someone that he had arrived.

"Richard, we haven't been able to contact you. We phoned the flat and your cell phone." Her voice was accusatory, but he ignored it.

"In the cafeteria, I heard such strange rumours about..."

"Richard, glad you are here" André's greeting was accompanied by Wil's snigger, especially when André wanted to speak to him in private. She directed them into a small interview room next to her office. Gosh, the woman was unpleasant. André closed the door.

"I believe nobody has been able to reach you this morning." He explained why that was. The faculty didn't know that he ran a coffee shop. He hadn't thought it would help his lecturing career.

"It was on the radio, but you didn't hear that either?"

"At what time?"

"During the news...at twelve, I think." André was flipping into his notebook. He felt like a criminal.

"Will you tell me what happened and why my lecture was again postponed? I feel as if I'm being interrogated."

When André didn't reply, he decided he could also play the game of silence. Gosh, he seemed such a nice guy.

"I was surprised that you were never notified about the bomb scare, but I suppose you were out of reach."

"You mean someone phoned in and threatened to explode a bomb during my talk?" He knew that someone didn't want him to give his lectures.

"We think they meant to during your lecture, yes. By 'they', we mean the same group that robbed Mr Brinks, kidnapped Ingrid, shot Toon, abducted Connie, assaulted you and beat up Mr Jaarsma. We don't want to add to the list, do we... I've stumbled on a case so full of holes. Never in my career have I encountered people who seem to have the means to vanish when we are tipped off. Then I learned that all you people communicate through telepathy. What's next?"

André was stressed out and in a foul mood, but what did he want from him?

"Before I return the two photos, which at least got us the old woman and the man whom we are now holding for other crimes, I want to study them further. I tell you, the sensations I got from them were something else. Do you have any idea where they were taken, or by whom?" The remark André made about his feelings about the photos surprised him.

"No, I haven't. I suspect Leo and Trevor know who stole them, but I haven't got a clue who left them for me." André looked up from his notes, surprised.

"What made you say that they were stolen?"

"Ben told me, telepathically..." Now, he felt silly, but Ben had mentally asked him to keep the photos in a safe place.

"Did Annelie's husband inform you that the items were stolen?"

"Yes."

"What exactly were his words, pardon me, his thoughts?" He was now thinking about what he telepathically heard. "These two photos have disappeared from Leo's laboratory, so please be discreet and always keep them with you." He verbalised Ben's words. André shook his head.

"I'm not sure if I can stay on this case. There is so much withheld from me. I like you all. I even feel I'm part of the group, but I also know that I have not been told everything. If I lose this case due to lack of evidence, the department will scrap the dossier or hand it over to someone else. I came to you because I feel you and I could somehow work together."

He decided to follow his hunch by telling him what Connie shared about her father and what Mien told him, but André knew most of it already.

"You are in constant contact with Trevor Zwiegelaar, not so?"

"Who told you?"

"Your girlfriend Sascia."

Of course, Sascia was to write an article for the newspaper on the whole kidnapping affair. He had suggested she should ask André's help.

"What did Sascia tell you?"

"That you are writing a journal on the findings in France." His journal was not like that at all.

"She later told me that she didn't think your journal could reveal anything to do with the kidnapping of her mother, but I disagree." He didn't know what to say. Annelies' ascension journal had nothing to do with this reality, or did it? Good grief!

"André, I...What do you know about the conspiracies through the centuries?" He was speculating about how events from ancient history could potentially be repeated in the future.

"I've read some books on the legend of the Holy grail. I think I became what is called an agnostic after reading about the Cathars. You people remind me of them."André replied

"Really? But I don't think that the Vatican has anything to do with what is happening, do you?" he replied sarcastically. He was sorry the moment it passed his lips.

"I know it sounds ridiculous, but...think about it. It all started with Pleasure Parks building a new complex. Something has been disturbed through the excavation to clear the area for the dome's construction. Somehow, someone wants it stopped. Why?" André's cell phone rang. In his mind, he saw the cave with the mummies, the golden foil sheets and Leo's laboratory. André's voice had taken on a different pitch, as if he had just heard bad news. He closed his cell phone and stared into space.

"You don't want to hear this, but...a bomb went off." A chill ran down his spine.

"Where?"

"Near the site where they are building the holiday resort."

"In France, Oh my ..." All he thought of was the Chateau and Sascia! He told André about Tieneke's workshop and how near the halfway house was to the site. His cell was in his laptop case, and he left it behind with Vinny and Debbie. Gosh, he had forgotten about them. He hoped they were still waiting for him.

André seemed to have the number of Peter and Helen's place. No one replied, which was weird. It was, after all, a business.

"André, can we....listen. I'll share all my interpretations no matter how far-fetched it might sound to you,...but promise me one thing."

André was making up his mind about something.

"I want to know all the police stuff you have gathered so far." He knew he was asking André to break an oath if such a thing existed, but he didn't care. He started to shake from worry that anything had happened to Sascia. He tried telepathy, but it felt like there was no band to project onto.

"Let's go. We have a lot to share."

They left the room and passed Wil, who completely ignored them...

Vinny and Debbie were still at the cafeteria. He wanted to introduce André to Vinny, but they seemed to know each other. Debbie knew André from her mother's kidnapping and the wedding, but neither Vinny nor André explained how they knew each other.

"Debbie, a bomb went off in France. We have tried to reach the Chateau, but there has been no reply." He hated sharing lousy news but couldn't accept the worst. Debbie's eyes turned into moist pools.

Vinny, who was totally in the dark about what they were worried about, put his arms around Debbie. Somehow, he knew that they were meant for each other. He was glad for them.

"Was it a big bomb? I mean, were people hurt?"

Debbie cried as André informed her that only two abandoned buildings near the site had been destroyed. When he returned to Amsterdam, he asked Vinny to go past Sascia's flat to collect the mail. Richard would join André at Mr Brinks' home and maybe travel to France, if necessary. All he wanted was to hear Sascia's voice.

André had reminded him of many conspiracy theories he had ignored. He now wondered where Trevor was.

"Richard, I'll go with you," Debbie said. "Remember that I have an appointment with Harry Brinks." Gosh, he had forgotten.

"Was it not with Tieneke's husband?"

"Yes, but I feel I have to be there."

When he returned, Vinny got up to pay the bill and said, "This time I'm not just waiting to hear that someone might remember I'm part of this family too." Vinny had not said a word before, which was totally out of character, but he also carried the name Jaarsma. When Vinny said something about the Jaarsma name, André replied that although it was common, he agreed.

"Richard, we will follow you. I'll take Debbie in my car." Vinny was not letting Debbie out of sight now that he had found her.

There were already two police cars in the driveway of Harry Brinks estate. André spoke to his colleagues. When they joined them, he overheard the last sentence. "We think it was the granddaughter."

Debbie and Vinny stood behind him when Harry Brinks opened the massive front door. His face was white. The man had aged. Debbie reacted to Harry's devastated expression with a hug. They all followed Harry inside to the sitting room. André told him what he knew. Harry asked if Debbie could stay until Annelies was told.

Vinny must have felt that he was intruding because he said goodbye to Debbie when they were all leaving. She walked them to their cars.

He was glad that Vinny, his best friend, had joined them. It's funny, but somehow, he probably was related to them. It increasingly started to feel like they were all pawns in a board game. Debbie arranged to meet Vinny later before returning to the house since it was her day off.

He heard André asking Vinny if he would come to his mother's dinner party. Vinny nodded and said he would take care of Sascia's post in Amsterdam.

He was glad for his friend's date with Debbie and was keen to know the connection between André and Vinny, but instead asked what André's next move was when they were alone in the driveway. The French police were on the hunt for the kidnappers of Ingrid; it was the older woman at the Apeldoorn station who had spilt the beans.

"We discovered that Connie's father, Piet, lived in one of the abandoned buildings near the Pleasure Parks building site. The rest of the criminals had made their headquarters nearby. One of the criminals was Hennie's boyfriend, who was used as a pawn."

"Hennie or the boyfriend?"

"Hennie. She was to become a go-between."

"Go between for whom"

"The woman didn't know who, but it must have been her grandfather." André flipped through his notes. The old established garden didn't entirely shut off all the traffic noises outside Harry Brinks's estate, making him realise that people lived in their own perceived realities.

"The old woman told us many things. She insisted that there are great treasures buried in caves under the site. A real estate dealer is after the property that is bordering onto the site of Pleasure Parks."

"Let me guess, Mr Nick du Toit?" André nodded.

"What happened to Hennie? Was she arrested?" André brushed his hair away from his forehead, reminding him that Niels, from his ascension group, and André looked very alike. Their mother was Indonesian.

"She was inside the building that blew up with Piet and another woman."

That shocked him. In a flash, he was back at the wedding reception. He saw Tieneke, who had asked her daughter to help the kitchen staff. Mr Brinks's face! That's why he looked so grey. He was in shock. Gosh, how would Connie deal with her father's death?

"It is possible that his daughter Tieneke has not yet been told of Hennie's death. Nobody had reached the Buttercup Chateau." André said as they strolled in the long driveway of Mr Brinks's estate. He again tried to reach Sascia, Liesbeth or Hans on a telepathic wave band, but there was no response.

"Everyone's cell phones are still off. We know that Toon Haardens, his wife Ingrid and Sascia are all at the Chateau. Ed Barendse and Yolanda de Wit arrived just minutes before the bomb. They must have heard the explosion since it was heard for kilometres. That's what a colleague just told me. He heard it from Mr Barendse, the steel tycoon."

"What happened to Nick du-Toit?"

"Not a sign. He disappeared into thin air."

"Maybe he got blown up as well?"

"We doubt that. He is a sneaky character. He seems to have many resources. The most intriguing thing is that all the mysteries seem to interlink with a specific bloodline of a family that lived at the Chateau during the Second World War." He got a weird feeling that his grandfather might have been involved, but he kept that to himself.

When André put his notebook away and unlocked his car door, he shared that one of his colleagues had an informer who tipped him off. He suspected it might be the same person who fed the radio station with bits and pieces. He told André about his Jaarsma Clan speculations.

André had spoken to Annelies and Ben about his surname but couldn't take it all in then. André shared that two nights ago, his mom had organised a meeting. She had been to Spain, so he thought nothing of it. When Niels arrived, he was pleasantly surprised to see his half-brother, but when Vinny and his dad walked in behind Niels and were told that Vinny's father was his father, too, he wanted to leave.

"Did you?"

André looked at his watch before he replied.

"At first Vinny behaved like a gentleman, but when he said something derogative to my mother,...I insulted him." With that comment, he climbed into his car.

He didn't know what to say. Gerrit from their ascension workshop was Vinny's dad. Gosh, so much started to fall into place. He remembered what Vinny once said about his dad's philosophy just after they attended Trevor's lecture on the chambers and passageways into the future.

He arranged to see André at the Pannekoek with Ula, his fiancée whom he knew from the coffee bar.

Before he drove home, he again tried to reach Sascia on her cell, but he only got a voicemail. Telepathy was still not working either. He phoned the Pannekoek. Jeroen answered. It had been hectic. Nel had just left, and he and Connie were clearing the tables. He asked how Zola turned out. Jeroen said he and Connie found her difficult to work with, but...it went fine.

"She left the coffee bar at three. Her feet were killing her...due to her stiletto heels."

"I'll be there in fifteen minutes. Jeroen, has Connie already heard about her dad?"

"What do you mean?" He was not sure what to say. Jeroen repeated his question and replied that he must not let Connie out of sight.

When he turned into Apeldoorn, he passed the train station and thought of the older woman and the young boy.

Connie was crying when he arrived. Jeroen was passing change to a customer, cleared the table and looked relieved to see him.

"Richard, my mom just phoned from France. Peter and Toon went to investigate when they heard the blast. Due to the workshop, All telephone lines were destroyed, and due to the workshop, their cell phones were switched off." Jeroen explained. Connie's tearful sob while he hugged her upset him.

He tried Sascia's cell again. This time he got through.

"Rich, Tieneke is in shock. Yolanda is fine. She is more worried about Connie."

He told Sascia that his lecture had been cancelled again, but this time due to a bomb scare that was thought to be directed at his lecture. Sascia was shocked to hear they didn't know about the bomb scare and wished more than ever that he had gone with her. He also regretted not going with her, but instead, he would be spending the whole day tomorrow at the Pannekoek because Jeroen and Connie needed a break.

"Debbie is with Mr Brinks. Oh, and I must tell you, I was there when Vinny met Debbie."

"Really?... And...did they know each other?"

"Oh, yes... You were right... he called her Cinderella."

"Oh, Rich, I'm so glad." He could hear a commotion in the background.

"Rich, Trevor has just arrived. Leo is missing. Something about a collapsing cave. I'll phone you later when I know more."

Jeroen closed the front door of the coffee shop after the last customer had left. He heated three Loempias, and they ate a meal together silently.

"You know, I'm glad for my dad in a way. I'm unfortunate for Tieneke losing Hennie, but my dad did want to die."

They sat quietly... absorbing Connie's comment. He told them about the bomb scare on the news when he drove to Utrecht. He got up to answer the phone.

It was Annelies. She and Ben had just heard from André. They had been out for the day and had just returned home. He told her that he had tried beaming her a message.

"Richard, like all of us, we have been sabotaged on a much higher level. Hans and Liesbeth are working on it. Please let me speak to Connie."

When Connie returned, she told them Annelies was going to Utrecht to be with Harry Brinks. Ben and Hans were on the way to France. He wished he could join him, but they had already gone, and he committed to seeing André the next day.

Back at the flat, he felt washed out and finished. So much had happened in one day; he fell on the bed, on clothes and all. He was about to drift off when a ... miaow reminded him that he hadn't fed Sascia's cat. He dragged himself off the bed. "My apologies, Ginger. Where are my manners?"... Miaow.

"Yeah, yeah, be patient." Thank goodness there was one tin left. Cat food had not been on his list. He decided to leave his emails for the next day. He was far too tired, strung up and bothered to read any mail.

• • • •

After the vibrations travelled over his whole body, he felt himself being sucked into a funnel. The spinning sensation created a detached feeling. Initially, this used to bring up fear, but now, he wanted to be free... He often wondered why others did not experience what he did or did not.

When the multi-coloured patterns suddenly spun around him, he was free. Theo was already waiting when a person in a long white robe strolled towards them and embraced Theo with joyful enthusiasm. He immediately recognised Leo from the wedding ceremony.

"I knew it. It had to be good for something! I've never been so unprepared. I always thought I would be." Leo beamed at both. He recalled something Sascia had said about the bomb blast: that Leo was missing! Did that mean he died?

"Richard, I'm honoured to meet you in this way. I'm temporarily stunned out of my physical body, but I can still attend one of POWAH's seminars." Just like that, he thought! Just like Toon when he had a heart attack.

"Are you not?"...

"Passed on? No. Richard, when people like us can consciously observe two or more realities simultaneously, it still does not mean that the one is more real than the other." That was a thought. He wondered where Theo had suddenly disappeared.

"He will join us shortly. Come, let's explore." Leo seemed to know his way around.

He tried to assimilate everything he saw next. The sun's rays bounced off the highly polished stone blocks from the Great Pyramid, which was a spectacle. The four sides looked like gigantic mirrors. He did not recognise the landscape except for the Great Pyramid.

"Leo, have you always been able to travel out of your body?" He was surprised that he'd never seen him before.

"*As you do, yes, only after the accident in the tunnel can I do it by will.*"He observed Leo wearing the same white robe as others who entered the Great Pyramid. Where were they? He knew it was not Egypt, although the pyramid was similar.

"*Richard I think that the more awake we are the faster the vibrational frequency. This could be anywhere. What were you thinking just before you left your body?*" He tried to remember. The Englishman. The cave where the mummies had been taken from. Yes, that's it. He had been wondering where the mummies had been stolen from. As he looked around he was mesmerized by the colour spectacle. It must be visible for miles around. The gardens with massive rock pools and the gold and silver ornaments seemed like a Hollywood set. As he marvelled at smelling the fragrance he suddenly heard it. Gosh, the light beams that bounced off onto the smaller pyramids seemed to create a sound. He looked up to see where the beams came from, but they must be the sun's rays. There was no other structure anywhere.

"*Leo do you also hear it?*" Suddenly in the distance, he saw more moving figures like them, all dressed in white robes. He spotted Theo who was holding on to a child. As they came closer he recognised Sammy! That was unusual and for a moment his dream consciousness got confused. Theo guided them inside a temple that reminded him of a massive stadium, except for the centre where the familiar monument of the Sphinx dominated the whole scene. Sammy jumped onto his knee while he looked around in absolute wonder. The luxury of the entire place looked like Neuschwanstein, the castle on top of a mountain in Germany.

"*Richie remember that our physical reality is often considered a dream, from which we are about to awaken. Because your thoughts, your mortal consciousness is linked and travels from the crown chakra and spirals down into the physical realms, your thoughts slow down."* What was Theo trying to say, that the colour spectacle was his thoughts?

"*Yes, physical reality is created by electromagnetic energy. As you see, electricity is a blueish colour. Magnetic energy is more reddish, together they form patterns. The sound you hear creates the colour yellow and the Dodecahedron facets makes it all what we call Ether.*" He could not comprehend what Theo was implying but Leo seemed to get it, for he smiled in acknowledgement. Suddenly a bright beam of light transformed the Sphinx monument into...what ...POWAH? Was this a mental trick? POWAH's familiar way of communicating through the Language of Light quietened his mind. They were all drawn to the energy beam coming from the forehead of the Spinx. It was a bright funnel of light with streams of blue and violet pulsations that appeared to act as speakers.

<*Many of us, as members of the family of light, have returned at this time as planetary midwives to assist Earth's transition into a new era of expanded consciousness. Over the past several years, many have found their unique niche, and in this process, we have been re-discovering one another*>

The celestial music penetrated his whole being. He knew that he still had to find what his unique niche was. *"You will soon"* Theo beamed.

<*We of the planetary council are chiefly concerned with your spiritual preparation for the next stage. We are delighted to contribute to your health, happiness, and prosperity. We are not indifferent to your success in all matters of planetary advancement.*>

"Richie, listen well to what POWAH has to say next."

<*I wish I could help achieve a better understanding and attain a fuller appreciation of the unselfish and superb work*

your higher-mind-guide living within you is doing. These monitors are efficient ministers to the higher phases of men's minds; they are wise and experienced manipulators of the spiritual potential of the human intellect. >

What was POWAH talking about?

"Richie POWAH talks about your higher mental body." Theo beamed.

< Your higher guide is engaged in one of the supreme adventures of the human race. We are very honoured. Your co-operation permits us to lend assistance in your dealings with time >

He tried assimilating POWAH's information and took a peep at Leo, who seemed to be in a state of meditation.

< The success of your higher guide in piloting your thoughts depends not so much on the theories of your beliefs but on your decisions, determinations, and steadfast faith. All these movements of personality growth become powerful influences aiding in your advancement. >

"Richie, I have taken you to one of POWAH's assemblies from the higher mental realm in preparation for your personality card." He wanted to know what happened to Leo, the one in the flesh.

< While the voice of your higher guide is ever within you, most of you will hear it seldom during a lifetime. Human beings below the third and second vortex cycles of attainment rarely hear their higher guides' direct voice except in moments of supreme desire or when the lower self relinquishes control. >

He suddenly realized that POWAH was directing his message to Leo. Leo bowed deeply, and then he was gone.

"Richie you might not remember anything from this level, but one day you will understand." He heard Theo's mental beam about not remembering, which made him aware that his body was shivering. He woke up cold and stiff with a headache.

As he moved he felt Ginger who was neatly curled up in a tight ball snuggled in the crook of his back. He must have gained his favour for feeding him last night.

The Pannekoek and the Bookshop

It was just after eight. The coffee shop opened at ten, which would give him nearly two hours to work on his journal. Gosh, his laptop was still in the boot of his car. He scolded himself for leaving it there.

When he returned, he turned the radio on, only to hear the tail end of the news that mentioned the bomb explosion in France.

"It has been reported that the bomb that went off just over the border in France destroyed at least two buildings. Both were occupied. We can not release the names of the occupants until all the families have been notified."The announcer moved on to other topics.

He wondered if Sascia was already up. Nothing had been mentioned on the radio about the bomb threat in Utrecht.

He tried Sascia's cell, but once again he got a voice mail. He hoped there would be an email from Trevor. He missed Sascia more than ever, especially now that so much was happening. He tried to remember his dream. He knew that he had been with Theo. He got a flash of Leo but discarded that as a fantasy for now.

There were three emails. One took a long time to get into his inbox because of an attachment with the title: When Souls are Gathering.

One was from Trevor and the other email showed the name the Cup of Gold as the return address with the title; miss you. His heart leapt....

——- Original Message ——-
From: "Cup of Gold"
To: <Richard de Jong:;>
Subject: miss you

Hi Rich

I just wanted to let you know we're all doing well, and I miss you. Tieneke has gone with Trevor to the site. They are supporting each other. Trevor is frantic about Leo, who was deep inside a cave under the buildings. Toon showed us the map Ben had. You would love to see it but I get the shivers thinking Leo could be buried alive! Ingrid believes it will help Tieneke to be with someone who might also have to accept a loss. We know that Ben and Hans are on the way by car. Everyone has been very supportive. So many people live at Half-way House. They are all preparing themselves to move up to Buttercup Valley when it is finished. Toon is still planning to fly there to see how far they are with the construction. If necessary my mom will stay behind with Tieneke. Ed, Yolanda and I will join him.

Rich, there is so much happening here. Liesbeth is now running the publishing side. She travels every second week to see everything. We are all going to meditate while drawing to help find Leo. Helen is taking over from Tieneke. We are all so sad for her. I'm glad for Debbie and Vinny. I hope that something comes of it. I told mom. Toon seems to think that many people who are on this ascension journey will find their soul mate! Sweety, it so feels like it to me, that we have. In my heart, I feel that you think the same way. I'm practicing remembering my dreams! Visit me tonight!

Lots of love

Sascia xxx

That was the best email ever. Richard instantly wanted to type back, but he was just as eager to read Trevor's letter and Theo's translations. He sent her an SMS instead.

——- Original Message ——-
From: "T Zwiegelaar"
To: <Richard de Jong:;>
Subject: please help
Dear Richard

Both Sascia and I knew that you would want to keep in contact this way. We are all still very shocked, and my heart goes out to Tieneke, who lost her only child. I never had any kids, but I would feel devastated if something happened to Hans. That way, I can feel what she is going through. The girl was apparently in bad company, and her father was not much help. He had a heart attack followed by a stroke, and they think he might not register what had happened. Tieneke hopes he is spared the grief. I think she is a fantastic woman with a lot of compassion. I'm very concerned for Leo. There has been no telepathic communication. Even Hans and Liesbeth had no success. It is alarming to us all. A wavelength seems to have been removed because of a lack of a better word. A search party has been digging in the rubble where the entrance to our underground laboratory has caved in. Toon, Ed, Peter and I will join them again after I send you this email. Please do what you can during your dreams. Phone me on my cell if you have anything, even if you think it's silly. I don't care.

Regards
Trevor

He was so sorry that he had never looked at his email last night. He clicked on Trevor's phone number in his address book.

"Richard, is it you?"

"Trevor I've only just read your email. I don't always remember clearly but....I dreamed of Leo, but he was travelling, as I do, I'm sure."

He heard people talking in the background. Somebody yelled. Noises of machinery told him that Trevor must be at the site where the bomb went off...

"Richard, I'll phone you back."

He remembered all the happenings ever since joining Annelies' ascension workshop. She had warned them that dark forces seemed to create obstacles. Every person would experience them differently. When individuals join together for a common goal, they make yet another reality that the whole group experiences.

The more he thought it over, the more he understood from a more profound level what had been happening: first Ingrid's kidnapping and Toon being shot, then the burglaries, not to mention the endless trouble at the Pleasure Parks building site. Their ancestral link with the Jaarsma clan started from two orphanages. The Star-map appeared in three places, including the resort in France, where Ingrid had been kept but still shrouded in mystery. The fact was that they all seemed to be related: Connie's abduction, the theft of the photos from Leo's hideout, wherever that was and The bomb that took lives! He could go on and on. Who was the scriptwriter of their lives? That is all he knew and experienced, but what about the others? He knew of many people, himself included, who had difficulty staying out of debt with the bank. Prices of everyday day-to-day commodities seemed to change over time. Then how about André's, Theo's and Trevor's theories? Was it all an illusion? Were they all playing a game but forgot that they did?

Ginger jumped on his lap and started purring. As he stroked him, he thought of the good things: how they all seemed to awaken psychic powers like telepathy, or how Toon and Ingrid, Fred and Quincy, Yolanda and Ed, Connie and Jeroen, himself and Sascia found each other. Even the last couple, Debbie and Vinny, seemed meant for each other. Then, the Tablets and his dream travel. The Halfway House project would be a springboard for the people who wanted to prepare themselves for community living, moving into a new paradigm, as Toon called it. Toon has made investments in various communities around the world. The Pleasure Park resort would now become known as The Garden of the Gods now that Toon had purchased it from Harry. Tieneke's and Annelies' workshops showed that they are all related in some way. Everything appeared to indicate a change of some kind.

He decided to send Trevor an email with all his reflections. As he was typing more ideas came to mind. Annelies' decoding method started to make more sense. It was not so much what they discovered about themselves that astounded him, it was more the qualities and potentials they all awakened within themselves that had started to create a different reality for them all.

The idea about the group soul, with POWAH as the spokesperson, was more accessible to grasp.

Something André had said about conspiracies triggered a thought. What was behind all the intrigue that involved people who did not turn away from violence? His cell phone announced an SMS. <We got him out. Leo is alive.>

What a relief. He phoned Sascia but there was only a voice mail. He sent them both an email, closed up and made sure Ginger could get to his friend next door and drove to the Pannekoek. He was looking forward to talking to André later that day.

All the tables were occupied! Thanks to Nel he could satisfy most of his customers with her fresh stroopwafels. He should suggest to his aunt Mien to change the name Pannekoek to Stroopwafel. When she returned at the end of the month he was hoping she would soon take over from him. He wanted to spend more time on his research, especially if his lectures took off. He knew that plenty of people had expressed their disappointment at the faculty, so who knows it might work in his favour.

"Hello Richard, do you need help today?"

"Zola! What, you want to work today? I can't pay you extra."

"Who said anything about more money?" Gosh, he felt terrible. Why was he so suspicious? Today her hair had purple streaks.

"I'm sorry. Thanks, I would appreciate it. Jeroen and Connie need a break. Especially, Connie, she lost her dad yesterday."

"Really, how?" She asked with childish sincerity, but something about the way she phrased it still triggered feelings of unease. Why was he so offish to her? Zola was wearing jeans, which was unusual. The high heels and massive jewellery looked creative. On Sascia jeans looked sexy, but on Zola they looked tartish.

Nel greeted her niece and asked for her help with a whole tray of packages that was to be displayed on the glass counter

A customer commented on the photo display. He explained the background of the prints and sold two unframed ones.

André phoned asking if he could get away from the Pannekoek for 30 minutes and meet him at the bookshop. Something had come up.

He told Nel that he would be at the Bookshop. After he had served three elderly ladies he told Zola that he would be out for half an hour.

The bookshop was closed but when he knocked on the glass door, Fred opened up.

"I'm glad you could come. André will be here in five minutes."

"I hope Zola will cope for 30 minutes."

"Who's Zola?" Fred was still reorganising books onto the shelves. He was casually dressed, not his regular dress code. It made him look a great deal younger.

"She's from our ascension group. I wish I could see her aura. I feel uneasy around her but I can't understand why."

"It could be that you have become far more sensitive. Some people have several agendas going. It's normal for them but in a sense, it can be confusing. When Annelies and I became aware of people's energy field I saw things in people I never suspected."

"Like what?"

"Mmm, difficult to put it in words. First of all, it took us some time before we could distinguish the difference between our energy field, and that of someone else."

"You mean you are looking through your own at another?"

"Exactly. We had to first learn to know where our boundaries were so to speak." Fred moved three to four metres away from him.

"This feels comfortable. By that I mean I can start feeling what is mine and what is yours energy-wise."

"You mean my aura is that big?"

"No, it's a lot larger. I mean from this distance I can attain some individuality. That is necessary to be more aware of what belongs to me and what does not." He wondered what Fred was seeing. When he asked, Fred had his eyes closed.

"I see more when I close my eyes When I open them again, colours flash past. I can see a great amount of yellow swirling just under your chin. There is a blueish tint behind it, so that tells me that you speak from the head." Fred closed his eyes again. While he was observing him, he thought of Zola and how she made him feel... Fred looked up again towards his solar plexus, and for a moment he heard...

"There are hooks with cords lodged into his heart chakra that are dancing in a frenzy." Fred grabbed something in the air, which gave him a slight tightness in his stomach. Then the feeling was gone. When Fred looked at him, he knew he was normal again.

"What did you just do?"

"You mean you could feel it?"

"When you did this...I felt it, like a slight cramp here." he laid his hand just under his rib cage.

"I pulled away from an attachment cord that was hooked around there. It was more to see if it would let go. If not, then it's your cords with Zola that are still in need of repair so to speak." Fred smiled as he shrugged his shoulders.

"This Zola, she tried to hook you. It is done without her consciously knowing. It created an uneasy feeling you became aware of now that you are getting more sensitive."

"You mean that most of us could trigger unease in each other?"

"It's a little more complicated than that. In general, when you feel like you say, uneasy, it can mean several things, but the bottom line is, there is something incompatible with your energy field. How well do you know her?" Fred's question made him listen to his body. He was aware of her needs and knew he couldn't give in to her. That made him feel uneasy because he wanted to please. Gosh, what an insight.

"When a stranger is compatible, we could also get into trouble, especially if we are searching for a partner," Fred commented when he put away some books from the counter.

"What kind of trouble."

"You can fall for a romantic love affair."

"Have you?"

"Twice. I had to learn the difference."

"Gosh, how do you know?"

"You always know. It's when people are truly lonely, then one ignores these warnings. That's why it is so important to feel good with your own company before sharing it with others."

He was mulling it over. Fred made a great deal of sense. He never even thought that becoming more sensitive could have all kinds of added insights and obstacles. He always assumed that when someone was more psychically aware, they had an advantage over others. He was now not so sure anymore.

"You've heard they found Leo?" Fred asked.

"Yes, Trevor sent an SMS. How is he?"

"Ben phoned me just before you arrived. He has been taken to a nearby clinic until he's stabilised. His lungs suffered the most. Leo has quite a few broken bones but otherwise...It could be worse I guess. It's Tieneke we are worried about. She's taking her daughter's death very hard."

André arrived. Fred made sure that the 'closed' sign was showing from the outside as he closed the glass door after him. André made himself comfortable in the reading corner. There was no news about any more casualties except that the remains of the woman had been identified.

"Who was she?" André didn't reply immediately, instead stared into space.

"That's the sad part. She happened to be a sister of a colleague of mine." Both Fred and he were thrown off guard by that remark.

"Has that discovery opened any other avenues in your investigations?" Fred asked. Gosh, he wondered if the criminals had an informer within the police force. It made sense. André didn't reply, instead, he asked them if they had ever heard of the Montauk Experiment. Both Fred and he were blank. It took them a moment to recall the association to the word Montauk.

"You mean the Time travel event about a ship that was transported through space and time called the Philadelphia Experiment?" He wondered what that had to do with anything.

"Yes, what are your opinions about the rumours of men travelling through time and the horror stories of men becoming stuck in bulkheads or even the ship's floor itself?"

He tried to search his mind for an answer while Fred took a book off the shelf.

"Theo had speculated that these experiments caused a rift in the space-time continuum. They apparently can cause parallel realities. At least that was his theory." Fred was still reading.

"You mean that this kind of technology was already known way back?" André asked surprised.

"Yes, I think so, anything is possible when all possibilities can be manifested." André mulled over his reply. He was still wondering whose body they had found.

"Okay, let me read to you about a sailor named Edward who claimed that he was transported in time to the future." They both waited, listening.

"Forty years later in the future, Edward was brainwashed by the Navy to believe he was someone else. When he discovered his true identity, he tracked down his brother who had also participated in the experiment." Fred looked up watching for their reactions. He had difficulty in establishing what André was leading up to.

"André, what most people didn't know was that Edward had a PhD in Physics, so he does have some technical experience," Fred added while reading further. He suddenly recalled having a long debate during his university days about the very same topic. He looked at his watch and asked if he could phone the coffee bar. Nel picked up the phone.

"It's me, is Zola coping on her own?" Nel said not to worry. She did the serving. There were only two ladies left with their coffees and cake.

Fred found what he was looking for and read out loud that this Edward (when the book was published) was a retired electrical engineer with thirty years of experience. Because of his obvious intelligence and skill, he couldn't entirely be discounted. Edward stated that the technology used in the Philadelphia Experiment was given by aliens called the Greys. However, the germanium transistor, which was what Edward said had been used, was invented by Thomas Henry Moray. Fred looked up over his reading glasses smiling.

"Gosh, I'm glad I can at least talk to the both of you. I believe the ship was gone from the harbour for about four hours, not just a few minutes. Several sailors were transported through a time loop into their future, to 1983." André added that he was interested in the background of the Philadelphia Experiment because of Interpol's interference. André shared an incident that had to do with a mind-control project. He was still questioning what those events had in common with their lives.

"As you both must know, in 1930, Nikola Tesla got involved with a group experimenting with moving through the Time/Space continuum. The University of Chicago investigated the possibility of invisibility through electricity." André told them as he was reading from a notebook.

"Yes, that could be true but both Tesla and Einstein had come to the same conclusion that this technology if developed would not be used for the benefit of mankind," Fred replied. André nodded his head.

"Also true, but you know as well as I do that this does not mean it was not pursued. It would seem that the American navy never did experiments on time travel at any other time, but especially the USA government has been known to cover up because of national security." They both agreed with André.

"Let's go back to what is happening in our lives. I need both your inputs to validate my detective work. It's so way off the beat that I can't share this with my colleagues. The Montauk Project centred mostly on how the mind reacts to inter-dimensional travel. Although much of the information is available, it's believed that the Montauk Project is continuing to this day. That is where we come in." Both he and Fred were waiting in gripping silence for what was to come. What possible connection could there be between what happened at the Pleasure Park project and the Time travel theory?

"I know you both wonder what all this has to do with what has happened, but I'm starting to see a link between the time travel experiments and Rennes Le Chateau in the south of France."

"Really? Gosh, I never even gave it a thought, but you know, it's possible." He remembered that there was a link like there was with the Holy Grail, the Ark of the Covenant or the treasures of the Temple of Solomon.

"Wait a minute, I read something about the lost gold treasures!" Fred looked for another book. His shop was a real treasure trove.

"Got it, the Prieure du Notre Dame du Sion, or Priory of Zion, is said to be the cabal behind many of the events that occurred at Rennes-le-Chateau." Fred read out loud. Richard got excited, recalling his student days.

"I remember that the story of Sion is linked in some way to the Hermetic or Gnostic society. The true secret of the village of Rennes-le-Chateau is that the extinct volcano Mount Bugarach leads down into the hollow earth to a realm of supermen." He said it with a grin.

"Really?"

"Yes, my brother had me doing a thesis on the Sion story. I read that the mother of Jesus, Mary, was known to the Gypsies of the south of France as one of the three "Maries-de-la-Mer," whom they call Sarah the Egyptian, the sun-burnt one." André stayed silent when Fred and he were recalling the Sion story that ultimately showed that the Rennes-le-Chateau may be a doorway into the invisible, a gateway to other dimensions.

"Gosh, I got it. The tablets! The tunnels under the Pleasure Park resort must be leading to the cave where the mummies were buried. Theo always said that the Copper Scroll of the dead sea sect, the Qumran Essenes, suggested that some of the Temple treasure was hidden before the Roman invasion. Now I know what happened to them!"

"What mummies?" André asked while Fred was looking for another book up high, using a ladder. He was very surprised that André didn't know. When he asked if André had not heard about the mummies from Ben, he shook his head. André told them that no police force has of yet been able to get near the so-called underground tunnels. The place is heavily guarded.

Ben, who is one of the private investigators of Interpol, seems to have an investigation going on for a while. André told them that Ben, who holds a degree in criminology, was his professor about ten years ago.

"Mmm...you say you can't talk to your colleagues about strange subjects because they would think you're whacko, right?"

"True, but there is more to it. Somehow, Interpol has got you all under surveillance, and I don't understand why."

"Really? What do you mean by under surveillance." Fred asked. André's face transformed into a severe frown.

"The secrecy techniques some chaps like to use is starting to get to me. I received a warning that if I pursue my interest in psychic phenomena, my career as a detective would be over." André's body language revealed embarrassment. Both he and Fred could relate to his dilemma.

"Richard, what were you going to tell me?"

Gosh, was it necessary to get André more and more in conflict with his apparent reluctance to open his mind? They were both waiting for his reply.

"Okay, let's see if I can share with you how I study ancient history or our future for that matter. Have you ever heard of astral travel?" André's expression changed from being attentive to stunned then with an almost despondent look he replied; "I heard rumours but do you astral travel?" André's expression spoke of disbelief. He'd half expected that.

"I seem to have an ability to stay consciously awake at the time that my body sleeps, but that does not mean that what I remember from my dreams is always accurate." André frowned. His Indonesian look added a touch of the mystical. Fred came down from the stepladder with yet another book.

"Let's speculate that the Ark was given to the Templars for safekeeping. But when it came into the hands of the Sion sect, they must have used it to blackmail the Church with some terrible secret." Fred speculated when he looked up peering over his reading glasses. He had to smile because he saw that André was mentally stretched.

"This conspiracy writer." Fred continued as he held up a book with the title 'Earth's power points' that has linked one powerful global elite, the Bilderberg Group, with the ultimate take-over of the world. Are you leading us in that direction?" Gosh, surely not...but André nodded.

"Yep, I'm afraid so. Remember that Toon was the target? So far this Bilderberg group holds control of the world economy through indirect political means. Toon is becoming a threat. His immense wealth, and the fact that he has partly financed the Pleasure Park group makes him vulnerable." André asked to see the book.

"Have you told him your suspicions?" Fred asked.

"Oh yes, and listen to this. A royal family member, who at the time was an important figure in the oil industry, and held a major position in Royal Dutch Petroleum (Shell Oil), as well as Société Générale de Belgique, which is a powerful global corporation knew Toon's father." Fred sat down resting his heels on the edge of his desk.

"Wow, I see where you are leading us. The Bilderberg group is made up of central bankers, press barons, government ministers, prime ministers and royalty. They are the most powerful people in the western world. You suspect they are behind all this?" Fred asked.

"Not quite yet. At the moment they are still using petty criminal pawns to do their dirty work, but all the signs leading up to that conclusion."

His mind scrolled past all the global events of the last few years. Were they living during the end times so often predicted?

"I heard that some $100 million was made by certain Wall street investors. Some speculate that there is a connection between them and Toon because of his immense wealth and because he had an office in that building. The rumour goes that his shares in the two airlines involved in the twin tower attack would plummet after that event on September Eleven."

André's remark gripped his gut. He was stunned. He never thought that the Jaarsma clan could be a threat to an influential group like the Bilderbergers. He thought of his talk to Ben after the last workshop. Now things started to fall into place for him.

"There is no proof, but Ben told me that he went underground because of suspicions that even Interpol was involved with Toon's project through the robberies of the artefacts. They might have done it to finance certain projects. This is very confidential. I never heard Ben mention what you just said. Ben only told me because he felt that I was being investigated because of my family connection. My grandfather lived at the Chateau during the first world war. My father grew up there. I only discovered all this lately myself. Leo and Trevor, a family friend, haveor had, a laboratory under the Pleasure Parks complex."

He could suddenly see the whole picture. Gee, he never suspected that such a powerful force was behind all the intrigue, but it made sense. Often people from websites he'd visited would keep you informed about common interests and iIssues, such as Iraq, Israel-Palestine, Iran, terrorism, the proliferation of weapons of mass destruction, and other longer-term issues, such as development, trade and even global warming. The papers were full of stories about people who are overworked, lost, or sought compassion through obscure causes. The world was in such a mess. Trevor had warned them that due to Internet networking, too many people now knew far too much and the scales would soon tip. He did not doubt that the Islamic extremists were involved in the attack on the twin towers in 2001, but why did the Bush administration offer them 'red carpet treatment' to accomplish their mission so successfully and even add extra terror of their own making for good measure? What is the close family connection between Bush and Bin Laden and why was the Bin Laden family permitted to leave the USA on September 11th when all other flights had been grounded?

In one of his emails, André reminded him that Trevor mentioned that the entire political administration depended on the Bilderberger crowd to keep them in the Oval Office. He never kept the email because his interest was more in ascension material.

Before he returned to the Pannekoek, André warned them both to take care. His mind was so occupied with all the information André shared that when he bumped into Niels in the street, all he was thinking of at that moment was the telepathic message; *"Remember that you are playing the prophet's game,"* that he suddenly heard."Gee, where are you?"

"I'm sorry. Gosh, it's you."

"Are you alright?" Niels' concern touched him as he walked inside the coffee shop. They were distracted by the argument Zola was having with a customer.

The very plain hefty middle-aged woman was quite a contrast to Zola's exuberant exterior. Zola had miscalculated the change. The woman had an instant dislike to her which he felt was unwarranted. He used his charm to settle the dispute. The woman left but by now Zola's eyes were flooded in tears. Her makeup had run all over, so she excused herself.

"That was a neat trick, you must teach me" Niels whispered.

"What happened?" Nel asked when Zola ran past her to the bathroom. He explained and she went back to see if she was alright.

"Toon told me that your computer in the shop could do with an upgrade."

"He did? It's working. Jeroen got it sort of going again."

"I'm here to have a look. Do you mind?"

"Not at all, but, what is the cost?"

"There is no cost if you can pay me in Talents."

"In what? You mean bartering?" Sascia had lately often mentioned it. While Niels ran a scan through his laptop he told him how Toon got them all involved in the Talent exchange program. Niels was surprised that he was not yet on their system and he showed a website he had created on his Laptop.

"It's the internal currency that is going to be implemented within the communities which Toon is building," Niels explained as he wrote down what he offered to do with the Pannekoek's PC.

When he looked at the bill he was surprised. He only had to pay in Euro for the electronic parts. He could pay for the labour in Talents. He asked what he could offer in Talents to him. Niels said that it didn't have to be paid to him at all.

"I pay you this amount in Talents and that upgrades this PC to Windows 11?" He helped Zola by handling the till while she served the drinks. She was very good at making coffees.

"No it's far too old, I can only upgrade it to Windows 2007, but that should be sufficient for the shop." They agreed and he promised to go online and add his name to Niels' list. He recalled Peter explaining to him about how they were trying out a new currency system amongst the people that worked at Half-way House.

When Niels left, he remembered forgetting to mention that André, his brother, was at the bookshop. Only two customers were having their lunch.

Zola was now fully recovered and had listened to their conversation because when Niels left she asked if they could look at Niels' website together since she wasn't good with computers. When it was quiet, he logged on to Cape Town Talent Exchange[1]. Niels told them about it From his laptop. Aunt Mien would be chuffed to find that her PC had a new hard drive with a modem installed. He felt good about that.

Between customers, they studied the community exchange system, especially Toon's community in South Africa. He wondered if it was worldwide. Many names on the offering list were known to both of them. Zola was excited when Yolanda offered her dressmaking skills and Ingrid her pattern-making skills. The rates were all calculated using Talents instead of Euro. Some were negotiable. Toon offered his gardening and landscaping service. Annelies offered 2-day intensive workshops teaching the philosophy and practice of sacred geometry. Tieneke offered her mind-drawing seminars; even Fred's name was on the list. He loved what he provided; if you have a problem, the solution to which defeats you, I will help you find the solution that, unknown to you, you already have by dropping your limiting assumptions. 100 Talents a session.

He spotted Niels' offer to help install computer software and provide support on almost any package.

"Gosh, you can join and offer whatever you want to earn Talents!" Zola affirmed. He was just as surprised, thinking what he could offer. He asked Zola what she wanted him to type in for her. He was curious what she'd come up with. Zola frowned into

---

1. https://www.ctte.org.za/

a severe look. He scrolled through the whole list to give them an idea of what others offered.

"Stop! I can do that!" Her long artificial fingernail indented his liquid Laptop screen. "Sorry," she said when he reacted. He read: companion/partner for any event: walking, driving, travelling, talking, dining, events, functions.

"Really?" He looked down at her high heeled shoes.

"Well... better take the walking out unless it is in shopping malls." She giggled. He started to warm to her.

"I'm sure you can do more than that."

"Mmm. I'm very good at making special coffees, or, I suppose I can cut people's hair. I'm a qualified hairdresser."

"That's it, excellent, what next?" Zola got the idea.

"I can offer a manicure or pedicure, including hand or foot massage." He typed all her skills and Zola's energy changed. He suddenly saw a woman who had something to offer;herself. The purple streaks in her hair and the long painted fingernails were who she was now. It was her emotional body that activated his unease. It was still very fragile. She could so easily be hurt. What did that reflect in him he wondered?

"What are you going to offer?" Two customers walked in which gave him time to think. After they served them, he came up with something.

"I can teach history or geography. I've been a travel organiser. I can work out the whole holiday tour that includes flights, hotels, etc. or scientific and business editing. That's it, but I can't think of anything more practical like you offer."

"Gosh, but you are so clever."

"Believe me not more so than you. Think about it if we were to live in a community. Who would be the most useful?"

"I suppose so. We offer very different skills."

"Yes, so stay who you are, long nails and all." He couldn't stop himself from saying that. Zola hugged him. He hoped that nobody was looking because his heart belonged to Sascia.

It had been warm and sunny for days, but now it was overcast, and the rain would come down at any moment. He wanted to be by himself to digest the things André had shared and what Fred had told him. It was quiet, so he said Zola he could manage independently. Zola flirtatiously suggested that they could go to the movies, but he had no intention of getting any more chummy than they already were. In a flash, he thought about the energy hook that Fred had mentioned. He mentally sealed his field.

He realized that Zola was lonely and she was looking for a mate. What Fred told him made so much more sense. Years ago he would have fallen for her charm.

He was about to close the coffee shop for the day when Annelies walked in. It was just on six. He had planned to warm up a Loempia at his flat and work on his journal tonight.

"Just in time, I see. Richard, Theo left me a letter I must give to you before you play the ascension game on the second level. I kept it and I'm not sure when we will play it now what with all the drama, but I thought to give it to you anyway." As he took the blue envelope he spotted the 1888 date on the top.

"This belongs to the stationery from the Prinsegracht Hotel, not so?"

"Yes, the date is quite significant. The Orphanage housed the children that belonged to the same group soul."

"I'm still battling with the idea. Has Fred told you what André has discovered?" Annelies sat on the high stool behind the counter. He turned the closed sign on the front door to the street. He didn't want to be disturbed.

"Yes, Fred came back to the Hotel in quite a state. We now realise more and more how vulnerable we all are if we don't release our attachment cords to people who are used as bait. Hennie and Piet are a good example."

"But surely there are millions of Piet's and Hennie's in the world. I can't accept that one has to be ruthless and cut off from people who are not at all interested in waking up!" he said it in dismay because of the threats directed at him and because part of him didn't want to cut all the cords. Annelies smiled.

"I remember saying the same thing to POWAH" Annelies stared out the window. He tried picking up on her thoughts.

"POWAH tried to make me understand over and over again that to wake up, we have to let go of programmed energy particles that are all around us." reflecting over Theo and his own beliefs. She shook her shoulders and straightened up.

"Okay, I can understand that in theory, but what about love and compassion, or our responsibilities towards others to name a few." He knew that she must have heard his questioning before, but he didn't want her to go just yet.

"Sweety it took me twenty years to understand the power beyond thought. Are you trying to grasp the wisdom behind it in 30 minutes?" He heard her think. Her eyes spoke the rest.

"Alright, I will brew over it. I'm sure I haven't got it all yet." Annelie's expression changed when she told him that Hennie and Piet's funeral was taking place on the spot where they both died. Peter's parents, who live in the Buttercup Valley community, were flying back with Toon and his party on the 7th. Ben and Hans were looking after Leo, who was slowly recovering. He wished he could be there, but someone had to look after the coffee shop.

"Toon's pilot is flying Connie, Jeroen, Harry Brinks and myself to France on Wednesday. We will stay at the Half-way

House and fly back the next day. Richard, we can't all be there. Fred has to open the book shop and Quincy is keeping an eye on the Hotel for me" She climbed off her high stool and looked at all Sascia's photos on the wall. Annelies mentioned the Talent exchange list. He told her that Niels had just shown it today. She gave him a great big hug.

"It's not easy hey, hang in there. Things will get better, they always do. I must go. Oh, how's your journal going?" Annelies suggested that he must let Liesbeth look at it after the workshop was finished.

He prepared a cup of soup at his flat and took the envelope Annelies gave him to the bedroom. He missed Sascia, especially when he suspected Annelie's envelope might contain Theo's 18th tablet. The file had a provoking title: When Distortions Take Over the Game[2]. Again, he had to click on the link to read it the content online. It is interesting how the titles of the tablets reflected the synchronistic events of the previous weeks.

Tablet 18

Translated by Theo

Richie, both Annelies and I knew that this tablet again mentioned how the separation from our higher self happened through the takeover of the persona. Even our oversoul started to experience life through nine ways of thinking controlled by a program. Annelies will share the nine aspects and give them to you for your journal. Even today, these nine personas have affected our planetary soul through the continents. Each continent has a distinct signature that is now being prepared for its reawakening. It is the resurrection our planet is involved with. This remarkable shift will affect any life form that merges in speed with Earth's energy changes.

Love Theo

He was too tired to open the USB port. He would rather wait until Sascia got back. It was a lot more fun to share it.

---

2. https://allrealityshifters.wordpress.com/tablet-eighteen/

Chapter 19
The Effects Fragmentations Create

The Valley of the Gods
It was only six days after Sascia left for France, but it felt like sixty days. He was about to leave the flat when the phone rang. Sascia asked how things were with him and his studies.

"When are you coming home?"

"Oh, Rich, I missed you too. How is Ginger?"

"Fine, we are great buddies. He sits on my lap the moment I sit down. I think he knows you are coming home. When is that?" He meant to ask how the funeral went, but then what could she say?

"Rich, have you heard anything from the faculty about a teaching post?" He hadn't, but then that could change overnight. Why did her sudden question mystify him? When he asked again, she replied that she was unsure how he would react to Toon's proposal.

"What do you mean by a proposal?"

"Toon wants you to be in charge of the design department when all the contractors arrive to build the Valley of the Gods resort."

"You are kidding me."

"No, I'm serious. Toon had been walking around with an idea for weeks. Mom said that he had spent hours on the phone getting artisans together from all over the world who could draw him a plan, like an artist impression of a health resort that looks like an Egyptian town." He was impressed. When the man had an idea, he indeed followed it through. Toon's reaction when he saw Sascia's poster on his birthday must have done the trick.

"That's a tall order. Does Toon have a plan?" A dream came to mind where he helped plan a city. Gosh, how uncanny that he had dreamed about it.

"Rich, when the rest of the group went back to Half-way House after the funeral, Toon and mom took me back to the site where the large dome was going to be positioned. It's about two kilometres away from where the explosion blew up the two buildings. There were lots of people around who are building a high wall to keep people out, but of course, we got in. Rich, what do you think? Are you up to it?" He didn't know what to say. Part of him was thrilled at the idea, but did he have the skill, the creative flair, the visions and the practical know-how to take on something like that?

"Moppie, I first have to see what Toon has in mind, and how far he wants to go," Sascia said that was all she needed to know. She would arrive with the others after lunch at Soesterberg airport.

When he opened the Pannekoek, he could hardly contain his excitement. He took the chairs off the tables and started the coffee machine in preparation for Nel's arrival. There were already a few customers when Niels delivered a new hard drive for the PC.

Toon flew him back to the Valley of the Gods later that day. They would start working on the outskirts of the park first. He never realised it was such a large estate. The project was fantastic, and he decided not to mention anything that André had shared a few days before. Toon was a man with a mission and had such integrity. Nothing would convince him that Toon was involved in global conspiracies.

Back in Apeldoorn the following evening he shared his dream over dinner with Toon, Sascia and Ingrid. His dream visions had become more apparent. When he described the time that he was the architect who together with Akhenaten, the Egyptian king built his famous city Tell-el-Amarna, Toon got so excited he practically dragged Ingrid to their office; so he could guide her into drawing a rough outline for the Valley of the Gods project. They loved his idea and he agreed to take on the task. Ingrid was amazing. How she managed to draw his visions with a 3-dimensional program was excellent. They would first start with the outskirts of the whole plan, while they were digging the massive lake. He had to hand it to Toon. Time or money was of no consequence.

Annelies' ascension workshop

"Rich, don't forget Annelies' assessment sheet with the questionnaire." He had left it on the table. There was so much to do now that Toon's project was in full swing, Sascia seemed to handle multi tasks better than he did.

"I'm so glad to be back with you", Sascia whispered in his ear on the way to Annelies' fifth workshop. So was he. The six days on his own were far too quiet.

"It must have been hard, hey, seeing Tieneke grieving."

"Dreadful, I can't remember ever meeting her, Hennie. She was her only child! Rich, I would hate to go through such pain, having a child and then losing them in that manner."

"Did she stay in France?"

"Yes, she and Harry, her dad, stayed on. Trevor will be around. He's in love with Tieneke. He's much older than her, but they seem to have something going for them.

"How is her husband doing?" He remembered that Roelof was a contractor who had a gambling addiction. He was the informer who told Ben all about the artefacts that were smuggled into France. The list of respectable art dealers was a mile long. It is shocking what people will do for money.

"I got the impression that Tieneke's husband, after his last stroke, had mentally withdrawn from the outside world. Harry said that Tieneke hadn't told Roelof anything since he wouldn't register it. Physically, I don't know. Debbie didn't tell me."

When they drove up Annelies' driveway, signs of autumn were in the air.

Class 5

SEEING THE WHOLE was written on her door. Annelies had changed her workroom. There were graphs on the wall he'd only seen when they had done their twenty-two decoding steps workshop.

"Our personality card has a vital role during the awakening game." She showed me some sample cards. Once again, Annelies handed them all the same questionnaires they had to fill out at the beginning of the decoding workshop. There were nine paragraphs, each marked with a number from one to nine. The nine paragraphs explained how each of the nine personality types would respond, react or feel in the same situation that was given above. All the charts on the wall were self-explanatory, especially since he had read the assessment sheet.

"As you can see, each of the nine numbers carries an energy that reveals the type of personality you have chosen to wake up with." By that, Annelies meant to awaken to full consciousness. He had chosen the number nine, the mediator. Sascia chose the numeral vibe of six, the devil's advocate. Toon was a seven, the adventurer. Ingrid chose a five, the observer. Annelies admitted that she had selected a numeral eight vibration, the boss. They were all surprised that Zola picked the energy of the two, the helper. Ed was also an eight, and Yolanda found it challenging to decide between three, nine, or six energy. The way Annelies explained why Yolanda found that difficult was very revealing. Niels was the perfectionist, the number one.

"Comforting thought, knowing you do all the electronic work for the park," Toon said to Niels with a grin. They were all keen to discover Hans and Liesbeth's personality types, whatever they were. Hans also chose the mediator, and Liesbeth said that she most related to the energy of the four, the tragic romantic.

"Really? I can't see you as a..." The others took up Sascia's comment, and a whole debate followed.

"All the personality types are presented in this room. That is going to be interesting." Annelies remarked. The time flew past. The stress and sorrow of the last few days lightened up. During their coffee break, Ben joined them. He still looked very bruised.

"How is your hand?" Annelies asked.

"Look, it's healing. I took the bandages off, and ever since you told me what to do, I have been talking to my body initiative. It worked!"

"Of course, it will. Always remember that, will you." Annelies' voice expressed such intent as if he had to be reminded. Did she know something he didn't?

"Richard, you are into anthropology, aren't you?" Gerrit asked.

"Yes, you could say that. At least I have applied for a teaching post on human evolution." He still hoped that the faculty would accept his application, at least part-time, now that Toon's project would bring him a steady income for quite some time.

"I didn't know that is what you want to do?" Toon remarked as he showed Annelies an article. He explained that he didn't want to teach full-time, but if the university asked him to write a paper on human evolution, he would have to be prepared to lecture on it. Toon nodded.

"Are you using the information that you learned through your dreams?" Yolanda beamed. He still wasn't sure how to differentiate between his dream consciousness and waking

awareness. He didn't want to become a fancy-ridden visionary. Yolanda picked up on his train of thought while Liesbeth's smile was directed to him or Gerrit, who was in a talkative mood. What a changed man after his disclosure last week.

"You know, Richard, getting past the half-century mark has its advantages," Gerrit said, whom he reckoned was around sixty.

"I've seen it all, done it all and experienced a lot. Now I can be free to explore territories most of the younger generation have no attraction for, except for you all here." Gerrit looked proudly at Niels.

"Most youngsters first have to grow up and do the family or relationship thing," Gerrit added as he drank his coffee. Sascia winked at him, replying that she wanted it all: family, work, material things, and a lot more soul awareness.

"I must admit, this hunger for the truth is both exhilarating and addictive, what do you say, Rich?"

"Moppie to have found you, who have the same drive and vision I have. Life has become an adventure," Zola commented, saying how lucky Sascia was. They were all thinking of Wim. Nobody asked if she still went out with him.

"Annelies, she's been invaded. Can you see it?" Liesbeth beamed.

Her mental comment made him think of what Fred had told him about attachment cords. What would it be like to be invaded, he wondered.

"Richard, most of us are. You must learn to recognise your energy particles and what is not yours." Annelies beamed at him. He knew that the other telepathists heard it, too.

"Zola, do you still see Wim?" Annelies asked. Zola sniggered; her whole body language showed inner anger.

"He must be interested in my lectures because I saw him twice, but he had gone before I could say hello."

"Believe me, he has another agenda. He is interested, alright, but for the wrong reasons." Zola had everyone's attention, Ben especially. In a very subtle way, he questioned her. What the man got out of her in five minutes would have taken him hours.

"What do you think of Zola's story?" Sascia asked when they were driving home. At first, he was stunned, but then it became very plausible.

"I think she has been used, but in such clever ways. As Annelies said, she has been invaded." He shared with Sascia what he had learned from André and Fred regarding Interpol's involvement, but he omitted the political or financial intrigue. Sascia had plenty of stories that came from Trevor. Still, Zola's comments had stirred Annelies into a different mode he'd never seen before while Ben practically interrogated her. They drove in silence for at least ten minutes. When they arrived on their street, he knew he had thought the same thing she had.

"Do you think Annelies will do it?" She asked.

"You mean to ask her to leave? Yes, for now, until she releases the cords that are corrupting her. We will know next week. Let's see if we have mail.

It had become a regular thing with them. At the end of the evening, they would look at the emails and reply to them the following day.

"It's your turn" Sascia called out. He knew what she meant. She gave him a cup of hot chocolate. It was getting chilly; the summer had gone.

They were both eager to read Trevor's emails. Next week he would fly to France while Sascia looked after the coffee bar. Trevor promised to take him on a tour underground. The linked title, The Effects of the Persona during the Game, was again amazingly coincidental...so they were eager to read the content online.

Tablet 19
Translated by Theo de Jong

Richie, as you read the nine aspects, you will soon understand the vital role personalities play in the scheme of things. Even throughout history, many ideas came from Europe and spread around the globe. Even the planetary soul experienced the division. The Atlantians understood certain root assumptions of reality that are not accepted today. Their mass consciousness held a unique system of beliefs. The Atlantians were trans-dimensional, meaning they could access this dimension as well as a multitude of others. They understood what was happening inside the Earth and their relationship to time, electronics, free energies, the power of the sun, and interplanetary and interstellar communication. They could move through time, forward and backward, and track their existence to some degree. They were, however, unable to control their physical existence during the last polar shift. Remember, Richie, The ability to jump time to see what probable futures exist does not mean that you automatically end up there.

Love Theo.

"How could Theo have known we were working on our personality card?" He was, as always, just as surprised by the timing.

"That reminds me, I haven't yet opened the UBS stick Annelies gave me. It was just before she left for the funeral. We must go to the office and use your mom's PC." Sascia was keen to see what was on the flash drive, so they took their mugs of chocolate to their study.

"Rich, have we not received this before? I remember the title,"

The Shattered World Ego Game

<u>The First characteristic</u> aspect of planet Earth was manifested through the continent of Africa. Initially, only the spirit of intuition could function through the instinctive behaviour of primordial animal life. Everything seemed to indicate a change of some kind. Richie, during the closure of the last cosmic cycle, that aspect became fixated on being number one, a starter or an organiser with solid ideas for excellence. It is a typical reflection of Europe, Australia, and China today.

The Second aspect of planet Earth was experienced through the continent known as Lemuria. As we observed the spirit of courage in operation, evolving animals developed a crude form of protective self-consciousness. During the closure of the last cosmic cycle, this aspect of the persona became fixated on being the keeper of truth. It is a typical reflection of the plant kingdom and the areas of Peru, Siberia, and Tibet.

The Atlantean civilization revealed **the Third aspect** of the planet. Higher types are differentiated, and the spirit of understanding grants creatures the gift of spontaneous association of ideas. When the spirit of worship first made contact with the female's mind, a bridge was crossed, and she soon shared it with the male. During the closure of the last cosmic cycle, this aspect of the persona turned into arrogance. It is a typical reflection of the areas called the USA and Asia.

The Fourth aspect is that the spirit of compassion started to manifest itself in increased measure. The evolution of the higher mind led to the development of group consciousness, resulting in the growth of the herd instinct and the beginning of social development during the Egyptian civilization. At the closure of the last cosmic cycle, this aspect was embraced by the people who globally had united to ascend. It failed due to the lack of compassion for others in some initiates who were less awake. Some suspect that many of these initiates embody the dolphins and whales of today.

The Fifth aspect is that the spirit of counsel can only begin to function again if a new order emerges willing to embrace unity within all. With expectation, we realised that the long-awaited hour was approaching; we knew we were upon the threshold of the realisation that our prolonged effort to evolve as human creatures on planet Earth would awaken during a following cosmic cycle. New communities would form where people from all walks of life can live and express their soul's passion.

The Sixth aspect is that the spirit of freedom must develop in increased measure while the shift of our awareness will make great leaps before the next cosmic closure. Most of us didn't make it in the last polar shift due to our need for personal power. Many of us left our distortions behind what today is known as the dark forces.

The Seventh aspect is that many Atlantians embraced the spirit of inner power during the closure of the last cosmic cycle, but in some, it had disastrous results. It was still not expressed for the good of all. Many souls were shattered and could only partly embody a human form. The DNA responsible for transmitting genetic information became dormant so that only 5% of our soul's wisdom after that could embody a human form. Using the symbols of the Language of Light makes it possible to activate the dormant DNA strands again.

The Eighth aspect also failed to awaken globally during the last closure. Before the spirit of Wisdom fully applies, acknowledging habit patterns is paramount to releasing distorted vibrations. We knew that some of us would have to incarnate again to replace these distortions with the tonal frequency of Forgiveness. The karma that had been created from all the landmasses on the planet would have to be transmuted through the soul quality of forgiveness. All ascending humans must embody the tonal frequencies of the Language of Light alongside animal and nature kingdoms. The human brain and hands are genetically programmed to create a map of the journey of ascension.

The Ninth aspect, the spirit of illumination, re-instates all the eight other aspects within the planetary soul. Each planet corresponds to a stage of universal evolution. Humanity's consciousness does not need to be limited to the environs of this solar system. Our space vessels are life manifestations of consciousness, not rockets. The spirit abides in one's inner self. All aspects must be transcended within, and this will be reflected in the external material life of every human being, opening the pathway to eternity.

Richie, as you start to remember that spiritual initiates utilised the pyramids on our planet to experience a consciousness expansion, we know that the emotional body of man had to evolve. Bringing the higher mental and emotional body in balance would affect the human physical cellular speed on an atomic level. This is necessary to transcend the programmed experience of death. You will by now have recalled that you had to conquer your external reality. The physical embodiment was converted to a new "crystalline." genetic code during this process. For many, their ascension failed during the closure of the last cosmic cycle. Our planet is now ready for a global reawakening, and the troubling times preceding this shift reflect the planet's resurrection. Naturally, this resurrection will affect every life form that merges quickly with Earth's energy changes.

Love Theo

"Wow! Rich, what does Theo mean by conquering our external realities?" His dream involving either drowning or being eaten alive by crocodiles flashed past him.

"It's to do with fear, I guess."

Well, I'm bushed. There is so much to take in. For now, I want to have a long, peaceful sleep." Sascia took their mugs to the kitchen.

His thoughts were so overwhelmed with information that had it started to flood his conscious mind, he would've become ill, but it still gave him feelings of nausea. He had difficulty falling asleep. He watched Sascia's rhythmic breathing, trying to imagine what the world looked like when the writer wrote the symbols onto the sheets so that his future self would find them. That idea still freaked him out.

In a dream, he could still see this cave where this old Englishman, his grandfather, dissects the mummy. The foil sheets were used as wrappings, so what was the man looking for? Was he just another archaeologist fascinated with ancient text, but why the mummies? Was the older man looking for something only the mummies could reveal?

• • • •

He tossed and turned. He knew that he wanted to be free, but he tried to decide where to go while sleeping. He wanted to hear more about POWAH. He wanted to visit the higher mental worlds, as Theo called them...

"What are you waiting for?" Leaving his body always felt joyful. To be able to perceive objects or beings of the spiritual world gave him a particular perspective on his physical reality. He was always glad to become aware of Theo, even when his mind made him appear wearing a long white toga. When he was out of his body following Theo, he instantly felt at one with his surroundings, as if he was part of it.

"Richie, in the physical world, all objects are perceived to be on the outside. You become a part of everything in the celestial or Astral realms. Let's observe what a temple looks like, built from

pure crystal." Gosh, he had only lately thought of how he would build a temple within Toon's Valley that would give the appearance of pure crystal. Was his mind extending that idea in his dream? Suddenly, he saw something indescribably beautiful, almost like what a life force might look like. Streams of liquid light beams formulated facets with brilliant sparkle-like mirrors. He was inside, being part of it!

"*These are the same forces that drive the sap through the organic form of the plant or cause the flower blossoms to unfold. Keep watching and listen.*" He heard it first, then as if a fog lifted, other beings surrounded them in light bodies. They were all sitting in a meditating pose, listening. Then, the repetitive melodies became words.

< *Your universe was created by a consciousness that manifests through a geometric blueprint in physical reality. What you see around you is the substance called Ether. In your physical world, the repetition of their movements, not seen by the bodily eye, creates the illusion of linear time.* >

As he translated the sounds into words, the melodies that seemed to move in synchronicity with the colourful patterns created a visual screen. In the mirrors, he saw himself merging with the stream of colours! An understanding emerged.

"*That's the idea. Mysteries and riddles lie hidden everywhere in the phenomenal world. Richie, a person born blind, can still successfully operate when surrounded by the objects he perceives. Likewise, the dreamer does not have to wait for his dreams to live simultaneously in another world.*" If Theo meant that he could be just as aware of his dream world while awake, he would not have experienced it as such. Whoever created all this of which he was part made him question how much he was influenced by mind control.

<In your age, when humanity is moving forward in all areas of science and technology, such as genetic engineering and the cloning of various sentient life forms, some feel that man has never walked on the moon or landed spacecraft on Mars. Men are starting to question what is real; they become analytical. Others question if some form of mind control is influencing them>

Gosh, he had just questioned that. How remarkable. How come?

"Richie, when one opens the files of the soul, one can perceive things that must remain concealed from the bodily senses."

<It is a time when many of you seek spiritual answers. Many are indeed in need of healing. Many dysfunctional souls are being abused or emotionally challenged in some way or another through the bodily senses. My beloved always remembers that to experience truth, your feelings of oneness, through the expression of LOVE, will direct the energy of the ethers.>

"Richie, there are many subliminal messages sent through television, radio, the internet, and other media that most people are unaware of." He wondered why or what purpose that would serve. Or was there some other force interfering with the mind of man?

"Yes. Many subliminal messages can limit people's consciousness and prevent them from functioning sufficiently to get through their day-to-day activities." Theo replied to his thoughts by making him think about the many people who went to work, ate, watched television, especially news bulletins, and went to bed, repeating the same pattern repeatedly. Was he not one of them?

<Each of you who answered the call from the far reaches of the universe and came before us, the Council of Nine, in all your glory. We observed your radiant bodies of Light, which

blazed forth your virtues, unique gifts and attributes gained through aeons of experience. That alone made you valuable and important candidates for the planned mission on planet Earth; I'm most honoured>

A warm feeling came over him. Who is to say what is real and what is not? If any information triggered feelings of love, understanding, joy, or inspiration, he would accept that as what truth was all about.

<After each of you awakened a particular assignment that would be the central theme in your incarnations via your Spirit I AM, you were also given free will, so it has always been up to you to take the high road, the fast lane, the middle path or the low road. Regardless of your decisions along the way or how long it takes, you are destined to return. You will soon accomplish your mission >

When he looked around, many light bodies started to sing in unison with the melodies that seemed to come from the central column of light where POWAH stood. Suddenly, Sammy, sitting on his knee, jumped off and started to dance. He had to reorientate himself by recalling that Theo had brought Sammy. Leo, who had been meditating beside him, grabbed his hand, and they joined in. Within the large circle, the light beam turned into a bright flame. POWAH's light body transformed into the monument of the Sphinx. He had dreamed this before! POWAH's message that everyone had been given a particular assignment stuck in his mind.

"*Richie, you will soon know yours fully. Whatever happens, remember that you accepted a particular assignment. This knowledge will help you in the months to come.*" For some reason, he intuitively knew that Theo was sad about something. Feelings of sadness clouded his mind as he seemed to move away. Theo became fainter, and he saw no more. The pressure on his eyes became quite intense from the heat.

He heard Sammy calling for him but...the heat...he felt like suffocating...gheeeeeeeeee...whoosh! With a heavy thump, he was wide awake....

• • • •

The sweat was pouring off him. Did he wake up from a nightmare? He remembered something about an assignment. He peeked at the clock radio. It said 6:00. Sascia was still fast asleep. He tried to remember what or where he had been. He knew if he tried to clear his mind and let the images pass him by, it would sometimes just come to him.

Without waking her, he got up. Ginger stirred but stayed on the bed. He might as well work on his journal. He got his laptop from the lounge and moved to the office. It was already light outside, and it promised to be a sunny day.

He poured himself some juice and settled down to study Theo's tablets that he had gathered so far. Ingrid had given him some idea of how to lay out his journal. He had started to write a daily diary to see if he could pick out events that made up his day-to-day realities. His thoughts drifted away...When Auntie Mien was back, he would try to spend some Saturdays with Sammy. Now and again, she would send him an email, usually with lots of cartoons. He would always consider Sammy his child, no matter if she...that was it. Sammy had been in his dream. In a flash, he remembered the rest. He was busy typing when Sascia appeared sleepily from the bedroom.

"What time is it, Rich?"

"Six-thirty, go back to bed. I'm just getting my journal up to date."

"Why, what is the hurry?"

"I just couldn't sleep."

Annelies' Decoding-workshop

"I can't believe it; they cancelled my fourth lecture again!"

"When now? But Rich, who is responsible for the bookings?" They were all cleaning and rearranging the coffee bar for his aunt's arrival next week. They had planned a welcome home party.

"Wil de Wit does the bookings. For some reason, she doesn't like me. I don't know why; I've never argued with her, but during the so-called bomb scare, she was unpleasant." He recalled her hostility, but André didn't seem to notice, so he thought it was him being over-sensitive. Nel was singing in the kitchen. Sascia explained to a smiling customer that the owner, a good friend of the cook, was expected to return home soon.

"Rich, you say her surname is de Wit. Could she be the family of Piet de Wit, Yolanda's ex, who died in the explosion?" Funny, but just now, it had crossed his mind. Sascia answered the phone while talking to a customer.

"Rich, it's Toon. He asked if you could fly to the Valley this weekend."

"Since I have no lectures tomorrow and if Jeroen and Connie are willing to work, why not? Then you can come too." he pulled a face.

"Yes, he can. Can I come too if there is space left?" She smiled at Toon's reply.

It was after five when Nel came to the front to say goodbye. She was all dressed up in rain gear.

"Hi there,... gosh, Nel, it's pouring. Do you want a lift?" Jeroen asked as he stepped inside. Connie ran in behind him with her bag over her head. He was glad Jeroen offered, even if only to the station. Nel always took the train home.

The windscreen wipers were doing overtime en route to Annelies. Tonight was to be their last evening. Time flew. Sascia had printed out Theo's Shattering of the Planetary Ego article. She wanted to share it with the others.

"Your mom and Toon just turned in behind us. Will Toon join us tomorrow?" Dirk, the pilot, would be leaving around ten in the morning.

"I think so. I'm keen to see how they progress unless it rains there like here."

"Hello there. Glad you can make it this weekend." Toon called out through the rain. Ingrid had started to wear looser clothing, but you could see nothing of the fact that she was pregnant.

Class 6

MAN AS A TRANSFORMER OF ENERGY was written in big letters.

"We are, aren't we," Toon remarked at the sign. They greeted everyone in the hallway that was now filled with rain gear. Again the workroom was creatively decorated with many charts. This time, there were visual drawings of how people interacted with each other on an energy level. It reminded him of Fred's explanation of the energy hooks.

Annelies was all dressed up in green. Ben came to say hello. He seemed more at home these days after the attack, and he started to look better. During their break, he would tell Ben about their suspicions about Wil de Wit. He didn't want to become paranoid, but something nagged him about her.

"Are you joining us?" Annelies meant mentally, as she was waiting for him to sit down.

"The nine different scripts we created for ourselves are divided into three equally important qualities of intelligence.

They are the intelligence of Thinking, Feeling and Doing." Annelies explained.

"You mean some people are more mental in their behaviour with others, while others respond through their feelings, and the third type does it with physical activity," Sascia confirmed. He knew that Sascia was warm and affectionate with a sharp mind.

"Yes, there are, of course, lots of variations within each type, stemming from such factors as maturity, our parent's types, birth order, cultural values, and inherent traits," Annelies added. Regarding their drawings, each had an opportunity to draw a symbol that they felt was their strength and weakness.

"Remember that only each person can decide on their type accurately according to their internal perception, but it helps to know that millions of people have the same coping strategy as you." That was a thought. He wondered if that program was more accessible to brainwashing. *"You have been dreaming again, have you?"* Liesbeth beamed. Where she got that idea from, lord knows....

Annelies told them that Zola would not be joining them anymore. It was her own choice when Annelies explained that she first had to make a graceful closure with Wim since he was not supportive of her aspirations.

Schiphol airport

They were finally on the way to Amsterdam. Richard closed the coffee shop after the last customer left. They would spend the night in Amsterdam at Schiphol airport early to collect Mien and his niece Sonja.

Six months ago, he decided to quit the tourist game and look after his Aunt's coffee bar while she spent six months with her children in South Africa. She had been doing that for years, living six months in Holland and six months in the Western Cape. It was a surprise that Sonja decided to work in Holland.

She had been a nurse at Groote Schuur Hospital in Cape Town. He tried to remember how old she was when he last saw her just before she went to college in Cape Town.

It was a great evening, but getting cooler. The summer was over. They had invited Vinny and Debbie around for drinks around nine. When Sascia heard yesterday that Debbie was spending two days with Vinny in Amsterdam, she asked them around. They were looking forward to the evening.

He was making good time on the freeway, with no congestion. The music from the old movie the Titanic played on the radio; still Sascia's favourite. He was excited to be seeing his aunt and niece but was glad to have Sascia with him when they arrived.

"Who ran the coffee bar for her last time Rich?"

"Ellie, with the help of a girlfriend."

"You mean your ex-wife?"

"Yes, she was looking for a job at the time."

"What did she do before, work-wise I mean?"

"She used to run a clothing boutique in Delft. When Sammy was born she stopped working."

"Delft! That's where Quincy's health shop and Oliver's offices are. Were you living there as well? Where did you meet Ellie?"

"At Carla's pottery show in Amsterdam believe it or not."

"Really. What's Carla's surname?" He grinned at her suspicions. Carla was a very creative woman but never seemed to make a go of things. She should have stuck to pottery. When she married Vinny, his friend encouraged her skills; he hoped Niels would do the same.

"No, no, I don't believe that the whole world is related. It's Carla Visser. Sascia was silent for some time. He could hear her think.

"I'm sure that Wim, Zola's boyfriend's surname is Visser and so is Nel's." He looked sideways at her in surprise, could it be?

What a reunion. Aunt Mien's big hug at the airport almost crushed him, but the small key with the chain around his neck broke. He caught it just in time, so it wasn't lost. Mien recognized the key from the safe. She insisted on having the chain repaired. He was reluctant to part with it, but his aunt had already put it away in her handbag. Sonja turned out to be a stunner. He forgot how tall she was. As tall as her mom, but still slender with an attractive smile. He knew that Sascia and Mien would get on fine. Sonja had already accepted employment at the hospital in Utrecht. She would even be starting the next day! She and Debbie had been in contact through email. His aunt would be back at work from the first of October.

· · · ·

"Daddy, can't you come?" Sammy pleaded over the phone. "But girly you will be there with all your classmates. What do you want me for?" Sammy's school had organised a day outing for tomorrow. The Prinsegracht hotel was one of the first stops and Sammy asked him if he could bring his poster and hang it on the wall so all her classmates would believe her story that her dad was a movie star. He was worried why Sammy needed to brag about him.

"Sammy you must not tell your friends that your dad is an actor. I don't know where you got that idea from."

"I know you don't play in movies, not like that, but you are in the poster picture. Oma said that people who are in poster pictures are special. I want everybody to see that you are."

"Are what"

"Special daddy, mommy says you are."

"Really?"

"Yes, mommy told me that many people come to your lectures about the dead people. Uncle Oliver said that I must ask you to come and be our tour guide." He was so surprised that Sammy spoke like this, 'about the dead people.' She must have heard that expression from an adult. He had explained often enough how the giant pyramid at Giza and the Sphinx were monuments left behind by very clever people from a civilisation that had disappeared. Why Oliver suggested that he give a guided tour of the hotel made no sense.

"Sammy I will be at the hotel when your schoolbus arrives, but I will talk to uncle Fred to see if someone like Connie can be a tour guide.

"Goody! Daddy, will you bring your picture poster?"

"No sweety I will not. Why not ask your teacher to tell the driver of the bus to make a stop at the Pannekoek instead, so I can offer you all an ice cream?"

"Really? Must I ask my teacher?"

"Ask if the teacher can phone me. Give her my cellphone number, you do have that?" Sammy rattled off the number by heart.

"Good girl, see you tomorrow."

The Prinsegracht Hotel

"Moppie, can you take over from us at the Pannekoek when Connie and I go to the hotel this morning?" Richard called from the shower. Sascia had been typing away in their study since six o'clock that morning. Ever since he had shared his idea about a book on symbolic languages, she had got into gear. It was great to do a project together. His research was in full swing with the Valley of the Gods. Sascia would type it out; she was a lot quicker at it.

"What time are you going, I want to finish this."

"Nine. The school bus will make a stop at the Pannekoek around eleven. Connie and I will be back before that time."

There is no rain today. The sun was even out. As he drove up to the hotel's parking bay, the school bus had already arrived but parked at a funny angle. Whoever was behind the wheel must have misjudged the kerb. Suddenly, someone jumped in front of his car from behind the school bus. Connie gave a yell.

"What the hell...What's going on?" He called out to a man in uniform. In the corner of his eye, he saw children sitting inside the bus while other groups were already inside the hotel's reception hall.

"Richard, they carry guns!" Connie cried in horror and fear.

"Get out, be quick, there is a hold-up, get inside," the man shouted while the hotel's parking bay was crawling with police and onlookers. He parked in front of the schoolbus. The man who seemed to be a policeman according to his uniform ...suddenly waved a machine gun at them. His heart was beating in his throat. Where was Sammy? He grabbed Connie by the hand and ran inside the Hotel. That was when he heard her.

"Daddy!"

"Sammy, where are you" he looked around. The sheer panic on Fred's face when he came from behind the reception desk shocked him to the core.

"Please, Fred, where is my daughter? I'm supposed to meet her inside the Hotel." A man with a mask suddenly grabbed Connie. Both Fred and he stared towards Connie in horror when Ed suddenly appeared from nowhere and hit the man from behind with a bottle.

"Daddy!" he heard again.

"He sprinted back out through the glass doors in the direction of the schoolbus. He was sure Sammy called him from that direction. When the first explosion went off, he felt a sharp pain from the shattered glass, but he ignored it and got up. Then, when Richard saw the school bus burst into an inferno of flames, he heard a gunfight, but all he could think of was Sammy. He ran back in through the shattered doors calling out for her. More explosions followed. He was thrown in the air... or so it felt like it. Kids were screaming everywhere. The sirens in the background made him regain his sense of direction but – when he was caught in the water spray he fell and started to cough. Suddenly the flames became a roaring inferno.

"Sammy, where are you?" He yelled. He could hear Connie was nearby vomiting. Why, he didn't know. He saw people climbing over the balcony rails on the top floor inside the reception. Oh no! Someone jumped only to land right on the flames below. He went rigid in horror when he saw some children near the fire. He grabbed at least two girls and pushed them towards the entrance. Suddenly, he was surrounded by flames, but the pain in his chest was nothing compared to the pain from the heat as he looked into the roaring flames up close. He covered his eyes and fell onto the floor, screaming.

"We're breathing soot and everything else right now." He heard Fred saying. The screaming had stopped. People were coughing....

"Fred, are you listening? Where was he?" a woman's voice called.

Out there, I see him, oh what can I do,... his eyes!" Fred cried. They were trying to do something to him. No...no...they were grabbing his hands away...

"Fred, flush his eyes with a large amount of water for at least 15 minutes" the woman called from afar.

Another explosion ripped through the building.

"Fred, are you with him?"

"Yes, but I must first remove his contaminated clothing and shoes because it could ignite at any moment."

"Annie, oh, his eyes...his eyelids are... oh..., It's his eyes."

"He knew that Fred flushed his skin with large amounts of water and occasionally lifted his upper and lower lids"...then he screamed...until it all became dark.

Sascia

When the explosions were heard from the distance, every person in the Pannekoek looked at each other. Funny, she'd felt suddenly hot and shaky. The feelings that rippled through her were an experience she'd never had before. Nel came from the kitchen asking if they heard it too.

Jeroen switched on the TV, but nothing was being announced. The sirens in the distance told them that something was going on. People in the street were all looking around to ask others if they knew what had happened. They all went about their business until a car came to a screeching halt in front of the coffee bar. Sascia saw Connie getting out of the car, then she ran inside, followed by her uncle Ed. Both looked dreadful...covered in black soot. Tears were streaming down Connie's cheeks as she slumped down on a chair sobbing. Ed was, like her, in an absolute state of shock. Everyone in the coffee shop was talking all at once.

Sascia felt like an ice block. Stiff and cold. Where was Richard? *"Rich where are you?"* she mentally screamed.

"Sascia it's on the news. The explosion we heard came from the Hotel!" Jeroen called out as he cuddled Connie who was shaking. They were all staring at the TV screen when the reporter got shot. The panic and screaming did not seem to prevent the cameraman from doing his job. There was an electrifying hush in the coffee bar as they stared in horror at a schoolbus exploding inside the parking bay of the Prinsegracht Hotel. The violent images were replaced by the studio staff, who were all in shock.

Sascia tried Richard's cell phone again to establish if he was one of the lucky ones to get out of the inferno alive. There was no answer.

"Sweety we both saw Richard enter the hotel just before the blast." Ed's voice trembled with emotion.

"No, no, I can't believe it. Richard must be alright, I know it." Sascia's panic almost choked her. Connie was crying.

"Jeroen I couldn't even say he wasn't there because I saw him, he was...." Sascia didn't want to listen, she repeatedly tried to contact Richard's cell to see if he would pick it up...Another very disturbed journalist broadcast the same images....

"The fires raged through the Hotel grounds like a tornado funnel and quickly spiralled out of control. They burned down all of the outbuildings of the old historical castle as if they were made of paper. The culprits responsible for the fire are yet to be identified. Fourteen people were admitted to the hospital, while three others were sent to the burn clinic in Utrecht.

"A total of four operating theatres at the two hospitals are devoted exclusively to the Prinsegracht Hotel survivors. People from throughout Apeldoorn, Hilversum and Utrecht General flocked to the scene.

"It's too bad that it takes a tragedy like this for people to start paying attention to bomb threats and safety issues," said Apeldoorn Fire Chief Dirk Jansen.

Sascia couldn't believe it. As she looked in horror with the others at the TV screen, she only had to look back at Connie, who had gone into shock. The fire inspector who was interviewed looked grim.

"Look, the doctors and nurses are working feverishly to maintain the victims' ability to breathe. For the survivors from the hotel, the battle is to keep their lungs working. This fire was started with intensely noxious fuel." The fire chief was replying to a journalist.

The cameraman was back on the scene where the hotel had been, and they all watched in dismay at the ruins of what was once a magnificent building.

"It's too dangerous for everybody. We're breathing soot and everything else right now. There are still ashes falling everywhere."

The cameraman reported the suspected arson with such vivid detail, Sascia was speechless. This did not happen to the people she knew. This could not be real. If only this was a dream, and she would wake up at any moment.

"Firefighters have been using the freeway and about 50 people helped to evacuate the children from the two school busses that were still outside, waiting to get in. It's a very difficult situation, people have been evacuated from their homes nearby just in case. We are doing what we can but methanol is very toxic."

"Uncle Ed, take me to the hospital, please. Jeroen was already on the phone when Toon's BMW stopped before the Pannekoek. She ran outside and jumped in. Toon said nothing; he just drove.

The entrance to the burn unit was crowded with people. Toon held her hand while he spoke to Debbie on his cell and firmly made his way to the closed doors. They opened to let them in. When Sascia saw her sister, the shock on her face said enough.

"Is he...Debbie...how bad is he?" she cried.

"My reaction is one of sorrow." Doctor van Dongen replied to Toon, who was his friend.

"What does he mean Debbie?" She wanted to know if he was still alive. What were they saying?" Toon had phoned Don van Dongen the moment he heard from Fred, who together with Annelies was at the nearby clinic, that Richard had been taken to the burn unit in Utrecht.

"Why can't I see him?" she pleaded. Doctor van Dongen shook his head. His eyes showed such hurt. She couldn't accept that there was no hope for Rich, her partner, her friend, her lover, and...the father of her unborn child. She had planned to tell him of her suspicion soon but wanted to make sure first.

Debbie embraced her, trying to prepare her for what? No way. She attempted to beam Rich a message. She sat down and concentrated but all she heard was Toon and the doctor whispering. "*Toon he's too bad. She can't be near him. It always is sad when I see somebody that's badly injured.*" Debbie cried with her.

Looking up at them, she heard Debbie asking the Doctor something.

"Debbie, you know that those kinds of burns set off a cascade of reactions deep inside the body, unleashing hormones and other chemicals that keep a healthy body in harmony, but in a burn patient? You know, in a burn victim, it's the nervous system disorder that can have a stroke-like effect, even temporary blindness.... she didn't want to hear anymore. Toon sat next to her, holding her."Sascia, don't give up hope. You've got to know from within that the road you both travel can end in an outcome that Richard finds valuable, that there is happiness for you both in the future."

Chapter 20
The Elemental Rules of Matter

The burn unit in Utrecht.
   Sonja

Her heart cried. Richard reminded her of the patients whose bodies had been so ravaged by flames that there was nothing left in some spots save for charred bone.

"Doctor, how is it possible that the injuries in four of the fourteen survivors are so severe?" she asked Don van Dongen.

"We found traces of methanol on their clothes. We have no idea how it got there.

"Methanol is extremely toxic, isn't it?" she whispered. Richard's face was in such a mess. "What is it used for?" Don peered up close at the dreadful mess where Richard's eyelids used to be.

"It's a liquid fuel. Someone sprayed with it. Who did it, or why is being investigated. Two patients inhaled the vapour but in Richard's case, we think that a small amount got near his eyes when he tried to save the children." They both stared in silence at Richard...who was heavily sedated.

"I learned that exposure to methanol, be it through inhalation of the vapour... or ingestion or indirect skin contact with this liquid fuel can be fatal. Is that what happened to Richard?" she asked softly. Don shook his head in dismay.

"You know a lot about burn injuries, where did you learn that?" Don asked with admiration as they walked away.

"In Red Cross Children's Hospital in Cape Town." Her reply almost triggered a flood of tears. Instead, she followed Don who had moved to another burn victim.

"Do you know if Richard ever found Sammy?"

"Nobody knows."

Sascia

Sascia's table at the Pannekoek was covered with letters sent by email, or post. There were so many good wishes. She would take them to the hospital.

Many people ask after Richard when they seen her. What could she say? Richard had not yet spoken a word since the fire. His injuries were severe. Thanks to Hans and Debbie, his healing started immediately, but they could not even reach him. Nobody knew if Richard knew about Sammy's death. They held the funeral at Toon's garden centre. Ellie and Oliver were heartbroken. Everyone was there, Quincy too. Nel had not been back to work. She was grieving over the loss of her granddaughter. Much to Mien's regret, her nephew was in complete charge of the kitchen, but for now, she made do. Richard's aunt was such a wonderfully warm person and such a storyteller. South Africa must be a wonderful place. Thank goodness that she was back to take over Richard's workload. Sascia helped her, but she spent most of her time with Richard. She knew he was in pain, and she felt so helpless.

Nel stayed with Ellie, who had been to see Richard as well. Oliver didn't seem to live with her anymore. Sascia hadn't told anyone she was pregnant, not even her mom. She suspected that Debbie somehow knew, but she wanted to wait until Richard snapped out of his state of shock so she could tell him first, hoping that her news might help him in some ways to deal with losing Sammy.

Mien had the TV on all the time. When the news at seven came on they were still talking about the fire.

Due to the smoke from raging fires billowing from the hotel near the shopping complex on Saturday morning, many shoppers quickly left the complex, trying to find alternate routes around the burning Prinsegracht Hotel that had now become a blazing inferno.

Thousands of viewers saw again in horror how the prestige hotel went up in flames. Housing developments within two miles of the hotel experienced difficulty entering the freeway.

There was an electrifying hush in the coffee bar as they once again saw how the schoolbus exploded inside the parking bay of the Prinsegracht Hotel.

"Oh please, I don't want Richard to hear about Sammy that way." She cried. She was so tired. Mien switched the TV off. Her usual dinner in the Pannekoek, which had become a ritual after her visit to the hospital, stood untouched in front of her.

"Sweety go home, have a rest, look after yourself, especially now..." Mien's face expressed so much. The moment they had met they liked each other....

The burn unit

It was a month ago that he lost his eyesight. His world was in total darkness. After the heat, he had landed in a dark pit. Now and then he would still get a panic attack, but he knew he had to climb out of this hell.

Today he was getting up and about. He had had enough of hospital beds. The pain as if millions of ants were crawling over him, eating him alive was still there, but he had to make an effort. If it was not for Sascia, who came every day... or Debbie, Hans and Liesbeth, who all gave him healing, he would have given up long ago. So many people were trying to help him. He knew their intentions were good but it brought on such cynicism in him. Like when Niels came around...his negative attitude...

"Since we agreed to forget our true identity and everything we knew the moment we were born, why not leave it at that." Telling him how he wished he had never had any awareness did not do anything. Niels reply was being sympathetic, which brought on more of the same response.

"Please, don't blame yourself, keep smiling you say. Niels, I hear cries all day long in this place. Most of us are having the same difficulties, trying to be joyful in this miserable world. To stay asleep is not so difficult since most of us when we entered as babies have a memory loss... with a few exceptions I suppose."

"That's true, but you of all people seemed to remember a lot more than most. The fire didn't wipe that away did it?" Niels replied. That was the trouble...he sometimes wished it did as he thought of a woman a few days ago, who wanted to pray for him....

"No it did not, but every institution in our culture supports this memory loss. I tell you for most people" thinking of the woman who wanted to save his soul... "It must have become easier as the years went on." He had chased the praying woman out of his room.

"Richard I hear you, but... Where is the person that shared his dreams with us, your insights that often came from your brother and the fact that you were asked to write the journal?" Gosh, he had heard it all before...what do they know. Nobody could understand what it was like to be in this darkness all the time.

"Niels you'd better dismiss all of my dream visions as the result of an over-active imagination." He wanted to sink lower away from this world, so he asked Niels to come back another time.

When Annelies told him a few days later in a clear voice that she would only come and see him again when he decided to take charge of his life, he knew that she had thrown a ball at him.

She had pointed out that his natural sense of humour was no longer accessible to his persona, which was true because next to him in the ward, Tom was able to joke and make light of life and their situations. Richard had to admit that he could only ever see through his cloud of seriousness, which kept him from having a meaningful attitude to life.

He started to understand why the world outside is a sort of circular hall of mirrors at the centre of which he, Richard's persona, sees himself reflected. He then understood that his shadow had conveniently projected his view of life onto others.

Utrecht Hospital

He was waiting for the nurse to take him for another skin graft on his shoulders. They were all amazed at his speedy recovery, but since he could not see the result of Hans' and Debbie's healing, to him, the days and nights were long and dark. To see no sunshine, no early morning daybreak, and not to see what the weather would be like for the day. Oh, he'd better stop this. He knew he had to find a way out of his misery. If only he could leave his body. Now, that would help.

"Good morning, Richard. How are you today?"

"Sonja, are you taking me to the repair shop again?"

"That's it. I asked you, how are you today?" He had no idea how to answer that.

"Like yesterday, the day before, and before that, miserable."

"Mmm, you are right... that's not a reality I would like to be in." Oh, why did he feel like a baby that only wanted to cry?

"I wish I knew how to climb out of it." He often lay for hours wondering why he had chosen such a tortured route to get to the truth. He couldn't accept that he had chosen this nightmare.

"Richard, maybe because we have been on this planet too long and have absorbed all of its dysfunctional thinking, only a good wake up call will do the trick. You are sure a good example....Come on let's go."

Sonja helped him out of bed. Of all the nursing staff, she and Debbie were the most gentle. The inside of his palms was not burned, so at least he could touch things. Gently he sat down in the wheelchair. He felt dizzy as she started to move, so he escaped into his mind. Sonja was a very loving woman who, like Debbie, was dedicated to helping people in need. Thank goodness he'd seen what she looked like, so he could visualise her in his mind. She was quite a stunner. Slender with curly long hair and big brown eyes. He could feel that they went into a lift.

"Richard, you know, this planet is no model for rational thoughts, butI learned by looking around here at all the people who end up like you, disfigured and broken, that no soul is permitted to enter our physical world to disarm its dysfunctional patterns without having lived them first. Think about that one will you." He had to mull over what she had said because he valued her thinking. He loved Sonja. She was witty, compassionate and genuinely cared. He was just a miserable sod.

Two months later

On the day that he was discharged from the hospital, he woke up with the memory of being somewhere. The hospital noises that he knew by heart – for the first time didn't bother him. For the past week, he had swallowed only half his painkillers. The rest he managed to flush down the toilet. He was suffering but he knew that he would not be able to experience out-of-body trips while any medication was still getting into his body. He was not entirely free from some of the stuff they fed him, but when he was at home, he would see to that.

Everybody was amazed at his recovery. He must have looked really bad. Sascia had come every day while he had been too knocked out to talk. The visions of the exploding bus, and the little girl that he didn't manage to save, kept haunting him. He knew that Sammy was gone, but during the last few days he somehow sensed her presence. He was sure because this morning he remembered the last time he saw her. It was in a dream. It was so clear now. She was sitting on his lap clapping with joy. Theo had brought her with him.

"Good morning Richard."

"Hi Debbie, you must be glad to get rid of me." He felt a slight pressure on his cheek. It didn't hurt.

"Did you kiss me just now?"

"Good, you felt it. Your skin is looking very good this morning."

"Do you kiss all your patients?"

"Only the special ones. Richard, I'm very worried about Sascia. She's very depressed but she is avoiding me." He ran through his mind what she had been like the last few days.

"Debbie...never mind. Thanks, I will find out."

"What are you going to wear?"

"Sascia hung my tracksuit in the wardrobe. She said it was...I can't yet wear anything too tight-fitting." He knew that he had lost a few kilos but anything against his skin, especially his shoulders, was still sore.

"Okay for the last time, I have to wash your eyes. How are they today."

"Very very scratchy." They were very sore, but he didn't want to let on that he had not taken anything for the pain. He knew that Sascia had been shown how to wash his eyes several times. Where was she?

He could hear from the clacking and rattle that Debbie was preparing things. He had to brace himself every time they took the bandages off. He held his breath and was about to grasp the side of the hospital bed when he felt Sascia's hand.

"Hi Moppie, I wondered where you were." *"What are you wearing?"* he beamed. *"Oh Rich,...you can do it again!"* He heard her weeping.

"Do you want to do it?"... Sascia must have nodded. He could smell her scent as she got closer to take the bandage off.

"Good morning, let me have a look " Dr Don van Dongen's voice filled the room. He squeezed Sascia's hand to cope with the stinging on his newly created eyelids.

"I think we'll leave it off for a while, let's say until you are home. Sascia I want you to change this layer at least twice a day for the first week." he started to relax for a while. His eyelids felt better without the pressure of the bandages, but the pain, when he was asked to try to open them was still torturous. He made an effort, but his memory of the incredible pain held him back. *"Richard, try to imagine that you are looking at a snowy landscape."*

"Hans! Are you there?"

"I am. Please, Richard, you have to do the reprogramming. While I'm giving you your last treatment at this hospital, I want you to visualise snow while bringing in feelings of a cold temperature." He did as Hans suggested. Every time Hans would send healing rays to his eyes he could feel the vibrations enter his forehead. He tried linking these sensations to cold air that came at him from an open fridge.

Slowly he opened his eyelids while he kept visualising and sensing the cold air on his face.... He knew that Dr. van Dongen was watching what Hans was doing.

"The pain...Gosh it's gone!"

"Hi, how does it look?" Sonja whispered. His room must be crowded with people. The total darkness was still depressing, but the love and care he received in such abundance pulled him out of his most profound misery. It was Annelies' comment about not coming anymore until he decided what he was going to do with his life that made him shift.

"Well Richard, all I can say again is that your recovery has been miraculous. I'm well aware that we have no idea about your eyesight as of yet. Give it a few months and we will take a good look again. For now, get stronger. Get up and about and learn to see with your mind."

"Richard of all people should not find that too difficult." Annelies' comment made him heave with emotion. She had come! He held his other hand out to her and gently she slid her hand under his hand palm. The top of his hands was healing, and still very tender.

"Sascia, do I have any hair?" he had never thought to ask before.

"Trust a man to wait this long to discover that he has the shortest crew cut ever," Sonja replied.

"Have I been bald?" He took his hand away from Annelies and touched his head. It was painful to lift his arm because of the burned parts in his neck and shoulder, but he could feel a soft furry bristle.

"Moppie, tell me honestly, do I look hideous?" he hoped that at least he didn't look scary and freaky. *"Rich apart from your eyelids and eyebrows that looked bad at first, your skin is almost back to normal in your face, with no scars."* As he heard her thoughts, he softly squeezed her hand.

"I'm ready to go home."

"That's the best news I've heard for weeks. Sascia get him home before he changes his mind." Dr. van Dongen's comment lifted the air. Hans moved away... so that he could get sideways off the bed onto his feet. Sascia helped him with his gym shoes. Then someone tucked a small chain with the key, that he had worn around his neck from the moment he was told to do so, in his hand.

"Aunty, are you there?"

"Yes, my boy. I will not stay long, but I hope that you can wear it again, now that your skin has healed." For some reason unknown to him, he was very happy not to have lost it in the fire. Mien put it gently around his neck. It felt O.K. A month before he would not have tolerated it, but now it could stay on.

He heard the others leaving his room, including his aunt.

When they were alone he groped in the air for Sascia, wanting to encircle her around her waist. When he felt her body pressed against him, he smelled apple fragrance when he pressed his nose close to her. *"I'm so sorry that I have not been there for you when you needed me, can you tell me what happened that made you so sad lately?"* He could feel her body shaking from trying to hold in her tears.

"Oh Rich. I could not tell you while you were so depressed."

"Moppie, tell me what?"

"Ten days ago I had a miscarriage." All the hurt that he felt for himself was nothing like what he felt now. He cried.

"Rich! your eyes, you have tears! Oh, love, now I know you are going to be better." He didn't know for how long they just held on to each other, but in those moments he felt for the first time grateful for what he still had.

At Ingrid's home

He woke up in a strange room. Sascia had gone, then he remembered. He was staying over at Ingrid's place. Sascia had left early with Toon to see to the progress in France. He wondered what time it was. Every day since he left the hospital he managed to do more for himself. He knew that Sascia had left his clothing on the chair in a way that was the easiest for him to dress. Never in his life had he ever thought that being blind was such a handicap. What he missed the most was reading. Toon was quite prepared to get him all the latest equipment for blind people, but he didn't want to accept that he would never see again. He went to the bathroom and washed at the basin. Soon he would try a bath. He couldn't yet think of a shower. The idea of water falling on his shoulders was too much.

"Richard, call me when you want to get down," Ingrid called from downstairs. "I'm already on the landing; I'm smelling the coffee." Slowly, he felt the stairs, and as he got his footing, he managed it quite well. *"One step, and you are down. See if you can find the kitchen."* He was so glad that his telepathic skills had come back. He practised daily with Sascia and the other telepathists that he knew.

"When is André coming around?"

"It should be any minute. You want to go through with this?"

"Wouldn't you?"

"I'm not sure. I was at first very angry with the people who mistreated me, who were so cruel and violent." Ingrid pulled up a chair and sat down. Her voice came from a lower direction. He started to direct his attention by facing people sideways instead of looking into their eyes as before.

"I know that when things seemed very bleak, I sort of let go. Richard, I filled my mind with visions of a reality I wanted to experience. That way I was able to let go. POWAH then showed me in a vision, that to participate in this ascension journey, I had to release all energy cords my mind still held with a link to this world."

"You mean even the good things you wanted to experience?"

"Yes, even those, because they only occupied my mind to externalise them. I had to steer away from what I perceived to be both good and bad experiences. When I was in a neutral space, that was when POWAH stepped in."

"You mean that was when you had a vision?"

"Sort of. I finally understood the saying, "to be in this world but not of this world." He had to mull the words over and over in his mind.

Away from the darkness of his external world, he suddenly saw with his inner eye a spider that was busy building a web. As he watched with fascination at the labour that was applied, he heard: *"A spider builds its universe without getting wrapped up in it."* He wasn't sure where that thought came from, but he could see how he had created a web of personal thoughts, dreams, desires and goals. What did his web look like? *"You built a prison with massive, thick interlacing threads around you."* Suddenly he saw the spider caught up in his web. The more the spider struggled, the more threads he spun that made his prison even tighter. He started to feel sorry for the poor bugger. He wanted to say to the creature *"Destroy your beloved web!"* then almost immediately a gust of wind hurtled at the spider who was trapped. It could not save itself, so it rolled into a tight ball and with the following wind woosh...the spider dropped onto the ground. At first, it was stunned, then, when it suddenly discovered that it was free, the creature ran back up the tree. He watched in awe when he became part of the world of the spider. This world was made up of many many threads that formed patterns of such splendour, never could he have created a better web. *"This is the true design I planned for you."*

"Richard POWAH led down a path that led me back to worlds I had left behind, where the law of Karma did not exist." Ingrid's words brought him back into his body, where darkness prevailed.

"I was shown that everything in the world of matter is governed by the law of karma, but when the mind becomes still you are in the kingdom of the infinite."

"But Ingrid, how do we free ourselves from this law?" His contemplation on the spider's dilemma was exciting, but he still needed to find his joy back while living in a body that was not functioning as he wanted.

"Richard...If we inherited our celestial code from the Universal Mind, then all the combined experiences in one's life will lead the soul towards the positive or negative manifestation. I remember that I was the one who drew the original Star-map. I am only now starting to remember glimpses of why my father, in a previous life, gave me this task." Ingrid's revelation on the Star-map was so unexpected, he was curious where she was leading to. She directed his hand to his breakfast, then moved about in the kitchen until they both heard a car arriving in her driveway.

"That must be André. I'll tell you another time about the Star-map." She walked out of the kitchen to answer the doorbell.

"He's in the kitchen, I'll be in my study if you need me." André needed his signature now that he could use his hand again. People often touched him on his shoulder to let them know they were there. He understood their need, but his skin was still tender.

When he heard his statements read back to him again, recalling why he was asked to go the hotel, repeating what Sammy had said that Oliver asked her, he sensed that André was in great stress, which reminded him of what Annelies had said; that humanity is moving through times of extreme turbulence, emotionally, politically, spiritually and socially. She called it the times of the Emergence, so he never asked if Wil de Wit was involved. As Ingrid said, let it go.

Soesterberg

"Rich, are you ready?" He was trying to get his laptop and other goodies in his bag. They were on the way to Soesterberg to fly with Toon's plane to France. He was still very clumsy in his movements especially when he wanted to do a simple thing like packing a bag. He tried not to get too impatient with himself. A week ago he had just got out of the hospital, now he was flying to France to be with the others who were all busy on Toon's colossal project. Oh, he so wished he could see what they were going to show him. Toon wanted him to be there at the weekly meetings. Toon believed that he would be valuable by just listening.

"Moppie did you hear from Toon that Trevor is going to be there?"

"Yes, he and Otto are back from the Paris conference on the future of politics." Sascia had driven to her mother's place, and Toon drove them to his plane in his BMW. He was getting used to being a passenger.

On the way, he reminded Ingrid, via a telepathic beam, to tell him about the Star-map.

"Kitty, haven't you shared yet what you think about the Star-map?" In the back seat, they listened to Sascia's mother's idea.

"This will shift anyone interested in heraldry," Toon added after Ingrid explained the Star map.

Sascia's body close to him in the back of the car started to stimulate his sexual needs that had been dormant for weeks. He softly explored the inner side of her thigh. She was wearing a wrap-around skirt that was very handy. She must have made sure nobody saw his fondling. He knew that the absence of sex had been a strain on her, especially after her miscarriage. He had consulted Vinny about how he best could help her over her depression since his injuries were so occupying his whole being. After that discussion, he insisted that she share her disappointment with her mother and sister.

"Mom, I have some ideas, especially about the meanings of the symbols found in heraldry and on coats of arms, and because of Annelies' theories, we'd love to hear more about yours."

Sascia always said that her mother, being such a private person, rarely talked about what was on her mind.

"Richard, remember that I told you that, like you, I sometimes have an out-of-body experience myself?" Ingrid had been going to tell him about the Star-map just before André arrived. After his visit his mind had been so occupied with André's stress, he forgot to ask her about how she concludedher story of being the artist of the Star-map.

"Ingrid, like you I was so startled by the painting, because it hit me with feelings of sorrow, why I don't know. Did you have that feeling?"

"*Gosh, Kitty,*" Toon interrupted. "Imagine if Richard and you shared a life while this map came into being? I don't think any one of us has the same reaction as you both seem to have. Curiosity, yes, but that's all."

He was waiting for Ingrid's response, especially after Toon's suggestion. He tried to feel in his body if it in any way somehow had genetically stored memories that would support such a claim.

"I have an uncanny feeling that Richard was my father in that life." Ingrid's suggestion somehow clicked with him.

"Gosh, Mom, how interesting. That backs up Annelies' theory. She told us(this was just after the fire) that whoever drew or knew what the star map represented must have known or had the knowledge about the energies of a group soul."

"I still have not been able to link Annelies' decoding of those stars that appear on this Jaarsma map."

"Richard years ago when Annelies had studied Astrology, especially everyone's housing system, she concluded that those stars are much more than dead rocks hanging there for the sake of beauty. In those days I was also then doubtful, but when Leo pointed out that 99.9% of the general population does not possess cosmic consciousness and are like robots that are influenced by the star's signature, as he called it; I decided to stop judging a science I didn't understand." Toon made sense, but he wished that he could free himself from his body and look into his akashic records with Theo's help.

"Rich, I overheard Leo saying that you will soon be able to connect with Theo again. I'm not sure why they said that but talk to Hans again when you see him." Sascia beamed as she kissed him.

"We are here. Dirk is waiting. Let's carry on with this fascinating conversation later." Toon suggested.

The Valley of the God's Resort

He was glad to be away from Holland. The shops' reindeer and jingle bell music drove him up the wall. The commercial bug had once again infected the material world's need for profit. It had many people in a frenzy which made him sad. He'd liked the evenings in the past with Aunt Mien's family when they shared presents, but the story of St. Nicholas, the Spanish Roman Catholic bishop and later declared saint, who fed the poor on his birthday had never clouded his mind. His dad saw to that.

Last weekend, when they came to France and visited the former Pleasure Parks site, he could hear how they were all frantically busy with the outskirt plan of the large resort. They described the various cottages, from tree houses to modern dwellings, reminding him of Annelies' board game. The large lake around the island was done in two stages. Toon had employed experts from all over who had the skill to pull it off. Two Egyptian-looking temples were scheduled to be ready for the opening of the first phase, as Toon called it. He said that, like Annelies' ascension workshops, it came to him in the dream how the resort would materialise over five stages.

He was not sure how he could contribute, but when he was taken to the subterranean underground laboratory where Theo, Leo, and later Trevor made their headquarters, they showed him through sounds, fragrance and touch and by him regularly going into a meditative state, what part he could play.

They left him alone after that.

In his mind, Richard saw himself leaning back in his chair while his brain waves were linked to the computer's mainframe. The computer used his visual images as the Valley of God's resort formula. His hands were folded behind his neck, imagining that he was staring at Sascia's photograph of Toon's eight-seater plane. In his mind, it was even more lifelike. For others, it would be a substantial holographic display projection.

"Thanks for the view", the computer's disembodied female voice responded. Trevor's communication network, which he designed with unlimited funds thanks to Toon, occupied the underground laboratory.

It had taken years to combine centuries of knowledge collected from books, articles and scientific and historical theses, plus Theo, Leo and Trevor's knowledge of metaphysical and quantum physics theories.

He knew he would soon join them permanently after selling his flat in Apeldoorn. Until then, they would commute between France and Apeldoorn. He was quite happy that this opportunity was valuable. He thought it was pretty weird that he would spend his time below ground like his grandfather must have done in the early nineteen hundreds.

Sascia was very happy, having found her niche. Before the fire, she had been helping him with the typing of the visions about the city of Akhenaten; now, he would soon travel in the world of his inner life again, as Leo called it, and translate it verbally through a mike, while the computer collected all the data from his mind. His senses of sight, smell, and hearing would all be recorded as he took over Sascia's typing with a unique keyboard.

The publishing business at Halfway House was growing. More people from all over had joined Toon's community scheme. The Talent currency operated exceptionally well thanks to Niels' extensive database, where everybody did their Talent-skill banking.

It was very quiet in the underground laboratory. All he heard were the sounds of electronic equipment. The imagery he recalled of the movie The Matrix came to mind.

Everything that had been written about in the hieroglyphs was visually available at the touch of a button, including images from the underwater archaeological findings that remained from the Atlantian times. On the screen, or in holographic media, visitors to the resort could become observers during the first two of the five stages of consciousness associated with planet Earth. This data was shown in a holographic format at Toon's resort. Lots of people would benefit from such visual exposure. It was needed to take them all into the third and fourth level of the ascension park project. He had to learn to see with his inner eye so he could project it into the database for others to see theirs.

The underground caves where he was hooked up had been repaired or rebuilt in parts. A link to the other tunnels that had caved in due to the blast would soon be reopened. Underneath the Valley of the Gods, they had a whole different world at their disposal. People from all over the world would quickly be able to experience what it was like to be in a timeless zone, as he called it.

The smell from the dryness and the stillness became apparent to him. Knowing that he was underground, away from the world on top, his mind started to wonder.

Recently, he learned that Leo had spent many years researching pyramid structures and using pyramid energy in everyday life. His interests also included the effects of natural and artificial electromagnetic radiation, ecology, and harmony in architecture and life. Leo only became aware of the symbolism of heraldry when he studied the documentation left by his grandfather, which included photos from the 1950s and 1960s that revealed fragile gold foil sheets. Together with Trevor and Theo, they studied the symbols that Tieneke referred to as the Language of Light and were able to decipher the tablets.

It was still incredible that ancient civilisations already knew that shapes, rather than numbers, generated the language codes of reality. Would they ever awaken to the mysteries beyond creation?

Lately, while surrounded by darkness, he has often tried to transport himself back to ancient times. He recalled Theo's discussion with a tourist.

They were inside the Giza pyramid, climbing the long tunnel to take them to the king's chamber. Often, they had to wait in between since too many people inside the king's chamber were no longer allowed.

"Mankind cannot duplicate this technology today because the blocks were moved by levitation and the secret of tachyon energy." Theo had replied to questions he was also wondering. Then everyone wanted to know what tachyon energy was.

He replied, "*'Standing Columnar Waves' deal with patterns that seem to influence energy for specific effects."*

Richard remembered vividly how that tourist group seemed more interested in the origin of the pyramid than most.

When a drawing of the temple dancers flashed mentally in front of him, he then remembered.

His sisters and young girls in the temples were taught how to use the resonating magnetic force field using rods and coil devices. They were able to manipulate them through the dance. They were the temple dancers who made the large blocks float across the desert sand on a resonating field of music. Then, the masters controlled these devices from the builder's platforms with their minds.

A noise from above snapped him out of his daydreaming. He missed Theo's presence, even if it was from a different realm but he knew that it depended on his projection abilities, which had come naturally to him before.

After the destruction wreaked by the bomb, there were only three mummies left of the twenty-two that had initially been hidden inside the deeper tunnels. Leo had been near the tunnel where the crystal skull had been found. Theo had insisted that they keep the crystal skull where it was until it was ready to come to the surface...So far, they have not found it but kept looking.

He had tried several times to have an out-of-body experience ever since he took himself gradually off the medication. With the help of Hans' healing skills, he was off any drugs, but somehow, his mind could not free itself, or he didn't manage to remember. Leo had explained to him that due to the trauma created by the feelings of terror, his self-created terror shadows had taken complete control of his external consciousness, which only operated on low awareness levels.

He felt really good after dinner. For the first time, he started to see how he could earn his keep.

"Significant karmic ties come into play within family groups" Leo replied to Helen's question about how they all seemed to be related, although not genetically.

"Being able to participate in choosing the family group before incarnating depends on the soul's level of evolution. Some of us have experienced that POWAH, on the soul level, is a significantly evolved being. That is how our mind translates POWAH to be."

"Leo, intellectually, I can accept that but if the mind is like a computer with a unique celestial program inherited at birth, does our DNA produce a genetic blueprint unique to each individual?" Helen asked.

"Absolutely, and it is based upon previous lives and karma. The physical connection between the mother and the child, or any of your family members, is also genetically programmed into our DNA. DNA is short for deoxyribonucleic acid, which is present in almost every cell in our body. So DNA produces a genetic blueprint, unique to each individual, except identical twins."

"Leo, has POWAH ever been or experienced being human?" Sascia asked. Leo smiled. "POWAH would reply to that question by saying: if you know yourself, then you know me."

"You mean all of us are a part of him? Do we belong to one large soul that divided its energy over several lifetimes, I have no idea how many, but to ascend back to where this great soul originated from?" Sascia's questioning was undoubtedly a way to see it, Richard thought. He loved these times when they discussed interesting topics in the lounge after dinner. He had missed them. Leo sketched the heliacal plane of the DNA molecule, which Annelies used in her decoding classes.

He started to be alright with the idea that he might never see again. Not that he had given up hope. No, on the contrary. He began to see that his wish for higher knowledge would never be sufficient. It would never be enough to resurrect his physicalness. All the knowledge he could gather would not raise the speed of his physical vibration or affect his health, abundance, or general well-being.

"Richard, so long as you doubt the importance of your inner life, the consciousness of your soul energy will not wake up from its slumber in these realms." As he heard Leo's thought beam while speaking to Helen and Sascia, he realised that his inner life, his inner world, had to be seen as more natural in every sense first. He was never a product of his outer world; it was reversed. The world around him was the product of his awareness on the inner levels.

"Leo, if people like Wil de Wit, her children Paul and Iris, or Wim Visser, Zola's boyfriend, all played a part in the corruption that even cost lives, were those people also part of the group soul POWAH that is reflected by the star-map?" Ingrid asked.

"It's hard to accept, I know. Through fear, we humans are capable of doing many bad things. However, any soul about to become incarnate is always placed in the best environment available for its evolution within the law of Karma. That alone makes me think we are experiencing darkness as a group soul."

They were all contemplating that one. Sascia took his hand in hers."Sammy must have played a critical role in the scheme of things, I'm sure." he squeezed her hand in acknowledgement.

"We are living through chaotic times but never has higher help been more available because of the profound transformations now being prepared on Earth. I have seen some of the workings Mom has prepared for the third initiation level, which confirms that." Hans said.

"Gee, can you share some of it?" Sascia asked. He had to grin at her eagerness. They had not even played the ascension game on the second level, and she wanted to know what was in store for them in the next round.

"Sascia, many highly evolved beings belong to very different spheres of existence or even other galaxies. However, they are part of the same group soul that oversees the human race on the Earth's surface. With their help, Mom will tackle why ailments come about and how to heal them in her third journal."

"Are you one of those beings?" He smiled at her forthright approach.

"Mmm, I know that some of you see it that way. Let's say that both Liesbeth and I had a soul change. As you know, we are what is called walk-ins, but for people to understand what that means, they have to first grasp the subtle facts through feelings that come from the heart rather than through the reasoning of their minds."

"Liesbeth, you will write about that in the fourth level, not so?" Helen asked from the dining room as she cleared the table. Liesbeth replied that she was glad to have still some time before she would have to document all her experiences.

"Like Ingrid and Richard, I too have first to awaken my understanding on all the subtle levelsLiesbeth inquired when he would finish his journal. It was nearly completed with Sascia's help, but he wanted to add more insights. Now that he has learned to see the world differently, he hoped to hand it to her early in the new year.

Before they all retired to their rooms for an early night, since they would fly back to Holland at dawn, Peter gave him a flash drive, saying that Trevor had handed it to him an hour ago just as he was leaving for Paris with Otto. He had found one of Theo's files inside a computer that had been retrieved from the rubble in one of the collapsed caves.

"Rich, I'm sure it is the twentieth tablet. I can't wait to read it. Let's use your laptop back in our room."

When they were walking back to their tiny cottage, which Sascia had described to him in great detail, they were greeted by people on the way. He would have to start remembering their voices to put a name to them. Their cottage had been occupied by a couple that moved to Buttercup Valley. It had a great view. Sascia set up his laptop as he familiarised himself with his surroundings.

"What is the title?"

"Wait, I'm still...He heard the music when Windows started.

"Yep, tablet twenty is called The Rules of the Human Game[1]. I'll read it to you."

Tablet 20

Translated by Theo de Jong

Richie, when I found this tablet, I knew my time was near. Because it was my job over many incarnations, as scribe, to see to it that these events were recorded through sacred texts and scrolls, or within the energies of crystalline bodies, or in stone formations carved out as hieroglyphs and pictographs, or even through channelled manuscripts and other art forms, I had to see and experience if I could awaken this DNA code while in my difficult physical state. I adjusted the factual translations with a group of words that still conveyed the same meanings, as you must have surmised. I left some of my experiences for Annelies to document her journey. On the physical plane, this new genetic code will result in the human body becoming more subtle; on the other astral dimensions, a transformation will happen according to the specific laws of the plane. Under the law of this new genetic code, individuals are no longer conditioned by their species' past karmic experiences.

love Theo

Now he understood! Theo had skillfully adapted the original group of words to a more modern idiom. Clever.

"Gosh, Rich, do you think that your brother managed it, creating a body that would be more etheric?" He had been thinking on the same levels, but his rational mind was often in the way when he contemplated such thoughts. Could it be that Theo became invisible?

---

1. https://allrealityshifters.wordpress.com/tablet-twenty/

"I want to meditate on it for a while; I will join you soon."

"Promise?"

"Yes, Moppie, I'll snuggle up soon."

"Rich, I love you."

He knew that she missed him... for he was, for now, more and more drawn into an inner world that seemed to affect his sexual drive. He trusted that in the greater scheme of things, he would understand the dynamic behind their sexual force. He needed all his energy to awaken into his etheric body while fully conscious.

"Moppie, my love, go to bed; I will join you soon."

He made himself comfortable in the lounge of their soon-to-be new home. He wanted to sit up straight so he had less chance of falling asleep.

· · · ·

After the vibrations started to travel over his whole body, he felt himself sucked into a funnel. The spinning sensation, like he had before, again created a detaching feeling. The excitement that he would be free almost jeopardised his release because he so wanted it to happen.

"Richie, the soul can do much even when imprisoned in the body. It makes the body its organ of sense, moving it invisibly and propelling it in its actions further than mortal nature can reach."

Theo's unmistakable essence implanted thoughts into his mind. He wanted so much to be true. Oh, he did it. He could see again! The colours were so transparent.

"Theo, I can see you! Theo?... Are you?" He remembered that he heard Theo's words before. It was during the endless fighting to perceive their faith. Why not die and let it be over with? He had often suggested it.

"Richie, we did, and during our cycle of around 65 years A.D., we had to start all over again." The misty substance cleared away for him to have a vision, and then the feelings to his vision made it yet another reality...

For years, they lived with their families within the boundaries of their fortress. He practically grew up there. He couldn't remember ever having been down the mountain. Only once did he accompany his father. He was ten years old. His mother insisted that he should experience what life was like down below. All he remembered was the ambush; now, the words were from Eleazar. He loved him. His hero, his brother, his mentor. Then they did it.

After the bombardment, when the Romans installed a ramp that put them into a position to breach the defences, they all took the poison. It was the fifteenth of April, his seventeenth birthday.

When he died, he saw how he left his body, his friends, and his younger brother. They all looked dazed back at their bodies. He saw how Eleazar was right. They were all free!

He saw how the army infiltrated their sanctuary, their impregnable fortress called Masada, which was situated at the southwestern corner of the Dead Sea. This magnificent natural fortress had been his home for ten years. Fluffy clouds still spread like a blanket over the mountaintop when the sun was up.

The Roman troops stabbed their swords into their bodies to make sure they were all dead. He strolled between them, but nobody took any notice. Some soldiers' aggressive expressions changed into shock. A tear rolled down a soldier's cheek when he turned the lifeless body of a young girl. Richard got such a jolt when he saw Sammy's face. He again heard Eleazar's words....or did he?

"Richie, I understood only part of the truth. My desire for immortal life compelled me to talk you all into committing suicide. I thought that if we showed true courage by regarding life as a kind of service, we must undergo it with reluctance and hasten to release our souls from our bodies. When the job was done, then I knew I was wrong." Theo was standing next to him, but not as Eleazar! The scene they were watching appeared like they were watching a movie. What did Theo mean by saying he only understood part of the truth?

"That it is the supremacy of spirit over matter, the union with the source of all that is, that is immortal." Every dream trip added more, or awakened in him more, transformed more of his soul's experience into the spirit? If he could walk into his soul's library and every book he read was a life his soul had experienced, then he was the author of each book... he could read as many books as he liked since there was no time involved?...but he had to learn how to read.

"Now you know that you must learn how to see and understand that the love force of spirit holds the key to immortality. Come, let's go and open another book from another cosmic age." As the visions disappeared, the feelings of immense sadness and sorrow lingered longer until they were gone.

He wondered which cosmic age they were approaching when he was in the physical. He pondered why he sensed that time in his reality was getting shorter and shorter. He noticed that Theo's light body had become more luminous. As he peered into Theo's energy field, another vision appeared. It became easier to stay the observer if he knew he was dreaming.

"Richie, astrologically, we are still moving into the Aquarian age but are at the end of our fifth evolutionary cycle." He recognised that Theo had transported him back into the underground laboratory, but it appeared drastically different...Leo had told him they found tunnels and chambers carved from a solid rock. So far, they discovered a total of 22 chambers, all intricately connected to an interior corridor, and each chamber held a specific wall painting, series of pictographs, written hieroglyphs, and what seemed to be dormant Atlantian technologies.

"Richie, the 22 separate chambers form a specific message. Trevor and Leo, who, as you know, are linguistic experts, had an insight into how to decode the symbols by reducing the symbols of *the wall paintings to their closest facsimile found in an ancient Sumerian text."* For a split second, he wondered if he was in some form of time capsule; the walls had changed. Together, they observed how what looked like monks, according to their dress, were enlarging the tunnels with a pick and axe. Suddenly, he recognised what had become their laboratory. It was their main hall. Richard marvelled at the decorated walls. It was bone dry. Along the walls, scenes that supported messages from a long time back suggested that the cave dated from what, about 500 AD? When he peered closer, the wall became transparent. The first drawings disappeared, and behind them, he recognised familiar drawings that he had often seen in tombs in Egypt! How old were they? About 5000 BC?

"Forget about time, Richie. I've shown you this through a capsule. During this life cycle, the soul bodies of these monks were still unaware. They could not see what we see. Your soul body must also first awaken more into your physical reality because it is still unconscious in these depths." Theo meant that his mental body might not interpret what he thought he saw justly, but what was a time capsule? Theo made him attentive to something that looked familiar. Deep within the rock, which appeared transparent, a stone figure of a man with his head turned to one side on his belly was holding a disk-shaped receptacle on which the crystal skull was balanced. Richard stared in pure astonishment. Theo fitted the key from the chain around his neck into the disk...A bright light came on, blinding him in the astral. How did the key he had only just begun to wear again stay around his neck in the Astral realm?

When he looked again, he saw what looked like mirrors! The third eye of the skull was projecting a hologram! Like they were doing when he was strapped to the mainframe in Leo's laboratory!

"Richie, in your physical world, you are experiencing what it is like not to see, but now you know what it is like not to see in the astral world. This time capsule and its contents will be available to the public at the appropriate time through the Valley of the God's reserve."

When Theo took him back to the Earth's surface, he could see the entrance hidden behind vegetation. For the first time, Theo had mentioned his blindness. Would he be there when it all was going to happen? Would he be there even when he was low and depressed? Was his soul trying to show him...through his mind...when he sat in the chair in the lounge of his new home...that the darkness was a time capsule?

"Richie, I am there when you look into an endless, empty, deserted abyss. I never left you, but you must learn to see again first." When he saw the man with the crystal skull, he also saw himself sitting in his chair...His body felt stiff but Sascia's soft, curved body next to his had a great appeal. He wanted to make love to her again.

Chapter 21
The Law of Karma & Love

France
Today would be a celebration. The opening of the Valley of God's first stage was broadcast on television. Sascia was already up and about in the shower. She'd run his bath while he was having a short meditation. Every morning for the last ten days, he would wake up with the memory of the same dream. Always the same....a stone figure of a man with his head turned to one side and on his belly, was holding a disk-shaped receptacle on which the crystal skull was balanced.

The radio interviewer was telling the listeners that at least 51000, primarily young people, who had come together for a conference on the future of politics were in an uproar.

"Sascia, didn't you say that Trevor and Otto went to Paris to attend a meeting about the future of politics?" He could hear her getting dressed.

"Yes, weeks ago. They took part in a European Social Forum conference in Paris, why?" he tried to listen to what was said further.

"Most young people have lost interest in politics, so they say." He was already dressed and packed.

"Trevor had said that the whole forum was a vast, messy, rambling affair," Sascia said while brushing her teeth.

"But wasn't Trevor rather pleased with the whole outcome?" Sascia was around him, picking up things.

"He was because thousands of people have worked out for themselves, and the world is collapsing. Otto, Peter's stepdad, is a real rebel. His motto is that until citizens can seize control

of global politics, we cannot regain control of national politics."
The interviewer had one last thing to say:
"Something big has begun. If there is no humane and democratic answer to what a world without capitalism would look like, what do we hope to replace it with? And could other systems be established without violent repression? Maybe the tycoon Mr Toon Haardens, who is building community centres worldwide where they use their currency systems, has the answer? It looks like our youth have not lost interest in politics; they have merely lost interest in our politicians."

The interviewer announced the opening of the first phase of the Valley of the Gods.

"This resort seems to have been inspired by Toon Haardens through provocative lectures on the lands of the gods. Throughout the year, two Egyptologists, Trevor Zwiegelaar and Richard de Jong, have made many people think. Mr de Jong, who was badly injured when the well-known hotel in Apeldoorn, The Prinsegracht, was destroyed by arson, is slowly recovering from his horrific ordeal where he lost his daughter Sammy."

Hearing Sammy's name reminded him of his dream before bed. Theo had brought her, and she sat on his knee. The announcer went on about the arson and what the police had come up with so far.

Sascia switched off the radio so they could join the others for breakfast in the main house.

As they walked into the dining room, he heard the same announcer still reporting on Toon's project, of which they were all very proud.

"A gateway to the lands of the gods will be the theme of the resort. In many legends in times long past, great heroes had gone to join their gods and passed through the gate for a glorious new life of immortality, but on rare occasions, those men returned for a short time with their gods to inspect all the lands in the kingdom through the gate. Will we ever find that gate?"

"Richard, did you hear on the radio that they made three arrests?" Peter mentioned this as Sascia helped him choose his breakfast from the self-service counter, and Sascia asked who they had arrested.

"Ingrid's sister's first husband, Oliver, gave himself up after the loss of his daughter in the Prinsegracht fire." He was sorry for him but didn't want to know what part he had played in the dreadful affair.

"Who were the other two."

"Our well-known Nick du Toit and a woman named Wil de Wit."

"Rich, we were right. Wil had something to do with it!" Peter heard that Wil had also lost a daughter named Iris. Both had paid a heavy price, which had made him again feel depressed. His emotional body was still unstable.

The opening was a roaring success. Richard was sorrowful that it was all hidden from his physical sight, but he tried to hide it as much as possible so the others would not be too aware of his sadness. He knew that Sascia had picked up on his lower energy, as she called it. She tried to cheer him up, but it only irritated him. His mood swings were getting to her, he knew. It also didn't help that they were financially not out of the woods yet. He also missed not being able to research his favourite topic through reading.

When they were back home in Apeldoorn the next day, they had their first big argument over nothing. She had left him at the Pannekoek for the next two days while she went to Amsterdam alone.... His aunt brought him home to his flat. He had a good time with her and Sonja, who was dating Dr. van Dongen but missed Sascia.

During those few days, when Sascia came back, he started to meditate regularly on his own. That had helped him overcome his depression about being blind.

New Years Eve
Annelies

All her favourite family and friends had come to celebrate New Year's Eve. So much had changed in life and the lives of everyone in the dining room. She looked at Ben, sitting at the opposite end. For a moment, their eyes connected. *"You look stunning as usual",* Ben beamed. With a deep fondness, she winked at the man who had saved her life and gave it meaning when she felt it was not worth saving. He would challenge anyone willing to research the most ungodly places to prove that there was a spark of divinity in everyone. That passion made him the perfect partner. Annelies could observe everyone on her left or right side from the head of the long oval dinner table.

Her attention was drawn to a conversation between Gerrit, her cousin, and his lady friend Adel, Niels' and André's mother. The genetic puzzle was coming together. The revelation of family ties through the web of karma had been unfolding right before her eyes. Dienie, the nun she grew up with when her parents ran a guest house in Leersum, always told her she would be the gatherer for the group soul. Not that she ever understood what that entailed then.

"Many people, at the last moment, confess to something they have been living with all their lives," Adel replied to a philosophical question from Gerrit. She admired Adel's Indonesian gracefulness. Teaching art in Spain and France for the last ten years must have done her good. When Gerrit introduced her, she instantly liked her. That was right after he had confessed to being Niels' father during her workshop.

"I have always known that there was something Kellie wanted to tell me over the years," Gerrit responded to Adel.

"Good grief! He is talking about his first wife's confession on her deathbed! What would have brought that up?" Annelies beamed to Ben on their private wavelength. She glanced at Debbie and Vinny across the table. Gerrit had told her that Kellie, his first

wife, Vinny's adoptive mother, could not have any children herself, so they adopted him from the orphanage that was to be closed down.

"Mom, was that when you and Dad adopted me?" Hans mentally replied. They had adopted Hans when he was three months old. His mother, Nicky, died during childbirth. It's funny that Hans, of all people, didn't know that. Toon got up to fill her guest's empty wine glasses. Gerrit shared with the group that he had been unfaithful to his first wife, Kellie. That confession sparked some remarks from Toon. His jolly character seems to need to see the humour in situations rather than avoid a severe conversation.

She knew that during the fire investigation, André looked at all the birth certificates from the orphanage in the archives of Apeldoorn's municipal offices. André knew by then that Gerrit was his father. Annelies didn't realise that Gerrit turned out to be her half-brother. Her mother had had a child at fifteen. In November, after Richard came out of hospital, lots of ancestral puzzles fell into place when she realised that Ingrid's dad had had an affair with her mother, resulting in the birth of Gerrit.

When she was fifteen, Dienie, a nun in the astral world, told her that Annelies would have to safeguard the Star-Map they had found while restoring the Prinsegracht hotel. She never understood what Dienie meant until Theo planted the seed in her mind years later.

"Hey, Gerrit! Let's hear the confession." She interrupted her train of thought. "Or is that not appropriate for me to ask?" Annelies hated severe topics at the dinner table, but she was intrigued.

"Annelies, I only now realised I have kept this confession from being exposed. What is it that makes us pretend something never happened? Would we rather forget a painful memory than deal with it? What is the worst that we are fearful of? She wanted me to expose it, but"...Gerrit was having difficulty revealing a secret. She was somewhat surprised. They would all play the ascension game on the second level next month; that must play on his mind. Everyone at the table waited in suspense.

"Gerrit, you know as well as I do that it's often out of guilt, shame, etc, that we hold on to secrets. If everyone knows our well-kept secrets, they might stop loving us. Or, sometimes harrowing memories are suppressed for self-protection." Admitting that was not easy.

"My love, can't you...you, of all people, should let it out!" Ben beamed. While some around the table agreed with her, she knew that she had never been able to admit to the one major trauma in her life. She still felt the guilt no matter what.

"You know Annelies?" Gerrit had everyone's attention. "Kellie was sixteen when she fell pregnant! That was no small thing in the fifties, and her parents threw her out of the house."

Gerrit's story hit her in the chest. That was how old she was when she gave birth to Tessa! The grief was still there, hiding behind her heart centre. Toon made a face to remind her of what Ben had beamed. She read his mind.

"Kellie told me that she had moved in with her boyfriend, who was the father. He was a sailor on the cargo ships that sailed between the ports around the European coastline. When he was ashore, he had rented a room at the sailor's accommodation in Rotterdam. Kellie was allowed to stay if she worked in the kitchen."

"That was in.....Nineteen fifty-seven?" Adel responded.

"Yes, love, before I met you," Gerrit responded as he munched on Nel's olibollen. Mien winked at her, reminding her of their young days in Cape Town. It all seemed so long ago.

How ignorant they were then, and how they had hurt each other. Now, at the age of sixty, it all seemed so trivial.

When the Prinsegracht burned down, Nel and Mien once again became her great friends in times of need. Gerrit was encouraged by his son André, the detective, to carry on. They were all waiting for the confession.

When she heard Richard beam. *"Gosh, when are we ever hearing the punch line?"* She smiled at Sascia, glad that he was getting on his feet. With the help of the latest computer equipment, Richard helped Trevor and Leo with their research on a genetic bloodline, explaining why some people retained the original DNA codes while others had new ones. It was eleven o'clock. Soon, they would send silver and golden balloons up in the air with their intentions for the coming year.

"Kellie told me that her boyfriend was abusive and had hit her on many occasions. She was eight months pregnant when he knocked her down after a fight and walked out on her. She had to leave the sailor's home and found a backroom in someone's garden. All this trauma brought on premature labour. She got herself to the hospital, and the baby was stillborn."

"How awful" Ula, André's fiancée, called out.

At least she was well taken care of when Tessa was born. Her parents supported her, and her mother was adamant that she kept her baby; only years later did she understand why. Her mother was pressured by her parents to give her baby up for adoption! She looked at Ben, who knew her every thought as if it was his own. He winked.

"I'm so glad you decided to quit Interpol" She beamed. André's files Oliver had given him in exchange for his freedom must have been profound. Piet de Wit had left them with Oliver, his lawyer, for safekeeping. It had shocked Ben enough to quit his connections with Interpol and take a well-deserved holiday

to visit an old colleague in South Africa. He hasn't shared the contents with her yet.

Suddenly, Ben got up and asked for everyone to raise their glasses. She knew that to break the heavy atmosphere due to Gerrit's morbid story, Ben would say something funny.

"*A toast to a lady who has given me the experience that a true love affair improves with time.*"

"*Kitty, I second that,*" she heard Toon's telepathy.

"Gosh Gerrit, how horrid; Kellie must have felt shattered after that ordeal." Ingrid sympathised while Liesbeth served more snacks. When Hans attracted Liesbeth into his life, she knew she was special like him. She was around five years older than Tessa would have been.

"*Annie, this time, I'm not going unless you join me, so I have booked two tickets to leave on the fourth of January.*" Ben's incoming thought surprised her.

"So soon? Really, wouldn't I be in your way?" Both Connie and Yolanda helped Liesbeth prepare the balloons. Toon stood up and gave a toast to the new year with a vision that they would all live or work together in Half-way House and Buttercup Valley. She hadn't made up her mind. Now that the Hotel had gone, there was nothing to keep her, and she wanted to travel again before settling down in a remote valley up in the Austrian mountains, no matter how lovely it was. Joining Ben on his trip to South Africa was not a bad idea. To revisit the places where she had lived for six years during the seventies would bring back many memories. Good and evil, but maybe that was needed before she was ready to write her journal.

"*When is the date for the opening of the second section, Toon?*" She'd wanted to join Liesbeth and Hans on their trip to South Africa, but she felt asking was inappropriate.

"*Why, mom, you never have before.*" Hans joined in.

"I know. I was not aware of it myself until now. Yes, that's what I would love to do. Ben, will there be time for you to join me to visit the places where Mien and I used to hang out?" She knew from experience that Ben's strange lifestyle as an undercover agent, especially when she had come along, often resulted in her exploring and sightseeing.

"Ben, why don't you show Annie where Jock and At have started their community and stay with them?" Toon telepathically joined in.

"Hey, dad, I'm still waiting for that big secret. Get it off your chest, man, before the year is out. You have half an hour left." Vinny urged. He had unknowingly interrupted their telepathic dialogue, but they were all still curious. Niels, André and their partners had joined them. She missed Harry, Tieneke, Mien and Trevor. They had gone away on a cruise before Christmas.

"Ben, we could meet with your sister in Cape Town." The idea of going on a trip to a warmer climate, even if it's only for a few weeks, suddenly seemed very attractive, especially since Mien and Tieneke would be there. *"I knew you would ask me that; I've already been in contact with them."*

Liesbeth, Yolanda and Connie returned to say that the balloons were ready. They passed everyone a piece of paper on which they would write, tie it to a balloon, and release it on the stroke of twelve. André again asked his dad what happened to Gerrit's first wife before he married her.

"Kellie was still not welcome to go home after she lost her child. She stayed on working at the sailor's accommodation because her boyfriend had run up a bill and left it unpaid. She must have got trapped into a major depression, and she was very lonely," Gerrit added with a sigh, "because of what she did next."

Everyone at the dinner table was now waiting in suspense. Annelies could very well relate to loneliness and despair. Would the pain of losing Tessa, her absolute bundle of joy, ever go away? Thinking about it now, I still feel numb after so many years. She had much to be grateful for, but Gerrit's story interrupted her thoughts.

"Kellie explained that she still hoped her boyfriend would come home. She told me that she had started to create a fantasy story about how he would be walking into the back room where she lived now, wanting to see his child."

"She told you all that just before she died?" Ula, André's fiancée asked. Toon and Ingrid had followed the whole conversation. She saw Toon was feeling Ingrid's baby; it must be kicking, as she observed Toon's expression of delight. How sad for Kellie. At least Ben wanted to marry her, but she was too proud to get married because she had his baby. She wanted to do it all on her own. When her parents moved back to Braband, she lost contact with Ben after Tessa had gone. He had joined his twin brother Leo in Tibet. Not many knew about her loss: only Toon, Fred and later, Ben.

There were ten minutes left. Gerrit had better get on with it and finish his story...She was also keen to go to bed to meet up with Theo.

"When she told me what she did after that, I was quite shocked!" Gerrit whispered. The sadness in his voice held everyone in a grip.

"Kellie had carried such incredible guilt for all those years! With great difficulty, she confessed to her crime. After that, she went peacefully."

The silence in the dining room was electric. They all wanted to know what this woman had done that was so terrible. Gerrit took a sip of his wine and carried on.

"One Sunday morning, when she had her day off, she was walking past the Central train station in Rotterdam. She had to buy stamps at a kiosk. She spotted a pram, and without thinking, she grabbed it and walked off with it as if she were the owner." Gerrit whispered.

Annelies went quite cold. Her mind went into a spin...back forty-five years ago... to the moment she saw that her pram had gone! All she remembered then was that she had just taken a newspaper and went inside to pay for it. It cannot have taken more than two minutes. When she walked back, Tessa and her pram were gone!

"Annie, are you all right?" Fred asked. Her tears were streaming. She couldn't stop. Gerrit's story had hit her so profoundly that the pain just gushed out.

"Please, Gerrit, carry on. I remembered something, and it overtook me somewhat by surprise. Please carry on with your story."

"Gerrit, what did Kellie do with the baby in the pram?" Fred's voice trembled.

"Kellie told me that she took it home with her and never left her back room. Then, about a week later, her mother visited her one morning." Gerrit paused. The party's mood had turned gloomy, and Annelies was sorry.

"Kellie did not turn up for work, so they contacted her parents. When her mother walked into her room, the baby was crying a lot, and she had run out of money to buy more food. Kellie was trying to feed it the last milk from a silver cup that she found in the pram."

Gerrit's voice gave such a vivid description of the whole scene; again, she felt as if a bullet had hit her! Tessa had a silver cup! Fred and Toon gave it to Tessa on her first birthday when they were about ten. They had her initials engraved on them. Fred got up and kneeled beside her, grabbing and squeezing her hand.

"What happened to the baby?" Ben asked in his detective mode while passing a box of tissues, trembling. The energy around the table was almost visible.

"Kellie told me, just minutes before she died, that her mother knew it was not her daughter's child because the kidnapping had been in all the papers. Her mother must have felt partly responsible for her daughter's predicament. After feeding the baby, her mother took it with her. Kellie knew kidnapping was a big crime. She was petrified."

"Did Kellie ever know what her mother did with the baby?" her heartbeat in her chest.

"Yes, her mother took it to the orphanage where she was raised. Kellie said that her mother was gone for at least a week. Her mother left the baby in an empty cot at the orphanage and walked out, hoping that someone would connect the kidnapping with the sudden appearance of a one-year-old baby."

"And did they?" Toon asked. His usual tone of voice sounded angry. Ingrid shook her head and knew something was very wrong with Annelies. *Toon, why are you... why the stress over this baby?* Ingrid projected wide open.

"Who's baby was it?" Everyone waited for Gerrit's reply.

"I asked her that question, too. No, Kellie never knew. She moved back home, and her mother told her never to say anything. She often wondered if the mother of the child found her baby again. I knew now how, for years, Kellie had been burdened by guilt for the grief she was responsible for. She told me that she had made a parcel about a year later, wrapped up the silver cup, and asked if her mother would send it to the orphanage where she had taken the baby. In her last words, she said the initial engraved was a T...then she died."

Annelies knew that her grief-stricken appearance made everyone emotional, but they didn't know why. Fred, Ben and Toon were the only ones who were openly distressed.

Annelies knew the moment Gerrit mentioned the initial T that it was Tessa, her child. Ben's arms were around her, and he was crying too. She wept against his shoulder. All the pain and anguish that she carried inside for so many long years came out. The intense hurt feelings she buried behind her heart centre had come free. For the first time, she understood what her grief-stricken shadows were capable of. They had manipulated her life's expectations. Gerrit was troubled knowing that his story had triggered great pain in Annelies.

When they all heard a cry of surprise coming from Liesbeth, who held her hands in front of her mouth, everyone's attention was shifted.

"Liesbeth, tell her!" Hans' excitement had everybody gasping. Liesbeth made a gesture of confusion, surprise and jubilation all rolled into one.

"Tell me what?" Annelies felt emotionally exhausted. She felt so drained.

"I was five when I was adopted. I had been living at the Jaarsma orphanage until that time. A silver cup came with me... It had the initial T and the letter L engraved on it. My adoptive mother was unsure if it belonged to me, but I have always wondered what the letter L stood for." Liesbeth whispered. Ben's mouth gaped.

"Laura..."Annelies uttered, "Tessa Laura were your names." She stared at Liesbeth as if she saw her for the first time. Why had she never seen it herself? Her intuition was usually so good! Even the comments that some people made should have already triggered her into some speculation. But it never entered her mind. Both Fred, Toon and Ben gaped at Liesbeth in amazement.

"Annelies, did you have a baby girl that was stolen from you?" Ingrid asked in horror.

Could it be possible? Oh... she realised that she wanted it to be true. How would she know for sure? She could suddenly see why Ben once remarked: *"Annie, when I saw Liesbeth for the first time, it was as if you walked into the room. Incredible, she reminded me of you when you were in your twenties."*

"But Liesbeth, that would make you forty-four years old?" She whispered, still unbelievingly and at the same time full of hope. Liesbeth got up from the table and embraced her. Almost everyone at the table cried in amazement for suddenly seeing the likeness.

"Not for nothing must my soul have selected to experience life through the body of a baby carrying your genes. It all makes a lot of sense to me." As she hugged her mother, the mood in the dining room returned to its original atmosphere.

"I'll show you the cup; I always kept it" Liesbeth beamed.

"Annelies, I have been keeping Kellie's secret for years! I never bothered to find out what happened to the kids that were fostered out. I had already left the orphanage before Liesbeth must have arrived. If only I..."

"Hey, you all, let's let our balloons up. Can't you all hear that it is twelve o'clock? Listen to the clock tower," Richard announced.

"Your hearing is better than ours." Sascia beamed....

Liesbeth made them all write their deepest innermost wish. She felt so blessed; there was nothing more she had any needs for except...that Richard's eye-sight would return. Intuitively, she knew that was what they all added to their list, but she, of all people, knew the best that he was the one that had to learn to communicate to his body initiate.

After the most eventful evening, Annelies looked forward to entering her second world, where Theo would be waiting for her at their meeting place.

Apeldoorn

After Annelie's New Year's Eve party, they were still mulling over the revelation Gerrit shared during dinner when they returned to the flat.

"Gosh, Rich, you should have seen Annelie's expression! Her surprise when she looked at Liesbeth was such an eye-opener."...He had followed the whole interaction between Gerrit and Annelies, but only at the end, when everybody was gripped by Gerrit's first wife's sad story, had he heard the clock tower announcing the new year.

"I'm sorry, Rich, I mean..." He could read her thoughts. Sascia was so worried when she realised too late that he can't see what she saw.

"Moppie, I know what you mean. Don't ever be worried about how you talk about something special to you in connection with what you saw." He held onto her shoulder as Sascia fumbled with their house keys.

Tomorrow, he will go for his regular check-up. Everything was healing, but his eyesight had not. With the help of Sascia, he regularly did the eye exercises that were prescribed to him.

On Monday, the removal company would come and pack all their belongings and transport them to France. The flat was sold to a car dealer looking for a bargain. He had not done anything to the flat since Theo left, so the fact that they could stay until after New Year's Eve was the deciding factor. He would be paid out and at least be able to pay off all his debt. That would at least make him feel free to leave Holland.

"Rich, you've got mail from Trevor. I think it's the twenty-first tablet." He got to the lounge with the same ease as if he could see.

"Maybe they found it. What is the title? What does it tell you?" Sascia told him that the attachment file was named Family Ties through the Jaarsma game[1]

"Wow, how uncanny," they both called out...when Sascia clicked on the link when tablet twenty-one appeared.

Tablet 21

Translated by Theo de Jong

"Gosh, Rich, that's it. Theo must have written it. Haven't you often visualised how Theo was during the last days before he left Leo and Trevor?"

"I now imagine Theo saying goodbye and physically disappearing inside the tunnels." He now wished he could himself read over the tablet text published online. Sascia read it slowly all out, but it was not the same.

In all his meditations, Richard tried to release any thoughts that would keep his rational mind linked to his human program. By staying in the null zone of his mind, he had hoped that the outcome would be that Theo would give him a clue, but he knew that even hoping that was an obstacle in itself.

"How far are you with my journal?" Sascia had helped him sort out the happenings, and Liesbeth or Tulanda would re-edit them into a novel as she had for Ingrid's journals.

"Almost finished. One tablet to go."

"Your mom showed us 22 excerpts, so there are twenty-two tablets."

"Wasn't the last excerpt mom received on the power of words?"

---

1. https://allrealityshifters.wordpress.com/tablet-twenty-one/

"No, it was about the observer's power." He thought. He had to finish his journal, but it felt somehow unfinished. What should he do with the minor key? He tried to make sense of the image of the man holding the crystal skull.

"Rich, the Eye of the Observer is the name of Annelie's ascension computer game?" Annelies! That's it. "She needs that key!" He practically smothered her with a big hug.

"What key? You mean the one that's hanging around your neck?"

"Yes."

"Why?"

"I have no idea. I know. I'll leave it at that. Let's go to bed."

"Rich."

"Mmm...what now."

"I want to do what you do, travel out-of-my-body. Can't you help me when you are out, as Theo did for you?"

"Okay, you know what, you go to bed, and I'll stay awake in the lounge. You do what I told you to. You have to be relaxed."

"Really. What will you do?"

"Pull you out."

"Can you do that?"

"That's what Theo did, so I'm going to ask him if I can do that since you seem sure you want to get out." Sascia didn't reply, but he could feel she was watching him. He knew what she was thinking, and it made him smile.

"Moppie, don't worry, I'll soon make you pregnant." He knew that she would carry his children one day. He heard her take a deep breath; in his mind, he saw how her emotional body quivered. He stayed silent. When she left for the bedroom, he prepared himself for something he'd never done.

He knew he was out because the lounge appeared very bright, as if the sun was shining in the evening, but he knew it was astral light.

The weird awareness as if he was seeing everything all at once always astounded him. Theo's strong, merry laugh from the grey substance took on a human shape.

"You are moving out like a pro; I'm proud of you" Theo's compliment made him glow. He went straight to the bedroom and asked Theo how he could help her.

"First, ask her body to initiate assistance."

"Really? *Do you mean the elemental being that controls physical matter?"*

"Whatever name you give to your super-consciousness is fine. Giving names to everything is a human thing to do." He watched with utter amazement how her thoughts formed a light body.

"Rich...something unusual is happening...I feel... loose!" He could see that Sascia was becoming aware of the tingling sensation because the energy he recognised as fear was developing in her throat area.

"Rich, what's happening?" He could see that the vibrational feelings that penetrated throughout her body freaked her out. He was about to reach her when Theo shook his head mentally. Then suddenly...she was suspended in space.

"Rich...I'm out... I can see myself...I'm still lying on the bed!" He could see that her heart was palpitating from pure astonishment. He so remembered how he felt the first time.

"Now is the right time to get her visual attention so her consciousness will not jump back into her body." Theo's advice came just at the right time because he sensed she was slipping back.

"Hi, Moppie. Are you going to join us?" He beamed, ensuring he dressed in something she would relate to.

"*Very good, you remembered. ...Sascia, I hear that you want to join us in exploring the mind of the crystal skull?*" Theo mentally probed. He observed with great amusement how she was touching him.

"*But, you are solid?*"

"*Moppie, what are you going to wear?*" He could see the confusion in her energy field; her etheric copy body, a replica of her physical body, was naked. Her other subtle bodies spun shooting colours, which represented feelings of great embarrassment. The love he poured at her had a soothing effect. With interest, he watched how her mind created a flowing, silky-long dress. They were still in the flat in Apeldoorn.

"*Come, you two, Annelies is waiting.*"

"*Theo, will I remember it as a dream, or will I remember it clearly like Rich?*" How could she have known he remembered his out-of-body journeys much stronger ever since he first meditated sitting upright?

"*Richie women have a much more developed emotional body. Hers is exceptional. Don't keep things from her. It will only stimulate her lower mind into action.*" Sascia peered at Theo as she held onto his hand. Her Etheric body was still quivering.

"*I like you. Where is Annelies?*" They both laughed. They followed Theo, who was still in charge of the subtle realms.

"*Yep, she is a girl to my heart. Richie, watch out; an eager astral traveller could easily take her away from under your nose.*" They both looked around in surprise when Theo pointed at couples who seemed to have just met.

"*Many people meet their soul mates in these realms. Especially when there was a strong physical bond between them.*" He also saw men and women looking for a date, just like in the physical. He never even thought relationships were established on other levels, but why not?

"*Do these people remember their meetings?*" Sascia's thoughts held the same questions as his. Are they asleep, meditating, or have they left their physical bodies through death?

"*All of the three options are possible. It depends on people's inner life development. If it is well established, they could live double lives.*" He thought that if someone could have an affair in the astral, while married in the physical, how would that affect people's relationships?

"*Depending on the soul's evolvement, it can help to heal or allow a person to work through karmic thought-forms faster.*" While they were following Theo, he never knew how they suddenly got to the building that became the Prinsegracht hotel. Many children were playing on the grounds where a school bus would explode years later. He wondered what Theo had in mind because his light body started to shake.

"*Richie, within the subtle realms, when our consciousness merges with the vibrations of the mineral world, we move to a different level of reality. But before we go there, we meet up with Annie. This is the place where I always meet her. Remember that on this plane, time is irrelevant.*" He was impressed when he read Sascia's thoughts that it must be the year that Annelie's baby was delivered. Where did she get that idea from?

"*Her emotional body is far more developed, so her sensitivity is also sharper.*" As Theo projected to him, he moved towards the reception hall, which now appeared more like an old-fashioned school gym. There she was. He smiled at her colourful Kaftan. Sascia was also admiring her familiar signature. With great interest, they observed how Theo and Annelies greeted each other.

"*Rich, are they twin souls?*" He'd thought the same because both their light bodies were merged and separated. He still wasn't sure if there was such a thing. Theo returned to him while Annelies greeted Sascia first.

"*Richie, twin-souls is more a word that the rational mind created to describe a wave-form pattern between two souls resonating so much that they have decided to divide the workload.*" When Sascia overheard their telepathic conversation, she, in her usual forthright manner, asked if she and he were twin-souls. Theo looked at Annelies, who smiled.

"*Sweety, believe me, I always see Theo as my twin-soul. Two souls rarely resonate on similar wavelengths on the physical plane, but like you, we shared many human lives. The fact that the four of us together tells me we belong to the same Over-Soul energy.*" Annelies beamed. Annelies looked at him and pulled away at his astral T-shirt.

"*Yes, he's wearing it as you said he would.*" Annelies' beamed at Theo. He was so glad he wore the little key Theo left behind around his neck.

"*I told you to keep it close to you so it would take on your energy.*" Sascia beamed but had a hunch so he should have given it to Annelies.

"*It was the right hunch.*" Theo beamed while Annelies was communicating with a child of about five years old. The girl took her hand and smiled. Annelies at first showed surprise, then she knelt, and a dialogue between them told them that it was Tessa just before Liesbeth's parents adopted her.

"*Theo, how can it be that Liesbeth is all grown up?*" Sascia seemed to understand. Theo explained that Tessa had given Tulanda, Liesbeth's real name, permission to use her body. Liesbeth is a walk-in soul. This means that Liesbeth did not have to go through the birth process.

"*Theo, mom told me that Liesbeth had told her where she and Hans came from. She has written it in her journal, but...Is there such a thing as a parallel universe?"* Theo looked at them both with a loving glint.

"Study the last tablet, especially next to the third symbol. When a Group-Soul has fully gathered all their experiences, they become one soul and join other soul-mates again." He certainly felt very down on the ladder of things. That also did not explain the parallel universe idea to him, but Annelies seemed to be in a hurry to take them somewhere. He held onto Sascia's hand because he still felt responsible for her when all four appeared to be falling inside the planet. He wondered if Theo would show him an even more fantastic scene from the planet's inner world.

"Theo told me that you have already been here, Richard." Annelies beamed. It felt that he was deep inside the cave again, where the stone man was trapped for eternity. Sascia and he gaped at the Crystal skull, projecting a brilliant light beam on the rock wall.

"What you see is a hologram that will be shown to many people in Toon's resort." Did Theo mean Trevor's simulator? Sascia wanted to know how a movie that looked like she was part of it would be shown at the resort.

"Sascia, our forefathers, already knew that this crystal skull could stimulate a part of the human organic brain, thereby opening a psychic door to the absolute. This crystal computer, once activated, will again continuously put out electric-like radio waves. Since the brain does the same thing, they naturally will interact."

Annelies suddenly asked for the key around his neck. What they saw next even had Theo flabbergasted. As Annelies held the key in front of the stone man, his human shadow hovering behind him looked almost evil…but, by peering closer, they could see that the face of the man had changed into a nearly glowing positive expression, and the shadow was no more.

The rock that held the man became even more transparent. At first, the sound vibrating from within the crystal skull alarmed them all. Sascia tightened her handgrip. Then they both saw how a light beam that had shot out from the area of the Crystal Skull's third eye pierced into Annelie's forehead.

"*Theo, is she alright?*" Sascia beamed with alarm when they saw how Annelie's light body radiated in a glow. Her light body seemed to accept or retrieve a message.

"*Richie, the priests in ancient times stored information to be found at a future date when planet Earth was to change its global destiny*" When Annelies stepped back away from the wall, the man inside the stone got up, moved out, and vanished.

"*Who was that? Where did he go?*" Sascia stepped closer, but only the crystal skull was visible. They were all looking for the man. He felt as if the man had stepped inside his own light body. He knew he was shaking because they were all concerned when they looked back at him. Theo smiled at Annelies, whose expression changed from worry to gladness. He had no idea why, but he felt as if a load had been lifted off his shoulders. Sascia asked many questions, which Richard also wanted answers to, but Theo and Annelies only had eyes for each other. They seemed to have accomplished something of which he was not aware.

"*Sascia, many people will start to receive these images when they awaken their inner sight. Some people, like you, belong to the Jaarsma clan, and you all have started to activate the senses of the inner ear first to receive messages that are not recognised by the physical ear.*" Theo was addressing one of her questions when Annelies joined in.

"*In people like Debbie or André, their abdomens are receiving messages that some will term as having a "gut instinct". What* is happening is an interaction between the physical and subtle realms."

"André, too? Is that why he is leaving the police force? He has to walk away from the undermining energies he can sense?" Sascia projected. That must have been the reason for the stress André was coping with.

"Yes, that's part of the reason. For many, this is a very spiritual experience. So remember that when we start experiencing the vibrations of the crystal skull, we are connecting to the vibrations of the life force." Annelies telepathically explained.

He suddenly became aware that they were walking in the gardens of the Chateau in France towards their cottage. Sascia asked how come she could not see the man in stone at first, only when the rock face became transparent in the astral.

"You were given a preview of the different layers of the astral realm. Both Richard and Annelies needed to connect with the even finer, more subtle realms of creation. This is where the core of our being is located, the very source of All That Is." Annelies seems to know other light beings because she left them. They stayed with them until they moved near their physical bodies.

"Richie, Annelies was the initiate who, through the fire initiation that I showed you, lost her life on the physical level; her Lightbody's Crystal Skull will now receive messages that will shed light on the situation at hand in the form of intuitive Christ impulses for her to take on the third level of the awakening journey." For some reason, his mind could take it all in without any doubt, as if the spirit of the man inside the stone joined his.

"Richie, when all these impulses are assembled and reviewed, the soul has to participate fully in the ascension journey before a clearer picture can be observedved. This information involves any soul's physical, emotional, or spiritual experiences on both the physical and the lower astral levels. A crystal skull is a vibrational *tool of the highest order."* Sascia had, as usual, millions of questions. By now, they were resting on the veranda of their wooden cottage.

"During the Atlantian times, priests usually used crystals to store the genetic DNA information, based on the grid program the soul resonates to. When people like you start seeing the spider web effect, they can see into their matrix or your collective unconscious." Sascia asked what the spider effect. He could only think of it when talking to Ingrid in the kitchen.

*"Theo, don't tell me that the spider is the oracle of the matrix? It was just a spider. It was the voice that "...*Had that been his unconsciousness?

Sascia asked him which people could see the Hall of Records advertised in one of the temples at Toon's resort.

"Through the hall of records, which is experienced as a hologram, this program, like Trevor's simulator, can transform brainwaves and translate the frequencies into images similar to the workings of the de la Warr camera. POWAH calls it a game. Many people are only comfortable awakening through a belief program or using the expression through the power of Jesus. They do not yet understand that it was Christ's force in him for the last three years of his life that he would sacrifice for humanity. Humanity could activate their etheric double while having a physical experience. Many would call a full resurrection a miracle, but they must experience it for themselves."

Sascia was so worried that she would not remember everything when she was back in her body, especially the last bit. Theo said that he could try to refresh her memory this time.

"Through decoding the spacings on your grid formation, geometry shows us that all things created on planet Earth, as reality, follow the same patterns or cycles we used when Annelies and I created the idea for the computer game. That is why creations

by the gods often have end-time scenarios that seem to have explosive endings. This pattern follows with tales of mythological places such as Atlantis and Lemuria, which had 'end times' when things came to an end due to explosions on the planet. These explosions are within us. They merge our polarities - yin/yang, male and female."...with that last note, Theo said goodbye.

They both felt the pull, him to his body in the chair and Sascia to hers in bed. As a sleepwalker, he joined her and snuggled up close.

The first thing he heard when he woke beside her in bed was how Sascia remembered everything. She must have been awake for hours thinking about things.

"Rich, do you remember why Tieneke or Annelies divided the awakening game into five stages?" He had to think about that one as he slowly woke up.

"I understand that an idea or desire should have a definite message-instruction that concerns things of the physical world like Toon and your mom do with their communities."

"And the second level? I can see that my mom and Toon's acts must be well-founded and thoroughly examined before they can build the resort, for instance, but..."

"Theo said that thoughts that bring increasing significance into a person's life must follow with outer action, but the awakening process must also be harmonious and conducive to the person's environment."

"I see. Now I understand what happened to Zola and why Annelies asked her to leave our ascension group for the moment," Sascia concluded.

"Yes, on the third level, life must conform with nature and spirit. Annelies has to write about the mental, emotional, and spiritual experiences she is going through, which are connected with her ascension ideas.

"Mmm... and simultaneously, she has to keep her body fit and healthy; that's what I overheard Mien say to Annelies and Tieneke one day in the Pannekoek. You were in the hospital."

I thought Annelies was very fit."

"She is, but Tieneke had lost many kilos through grief, and Mien was trying to make her eat a healthy meal."

He had asked Hans what the fourth level would be like regarding their awakening. Sascia heard his thoughts because she replied,

"Every endeavour will gather and add a valuable experience to their life."

"That's correct. Hans also said that all gathered experiences must be internally counselled to test the subtotal of the content and aim of the embodied soul in this life.... Phew!" Telepathically, they heard Theo beaming their thoughts on how the fifth level would be experienced.

"On the fifth level, the blueprint of your biological creation is held into the third eye. For each fully embodied living soul, this has to be activated to be motivated to awaken to full consciousness."

"Rich, do you still have that key around your neck?" he looked...it was gone....

Chapter 22
The Prophet's Orphanage of Souls

Buttercup Valley

As he turned his head towards the window, he felt a cold breeze from the cottage window. It must be open because he thought he saw a glimmer of lighter shades. Dr.van Dongen had explained to him why he might never see again...He could have gone for the operation, but there was no guarantee.

He felt Sascia's hand stroking him softly on his cheek. Her legs were snugly intertwined with his. Their cuddles in the morning made each day extraordinary. He knew that his scars had been bad. Thanks to Hans, his skin grafts were still very tender but had healed fast. Sascia seemed to know what part of his body was still painful. She always very carefully touched and explored him where there was no tenderness. The palms of his hands were delicate, so at least he could feel her curves.

"Rich, what time did Dirk say we will leave for Buttercup Valley?"

"What is the time now?" He was trying to guess the time by the faint light, assuming that the sun must be up. Sascia had to switch on the light to see, so it must still be dark. She got out of bed, and he heard her close the window.

"Gosh, Rich, a lot of snow has fallen at night. That's why it is already so light outside. The spotlights are still on because it's still early, just after seven."

"Then come back to bed for a last cuddle before we join the others for breakfast." He could distinctly see different shades.

Sascia's warm body, close to his, ignited his passion. He explored her curves, and as he stroked her near her pleasure points, her reaction to them did the rest. For the first time, he truly wanted to make a baby. The dream of seeing Sascia heavy with child months ago kept his spirits up. He knew he could materialise a reality if he often saw it in his mind.

It took some convincing before he realised that he was seeing the vague outline of the furniture in the bedroom! As he peeked into the bathroom, the noise from the shower felt tempting. He would love to take a shower, but the thought of the pressure from the spray on his skin still put him off. When Sascia stepped out of the shower, he saw her naked!

"Rich, can you...Are you seeing something?"

"I think...I start to see different shades of darkness."

"Really?"

"Yes, I think so. I can see your nakedness. It's all one..." he got up and reached for her face to feel if his seeing her shape was correct. The wetness on her cheeks told him that she was crying. Her reaction to his possible recovery made him aware of her need for his well-being. They held on to each other for eternity.

"Oh, Rich, everyone will be so happy to see you again." He understood their wish, knowing that only in his mind he could create that reality. His love for her mounted as he licked salty tears away, beaming;

"Your tolerance, determination and unconditional love brought me back to a reality I want to build on. To have had you in my life during these last few months has had a healing effect on my eyesight; I truly believe that."

"Rich, I know in my heart that you will fully recover, but... if you didn't, it would not have made any difference. I want for you what I want for myself." she beamed further. Her naked body told him that he already had received that."

"I love you."

"I adore you too. Let me wash before I change my mind and again plant my seed in you to get you pregnant." It was out before he knew it.

"You want us...to have a baby?"

He had told her about his dream months back when they just met, so her miscarriage just before he left the hospital had truly made him sad for the loss.

"How do you feel about it?"

"Rich, I do want your baby or babies, but I also want to help you with your research, to work with you to build Toon's park and here at Half-way House...I suppose I want it all?"

"Well, we accept that we already have it all." He opted out of having a shower and ran the bath instead.

"Moppie, when we get to the dining room for breakfast,..."

"I know; let's see how long it takes for your sight to get back to normal. But ...won't they know it anyway?"

"Probably, let's just play it by ear."

He was getting used to the surroundings, and now that he could genuinely see distinct shapes, walking to the main house became a new experience. They met quite a few people on the way whom he only recognised by voice. Their shapes were still too vague to recognise but he knew that André had joined them.

"Sascia, what time do you both fly to the Alps?"

"Before lunch. Aren't you joining us?" André had arrived last week with all his belongings. Richard was still amazed at his decision to leave the police force. Ula, his fiancé, would join them soon. The whole conspiracy drama that he uncovered must have been his wake-up call. They were planning an April wedding at the Cup of Gold Half-way House.

"Yes, I was just making sure if I had the time right. You seem to walk very steadily for someone who sees nothing at all. Hey! Are you sure you are completely blind?" André remarked as they stepped through the double doors that led to the breakfast counter.

The light through the large glass windows took on a colour spectrum. They walked hand in hand, and as they approached a large corner table, he knew that Leo had pulled out a chair for him. Sascia went to the serving hatch. He decided to join her to see how well he could manage.

"Richard, your eyes, there is a different look about them!" Helen said as she was dishing up for herself. He was unsure what to make of the images floating before him. It was still touching and smell that told him what was before him. Sascia gave him a plate and helped him. Turning with his plate back to his chair, he held onto Sascia's shoulder so as not to bump into things.

"It's returning, isn't it?" Leo asked. He turned to face him because he could see the shine on his bald head. As he sat down, he turned in the direction of what he thought was André, who was wearing a checked shirt. André walked back from the buffet carrying something, but he could still not see. Suddenly, he was embraced by a female from behind him. The distinct fragrance told him it was Ingrid.

"Oh, sweety, Hans was right." Ingrid kissed his cheeks.

"Your sight will return. Everyone will be so glad for you" He kissed her wrists. He could never see her as his mother-in-law, more a great friend. Toon's tall shape appeared in the corner of his eye. He wondered if his mind was just gathering all the files that had been misplaced in his brain. Was his mind reorganising his database and sending messages back to his eyes?

"That's just what Hans did when he covered your eyes with his hand. He rearranged your filing system. When he did a healing on me, that's how he explained it. Hans communicates with the body initiate." What Toon projected started to make sense. Annelies

called it the elemental Deva that controlled the body, which does the healing.

"Annelies will write about how we must learn to communicate with our body. In her journal," Liesbeth said with a hug. It felt like it was his birthday. He always loved the breakfast sessions at Halfway house.

"Richard, when will you be handing me your journal?" He was still wondering how he was going to finish it. He had tried typing his thoughts down since Sascia constantly nagged him to get active again through writing. He had to admit it had helped. He knew she had to retype most of it since he had never been the best typist, but according to Sascia, his journal was getting into shape.

"Mom will be pleased," Liesbeth replied to his thinking. He had to get used to the idea that Liesbeth was her daughter. He buttered his toast and tried to see what he knew was on the table. Leo and André were in a deep scientific discussion.

"André, we speculate that our entire DNA structure is linked to a time-release capsule."

"So when Annelies speaks about our original blueprint, what is she referring to?" Sascia mentally asked

"Annelies sees the genome as the essence of the person, a secular equivalent of the soul. She explained that when we were originally programmed, our DNA coding was limited to a double-helix strand."

"How do you think she knows about genes? She's no scientist?"

"No, but Leo is. Come on, Leo, can you satisfy the girl's curious mind?" Toon asked, knowing that he needed answers.

"The gene is seen as a computer program coded with our instructions, as a sacred text which will reveal the secrets of human existence. Richard correctly sees DNA coding as a surrogate for the soul."

"Leo, I'm not sure if I can follow you. You mean that the DNA coding is like... a monument ... keeping the original blueprint of physical immortality?" André questioned. They were all waiting for Leo's explanation.

"The triggering mechanism that enables us to function as we do now is affected by stellar solar system radiation," Leo replied to André. He noticed that Leo still walked with the help of a stick towards a map on the wall. His recovery from being trapped inside the underground tunnels also took a while. When the blast from the bomb had caved in the top tunnels, nobody knew that under these were lower tunnels linked to the Half-way House estate. Trevor had found old maps dating back to the middle ages. It reminded them all of Paris and London's subways. The bomb went off at the time when they were still searching for the entrance of the lower tunnels. They hoped these tunnels would eventually link with the chamber that had been discovered below the centre island in the Valley of the Gods park. The first phase of the large project was a great success. The outskirt dwellings were fully booked. People were streaming in from all over the world.

"What is stellar radiation?" Sascia asked.

"Ever heard of solar wind?" Leo asked.

"No idea."

He knew that it was an astrophysical subject he had never really studied. Theo had, and he wanted to learn all the phases of the life of a star. He was all ears.

"Sascia, when I was studying genetic science, I concluded that, like the atom and the nuclei our physical bodies consist of, the life of a star is no different. To understand the properties of stars and their evolution, I started to understand how the universal mind works."

"I'm glad you do because it's all too scientific for me. Rich, what is your idea about solar wind, whatever that is?"

"Moppie let Leo finish his explanation first. I'll see if I can link it to my theories." Leo had been scribbling on his serviette when Toon reminded them that they had to leave for the small airport where his plane was waiting in a half-hour.

"We are now at a place in the orbit around our central galaxy where the radio frequencies of the galaxy's centre, as well as many other star systems, are communicating new information to our planet."

"You mean...we are within a program of the planet?" André asked. "I'm no scientist, so what you're trying to say is..."

He could see that André's arms were crossed, his legs stretched out in front of him, and he leaned back from the breakfast table. His sight was indeed coming back! Stunned by the flames' heat, it was as if his mind gathered all the data back again to see into the dream. Sascia's squeezing hand confirmed the world of the five senses.

"Rich, I told you, you will fully recover, you hear? Every day, we will do your eye exercises." Ever since he cried to sleep each night, he had finally understood what it meant to be trapped in the matrix. To be free from all pain, misery and unhappiness, he had to let go of thinking about it.... Sascia's warm hand on his lap returned his attention to the discussion between Leo and André.

"Notice how threads weave the patterns together in the same geometric shapes! Focus your mind on geometry. Note the six pyramids. You should also see the cubes, which is explained through geometry." Leo's excitement was heard in his voice as he was drawing something. It inspired him to think back to his out-of-body experiences. If he wanted to travel out of his body consciously, he had to stop taking any medicine. It took nearly six weeks until he woke up one morning with a clear memory of an astral travel journey.

He could see that André studied Leo's drawing with interest. He asked Sascia to describe Leo's drawings.

"Leo has drawn two circles, one within the other. The outer circle is divided into twenty-two sections." Sascia explained. In an instant, a memory of a dream came back when he had astral travelled towards the centre of the eye symbol. To him, it had been the most bizarre dream ever.

"This is a star-gate linked to the Creator Gods." Leo pointed out as he held up his serviette drawing. All he saw was a solid white image.

"That looks like what they used in the movie Stargate!" Helen exclaimed as she served coffee. He could just imagine what Leo's drawing looked like. In the centre was Horus's eye. If it was the right eye, it represented their left hemisphere, a logical sight that turned thought into external physical reality. The left eye then gives the right inner mind a passage into the multidimensional universes. The silence around the table because of what had been discussed brought his attention back to Leo and André's discussion.

"Leo, I counted the sections around this image that you have drawn. I can't see your drawing, but your explanation made me remember that the sensation of travelling into the eye in one of my dream journeys was quite a revelation."

"Let's hear it, and then we have to make a move," Toon responded. He could feel Sascia's face suddenly very close. The laughter from the others distracted his attention from what he was about to say. André told Sascia to give him some space to breathe.

"Theo explained that thirty-six doorways represented the thirty-six creator forces which connect each soul back to the source." He added to the conversation.

"Gosh, your astral travels must be something. How often do you do it?" André asked. He said nothing for a while. Richard had difficulty falling asleep in the last months, and when he finally did, he always woke up with no memory whatsoever. Still, he recalled his dreams through his inner mind's eye when he meditated before sleeping. He always thought that his out-of-body journeys would never stop because he had had an amazing second life. He felt Sascia's hand sliding into his.

"André, for quite some time, I had no recollection of any dreams until a few weeks ago, just after the opening."

"Snooks, what do you know about this eye symbol connected to our park?" Ingrid beamed at Toon.

"Kitty, all I know is that a group of people with lots of political power are snooping around to do with discovering the Eye symbol."

During his blindness, their telepathic dialogue had become more and more vivid. He learned to respond to verbal communications at the same time while he was listening to people's inner dialogue. He beamed back.

"Ingrid, thousands of years ago, people knew about the thirty-six portals! They certainly were more 'in the know' than we are! During my dream journeys, Theo showed me that there are nine rings around the iris. He speculated that they had to do with time linking the nine perceptions through which we oversee this reality."

"You mean because we are living in the age of closure, this inner eye has to be activated?" Sascia replied to his projection.

"Rich, our out-of-body trip now starts to make sense." she beamed on a private line.

"Mmm, Yes, Theo said that the gods who walked on our planet used the Eye of Horus as a device to oversee their creation, then they stored it away like we stored our data in our computer; only their computer was in the shape of a human skull."

"Really? Is that what the ancient texts reveal?" André queried. He knew that André still had difficulty with him deriving his information during sleep. Sascia squeezed his knee. She still could not stop talking about her out-of-body journey. He hoped many would follow.

"Come to think of it, yes. The science behind the Eye of Horus device completely eludes me, but this eye device is a sort of a filter or a program."

"You mean the eye could hold the code of our creation?"

"Of course, that makes sense," Leo exclaimed with joy. He felt rather chuffed to have inspired Leo with his theories.

"Eyes are to be understood as inductive filters. Richard describes the device used in other universes as a platform or a station." Nobody had noticed that Hans had arrived at their table. Hans told them all to get going, for Dirk had the plane ready for their departure. They were all sorry that the conversation had to stop. They said their goodbyes.

As he sat snuggled up close next to Sascia in the plane, he recalled the first time he sat beside her, looking for her mother. So much has happened since then.

His thoughts took him back to when he was a very young child. Theo was twelve when he was born, and he was often left with his big brother when their parents were absorbed in their research. Theo had been fascinated with science fiction stories and was introduced to many wonderful theories early on. Later, the re-birthing practices replaced the way-out sciences until Theo decided to make it his business one day to ensure they would both find their true purpose in life. ...The apple fragrance from Sascia's hair took him back to when he held her in his arms.

• • • •

When gooseflesh spread throughout his whole body, he knew what was happening. He stayed in his position while Sascia slept. When he saw Theo nodding, his familiar face brought on feelings of gratitude.

"Richie, truth is often relative to the setting of one's consciousness. That is why an awakened person always updates his standards and perceptions." Hearing Theo's thoughts reminded him of their conversation back at Halfway House. Lately, his perceptions had gone through such shifts about life and who or what he was; he was far more open to the inexplicable. As they moved away from their cottage, the sensation of standing in a crystal cave resembling a theatre became a reality. It took him completely by surprise. He was looking down over rows of flat crystal seating arrangements. He recalled that he had been there before. What would POWAH reveal?

"Listen to what is being addressed so that you can end your journal with it." He saw many light beings gazing towards the cave's centre, where a collection of Crystal Skulls was being prepared to receive the planet's memory data. Brilliant laser ray light beams from at least five directions were projected towards them. Then, a massive water feature took on the appearance of POWAH, who was scanning the gathering. Richard knew that his gaze reached into the very depths of each light being that was present. Sounds of clear voices in perfect unison charged the area. For one moment, POWAH's sky-blue eyes connected to his, and the familiar tones formed the words in his mind....He knew he had experienced this before!

\<Dearly beloved, when you all embrace and work in unity, silently and freely, each one in their particular way will experience liberation within. You are all here to prepare yourselves and your fellow beings for the space-time overlap intervention soon upon you. You are preparing a pathway so others can follow.\>

The most awe-inspiring spectacle of blinking stars reaching out into the silken darkness of fathomless space appeared. The Milky Way, in all its glory, surrounded them all. As he gazed up, he saw planet Earth in the prime of her life-span, home to various kingdoms.

\<The resurrection for a New Earth is already in process. Many souls have chosen to come into this incarnation to gather lost knowledge. Those who seek the light will directed by colour, and the sounds you know are the primordial basis of all matter.\>

Everything came back to him. Streams of soft rose-red flares burst into a firework display, forming brilliant layers of colours around the lonely planet like an onion. When the sound of harmonic vibrations penetrated his light body, layer upon layer of colours of intense beauty settled around the floating sphere. A division had taken place.

"Richie, this is our last journey. With Sascia, you will explore your inner worlds until you can observe what I will show you now as a preview."

An immense sadness flooded his mind when he thought of saying farewell to Theo. Where...Why does it have to end? There was no reply. Instead, Theo took hold of him, and suddenly, with a minimum fuss, they observed the solar system from afar. It was as if...planet Earth was reflected through a mirror!

"Theo, am I looking at separate realities?" Nothing was natural to him anymore. He wasn't sure he was seeing anything at all!

"Richie, when you think of seeing, you expect to look at something familiar, am I right?" Right, he got it. He was trying to look at something he'd never seen before. He thought back to when he was in his body, the two months of misery because he couldn't see. Now, he realizes that true sight does not rely on physical eyes.

"Richie, I'm preparing you for a journey into an anti-universe. The reason is so that you will understand why some people seem to do anything to stop people from becoming fully awakened." They certainly had. A trail of destruction had followed. Did it all have a connection to the Jaarsma clan? Or were they mirroring the world where wars, corruption and destruction raged?

"Do you remember POWAH previously instructed us on repositioning the Crystal Skulls over the inter-dimensional passage to reopen the sound-wave-spheres?

He remembered something POWAH had said about how these crystal skulls can re-activate the magnetic force field around the planet's inner sun, and that porthole will re-open. Was it really from another dream?

"Yes, I'm glad you remembered. That is how matter and anti-matter created a passage through time and space, through sound and colour!" What had that to do with the corruption and destruction in the rest of the world? Or...was it to stop the completion of Toon's park, The Valley of the Gods?

"Destructive fear-based thought forms have formed what is called Metatronic creations. They originally came from the Outer worlds."

He had no clue what Metatronic creations were, but as he thought it, an image of a big-eyed Grey alien crossed his vision. Was Theo implying that any thought forms he had seen as shadows were Metatronic creations? What it had to do with an anti-universe puzzled him. He gazed at both linked universes like two balloons tied to a string opposite each other. He wondered if he was looking at a vast, expansive, three-dimensional movie screen. He saw weird-looking intra-oceanic vessels coming from out of planet Earth. He knew he was not watching a movie, but it looked like he was. Space vessels travelled through what seemed like space freeways from one universal bubble to the other.

"*What does it remind you of?*" Gosh, science fiction movies or...an hourglass model of the cosmos?

"*Okay, if that is how you see it, then explore further. Let your higher mind create the files you need to expand your perceptions.*"

He gazed back into space. He observed how one universe, with many galaxies, was trapped into one side of a figure-of-eight-shaped hourglass while another universe with identical galaxies was on the other side. Both halves seemed to rotate in opposite directions. The narrow part that linked them looked like an umbilical cord.

"Very good. This umbilical cord or thin stream is a magnetic field, a timeless passage linking different parts of our universe to a parallel universe. For one moment, think of the two hemispheres of the human brain. Think of the neuron pathways." For one moment, he wondered if he was inside the human brain. He zoomed up close, which intuitively gave him an idea.

"You mean this link or bridge is like a time machine?"

"*Sort of. In ancient times. Liesbeth and Hans will explain the Outer worlds and their place in the greater scheme of things.*"

The vision of space seems replaced by celestial sounds that appear far away. When they got stronger through Richard's inner eye, the sound formed the colours he saw into shapes. He recalled seeing this before.

"*Richie, I showed you the two matter and anti-matter universes so you can synchronise both your brain modes. I will be with you through this balancing process, helping you obtain the highest vibration possible within your physical body. That is the ultimate aim of the evolution of the human species."*

When Theo mentioned the brain hemispheres, he thought of the second level of Annelies' ascension card game, how the Left and Right palms of their hands were encoded. It always came back to the balancing process.

"Richie, each realm is divided by energy veils, and every human being unknowingly adds to this energy veil from moment to moment. The inhabitants of the Outer worlds knew this. Remember the vortex where you saw many eyes?" How could he forget? Eyes had a rather strong influence on him. So the human thought process, especially when it was fear-based, was like food to these Metatronic creations?

Theo did something, and suddenly, he became aware of the symbol of the eye again. Months ago, Theo showed him how, through a crop circle, an image of an Egyptian eye symbol looked from a great distance.

"There is no such thing as time. The Metatronic creations that occupy the Outer worlds have programmed that illusion! Remember that this eye shape represents the beginning of all creation." In a flash, he saw all the journeys he'd experienced. He remembered that Theo had speculated that they lived or had their being in POWAH's mind field. Then, how real would it be if all of it was in POWAH's creation?

"Richie, unexpected genetic distortions occurred when a very evolved species from an Outer universe started to program all their soul's wisdom on cosmic alchemy into their Metatronic creations. A virus we now know as the 'false self effect' within the humanoid creations took over. On a soul level, complete forgetfulness trapped our spirit into a cycle of reincarnation " Richard wondered what Theo meant by a humanoid. Robots?

"I thought that a serpent or reptile creation did that, mixing with other creations. What are Metatronic creations?" His dream journeys were starting to feel very...unspiritual.

"They are mechanical shadows. They have lost their emotional body. That's why they were the fallen offspring of a genetic experiment during the Atlantian times. Their technology for attuning the cycles of matter and anti-matter using crystalline structures failed. Or let's say the physical and the non-physical world. Remember the movie Matrix Revolutions, when Neo merged with the machines at the end? He had won the battle with his dark side, Mr Smith." Good grief, he got it. Suddenly, many things dropped into place. It reminded him of the Observers in the Fringe series. The possible time warp areas, the planet's meridians, and the solar flares all returned to the Great Pyramid at Giza. Who built it? Was it the humanoids, the giants, or humanity from long ago? When he was inside the King's chamber, it often felt like he was inside a machine.

"Richie, scientists today know that stepping up or slowing down the energy between two cycles causes a shift in time and space. They discovered that in the Philadelphia experiments."

The visions Theo showed them again looked familiar. Did he remember flashes from his past?

"Richie, some evolved souls, who were then seen as 'Gods' by our ancestors, were Oversoul beings who tried to return home through the force field of others. It is even happening now, as you will know."

He now started to understand how difficult it is to translate energy images into words. Words make forms out of what is formless, but then whose words are describing truth?

"Words and symbols are tools in the law of evolution. Spiritual knowledge must be developed in man, not used to preserve unfavourable conditions of dense matter." He must have

misunderstood Annelies when she kept saying that it was all in the intent to ascend. Did she not say that we could achieve freedom from the law of birth and death? Theo's compassion and love flooded through his light body.

"Richie immortality is about consciously leaving when you want to, not to achieve a perfect long life free of illness. When humans today have reached a far greater knowledge of how to coexist with the harmonious laws of nature, they can expand their life spans that exceed 650 to 800 years of the Earth's calendar. I will show you what the spokes being looks like and can tell you how to coexist with the harmonious laws of nature. Ask Aunty Mien; she will tell you." Theo covered his eyes because he felt an energy streaming into his astral eyes. When Theo removed his hands, he saw a massive, tall tree with a wooden walkway built around this majestic big specimen. Tree ferns, hanging mosses, ground cover ferns, and many more tropical plants gave off a fragrance only a dense forest gives. He wondered where he was.

"It is here where I will see you again. Remember, there is no such thing as time…. To learn how to conquer matter, we must incarnate in a physical body." These were the last thoughts he translated into words when he felt someone was shaking him.

· · · ·

"Rich wake-up, we are at Buttercup Valley." He saw a bright window where the sunrays danced on the plane's wing. He looked further outside as the small plane was taxying to a halt. He admired the view…There was lots of snow…What beautiful scenery. Gosh! He could see! The snow… how white it was. He could see the mountains in the distance. He turned to Sascia and saw that her eyes were moist; a tear rolled down her cheeks. His happiness made him take deep breaths.

He had to pull himself out of his inner world, but Theo's last words were still ringing in his inner ear. Where did Theo say this massive tall, sizeable old tree was?

"Oh, Rich, your eyes. There is no more redness. How amazing." Sascia cried with joy.

Upon landing, Otto, the half-brother of Fred and Annelies, greeted them and urged them to disembark the plane.

"This must be André the detective who has decided to learn about permaculture. Peter told me all about you. We are proud to have you onboard." Otto slapped him on the back. That was the first time he had heard that André went in for gardening.

"Well, well, Sascia, welcome again to Buttercup Valley. Every time I see you, I see your mother again." Otto gave Sascia a big hug.

"When your mother stepped out of the plane, I knew Toon had found his soul mate. Now that I see you, I want to see that man of yours I heard so much about." Otto's intense gaze inspected him as if at an auction.

"I thought you were blind." He forgot that they were all telepathic up in Buttercup Valley.

"I was, temporarily. You are the first man I can see with a completely returned vision." Otto stared, and then a smile appeared. The change that came over Otto's face was truly remarkable. He had heard that Otto saw everything as one big joke.

"Richard, a man who sees visions, now I call that seeing. Not many admit they were first blind until they know what seeing entails. So you are the dreamer." Otto shook his hand and told his party to follow him down to the valley where Jill had the coffee pot brewing.

It started to snow as Otto stopped and pointed to a domed wooden house in the distance.

"That's Peter and Helen's house. They're almost finished. Tomorrow I will take you on a tour of the Valley. André, I believe that you can measure psychometry from items in nature?"

"I seem to, yes" André replied as he shifted his backpack.

"Really, like Debbie?" Sascia reacted with surprise.

"I have more luck with plants, trees, and stones."

"That must have been handy in your detective work." He never heard André reply to Dirk, who would fly back to France in two days. Jill and Otto would join them to see what had been done at the Valley of the Gods.

On the 18th, they would all fly back to Holland. He had an appointment with Dr. van Dongen in Utrecht.

Otto's wooden cottage was surrounded by pine and cedar trees that were laden with snow. They tapped the snow off their shoes on the wooden veranda and stepped into a warm hallway where Jill, Otto's wife, greeted them.

"I heard from Helen that your sight is back," Jill said with joy, he hugged her. Dirk reminded him to look at the DVD Trevor passed him at the last minute.

"Rich, it must have the twenty-second tablet on it." Sascia guessed. After they had coffee and warm strudels, Sascia wanted to change her clothes for hiking gear before they explored Toon's community in the Alps. They would spend a long weekend in the snow; what a treat.

"Moppie, did you bring my journal file?"

"Of course I did, but let's first read what the last tablet says. I'm so curious. It might tell us more about the Outer worlds." He had told her all about his visitation during their flight.

Their room was great. A big double bed made from pine wood was inviting, but Sascia wouldn't hear his suggestive strokes. The Man in Stone was written on the DVD. Sascia wanted to read the last tablet. They both reacted as she entered the DVD file titled The Game of the Prophet[1]. They clicked on the link and entered cyberspace.

Tablet 22

The last translation by Theo de Jong

The sadness overcame him, reading the last sentence. He missed Theo already, but he also knew that a kind of initiation had happened on a higher level.

"Rich, I understand now that the symbols from one to ten are quality keys! Tieneke says that when people bring these soul qualities into their realities through feeling and experiencing them, they will see great happenings.

"So they shall, or we will. Moppie, let's explore. That's why we are here. Later we'll watch the movie about the Stone Man.

Amsterdam

Through the curtains of Sascia's hideaway in Amsterdam, he saw that the clouds allowed a few rays of sunlight to shine. He snuggled close.

He would soon have to get up and drive to Utrecht, where he would give his first lecture for the year. Straight after that, they flew on Toon's plane back to France. He would travel to Utrecht twice a month to give his lectures. His work was with Leo and Trevor at their underground laboratory.

He tickled her earlobe to wake her up.

"Yeeeee, that is ticklish." He slowly pulled her nightie away, enjoying the view while receiving the treatment dreams are made of.

Sascia insisted he wears his black polo neck jersey under his beige corduroy jacket. She declared that it made him the sexiest man around. His vision was almost back to what it was before. He still needed to use his eye drops when he felt a burning sensation, but Hans maintained that it was still a memory of the

---

1. https://allrealityshifters.wordpress.com/tablet-twenty-two/

pain he had not been able to release entirely from his energy field. According to Hans, Annelies third genetic decoding workshop will handle that.

Next month, they would play the second level of the awakening game when Annelies and Ben, along with Aunt Mien and Harry Brinks, returned from the opening of his cousin's Monkey Valley community in South Africa. His aunt had shown pictures of a lush tropical forest, reminding him of his last dream with Theo. It was something about the big tree.

Together with Sascia, they explored regular out-of-body journeys. They both missed Theo, but so much was happening in their new environment and work that their life in France would soon bring new challenges. He never did find out what happened between Annelies and his aunt years ago. After Annelie's party, when she discovered Liesbeth was her daughter, there was a large family reunion. Sascia went, but he wanted to be by himself.

It was the first time he drove after the accident. What a blessing.

"I told you it would all return to you, didn't I?" Sascia squeezed his thigh. He was looking forward to his first lecture in Utrecht on the resurrection of matter. Trevor's and Leo's efforts to produce a movie that would enhance his talk would make all the difference, especially the movie clip about the stone man.

They greeted many familiar faces in the parking bay of Utrecht's Parapsychological Institute. Niels and Carla had just arrived.

"Sascia, will you be joining us?" Vinny asked through the car window when he parked his sports car next to them. Debbie was still in uniform.

"Hi, sis; I'm glad you could make it. You are coming with us after the lecture, aren't you?"

"You're kidding! I've been looking forward to the plane trip for days. I just finished my last shift. I'm all packed." Quite a few people from the faculty came to greet him. Annelies and Ben would be in the audience with Trevor and Tieneke. Niels waved, and it was the first time he could see Adel, Niels' Indonesian mother, when Gerrit introduced her.

"I'm honoured. So many people are here."

The seats were filling up. Sascia joined the others in the second row from the front. He waved at Mien, who was with Harry Brinks. Higher up he spotted Annelies, Ben, Trevor and Tieneke. Leo, Hans, Liesbeth and Ingrid were in France with Ed and Yolanda.

Just before the door closed, Toon arrived. Instead of joining the others, he came towards him at the podium. He grabbed the microphone and gave a very flattering introduction in his deep voice.

"Richard, I'm leaving the rest to you. I know that we are all in for a treat." Toon joined Annelies as she waved, pointing at the empty seat beside her.

The Resurrection of Matter

An electrifying wave transfixed the audience as Richard's mental grip held his audience.

"Ladies and gentlemen," There was no more flutter of nervousness in his Solar Plexus. There was nothing he needed to prove, teach or reveal to anyone. When he saw Sascia, he gave her a very obvious acknowledgement by sending her a kiss, to which most heads turned. The laughter settled the tension.

"I'm going to take you on a journey to show you all that we truly live in the most important times of our human evolution." Everything was set up, but he liked to stand next to an image that supported his talk.

"If we hold on to the idea throughout my lecture that the element of Ether is a unified electromagnetic field, then there is no such a thing as space. Let's make it more graphic by drawing a large circle" He used a large whiteboard for everyone to see.

"Ether is pure energy that links our physical sense-organs and our subtle organs called chakras into the intercellular substance of the core crystal of our planet." He had everyone's attention when he showed a giant crystal buried deep within the Earth, more than 5,000 Km down at the very centre.

"Scientists discovered it in 1995 with a sophisticated computer model that could reach Earth's inner core. This remarkable finding offers plausible solutions to some perplexing geophysical puzzles." He was preparing his audience for yet another theory that might set some tongues wagging, but so what?

"Let me explain that these Hexagonal crystals have unique qualities that are also used in our microphones. This crystal core is the brain of our planet that controls her magnetic field." In the next slide, an image of the well-known Mitchell-Hedges Crystal Skull, enlarged within Earth's inner core, enhanced his talk's crucial direction.

"Let's go back to the element of Ether. It's the same force we know as cosmic life force, prana or Chi. Keep that in mind.

"It was through the translations of the twenty-two tablets that were discovered in deep underground caves that brought to life a technology so advanced, so profoundly awesome; it made Tesla and Einstein look like kindergarten students when it came to their time travel theories." He knew the following slides would help the audience translate his lack of words. The slides of Ramses and the massive hall of 24 columns did the rest.

"Our modern mind is still baffled by the evidence that advanced beings imbued with sacred wisdom visited our planet.

They were like the gods to the local population. Their technology, which was used to construct the many sacred monuments worldwide, was lost when they left our solar system." He was leading his audience further into the core of his topic.

"On my last visit to Egypt in October, I again visited all the well-known sites, especially the Giza pyramid. The resonance within this stone monument in most people causes a vibration in our cerebral-spinal column, especially at the nape of the neck."

When Trevor's movie showed how the crystal skull within the planet's core started to send sound waves into the far regions of space through the famous pyramid, he had the audience spellbound.

"Let's move back to our beginning. In all the ancient books and writings handed down from the time of Osiris and Horus, to name a few deities, it seems that the creation of our world began here."

His next slide created a tremendous stir. The display of opulent scenery did the same with him when he saw it in his dreams.

"Richard, who were the first people who could build like that?" The man up front could not wait for question time.

"Please, sir, I will answer all questions after the slide show." He showed the photos Leo had found of the gold foil wrappings with the Language of Light symbols. Trevor made beautiful-looking golden slates that showed Tieneke's mind drawings, with translations next to the symbols.

The following slide showed an image of what it could have looked like during the flood.

"During the destruction of Atlantis, when all seemed to disappear into the depth of our oceans, scientists of those days had programmed their secret knowledge in the crystal skulls around the planet, with the intention that their knowledge would be rediscovered before the next polar shift that has been predicted during our age." The same man jumped up again.

"I'm sorry, Richard, but I will forget my questions if I don't ask them now." Gosh, he hated to lose his control like that.

"What is your name."

"Piet Boshof."

"Okay, Piet, I have not forgotten your first question, but let me carry on." Piet sat down, and the woman beside him told him off because he had shrugged his shoulders.

He impressed his audience by saying that all the assumptions Egyptologists, archaeologists, astronomers, and various other writers have about the ancient mysteries to do with our planet must be listened to but not necessarily taken as fact.

"There are too many diversities. My job is to present a possible scenario, nothing more." He explained that he would take his story from the time of the great flood in this lecture. It was too vague to speculate on what happened before the flood. He would instead publish his articles on the internet.

The following movie clip was created to enhance his storyline.

"It was Thoth, who supposedly left Atlantis in a spaceship during the destruction." He loved the way Trevor had portrayed the flood scene.

"As you see, many are left in different-looking crafts." The dramatic cataclysm was well presented. It was so rewarding to tell a story in this manner. The humming from the whispers died down with the following movie clip. He narrated Trevor's movie. Many people gasped at the great Sphinx rising from the declining water levels. He always thought that the Sphinx and many other monuments survived the flood.

"We pick up our story again with the great Sphinx who sits in front of the Great Pyramid. At that time, Thoth moved back into the realms of the physical and brought those who would walk upon the land." He paused the movie as he faced the audience.

"We all know the story of Noah, who also survived the Great Flood. In many other religious-orientated literature, a flood story is told, so there must be another meaning to having survived the end times, so to speak."

He pressed the start button again, hoping his audience was following him.

"Now, I want you all to remember that I started my talk with the element of Ether. Because we have now, on Earth, time has entered a new epoch through the element of water, which means consciousness. Soon, the stage of our evolution will shift into a higher dimension."

The following slide takes Leo and Trevor endless hours until Annelies comes on the scene after her experience with the crystal skull. She guided Trevor through what looked like grid programs projected by the centre core into twenty-two crystal skulls, just as we do today when we write a program. These crystal skulls, found worldwide, store all of planet Earth's experiences." Again, he narrated Trevor's movie.

"During the fall of Atlantis, awakened souls created subterranean cities and moved underground. As you can see, their pictorial language described how they were guided by a golden light, which came from the inner core crystal of our planet. Many of you have seen the movie The Matrix and the two others that followed. Where do you think they got their idea from?" When he clicked back to Annelies' grid program, he knew by the silence that he had everyone's attention.

"As you can see in the next movie clip, when the Gods and Goddesses returned to the planet in their craft because they were space travellers, they stepped into another program or reality.

Remember that these beings could embody a human form while staying fully conscious. For them, they participated in a simulation game we've all seen on Star Trek. Their knowledge of alchemy was all about how to create physical matter. Their knowledge affected the following events as they moved through passages of time."

What drew breath was the next scene. He had told Trevor and Hans in detail what he remembered from his dreams. At the time, his sight was gone, but the images were riveted to his mind. They managed to get it to almost look like the way he saw it with Trevor's brainwave simulator. His movie showed how the brain of the planet used the significant stone pyramid monument as a huge transmitter and projector simultaneously.

"In ancient times, large polished blocks covered the Great Pyramid so they acted like gigantic mirrors and could be seen for miles around." He had heard a most unusual sound in his dream when the colour rays bounced off onto the smaller pyramids. He tried to describe it, but Trevor's brainwave program could not capture his description. It did not reach the profound pitch they had hoped for, so they left it out.

"You will now recognise why there is evidence all over our planet of a civilisation that possessed a piece of knowledge far beyond our present capabilities. They were much further advanced in the science of creating the holographic realities we only see in science fiction movies. We are in our infant stage of projecting thought-waves.

He soon knew, by the questions asked, what the audience's level of perception was.

"Richard, how were the pyramids built?" Piet almost shouted before other people got a chance to ask. He always got that question. It reminded him of the days at university when students asked how the brain worked. He would never forget how the lecturer replied.

"Piet, we do NOT know how the pyramids were built, we do NOT know why they were built, we can only speculate. There is no evidence that the pyramids of Giza and Dahshur ever served as tombs. We do NOT know how the 200-ton blocks of the Sphinx and Valley temples and the paving blocks surrounding the Khafre pyramid were moved and put into place. Most are only speculations. Still, the energy of the pyramids forcefully reminds us of their enduring power as monuments to the spirit of human creativity. It stood the test of time." He hoped that would somewhat clear the air and satisfy Piet, who seemed nice.

"Richard, where does God fit into all this?" A tall, businesslike woman asked. He always knew when he had people in his audience who were still hooked into the religion program and that he had to be careful about how he replied.

"Thank you for that question. Almighty God or the divine Source of all Sources is neither male nor female nor ever manifest in any personal form." He turned and pointed at the circle he had drawn on a large whiteboard at the start of his lecture.

"I know that our scientists will soon agree that the gods who created our holographic realities used basic geometry to create the endless grid programs. I will show you how these grids form many realities through a mirror effect."

He again showed the movie about how the heart core crystal of the planet vibrated its thought waves into the giant pyramid of Giza. As he was drawing on the whiteboard, he could hear people whispering. While he used Leo's ideas, the dreams and interactions with POWAH flashed through his mind.

"Richard, as I understand it correctly, we are still part of one soul throughout our many incarnations?"

"Yes, from Jesus to aliens to Thoth to any teenager today, the chronology of events all happen in the mind of one supreme being. We are multidimensional beings participating in a game of evolution by creating our realities on many inner planes; the truth is relative to the setting of one's consciousness. I hope that answer will satisfy your question."

While he said that, he turned to the massive whiteboard and drew a colossal sphere, he wrote in big letters: let there be light...life...

"There is nothing outside the divine creation of the Source of all Sources. There is no experience beyond consciousness." Underside his sphere, he drew a pyramid.

"Richard, the world is full of events which do not appear in my consciousness. Can you explain that if there is nothing beyond consciousness?" He was glad for Vinny's question; it helped him along in his reflection.

"We all know that our physical body's maintenance is guided by an intelligence not part of our conscious awareness. To have that ability, we must have a consciousness of super-consciousness. To awaken that kind of pure awareness, we have to surrender the program of our ego, which is a requisite for the liberation of the spirit." His audience was silent.

"Our consciousness is full of gaps. The architect of the pyramid knew this." He allowed his contemplations to sink in before he carried on.

"Let's say that the pyramid is the mind of the matrix, expressed in stone, portraying the creation of man. Within its mass is exposed the secret of the Universe...and we are within its creation." He turned to his whiteboard and drew a circle in the centre of his previous sphere.

"Our mind seems to use, as a pointer to an experience, the word I." Again, he drew a smaller circle so that the symbol of the eye appeared. The profound stillness in the audience created a feeling of unity.

"This eye symbol stands for the awareness of the observer." When he blackened the centre pupil, he got an insight.

"The Godhead, our large Group-Soul that the many different religious teachings refer to, is the architect of our universe, the dreamer of our reality." He knew that he was on to something. The dreamer seemed to sidestep their mortal mind.

"Richard, what would have been the reason, plan or idea to establish religions?" the same woman asked upfront as he was about to continue. Like her, he knew that everything had a purpose for the good of all, no matter how distorted the result might have been.

"We often try to step into the shoes of another to understand their reasoning, but not so? So allow me to be so bold as to do the same." He paused for a moment until the buzz died down.

"Don't forget that it's just my idea. Like you, I'm the seeker who links with other seekers. We are joined with our minds into a dream of our creator. During recent months, I've had to learn to let go of the reality of my dream through blindness so I could become much more the inner observer of this illusion we call reality." He pointed at the eye symbol on the large whiteboard.

"To return to the lady's question of why religions were formed. If the Archangel, or architect who created our universe, wanted to return to the almighty source, this Archangel, like us, has to go within, away from its universal mind, back into the absolute, all-pervading, eternal, ever-present timeless moment of now." He turned back to the whiteboard and pointed at the eye pupil. He knew that his audience was at the end of their concentration span. He had to wrap it up soon.

"Our biological bodies were seeded on this planet by a universal mind integrated with the mind of Gaia, our planet."

On his screen, he showed the image of the well-known drawing of a human body by Leonardo da Vinci.

"Richard, this polar shift that you mentioned before, is there any evidence that justifies all the speculation we might face on a global scale?" Adel asked. There was tension in the air as if many others had wanted to ask the same question.

"The following statement was published on a known website a few years ago. It said: Sometime after May, the earth's rotation will stop within a day and hold for several days just before the pole shift. This is when you and your loved ones should be situated at a safe location". There was complete silence...then a giggle...He waited until they got it.

"We are still here!" he said, waving his arms. The laughter cleared the air.

"Okay, let's tackle that interesting question properly. Plenty of evidence proves that the poles were in different positions during the Pleistocene era." His database had some very visual images that helped his following explanations.

"A polar shift can mean that the Earth's outer shell moves and tumbles occasionally.

"Richard, what happened to Atlantis?"

"I think so. It would support the abrupt disaster that befell Atlantis. I think there have been many pole shifts in the planet's history. There are all kinds of theories as to why pole shifts occur, and nobody knows what triggers the process. However, I strongly feel that when we shift our perception about something on a global scale, a pole shift is like a shift in global consciousness." As he recalled from his dreams, he showed the impressive statue of Akhenaton, the Egyptian king aware of the three grids for human consciousness around the planet.

"For now, let's stay within the boundaries between the two consciousness concepts... the inner and the outer world of our realities. As we all know, the Sphinx marks the oldest object on the planet, an external reality left by a very advanced civilization. We can all agree on that. Now, both Sumerian and Egyptian cultures seemed to flourish overnight. Still, as soon as they were at their most awakened or advanced state or reached full consciousness, both cultures began to degenerate." He let that sink in, hoping they would follow his drift.

"Richard, why would that be?"

"Let's speculate about three levels of inner consciousness linked to our outer world. Most people are only aware of the state of physical reality. In meditation or creative visualisation, we move into our inner world of lucid dreams and deep dreaming states."

He showed a person surrounded by a colourful audio field that interacted with nature on the screen, which Annelies used in her decoding workshops.

"However, many people today are moving into lucid dreams while awake, where they can materialise physical matter or events by pure intent and thought. They are moving into the fourth dimension.

"Then there are a few people on the planet who have reached the fifth dimension, or the deep dream state while awake, sometimes called Christ consciousness. Could it be that when enough people move into this fifth level of consciousness, the external world disappears to people in the normal awake state because these people we hope to be amongst are moving into an inner existence?"

When he looked up and gazed straight into the spellbound assembly hall, he knew why the dream kept surfacing into his conscious awareness. Now, he knew how to close his journal and end his lecture.

"Let me disclose a personal experience that humbled me."

He turned and loaded his last DVD on his laptop. A buzz of bewilderment filled the auditorium when he showed the image that had plagued him for weeks. He waited for people to quiet, then narrated Trevor's last movie clip.

"Ladies and gentlemen, I'm not here to convert anyone. There is nothing to convert to. I want to close this lecture with the following material and let each absorb it as they choose." There was a buzz in the auditorium when he thought he heard what could be a warning.

"We warn you, if you continue, the Jaarsma clan will come up for trial." He shrugged it off. He had already started and strongly felt that his audience needed to be warned. He showed them all the 22 tablets up close.

"My brother and two other colleagues had knowledge and expertise in languages and ancient texts. Theo was able to speak over 30 different languages fluently and another 12 or so languages that are officially extinct. He was my teacher, and because of his skills in linguistics and my ability to decode symbol pictures like petroglyphs or hieroglyphs, during my dream state, I, together with two other colleagues, was chosen to disclose the following discoveries." He could feel that an energy force was closing around him, but somehow, he knew that Theo was near.

"I tried every conceivable combination to create an access code to access the disk. As you can see in the movie clip, the Crystal Skull had spoken to the man in the stone, and while his body was altered to tolerate the skull's presence to accomplish what needed to be done, he was both awed and terrified." In a flash, Trevor had captured the memories from the planet's mind. He now saw why the many shadows around the man reminded him of cockroaches scuttling away from the light.

"You see, the skull could resonate tones like God himself speaking. The man leaned over the centuries that these Crystal skulls abide organically within each person's head." The movie showed Annelies' Lightbody.

"Richard, is that me?" Annelies beamed. The audience saw how the planet, through the Crystal skull, spoke to a human light body that radiated while accepting a message.

"When the individual soul and spirit unite and remain in unity, the man in the stone will forever be free." In the movie, the man of stone moves out of the stone and vanishes.

"Like Man who feels trapped in the illusion of Time and Space, his spirit is immortal, but man alone can resurrect physical matter and allow it to ascend. How fortunate we are to experience these times."

The energy force that came from all sides dissipated. It was gone. It seemed that the silence in the hall swallowed it.

"I was convinced that the Language of Light was deliberately made difficult to awaken, at least by our present-day modes of thinking. It was almost like I had to decode this symbolic Language of Light. In my case, I saw mental images of how to use the Sumerian language to decode these symbol pictures, but I had first to learn to communicate telepathically.

"I'm so glad you said that. You've made my task so clear to me. Thank you." Annelies beamed. He acknowledged her by nodding in her direction. He knew he had somehow crossed a boundary when he decided to show the movie about the man in stone holding the time travel disk. He also knew that any thoughts, feelings or actions influenced by fear would disempower them all, so stuff them whoever they were.

"I will add additional documents and artefacts from the ancient underground tunnels to the Ascension workshop website when I feel it is safe to do so, but for now, there's enough material on the website to introduce anyone to the time travel culture of Akhenaten" he concluded. Someone jumped up and waved for his attention when he was about to give his closing speech.

"Richard, I refer to Mel Gibson's movie about crop circles, Signs, which came out years ago. For a Hollywood movie to touch on crop glyphs, they must have had a reason. Why was it then that the movie does little to reveal any educated information about the subject, but you have? Was there more, but were they silenced? " Good grief, he never expected such a question.

"Many respected scientist square/straight types take the crop circle appearances very seriously, as do mystics and occultists." What more could he say? He wanted to end his lecture with a more spiritual note. How would he get his audience back to where he left them with the eye symbol, which he could see as a type of Stargate?

"Due to the many movies about our topic, people might foresee a frightening future, which may be the reason for it: to spread fear, who knows."

That is what Theo meant during his campfire dream! "When the shadows come out to play, chaos will have its way." That is why today, there is so much turbulence worldwide. He wondered if the writers of movie scripts were aware of this.

"Hollywood is therefore also using the idea of man and alien being from the same gene; creatively combining the DNA tampering Nephilim/Anunnaki theory of ancient history, with star-gates and crop circles."

"Richard, what are Star-gates?" A girl right in the front yelled out. He wondered if he ever was going to finish.

"Mmm...Stargates, like the 'Stargate' movie, can be called water-doors since we are talking of movies. I remember that in the film Cocoon, during the eighties, the C-shaped wormhole symbol of the crescent moon was present. This film is about aliens who came to earth, founded Atlantis, and are trying to return home."

"Is it not mind-blowing how the Stargate theme kept cropping up during the eighties?" An older man said out loud to everyone.

"In the movie 'Stargate,' they also describe this transportation device as the Atlantis water door that can transport your body to another planet, like when a fully activated chakra funnel allows man to travel astrally. The physical door or wormhole might be our Westernized way of allowing us the same technology the ancients already had. Only one more question, please." He nodded at the man three rows back who'd been waiting patiently, trying to get a word in while holding up his hand."

"Richard, you mean that during the time of Akhenaten, they were already able to Travel in time?"

"That, we don't know, but physicists have strived to develop plausible mechanisms for time travel for decades. So far, it has only happened in Hollywood."

People started to applaud when he switched off all the equipment he had used to make his talk memorable. He made a perfectly timed dramatic pause he learned from Trevor, turned to his audience and made eye contact with all the people from the Jaarsma Clan. By lowering his head as if deep in thought, he knew that his audience would still be waiting in suspense. They did, for everybody became still.

"I think that the greatest secret about our human species still lies in the eye of the observer, who is seen by the inner eye of everyone in this assembly hall. Let's say that the symbol of the eye is our stargate. From the ONE and to the ONE, we shall return. The rest is pure contemplation". He winked at Sascia, who smiled.

"We are all Souls and Planet Earth is our Orphanage."

He made the Namasté sign to his audience and walked off.

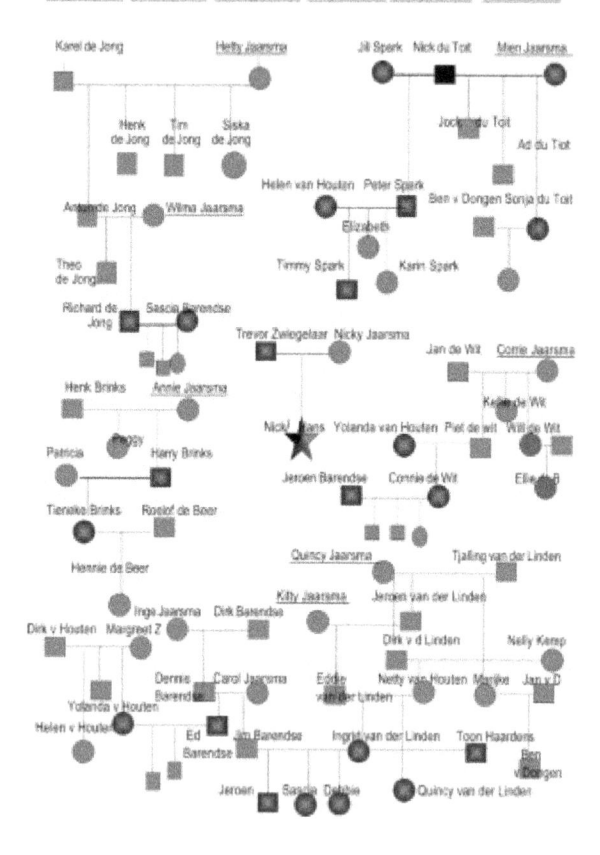

The Jaarsma Tree

Chateau / Half-way House

The Jaarsma Tree - Chateau / Half-way House

Hetty Jaarsma, Mien Jaarsma, Anna Jaarsma, Corry Jaarsma, Quincy Jaarsma, Wilma Jaarsma

Karel de Jong — Hetty Jaarsma   Jill Spark — Nick du Toit   Mien Jaarsma

Henk de Jong   Tim de Jong   Siska de Jong   Jockey du Toit   Ad du Toit

Helen van Houten   Peter Spark   Ben v Dongen — Sonja du Toit

Antonia de Jong — Wilma Jaarsma   Elizabeth

Theo de Jong   Timmy Spark   Karin Spark

Richard de Jong — Sascia Barendse   Trevor Zwiegelaar — Nicky Jaarsma   Jan de Wit — Corrie Jaarsma

Henk Brinks   Annie Jaarsma   Kees de Wit

Patricia   Peggy — Harry Brinks   Nick/Hans   Yolanda van Houten   Piet de wit   Willie de Wit

Jeroen Barendse   Connie de Wit   Ellie de B

Tieneke Brinks   Roelof de Beer

Hennie de Beer   Quincy Jaarsma   Tjalling van der Linden

Kitty Jaarsma   Jeroen van der Linden

Inge Jaarsma   Dirk Barendse

Dirk v Houten   Margreet Z   Dirk v d Linden   Nelly Kemp

Dennis Barendse   Carol Jaarsma   Eddie van der Linden   Netty van Houten   Marijke   Jan v D

Yolanda v Houten

Helen v Houten   Ed Barendse   Jim Barendse   Ingrid van der Linden   Toon Haardens   Ben v Dongen

Jeroen   Sascia   Debbie   Quincy van der Linden

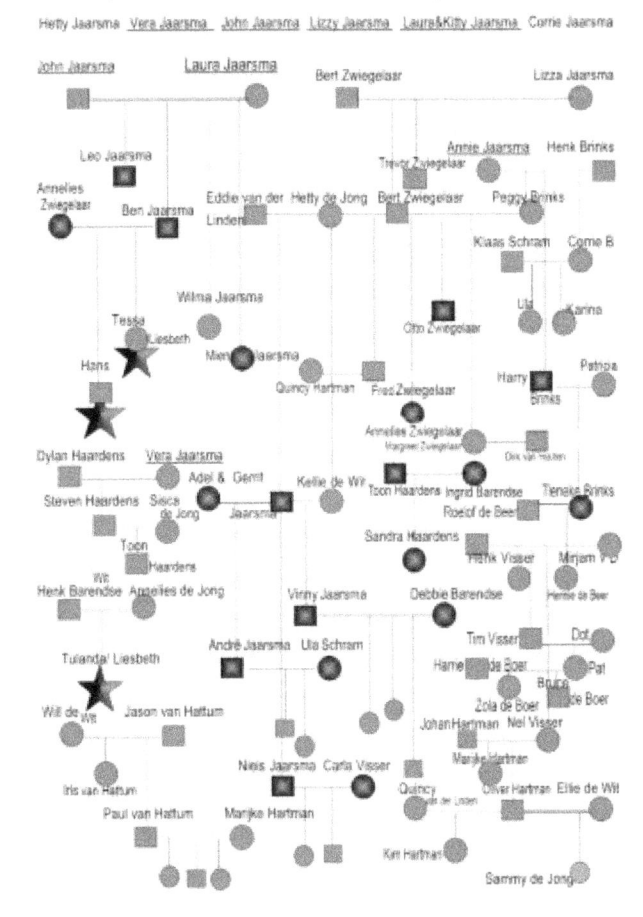

The Jaarsma Tree

The Prinsegracht Hotel

The Jaarsma Tree - The Prinsegracht Hotel

Hetty Jaarsma Vera Jaarsma John Jaarsma Lizzy Jaarsma Laura&Kitty Jaarsma Corrie Jaarsma

About the Author

The Ascension Journals

I was told during the mid-1980s and 1990s that there would be a great awakening during a period of chaos on Earth, leading to the evolution of humanity.

Dreams and a few out-of-body experiences inspired the second ascension novel, but I used a lot of creative writing to make the astral planes an inspiring adventure for my readers.

During the last twenty-plus years, the idea that five levels of awakening (as written in my Language of Light workbook) would be the correct process for sharing spiritual sciences was allowed.

I had no idea about the 'timelines' when I started to write the Second Level Two Richards journal. Sharing my understanding can change, so I hope that with Annelie's journal, Vanishing Worlds, sharing more about my ideas about our ascending journey will be an awakening.

About the Publisher

In 2001, I published my first novel with Kima Global Publishers. Over the years, I published 12 more titles with the same publisher, who eventually became my husband. Sadly, he passed away in 2023. After much consideration and weighing my options, I have published my two-book series, "The Dairy of a Foreigner", and the five-book visionary fiction series, "Awakening to our Ascension", under the name 'The Power of Words' through Draft2Digital. I plan to include my workbooks and journals at a later stage. For now, they are still only available locally in SA.

Read more at https://nadinemay.company.site/.

Milton Keynes UK
Ingram Content Group UK Ltd.
UKHW011122050624
443649UK00006B/479